The Last Open Road continues…

MONTEZUMA'S

FERRARI

…and other adventures

written, produced, and directed by:

Burt "BS" Levy

Art Direction by:
Art Eastman
Olga Lindsay
Robert Gillespie

Executive Producers:
Carol Levy
Karen Miller
Adam Levy
June Fredlund

Edited by:
Bill Siegfriedt
Tara Treacy
David Whiteside
Bob Woodward

Website by:
Dick Carlson
www.lastopenroad.com

THINK FAST INK L.L.C.

Oak Park, Illinois

1999

<u>published by</u>:

THINK FAST INK L.L.C.
1010 Lake Street
Oak Park, Illinois
60301
www.lastopenroad.com
e-mail **thinkfast@mindspring**

Written and manufactured in the United States of America.

First Edition
October 31, 1999

<u>Library of Congress Cataloging in Publication Data</u>:

Levy, Burt S., 1945–

Montezuma's Ferrari and Other Adventures

1.   Sportscar racing in the 1950's. 2. Automobile mechanics. I. Title

LIBRARY OF CONGRESS CATALOG CARD NUMBER: 99-093834

ISBN: 0-9642107-1-1

Dedicated to the fond memory of

Mike Belfer and Bill Parish

gentlemen, racers, family men, friends

two guys who took the good line through life!

Chapter 1: Montezuma's Ferrari

Big Ed Baumstein wanted a Ferrari in the very worst way. In fact, he *needed* one. Big Ed figured if he had a car like that, those snooty Mayflower Money assholes on the S.C.M.A. membership committee-including their head man and chief committee-chairman-in-charge-of-just-about-everything Mr. Charlie Winthrop Martingale Priddle-would pretty much *have* to let him in. Even if he was half-Jewish (although damned if you could tell which half) and ran a bunch of New Jersey scrap yards for a living. But if he had something as rare and fast and hard to come by as a hot new Ferrari, well, how could they even think about keeping him out? Or at least that's the way Big Ed had it figured, his dollar-plus Cuban stogie doing its usual, deep-in-thought Dutch Roll as he mulled it over.

Me, I wasn't so sure. The way I sussed it out, Charlie Priddle had developed a deep personal dislike for Big Ed that went well beyond your standard-issue, Old Wasp Money snob-grade considerations like occupation, religion, and family background. The truth of it was that he considered Big Ed a loud, obnoxious jerkoff with no sense of manners, breeding, or which fork to use at a fancy dinner table. And it didn't help that Big Ed had threatened to leave the multi-faceted impression of his pinky ring on Charlie Priddle's upper eyelid the first time they met in the S.C.M.A. registration tent at Bridgehampton in the early spring of 1952. I was there when it happened, and almost wished that Big Ed had just said "the hell with it" and laid the little pipsqueak out cold. In fact, I've always felt a little guilty that I was the guy who pulled Big Ed off and led him away-steam rising from both ears, hands clenched into fists the size of petite Easter hams-before he could take a proper swing. I mean, the little jerk really deserved it, you know?

Charlie was also highly peeved about the way Big Ed simply refused to give up-not ever!-and finally, after trying all the usual pressing of flesh and buying of drinks and fluffing of already dangerously over-inflated egos, managed to weasel his way sideways into the S.C.M.A.'s most important race of the year at Watkins Glen by coming up with a competition license from the Triple-A club, who ran most of the oval track racing in the country-including the Indy 500-and co-sanctioned the event. I think it must have cost Big Ed a bundle (or at least a bundle of favors) but he'd grown up on the streets and sidewalks of New Jersey and knew how things got done. If the front door was locked, maybe there was a back way in. Or at least a basement window with a busted latch....

And it was worth it. Rolling his creamy white XK-120 up to the grid at Watkins Glen next to all the golden boys from the Lucky Sperm Club had really given Big Ed a taste for it, what with the crowd whooping and cheering and ooh-ing and aah-ing and churning around ten- and twelve-deep along the curbsides-their camera shutters clattering and tongues clucking like a blessed marimba band-while he sat there in the middle of that enormous pool of attention like a full page magazine ad for Stylish Danger, casually fastening the strap on his freshly painted and perfectly color-matched creamy white racing helmet, pulling down those fresh-out-of-the-box split lens fighter pilot goggles, and tugging at the wrists of those fancy string-back driving gloves he'd bought from that sportycar mail order outfit in California. It was pretty heady stuff, no question about it. Even if he didn't exactly set the world on fire as a race car driver. Fact is, Big Ed got so damn excited he forgot to shift and blew that poor Jag's motor sky high before they even finished the warm-up laps. But that didn't matter. Not to Big Ed. Hell, you could always fix the metal stuff. All that took was a little time, another car or two to drive, a largish pile of money (all of which Big Ed had) and some starry-eyed working stiff at the local corner gas station-like me, fr'instance-who'd be only too happy to put that wonderful lump of British iron right again. And reasonable, too (at least the labor part, anyway) because it was a lot more interesting than doing a muffler job on some up-and-coming tax accountant's Oldsmobile or fixing the wiper motor linkage on a clapped-out Henry J.

Besides, it was occurring to me that there might be a genuine future in the foreign sports car business, seeing as how most of those guys had real folding money in their pockets, beat hell out of their equipment-especially on race weekends!-and had come up the hard way doing business with notorious Manhattan MG/Jaguar dealer and all 'round British Sportscar Shylock Colin St. John over at Westbridge Motor Car Company, Ltd. So they were more than willing to pay what it took and even *thanked* you if you managed to get it right and done on time. And that was pretty much the exact opposite of your rank-and-file Ford, Chevy and Plymouth owners.

The way I had it figured, Big Ed Baumstein was the key to the whole thing, since he had deep pockets, really loved automobiles, and wanted all his cars to look and run perfect all the time. Better yet, he trusted me completely ever since the day I fixed that ugly, now-you-hear-it/now-you-don't grating noise behind the dashboard of his white Caddy convert-it was just the blessed speedo cable, for gosh sakes!-and only let Old Man Finzio charge him a dollar for it. That was the day he palmed me the first of countless five buck tips (which was one *hell* of a lot of money in 1952!) and things only got better when he bought that creamy white XK-120 from Colin St. John. And even better yet when he started trying to race it. Truth is, I really liked Big Ed, even though he'd get loud and pushy and overbearing sometimes and, the more you hung around with him, the more you realized that things were either going to be His Way or No Way At All. But underneath all the bluster and bullshit, Big Ed was a regular guy. Or at least the way we think of regular guys over here in Passaic, New Jersey, where, on a clear, early morning, you can see the shadow of the Manhattan skyline through the mist rising off the Hudson and yet know in your heart that it's a whole different world over there. A regular guy on our side of the George Washington Bridge simply means a guy you can trust with your life (if not always your wife) and who'll back you up even when you're wrong and argue like hell with you even when you're right. A guy you can count on (so long as you don't count on him too much) and a guy who'll take care of you so long as you remember to take care of yourself. And, if you ever get yourself in a jam-and I mean a real *serious* jam-he'll do his level damnedest to get you out of it.

Once.

But the best part was when Big Ed started taking me out to the races to look after his Jag. That started the old heart pumping and juices flowing like nothing I'd ever experienced before and pushed buttons I never even knew I had. Plus it introduced me to promising young hotshoes like my perpetually broke rich-kid friend Cal Carrington, who could drive like the wind that was forever blowing through his wallet, plus genuine racing heroes like ace Allard driver/ex-English fighter pilot Tommy Edwards. Or Phil Walters and John Fitch, who drove for the Cunningham team here and over in Europe. Or hopeless wannabes like Carson Flegley, the pale, stuttering, fourth-generation undertaker from East Orange who couldn't find his ass with both hands when it came to race car driving but loved it anyway, lived not too far from Old Man Finzio's gas station in Passaic, and always seemed to want something done to his MG to make it go faster. But the real goldmine was Big Ed. Like I said before, he wanted his cars to be *perfect,* and the beauty part was that if you turned him loose on a racetrack, you could be absolutely rock-solid certain he'd find a way to break, bend, burst, burn, blow up something, or fling his XK-120 into the trackside scenery. In fact, you could just about bank on it.

And I did.

So I had a lot of important reasons for wanting Big Ed to continue his racing career. The problem was getting him *in* with those snooty S.C.M.A. people so's he could go out and do it all over again once I got his Jag put right again after the blow-up at Watkins Glen. No question Big Ed had the racing bug. Had it bad. I don't think he'd done anything in his whole blessed life that made him feel so, well, *extraordinary.* And there's a lot of magic in that, believe me. Even if you're not much good at it-not much good at it at all!-it's still awfully damn intoxicating to sit there on the grid in a sleek, shiny imported sports car that can

3

top two miles a minute and costs more than most of us rank-and-file dirty fingernail types earn in a year, gazing dramatically off into the distance like a lighthouse beacon on a foggy night while all of the slack-jawed, bug-eyed Ordinary Slob Citizen drools huddle fuzzily in the shadows on the dull side of the fences. No question it was hardly the sort of sensation a guy like Big Ed Baumstein wanted to give up.

Would you?

But Big Ed was savvy enough to know he was on a dead-set collision course with Charlie Priddle and his wolf pack of armband types on the S.C.M.A.'s membership committee-sooner if not later-and that's exactly what Big Ed had in mind when he rolled into the Sinclair the Tuesday morning after I proposed to Miss Julie Finzio inside that oversized, lardass model coffin at the big end-of-season racer's Halloween costume party over at Carson Flegley's family's funeral parlor in East Orange. I remember it was Tuesday on account of it was also election day, when the voters of this great country swept World War II hero General Dwight D. Eisenhower into the White House in an absolute landslide over that egghead Adlai Stevenson guy with the hole in his shoe. The bad news was that Richard Milhouse Nixon of the shifty eyeballs and sweaty upper lip was Ike's running mate and got the vice presidency. Now Cal Carrington's folks (who were genetic Republicans and even flew in from Bermuda or someplace to cast their votes and check up on their top-shelf Scotch supply) thought Nixon was a fine specimen of a right-thinking young Republican, and allowed as how the big problem was he didn't see eye-to-eye with all the Hebe Liberal Pinko communist sympathizers in the press so they tried to make him look bad all the time. Which is not hard to do when a guy has five o'clock shadow by 10:30 in the morning. And many of the good people who lived in the manor houses and estates out around Castle Carrington felt much the same way. Except for the hired help, maybe. But what most of the people around our neighborhood couldn't figure out was, if he really *did* have this big hush-hush slush fund like the papers all said, why the jerkoff wouldn't buy his wife anything better than a cheap cloth coat. Personally I didn't much care, seeing as how I was only nineteen and still too young to vote.

Anyhow, the first thing I noticed when Big Ed wheeled into the Sinclair is that he was behind the wheel of a brand-spanking new Cadillac Eldorado ragtop-creamy white with red leather interior, natch-which was for sure the first one in Jersey and very likely all of New York, too. You have to understand that the '53 Eldorado was a certified Big Deal And a Half and trumpeted to be a very special automobile and certainly lots more than just a few extra flashes of chrome trim and that nifty new panoramic wraparound windshield. Or at least that's what the advertising people at Cadillac were working overtime to make everybody believe. Otherwise, why the hell would anybody pay almost *eight thousand dollars*-why, it was more than a damn Jaguar!-for Caddy's new Eldorado when they could buy a highly similar Series 62 convertible for a little over four grand? It made no sense. But, in the ceaselessly overblown and regularly incomprehensible world of bigtime automobile merchandising, a ridiculous price could become a reason to *buy* just as easily as a reason not to (at least if it was high enough) on account of it made sure you wouldn't see some working stiff butcher, baker, or candlestick maker tooling down the pavement in the same kind of car. It also guaranteed that anybody who reads the funny papers would swivel their heads and blink a few times whenever you cruised down Main Street, marveling at the enormous stack of simoleans it must have taken to drive a beauty like that one home.

For sure it did in Big Ed's case. But then, he'd been buying fancy cars for a long time and knew exactly how the game was played. In fact, I heard the commissions on Big Ed's deals were enough to put the fat, ugly daughter of his favorite Newark Cadillac salesman through beauty school (not that it helped much), buy a mink coat for his fat, ugly wife, cover a few months rent on the apartment he kept for his side girlfriend over in Paterson, and pick up the lawyer's fees and a sizeable chunk of the divorce settlement when his wife found out. In any case, this guy was deep into Big Ed's pockets, and made extra double sure Big Ed got the red carpet treatment whenever he happened by the dealership. I figure he must've slipped the Caddy zone rep a large wad of greenbacks under the table to land Big Ed the absolute first 1953 Eldorado convert in the entire metropolitan New York area. But he could afford to. Like his sales manager and the owner of the dealership and even Colin St. John over at his Jaguar agency across the bridge in Manhattan (or just about anybody else in the retail automobile business) he understood the laws of supply and demand and that there were times it turned your pockets inside out and other times it stuffed them full to overflowing with gold.

This was one of those.

As a seasoned and battle-scarred automotive customer, Big Ed understood those laws, too. There were times-like when Big Ed bought his new black Sixty Special sedan every year-when you dickered and clawed and scratched down to the last, flinty nickel (including threatening to walk out the door and buy a new Lincoln instead or, worse yet, taking your damn business to the *other* Caddy dealership in Weehawken) and there were times you had to pay Full Pop Plus in order to get what you wanted. Which is precisely what Big Ed had to do to get that first Eldorado convert. And he was happy to do it, too, on account of the way it made people's heads rotate and tongues cluck and eyes bug out. That was a nice kind of feeling, knowing you could buy respect with money.

All of which is what brought Big Ed over to the Sinclair that particular Tuesday afternoon. I figured he just dropped by to show off the new Caddy and maybe check up on the engine job on his XK-120, which was still scattered all over the shop in cardboard boxes and coffee tins, waiting for a few more overpriced parts to arrive down at Westbridge and then for me to find the time to actually put it back together. That's one of the toughest problems in the car shop business, when you rip something really complicated into a billion kazillion pieces and then have to wait a few weeks-or more-for parts to arrive and stuff to be finished over at the machine shop before you can put it back together. You worry that maybe you'll forget how it all came apart, you know? And then, even when you've got everything you could possibly need lined up and ready to go, it's hard to peel out of your regular, Ready Cash grind of tune-ups and brake jobs and rusted-out muffler replacements that put money in the till every night and embark on a long, complex project that you're not even sure you can do and that furthermore won't yield nickel number one until it's finished and purring out the door. Of course, all I had to do was *ask* and Big Ed'd peel me off a few more Franklins-just like that!-but he'd already given me a $200 deposit for parts and that was long gone, and it was a matter of professional pride that I wasn't about to put the squeeze on him for more until that engine was all back together and buttoned into the car and growling through the tailpipes like a well-fed tomcat. Besides, Big Ed always had his *other* Jag roadster-the lumpy, oft-crashed and abused ex-Creighton Pendleton, ex-works XK-120*M* he'd bought off Skippy Welcher (against my better judgement) just to run that one stupid airport race down in Georgia while his own Jag was laid up with a compound fracture of the #6 connecting rod and a little attendant valve rash on the piston domes.

"Hey, good t'seeya!" I grinned, running my eyes down Big Ed's new Eldorado. "That's a pretty classy lookin' automobile you got there."

"It's OK," Big Ed allowed casually, unwrapping himself a fresh dollar cigar. "But it ain't no Jagwar."

"Oh?"

"Nah. Not really," he shrugged, "but it's nice." He brushed an imaginary wisp of cigar ash off the red leather upholstery. "I guess I like it pretty good."

"Well," I said carefully, "you probably stopped by t'find out how that Jag engine job of yours is coming along. And it's doing just fine," I lied. "Honest it is. Why, we got the cylinder block back from Roman Szymanski's machine shop the other day and it looks just great. Unbelievable, in fact. That guy does one hell of a job, you know?"

"I thought you had the block back two weeks ago, didn't you?" Big Ed asked, sounding a little puzzled.

"Well, uh, yeah. We sure did. But, see...."

"Lissen," Big Ed broke in, not the least bit interested. I noticed his fancy Cuban stogie was rolling from one side of his mouth to the other, and that was always a sure sign that Big Ed had something Major League Colossal on his mind. "That's not what I came by about."

"It isn't?"

"Nah. I need to talk to you about my Ferrari."

"Your *what?*"

"You heard me. My Ferrari."

Now, this all sounded pretty strange to me, since I knew the sole Ferrari importer for all of North America from the polar ice cap clear down to the isthmus of Panama was Carlo Sebastian over in Manhattan, and he'd already refused to sell Big Ed any of the Ferrari racing models that came through his hands on account of he knew Big Ed would try to enter it in S.C.M.A. race events, and, since a lot of the young, wealthy, black sheep S.C.M.A. bluenoses were his very best customers, that would never do. Besides, Carlo Sebastian had seen and heard enough about Big Ed's skill and talent behind the wheel to realize he was highly unlikely to reflect undying glory on the hallowed Ferrari name. Not to mention that Carlo had pedigreed, well established, cash-heavy people like Creighton Pendleton III lined up with checkbooks in hand for all the hot new cars from the Ferrari race shops in Maranello. Who needed Big Ed?

On the other hand, beneath all the class, charm, opera capes and continental style, Carlo Sebastian was still just another automobile salesman-same as Colin St. John over at Westbridge and the guy with the baby blue sport coat, white leather belt and matching white leather shoes who sold Big Ed his Caddies at the big, glass front Caddy dealership in Newark-and it went against his basic car salesman's nature to turn down a financially pliable guy with a fat wad of cash in his pocket. Especially when he had That Look in his eyes. When it came to buying a Ferrari, Big Ed was what car dealership insiders call "a laydown." I don't believe I need to explain. So there was no question Carlo Sebastian wanted to do a little business with Big Ed, on account of it would be good for both of them. Only he couldn't do it directly. That would never do. But there were ways of getting around a little problem like that. Especially for a clever, shrewd, and stylish little showman like Carlo Sebastian.

"You ever been to Mexico, Buddy?" Big Ed asked, like it was the sort of thing people ask a nineteen-year-old New Jersey garage mechanic every day.

"Huh?"

"You know, *Mexico*. The place with the big hats."

"Sombreros?"

"Yeah. Some *breros* and some *burros* and maybe even a bullfight or two. And that stuff they drink afterwards that can take the shine off galvanized pipe."

"Tequila?"

"No, the other stuff. With the worm in the bottom."

"What worm?"

"Nevermind." Big Ed took a long, thoughtful suck off his stogie and blew two perfect smoke rings in the general direction of the Eldorado's hood ornament. "Anyhow, I was kinda thinkin' you and me maybe oughta fly down t'Mexico together to pick up my new Ferrari."

You could've dropped the engine block of Big Ed's XK-120 on my toes and I wouldn't have so much as blinked.

We wound up going across the street to the little sandwich shop where Big Ed ordered us a couple hefty meatball sandwiches and between mouthfuls explained as how there's this unbelievable open road race called the *Carrera Panamericana* that runs up the central spine of Mexico from the Guatemalan border all the way to Ciudad Juarez just across the Rio Grande River from Texas-damn near 2000 miles all told!-and also about how a slightly used late model Ferrari racing coupe might just become available at the finish line this year. Or at least that's what one of the Muscatelli brothers casually mentioned from the next urinal over when he made a brief pit stop during the big, blowout Halloween costume party at Carson Flegley's family's funeral home in East Orange the night I proposed to Miss Julie Finzio.

Turns out the first *Carrera Panamericana* was held two years before to celebrate the grand opening of the newly finished Mexican section of the Pan American Highway, which someday planned to stretch like a paved zipper from the southernmost tip of South America to the frosty top of Alaska. Anyhow, this was quite a big deal south of the border, on account of there weren't all that many paved roads down in those parts. Not to mention that they'd been working on that particular stretch since about 1935, and a lot of the major league Mexican politicos, industrialists, and merchant trader types figured it might someday lead them all the way to Wall Street. But first they had a little image problem to overcome, on account of most Americans regarded Mexico as a poor, dirty, backward sort of country known mostly for cactus, buzzards, hot food, high octane liquor and donkey shit, and that sort of thing is hardly conducive to high level commerce. And I could understand that, seeing as how if you asked anyone around our neighborhood what they thought about Mexico, they'd most likely conjure up mental images of little dust-collector wooden statuettes and ceramic figurines featuring long-eared *burros* piled up with bundles of stuff like four-legged delivery trucks parked next to fat, swarthy Mexican peasants (dressed in what appear to be white linen pajamas) leaning back against a large Saguaro cactus with a multicolored *serape* (Mexican for bath mat, I think) draped over their shoulders and a big straw *sombrero* pulled down over their eyes, snoozing their way through their traditional afternoon *siesta.* Of course, that's a pretty insulting way to look at an entire nation of industrious, patriotic, hard working, church going people. I mean, who the heck do you think *made* all those little carved wooden statuettes and ceramic figurines of fat, swarthy Mexican peasants in white linen pajamas curled up to take their afternoon naps? Besides, who in their right mind would ever try to take a snooze leaning back against a cactus?

So the Mexican bigwigs were eager to show the rest of the world-and particularly American businessmen and free-spending tourists from north of the border-that their country was as modern and up to date as a hi-fi phonograph, and that you could furthermore drive your way up and down the whole blessed country as easily as you could drive from the Jersey Shore to Lake Shore Drive in Chicago, enjoying a lovely climate, magnificent scenery, beautiful *mariachi* music, friendly, warm-hearted people, and dirt cheap prices on food, lodging, *serapes, sombreros,* tequila, bull fights, all manner of silver-and-turquoise trinkets, a few unusual animal acts, and as many of those little Mexican-peasant-sleeping-against-a-cactus wood carvings and ceramic figurines as you wanted along the way. At least if you didn't mind a few blowouts from the volcanic rock paving surface down at the southern end or fording the occasional stream or crossing the occasional desert not to mention the risk of coming down with a case of Montezuma's Revenge from eating the local food or drinking the local water, either of which could turn your intestinal plumbing into a sort of heavily greased chute with no stops or restrictions along the way.

In any case, the whole *Carrera Panamericana* thing started after some hotshot Pontiac dealer from Mexico City named Antonio Cornejo dreamed it up as a great way to show the rest of the world the new Pan American Highway and everything else Mexico had to offer. The Mexican government thought it was a swell idea, too, and ponied up 250,000 pesos for prize money on top of the 500,000 pesos Cornejo sweet talked out of a bunch of Mexican businessmen.

That instantly made *La Carrera* one of the richest races in the whole damn world. Can you imagine trying to pull a deal like that off here in the States? Fat chance. Why, you'd have politicians mounting their soapboxes and preachers thumping their pulpits and damn newspaper columnists-they're the *worst!*-spilling gallons of ink about the *speed* and the *danger* and the *risk to life and limb.* All the things, in fact, that made *La Carrera* irresistible and earned it fat headlines and plenty of column inches from those same newspapers when they pulled the first one off in 1950. Puffy-eyed scribes running on a diet of bottled water and tequila called it *"the toughest race in the world," "five days with the devil,"* and *"two thousand miles of flat-out hell!"* It was enough to capture people's imaginations all over the globe.

Why, you could even read about it in the *New York Times!*

Most of the cars in that first *Carrera* were standard-issue Detroit sedans like Buicks and Fords and Hudsons and Cadillacs driven by standard-issue American stock car and Triple-A stars who learned their racing on the hard packed dirt and clay at county fairs and Saturday night bullring ovals from Syracuse to San Diego. Several of them had even raced in the Indianapolis 500. There was even one of those bulbous, bustle-backed Nash Ambassador things that reminded the locals of an ironclad armadillo hustled along by two back alley stock car guys from Daytona Beach named Bill France and Curtis Turner. You may have even heard of them. But the ringer in the mix was this team of Alfa Romeos that came over from Italy. They were just sedans, really-not out-and-out race cars-but what with their light weight and better brakes and nimbler handling (not to mention a few genuine international racing stars who had driven in the famous European open road races like the *Mille Miglia* and the *Targa Florio* before) the Alfas did really well-even winning a couple of the mountain stages outright from the bigger American iron. So afterwards they all went back to Italy feeling pretty smug and one of the drivers, an experienced Italian ace named Piero Taruffi (who was known as "The Silver Fox" on account of his silvery-white hair and the fact that he was a pretty shrewd customer behind the wheel of a racing car) casually mentioned to his sometime boss Enzo Ferrari about how well Alfa had done with just some dinky 1900cc sedans, and how, moreover, Mr. Ferrari could really clean up if he sent over a team of his latest, fastest V-12 sports cars for the next one. With, of course, Piero Taruffi "The Silver Fox" as one of the key Ferrari drivers. That went without saying.

Old man Ferrari saw right away that it would be a heck of an opportunity to show how strong, tough, powerful and fast his cars were. Especially since none of the other major European teams knew or cared about *La Carrera* yet and so the opposition figured to be mostly lardass American sedans with lumbering pushrod engines, squishy suspensions and flaky brakes. Not to mention that there was a huge bag of gold in prize money and lots of newspaper ink involved-in a wide assortment of languages!-plus a huge market for fast, exotic sports cars over on this side of the Atlantic. So old Enzo decided to roll the dice and sent two of his latest 212 coupes over to the '51 race for Piero Taruffi and fellow Italian grand prix ace and reigning World Champion Alberto Ascari to drive, and, just like "The Silver Fox" had it figured, they steamrollered the opposition in no uncertain terms. Taruffi's Ferrari took the overall win in just under twenty-two hours (knocking a full *five hours* off the winning time Hershel McGriff's Oldsmobile set the year before) while Ascari put an exclamation point on the whole deal by finishing a solid second. And that was after a bunch of blown tires on the first leg dropped Ascari way back in the pack. It was a hell of a victory for Ferrari no matter how you looked at it. Better yet, there were rich, aristocratic Mexican guys lined up with cash in hand to buy the two team cars after the race was over (at Full Pop Plus, natch) and that surely made more sense than paying some of that substantial prize money to ship two very tired Ferrari coupes that had just been flogged up the entire length of Mexico back to the Ferrari factory for refurbishing.

As you can imagine, Carlo Sebastian made all the arrangements and handled all the cash-it's important in those sort of exotic, aristocratic, high society deals that they appear totally effortless and the money stays invisible-and the two rich Mexican guys who wound up with the cars, Paco Ibarra and Javier Premal, were pleased as hell with their new toys. Wherever they drove them, their country-men shouted and whooped and shook fists in the air, and both of them planned from the beginning to run the cars in the following year's *La Carrera.* Better yet, part of the deal was an under-the-table option on the special, top secret *new* cars Ferrari was planning to build and send over for the '52 race. At least after the factory drivers were done giving them a gentle little two-thousand-mile break-in run from Tuxtla Gutierrez near the Guatemalan border all the way up to Ciudad Juarez on the Rio Grande. All of which meant that a couple reasonably low mileage '51 Ferrari racing coupes might suddenly come on the open market at the end of the '52 race (although it's worth mentioning that most of that "rea-sonably low mileage" was accumulated during two desperate, full-bore runs up and down the mountains and flat out thrashes across the deserts from one end of Mexico to the other).

Not that Carlo Sebastian had changed his mind one bit about doing business with Big Ed Baumstein or what Big Ed could or couldn't do with a race car. But, seeing as how Big Ed had his heart set on getting himself a Ferrari and likewise seeing as how his money was as green as anybody else's, this looked like a perfect opportunity for Carlo Sebastian to dispose of one slightly used-and-abused Ferrari for his fine Mexican customer Javier Premal (who would incidentally be paying a golden left nut for his *new* slightly used-and-abused Ferrari in Ciudad Juarez), get Big Ed what he wanted without actually selling him a car (or at least not directly, anyway), and, most important of all to a car dealer, make a few dibs off the deal on both ends.

Typical of most everything I'd been through with Big Ed since the first day he drove that shiny new XK-120 into the Sinclair, it sounded like one hell of an adventure. But I wasn't real sure I could go. Or wanted to, for that matter. Especially seeing as how the first thing we'd have to do is fly down to the southern tip of Mexico in a series of airplanes. Like most 19-year-old grease monkeys from our part of Jersey, I'd never exactly been up in an airplane before, and, although I had the greatest faith in the smart, serious minded and hard-working gentlemen who design and build things with wings and motors, I'd had enough bad experiences with automobiles to worry a little about being way up there in the sky where there isn't exactly anyplace to pull over and have a little looksee if something decides to go wrong. In fact, even though I could gaze up from my little pump island in Passaic and see airplanes coming in for landings and taking off from airports around New York City at virtually any hour of the day, I still wasn't convinced that anything that big and heavy and made out of metal should really be able to fly. At least not without some sort of guywires or invisible supports or something.

Besides, I had things to look after now, what with more and more sportycar work coming into the Sinclair every week and Old Man Finzio taking his coughing jags off to see the doctors every other afternoon. He wasn't much good when he was there, either, mostly just sitting on the stool behind the cash register, looking out the window through a soft haze of cigarette smoke at the cars and delivery trucks passing by on Pine Street. Oh, he'd still shuffle out to the pumps when a customer rolled in or maybe go back by the workbench and spend an hour or two going through his old Maxwell House coffee can full of nuts and bolts and miscellaneous hardware, carefully sorting them by size and thread pitch and painstakingly straightening out all the used cotter pins in the bench vise. *"Ain't no sense spendin' hard-earned money on new when we got perfectly good right here,"* he'd mutter to nobody in particular while squinting down at a grease-blackened cotter pin the general shape of a seahorse's spine like it was that special, prize needle everybody's always been searching for in all those haystacks.

I never thought I'd come to feel this way, but I really sort of missed the Old Man Finzio who used to yell and kick stray dogs and spit on the shoes of down-on-their-luck customers who asked for credit. Then he'd generally chase them off the property with the sawed-off baseball bat he kept hidden behind the counter. *"Y'kin come back fer thet automobile when y'got cash money in hand, unnerstand?"* he'd screech, shaking his baseball bat in the air like a Hollywood Indian brandishing a tomahawk. *"An' remember, I allus charge fitty cents a day fr'storage, too...."*

But that Old Man Finzio hadn't been showing up too often anymore. At least not since all those doctors' appointments started up a few months before. Fact is, it looked like most of the air had leaked out of the Old Man, and a lot of the piss and vinegar had gone right along with it. Sure, I had old Butch dropping by most afternoons to help out with the phones and order parts we needed and even do a little unit work on the tool bench with carburetors and distributors and stuff. But, no matter how much a guy knows about mechanics-and I mean real, hands-on *fixing,* not just taking stuff apart and putting it back together-there's only so much you can do when you're stuck in a damn wheelchair and your best hand isn't much more than a blunt lump of meat with a couple little stump-end fingers sprouting off of it. Not to mention I worried about leaving Butch and the Old Man alone together. Even for a few hours, let alone a week or more. They just weren't the chummy, pallsy, easy-to-get-along-with type. Either one of them.

"Y'know," I told Big Ed, running it around in my mind, "I'm not real sure I can just, y'know, *take off* and go traipsing down t'Mexico with you. I mean..."

"Sure y'can, Buddy," Big Ed nodded, rolling his cigar over to the side of his face. "It's a *business deal,* see. I'm plannin' t'*pay* ya t'go with."

"Pay me?"

"Absolutely. Howz a couple hunnert bucks sound?"

As you can see, Big Ed could be pretty damn persuasive when he put his mind to it! And I knew precisely what I'd do with an extra two hundred dollars. See, the night I asked Julie about getting engaged there in the warm, satiny-smelling darkness of that oversized coffin in the middle of Carson Flegley's family's funeral home's casket showroom, it wasn't exactly something I'd thought over much in advance. Not hardly. In fact, I just more or less *did* it, you know? Not that there's anything wrong with acting on the spur of the moment. I mean, there's things in life that you think and plot and plan and worry and agonize over, carefully evaluating and re-evaluating and re-re-evaluating every little pro and con until you're head's spinning around like a short-necked dog chasing a polish sausage tied to the end of its own tail. It's like you've got so damn much information you don't know what to do with it, you know? And then there's the times, almost without thinking about it, that you say "oh, well, what the hell" and make some blink-of-an-eye decision that will, in a single, strangely unremarkable moment, change your life forever.

Proposing to Julie was like that. It had to be. Otherwise, I don't think I ever could've mustered up the stones to do it. And it helped that it was real dark and soft and quiet in that coffin, and I could feel her skin all smooth and warm and comfortable next to mine and smell the perfume off her hair. *"So lissen,"* I remember whispering up into the darkness, *"y'think maybe you an' me oughta get engaged or something?"*

I counted a few heartbeats.

"To be married?" Julie whispered back.

I counted a few more thumps. *"Well, uhh, sure to be married, Julie. I mean, what the heck else do people get engaged for?"* I swear I could hear the blood pounding against my eardrums.

"You sure you've thought this over?" Julie asked, measuring every word.

"Sure I did," I lied, not even pausing to think about it.

Then it was quiet for a minute.

"Do you love me?" Julie wanted to know. I guess girls always want to know that stuff.

To tell the truth, I hadn't really thought about it. I mean, not in those exact words. Guys just aren't real comfortable using words like that, you know? *"Yeah. Sure,"* I finally told her.

"Yeah, sure what?" Like I said, girls always want to make you say it.

"Yeah, s-sure I love you," I told her, my guts going all hollow in the middle like when an elevator takes a sudden drop.

Julie took in a long, slow suck of air. *"OK then,"* she finally whispered, easing in a little closer next to me. *"Sure. Why the hell not? You got a ring, Palumbo?"*

"Well, er, ahhh..." I mean, there was no way I could admit that this was just some sperm-of-the-moment whim, *"...see, I thought maybe, well, everybody knows how, umm, artistic you are and everything..."*

I could feel her eyes narrowing, even in the darkness.

"...and so I figured maybe you ought to, uhh, maybe come along and help pick it out yourself, you know?"

"Really?" Julie whispered through her teeth, making sure to add that little wisp of frost girls use to let you know precisely how full of bullshit you are. But then she gave my hand a nice, warm squeeze. *"That's one of the things I like best about you, Buddy."*

"How's that?"

"You're such a lousy liar. You just can't help yourself."

She made it sound like a real plus, you know?

In any case, Big Ed's two hundred bucks figured to do the trick on the ring, since everybody in the civilized world knows you either need a dead lab rabbit or a diamond ring that costs about what you make in a month for any engagement to become truly official. Or at least that's the way it always worked around our neighborhood. In fact, Julie was real specific that we shouldn't say anything to anybody until I came up with a proper sparkler, because she wasn't about to get embarrassed like her cousin Louise DeFazio, who worked as a hat check girl in a club over on the New York side and told everybody she'd gotten engaged to this big fig, nut, and date importer named Tony Provalone. Only it turned out Tony Provalone wasn't his real name, and what he really wanted was to more or less play house every Tuesday and Friday evening and string her along, on account of he was already slightly married to this overweight Sicilian girl from Brooklyn Heights who thought he was in a bowling league. At least until the day she got suspicious and went into his bowling bag, where she found the beautiful custom monogrammed gold metalflake bowling ball she'd bought him for Christmas didn't have a single pin mark or gutter scuff on it-not even under a magnifying glass-and the handsome new bowling shoes that went with it still had the laces stuffed in the toes. She also probably wondered what the little box of Sen-Sen and the crumpled-up receipt from the slinky lingerie department at Gimbels were doing down under the seam in the bottom.

Unfortunately for this Tony Provalone character, his overweight Sicilian wife turned out to be a first cousin of the Muscatelli brothers who spun wrenches on Ferraris for Carlo Sebastian, but used to fix getaway cars for some of our more celebrated local ex-cons and union organizers out of a windowless back-alley garage in the old neighborhood. Although I'm sure none of them had anything to do with it (perish the thought!) nobody seemed much surprised when the steering and brakes apparently failed on this Tony Provolone's year-old DeSoto just about the time the throttle stuck wide open as he was tooling down a one way alley in the Bronx with a brick wall at the end of it. Of course, there were a few muttered questions about where the big dent in the *back* of his head came from, but what with the fire and all and the fact that the investigating officer's sister-in-law lived directly downstairs from the grieving widow, nothing much ever came of it.

Although everybody agreed it was a real damn shame about the DeSoto.

Anyhow, it was quite a scandal, and no way was a girl like Julie Finzio about to leave herself open for anything like that. Not in this lifetime. So when she dropped by the Sinclair later that day-like she always did on Tuesday afternoons to put a few numbers in Old Man Finzio's books and straighten the place up a little-I was all set with this well-rehearsed spiel about Big Ed's trip to Mexico to buy his new used Ferrari and the two hundred bucks and of course the big diamond engagement ring shopping spree payoff at the end of it. But Julie didn't let me get much past the Texas border before her eyebrows shot up like window shades. "What the hell are you telling me, Palumbo?" she snorted. Judging by the way she had her head cocked and arms folded, I was not about to get the chance to answer. "Just what kind of frickin' idiot do you take me for?" she demanded, flicking her forefinger out like a switchblade and tapping it against my chest. "What the hell kind of jerkoff asks a girl to marry him-doesn't even have a frickin' *ring*, can you believe it?-and two days later there's *still* no frickin' ring so she can't tell anybody-not even her mom, fr'chrissakes!-and the bozo who asked her's talkin' about takin' off for frickin' Mexico with some rich hebe who's been *married* more frickin' times than she's been kissed!"

"Aw, Julie. It's not like that. See..."

"Look here, mister Buddy Palumbo," Julie snapped, "there's proper ways you do things and then there's the way slobs, finks, jerks, rats, and stinkin' filthy road gypsies who live in frickin' tents do them. And I'm not gonna stand for that kind of crap from *anybody*, see. Least of all *YOU!*"

"But Julie..."

"Lissen, Palumbo, in a weak moment I said I'd consider maybe gettin' engaged t'you. But I'll be damned if I'll be made a frickin' fool of."

"Lissen, Julie," I pleaded, "I'm not trying to make a fool out of you. I *love* you." Just like in that dark, close, satiny-smelling coffin at Carson Flegley's funeral home, the words came out all by themselves.

"Hmpf," Julie snorted. But I could feel her softening up a little. "Look, Buddy, I was really, you know, flattered and all when you proposed. And I may even be a little bit in love with you, too. Maybe. But don't ever think that means I *trust* you." She looked me right in the eye. "Face it, men are finks. They just can't help themselves."

I couldn't believe what I was hearing, you know? I mean, far as I could tell, I was about the most trustworthy guy on the whole damn planet. At least most of the time, anyway. "You're saying you don't *trust* me?" I said, sounding all hurt and horrified about it.

And that's when Julie looked at me a brand new way, and when she spoke, she all of a sudden didn't sound angry anymore. In fact, she sounded almost a little sad. "I didn't say you weren't trustworthy, Buddy," she said, forming the words slowly and carefully. "But I don't *know* that you are, either. All the married girls I know say the love is the easy part. You can whip it up out of thin air. But trust is something else. It's something you've got to build and earn and prove over the long haul...."

To tell the truth, I felt a little insulted. I mean, I'd been absolutely cross-my-heart-and-hope-to-die True Blue when it came to Miss Julie Finzio. At least if you didn't count that surprise, one-night-stand charity hump up at Elkhart Lake with Sally Enderle. And she was only doing it to bust Creighton Pendleton's balls, anyway. Besides, I didn't enjoy it one bit. In fact, it made me feel heart-sick and miserable and scummy all over. Not to mention that was almost two whole months before and Julie and me weren't really even going out with each other at the time. All of which goes to show that it's a very easy thing to be trustworthy so long as you don't get tested on it. Which, if you are an extremely fortunate individual, doesn't happen very often.

Anyhow, I suddenly got this brainstorm about how I could put this whole deal together, keep everybody happy, and even dodge a few bullets in the process. "Look, Julie," I told her, "I was dead serious when I asked you about getting engaged. Honest I was." I swallowed and looked her right in the eyes. "And that's why we're going out on Saturday afternoon to shop for a ring."

"We *are?*"

"Yup," I nodded. "You and me."

"Really??!!" It's amazing how great it makes a guy feel when he says the exact right thing and turns loose the gushy little girl hiding behind the eyes of the woman he loves.

"Cross my heart," I told her.

Julie took hold of both my hands, leaned her face up into mine, and gave me a nice, soft kiss. Right on the lips. With her eyes all closed and dreamy, too.

It was too good an opportunity to miss. "Uhh, Julie..." I whispered into her cheek, "...then I'm gonna need you to help out a little when I go down t'Mexico with Big Ed. Keep an eye on things, y'know? See that Butch and your uncle don't kill each other."

She eased back away from me, her lower lip rolling out into a little girl pout. "I still don't see why you have to go to Mexico."

"Because Big Ed's paying me two hundred bucks to do it. It's a *professional* deal, see. And that two hundred is what's gonna buy us your diamond ring." I kind of looked down at my shoes. "I didn't exactly, um, have the money, er, *set aside* for one when I asked you..."

"I know," Julie laughed. It was one of those great little laughs she had with sleigh bells hung all over it. "I can see through you like a pane of glass, Palumbo."

Believe it or not, it felt really nice being that transparent. Like I had nothing to hide, you know?

"So, we're going ring shopping Saturday afternoon, huh?"

"Yup," I nodded.

"This Saturday afternoon?"

"Um-hum."

"You *sure* about this, Palumbo?"

"Wanna shake on it?"

"Shake on it?"

"Sure. That's what guys do."

So we shook on it. Like guys do. And then she gave me the nicest, warmest, softest sort of hug. Like girls do even better.

This was starting to feel like the best damn move I'd ever made.

So, come Saturday afternoon, Julie and me went looking for an engagement ring. After, of course, I explained to Big Ed as how I kind of needed that two hundred in advance. "What for?" he asked, not really sounding too interested. I think his mind was off someplace in Mexico thinking about his new Ferrari.

I stood there all tongue-tied for a moment, trying to get the words organized. I mean, it was amazing how easy they came out when I was alone with Julie. Fact is, I hadn't really talked about getting engaged with anybody but her. At least up till now, anyway. "Uh, see," I started out, noticing a strange and uncomfortable waver in my voice, "I, uhh, sorta need to buy this diamond ring, see...."

Big Ed looked up at me from the driver's seat of his new Eldorado like he was evaluating a piece of used machinery he was thinking about buying. Only now he was maybe noticing a few stripped gears in the drive mechanism. I guess I looked a little uncertain. Maybe a little bit scared, even. Very slowly, Big Ed's face spread out into a beaming smile. "Hey, don't worry about it, kid," he laughed. "It'll all work out. It always does, one way or the other. Take it from a guy who's been married a few too many times."

"Oh, I'm not *worried* about it," I lied. "Just a little, you know, *concerned...."*

"Oh, *suuuure,"* Big Ed sneered. "Lissen, you show me a 19-year-old kid who ain't worried shitless about gettin' hitched and I'll show you a guy who's lettin' the *little* head do all the thinkin'."

"Aw, Geez, Ed, it's not like *that."*

"Suuure it's not," Big Ed snorted, punching the dash lighter to re-fire his cigar. But then he stopped and looked up at me again. "Lissen, Buddy, are you absolutely, positively *sure* this is what you wanna do?"

I took a big gulp of air and nodded. "Yeah, I think so," I answered with that strange, shaky waver in my voice. "I s'pose I feel pretty sure about it."

Big Ed looked me up and down one more time and sighed. "Well, I guess it's time fr'congratulations, then." He stuck out his hand and we shook on it. "I really mean it, too."

"Thanks."

Then he kind of sagged back into the upholstery of his new Eldorado and slowly shook his head. "I've heard there's such things as decent marriages out there," he mused, re-firing his fancy stogie and blowing out a single, perfect smoke ring, "even if you couldn't prove it by me." You couldn't miss the sad, faraway look in Big Ed's eyes. "So Buddy's gettin' married…." he said softly into the end of his cigar.

"Uh, and about the two hundred bucks?"

"Ahh, why the hell not?" Big Ed pulled out his money clip, which always held a fat, disorganized wad of Washingtons, Lincolns, Hamiltons, Franklins, and the occasional Ulysses S. Grant, and weeded out two fifties, four twenties, and two tens. "And here," he said, peeling off an extra twenty, "here's one for good luck, too."

"Geez, thanks," I told him.

"Think nothin' of it, Buddy. You're prob'ly gonna need it."

"Say, you got any tips for me?" I mean, if experience was any sort of teacher, Big Ed figured to be one heck of an expert on the subject of marriage. Why, he'd been married more times than anybody I'd ever known.

Big Ed answered me with a low gut chuckle. "I don't know as I'd be the guy to give you any hot tips on the institution of holy matrimony," he laughed. "Besides, you don't gotta go looking for advice once word gets around you're planning t'get married. Believe me, advice'll find *you*…."

And of course he was right, as I discovered that very afternoon when I took the Old Man's tow truck across the George Washington into Manhattan to pick up the last of the parts for Big Ed's engine over at Westbridge. "Bully for you, old chap!" Colin St. John beamed when he heard the news. "Bully for you," he repeated, tweaking the ends of his mustache. Then he took me aside for a quick snort of that phony single malt scotch from the fancy Glen-Something-Or-Other bottle and the two little Niagara Falls souvenir shot glasses he kept hidden behind the parts counter where everybody and his brother knew exactly where they were. "Wonderful institution, marriage," Colin enthused as he poured a scant finger-and-a-half of whiskey down Niagara Falls. "Can't recommend it highly enough. Plants a man's feet square and solid on the ground and puts reason and purpose in his every step."

Which is when it occurred to me that I'd never exactly seen a *Mrs.* Colin St. John around anywhere. "So," I asked him, "have *you* ever been married?"

"Well..." Colin fumbled for the flicker of an instant, "...actually not." He tossed off his half-inch of scotch and, in true master salesman fashion, came roaring right back in a heartbeat. "But that doesn't mean I'm *against* it. Not one bit. Just haven't been, umm, *lucky* enough to find the right one. Why, when I think about how my old mum and dad got on together...." he dabbed a white, bony knuckle at the corner of his eye and poured us each a bonus quarter-inch snort of Scotch. "Here's how, young man. All the best," and he clinked our glasses together.

"I been married twenty-eight bleedin' years," Barry Spline sighed as he wrote out a receipt for Big Ed's new engine hardware. "Got married back in England when I was just a young pup like you. February of '24 it was. Bloody first labor government just got itself elected. Remember it well. Fat lot of good it did anybody, though."

"And you're still married?"

"Aye. We're still puttin' up with one another."

"Twenty-eight years, huh?"

Barry nodded. "Not much to it, really. All yer really need is not too much ambition and t'stay the bloody hell out of each other's way. That's 'ow me an' the missus always done it."

It wasn't exactly the kind of advice I was looking for, you know?

"And let me tell yer another thing," Barry added, leaning in across the parts counter and dropping down to a whisper. *"Yer wanter see what she's gonna look like twenty years on, just lookit the bleedin' mother...."*

A vision of Mrs. Finzio in her flower print pattern housecoat and the puffy pink snowball slippers she wore around their apartment flashed into my head, complete with her piled-up, spray-paint black hairdo, those overly powdered cheeks and penciled-in eyebrows, and the long, thin, pastel-colored Vogue cigarettes with the shiny gold tips she'd fire up and parade around with on special occasions like when the plumber came over to fix the toilet. It was not the kind of image a young guy freshly on his way to get married should have to carry around with him. But it was hard to shake, you know?

Thank goodness Sylvester Jones was around to straighten me out. Like always they had him hidden way back in the shadows of the Westbridge shop where the paying customers wouldn't see they had a colored guy working on their Jags and MGs. "Shee-it, look whut th'cat dragged in," Sylvester grinned, leaning hard into the scraper he was using to get the residue of an old head gasket off an MG cylinder block. Like always he had the butt end of a Lucky dangling out the corner of his mouth and dribbling little puffs of ash down into the cylinder bores.

"So," I asked, "howz things with you?"

"Aw, same ol' shit ever' day. You know how it goes."

"Yeah. I know. And how're old Colin and Barry treating you?"

"Like a five gallon bucket of shit, same's always. How 'bout you? What's the hot news from over on th'frontier side of the Hudson?"

"Aw, it's goin' OK I guess. Workin' my ass off."

"You makin' any damn *money?*"

"Too early to tell, really. But I'm busy as hell. We're gettin' lots more Jag and MG business, and the Old Man's been sorta sick so he's not around much."

"Thass good."

"Yeah," I nodded. "And I sorta got myself engaged...."

Sylvester froze solid in mid-scrape. *"Engaged?"* he gasped. *"YOU?!!"*

I shrugged and gave him a feeble nod. "Yeah. Me. To Julie Finzio."

"Hell, son. You isn't even twenty yet."

"I'll be twenty next month...."

Sylvester looked me in the eye. "You sure it's what you wanna do?"

It struck me that's exactly what Big Ed wanted to know. So I gave Sylvester the same answer. "Yeah, I'm pretty sure. I mean, I didn't really think it over or anything. I just kind of, you know, *did* it."

"Hmm. I see. And did it feel *right* t'you when you did?"

I thought it over. "Yeah. I guess so," I told him. But the image of Julie's mom in her housecoat, slippers and cosmetic war paint kept rotating through my head like a ghost in a revolving door. "So far, anyway...."

"Aw, don't worry over it, son," Sylvester said, putting his hand on my shoulder. "It'll work out. One way or th'other. Hell, ah got married myself th'fust time when I was only but eighteen."

"You did?"

Sylvester nodded and went back to his scraping.

"How'd it work out?"

"Terrible." He paused to wipe off the scraper blade. "Finally had t'kill her t'get m'self the hell out of it."

"What?"

"Shit yeah." He said, leaning into the scraper again. "Set her on fire with a damn blow torch. Boy, you ever wanna smell something *bad....*"

Sometimes it took awhile to catch on when Sylvester was pulling my leg. "C'mon, that's a bunch of bullshit," I told him. "You were never married when you were eighteen."

Sylvester raised his eyes up from the MG cylinder block and focused them directly into mine. "Yes ah was," he said softly.

"You were? Really?"

He gave me the faintest of nods.

"Then tell me what happened. I mean what *really* happened."

Sylvester slowly straightened and set the scraper down. "It was back home in Al'bama. She was hardly sixteen then, and the prettiest little thing y'ever saw." He paused to take the last quarter-inch drag off his smoke. "She loved me, too. Hones' she did. Ah still can't out figger why." A little glow of a smile warmed his face. "Hell, her an' me just about wore mah dick out durin' them first few weeks." Then the smile faded. "But it was during th' d'pression, see, and there wasn't no work a'tall down home. So we d'cided t'come north t'find work up here. Ever'body said you could find plenty a'work aroun' New Yawk City. Plenty a'work. But it *scared* her up here, all alone and away from her people an' all...." he fished another Lucky out of his pocket and fired it up. "Ah did my bes' back then. Hones' ah did. Haulin' boxes. Sweepin' floors. Fixin' cars here an' there. But it was tough an' we was allus down on money. B'lieve me, son, it's harder n'hell t'stay in love when you's poor."

"Why's that?"

"'Cause bein' poor takes up all yr'damn time, that's why."

"So what happened?"

"She wanted t'go back home, see. But I knew there wasn't nothin' fr'us down there. Jus' mo' poor family and mo' mouths t'feed. An' then she up an' died up here with the first chile..." his chin sagged down towards the floor, "...th' baby died, too...."

"Oh, God, Sylvester, that's awful. Really it is. I'm sorry."

"You got nuthin' to be sorry about," he shrugged. "It wadn't none of your fault. Besides, it was a long time ago, Buddy. A long, *long* time ago."

"I mean, I never knew...."

"Hey, don't worry over it, son. Prob'ly shouldn't even a'toldt you. It ain't none of your business anyways." Then he looked me square in the eye. "But ah swear ah'd do it over again."

"You would?"

"In a minute, Buddy. In a minute." He took a long last drag off his cigarette and snubbed it out. "Oh, it was pure fuckin' hell a lot a'th' time. Most a'th' time, in fact. But I surely b'lieve I would." Then he picked up his scraper and leaned back into the MG's engine compartment.

"So you think it's a good idea I get married?"

"Sure it is, Buddy," Sylvester answered without looking up. "Why th'fuck should *you* be happy?"

There was another dose of sage marital advice waiting when I went over by my folks' house that evening to raid the refrigerator, drop off some laundry, tell them about my upcoming trip to Mexico, and casually mention as how Julie and me were getting engaged. And of course my old man was his usual helpful and supportive self about it. *"Married?"* he gagged, almost choking on it. *"YOU??"* Then he went into one of those rolling, evil, *"ho!-ho!-ho!"* cackles that always made me want to bust him one in the nose. "Boy, *that's* a rich one," he laughed. "The little pissant who can't even hold down a job as a stinking gas station mechanic is gonna be the head of a goddam family. *Ho!-ho!-ho!"*

He was of course referring to the time Old Man Finzio fired me for playing tonsil hockey with Julie during regular business hours. And getting fired from the Sinclair was a pretty terrible thing to go through, no doubt about it. But that led to my summer job as a racing mechanic for Colin St. John and Barry Spline over at Westbridge, and, even though I knew my dad would never take me seriously until I threw the last damn shovel of dirt in his grave, I believed that all the stuff I'd learned and all the people I'd met would someday blossom into a nice, tidy little business right there at Old Man Finzio's gas station in Passaic. Only it wouldn't be the Old Man's anymore, it'd be *mine.* Or mine and Julie's, anyway. But there was no point dragging dreams like that out in front of my old man, because he'd just shit all over them. He'd never forgiven me for bailing out of that stinking, no good, punch-the-damn-time-clock union job he set me up with over at his beloved chemical plant in Newark, and especially for how it made him look bad in front of all his lazy, overpaid union buddies when I quit. And if there's one thing my old man held dear to his heart, it was a grudge.

"Tell me, son," he asked through a smile like a gleaming cutlass, "exactly how do you plan to take care of this girl?"

"Well, uhh, I've got a job and she's got a job and..."

"Oh, *sure!*" he sneered. "Let your *wife* work to support you." He shook his head like it was the most revolting thing he'd ever heard.

"But mom said *she* used to work when you first got married. Over at the bakery on Center Street."

"That was *different!*" he snapped. "That was during the damn *depression,* you little shit. Anybody who was lucky enough to find a damn job worked during the depression...."

And that's about when I stopped listening, since no question my dad was about to launch into his Great Depression speech, which I had already heard about fifty kazillion times dating back to the first time I spilled my tapioca pudding out of my high chair when I was six months old. Although I must admit he'd made it more dramatic over the years, what with the part about boiling out tablecloth stains to make soup and the year they ate street pigeons for Thanksgiving dinner (which always made my mom squirm on account of the way she felt about birds-even street pigeons).

Speaking of my mom, she was a lot more understanding about my engagement plans with Julie Finzio. But of course, just like my sister Sarah Jean and all the girls who worked with Julie up at the Doggy Shake on Fremont Avenue and, in fact, just about every other female human being I've ever met, my mom had a terminal case of The Wedding Disease. Right away she wanted to know if we'd picked out a ring yet or set a date and what about going to the church and meeting with the priest and renting a hall and what color satin sashes the bridesmaids were going to wear (it absolutely *had* to match the flowers!) and when could we have Julie over for dinner and, oh, what about her mom, too, and did we plan to have that nice Mr. Finzio from the gas station give her away at the wedding since the poor girl's father got killed in the war....

Naturally that's something I'd never even thought about. In fact, I'd never thought about *any* of that stuff. And that's when-for the very first time-I got this mental picture of the wedding, what with everybody dressed up in satin gowns and cheap rented tuxedos and my old man carrying on at the bar with his union buddies about what a wet-behind-the-ears little dipshit I was and Julie's mom smoking her gold-tipped, pastel-colored Vogue cigarettes while glaring at everybody from under those penciled-in eyebrows of hers and Old Man Finzio, still with the customary three day growth of stubble on his chin and wearing the same exact furnace-black coveralls and cap he wore every day at the Sinclair (only this time with a silk bow tie) pulling his rumpled-up pack of Camels out of his back pocket and lighting one up off the slender white candles in the silverplate candelabra on the corner of the altar. Strangely enough, the only people who *weren't* in the picture were me and Julie!

Anyhow, the upshot of the whole evening was that my mom said she'd be happy to call Julie's mom (*after* we got the ring-I made her promise!) and invite them over for Thanksgiving dinner. And she'd make sure and invite all my sisters, too. Even the youngest one, Mary Frances, who worked across the bridge at some beauty shop in Manhattan and hardly ever came home on account of she was busy sharing a second-story walkup apartment with three other girls on Bleecker Street in Greenwich Village and hanging around with a bunch of scruffy, egghead literary/political types from N.Y.U. I think some of them were even communists (or at least Fellow Travelers) and so our family most usually spoke in whispers whenever they talked about Mary Frances. And then there were the two married sisters who lived out of town, Tina and Ann Marie, who would try to come depending on what they had to do and where they had to be to properly satisfy "the other side of the family," but they'd be sure to drag their kids and husbands along and bring their favorite side dish if they could make it. That was good news and bad news, since I always liked seeing my sisters but noticed as how they'd grown into sort of familiar strangers since they'd moved away. I didn't especially care for the guys they'd married, either. One was a wholesale paint salesman with a big gut who turned bright red after a couple drinks, knew a lot of really disgusting off-color jokes, and thought he was funny as hell. The other guy worked as a raw materials inventory clerk at some big pharmaceutical plant near Albany, and he was so quiet you wanted to check his pulse every now and again to make sure he was still alive. But then I guess nobody's ever good enough for your sisters, you know? Plus I always had trouble keeping track of who was who in that bunch since I only saw them once a year at Christmas and they were both in the habit of popping out a new batch of toddlers every summer the way some people grow perennial flowers. And then there was my sister Ann Marie's signature cabbage, bean, and peanut butter casserole side dish, which looked and tasted like a sickly sweet turd paste and always gave you the farts something awful. But you had to eat it. And then you had to say nice things about it, too. That's part of being a family.

My third sister Sarah Jean would definitely be there on Thanksgiving on account of she'd been living at home ever since she got jilted by that no-good greaseball whose family ran a trucking company over in Jersey City. She'd always been sort of the shy, quiet, stay-at-home quilting and baking type, and, what with the aftershocks of how this guy treated her, she was seriously thinking about becoming a nun. Personally I couldn't see it, because she was neither fat enough or skin-and-bony enough to meet the usual, nun-type physical requirements, didn't really have the guts or know-how to rap somebody's knuckle with a ruler, and figured to make some lucky guy a fine wife and mother one day if she just hung in there and gutted it out. Or at least that's what I thought, anyway. And I told her so. Of all my sisters, I guess she was the one I felt closest to. Even though we didn't have much in common. Or maybe I just felt, you know, *protective* about her. Not to mention that she was the only one who never gave me razzberries, noogies, pink belly, or a Dutch Rub when we were growing up. And it always seemed real comfortable just being around her-we didn't have to talk or anything if we didn't feel like it, you know?-and I really wanted things to work out for her. Sometimes I even thought about praying a little about it. I mean, it couldn't hurt.

Among the many, many things concerning marriage and engagements I knew nothing about, picking out a ring was right up there at the top of the list. I'd asked around about where to shop for a ring-I mean, what the heck did *I* know about jewelry?-and was surprised to find that everybody seemed to have their own favorite jeweler who they were absolutely certain would "take good care of me" and give me the very best deal on the planet. And I needed somebody like that, because no question I was lost as one of Colin St. John's first-time Jaguar customers when it came to diamonds, gold, or anything else where price was proportional solely to the quality and quantity of reflected light. In fact, Colin himself suggested an English jeweler he knew who operated out of a narrow, dirty little storefront on Broadway in Manhattan with big, cheap, hand lettered signs plastered all over the front windows that read: *"INCREDIBLE BAR-GAINS!!! 30%-40%-50% OFF!!!"* and *"LOST OUR LEASE!!! EVERYTHING MUST GO!!!"* That didn't exactly fill me with a sense of confidence or permanence, so I asked I asked Colin St. John about it. "Oh," he explained airily while casually tamping a fresh wad of Cavendish into his pipe, "that's just for the tourists, don't you know. He's been there for bloody ever. This month he's lost his lease, next month he'll be going out of business, and the month after that he'll burn a couple roof shingles in the back room-just for the odor, you understand-and celebrate with a fire sale. It's all part of the game." I could see where Colin and his jewelry store buddy had maybe gone to the same business school together back in England. And it wouldn't have surprised me if there was maybe a quick phone call and a small finder's fee involved if Julie and me wound up buying our ring there.

My mom went on and on about the store where she and my dad got their rings back in '29-why, it was just a month before the market crashed-and about how clean and elegant it was and how pleasant and polite and distinguished the nice older gentleman with the gray mustache who waited on them was-I'm sure he's dead by now-and weren't the rings all lovely and wasn't it nice to be treated that way, like you were almost royalty or something and had a genuine sense of style. The way my mom made it sound, it was exactly the kind of place I was looking for. So I asked her where it was. "Oh, it's long gone now," she said with the usual bright, empty sparkle in her eyes. "I suppose the jewelry business must've gone downhill after the crash and I think they lost their lease or some- thing and then the building burned down a few years later. I think there's an apartment building there now," she smiled like it all made perfect sense, "but there's a florist and a nice little dressmaker's shop on the first floor...."

As usual, Big Ed Baumstein had some slightly more practical advice. "There's only two places t'go shop fr'friggin' jewelry," he said, leveling his cigar at me like a hunting rifle.

"Oh?"

"Yep. Tiffany's or a pawnshop. That's it."

I told him I didn't get it.

"Lissen, Buddy. If she's goin' with, you take her to Tiffany's. Go first class. Dress up a little, even. Put on the dog. Let her feel that warm, stinking glow women get from being extravagant."

"But aren't they kind of, you know, *expensive?*"

"Look, you're gonna spend the same two hunnert no matter where y'go, right? I can even put in a call if y'like. I think I still maybe got a little drag left over there thanks to th'second Mrs. Baumstein. She had herself a real thing about emeralds...."

"And the pawnshop?"

"Well, that's only if you're goin' *alone,* see. I mean, they got a lot of the same stuff as Tiffany's, only at, uhh, *distressed* prices." Through his many years' experience buying and selling scrap industrial machinery, Big Ed knew all about distressed prices. "Just be honest with the guy. Tell him yer lookin' to buy a $300 engagement ring for a hunnert and fifty bucks. Y'always gotta start on the low side, see. Then tell him the girl's got a brother-in-law who's a jeweler an' you'll come back and put a damn dent in his forehead with a tire iron if the brother-in-law thinks that ring's worth a penny less'n three bills."

No question Big Ed knew how business was done.

But, come Saturday afternoon, Julie and I found ourselves at the same old family jewelers up on Fremont Street that we'd passed a million times since we were kids, gawking at velvet-covered platters lined with perfectly regimented rows of sparkling diamonds winking up at us out of slender gold bands, none any bigger than a 3/16ths flat washer and every one worth more than a damn cylinder head overhaul on a Jaguar twincam. I felt kind of uncomfortable about it, to tell the truth. I mean, those diamonds didn't *do* much of anything except sit there and flick light at your eyes and cost a lot of money. But it was nice any- way, being there with Julie and seeing how her eyes sparkled right back at those diamonds and how she squeezed my hand when she saw this absolutely special and perfect one that looked pretty much like all the rest to me. Until she slid it gingerly onto her finger, that is. That made it really stand out from the others, no two ways about it.

Naturally it was more than I'd planned to spend-two hundred and thirty five bucks, in fact-but I think that's sort of an unwritten law about buying engagement rings. Or wedding rings. Or dining room sets. Or carpeting. Or station wagons. Or home appliances. It's a test, really. To see exactly what the prospective bridegroom will do when his loving wife-to-be holds up a finger wearing the ring she absolutely adores and cherishes and never wants to take off but that perhaps costs a little bit more than he'd planned to spend. That's when she looks him right in the eyes with her face all lit up with joy and expectation and waits for no more than a few fleeting heartbeats to see what he'll do. And I'm proud to say I passed that test with flying colors, as the same voice that proposed to Julie in the first place piped up again and told the guy with the oh-so-attentive smile that, yeah, sure, we'd take it.

As you can imagine, I was a couple bucks short, but fortunately they had to size it down a little so I gave 'em a two-hundred-and-twenty dollar deposit and said we'd be back to get it on Wednesday. It was actually worth the extra thirty-five bucks just for the way Julie put her arm around my waist and leaned her head into my shoulder as I walked her up the street to drop her off for the early dinner shift at the Doggy Shake.

Chapter 2: Terror in the Sky

You'd have thought that buying a ring was the end of it and that afterwards I could just slide back into my regular routine of being an up-and-coming sportycar mechanic and one of the most promising young garage operators in the greater metropolitan New York area. But that's not the way it worked-not at all-and without warning my life turned into a stupefying roller coaster ride of dates, times, commitments, arrangements, complex interconnected family relationships and dumbass social details that I'd never so much as paused to think about when I oh-so-casually asked Miss Julie Finzio to get engaged. It wasn't that I didn't love my family (well, except for my dad a little, maybe) but there is simply no way to be involved with families just slightly. Especially where engagements and weddings are concerned. And everything was getting so damn *complicated!* We absolutely *had* to have Julie and Mrs. Finzio and maybe even Old Man Finzio over for Thanksgiving dinner on the 27th so they could meet the whole family (at least if my two far-flung married sisters and *their* families could make it) plus even my nervous old maiden Aunt Rosamarina, who'd more or less been on the outs with my folks ever since she let me move into the leaky, drafty little pup tent of an apartment over her garage that Cal and me damn near burned down during our ill-advised and thoroughly inebriated fireworks extravaganza on the Fourth of July. But, now that I was getting *married,* well, all was forgiven and wasn't it all just *so* wonderful and have yourself a nice glass of Asti Spumante and another slice of *calzone.* I have to tell you, the thought of having all those people crammed together in my folks' living room with their attention focused directly on Julie and me was making me more than a little nervous. Especially my old man and Old Man Finzio, seeing as I sensed those two would be on a direct collision course over something (damn near anything would do) before the evening was over. Not to mention that the looming probability of becoming a blood relation to Old Man Finzio and Julie's mom-complete with her nasty disposition, fancy pastel cigarettes and penciled-in eyebrows-was giving me regularly recurring daydreams that were more like nightmares.

So all of a sudden I was really looking forward to that trip down to Mexico with Big Ed for the *Carrera Panamericana,* even if it did involve climbing on an airplane for the first time in my life. A whole series of airplanes, in fact, since no airline flies direct from New York or Jersey to the southern tip of Mexico. And I was more than a little worried about the prospect. Even so, I was more than ready to make my escape when Big Ed pulled up the driveway to my Aunt Rosamarina's garage just before sunup on Saturday, November 15th. He was driving the black Sixty Special Caddy sedan with the suspiciously thick glass in all the windows-no way was he gonna leave his new Eldorado parked at the airport!-and I had all my stuff packed in a thoroughly presentable, genuine leather suitcase that Cal Carrington had borrowed me for the occasion. No way was I going to use the mangy old straw one up in my folks' attic or the darling little pink one with the Cinderella design that my mom used to pack my sisters for sleepovers when they were kids, and the old cloth laundry bag I'd pressed into service for my drive to Elkhart Lake with Tommy Edwards in the two Jaguar C-types just didn't seem appropriate.

To tell the truth, my friend Cal Carrington was jealous as hell that I was flying down for *La Carrera,* since he was absolutely dying to go himself on account of all the big international factory teams he dreamed about driving for some day would be there. Being stuck on the road and palling around with them for five solid days in the middle of nowhere might offer an opportunity to chat himself up with the team managers and maybe even bullshit his way behind the wheel of something (as only Cal could do) so he could show them what he could do. Which was plenty. Really it was. But Cal didn't have anything to drive since his folks took away his ratty '47 TC (not that it would've been much use on a race like *La Carrera)* plus no way to even get there since they'd likewise pinched off the old cash flow over at Castle Carrington. Then again, Cal had embezzled a large wad of what was supposed to be college money to buy that TC on the sly and go racing in the first place, and he hadn't been above going through every purse, pants pocket, top dresser drawer, and beaded evening handbag in the house to finance his dirty little habit throughout the summer. And now it was all coming home to roost. Which was really too bad, since I'd seen Cal drive and knew for certain that he was one hell of a talent behind the wheel of a racing car. The pitiful part was that his family could've easily afforded to turn it into a career for him if they only wanted to. But they thought it was all a thorough waste of time-not to mention foolish, dangerous, frivolous, extravagent, showy and outlandish-although I personally couldn't see how it was any worse than traipsing back and forth between all those fancy places they went to in Europe, the Hamptons, the Carribean, and Palm Beach, always with the same rich, dull, perfectly dressed crowd who sucked up six or seven tumblers of top shelf hooch every day just to make each other seem interesting. Is that the kind of life you'd want your kid to aspire to?

Typical of my well-to-do but forever broke buddy Cal, he needed a way to vent some of the envy and frustration he felt about me flying off to *La Carrera* with Big Ed while he sat home thumbing through old copies of *Road & Track,* reading up on how to hot-rod the engine in the raggedy old MG he no longer had. So he borrowed his mom's new two-tone Packard the morning after they took off for Bermuda (foolishly thinking they'd hidden all the keys, but not counting on the spare set he'd had made at the Packard dealership to replace the ones his mom had "lost" when she dropped her clutch purse over the railing of the Queen Elizabeth as it set sail for Southhampton earlier that summer-or at least that's what Cal told the service counter guy) and cruised over by my Aunt Rosamarina's garage while I was off working at the Sinclair. I figure he must've spent half the day there, carefully going through the bundled-up copies of the *New York Times* she was saving for the next paper drive at the local grammar school. Then he came over by the Sinclair to drop off that smart-looking leather suitcase, cadge a few gallons of gas, and tell me every gory detail of all the Major Air Disaster horror stories he'd dug up in those old copies of the *Times*. He'd even torn out a few particularly grisly photographs and stuck them up here and there while I was out at the pumps taking care of customers. I'd go to take a whiz and taped to the mirror there'd be a grainy picture of this military C46 that came tumbling out of the sky not too far from us back in December and landed with all the effortless grace of a watermelon dropped from a second story window. In fact, you couldn't even tell it was an airplane any more, since it looked more like a crushed eggshell surrounded by what they sweep out of the grandstands after the last game of the World Series. I found another cheery shot inside the top of Butch's toolbox, right behind the set of deepwell sockets, featuring the scattered remains of a cargo plane that had run itself into the side of a mountain way out in the middle of nowhere. It looked pretty damn bleak, no two ways about it. And when I hit the cash register key to make change for the pop machine, what should I find inside but Cal's absolute favorite, that famous wire service photo of the Hindenburg going down in flames over by Lindenhurst. Naturally Cal was following right behind me so he could see my reactions and maybe even add a little audio embellishment, and it got to where I was ready to pop him right in his handsome, all-American kisser if I caught him whimpering *"Oh, the humanity!"* one more time.

"Hey, knock it off, OK?" I told him. "I don't think that's funny at all."

"Of course it's not funny," Cal agreed, an evil gleam dancing in his eyes. "After all, this is serious stuff. And I'm not doing this just to scare you or anything. That would be pretty rotten, wouldn't it."

"It sure would."

"Ah, but you need to *know* these things, Buddy. Because an *informed* air traveler is an *aware* air traveler, and an *aware* air traveler is the one who's going to be smart enough to get a seat close to the door so he can get the heck out of there if an engine catches fire or the wings falls off."

"Look, that's enough, OK?"

I might as well have poured gasoline on a bonfire. "Of course, the problem with jumping out of an airplane is that it doesn't do much good unless you have a parachute. You *do* have a parachute, don't you?"

This time I just glared at him.

"Oh, no. That's right. It's the *pilot* who gets the parachute. And maybe the co-pilot, too. Or maybe not. I'm not sure how their contract reads." He furrowed his brow. "Maybe you should pack a bed sheet?"

"I'll be sure to."

He knitted his brow even tighter. "But that won't help either, will it? After all, your suitcase will be down in the cargo hold where you won't be able to get at it...*WAIT!*" Cal snapped his fingers. "Maybe you could carry it like a large pocket handkerchief!"

"That's another swell idea."

Cal pointed sadly to the picture of the Hindenburg going down in flames. "Poor devils," he choked. They never had a chance."

"Hey. I said *stop* it!"

"Oh, don't take it so seriously, Buddy. After all, there *were* survivors. Plenty, in fact. Why, one of them lives right down the road from a cousin of mine in White Plains. Of course, he was horribly disfigured. Lost both his arms and legs. And his ears, nose, and lips were burnt right off his face. But he *survived!* Isn't that wonderful?"

"You're a sick individual, Cal Carrington."

"No, I think it's *inspiring,"* Cal continued, not missing a beat. "He not only survived, he went on to go land himself a top government job, doing something vital and worthwhile for the whole community."

"Oh, really?" This I had to hear. "What's he do?"

"You mean you missed it in the newspaper? He moved down to Allentown and serves as a key sandbag whenever the river floods."

"That's genuinely disgusting, Cal," I groaned, trying not to laugh.

"Of course, they have to remember to put him in one of the top rows."

There was nothing for it but to join in. "Hey, come to think of it I *did* see that story in the newspaper."

"You did?"

"Yeah. I read where he plays sports now, too."

"He does?"

"Sure. Didn't you see the picture? He plays baseball."

Cal instantly fed me the straight line. "Oh? What position does he play?"

"Second base!" we chimed in unison, and that was the end of it.

My case of the jitters got even worse when Julie and I went to the movies Friday night in the Old Man's tow truck. She wanted to see Rita Hayworth and Glenn Ford in some picture called *l'Affaire en Trinidad,* which was actually some sort of foreign espionage story but sounded like one of those dumb, smarmy "women's movies" about tragic love affairs in faraway places between breathtakingly beautiful yet hopelessly sweet and sensitive female leads who dress well but never seem to work and their square-shouldered, smoldering-eyed, a-man's-got-to-do-what-a-man's-got-to-do leading men, who inevitably also dress well but likewise don't seem to hold down a regular job. This lack of a 9-to-5 occupation leaves plenty of time for sitting in romantic seaside cafes and leaning against fancy wrought iron railings overlooking the Mediterranean and tooling top-down along the French Riviera in the most amazing open cars that never seem to muss their hair or flutter the stylish, devil-may-care silk scarves a lot of those leading ladies favor wearing around their necks. Not to mention some of the leading men, too. I can never follow the plot lines, but most of the chatter is generally about how *impossible* it all is for them to be together. Even though they are. You figure it out.

Like I said, those kind of movies don't do much for me-hell, they're even too boring to sleep through-and I doubt I'm the only male person on earth who feels that way. So I told Julie I'd much rather see *Battle Zone* with John Hodiak. But Julie made it clear she wasn't about to sit through any grisly, blood-and-guts war movie on our last night out together. So we compromised on taking in *The Crimson Pirate* with Burt Lancaster, which was playing over at the Tivoli on Fremont Street. But there was a long line on account of it had just opened and neither of us felt much like waiting out in the cold for an hour just to get the last two seats in the front row where you spend the whole time looking directly up Burt Lancaster's nostrils.

It was getting late and I knew Big Ed would be around for me bright and early next morning, so we decided to cruise over to the outdoor drive-in on the edge of town where Julie and I had kissed for the very first time in the spacious front seat of Big Ed's black Caddy sedan. Normally Julie wouldn't think of going to the drive-in movies in the Old Man's tow truck, but, now that we were officially engaged with a ring and all to prove it, and furthermore seeing as how I was getting ready to leave on this big, faraway airborne adventure to Mexico, she was willing to make an exception. So long as we parked well towards the back, anyway, where none of her girlfriends from the Doggy Shake were likely to see us. That actually sounded pretty good to me. But, wouldn't you know it, the drive-in had a twin bill that night, and, after getting ourselves comfortable during the last fifteen minutes or so of a western called *The Big Sky* with Kirk Douglas, what comes on the screen but *Breaking The Sound Barrier* with John Richardson. If you've seen that particular movie, you know it's hardly the sort of thing you want to see before taking off for your first-ever trip in an airplane. It's mostly the usual old Hollywood Test Pilot stuff, and of course there's the inevitable Sidekick Buddy who gets killed right on schedule at the end of the second reel. *"There's a little buffeting now,"* he crackles calmly through the static while the stick jumps around in his hands like the business end of a jack-hammer. Then it won't respond to the controls. *"She's not responding to the controls,"* he crackles through the speaker again, only not sounding quite so calm this time. Remember, he's just the Sidekick Buddy, so he's allowed to show fear. In fact, it's pretty much mandatory. Meanwhile, everybody in the tower is staring into the radio speaker and looking back and forth at each other with sad, knowing eyes and then there's this horrible, pilot's-eye view of the desert floor rushing up at the screen like a semi with failed brakes and then you're back in the tower staring up at the radio speaker when the static suddenly shuts off like somebody pulled the plug.

Like I said, it was hardly the sort of movie you'd want to see the night before your first plane ride, and even having Julie there next to me didn't much help. Not even when she nuzzled up against my neck and did that thing she does with my ear whenever she wants to make sure she has my undivided attention. But I was frozen wide-eyed at the wheel of the Old Man's tow truck, watching pilot after pilot lose control and crash into that suddenly silent radio speaker (I guess they didn't have a big enough budget to include an actual experimental jet fighter crash) but at least I was picking up a little insider, supersonic pilot-type infor-mation about what to do if any of the airliners I'd be riding in the next day accidentally ran smack dab into the sound barrier. According to the movie, the whole trick was to "reverse the controls," and then the plane would slip past Mach 1 like a quarter-inch lock washer falling into a tub of gearlube.

I sure hoped the pilots I'd be flying with the next day knew that!

After the movie Julie and me went over to Weederman's for a couple sodas and an order or two of fries, and of course she could tell I was a little tensed up. "You're worried about that trip tomorrow, aren't you?"

"Nah," I lied. "I'm just a little, you know, *preoccupied.*"

"'Preoccupied,' huh?" Julie grinned through an insider smile. "That wouldn't be anything like 'scared shitless,' would it?"

Truth is, it'd gotten to be like one of those deals back when you were a kid waiting for some huge, earth-shaking event to arrive. Every minute drags by like it has anchor chains hanging off it-especially when you're alone in bed in the middle of the night-and then, sudden as the snap of a thumb and forefinger, it's the night before and you're alone in bed on the far side of midnight, frozen with anticipation and feeling like it's not really real-it *can't* be!-and worrying that you're not nearly prepared. Only when you're a kid, it's usually fun stuff like Christmas or your birthday or the circus coming to town. Then you start growing up and it turns into things like algebra exams and report cards and dental appointments and the day the rent comes due. Or bone-headed plane trips that will take you halfway down the hemisphere, much of it on Mexican airplanes flown by Mexican airline pilots and serviced by south-of-the-border Mexican airplane mechanics who don't even speak English and perhaps don't know all the little insider tricks required to keep a few hundred tons of wings, engines, fuselage and tail section up in the air. In fact, you're not even convinced of that when it comes to our own home grown, English speaking, right-here-in-the-United-States-of-America airline pilots and airplane mechanics. Even the ones with New Jersey accents.

So I was feeling very nervous indeed by the time Big Ed and me found ourselves tooling towards Newark in the black Caddy sedan around dawn the next morning. In fact, I was damn near frozen paralyzed by the prospect of climbing aboard the first of several different airplanes and airlines we'd have to fly (some as I mentioned neither piloted nor maintained by people who spoke English) to get down to some primitive little airport on the outskirts of Tuxtla Gutierrez near the southern tip of Mexico, not all that far from the Guatemalan border. I'd actually gone down to the library and looked it up in a world atlas. I also did a little studying about what kept anything as big and heavy and made out of metal as an airplane up in the sky, and, although it seemed an overwhelming majority of intelligent people agreed it was simple physics and aerodynamics, a large portion of me still wasn't convinced.

And it didn't help at all that the Newark airport was just "reopening" that very day on account of it'd been closed for awhile because of all the airplanes it'd recently been depositing in downtown Elizabeth, which was just a hop, skip, and jump down the flight path from the end of the main runway. I'd read all about it in a *The New York Times* article while I was laying wide-eyed awake in my apartment somewhere around two ayem the night before. The story went into great detail concerning the events leading up to the airport's closing. Seems the previous December, a military plane trying to make an emergency landing had crashed into Elizabeth and killed all 56 people on board. Then, barely a month later, a commercial airliner on a routine approach fell out of the sky and again killed everybody on board (including ex-Secretary of War Robert Patterson, proving air disasters never play favorites) not to mention seven poor slobs on the ground who certainly must've thought in those last, terrifying moments that the commies had finally launched that nuclear missile strike Senator Joe McCarthy had been warning everybody about and that the world was coming to an end. Then-less than three weeks later, can you believe it?-there was yet another terrible air crash and the citizens of Elizabeth got pretty damn vocal about all the scrap metal, busted luggage, and assorted human carcasses the Newark airport was dropping in their laps. So the place was closed for "renovation," and, wouldn't you know it, Saturday, November 15th-*that very day!*-was when the Newark airport officially reopened. But the worst part was what I'd read about the changes they'd made to "renovate" the Newark airport and make it safer-most of which amounted to building a brand new runway that pointed the other way so it was no longer aimed like a cocked pistol towards the citizens of downtown Elizabeth.

"Ahh, don't worry about it," Big Ed advised as we wheeled into the airport parking lot. "Those planes all crashed trying to land. We're just taking off."

Somehow I didn't feel exactly comforted.

It was pretty busy inside the airport terminal (couldn't they maybe call it something else, like a "station" or a "depot?") and I was frankly amazed at how nonplussed and nonchalant all the people there seemed about flying. Even the little kids and old ladies. We checked our bags across from a coffee shop area where a few pilot, co-pilot and navigator types were having coffee and smoking cigarettes and talking about sports and good looking stewardesses, and right behind them were a bunch of stewardesses chattering about the latest new hemlines and lipstick colors and good looking pilots, co-pilots and navigators, and all around them were tables full of soon-to-be airborne airline passengers drinking coffee and munching on sweet rolls and reading the morning papers and chewing the fat as if climbing on a damn airplane was nothing to worry about at all. It made me feel like I was spray painted yellow and the paint was still wet.

Big Ed bought us a couple cups of coffee and a half dozen glazed doughnuts, but I couldn't eat much of anything and just stared at my plate like it was the last meal of some guy on death row in an old Jimmy Cagney movie. So Big Ed ate mine after he'd finished up with his. "There's no point lettin' 'em go to waste," he explained, pushing yet another doughnut into his kisser. "After all," -this part came out kind of muffled since he was talking directly through the hole of his fifth doughnut- "children in Europe are starving." Watching Big Ed eat was like watching a train wreck. You wanted to turn away, but you just couldn't. On the other hand, it was usually enough to kill your appetite, so it might make a pretty good idea for a diet.

Then it was time and we headed towards the gate, and Big Ed noticed right away that I was looking a little green around the gills and shuffling along on my pants cuffs like I was taking that final, Jimmy Cagney movie hike towards the gas chamber. So he bought us a pack of Beeman's chewing gum and a fresh copy of the *New York Times* and suggested maybe I should read a little to take my mind off things. Sure enough, right there on page one was this story about a C-119 Flying Boxcar that crashed into a mountainside in South Korea and killed forty-four unlucky G.I.s who had been fighting their asses off and thought the were on their way to a little well deserved R&R in Tokyo.

Big Ed must've seen how my eyes bugged out. "Here. Gimmie that," he said, and flipped through a few pages until he found a story about a collision at sea between a tanker and a troop ship that killed seven and injured 33. I'm not sure exactly what his point was, but for me, it only served to underscore the notion that you could possibly survive most of your standard issue land- and sea-based transportation disasters, but, when it came to air crashes, they killed people in crowds and without exceptions, and the only real uncertainty was if they'd be able to separate enough of you from the surrounding scenery to give a proper heft to the casket.

We were flying Pan Am, and the plane turned out to be one of those enormous Boeing Stratocruisers, which were really converted military cargo planes and looked like a gigantic tin guppy. With wings. Attendants in dark blue caps and coveralls wheeled this tall, naked metal staircase that didn't go anywhere over to the fuselage and opened the door, and I swear I almost got a nosebleed just climbing to the top. I must admit, that Boeing Stratocruiser was pretty damn plush inside, what with recliner seats that were almost even big enough for a guy like Big Ed, plus this nifty "conversation pit" down on the lower level that looked more or less like a railroad club car stuffed into a walk-in closet. "We'll go down there later," Big Ed said. "After we reach cruising altitude." It was reassuring he sounded so certain we'd make it to 'cruising altitude.' We found our seats and strapped in-I naturally had to take the one by the window since it was hard enough for Big Ed to stuff himself into the one on the aisle-and then I thumbed through the *Times* a little more while we waited for everybody else to do the same. Believe it or not, this is the first story I found:

COCKER SPANIEL CLINGS TO PLANE 2000 FEET UP!

It was just a routine flight for Roy Aitcheson as he gunned his seaplane along at 2000 feet. Until he looked out the window. Then he nearly froze with fright. What the pilot saw was the Aitcheson family's cocker spaniel pup, Curly, clinging to a pontoon. The dog's tail was towards the front and his fur was blowing like crazy.

Mr. Aitcheson throttled the plane down to 60 miles an hour. Then, making a slow, flat turn, he flew back to Lake Sammamish with Curly still hanging on and everything turned out all right.

And that's about when the engines fired up and my ass sucked a cocker spaniel pup-sized wad of upholstery up out of the seat cushion. Believe me, there is no sound on earth like the wild, oscillating drone of four supercharged, 18-cylinder Pratt and Whitney rotaries as heard from inside the enormous tin cigar tube they're about to drag into space. When a Hemi-powered Allard hauls past at Bridgehampton or Watkins Glen, you can feel it throb right up through the ground you're standing on. But then it melts off into the distance and the only thing left is the echo reverberating in your eardrums and a few hairs standing on end that will eventually ease back down. But in an airplane fuselage-and especially a big, lumbering, oversized, overpowered monster like that Boeing Stratocruiser-you're *inside* that noise. Swallowed. Surrounded. Engulfed. And the scary part is that it's not a *regular* sort of sound-not a steady mechanical buzz or a regular motorized heartbeat or a finely meshed machine shop hum. Not hardly. No, it's more like eight or ten of Big Ed's dump trucks clearing their throats to do a little barroom singing someplace down in a subway tunnel on the night of a full moon. Or at least that's what it sounded like to me, anyway.

That's when Big Ed leaned over and hollered over the noise, "You grip those armrests any tighter and you'll leave dents."

"Huh?"

"I said take it easy, OK? Hell, we haven't even started to taxi yet."

Right on cue the engines picked up in ragged unison and that big Boeing Stratocruiser lurched forward towards the runway. Which is about when I left the first of those dents Big Ed warned me about in the armrests. They would not be the last. I peered desperately out the tiny, round-cornered window that had been carefully placed so you had to crane your neck at a strange angle in order to see anything-I wondered just who the hell designed these things, you know?-and watched the airport terminal and flight apron and fuel trucks and luggage carts slowly peel by. You could feel the jounce and rumble of the wheels over the uneven concrete slabs (what was this thing riding on, bed casters?) and hear the engines lift and fall irregularly like they were gargling too much fuel. For some reason, it reminded me of when Julie and I were stuck on top of the Ferris wheel at Palisades Park the night we went out for the very first time. God knows it opened up the same cold, empty hole in my gut between my belly button and bladder. On the Ferris wheel, all I could think about was the jerky, unsteady way it moved and all the rusty, long neglected cables, turnbuckles, clamps, and clevis pins that held it together. Only this was much worse, since a Boeing Stratocruiser has so many more nuts and bolts and seals and rivets and parts and pieces and switches and gears and gigantic, heavily rotating gizmos to keep happy and organized if the damn thing is going to have any chance at all of climbing into the sky and staying there. Sometimes a grease monkey's understanding and sympathy for mechanical things can be a real blessing. Other times....

But remembering that night at Palisades Park actually helped. I closed my eyes and I could see it almost like I was there. That was our first real date, and even though it was only back in May, it seemed like a lifetime ago. Maybe two lifetimes. Why, I couldn't even recognize the goofy, gawky, fumbly little kid sitting beside her on the Ferris wheel, desperately trying to figure his way into a kiss. So much had happened since then, I could damn near write a book about it. But I kept thinking back to what it was like that night. And not so much about when she got sick over the side and upchucked on the poor slobs in the next gondola down or how I made a point of giving her a hard time about it for months afterward. Or maybe longer. No, I thought about what it felt like when we cruised up the parkway from the Doggy Shake on our way to the amusement park, and how she slid over next to me in the front seat of Big Ed's Caddy white convert and how I could feel her body all warm and soft against me and the pulse beating just under her skin and smell the perfume off her neck and hair. Hell, I didn't even know her then. But even so I knew something special was happening, and especially how easily we fit together and how comfy it was when we did. And now we were engaged to be married. Like my mom and dad and Butch and Mean Marlene and all the other miserable, hateful, angry, disappointed, disgusted and disillusioned grown up married couples I knew.

But we weren't going to let that happen to us!

Were we?

Then the plane did a slow, cumbersome U-turn and I felt a solid elbow dig from Big Ed. "Here, chew this," he said, waving a stick of Beeman's under my nose. "It'll help your ears pop."

"Huh?"

"Just chew it, OK?"

So I folded the gum into my face while the engines all rose up in unison like a fanfare for the end of the world and that enormous Boeing Stratocruiser started lumbering slowly down the runway. It gained speed almost painfully at first, but then kept going faster and faster and faster like a runaway locomotive until, without warning, I felt the nose tilt upward and we lurched into the sky. If I'd had any sort of proper control of my bodily functions, I would've shit my pants. Outside my window, Newark fell away from us like a life raft floating off into the distance in the middle of the Pacific Ocean and that cold, empty hole in my gut opened bigger and bigger as it drifted further and further away. Then came this deep, anchor-chain shuddering noise right up through the floorboards followed by a heavy metallic clunk that made the blood freeze solid in my veins. *"Jeezuschristalmighty!"* I whimpered through a perfectly matched set of perfectly clenched teeth. *"WhatthehellwasTHAT??!!"*

"Hey, take it easy," Big Ed laughed. "That's just the gear coming up."

"The *what?"*

"The landing gear. You know, the wheels. We don't need 'em anymore now that we're up in the air."

Personally, I would have preferred that the pilot kept the wheels down, just in case a few of the engines caught fire or a wing fell off and we had to make an emergency landing. And about then we passed through a cloud layer and hit the first serious air pocket of my life and I about crushed both of those armrests like so much tinfoil.

"Hey," Big Ed hollered over the engine drone. "It doesn't do shit for good to hang on t'those armrests so tight."

"Howz that?" I answered in a weak falsetto.

"To hang on so tight," he repeated, tapping on my knuckles. They were bleached about white from their death grip on the armrests. "If the damn plane goes down, that seat you're sittin' in is gonna go right along with it."

"Oh. Yeah."

Flying didn't seem to bother Big Ed at all. But then he'd done his share of it, taking business trips every now and then or jaunting off to Miami or Miami Beach in the wintertime with whoever the current Mrs. Baumstein might be or even all the way down to Havana on his own when divorce proceedings were going on. So Big Ed was pretty comfortable in an airplane. But while he just sat there and calmly read his paper, I spent the first couple hours aloft with my neck craned forward to the window and my nose pressed flat against the glass, staring at the wing and those two huge, droning Pratt & Whitney engines in their shiny aluminum nacelles. It was like I figured as long as I kept an eye on them, they wouldn't dare to explode in flames or have a prop come loose and shear the fuselage in half like a buzzsaw. I didn't even dare blink. And I hoped that somebody just as mechanically sharp and scared shitless as me was likewise doing no-blink sentry duty on the other side of the plane.

But you can only hold a hard edge of fear like that for so long, and eventually even self preservation gets boring. Besides, we were up above the clouds now, and, even though I knew it was only an illusion, they looked like a soft, cottony, comfortable place to land if anything bad happened. I'd never seen the topside of clouds before, and being up there in the sky in that droning Pan Am Stratocruiser filled me with a giddy sense of power and an overwhelming feeling of helplessness all at the same time.

"Hey," Big Ed grunted as he finished the sports section of the *Times,* "let's go down for a drink, huh? Whaddaya say?"

"A drink?"

"Sure a drink. Why not?"

"Well, ahh, I'm not, um, exactly twenty-one yet, see...."

"Hmpf." Big Ed snorted. "Nobody'll give a shit up here."

"You think?"

"Sure. C'mon."

I wasn't entirely convinced. After all, I had my wing and engines to look after. Besides, it seemed a little early in the day to be sticking my nose in a liquor bottle. I mean, I hadn't even had breakfast yet, you know? I looked at my watch. "Geez, Ed, it's not even 9 o'clock."

"So? It's midnight in Moscow. I'll bet they got the bottles out and the vodka flowing over there."

He had a point.

"Besides, you got anyplace special t'go for the next five hours?"

I had to admit I didn't, so I gave my wing and engines one final Stay Put stare and followed Big Ed's massive backside down the narrow spiral staircase into the lower lounge. It was tough going since Big Ed was a good six inches wider than the staircase, and he had to kind of suck in his gut and turn half sideways to make his way down. The "lower lounge" on a Boeing Stratocruiser was more or less a busy, smoky little cocktail den crammed into a long, narrow crawl space, what with upholstered benches along both sides trying their best to look like luxurious couches (except that they weren't all that luxurious and your knees kind of met in the middle) and these matching café curtains to dress up the windows. We managed to find about a yard of seat space down at the far end, and of course Big Ed had to steamroller every knee in the place- *"S'cuse me.*

41

Sorry. S'cuse me"-before we finally landed. But it turned out to be kind of an icebreaker. Especially when Big Ed looked back at everybody and said, "Lissen, I'm goin' on a diet next week, folks. Honest I am." Then he ordered us up a couple Bloody Marys-the stewardess looked right at me and didn't even bat an eye-and it occurred to me all over again how the rules that apply to all the clock punchers and working stiffs of this world tend to evaporate when you start running with *real* money.

It took us about five or six Bloody Marys to make it down to Texas, and along the way we got pretty chummy with everybody in the lounge. Of course you had to holler if you wanted to be heard on account of those big Pratt & Whitney radials churning the air just outside, but there was a little gin tournament for some fairly serious money going on at one end of the aisle, and Big Ed finessed his way in by flashing his usual fist-sized wad of greenbacks and acting drunker than he really was so this self-styled card sharp in a big, cream-colored Stetson and one of those wild west string ties would consider him a likely pigeon and take him on. Big Ed hustled him good, too, purposely dropping a couple dumb cards and losing the first two Hollywoods so he was down about twelve bucks and then drunkenly asking if he could maybe raise the stakes so's he could catch even. You could see the guy in the Stetson figured he'd hit a main vein. "Aw," he kind of drawled out the side of his mouth, "ah don't rightly know if ah'd feel right and proper about takin' yer money like that, friend."

"Don't worry about me and *my* money, Bub." Big Ed snorted. "Y'know, I remember hearing someplace they got th'balls t'play for *real* stakes down in Texas." Big Ed drained the rest of his most recent Bloody Mary. "But I guess that was just a bunch of that typical Texas bullshit, huh?"

The guy's eyes narrowed down like gunslits. "You just make yourself happy, friend," he said between his teeth. "Play for whatever stakes y'all like. Ah 'spect ah kin handle it."

So Big Ed bumped him from penny-a-point to a dime, and, as anybody who's played Hollywood gin can tell you, that can add up to a rather substantial pile of dimes. Especially when you put some poor fish on the Schnide and run a triple blitz on him, as Big Ed proceeded to do. With the Texan keeping score, too, just to make sure there weren't any mistakes. I had to admit, it was a pretty impressive performance. Mostly when I thought about Big Ed, it was about how he was this hulking, loud, bullish, loyal, well-meaning sort of slob who just happened to have made himself way too much money and wanted to race sports cars but wasn't very good at it. But this was a good look at the Big Ed who actually *made* all that money, and no question he could be one shrewd, ruthless, and predatory customer on his own home turf. No two ways about it. Especially up in an airplane, since most of the air travel he'd done involved taking off at a moment's notice and circling like a vulture whenever poor management, stiff competition, the kids taking over the family business, or the odd insurance fire or natural disaster caused some company with an inventory of interesting industrial equipment to go tits up. Big Ed explained that it was always a good idea to be there first with a wad of ready cash in your pocket, but also not to look too interested or like you were in any kind of special hurry. Totally unlike the Full Pop Plus deals he'd made on his new Caddy Eldorado or Colin St. John's Jaguar 120 or the one he was dying to make on one of Carlo Sebastian's rare-as-angel-farts new Ferraris, industrial scrap was almost always a buyers' market. The harder times were, the more of it there was around, the guys who had it needed cash and needed to get rid of it, and they'd already made up their minds (or the banks had made up their minds for them) that it wasn't worth anything sitting where it was. And guys like Big Ed were rare-guys who could run their eyes over some aching pile of rust and gears and grommets and gadgets and figure out how much it weighed and how much it would cost to move or dismantle (or move *and* dismantle) and how many usable parts and pounds of scrap steel and iron and brass and aluminum it would yield at the far end of the deal. You need a special kind of eyes to see that far ahead, and Big Ed had them.

Anyhow, Big Ed spent the rest of the flight drinking Bloody Marys and turning the Texas guy's wallet inside out (I think he went up over a hundred bucks by the time we landed!) and I struck up a conversation with this guy next to me who turned out to be a Pan Am pilot on his way down to Texas to meet some stewardess-he called her "a stew"-for a little free form R&R before he had to fly back to Newark just so's he could pilot another plane down for the company. I guess flight crew people get to fly free if there's room on the plane, and I noticed right off he had those same faraway, gunfighter eyes like Tommy Edwards and Cal Carrington. So I asked him and sure enough he'd flown for the air force, but mostly cargo planes carrying supplies "over the hump" into China. "That's where these things came from," he told me, kind of pointing around the cabin.

"How's that?"

"Boeing Stratocruisers." He took another sip of his 7 and 7. "They're really just B29s converted for civilian duty."

Even I had heard about B-29s. "That's the plane that dropped the bomb on Hiroshima, isn't it?"

"Yep," he nodded. "Nagasaki, too. Damn fine aircraft. Built strong, too."

That was a comforting thing to know.

"Boeing took the wings, tail unit, landing gear, and engines off the B-29 and put a fat body on it to make the C-97 military transport. Then peace came and they stuck a couple rows of seats inside and this lounge unit downstairs and called it a 377. That's a Stratocruiser to guys like you."

I liked the idea that I was riding inside something with such a distinguished war record. It made me feel a lot more confident. All those Bloody Marys were helping, too.

"Yep," he said, taking another swallow, "only trouble is the engines."

"The engines?" That wasn't exactly what I wanted to hear.

"Yeah," he sighed. "They haven't been the most reliable things around. In fact, one of my pilot buddies calls these things 'the best damn three-engined airliner since the Ford Trimotor.' But he flies mostly Constellations, so what do you expect."

I casually peeled the café curtains back and took another quick peek at my Pratt & Whitneys. They were doing just fine.

We landed in Brownsville a little after lunch local time, and had to wait around the airport an hour or so for a bus to take us across the Rio Grande to the Matamoras airport on the Mexican side. It was a hot, dusty, uncomfortable ride, and I don't believe the people who looked after that bus would recognize a bad shock absorber if you threw one at them. Or even four. Then again, maybe there just weren't any shocks on that bus for them to recognize in the first place. For sure that's what it felt like.

But at least I didn't have to worry about wings falling off.

At the Matamoros airport we were loaded on board a C.M.A. *(Compania Mexicana de Aviacion)* DC3, and it seemed small and dark and cramped inside after the Pan Am Stratocruiser. It felt especially strange to enter at the back and have to kind of climb uphill to find your seat. That's because the DC3 is a tail-dragger and sits on the flight apron kind of like a frog on a lily pad. But they're good, rugged planes-the pilot I met on the Stratocruiser told me that-and per-fectly suited to the kind of Frog Hop travel we were in for the rest of the way down. That first hop took us to Monterrey, which surprised me when I saw it out the window on account of it was a big, ugly, smoky, industrial city a lot like we have up north of the border. Although, to be fair about it, Monterrey wasn't nearly as big or ugly or smoky as Newark. But what would you expect? Any-how, it was coming on dusk when we landed in Monterrey and transferred to a four-engined DC6 for the night flight to Mexico City. That pilot told me you pretty much need four engines to carry any kind of decent payload in or out of Mexico City, since it's way up in the mountains -over 7000 feet!-so the air's pretty thin under the airfoils and the engines start running out of breath. In fact, the CMA DC6's had special, uprated engines for exactly that reason. But I was getting to be a pretty cool customer when it came to flying and didn't much worry about it. After all, guys like my pilot friend had been frog hopping in and out of Mexico City since 1928, and I felt a certain confidence in the steady, even drone churning out of those four big engines as I chewed furiously on another stick of gum to help my ears pop. Besides, I'd never witnessed a sunset from the sky before, and down below I could see street lights and work lights on factory buildings and headlights on cars scratching through the dark, purplish evening haze while off to my right a blood red sun splashed its colors across the whole blessed curvature of the earth, painting the flat layers of clouds between us orange and gold and violet. When the darkness finally came, it was so clear and pure and deep I felt like I could've reached right through the window and picked stars clear out of the sky.

And that's when we hit the first really rough patch. I guess there's always a lot of turbulence when you cross the mountains into Mexico City, but it made me kind of uneasy when the plane would unexpectedly rise up like a Coast Guard cutter going over a big swell, and it was even worse when it suddenly dropped a few flights like an elevator with a sheared cable. I thought we were falling out of the sky. And then there was the plain, ordinary buffeting like I remembered from that *Breaking the Sound Barrier* movie I'd seen with Julie the night before. Geez, it seemed like ages ago. I sure hoped the pilot had seen that film, too, so he'd know enough to reverse the controls in case we accidentally went into a plummeting nose dive and bumped up against Mach 1. Plus all the bouncing and the after effects of a long day and too many morning Bloody Marys and not eating much more than two candy bars and a greasy airport hamburger in Brownsville were combining to make me feel a little green around the gills. Big Ed didn't look all that much better, but at least he wasn't into his second round of barf sacks by the time the plane touched down in Mexico City.

I wasn't the only one, either.

Big Ed's travel agent had us booked into a fancy hotel called the Monte Cassino that was supposedly "just a short taxi ride from the Mexico City airport," but obviously this particular travel agent had never personally been to Mexico City and didn't know all that much about cab rides and the general state of traffic management there. At the airport, a very agitated looking guy in an official-looking hat with a brass badge on it took ten pesos off Big Ed at curbside and then, with much gesturing and windmilling of arms, directed us and our luggage into this strange, shopworn sedan with no Taxi markings of any kind on it and a kid in a string T-shirt who didn't really look old enough to drive behind the wheel. It looked a little like a Nash, but it wasn't, and I was surprised to hear the engine noise coming from *behind* the fuzzy cloth upholstery of the back seat. Which, incidentally, smelled a lot like the litter box my Aunt Rosamarina's cats use. Especially when she hasn't changed it for awhile. Big Ed disagreed, though. He thought it smelled more like a goat.

Turns out the car was a Tatraplan, which come from Uncle Joe Stalin's side of the Iron Curtain-Czechoslovakia, I think-and have an air-cooled V-8 mounted way in the back end, kind of like a cross between a Plymouth and a Porsche (although why any car company would want to do such a thing is beyond me). Anyhow, the guy in the cap told the kid where to take us in Spanish-I thought I heard him say something about *La Carrera* a few times, too-and turned him loose. And right there began the single most terrifying automobile ride of my life. Or so far, at least.

First let me explain that Mexico City traffic makes New York City traffic look wondrously organized. It's essentially a free for all down there-every man for himself!-and they have these places where four, six, or even eight streets dump into these big traffic circles that are sort of miniaturized versions of the Indy 500. Only mostly in old beat-up American sedans and more sickly, rickety Model A Fords than I'd ever seen in my life. Plus a lot of oddball European stuff like Fiat and Mercedes and Austin 4-door sedans that you really never got to see in the states. And every single one seemed to be going flat out and Wide Fucking Open, in spite of tight quarters and squealing tires and countless meandering pedestrians who were apparently counted on to leap out of the way at the last possible instant-matador fashion, you know?-to avoid being crushed under the wheels. I was sure our young driver was going to kill a few at every intersection, because he was really *flying!* I guess he picked up that Big Ed and me were down for *La Carrera,* and whether he thought we were important American team managers who might want to sign him up or just a couple rich gringo racing types to impress, he was going like hell and only resorting to the brakes when he'd used up all the possibilities offered up by the accelerator, steering wheel, and horn button. It was like the spook train ride at Palisades Park, honest it was. The only thing that saved us from a terrible wreck is that *everybody* seemed to drive like that down in Mexico City. The kid taxi driver in the Tatraplan was just a little better at it than most. Lord knows he was always leading the pack by the time we came out of those traffic circles....

If he lived, he might have a real future, you know?

The Hotel Monte Cassino was a pretty posh address, and Big Ed offered to buy us a late dinner when we finally got in. But my stomach was still doing a slow roll from the plane ride and the slide-for-life taxi dash across Mexico City, so I took a pass and went upstairs for a hot shower. I felt a little better when I got out, so I put on a fresh shirt and went downstairs again, and naturally caught up with Big Ed in the bar, where he was well into his fourth bourbon and water. Big Ed bought me a Rusty Nail-he said it was just the thing for a bum stomach-and even offered me one of his fancy Cuban cigars. Now I've never been much of a cigar smoker except at weddings and stuff or when I was at the hospital when my oldest sister had her first kid, but me and that Rusty Nail (or maybe it was two Rusty Nails?) thought it might be just the thing to celebrate surviving my first ever plane rides and that hell-for-leather drive across Mexico City. Besides, it was strange and exciting to be down in a foreign country where you were the odd man out if you spoke Jersey English and spun wrenches in Passaic for a living. All around us, people were jabbering away in Spanish and English and even a few other languages about *La Carrera,* and how it would be coming right through Mexico City on Thursday. Which was, by the way, the forty-second anniversary of the Mexican Revolution, guaranteeing a blowout fiesta extravaganza of truly massive proportions. You could feel the buzz and pulse of it building in the air. This was really going to be something! After another Rusty Nail or two I went to bed and slept pretty good in spite of all the strange, ugly noises coming from Big Ed's side of the room. Geez, you would've thought there was an oil tanker rubbing against some dock pilings over there.

In the morning we got up early, grabbed some toast and coffee downstairs, and headed back over to the airport in a wheezy, heavily dented 1940 Hudson Straight 8 that the Mexican driver was extremely proud of. He spoke a little English, too. "I have it four years now, *si?* And my father before me five more than that. She come all the way from Nueva Jersey."

"From Jersey? Really?" Big Ed said, sounding mildly impressed.

"Oh yes," the driver nodded. *"Si. "* And that was just enough English to earn him one hell of a tip.

At the airport we boarded a C.M.A. DC3 for the frog hop from Mexico City to Oaxaca, and it was pretty full up because of the race and those two engines were really straining to lift us off into that thin Mexico City air. It took just about the whole damn runway to get airborne, and it wouldn't surprise me if the landing gear came up just in time to avoid getting sheared off on the mountain ridge we just barely cleared on our way out of town. You could tell the plane was full of racing people, including a couple Lincoln engineers from Detroit and two German speaking suit-and-tie types from the Mercedes team. There was only one empty seat, and Big Ed palmed his way into getting the one next to it so he could get a little more shuteye on the trip to Oaxaca. I wound up sitting next to a skinny young guy from California named Henry Lyons, who was a cub reporter for the *Los Angeles Herald Examiner* and about as sick with the racing bug as I was. He wore thick glasses with heavy black rims and he was kind of a nervous type-always lighting up a cigarette or gnawing on his cuticles or folding and unfolding his eyeglasses or picking at the spiral binding on the notebook he was carrying because he wanted to be ready at a moment's notice to jot down any hot new story angles he might think up for the race. Turns out he was on his way down to help cover *La Carrera* for the Associated Press, acting as gofer, sidekick, and second-rate interpreter (he'd had a little high school Spanish and grew up with a housemaid from Cuba while his mom was working as a weld inspector at a defense plant during the war) for about the most celebrated damn sports columnist west of Red Smith: the one and only Skip Stryker.

"Geez," I said, *"the* Skip Stryker is coming down for the race?" After all, Skip Stryker did mostly only major league stuff like the Rose Bowl and Heavyweight Championship boxing matches and the World Series.

"Yup." Henry Lyons nodded. "In fact, he's sitting just a couple rows up."

"How come you're not sitting with him?"

Henry Lyons started to say something, but picked at the binding of his notebook instead. "Aw, I guess I just felt, I dunno…."

"I mean, he's *famous*. We've even heard of Skip Stryker back in Jersey. My dad always reads his baseball stuff in *Sports Illustrated.* Unless it's something nasty about the Yankees, that is."

"Hmpf." Henry snorted. *"Baseball!"* He shook his head. "I think it's about the most boring damn game there is."

My eyes opened wider. "You think so, too?"

"Absolutely! It's mostly foul balls and waiting for the damn catcher to throw it back to the pitcher and watching the third base coaches make little finger signs and scratch themselves."

"Boy, that's how I feel. Exactly."

"Car racing's a *lot* more interesting. You need *real* balls to do that sort of thing. And I don't mean the stitched leather variety."

"Yeah. But in car racing, y'gotta be cool, too. Y'gotta be patient. Y'gotta *think…"* I could see he was hanging on every word "…but most important, y'gotta listen to the car and let it tell you what it'll let you get away with." Of course I didn't make any of that stuff up myself. I was just repeating back what my English racer friend Tommy Edwards had told me.

"I guess you must hang around with a few drivers."

"Yeah. I do." I said like it was nothing special. "I twist wrenches on a few Jaguars and stuff back East."

"Really?"

I nodded. "In fact, we're on our way down here to pick up a new Ferrari for B-er, one of my customers." You should've seen how his jaw dropped. In fact, I decided it was maybe time to backpedal a little. After all, sooner or later, he was going to meet Big Ed. "Uh, to be honest, it's not really what you could call a 'new' Ferrari. It's one of the team cars from last year."

"That'll do. Heck, they finished one-two."

"Geez, did'ja see it?"

"Nah. Just the end up in Juarez. That's when I decided I just *had* to do the whole race this year. I just hope I can sell enough stories to pay for the trip."

"That shouldn't be hard palling around with somebody like Skip Stryker."

My new friend looked down at the floor. "If you say so."

So we shot the breeze together the whole way down to Oaxaca. I told him all about Bridgehampton and Watkins Glen and Colin St. John and Big Ed's Jaguar and Cal Carrington's woeful TC and most especially the trip Tommy Edwards and me made to Elkhart Lake with those sleek new Jaguar C-Types, and he told me about the races at Torrey Pines and Paramount Ranch and Golden Gate Park out in California along with a few stories about some of the neater cars and more colorful racing characters they had running around on the west coast. Then he told me about the super duper, top secret new Ferraris the factory in Maranello was sending over for this year's race. "It's all real hush-hush," he said, drawing in close and dropping his voice down to a whisper, "but the word on the grapevine is that Ferrari built some really special cars for just this one race."

"Honest?"

He nodded. "They're supposed to be coupes, like last year's cars, but with great big honking V-12s under the hood. Biggest and most powerful damn motor Ferrari's ever built. Rumor is they're close to 300 horsepower on pump gas and good for 175 miles-an-hour. All day long."

I let out a low whistle.

"Ferrari's got the drivers, too. Villoresi is real good and Chinetti won Le Mans and Alberto Ascari, well, he's the world champion. You can't get much better than that."

I was impressed with how much this Henry Lyons knew about the international racing scene and all the bigtime European teams that were coming over for the glory and prize money at this year's *La Carrera*. "It's a really big deal now," he told me, chewing on a cuticle. "First place pays 150,000 pesos. That's *seventeen thousand dollars* in American money. Plus all the other manufacturers saw what it did for Ferrari to win this thing last year. Now they all want to come over and scramble for it."

"Like who?"

"Well, you've got to figure Mercedes will be tough." He moved to another finger. "They're typical krauts. Really smart. Really well organized. They won Le Mans that way this year, even though Jaguar probably should've walked away with it."

"How's that?"

"Well, Jag had the best car last year-the C-Type, like the one you and that English guy drove to Elkhart Lake-but they got wind that Mercedes was building these special new lightweight coupes called 300SLs and heard all these bullshit stories about how powerful the motors were and how fast and aerodynamic they were supposed to be. So they tried some new engine stuff and a special new nose to make the cars more streamlined, and all the factory Jags dropped out with overheating because of it. Every single one."

"Geez. That's a shame."

"Yeah. But it's their own damn fault. They fell out and Mercedes wound up winning with cars that maybe weren't really as fast as the Jaguars. But racing's about a lot more than just sheer speed. Especially endurance racing."

"I know that," I told him.

"The 300SL Mercedes coupes won a couple other races, too, at Bern and the Nurburgring. Finished second to Bracco in the *Mille Miglia,* too, right on Ferrari's back doorstep." Hank finished up with his fingers for the moment and lit up another cigarette.

"So what makes them so good?" I mean, I had a hell of a time imagining anything *better* than a Ferrari or a C-Type Jag.

He thought it over while blowing out a long, slow stream of cigarette smoke. "Everything," he finally answered. "They're not the fastest and not the lightest and not the most powerful and probably not the best handling, either. But they've got *no weak links."*

"No weak links?"

"Everything about them is *strong.* The engineering is excellent. The materials are the best available. The design is brilliant and yet still practical and conservative. The construction quality is flawless. The mainenance and race preparation are topnotch. The driver lineup is fast and well disciplined-they *won't* make mistakes or over-drive the cars-and the team organization is far and away the best in the world." Hank looked me in the eye. "Have you ever heard of a guy named Alfred Neubauer?"

I couldn't say as I had.

"Then you'll see," he said through a knowing smile. "You'll see."

We changed planes one final time at Oaxaca and I asked Big Ed if he would mind if I sat next to Henry (although by now it was Hank, of course) on the final leg down to Tuxtla Gutierrez. "Suit yerself," Big Ed said, looking slightly hurt but not really giving much of a damn one way or the other. I also got to meet Skip Stryker while we were waiting to board, and it easily ranked as one of the most underwhelming experiences of my life. I'd imagined that anybody with a moniker like Skip Stryker and a byline column that dealt with bases-loaded home runs and one-punch knockouts would be lean and tough and hard as the turn four wall at Indianapolis. But Skip Stryker turned out to be a pale, puffy-looking little guy who waddled around behind a substantial beer gut and had a kind of perpetual, high-pitched whine to his voice that made you glad he was a writer rather than a broadcaster. "I'm sick of these pissant little Mexican airports," he said loud enough that the proud looking attendant at the ticket counter couldn't help but hear. "It's hot and it's sticky and there's goddam dust everywhere and the water's full of stuff that'll give you the shits if you even so much as bathe in it." He looked up at Big Ed, who happened to be standing next to him. In fact, Skip Stryker's eyes were about dead level with Big Ed's armpit stains. "And I'm sure it's even worse where we're heading. Absolutely sure of it." Obviously Skip Stryker was not very fond of this particular assignment.

"Nah," Hank told me on the plane. "He doesn't much like racing. Oh, he'll do the Indy 500 where he can sit up in the press box and push free food in his face all day long. May even get to see somebody killed, and that always makes for a good story. Plus it's all laid out right in front of you. But he doesn't much like being hot and uncomfortable for more than nine innings or fifteen rounds at a stretch. Besides, he really wanted to do the big Southern Cal/UCLA football game that decides who gets to go to the Rose Bowl this weekend. Tickets are rare as hen's teeth, and I think he knows a girl up there who'll swap a whole bunch of tongue favors in return for an afternoon in the press box. At least I hope it's a girl, anyway."

I shook my head. "Geez, I never would've imagined him like this. I mean, he's *Skip Stryker,* fr'chrissakes?"

"Well, feast your eyes."

"I just can't believe it, you know?" I shook my head again. "Wow, what a shock. *Skip Stryker....*"

"And that's not his real name, either."

"It isn't?"

"Hell no. That's his byline name. He made it up. Just like all those phony high school football hero stories from before he supposedly hurt his knee."

"No kidding?"

"Yup. His real name is Chester Deetle, and the only thing that whiny little sonofabitch ever carried into the end zone was a water bucket."

Chapter 3: Loaded for Bear

Hank Lyons took his cub reporter newspaper job pretty seriously, and he had that necessary and thoroughly contradictory news reporter combination of optimism, pessimism, baffled innocence, and world-weary cynicism that make for great column-inch prose and fidgety personal habits. Besides wearing a Jimmy Olsen Signature Edition cub reporter hat with the brim turned up and an all-purpose *Los Angeles Herald Examiner* press pass stuck in the headband, he carried a little canvas duffel bag stuffed with spiral notebooks, plenty of pens and sharpened pencils, a few emergency changes of socks and underwear, his prized 35mm Leica camera with two lenses that some Army friend of his mom's had "liberated" from a bombed-out office in Berlin in 1945, and an assorted hodgepodge of reference materials like the fat little Mexican tourist guide book that told us Tuxtla Gutierrez was the capital of the Mexican state of Chiapas and sat in the middle of lush equatorial jungles full of screeching birds, slithering snakes, jabbering tree monkeys, and a bunch of far flung coffee and tobacco plantations that pretty much supported most of the local Zoque Indian population. But not all that well. Like the rest of Mexico, most of the heavy duty land ownership and business and government positions belonged to descendants of the Spanish Conquistadors, who were genuinely severe guys in their day and made what the Pilgrims did to our own homegrown American Indians look pretty damn tame by comparison. So it's no surprise that there's always been a little free form tension between the Spanish-descended ruling class and the Indian peasants down there, and, according to the guide book, it all came to a pretty nasty head a few times in Chiapas (particularly in 1693, when the locals residents stoned the appointed Spanish mayor to death and set fire to a couple of his village official sidekicks for good measure). In any case, the first thing I noticed heading into town from the airport was the quantity of Mexican Army types with prominently displayed WW2-issue rifles slung over their shoulders meandering around just about everywhere. They weren't directing traffic or giving out directions or helping little old ladies across the street or anything, and you got the idea they were mostly there just to look menacing. Which they did.

The other thing we noticed was the heat. Tuxtla Gutierrez is way down near the Guatemalan border and not all that far above sea level, so it's generally hot and sweaty most all the time-I guess the coffee beans and tobacco leaves really like it that way-and maybe even a little on the unsanitary side for someone used to normal New Jersey standards, what with jungle bird poop all over the place-even in the hotel rooms!-and happy little bugs doing the backstroke in your water glass at most of the local restaurants. Although that didn't really bother me, since everybody back home already warned me not to drink any water down there unless it came in a sealed bottle.

To tell the truth, Tuxtla Gutierrez was not one of those beautiful tropical getaway destinations you read about in the travel section of the Sunday *Times*. Not hardly. In fact, it's about as scenic as Harlem. But it turns into a pretty amazing place when *La Carrera* rolls around. The whole town-Hell, the whole blessed country!-turns inside out to accommodate all the racers, crews, tire guys, oil guys, photographers, press pass types, Mexican Army squads, and free form hangers-on like Big Ed and me. It's really quite a spectacle-a colorful, week-long fiesta celebrating all the speed and noise and excitement and especially the way it all rolls in on a sweet, frothy tidal wave of American greenbacks, German marks, Italian lira, and homegrown Mexican pesos.

Big Ed's travel agent had made us reservations "at the second best hotel in Tuxtla Gutierrez" because the best one was long since booked, and a quick look at the room (or, more accurately, a quick sniff) made you wonder what on earth the third and fourth place accommodations might be like. According to the travel agent, we were damn lucky to get anything at all, since Tuxtla Gutierrez was really bursting at the seams during race week and we only got in because she knew someone who had a friend with a brother-in-law in the State Department who knew who the hell you had to pay off to have somebody else's reservations mysteriously disappear from the bookings.

Still, it all seemed wonderfully foreign and exotic to an odrinary young guy from New Jersey who'd never been any further from home than Elkhart Lake, Wisconsin, or anyplace at all where the standard-issue language wasn't English. To be honest, the only Spanish words I knew were *tamale, adios,* and *cucaracha,* while Big Ed couldn't do much more than order a round of drinks or negotiate the price of a blowjob, both of which he'd picked up in Havana somewhere between Mrs. Big Eds two and three. But the travel agent had given him a fat little paperback English/Spanish dictionary, and Big Ed was down in the lobby trying it out just as soon as we'd dropped our luggage off in the room. "Say, lissen," he said to the smiling and attentive little Mexican guy at the front desk, *"DOAN...DAY...ESS...TAH..."* he fumbled through the pages, then looked at me. "How the hell do you say 'registration' in Spanish?"

I shrugged.

He looked back at the guy at the desk and tried again, speaking real loud and slow like Americans always seem to do when they're trying to convince people from other countries that we have a serious national hearing problem.

"DOAN...DAY...ESS...TAH...the...REG...ISS...TRA...SEE...OWN?"

The guy grinned from ear to ear and fired off a machine gun burst of friendly, helpful, and totally incomprehensible Spanish. Big Ed and I looked at each other, then back at the counter guy. "Ahh, thanks," Big Ed told him.

Then, almost as an afterthought, he fished around in his pocket and slipped a rumpled ten peso note across the counter and under the guy's palm. It was like sending him to Berlitz. Honest it was.

So we followed the little desk guy's instructions (in very passable English, natch) and headed down the street in the bright afternoon sunlight towards the plaza where registration was being held. There were banners flying and people milling around everywhere waving and shouting and wherever you looked there were race cars and race crews and swarms of eager, wide-eyed, finger-pointing local citizens-everybody from shop owners to shit haulers and eye doctors to donkey washers-who were obviously thrilled as hell that the race was in town and regarded anybody involved with a combination of awe, envy, and deep, gleaming admiration. No question *La Carrera* was the biggest damn thing to ever hit these parts, and the locals absolutely loved it.

We found the central plaza of Tuxtla Gutierrez without too much trouble, and it was chock full of Oldsmobiles and Cadillacs and Chryslers and Packards and Hudsons and such with auxiliary fuel tanks and extra spare tires crammed in where the back seats should have been and racing numbers and sponsor signs painted all over them. The year before, all the cars ran in the same class, and it surprised no one-least of all the American stock car and Triple-A guys driving the big Detroit sedans-that those fancy $7000 Ferraris cleaned their clocks. In fact, there was even talk of a boycott. So, for 1952, the organizers added a "Standard Category" for volume produced American sedans. And it was hardly a minor league deal since the stock car winner got a 100,000 peso bonus. That was Big Time Money to anybody running the bullring oval circuit back home, and every racer who could scrape together a car and a tire and gas money deal or find some starry-eyed sucker to pony up the hefty $500-plus entry fee was down there on the streets of Tuxtla Gutierrez getting ready to roll for the gold.

In fact, who should I see over in front of a little bakery shop but Sammy Speed and Spud Webster, the two oval track guys I'd met at the coffee shop in Breezewood, Pennsylvania when I was driving Tommy Edwards' C-Type Jaguar back to New York after the race in Elkhart Lake. "Hey, how the heck are you guys doin'?" I asked.

Sammy Speed looked at me kind of funny, trying to place me, but Spud's face brightened immediately. One race mechanic to another, you know? "Say, you're the kid who was drivin' that Jagwar thing, aren'cha?"

"Yeah. But it wasn't actually *mine* or anything…."

"Hell, we knew that," Spud grinned around the last two cents of a five cent cigar. "Not unless y'*stole* it, anyways."

"That thing run pretty quick?" Sammy Speed asked, not really sounding particularly interested.

"Well, the guy from the Jag dealership says it'll top 150 easy."

Sammy Speed didn't look too impressed.

"They really handle great, too," I added, trying to sound like I knew what I was talking about.

Spud looked at Sammy and Sammy looked back at Spud. "That's really a damn shame then, isn't it," Spud said, and Sammy nodded.

I didn't get it.

"Just look over there."

Across the street all I could make out was a bunch of Mexican backsides crowded in three or four deep around a car I couldn't see. Then I heard the unmistakable, clearing-its-throat growl of a lightly muffled Jaguar six coming to life, and who should come lurching out of the crowd with a typically spastic clutch release (and running over a few toes in the process) but Reginald "Skippy" Welcher and his doofus sidekick Milton Fitting in the exact same Jaguar C-type I'd driven back and forth across the country for Tommy Edwards and that Skippy'd bought off Creighton Pendleton at Watkins Glen and then caused the terrible accident that killed that poor little seven-year-old boy and got Tommy's S.C.M.A. license suspended.

"You know those guys?" I asked.

"Nah," Spud groused. "We just met 'em at the hotel bar last night. What a flaming pair of assholes."

I knew from the first time I met them that I liked these guys.

"Yeah. It just don't seem fair," Sammy muttered under his breath. "That's one hell of a racecar, and I bet that guy behind the wheel can't drive a lick."

So I told Sammy and Spud a little bit about Skippy Welcher-about how he was a longtime Major Member of the S.C.M.A. and they couldn't kick him out on account of he was rich and had been there about forever and that his greatest qualification as a racing driver was that he was sole heir to the Welcher Waxout ear swab fortune and could afford to buy any damn sports car he wanted. Then I finished up by quoting my friend and part-time hero Tommy Edwards, who once said that Skippy "couldn't pee a hole in the snow when it came to driving a race car."

"Damn shame," Sammy snorted.

"Amen to that," Spud agreed.

"It's one of the things you've just got to try to get used to around the sportycar crowd," I tried to explain. "We've got some really great drivers. Honest we do. Guys like Tommy Edwards and Phil Hill and John Fitch and Phil Walters and my friend Cal Carrington. Those guys are *good.*" I knew Cal would've appreciated being mentioned in that group. And I was pretty damn sure he belonged there, too.

"But what about guys like this Welcher character?"

"Well, see," I was working it over in my mind, trying to find a way to put it. "You've got to understand that the S.C.M.A. is really a club, see. Like a big college fraternity or something. They don't allow prize money...."

"Don't allow prize money??!!"

I shook my head. "Nope. That's not the point, the way they see it."

Spud and Sammy shook their heads. "It's all about sportsmanship and playing the game, see. Or at least that's what they tell you. Plus they have these, uh, *standards of admission* you need to meet before you can join."

"Like what?"

"Well, like you gotta be rich-even better if it's old family money-and it gets a little tough if you don't belong to the right church or come from the right kind of neighborhood, if you know what I mean."

"Sounds pretty snobby and stuck-up," Spud observed.

"Yeah, I guess it is. But, like I said, there's a lot of neat people, too. And the race weekends are a lot of fun. But maybe the best part is getting to work on the cars. Like the Ferrari that won here last year or the C-type Skippy Welcher just drove off in."

"But he's such an *asshole.*"

"Well, I guess that's the hard part. You gotta get used to the idea that great cars don't have any control over the jerkoffs who own them." I looked up and gave Spud a wink, "I reckon it's one of the great inequities of our time."

"Amen to that." Spud agreed.

"Shit," Sammy muttered under his breath. "When I think what a guy like me could do here in a car like that..." His voice trailed off like an echo.

"Aw, don't take it so hard," Spud told him. "At least we're *runnin'* this thing, aren't we?"

"Say," I wanted to know, "what kind of car are you guys in?"

Sammy looked at Spud. *"You* tell him."

"Well, uhh, actually," Spud mumbled, "we're runnin' a, um..."

"Actually," Sammy cut in, kind of clearing his throat and trying to sound confident and proud about it, "we're running a Nash this year."

"A *Nash?"*

"Sure a Nash. Why not? Hell, I heard Curtis Turner and Bill France damn near won this thing with one in 1950. And Bob Korf finished up tenth overall in a Nash last year...."

"But a *Nash?"* I mean, I'd worked on damn near any kind of American sedan you'd care to mention, and I couldn't figure any way that wheezy Nash 6 would have a ghost of a chance against the big, modern V-8s under the hoods of the Oldsmobiles and Lincolns, let alone that hulking, King Kong of a Hemi in the new Chrysler Saratogas. And I told them as much.

"Well, I gotta admit that the competition's bound to be a little tougher this year," Sammy offered, sounding just a wee bit lame.

"See, we met this Nash dealer at the Triple-A race in Denver," Spud started to explain, "and Sammy here was puttin' on a real good show-leading his heat by a mile until the pinion gear broke and put us on the trailer 'cause our spare was no good either and it's some morphidite old truck rear end nobody uses any more so's we couldn't even borrow one, either."

"Tell him about the Nash deal, OK?" Sammy said wearily. I was getting the idea that Spud maybe tended to run on about things.

"Oh yeah. The Nash. Well, we wound up havin' a drink or two with this Nash fella and Sammy happened to mention about this race down here in Mexico, and before you know it he'd talked him into lending us one of his demos and paying the entry fee and even fronting up a couple extra bucks for tires and expenses. So we just kind of..."

"So we just headed off down here to Mexico in this Nash since we really didn't have much of anyplace else to go. That's just the way it is sometimes in this business. When you get an opportunity, you gotta take it."

"Yeah," Spud agreed. "Even if it may not be the best opportunity around." Then he brightened. "At least it gave me a chance to check in with my wife and kids in Fort Worth on the way down. Don't get t'see 'em more than a couple times a year anymore. At least during racing season, anyways. Hell, that's why we're probably still married."

For the first time since I'd arrived in Mexico, I thought about Julie. But she seemed awfully small and a million miles away. "Well listen," I told them, "I prob'ly oughtta go catch up with my friend. We'll see you around, OK? And good luck!"

"That's what you really need for this deal," Sammy allowed, the leathery crows feet wrinkling at the corners of his eyes. "If you're lucky enough to keep your nose clean, not make too many mistakes, and hang around for the finish, you'll most likely get a bag of cash at the end. Even in a Nash."

"Amen to that," Spud agreed.

I managed to locate Big Ed over on the far side of the plaza, where he was trying to get directions he could halfway understand to the official Ferrari team garage a few blocks away. But just when he'd about run out of *"DOAN...DEY...ESS ...TAHs,"* who should come wandering out of the crowd but Hank Lyons on the heels of a very angry, sweaty, and agitated looking Chester Deetle (a.k.a Skip Stryker). *"I just can't believe it!"* the ace sports columnist snapped in a high, grating whine. *"Just fucking can't BELIEVE it!"*

"What's that?" Big Ed asked, not sounding particularly interested.

"The goddam hotel lost our goddam reservations! Can you believe it?"

Big Ed and me looked at one another sort of sheepishly and allowed as how we couldn't.

"Well I'm not about to take it!" he continued, jutting his pudgy little jaw out over his bow tie and curling his lower lip forward for emphasis. *"I'll be damned if I'm gonna sleep with the damn bugs and lizards out in a damn bean shed! They gotta know who the hell they're dealing with here!"*

I looked over at Hank and saw he was kind of sucking in his cheeks to keep from laughing. "Hey, take it easy, Skip, " he finally said, trying to sound all calm and reasonable. "We'll get it sorted out. We'll find something. Besides, we're only in town here a couple days...."

Skip answered with a scowl that would curdle milk.

I looked over and made a face at Big Ed when I was sure neither Skip or Hank could see it. He answered with a helpless shrug and a quarter-turn New Jersey palm roll that they couldn't see either. "Listen," I offered hesitantly, "maybe you guys could bunk in with us..." I saw Big Ed's eyes narrow, "...at least if you don't mind using a piece of floor, anyway."

Big Ed gave a near invisible nostril flare of approval.

But there was no compromising with Skip Stryker. *"Bullshit!"* he snarled. "They sold that goddam room right out from under us! I know how these things work! And I don't have to take that kind of shit. I'm syndicated in twenty-seven goddam newspapers. *TWENTY SEVEN, do you understand?"*

I looked at Big Ed and he looked back at me and it was hard to hide that we were both about ready to burst out laughing. And I had a feeling Hank was about ready to join us, too. Since there was no apparent sympathy coming from our side of the conversation, Skip leveled his eyes menacingly at Hank. "Listen, boy reporter, I'm out of here."

"You're *what?"*

"Out of here. Vamoosed. *Leaving!* Do you understand?"

"But how can you?"

"You just watch me, kid. I'll be on the next damn plane up to Mexico City. Count on it." He stuck his chin out even further. *"You* can stay down here with all the damn heat and noise and these loony car people."

Hank just stood there for a moment, looking more confused than stunned. "But what about the stories we're supposed to file?"

"You're supposed to be the up-and-coming hotshot reporter, right? So *report.* I'll keep track of the Big Picture up in Mexico City and you just send in a field report every day along with some human interest shit if you come across anything interesting. Wire it up to me in Mexico City and I'll file it from there. I'll be staying at the *El Presidente.*"

Hank started to say something but thought better of it, and I was getting a quick whiff that maybe this is what Skip had in mind all along.

"Adios, amigos," the famous syndicated columnist sneered like he was giving us all the finger, then spun on his heels and stalked off into the crowd.

"Geez," I said. "He sounded pretty pissed."

Hank laughed. "He's happy as a pig in shit, believe me. He'll fly up to Mexico City and get himself a nice expense account room at the *El Presidente* with plenty of booze and room service breakfasts and hot and cold running hookers. He'll do all right."

"But what'll *you* do?"

"Me?" Hank thought it over. "This is probably the best damn thing that's ever happened to me. I'll get to follow the race the way *I* want to follow it and write the stories *I* want to write without that asshole looking over my shoulder and griping and grousing and deciding what we're going to do all the time."

"But won't he put that stuff under his own byline?"

"Oh, sure he will." A little grin started sneaking up the sides of Hank Lyons' face. "But I may just file a copy of my stuff directly with the paper and the AP every day." His grin blossomed out into an enormous smile. "Just by accident, you understand. That offer on the piece of floor still open?"

I looked over at Big Ed and he nodded. "Sure. Why the hell not?"

And now we were three.

Better yet, one of us spoke a little Spanish, and that made it a lot easier getting and following directions to the Ferrari compound where Big Ed was supposed to meet Carlo Sebastian and Javier Premal, the mysterious rich Mexican who owned and was fixing to race the car Big Ed planned to buy when it was over. As we walked through town, my head kept swiveling around like a kid on a carnival midway, taking in all the cars and people and activity going on all around me. Besides the American stock cars and European sports cars, there were a few fascinating "specials" whipped up by some homegrown Mexican competitors to run in the open class. They were mostly hot-rodded American sedans like Fernando Duran Mejia's strange '52 Cadillac, which looked pretty standard to me except for a few extra carburetors, a wildly colorful paint job, lightening holes drilled in the chrome grille trim, and no less than eight hood scoops. Personally, I didn't see how something like that had much of a chance against the Ferraris (or even Skippy Welcher's C-type) but Hank said you never really knew in a race like *La Carrera.* Especially when the driver was a genuine local citizen and might actually know which way the road went over the next rise or around the next blind bend. That could count for a lot at a race like this.

We found the Ferraris bivouacked in a big heavy equipment garage that I think belonged to the Mexican government, and it was a pretty decent setup because they had lots of room and a solid roof overhead plus plenty of electrical outlets and an ancient compressor that dated back to around the conquest of the Aztecs. After their utter domination the previous year, a lot of people figured Ferraris were the car to have, and there were no less than nine of them entered. The most interesting, of course, were the three wicked looking "Mexico" coupes entered by the factory team. They had big 4.1-liter engines and the sleekest, meanest, most sinister looking bodywork you ever saw. But I didn't much care for the way they were slathered all over with advertising like the American stock cars. That's the first time I'd ever seen something like that on a sports car, and it just didn't look *right* to me. The way I had it figured, any self-respecting Ferrari ought to be bright blood red with plain white number circles and plain black numbers inside them. Period. But that's not the way things worked down at *La Carrera.* There was big money and prestige at stake here, and no question the eyes of the whole damn country (not to mention a goodly portion of the rest of the world) were squarely focused on these cars. What better place to tack up your ad? I guess Carlo Sebastian had a hand in setting up the deal-what else?- and no question a healthy pile of pesos were pushed across the table to get *"Productos 1-2-3"* splashed all over the nose and sides of the three team Ferraris. Ugh. But you kind of forgave it because *La Carrera* felt like some kind of costume theme party anyway. Besides, I was proud as hell to see the name of my own personal gasoline brand, "Sinclair," painted in large letters over the front wheels of the Ferrari team cars. I pointed it out to Hank and asked him to be sure and take a picture so I could show Butch and Julie and even Old Man Finzio back home.

Turns out *Productos 1-2-3* was a Mexican company that distributed oil and laundry soap and stuff like that, and there was a lot of nudging and winking going on in the Ferrari garage about how that's exactly how those dangerous new Mexico coupes figured to finish. And why not? After all, they'd finished 1-2 the year before with some pretty standard cars sporting little 2½ liter engines, and the new, big motor Mexicos figured to be one hell of a lot stronger climbing up-and-down through the mountains and hustling north across the straight, flat, high speed legs through the desert from Leon to the finish line in Ciudad Juarez. Plus they had the best damn drivers in the world, as any one of them would cheerfully tell you. Alberto Ascari was World Champion, plain and simple, and he very likely would have won *La Carrera* outright the year before if he hadn't run into some serious tire trouble on the very first leg. The asphalt was made out of volcanic rock down at the southern end of Mexico, and it cut hell out of those high class European tires. Especially if you tried to go fast. Ascari had to stop *four times* to change shredded tires, and that put him all the way down to forty-fifth position at the end of the first leg. But he stormed back to win four of the next seven legs outright and finished a solid second to the more conservative "Silver Fox" Piero Taruffi in the other Ferrari. So no question Ascari could drive and also knew the course, which, like I said, could be a huge advantage at a race like this one. His teammates in the other two factory cars were Luigi Villoresi, who also drove on the Grand Prix circuit for Ferrari and rode shotgun with Ascari in *La Carrera* the year before, and the smooth, experienced Luigi Chinetti, who had won Le Mans for Ferrari in 1949. You could sense a lot of confidence brewing around the Ferrari garage. Cockiness, even. But then, who was going to beat them?

"You ought to see Mercedes' setup on the other side of town." Hank told me. "Their cars look like they've been beamed down from outer space. And they're built like tanks, too. I don't reckon they're as flat-out *fast* as the team Ferraris, but I heard the Mercedes importer in Mexico City lent them a few sedans and their drivers have been practicing all up and down the course for three solid weeks. Neubauer even hired a pair of Douglas DC3s to act as air scouts and follow the practice squads around to pick out likely places for tire service stops along the way." The way the rules read, only the driver and riding mechanic could work on the car while the race was on, but that didn't prevent teams from setting up convenient places to stop all set up with jacks at the ready and ply-wood sheeting on the ground so the jacks wouldn't sink into the sand and every possible tool or part that might be needed (plus safe food to eat and plenty of cold bottled water) just a short reach away. Between legs and at the overnight stops, anybody on the crew could work on the cars, and Mercedes had brought along enough manpower and hardware to damn near rebuild the cars from scratch every night if necessary. Or change them a little to make them more suitable for the legs that lay ahead the following day. They were way ahead of Ferrari-way ahead of everybody, in fact-where that kind of thing was concerned. "They may have lost the damn war," Hank said with grudging respect, "but the Germans sure learned how to prepare for and organize mechanized military campaigns just about anywhere in the whole blessed world. And they sure haven't forgotten any of it, either."

And that was the big behind-the-scenes deal with Mercedes. Sure, it was 1952, but nobody on either side had really forgotten the war. Not hardly. On the one hand, the guys on the German side (and particularly companies like Mercedes Benz, who hoped to sell cars to many of the same exact folks the Germans had been lobbing V2 rockets at and dropping incendiary bombs on only a few short years before) wanted to put it all behind them and get on with their lives and find their place in the world. But they also wanted their pride back. Hell, they'd damn near kicked the whole damn world's ass with a country you could fit inside the state of Texas and have plenty of room left over, and no question they'd done it by being organized, scientific, and disciplined, and by building some of the most incredibly terrifying hardware the world had ever seen. I remember Tommy Edwards telling me about a friend of his who was a tank commander during the war. "The German Tigers and Panzers were always better than our stuff. *Much* better. The only reason we ever beat them is that we could build so many. In the end, we simply crushed them under the sheer weight of our numbers." And the hungry, shell shocked German welders, fitters, and drill press operators who crawled out of the rubble and went back to work in the bombed-out factories after the war knew all about the kind of stuff they could build. And they wouldn't be satisfied until the rest of the world recognized it, too.

That, at long last, was a war they could win.

But the suit-and-tie types at Mercedes knew they had to be careful. Even if they'd succeeded in building a better mousetrap, they couldn't just go goose-stepping over the opposition without bringing back a lot of ugly memories and maybe accomplishing the exact opposite of what they had in mind. So they made sure to act a little humble and have some semblance of a sense of humor about things (or, as Hank put it, holding a pocket comb under his nose: *"YOU VILL LAFF! IT IS AN ORDER!"*) and tried to ingratiate themselves with all their old WW2 sparring partners by inviting Local Heroes from all their old foe Allied countries to drive with the Mercedes factory team. Sure, the core was still regular German drivers like Karl Kling and Hermann Lang, who'd both been with Mercedes before the war when they, you should excuse the expression, annihilated the opposition, but for *La Carrera* they were joined by American racer and regular Cunningham team driver John Fitch. And it was more than just a token gesture, since Fitch had won a lot of races and done a lot of the development work on the Cunninghams, plus he'd run *La Carrera* in a Chrysler Saratoga the previous year so he had some idea which way the road went and could let the other Mercedes drivers pick his brains. In fact, Hank heard John had a lot to do with bringing Mercedes Benz to *La Carrera* in the first place. Based on his success in the United States and the fact that he was the kind of cool, patient, and technically sharp "thinking man's" driver Neubauer favored, he'd been invited to drive a fourth 300SL in their home race at the Nurburgring earlier in the year. And that's when he casually mentioned what a great race and test of equipment *La Carrera* was, and also allowed as how the fast, strong, and reliable 300SLs had an excellent chance of winning. Neubauer and the rest of the Mercedes brass liked that kind of talk, but they also knew that you didn't just send some fast cars and a few good drivers over to run a race like *La Carrera*. No, sir. You sent a *team*. And a *plan*. Although winning outright was a hope and even a genuine possibility from the beginning, Neubauer's main goal was to have all three Mercedes finish the race. If they did that, he reasoned, the results would take care of themselves. After all, the new 300SLs had come home 1-2-3-4 in Germany along with second and fourth out of three cars entered in the *Mille Miglia* and 1-2-3 again in Switzerland and a lucky but impressive 1-2 at the 24 hours of Le Mans. And those were the only blessed races they'd run!

No question Neubauer intended to keep that record going at *La Carrera*.

So he and John Fitch wrote a whole bunch of letters back and forth, with Neubauer asking questions about the route and the climate and the altitude changes and the road surface and the average rainfall and what sort of tummy medicine you ought to bring and whether you should pack Bermuda shorts or earmuffs. Fitch did his best to give detailed answers-in complete secrecy, of course-and also ran interference on all the travel arrangements and flight connections and such. So when the Mercedes team arrived in Mexico a few weeks before *La Carrera,* they figured they'd done whatever they could. They were loaded for bear.

According to Hank, there was also a dark horse team in the Open Sports category in the form of the tiny, flyweight little French Gordinis. "They're really just Grand Prix cars with a passenger seat, headlights, and fenders," Hank explained. "And I'm not even sure why they put the extra seat in, since they're planning to run without riding mechanics in order to save weight."

That was an intriguing idea.

"But I don't see them lasting the distance. They're just not built for a grind like this. They're too light and wound a little too tight. But they'll go like stink until they break. Especially in the mountains. And especially the one with Jean Behra behind the wheel."

"Who?"

"Jean Behra. French motorcycle champion a dozen times over. Switched to cars a few years back and picked right up where he left off on bikes. On his day, I'd say he's as good as the best in the world. Maybe even better. But he crashes a lot." Hank shrugged. "Doesn't seem to bother him, though. Way I hear it, he's braver than Dick Tracy."

There were also some pretty impressive privateer Ferraris bedded down with the factory team. Of course we had the two ex-works Mexican cars that finished 1-2 the previous year (including the one Big Ed hoped to buy at the end of the race) along with a similar 2.5-liter model (unfortunately with a big orange Gulf Oil logo on the side) with *Piloto: Phil Hill* lettered in over the door. That had to be the same Phil Hill who raced so well against Tommy Edwards at Elkhart Lake, driving for that California wine guy Ernesto Julio who lent me the snazzy silk pirate shirt and the pair of brown pants I later took off to go skinny dipping with Sally Enderle what seemed like a dozen lifetimes ago. We noticed this pair of shoes sticking up out the window of that Ferrari, and a closer look revealed none other than Phil Hill himself growing out of them. He was all folded up into the driver's side footwell with his shoulders pretty much jammed in solid underneath the big woodrim steering wheel. "Hi, Phil," Hank said into his insteps.

"Oh, hi there," a voice echoed up softly from down in the footwell.

"What'cha doin' in there?" I asked, craning my neck in for a looksee.

There was the sound of a ratchet wrench clicking off those last few rounds, followed by a bunch of grunting and banging as Phil worked his way out of the car. It was like somebody who was half-swallowed by an alligator trying to crawl back out. But eventually he sprawled free and wound up sitting spread-legged on the floor with his back against the rocker panel. "Hi, Hank," he said, like there was nothing much unusual about his position. Then he looked at me, and although the spark of recognition was there, he obviously couldn't place it.

"Buddy Palumbo," I said, sticking my hand out and then leaning over so he could reach it. "I met you at Elkhart Lake. I was the guy…"

"I remember. You and Tommy drove the C-Types out from New York."

"Yup. That was me."

"And you worked for Colin St. John, didn't you?"

"Guilty as charged," I admitted. "But no more. I got my own place now."

Phil gave me a little nod of approval. "That's probably a good idea. Colin can be, er," he thought about it for a moment. "I'd better not say anything."

"Wouldn't bother me."

"Yeah, but it might bother me." You had to respect a guy who thought twice about saying stuff behind people's backs. Even double dealing, now-you-see-it-now-you-don't automotive car con artists like Colin St. John.

"So, what were y'doin' down in the footwell?"

"Just checking the free play on the clutch and brakes. You'd like to think you've got everything pretty right before you start a race like this."

Hank and I nodded like we both understood.

"So," Hank asked, "how do you rate the competition?"

"You mean all of it," Phil answered with a perfectly straight face, "or just the cars in this garage?"

Hank's eyes panned around the shop. "Might as well start right here."

"Well, the works cars ought to be in a class of their own. Or that's their plan, anyway. But they're new and it's a long race and anything can happen. And you've got Lancia over from Italy to reckon with. They're wonderful little cars-I heard one of them is even supercharged-and there's nothing they'd rather do than knock off Ferrari. Their drivers are real experienced at this open road stuff, too. It's a whole different ball game from circuit racing."

"Like how?"

"Well," he allowed, sliding behind the wheel for one last check on the pedals, "you run a typical race track and it's the same three or four miles over and over again. You get to work on each corner and braking zone and get yourself into a rhythm. Here, each crest and bend is a stranger you've never met before. Plus you never really know how you're doing."

"How's that?"

"In a closed circuit race, you can generally see the next guy ahead or the guy filling up your mirrors. You know where you are. But here they start the cars at one minute intervals, so by the time the next guy catches you, he's already a minute ahead of you on the clocks. You may not see some of the people you're racing against all day."

"So how do you know how fast to go?"

Phil's brows knitted together over a helpless laugh. "That's the trick then, isn't it? On the one hand, you want to be easy on the car, because if you run it hard you'll break it or wear it out long before you reach Juarez. Plus you really can't drive flat out because there's farm animals wandering across the road and buildings to hit in the villages and sheer cliffs with thousand foot dropoffs that you'd really rather not fly off of up in the mountains. Far as I can see, you only get one mistake per car at a race like *La Carrera."*

"So what'll you do?"

"Oh, we'll mostly run our own pace and try to be around at the finish. But it'd be nice to beat the *other* 'American' Ferrari." He pointed over to another last year's model Ferrari coupe that was painted up differently from the three team cars. "Your friend Creighton Pendleton is in that one with one of Carlo Sebastian's mechanics as navigator. It's got a big engine, just like the factory cars, and they've got it pretty tweaked up. Take a look." We walked over and looked into the engine bay. Under the air cleaner you could see no less than *six* downdraft Weber carburetors down the center of the vee. I let out a low whistle and Phil nodded. "Wouldn't surprise me one bit if it's the most powerful Ferrari in private hands in the whole dang world."

"Figures." No question Creighton Pendleton had developed a fine knack for landing the good rides. But of course he could afford to. Not that you ever got a whiff of the cash money that was undoubtedly changing hands under the table. Whenever he showed up in someone else's car, it was always "so-and-so rang me up to see if I wanted the drive," as if it was all free and casual and the only reason they asked him was because he was such a gifted chauffeur (which, to be honest, he was) and not because he had so much money that he could keep everybody smiling even if he drove the damn thing off a mountainside, blew the motor to smithereens, or fetched it up against a white stucco wall going through one of the many small villages along the way. It made you sick, you know? I mean, not only was the sonofabitch rich as hell and handsome as a movie star, he also got to drive all the best cars and had a girlfriend so beautiful and sexy she made everybody drool on their shoes. It just didn't seem fair, you know? Especially since he was such a stuck-up prick. "So, you think you can beat him?" I asked. To be honest, it'd become pretty important to me that, no matter who won, I wanted to make sure Creighton lost.

"Well, he's in about the same boat I am. Neither of us ever saw the road before we drove down a few days ago. And that was doing it backwards."

"How is it?" Hank wanted to know.

Phil shrugged. "When we started, I figured we'd have time to turn around and run through the difficult sections a few times and try to learn them."

"And?"

He offered up a hopeless little smile. "Oh, it was a swell idea for the first couple hundred miles. But that's all flat and straight. Once we got into the mountains, forget it. It's all climbs and dives and blind hills and ess bends and hairpin turns. If you tried to go back over every tough stretch, you'd never make it down here for the start.." He pointed to the number 8 Ferrari coupe, which was not one of the new Mexico models but was painted up with the same *Productos 1-2-3* and *Sinclair* lettering like the team cars. "Bracco and his riding mechanic have been down here practicing for a week."

Later on, Hank filled me in on Giovanni Bracco, who was a rich, suave, sleek looking Italian guy who owned his own cars and brought along his own mechanic but pretty much traveled as part of the Ferrari works team. That was a pretty special kind of deal, but Giovanni Bracco was a pretty special kind of person. After all, he'd won the *Mille Miglia* for Ferrari earlier in the year, not only finishing ahead of all the official factory cars but also keeping the enemy Mercedes team from winning on Ferrari's home turf. That was worth a lot in a country like Italy. The number 8 coupe was the same car he'd driven in the *Mille Miglia,* and it was pretty special, too. Bracco'd had it built for him, and it had all these special lightweight parts and a hopped-up 3-liter engine with three four-barrel carburetors that produced damn near as much power as the big 4.1 liter engines in the factory cars but weighed a lot less. And the guy could *drive.* Plus he was competitive as hell and took winning-and especially beating all the factory types with his lowly 'privateer' entry-very seriously indeed. So he'd been down in Mexico with his personal Ferrari race mechanic for over a week, running the course from dawn to dusk and from one end of Mexico to the other in rental cars (at least two of which he'd crashed), learning the twists and curves and blind brows, making all sorts of notes, and even taking a can of bright yellow paint along to make strange, indecipherable markings on the pavement and assorted roadside scenery that only he would understand when he ran the route in anger come race time.

No question this Giovanni Bracco character was someone to reckon with.

"Hey, Buddy!" Big Ed's voice boomed from the other side of the garage. *"C'mon over here. There's somebody I need'ja t'meet."* So I walked down the line of blood red Ferraris with *Productos 1-2-3* and *Sinclair* signs painted all over them and found Big Ed and Carlo Sebastian leaning up against a tool bench in deep conversation. And right there between them was the single most dangerous looking Mexican I have ever met in my life. He was short and dark and wiry, and his tailored linen jacket, highly polished shoes, and gleaming gold cufflinks left no doubt that he had a few pesos in the bank. But there was no

trace of the easy life in his face. He had eyes like a pit viper and a crooked, evil little half-face smile that flashed open like a switchblade knife and closed just as quickly. It was almost like you could see his skull coming through his skin when he smiled like that. "Buddy," Big Ed said, sounding unusually formal, "meet Javier Premal."

He stuck out a small, dark hand that felt like it had steel knuckles and wire cable tendons inside. *"Con mucho gusto, mi amigo,"* he said in a hard, wary voice. "Did you have a pleasant flight down?" He spoke pretty decent English, but with a heavy accent and sometimes a little Spanish mixed in.

I allowed as how it was just a little bumpy in and out of Mexico City.

"Our Mexican *pilotos* are the best in the world," he said, holding up his index finger. "They have to be!" The smile flashed open on one half of his face. "Do you know how our airline started, *amigo?"*

"No. Not really."

"It was the *banditos.* They kept robbing the payroll shipments going into Tampico for the men working the oil fields. It was very bad. So our airline was started to deliver the gold. It was 1924."

I made sure to look impressed. "And that took care of it?"

"That and the *Federales,"* he laughed, and then looked me square in the eye. "When they caught those *banditos,* they made them dig their own graves before they shot them."

I was beginning to understand that they did things a little differently down here in Mexico than we do up in the states.

"Señor Big Ed and my friend Carlo have told me you are a fine racing mechanic. Is this so?"

"Aw, I dunno if I'd go that far," I answered, feeling the old heat starting to creep up my neck.

"No, please. Do not be shy about it. This is something of which you should be *proud,* my friend." He flashed that switchblade smile again, where only one side of his lip curled up and you could almost see his skull coming right through the skin. This guy could've made himself a fortune playing threatening villain types in Hollywood. He wouldn't hardly need makeup.

But of course he already *had* a fortune. And I got the distinct impression you didn't ask where it came from, either. But all that money was the reason he was down here in Tuxtla Gutierrez, getting ready to run the 1952 edition of *La Carrera Panamericana* in last year's winning car and planning on buying this year's winning car (assuming it was one of the new Ferrari Mexicos, anyway) just as soon as the factory guys got done filling the gas tank, checking the oil and water, and wiping all the dirt, dust, bug splats, and *Productos 1-2-3* and *Sinclair* lettering off of it.

"Gee whiz," I said, just trying to make a little conversation, "that's a hell of a car you've got there."

"Gracias, señor. But it's really nothing compared to the new ones." He nodded in the direction of the three new Mexico coupes lined up on jack stands with a half dozen factory mechanics swarming all over them. "And *I* am nothing compared to men like Ascari, Villoresi, Chinetti and Bracco. They race all the time. At the greatest tracks and for the biggest prizes." His voice dropped down to a whisper. "I only get this one chance a year." Then he looked directly into my eyes, and when he spoke it sent a shiver up my spine. "But this is my country-*mi nacion!*-and I can close my eyes..." he closed his eyes, "...and feel the rise of every mountain and the sweep of every curve from where we are standing to Ciudad Juarez. It is like the very blood in my veins." There was something almost terrifying about the way he said it, and it got even scarier when he opened his eyes and I saw the kind of cold, ruthless determination you usually associate with ax murderers, religious fanatics, and life insurance salesmen. Geez, did he ever give me the creeps.

Carlo Sebastian reached out and put a calming hand on Javier Premal's shoulder. "You make it sound so serious, my friend. It should be more enjoyable," a smile spread across his face. "Like a beautiful woman, eh?"

The Mexican's switchblade smile slowly re-opened.

"Come," Carlo Sebastian grinned, putting his other hand on Big Ed's meaty shoulder, "the three of us have much to discuss and many important meals to eat today." And with that he whisked them out into the gathering dusk. "We will meet you later at Boliches," he called back over his shoulder, making it abundantly clear that scribes and wrench spinners were very definitely on their own as far as dinner was concerned.

But that was OK. It was coming on dark and you could hear the *mariachis* firing up their guitars and accordions in the courtyard cafes and it seemed a swell time to be out on our own in a faraway sort of town like Tuxtla Gutierrez just a few short days before the start of *La Carrera Panamericana.* "You got any special preference for dinner?" I asked Hank.

"Yeah. Cheap."

"Clean wouldn't be bad, either," I observed.

"That might be a little bit harder to find."

So we started off down the street together, heading for the plaza. It was full dark now-they don't have much in the way of twilight once you get down near the equator-and it seemed like there were race cars being fussed over in almost every driveway and behind every gate and overhead door in town. We passed a rickety little café with a few tables outside and who should I see in there sharing a plate of mystery meat, rice, and refried beans but Sammy Speed and Spud Webster. "Are you guys being careful about what you eat?" I asked over the hedge. I mean, everybody'd heard all the horror stories about what the local food could do to your insides.

"No problem," Spud grinned. "We got pills." He reached into his shirt pocket and pulled out a little prescription vial he'd got off a doctor friend of his in Fort Worth. "Take these babies and you can eat damn near anything."

"You can even do it with the local girls and not get sick," Sammy added, shoveling hard through his beans.

"Mind if we join you?"

"Help yourself. It's a free country. But you maybe want to take one of these first." He passed the little pill bottle around.

"You sure you got enough?"

"I brought plenty. I got three more bottles in the glove compartment. The doctor's a friend of mine. In fact, lemme wrap you some in a napkin so's you can take 'em with you." Spud shook about a dozen pills out and handed them over. "It's no fun if you get the drizzly shits down here."

"Yeah. It can get pretty serious." Sammy agreed. "Who's your friend?"

So I introduced Hank Lyons and we all sat down together. "Where you guys staying?" I asked.

Spud and Sammy looked at each other. "The hotel Nash," Spud answered.

"Yeah," Sammy nodded. "The town's booked up solid. Besides, we're on a little bit of a gas and tire budget right now."

"I 'spect we'll be switching to campfire beans for the rest of the trip after this meal," Spud added. "But we thought we'd maybe splurge a little tonight."

"Just this once." Sammy said sternly. But then he shot us a wink.

Sharing one dinner didn't sound much like splurging to me. "Lissen, I got a little money in my pocket," I said. "Lemme maybe buy something for the table. You know, an appetizer or something." Even though I'd already blown out Big Ed's two hundred bucks on Julie's new engagement ring, he'd slipped another ten into my shirt pocket for walk-around money. Just like that. Ten bucks could buy one hell of a lot of food, drink, or whatever the hell else you had in mind down in Mexico.

Spud looked over at Sammy. "That'd be great," he said carefully. "Thanks. Only nothing with fresh fruit or raw vegetables in it, OK? I got pills, but there's no point pushing fate now, is there?"

We had a nice meal together in that outdoor café. The food was good and cheap and there was plenty of it, and we were careful to drink beer instead of the local water (after all, it was a health issue!) and the main hot topic of conversation was the factory-backed team of Lincoln Capris that'd come down to run the stock car class. Or run away with it, to be more accurate. Lincoln was introducing a brand new, 205 horsepower V-8 for the '53 model year-it was supposed to be the most powerful engine in Detroit!-and they figured a good way to show it off would be to win *La Carrera Panamericana* with it. And they didn't leave much to chance. First off they hired some of the very best drivers available-Triple-A stars Walt Faulkner, Chuck Stevenson, and Johnny Mantz, plus semi-factory privateer entries for Ray Crawford and Duane Carter, and then they had a pair of California wrench wizards named Bill Stroppe and Clay Smith build them no less than *seven* heavily breathed-upon 1953 Lincoln Capris for the race. "I know both those guys," Hank said. "They started out racing hot rods, doing speed runs across the dry lakes with the S.C.T.A. plus a little informal stoplight-to-stoplight stuff on Sepulveda Boulevard. Smith got pretty famous for building cars and grinding camshafts. He's the guy with the cigar-chomping Woody Woodpecker decals."

"Yeah," I said. "I've seen those."

"He did the car that won the Indy 500 this year," Spud said respectfully.

"Our buddy Troy Ruttman drove it," Sammy added. "But he was lucky as hell. Billy Vukovich was clobbering everybody in that new Kurtis. Nobody could touch him."

"Yup," Spud agreed. "But then he broke a steering arm and hit the wall with less'n twenty-five miles t'go." He shook his head. "Damn shame. He sure as hell had the better mousetrap this year."

Sammy let out a long, slow sigh. "Looks like everybody will be wantin' one of those new Kurtis roadsters next year. They'll be the car to have."

"No two ways about it."

You could feel the realization settling in that Sammy's old upright sprinter was turning into an antique even as we sat there over our plates of beans at that little café table down near the southern tip of Mexico.

"How about the other guy?" I was just trying to spark up the conversation.

"Well, Bill Stroppe started in hot rods, too," Hank explained, "and he's done pretty well in a few road races out on the west coast driving one of those new, 2-seater Kurtis chassis with a hopped-up Ford flathead stuffed in it. Fact is, he pisses off a lot of the Ferrari and Jaguar people pretty regularly with that thing. It's a monster."

I'd never seen one of the new Kurtis sportscars in person yet, but I'd heard about them. They really weren't much more than one of Frank Kurtis' full tilt Indy chassis stretched wide enough to hold two people (at least so long as they were friendly) plus a couple of headlights, two taillights, and a set of cheesy little cycle fenders to make them road legal. They were about as graceful as a fire brick, but fast and powerful and really nicely built. Or at least that's what Hank thought.

"Anyhow, they both raced down here before," Hank continued. "Stroppe rode with Johnny Mantz in a Lincoln Cosmopolitan in the first race in 1950, and they damn near won the thing. In fact, they were leading by a pretty fair margin at Mexico City, but then the brakes went out in the mountains and they had to stop to fix 'em-I think Bill had to crimp off a line and they only had the fronts working after that-and right about the same time Johnny came down with about the worst case of Montezuma's Revenge in recorded history. Man, he got sick. Said he'd have to start feeling better just t'die."

We all looked down at the empty plates in front of us and Spud tapped the prescription vial in his pocket like it was one of those little Vatican-blessed religious mementos that nuns carry around.

"I think they came ninth at the end, which was still pretty good. But Clay Smith did even better. He came down last year with a plain old 1948 Mercury Club Coupe he'd bought off some used car lot in Los Angeles. But he went and hopped it up a little with Edelbrock heads and a twin carburetor setup, and believe me, even though it looked stock, it went like no '48s Mercury you ever saw. Plus he had Troy Ruttman to drive it for him. They wound up fourth over-all, and even the Ferraris were amazed by how fast they went."

"But you can't get away with that stuff this year, can you?" I'd read the rules, and the Standard Category cars were pretty much restricted to the way they came off the assembly line. Or at least that's what it said in the official race regulations, anyway. But it turned out there were a lot of things you could do. Especially if you had two sharp hot rod wrenches like Stroppe and Smith, a big bag of Lincoln's money, and a car manufacturing company that was willing to rewrite their option book to make the parts they needed legal on their cars. Like fr'instance that rule about only having one carburetor. All of a sudden the Lincolns showed up with four-barrel carburetors, which was essentially the same as having two carburetors, only put together as one. And it was *legal.* Rumor had it the Clay Smith/Bill Stroppe Lincoln V-8s put out close to *three hundred* horse-power! Even on that weak Mexican gas. They had special dual-range automatic transmissions and a lot of the chassis and suspension stuff under those cars came from heavy duty Ford trucks rather than ordinary passenger cars. But it was all in the option book....

And it didn't end there. Even though the Standard Category cars were all supposed to be strictly rank-and-file production line models with no fiddling or finagling going on, a sharp wrench could do a lot of things to make their cars just a tad better than the one your Uncle Tony drove off the showroom floor. The rules were pretty strict about how you could only have one carburetor and a stock camshaft and no tricked-up speed equipment under the hood. But rules in racing are never any sharper than the people who have to enforce them, and it's been my experience that your average race mechanic is a lot smarter about that stuff than your average race official. And your really *good* race mechanics? Well, it's simply no contest. The only trick is that you cannot afford to get caught with your thumb and forefinger in the cookie jar. Reflects badly on the manufacturer. So you gotta be clever about what you're doing and keep a perfectly straight face even when you're looking at the rulebook cross-eyed. In fact, that's become a sort of respected tradition in the world of Stock Car racing. And a lot of it started right there with the Lincoln team in Mexico in November of 1952.

After dinner Hank and me took a walk to the Tuxtla Gutierrez Ford garage a few streets over to have ourselves a firsthand look at the Lincoln deal, and no question they'd come down loaded for bear. The three team cars were lined up in a neat row, all polished and ready to go, and behind them were evenly spaced stacks of mounted wheels and tires-it looked like hundreds of them, no lie!-plus all sorts of spare engines and transmissions and rear ends and, if you got right down to it, enough stuff to build two or three more cars! Meanwhile the team drivers were out learning the route in a couple fully prepared "practice mules" that the Lincoln team brought for just that purpose. The actual race cars came down in a transporter so's they'd be absolutely fresh when race time finally rolled around, and parked right next to it was this big delivery truck chock full of tools, parts, hoists, jacks, welding tanks, fuel rigs, pots, pans, pit equipment, and Lord only knows what else. And hitched behind *it* was a damn sleeper trailer. But they needed all of it, since Stroppe and Smith's Lincoln crew included a virtual army of mechanics, body men, tire guys, engineers, ad photographers, and even their own cooks and food supplies so that nobody on the Lincoln team'd get the trots from eating the local cuisine plus their own, in-house doctor in case somebody did anyway.

They were *ready!*

Chapter 4: The Worm Turns

Hank and I met up with Big Ed, Carlo Sebastian, and Javier Premal over at Boliches Bar on the plaza around 9:30, and, as you can imagine in a little backwoods burg like Tuxtla Gutierrez when the whole blessed American and international racing circus comes to town, the place was packed and noisy as a New York Central club car during rush hour. It was obvious the three of them had been into the sauce pretty hard for awhile already, but that was mostly because they'd run into a major snag in the negotiations and Carlo was off to the side with Big Ed trying to lubricate the situation with an ample oversupply of Mescal. I don't know if you're familiar with Mescal, but it's made out of some special brand of cactus and is more or less the rowdy black sheep of the tequila family. But it's very popular down in Mexico because you can use it to strip paint, run small farm machinery, or turn yourself and your *compadres* into the wild and wooly sort of individuals who empty pistols into the nighttime sky and howl dirty poetry at the moon. Plus each and every bottle comes with its own little petrified (or perhaps just perpetually inebriated?) cactus-type caterpillar floating in its own gritty little haze of Mescal embalming fluid and petrified cactus caterpillar poop. Or at least that's what it looks like. In any case, local tradition dictates that the person who takes the last swig out of the bottle gets to eat the caterpillar as a sort of triumphal snack. You'll do it, too, after polishing off a bottle of that stuff.

Anyhow, the problem on the front burner was that Carlo wanted Big Ed to fork over a sizeable chunk of the used Ferrari money *before* the race, while Big Ed hadn't exactly just fallen off the turnip truck and was not about to put some very serious cash down on any car that a dangerous-looking, hot tempered Mexican who could stare holes through eight gauge sheet steel was planning to flog from one end of Mexico to the other. Unless, of course, Big Ed could go along for the ride to look out for his investment. As you can imagine, that didn't go over well at all with Javier Premal, who looked at Big Ed as not only a huge, fat, graceless and poorly born American pig, but also as about 300 pounds of useless ballast he really didn't need (especially hauling uphill through the mountains) and that would moreover occupy a goodly percentage of the Ferrari's available cockpit space.

So there was quite a discussion going on between Carlo Sebastian and Big Ed when Hank and I rolled into the bar, and it was pretty entertaining stuff if you accidentally happened to eavesdrop. *"After all,"* Carlo was telling Big Ed in that confidential, behind-the-hand whisper traders in expensive merchandise always use, *"there are always other parties interested in a car such as this-I was approached this very afternoon by a gentleman from the local government-and one never knows when another opportunity such as this might ever come around again...."*

Big Ed stood his ground. "What if this guy blows it up or runs it off a damn cliff, huh? What happens then?"

Carlo sighed like he was terribly, terribly disappointed. "I have known Javier Premal personally for many, many years," he explained, putting a fatherly hand on Big Ed's shoulder, "and he is a man of impeccable honor. Any damage would be fully repaired by authorized factory technicians. At his complete expense. You would have his word on it."

I noticed that Carlo gave Javier's word rather than his own, and, in any case, Big Ed had been around the block enough times to know that it was extremely difficult to put honor into your bank account. "Howzabout if I ride with him?" he asked for probably the tenth or twelfth time. It was, you should excuse the expression, a real Mexican Standoff. But Carlo Sebastian was an experienced hand and knew how to maneuver with equal parts grace and guile in such situations, and so he poured Big Ed another drink, took a slow breath, and started in again. This was obviously going to go a few more rounds.

Javier Premal was up against the bar on the other side of the room, trying out his switchblade smile on a few highly likely looking *señoritas*. He waved us over as soon as he saw me. *"Buenos noches, amigos,"* he said like we were great old chums. "And how is the young American race mechanic and his fine journalist friend this evening?"

I allowed as how we were doing pretty well, although obviously not so well as he and Carlo and Big Ed. I happened to recognize the familiar jet black hair, perfect Bermuda tan and Colgate smile of Creighton Pendleton III down at the other end of the bar, and, although he made the usual point of thoroughly ignoring me (what else?) I noticed he did have a condescending nod of approval on tap for Javier Premal, obviously recognizing him as a fellow patrician-albeit from a vastly inferior nation. Then he went back to work on a dark, bosomy local beauty who looked quite a bit younger, prettier and classier than the two high mileage utility models next to Javier.

"Have you had dinner yet?" Javier asked. "It would give me great pleasure to introduce you to our local cuisine. It will put tears of joy in your eyes and hot, raging fire in your bellies."

"Ah, actually, we've sort of eaten already." I told him. "At that little café a couple blocks over. With some of my stock car friends."

Javier's eyebrows climbed slowly up his forehead. "You are not afraid to eat our food? You do not worry about the *touristas?*"

Somehow I didn't think it would be such a great idea to tell him about Spud's little prescription bottle, so I just shook my head.

"That is good!" he nodded, the switchblade flashing open. *"Bueno!"* Then he leaned in close and whispered: "Most *gringos* believe we are unclean here in Mexico. They think we have rats in our beefsteak and worms in our corn." He looked me right in the eyes. "Tell me, *amigo,* do *you* think we have worms in our corn?"

I gave him a patented New Jersey shrug.

He leaned in even closer, so I could smell the high octane hooch on his breath. *"Of course we do!"* he rasped. "We are an old, poor country. But look around you," he swept his palm past the grinning bartender with half his teeth missing and the two very patient looking working girls next to him at the bar. I think maybe he had them on retainer. "Do *we* look sick to you? Do *I* look sick to you?" You could see he was getting pretty worked up about it.

Hank and I shook our heads in unison.

"No. Of course not. *Absolutamente!"* He held up an important forefinger. "It is the *gringos* with thin blood and weak stomachs who come here and become sick. They have no *cojones!"* He leaned in close again and rasped, "But I can look into your eyes and see that your blood is dark and thick like mine. You will be able to eat our food and enjoy it as I do." The switchblade flashed again. "Especially if you remember to take the secret medicine."

"The what?"

He grabbed the bottle on the bar and slid it over in front of me. "The secret medicine, *mi amigos.* The secret medicine that keeps us strong and healthy in every way." He leaned in so close our noses were almost touching. "It also wards off sickness, sadness, evil spirits and despair."

"It does?"

Javier nodded and ordered up a couple more glasses. Then he poured Hank and me each our first-ever shot of Mescal. And that's about when I noticed the caterpillar and his little cloud of caterpillar poop floating around behind the label. *"Geezsus! What the hell is THAT?"* I wanted to know.

"Oh, he is very important, *amigo,"* Javier explained. *"Muy importante!"*

"Oh yeah? Whyzzat?" I wasn't so sure I liked the idea of cactus worms floating around in my hooch.

"Because if you leave the little fellow alone, he will always make *more!"*

"Make more?"

"Si!" Javier grinned. "If you do not drink the whole bottle-if you leave even a tiny bit-and put it away in a dark place where no one can see what he's doing or learn how he does it," Javier raised his glass and no question expected us to join him, "the little worm will make *more!"* And with that he tossed his off. I looked at Hank, Hank looked back at me, and we had no choice but to go bottoms-up ourselves. What else could we do?

Javier poured us another round. "I think we need to drink one in honor of the little worm, eh?"

Like I said, what else could we do? Besides, the second one went down a lot easier than the first. And the third easier than that.

"Say," I wondered out loud, "what happens if you don't leave any left for the worm in the bottom?"

"Oh, that is the subject of a fine tradition, *mi amigo.* The fellow who takes the very last drink from a bottle of Mescal gets to eat the worm."

"Eat the worm?" It didn't sound particularly appealing.

"Why, of course eat the worm!" Javier shouted, thumping a fist against his chest. *"Absolutamente.* That way he can keep making more inside of *you!"* He pounded his chest again for emphasis. "It gives you the strength of ten and the courage of twenty. Believe me," he continued, drawing in close again, "you will never get sick here in Mexico if you eat the worm."

"Really?"

"I swear it is so. *Verdad!"*

He poured us another round. Like we needed it, right? We tossed that one off and banged our glasses back down on the bar. "I am being a poor host!" Javier suddenly announced. "Would either of you like company?" He nodded in the general direction of the two bored-looking pros sitting next to him at the bar, waiting quietly like horses tied to a hitching post in spite of all the highly eager racing types teeming in around them. The less ugly one smiled at me-she was missing a few teeth herself-and suggestively formed the letter "O" with her mouth. That kind of startled me. And I guess it made me blush, too, because Javier and the girls enjoyed quite a laugh over it.

I didn't want to be rude or anything, but I wasn't really comfortable at all with the idea of bedding down either one of Javier's companions. They both looked a little, well, *earthy* compared to your normal New Jersey standards. Besides, I'd heard all the horror stories about Army guys coming back from Tijuana with an unexpected little surprise in their pants. Not to mention that Julie would *know.* Even if nobody ever breathed a word to her. All she'd need to do was look in my eyes.

Or at least that's what I thought, anyway.

So I thanked Javier with the greatest respect but allowed as how I was really pretty tired and had just gotten myself engaged back home and wasn't much interested. Hank felt pretty much the same way, even though he didn't have a girl back home. "Very well then, *amigos,*" Javier laughed, "we will have another round and see if the girls get any prettier."

He drained the last of the bottle into our glasses, and guess who wound up taking the last slug-worm and all-and even showed it back through my teeth for a quick curtain call before crunching it up and swallowing.

"Well done, *amigo,*" Javier nodded. "After all, it is only fair. The worms get all of us back in the end."

Truth is, I don't remember exactly how we got back to our hotel that night, but for sure it was one of those bank shot deals where you're ricocheting off shop windows and stumbling off of curbs and constantly saying "Excuse me," to all the lamp posts you bump into. I do recall there was still *mariachi* music playing in some of the courtyards and lots of people still out on the streets, and I especially remember the serious looking young Mexicans gathered quietly around the racecars gleaming in the moonlight. Sometimes, if they thought nobody was looking, one of them would reach a cautious hand inside and actually touch the steering wheel. You could almost hear it sizzle and snap like bacon in a fry pan when they made contact.

That night I slept like a man who'd been hit by a thousand-pound wrecking ball, and woke up in pretty much the same shape the next morning. Only without any anesthetic in my system to ease the pain. Plus I swear I felt hundreds of dirty, tiny little caterpillar footprints on my tongue. And then it was like I started to shake and jiggle and rumble all over. Geez, I'd never had that kind of reaction to hooch before. Maybe it was the worm? Only then I heard the glassware rattling on the dresser and opened my eyes to see that, yes indeed, everything that wasn't nailed down was doing a little vibratory dance like those magnetized miniature Scottie dogs you can buy at your neighborhood trick store. It occurred to me that this might indeed be the End of the World (although I remember wondering why even the dirtiest of commies would want to waste an expensive nuclear missile on a godforsaken place like Tuxtla Gutierrez) but when Big Ed and I ran out into the hall, we saw the toothless old Mexican housemaid going about her business as if nothing special was going on. And that in spite of the fact that the whole blessed hotel was jiggling and juggling like a bowl of jello on a window fan! Turns out it was just the normal, everyday morning earthquake that rumbles through that general region as regularly as the local bus service. More regularly, in fact. About then the shaking stopped and Big Ed and I looked back and forth at each other and it slowly began to dawn that we were both feeling pretty damn awful. So we went back in the room for a little Aspirin and Alka Seltzer morning-after cocktail. Only I made mine with some leftover bottled mineral water while Big Ed couldn't be bothered and made his with the standard local tap-issue stuff. And we couldn't help noticing that old Hank had slept right through the earthquake without so much as fluttering an eyelash. Then again, he comes from Los Angeles, so what do you expect?

We went down a little later and had a breakfast of red eggs, rice and tortillas, and of course Hank and I made sure to take one of Spud's pills apiece. But Big Ed waved them off. "I don't need that stuff," he said, peeling himself one of the strangely green local bananas. "I got a iron constitution...."

It was the day before race day, and you could really feel the tension building all over town. Ferrari privateer Bracco and the Mercedes drivers were back from their reconnoitering trips to check things over one last time and go over their route notes, and Hank and I decided to stop over by the Mercedes garage to take a firsthand look at the only team the Ferrari people seemed to be worried about. They were set up in a building on the far end of town with a grass airstrip behind it and the pair of rented DC3s at the ready, and it was amazing how quiet and well organized it seemed out there away from all the noise and hubbub on the plaza. There were three team cars lined up with military precision in the exact center of the floor, two 300SL coupes for regular drivers Karl Kling and Hermann Lang, plus an open roadster version for John Fitch. Apparently the Mercedes engineers hadn't come to a satisfactory conclusion as to whether a coupe or an open car would be more advantageous in the heat, wind, weather and dust of Mexico, so they decided to bring both and cover all bases. A closed car might be a little more streamlined and faster on the top end and also figured to protect the driver and riding mechanic better from the elements, but they'd also be trapped in there with the heat and noise and engine fumes, while an open car could be a little lighter without the top and the window glass and the weight would likewise sit a little lower, but the crew would be exposed to the sun and wind and grit for the entire two-thousand-mile run from Tuxtla Gutierrez to Juarez. At least they'd have plenty of fresh air.

To be honest, I'd never seen any race cars like the 300SLs before. Nobody had. They looked like what they were-machines-and were painted the same dull, cool silver as a raw aluminum casting. They were shaped like something out of a flying saucer movie, but with that unmistakable three-pointed star glinting ominously in the center of the grilles. I noticed it was the only brightwork on the whole car. Although loosely based on the engines and drivelines Mercedes had hanging around from their big, lumbering sedans, the way those 300SL race cars were designed, built, and developed set brand new standards. It started with the frames, which were welded up in three dimensions out of small diameter steel tubes and figured to be both considerably stronger, stiffer, and lighter than what anybody else was using. But the frames were pretty tall, and that's what made Mercedes come up with those strange, hinged-at-the-top gullwing doors that only came about halfway down the sides on the two coupes. The cars had independent suspension all around, which figured to make for better road holding over rough, uneven surfaces than the solid rear axles favored by Ferrari and the rest, and the 3-liter straight six engines were fuel injected and tipped way over on their sides to keep the weight and hood line low. Hank said the rumor mill pegged them at around 200 horsepower, and while that was nowhere near what Ferrari claimed for the big 4.1 liter V-12s in their new Mexicos, you got the idea those German horses might be a tad more robust than the ones prancing out of the Ferrari race shops in Maranello. Besides, the fast and original 300SLs only amounted to one component of Mercedes' assault on *La Carrera*. Hank pointed out team manager Alfred Neubauer, and I must admit he wasn't at all what I expected. He was just this big, lardy looking German with a whole collection of chins and a suit shaped roughly like a burlap potato sack. Fact is, he looked like an unmade bed, and no question he'd been pretty chummy with the knackwurst and dumplings when he was growing up. You couldn't miss how he sort of overflowed his folding chair on either side. But he was all business when it came to running the Mercedes racing team. Far as Alfred Neubauer was concerned, it was preparation, organization, teamwork, and tactics that won races like the *Mille Miglia* and *La Carrera*. It went without saying that you brought a good machine, but that was only the first little part of the equation.

Anyhow, Neubauer was deep in conversation with his lead driver, Karl Kling, who, unlike his boss, really looked the part of a crack German racing driver. In fact, you could squint your eyes and very easily imagine him climbing into a Messerschmitt with a row of little British target emblems under the canopy. Somebody in Washington apparently thought so, too, since the FBI nabbed Kling between planes at the New York airport on account of somebody pegged him as some sort of bigshot Nazi war criminal who'd slipped through the net at the Nuremberg trials. Eventually they got it straightened out and decided he wasn't who they thought he was (or at least that he wasn't such a bigshot after all) so Kling could take the next plane down to Mexico City to start practicing with the rest of his teammates.

I noticed John Fitch over to one side, looking lean and clever as a hungry fox, and it was nice that he remembered me a little from Elkhart Lake and Watkins Glen. "So howzit goin'?" I asked.

"Pretty well," he allowed through a cautious smile.

Hank pulled a little spiral notebook out. "You guys have been out practicing for the past few days, right?"

"For almost two weeks, actually," he said matter-of-factly. But then his eye kind of peeled around to see if Neubauer was watching us-he was-and you could tell John Fitch started picking his words pretty carefully from there on. "Mr. Prat, the Mexican Mercedes importer, was kind enough to provide a couple 200 and 300 series sedans so we could go over the roads together. Of course neither Karl nor Hermann have been here before, so that was absolutely necessary." Then he added with a sheepish smile, "I'm afraid we beat on those practice cars pretty mercilessly."

"But it went all right?" Hank continued, scribbling furiously away in his spiral notebook.

"It went very well. The Mercedes sedans held up beautifully under some hellish pounding and dreadful weather conditions." Like any good driver, John Fitch couldn't resist giving Mercedes a plug within earshot of the boss. "Then we switched off to the 300SL practice mule so each of us could get a feel for the actual race cars."

"The practice mule?"

"It's already loaded back into the transporter. I'm afraid it looks pretty disreputable now."

"What happened?"

John Fitch looked at him funny. "Nothing 'happened.' We're just finished with it. I'm sure they'll send it back to Germany and strip it down to the last nut and bolt to see what needs to be improved upon next time."

You had to be impressed with that kind of precision and forethought. But it kind of bothered me that one of the best *Carrera* cars in Mexico was being loaded up and shipped off before the race even started while talented guys like Sammy Speed were stuck driving Nashes.

It didn't seem fair.

"So the practicing went well for you guys?" Hank prodded again, eager to get in a little more scribbling.

Fitch gave a half nod. "I'd say so. Of course, there's no way you can memorize the whole route-not in a dozen years-but we made good notes and I think we'll be at least as well off as the rest."

"I see. And how about team orders?"

John hesitated for a second, his eye peeling around in Herr Neubauer's direction. "There aren't any team orders," he said so that you almost believed him. Then he added, "But of course we want to maximize the team's chances of doing well…."

"And what exactly does that mean?" Hank continued, pressing a little as members of the press invariably do.

"Herr Fitch!" Alfred Neubauer called out in a surprisingly high pitched, singsong voice. He heaved up out of his chair and pork-waddled over to where we were standing. You couldn't miss the stern, preoccupied look on his face. But when he reached us, that suddenly switched to a smile that hung like a big, toothy sash beneath two of the clearest, most calculating eyes I have ever seen. *"I am zorry,"* he said to us in that same singsong voice, sounding genuinely apologetic, *"but ve need to dizcuss der fuel undt tire schtops."* He turned to John. *"Please excuse vfrom your friends."*

End of interview.

"Could I at least get a picture?" Hank asked, fumbling for the camera in his duffel bag. You could see his stock went up with Herr Neubauer the instant he saw the Leica, and nothing would do but that the whole team posed for Hank in front of the cars. Neubauer even asked if the light was all right, since it would be no problem at all to push the cars outside. Which they did.

With the Mercedes team cars out of the garage, I noticed two runty, familiar shapes off to the side, all by themselves, and recognized them immediately as Porsches. On the one hand, it seemed perfectly natural to see Porsches at a car race-no matter if they looked like ripe tin fruit and sounded like a fart in a bathtub, I'd grown to appreciate what those cars could do after seeing them beat the crap out of all the other smallbore cars at Bridgehampton and Brynfan Tyddyn. But there was no smallbore class at *La Carrera* in 1952, and it struck me as sort of futile to send a couple anemic little 1500cc fours-they were nothing but hot-rodded Volkswagen engines, really-all the way from Germany to do battle against Ferrari Mexicos and Mercedes 300SLs. I mean, no way was light weight or nimble handling going to even things up against those big guns. Even through the mountains. Turns out it was actually sort of a winter lark for some rich, old school German aristocrat types who had managed to come through the war (as the really *upper* upper crust always do) with their families, fortunes, and facial features in tact. The guy behind it was a certain Prince Alfonso von Hohenloe, who, in spite of being as German as a bratwurst, lived in Mexico City (it was so much nicer than Berlin towards the end of '45) and ran the local Volkswagen and Porsche distributorship. He figured running a couple of the new Porsche 356s in *La Carrera* would be a great way to show them off to his high class, upper crust Mexican clientele (most of whom were rich, aristocratic types themselves) and what could be better than having a couple more genuine princes, barons, etc. over to drive them. So von Hohenloe rang up his cousins Prince Furst von Metternich, Baron Effee and Graf von Berckheim (Hank explained as how a "graf" is a lot like a British "earl," only with dueling scars) to come over and join him for a jolly good time and not incidentally enhance the snob appeal quotient of the whole effort. How they wound up finishing was never an issue.

Not having hung around much with genuine bluebloods in my time, I was surprised to find out how much prestige and privilege goes along with being an old line, Old World member of the Lucky Sperm Club. Why, even Creighton Pendleton cowtowed to those guys! And they gave him the same old condescending, down-the-nose "thanks" when he bought them drinks just the way Creighton did to people like Big Ed and me. And that's when I realized that this whole snoot appeal thing is just a big house of cards, and if you want to keep your place on the first floor and sneer down at the folks in the basement, you've got to let the fellows on the second floor do the same to you. And it goes on like that all the way to the penthouse, which was really only one short flight up from where these prince and baron guys lived. Seems like no matter how much old, old American money you had in the family strongbox, it was never as good as old, old European money. And none of it-not even a million kazillion dollars-was as good as having a noble title and a family coat of arms over the mantlepiece and a bloodline you could trace back to some old medieval castle (even a bombed out one) because those were the absolute highest of high end snoot appeal trappings and things that all the new money in the world could never, ever buy.

But being born so high carried a burden of attitude with it, and these guys made people like Creighton Pendleton look like amateurs when it came to being snooty, snobby and arrogant. Oh, they were perfectly friendly and chummy and even a lot of fun with each other, but you couldn't miss the sense that the ground was just a little bit higher and the air was just a little bit sweeter wherever they happened to be standing. The amazing thing was how they didn't have to *say* or *do* anything special to carry it off. It must take a lot of generations and some special, top secret training to develop something like that. Of course, it probably helps that, all your life, people have been bowing and scraping and calling you "your majesty" or "your highness" instead of giving you a swift kick in the backside, not to mention the family retainer toadies who are always there sweeping up behind you no matter where you go, what you do, or to whom you do it.

No question that kind of treatment could easily lead a person to believe that their ass is made of cake, their shit doesn't stink, and that their blood is truly of a different color and viscosity from yours and mine. Plus there must be genuine comfort in knowing that your ancestors could have sent the ancestors of most anybody you meet to the gallows or the dungeon or the old chopping block if they didn't like the cut of their jib or the color of their waistcoat. And probably did. We talked a little about it, and Hank and I came to the conclusion that the well born couldn't help it any more or less than anyone else. It was okay to hate their guts, though. In fact, they rather expected it.

On our way back to the plaza, Hank and I engaged in a little free form handicapping, and agreed that Mercedes looked by far the most serious threat to the Ferrari team. We also agreed that it made for an interesting match, seeing as how the Italians were dramatic and hot and passionate about their racing and you could almost feel the animal pulse throbbing through their cars. They figured if you built the fastest, sleekest, most powerful racing cars in the world and put the world's most daring and skillful drivers behind the wheel (who were all Italians anyway, natch) the "friendly" rivalry between them and the superior performance of the automobiles would ultimately lead to victory. By contrast, the Mercedes cars were War Machines and *La Carrera* was just another far-flung campaign waged in a far off country by people who, based on history, were accustomed to winning such things. There was a cool sense of purpose and patience in the Mercedes camp that went along with that. They weren't loud or cockily confident like the guys in the Ferrari garage. But they weren't exactly scared of them, either.

Not one bit.

Then who should we see in town surrounded by a horde of open mouthed local gawkers and a squad of Mexican Army types but that asshole Skippy Welcher and his eternal squire/sidekick with the Coke-bottle-bottom glasses Milton Fitting. Of course the crowd was really there to see the Jaguar C-Type, which drew people like steel filings to a magnet no matter where you parked it. But Skippy was convinced it was *his* crowd, and so he was rambling on as only The Skipper could, waving his arms excitedly in the air as he told heroic tales of all his great racing adventures, his face popping and flinching like pea soup coming to a boil while spit and sweat showered off in all directions. Fortunately nobody in the audience spoke English except Hank and me, and we only stayed long enough for Hank to snap a picture. "I gotta remember *this* guy!" Hank mumbled as he focused the Leica.

"Believe me, there's no way to forget him."

We found out later that Skippy didn't much fancy the idea of driving his C-type down, so he had Milton take it on a boat to Veracruz and then drive it through the mountains and jungle to Tuxtla Gutierrez. Although Milton didn't say much about it (he never said much about anything, to tell the truth, and you got the idea that if you looked hard into one of Milton's ears, you'd very likely see light coming through from the other side) but I understand it was quite an ordeal. Unlike the new Panamerican Highway, which was supposedly all paved, the road through the mountains and jungles from Veracruz was gravel at best and rocks, boulders, wild animals, farm animals, poisonous reptiles, and opportunistic local bandits at worst. My understanding is he had six flat tires, got charged by a wild pig, bitten by a kinkajou, shit and pissed on by a band of playful tree monkeys, robbed at least twice, and arrived in Tuxtla Gutierrez driving on four naked wheel rims and looking pretty naked himself, since the last group of *banditos* had taken all of his clothes except for one pair of wool socks. Which, as you can imagine, he was wearing in his lap.

But I've got to hand it to Milton, because he bounced right back and got himself and the car back into racing shape after The Skipper wired him some money and a few of the race officials put him in touch with a group of talented local mechanics who were accustomed to *fixing* things that you or I would normally throw away. I guess that comes from working way out in the Mexican boondocks where it's hard as hell to come by spare parts and harder still to find money to pay for them. To a man, the Mexican mechanics were true *maestros,* and I developed a genuine respect for them after I saw how they resurrected The Skipper's Jag (not to mention a host of other cars) during *La Carrera.* Those guys could even *make* stuff rather than simply buy it over the parts counter and stick it on like we do up in Jersey, and I was amazed at the way they could fabricate a motor mount out of scrap metal or pour a new carburetor float bowl casting out of pot metal cooked up on an outdoor fire or re-weld a broken spring and then temper it so it wouldn't break again or straighten out and re-lace The Skipper's thoroughly pretzelized wire wheels so they looked and worked good as new again. And they were sheer magic when it came to bodywork (even though it didn't look like they did much practicing on the local automotive population) including the delicate aluminum alloy panels on the C-Type. By the time Skippy arrived by plane three days before the race, that Jag looked as fresh as when Tommy Edwards and I took off from New York to Elkhart Lake.

You had to be impressed. The bad part was that Skippy had never seen so much as a foot of the Panamerican Highway any closer than on a map in his lap, and spent the days before the race drinking Margaritas, playing to the street crowds, and pumping money into the local hooker's union retirement benefit fund rather than trying to learn anything about which way the road went over the next rise. So it was a pretty safe bet that all the fine work put in by those excellent local Mexican mechanics would get undone and go for naught by the time the first leg was over. In fact, I tried to get Hank to lay me a bet on it. But after seeing The Skipper in action-even for the very first time-he was too sharp to go for it.

We couldn't find Big Ed or Carlo Sebastian or even Javier Premal back at the hotel or down the street at Boliches Bar, and, seeing as how I'd already about run through Big Ed's tenspot, we wandered over to see how the final preparations on Sammy Speed's Nash were going. The race was due to start around daybreak the next morning, and you could feel a hard new edge in the air as we made our way across the plaza. Everywhere you looked, people were either fiddling with their cars or standing nervously around trying to figure out what they ought to be fiddling with. It didn't feel much like a fiesta anymore. No, this particular evening Tuxtla Gutierrez was a race paddock, pure and simple, and you could feel the tension, fear, excitement, and giddy anticipation all swirling around like a cold wind through your gut.

Sammy Speed was trying about his forty-seventh different arrangement of tool box, jack, lug wrench, parts and spare tires in the back of the Nash-even though he knew it'd be a total, disorganized mess after the first flat-while Spud was sitting on the rear seat cushion in front of a small campfire, cooking up a can of beans and a few slices of Spam in a black iron frypan. "Hey, how's it goin'?" he grinned. "You guys want a little dinner?"

I was hungry, but I felt a little funny about sharing their food. I mean, it didn't look like they had all that much.

"Sure," Hank agreed. No question he was tailor made to be a reporter.

"You been takin' those pills I gave ya?"

"Absolutely."

"They workin' for ya?"

I shrugged. "I guess they're the kind of thing you only find out about when they *stop* working."

Spud laughed. "I s'pose."

We had a nice little dinner of Spam and beans and bottled soda out there under the stars, and Spud encouraged us to eat hearty since there was no way to put the Spam back in the can once you'd cooked it and Sammy was still fooling around in the back of the Nash and apparently not all that interested in eating. Spud leaned over and whispered, "He's nervous. I can always tell."

87

"He's nervous about the race?" I mean, that didn't sound much like the Sammy Speed I knew about.

"Shh." Spud whispered. "Y'don't want him t'hear ya." He leaned in even closer. "A'course he ain't nervous about the race. Hell no. He's nervous about the damn *money!*"

And it occurred to me all over again that *La Carrera* was a monumentally big deal to a guy like Sammy Speed. He knew going in that if he could keep his nose clean and maybe get a little lucky and, most especially, take that dumb old Nash right out to the edge of what it could do and keep it there for five solid days and two thousand grueling miles without screwing up even once, he'd be in for the biggest damn payday of his life. Plus enough notoriety to land him some better rides in better cars like those new Kurtis Indy roadsters he coveted so much. It was a lot different situation from those well paid factory team drivers in the Ferrari and Mercedes Benz camps or those blue-blooded German play-boys in the two Porsches or rich dilettantes like Creighton Pendleton III, Giovanni Bracco and Javier Premal in their fancy privateer Ferraris or even Welcher Waxout ear swab heir and full-time professional jerkoff Skippy Welcher in his freshly rebuilt C-Type Jag. No, for guys like Sammy Speed, this was more than serious.

It was life or death.

We wandered back over to the hotel after dinner, stopping along the way to buy a couple cold *cervezas* with the last few coins in my pocket. By this time I'd come to realize that Hank Lyons hardly ever reached into his pocket except to pull out a kleenex when he had to blow his nose. Now don't get me wrong. I liked Hank a lot and he was really good company to have down in Mexico. Especially with Big Ed off gallivanting around with Carlo Sebastian and Javier Premal, not to mention Hank knowing just about everything there was to know about the cars and characters we saw. But he was cheap as hell. Or maybe "cheap" is the wrong word, since it seems to be something of a tradition among press pass types that they never expect to pay for anything so long as either *(a:)* they are in the company of somebody they are likely to write about, thereby bestow-ing radiant celebrity status in front of the teeming multitudes who read their stuff, or, *(b:)* they find themselves in the company of people who earn more or have higher lifestyles than they do (which, to hear most reporters talk, includes just about everybody), or, *(c:)* the poor drool they're with keeps reaching for his wallet and never gets up the stones to say anything about it.

But I didn't mind, since it was really Big Ed's money we were blowing and Big Ed always told me (and showed me by example) that's precisely what money was printed and minted for-to buy neat things and good times in equal measure. Unlike the Princes, Barons, Grafs, and Creighton Pendletons of this world, Big

Ed worked hard for his money. But he laughed like hell when some of it slipped right through his fingers, so long as he was having himself a fun time while it happened. You had to appreciate an attitude like that.

Speaking of Big Ed, we heard him in the bathroom just as soon as we opened the door. No question Javier Premal's nonstop, high profile tour of the local restaurant scene had produced the desired effect and now there was no question of Big Ed riding with him in the race tomorrow. In fact, it sounded like there was little chance of Big Ed riding anything besides the commode for at least the next 24 hours. We heard him squeeze off another burst (imagine a load of grapeshot blasting through thick mud) followed by soft, sad groaning like a milk cow with her head stuck in a fence. I looked at Hank and he looked back at me and in an instant we were flipping a coin to see who got to sleep out on the narrow little strip of balcony outside the window.

"Buddy?" Big Ed called forlornly from inside the bathroom.

"Yeah?"

"C'mere. I needa talk t'you."

I took a few cautious paces across the carpet and hesitantly swung the door open a few inches. Big Ed was about doubled up on the toilet, his eyes red and puffy, complexion pale and sweaty and not looking too well at all.

"What's up?" I asked, prudently staying well back from the door.

Big Ed feebly cleared his throat. In fact, he cleared both ends. "I'm sick," he groaned miserably.

"I can see."

"I think I'm gonna die." He was almost crying, you know? It tore your heart out. Your nostrils, too, for that matter.

"I'll send Hank down to find a doctor."

"Make sure it's an American doctor, huh?"

I promised.

"An' one more thing."

"What's that?"

"We made a deal tonight."

"Oh? What kind of deal?"

"You're riding with Javier tomorrow."

Chapter 5: The Stallion and the Star

As you can probably imagine, I didn't sleep too well in that stuffy little hotel room in Tuxtla Gutierrez the night of November 19th, 1952. In fact, I didn't sleep at all. Hank won the toss for the balcony, but he came in after awhile and tried the floor seeing as how that balcony was about the size of your average bookshelf and not particularly accommodating. I told him to help himself to the bed since my eyes were frozen W.F.O. (Wide Fucking Open) at the prospect of riding shotgun in that Ferrari with the skull-faced Javier Premal the next morning. Not to mention that the sounds coming out of the bathroom barely two feet away were not exactly lullaby music. So I tried the balcony, and, just like Hank said, it was really more of an overgrown half-flat window box without any flowers (although it was doing fine when it came to dirt and fertilizer) and there was no way you wanted to lie down even if there had been room to do so. The chair wouldn't fit through the glass doors either, so I wound up putting the chair cushions and Cal Carrington's genuine leather suitcase together to make a kind of impromptu beach-style recliner on top of the regular-issue local base coat layer of insects, dead lizards' and tropical bird poop. It was about as comfortable as the back seat of a Morris Minor.

Still, it was a beautiful night. There was a soft breeze wafting in from the jungle scented with palm oil and tobacco and drying coffee beans, and, if I looked up, I saw more blessed stars than I'd seen anywhere except maybe Elkhart Lake. But I just couldn't get comfortable. Not to mention the noise from the street, since there were race officials and race crews and army guys and leftover drunks and occasional between-engagement hookers wandering by all night long. Voices carry in the middle of the night, and it was all the more fascinating since it was all in Spanish and totally incomprehensible to me. Plus we had a very vocal group of local Tuxtla alley cats down by the kitchen trash who had apparently eaten their fill and were now on the lookout for a little companionship. I swear, it was worse than Jack Benny's violin. Or maybe it was just the same, only louder. But it was a sad, lonely, mournful sort of noise, and it made me wish I'd called Julie earlier in the day. Not that I didn't try once or twice. But there were all sorts of people trying to call long distance out of Tuxtla Gutierrez that afternoon and precious few operators (including none that spoke English as far as I could tell) plus actually managing to get a live operator on the line was still no guarantee of getting a long distance connection to New Jersey. To be fair, the Mexican telephone service was certainly better than two Dixie cups and a string. But not by much.

If you strip it down to the bare essentials, my problem that night was simple. I was *scared.* Well, maybe "scared" is a bit too strong. Let's just say I was "concerned." Concerned that rich, crazy, skull-faced sonofabitch Javier Premal was going to kill me. And the weapon he was going to use was Big Ed's presumptive new Ferrari (assuming it made it all the way to the finish line in Ciudad Juarez, which didn't seem too likely based on the cold, dangerous glint in Javier's eyes). Although I had to admit it sounded like a glorious sort of way to exit this life, I couldn't say I was actually ready to go. Besides, I was newly engaged to get married, and Julie would absolutely murder me if she found out I'd gotten myself killed. Not to mention that I didn't really know this Javier Premal character all that well, and what little I did know convinced me even more that I was doing the right thing by being terrified.

So I sat up on that little balcony all night, alternately thinking about how furious Julie would be when she heard I was coming home in a pine box with a few leftover Ferrari parts and failing miserably to convince myself that this was going to be a great adventure and that Javier Premal was actually a safe, sane, and skillful sort of driver. I mean, he'd somehow made it this far, hadn't he? And there was an undeniable buzz in my gut about getting to ride in a Ferrari. Hell, I'd never even sat in one before. Let alone ridden shotgun in one being driven right out to the limit of its capabilities by a rich, crazy, skull-faced Mexican who…and then I'd be right back on Julie's mom's doorstep in the pine box with the Ferrari parts again.

The sky in the east was just beginning to turn pink when I packed up my makeshift recliner, washed my hands, splashed some water in my face, put on the cleanest T-shirt I had, and headed downstairs. Big Ed had finally fallen into a deep, druggy sort of sleep from the shot the Lincoln team doctor gave him with a hypodermic needle big enough to be a prop in a vaudeville show, and I didn't see any reason to wake him. He'd be up soon enough when the engines started firing.

I located Javier Premal backing Big Ed's soon-to-be new Ferrari into its assigned position on the street across from the plaza, and I knew it must be getting close to the seven ayem starting time on account of there were race officials and Army guys and an enormous, seething crowd of local citizens gathered around the long line of race cars parked along the plaza and pointed north towards the mountains on the one paved road leading out of town. I felt a chill breeze go through my gut when I noticed some of the drivers and co-drivers up towards the front were already putting their helmets and driving gloves on. The Sports Category cars would go first, with that wild Mexican hotrod Cadillac with the eight hood scoops in the leadoff position (I wondered how many pesos changed hands under the table for that particular honor?) and the other "sports" cars following at one minute intervals. Then there'd be a five minute break and they'd turn about twice as many Stock Category cars loose, also one minute apart. Don't ask me how, but Javier's Ferrari had somehow drawn the 13th starting spot out of ninety total entries. Oh, great. Lucky 13. All I needed now was to have a black cat cross my path. Right on cue, one of the loud, raggedy felines who'd been serenading me from the kitchen trash all night came scooting out from under the Ferrari's fender and shot right between my legs. I jumped back-hey, it startled me-and Javier laughed. "I hope you are not superstitious, *amigo?*"

"Nah," I told him. "Being superstitious brings you bad luck."

Javier lit up one of his skinny black Mexican cigarettes and took a long, thoughtful drag. He was looking right past me at the first little sliver of sun breaking up over the mountains. "And how is Señor Big Ed this morning?" he asked, his eyes focused far off in the distance.

"He had a pretty rough night," I allowed, "but he got some kind of shot from the Lincoln team doctor around 10:30 and he's sleeping it off now."

"Good." Javier said absently, still watching the sun inch its way up out of the horizon. I don't think I'd ever seen such a faraway look in a man's eyes before. "There is a helmet for you inside the car," he said softly. "Try it on."

Sure enough, there was a dinged-up, pudding bowl-shaped helmet with black leather earflaps sitting on the passenger seat. But my brain must've been a little bigger than whoever originally owned that helmet, because it more or less sat way up on top of my head instead of coming down around it. It was pretty beat up, too, and you couldn't miss the nickname *'Poco Loco'* painted across the front. "Say," I asked, "whose is this?"

"It's mine, *amigo*. I bought a new one for *La Carrera.*" He pulled a shiny red helmet out of the driver's seat and strapped it around his chin. The new one had a small Ferrari emblem above his eyebrows-the famous black stallion reared up against its bright yellow background-and when he turned around, I saw Javier had *'Poco Loco'* painted on the back of that one, too. Oh, great. I was about to climb into the suicide seat of perhaps the fastest car I'd ever been in alongside some crazy-macho Mexican guy with a demonstrably tiny brain, an oversupply of nerve, and *'Poco Loco'* painted on his helmet. Swell.

Engines fired at the far end of the line.

Just then who comes screaming past but The Skipper and Milton Fitting in their locally rebuilt C-Type. I guess they must've overslept or something. Wouldn't you know it, they were slotted in four places ahead of us. "Watch out for that guy," I told Javier. "He's kinda nuts."

Javier flipped open the old switchblade smile. "No, my friend. You have it wrong. It is *he* who should be watching out for *us.*"

"Yeah, okay. But watch out for him anyway. He's, umm, a little bit *unpredictable.*" That was about the nicest word you could use for it.

We heard the sound of that big, unmuffled Caddy engine revving up at the head of the line and a huge cheer went up as the starter's flag waved and it took off for Oaxaca, some 330 miles away.

"Might as well get in, *amigo.*" Javier advised. So I opened the door and slid down into the passenger seat, damn near knocking that stupid helmet off in the process. I had to tilt my head way over to the side to put it back on, and then realized that it stuck up so high that it pressed into the headliner and I had to kind of kink my neck to one side to make it fit. No question this would not be very pleasant for five days and two-thousand miles, and I resolved to take some of the stuffing out of the seat cushion as soon as I got the chance. Then Javier reached for the key and I watched him rotate it a quarter turn to the right to switch the juice on-you could hear the electric fuel pumps clicking behind the seat-and then push it *in* to engage the starter. That was about the cleverest, most magnificently designed ignition switch I'd ever seen. But the best part was the noise it was attached to: a smooth, metallic whirr followed by this wonderfully complex and perfectly meshed explosion of power. I'd never been inside a Ferrari before, and, for a moment, anyway, it was enough to make me forget about the dangers of the road ahead or the nickname *'Poco Loco'* painted on the helmet of my driver. Hell, that sound was enough to make you wet your pants!

Javier smoked another of those skinny black cigarettes while waiting our turn, goosing the throttle every now and then and unleashing a chorus of high caliber sewing machines in the valve gear coupled with that unmistakable 12-cylinder snarl out the tailpipes. It gave you goosebumps. Directly in front of me was a simple rolled metal dashboard painted a deep, lustrous silver, with an oversize speedo and tach and a bunch of smaller gauges for temps and pressures and anything else you might want to know. Underneath were a row of unmarked, bat-handle toggle switches. I guess if you owned a car like this, it was pretty much *assumed* you knew what the hell they were for. Like you were born with it, right? Arms-distance in front of Javier was this beautiful woodrim steering wheel with slotted aluminum spokes and a bright yellow horn button featuring that proud, undeniably thoroughbred Ferrari stallion reared up in the center. Just a fingertip reach away, somebody'd fastened a gold St. Christopher's medal with two brass machine screws, and you couldn't miss the little magnetic Holy Mother kind of teetering off the curve of the dash under the rearview mirror, hands spread benignly to either side and eyes cast sweetly downward like she was saying a blessing over the tall, slender gear lever with the polished aluminum ball on top. On top was this nifty button to control the reverse lockout so's you couldn't accidentally grab reverse in the heat of a desperate downshift. To tell the truth, I'd never been in a car like that Ferrari before, where every single piece was handsome and elegant enough to hang on your living room wall.

About then Hank Lyons wandered out of the crowd and knelt by my window. "How y'doin' in there, Buddy?" he asked, chewing hard on his nails. Hell, he looked more nervous than me.

"Just ducky," I told him, hoping my voice wouldn't crack.

"You guys be careful on this first leg. They had three fatals on it last year."

Like I needed to hear that, you know?

"The pavement's real hard on tires, too. Mostly volcanic rock, I think."

"Thanks. I'll keep it in mind."

I heard the painful howl of a Jaguar engine being taken right to the redline with no load followed by a mournful screech off the tires as Skippy and Milton took off in their C-type. Four minutes to go….

"How'bout a picture, Buddy?" Hank said. "You know, for posterity." He pointed the Leica at me. "Say 'cheese.'"

I did my best to muster up a smile.

Then I looked over at Javier. His face was perfectly still, but I could just about hear his heart pounding inside his chest. I know for sure I could hear mine. We watched John Fitch pull neatly away in the open Mercedes and we eased forward another dozen feet. I closed my eyes and instantly saw Julie's face on the inside of my eyelids. God, why hadn't I called her?

God, why hadn't I taken another piss?

"Ready, *amigo?*" Javier asked, flicking his switchblade open and shut. He was trying to seem calm, but you could see how tense and determined he was.

"I guess I'm ready as I'll ever be." *Jesus, what was I doing here?*

"*Bueno, mi amigo,*" Javier grinned as the last car in front of us-another of those hotrod Mexican sedans-chirped the tires to yet another roar from the crowd and took off towards the mountains. I remember feeling very small and cold and empty inside. Then one of the Mexican officials stuck his head in the window on Javier's side. *"Poco Loco!"* he grinned, showing off a nice assortment of gold teeth. *"Esta bien?"*

Javier nodded.

He gave Javier a playful slap on the helmet. *"Bueno. Vaya con Dios!"*

As the starter stepped back to his post, I saw Javier whisper something, reach out, touch his St. Christopher's medal, and very quickly cross himself. That looked like a pretty good idea, so I touched the St. Christopher medal and crossed myself, too. Hey, it couldn't hurt.

The starter held up his hand and began slowly peeling down the fingers: *"Cinco...quatro..."* with every number the engine revs rose another thousand, *"tres...dos...ANDALE!"* Instantly the Ferrari squatted down on its haunches and we were rocketing towards the mountains. Javier took it right up to 7000 in first gear-*seven blessed thousand!*-banged a quick shift into second and the rush just kept on coming. I was aware of a sea of people crowded in on either side, and the faster we went, the narrower the path between them seemed to be. Javier grabbed third and once again buried the throttle. For sure we were going to kill some of them. Maybe all of them. And then suddenly we broke free just as Javier upshifted to fourth. We were going over a hundred already and he still had one gear to go! I was hanging onto the little chrome grab bar in front of me with the same exact death grip I'd used on the armrests in that DC6 coming through the air pockets into Mexico City. Out the windshield I could see the road gently rising and falling over the low foothills leading towards the mountains and that hotrod Packard that had started ahead of us slowly drawing closer. We came to the first serious bend in the road-a sweeping left-hander that you could see all the way around-and I gritted my teeth as Javier kept the pedal buried and didn't even flinch towards the brakes. *Jesus, this was going to be over pretty quickly after all.* But Javier set his jaw and turned in with fierce determination-*daring* the car to get away from him!-and damned if we didn't just scoot around like we were on rails. Made up a good fifty yards on the Packard, too! Maybe this *'Poco Loco'* Premal wasn't such a bad 'shoe at all. For sure he wasn't afraid of anything!

I'd been on my fair share of scary rides before, and my comfort level was always more proportional to how calm and collected the guy behind the wheel seemed than how fast we were going. Like that rainy midnight charge through the Poconos in Cal Carrington's TC on our way to Giant's Despair. Cal always looked so relaxed-almost serene-even when we were skating towards a sheer edge with nothing but a thousand feet of pitch-black emptiness on the other side. Even so, I felt more at ease than doing a white-knuckled 85 or 90 down a straight stretch of road with Big Ed Baumstein at the wheel. But Javier wasn't like either one. He drove with a sort of grim, sustained fury and an unforgiving, almost threatening touch. Thank goodness the car was good enough to let him get away with it. But he didn't know how to use the road the way Cal did. Not hardly. With Cal you could feel a flow and rhythm as he swooped late and deep into the corners and made the absolute most of the available pavement coming out the other side. Javier tended to turn in much earlier-usually as soon as the road started to bend-and then just more or less fought it out from there. Fortunately for both of us, he turned out to be a pretty good fighter. No question he had plenty of instinctive, seat-of-the-pants steering savvy. He needed it. In fact, he reminded me of what Tommy Edwards always said about wild drivers: "He's gifted with all the car control he needs to get himself out of all the filthy situations he'd never be in if he drove with his bloody head instead of his behind."

We saw that hotrod Mexican Cadillac that was first car off pulled over to the side with driveline problems-*finished!*-not ten minutes out of Tuxtla! Poor guys. I caught a glimpse of the driver's eyes as we flashed past at a hundred or so, and I swear it looked like he was crying. But who could blame him? Javier caught the Mexican Packard in another couple miles and the guy left us plenty of room to pass and even waved and shouted as we went by. That actually made me feel pretty good. The road climbed up towards the mountains in smooth, easy swoops at first, but then it got steeper and more difficult and naturally that's precisely when we caught up to Skippy Welcher in the C-Type, who, as per usual, was tooling along right down the middle of the road, blocking like hell and not leaving room enough on either side to get past. Javier gave him the horn and the lights and finally even gave him a few modest love taps, but he might as well have thrown sand at a crocodile. You could see Skippy had his head scrunched down between his shoulder blades and was working the wheel something fierce-he obviously thought we were *racing* each other!-and it amazed me all over again what a complete doofus that guy was. I mean, if somebody catches you from four minutes back, the obvious conclusion is that they're faster and it would be the righteous thing to let them by. The smart thing, too, since then you could maybe try to slide into their slipstream and pick up a few pointers. But not our boy Skippy. No, sir.

I must admit that right about then I was as terrified as I have ever been in an automobile. But it was exciting, too, and even while I was hanging on for dear life as we went feinting and dodging and skittering around these wild mountain curves, I was rooting like hell for Javier to get by. Then The Skipper finally left an opening. We'd come up to a hook-shaped left hander with a bare rock wall on our right and a dropoff the general profile of a two thousand foot ice cream cone on our left, and Javier stayed wide for once while Skippy entered from his usual position smack dab in the middle of the road. Naturally the C-Type skittered wide as the corner tightened up and Javier instantly went for the opening on the inside. I swear there wasn't anything but air and flying gravel under our left side tires in the middle of that bend! Skippy saw what was happening and tried to come down on us, but Javier held his line and I looked over right into the Coke-bottle-bottom glasses and terrified, fried egg eyes of Milton Fitting as the two cars banged off each other. But Javier kept his foot in it, and the Jag kind of glanced off and I wheeled my head around just in time to see it whack hard against the rock wall, do a bank shot sideways across the road and disappear down into the gully. I thought sure I saw Skippy's fist shoot up-middle finger extended-just as they catapulted over the edge. *"JeezusChristAlmighty!"* I shouted. *"Did'ja see THAT??!!"*

Javier nodded and crossed himself. But he kept his foot down.

We crested the first ridge out of Tuxtla Gutierrez at Ocozocuautla (2,528 feet above sea level, and no, I can't pronounce it either) where Hank's guide book said there were some really interesting old ruins from the days before the Spanish *Conquistadors*. I guess the local Indian population had themselves a pretty high culture back then, what with grand stadiums for favorite weekend sporting events and even grander temples for favorite holiday religious ceremonies and the odd human sacrifice or two. But I missed it all on account of I was more than a little preoccupied with Javier's driving, and even a little worried about what had happened to The Skipper and Milton Fitting. I mean, that cliff they went over looked like a *long* way down.

On the other side of the mountain we headed into a long downhill to the lowest point of the whole race at Tehuantepec, just 328 feet above sea level. It was mostly dry, dusty jungle down there, and along the way we passed one of the little blue Gordinis off to the side. Like I said, they were running without riding mechanics to save weight, so the driver was stretched out on the gravel all by his lonesome, peering under the back end. "He should be more careful." Javier said through clenched teeth. "Scorpions...."

That was the other thing you had to watch out for. The Mexican wildlife. It came in all shapes and sizes, from farm-issue stuff like scrawny, concentration camp-issue cows and flea-bitten dogs and donkeys to free roaming local critters like lizards, snakes, armadillos, coatis and kinkajous, and every blessed one of them was accustomed to waltzing right across the Panamerican Highway whenever the hell it felt like it. They were just not expecting a Mercedes or Ferrari or Lincoln or Cadillac to come hauling over the next crest or gunning around the previous bend at a hundred-plus miles an hour. A certain amount of bestial carnage was bound to occur, and it was the rare entry (or the very early retiree) who didn't pick up a few bloody dents and hair-raising animal stories along the way.

But by far the worst of it was the buzzards. They followed *La Carrera* like they knew in advance what was going to happen, circling lazily in the sky over the Panamerican Highway and just waiting for the pulpy thump-and-crush mismatch of four wheels colliding with a similar number of legs. Then it was banquet time. So you'd crest a hill and there would be a big old buzzard or two picking through a tasty appetizer of armadillo guts right in the middle of the blessed road. And they'd just *stay* there, smacking their beaks and commenting in buzzard talk about "have you tried the eyeballs?" or how delicious the spleen was and meanwhile you'd be bearing down on them like a guided missile and maybe even leaning on the horn and flashing the lights to try and get their attention. Of course, the local buzzard population was used to occasional truck and auto traffic interrupting their picnic luncheons, and knew instinctively how to spread their wings at the last possible instant and struggle up into the air. Unfortunately, just like their four footed entrees, they were accustomed to bumpers and grille hardware approaching at speeds of well under a mile a minute. So it was really no surprise that they tended to misjudge things a bit. And believe me, even under the best of circumstances, a buzzard's lift-off time is nothing special at all. So it went without saying that there would be a few, umm, *incidents*....

A little further on, the road started to climb back up into the mountains, even steeper than before, heading up towards the highest pass of the day at Totolapa, some 6,560 feet up. Right about then Javier recognized World Champion Alberto Ascari's Ferrari looming up in the mirrors, and he wisely lifted for an instant and waved him past on a short uphill straightaway. The big 4.1-liter Mexico roared past, exhausts booming with a deep bass version of the trademark Ferrari howl, and Javier slotted right in behind, trying to stay on the World Champion's tail. But it was no contest. The Mexico had us on power and acceleration-especially going uphill-and Ascari was simply in a different class when it came to driving. Plus he obviously knew a little something about the strange yellow "Bracco Dots" that Giovanni Bracco and his riding mechanic had painted on the pavement and roadside scenery when they reconnoitered the course in the weeks before the race. Some were just round circles, some had arrows attached, and others included odd, indecipherable hieroglyphics understood only by Giovanni Bracco and a few other people on the Ferrari team. In any case, Ascari was able to flat foot it over blind crests where any normal human being would lift and commit the car into wild, tire shuddering slides around hidden curves with Who Knows What lurking on the other side. It was absolutely terrifying to watch. Thrilling, too. But the show didn't last very long, as the Mexico drew steadily away from us and was gone completely within only a few short miles. *"Madre de Dios,"* Javier muttered, shaking his head. "The man casts no shadow."

As we climbed towards Totolapa, I noticed Javier was checking the rearview mirror again, so I swiveled my head around and saw the second French Gordini, the one with ex-motorcycle champion Jean Behra at the wheel, furiously reeling us in. He'd been the very last sports car off, so no question he was really flying and the powerful, handy, and lightweight little Gordini was really in its element up here in the mountains. When he got right up behind us, I tapped Javier on the sleeve and nodded for him to give way. I mean, there was no point being a Skippy Welcher about it. Javier held him up for another couple corners-just to show me who was boss as much as anything else-and then swung graciously aside and let Behra's Gordini through at the next bend.

Our Ferrari was no match for the Gordini up here, and Javier was certainly no match for Jean Behra. The little blue car vanished in a few corners. We passed Fitch's Mercedes roadster changing a blown tire, and not much further along Lang's 300SL coupe doing the same. *"Hah!"* Javier snorted. "They should use Mexican tires!" And he knew what he was talking about. Seems the Mercedes team was running special, thick-tread Continentals-they'd brought over three hundred of them!-and they just weren't up to the abrasive volcanic rock surface on the Tuxtla-Oaxaca leg. We, on the other hand, were on homegrown Mexican Goodrich treads that were almost 100% pure gum rubber and built for coping with the local roads and driving conditions. I think we were about the only car that didn't have a flat that day! But the Mercedes team had anticipated things-as usual!-and had a ready-made tire stop laid out about halfway through the stage, complete with quick-lift racing jacks and an extra knockoff hammer for the driver. But none of that did much good if you had a blowout before you got there, like happened to Fitch and Lang.

The Lincoln team even went them one better. Crafty old Bill Stroppe had found a little pop stand on a wide spot in the mountain road leading up to Totolapa, and that's where he'd hidden fresh sets of tires for all the Lincoln team cars behind the bushes and then had his guys dig a big hole and bury a compressed air tank and a shop lift. When Stroppe's cars pulled in, all the riding mechanics had to do was hook up the air hose and the cars would leap off the ground for them. Then they'd change the worn tires all at once. With air guns! You had to admit, that was even slicker than the Mercedes deal.

A little further on we came charging up this steep, blind rise at a hundred-plus and all of a sudden we see this guy in coveralls running towards us over the top, waving his arms in the air. It was Ascari's riding mechanic! Javier lifted off and we shot over the crest to find Ascari's Mexico flopped over on its side and stuck nose-down in a ditch with the back end still hanging out into the road. It looked pretty banged up-I figure it must've rolled a couple times at least-but thankfully Ascari was standing next to it, disgustedly smoking a cigarette and looking very depressed indeed. Scratch one World Champion....

To be honest, I figured we were looking pretty good. Or a lot better than I expected, anyway (which wasn't really saying much, seeing as how I more or less expected us both to be dead by then) but, as always in the racing world, a sense of confidence and well-being are generally a rock-solid tipoff that something awful is about to happen and the shit is about to hit the fan. Right on cue, the Ferrari's engine started gagging and coughing and spluttering. I looked over at Javier and he looked back at me. Out of gas? No, we should have plenty. Maybe the altitude? No, it came on too suddenly and was way too severe. The car was really stumbling now, hardly able to make it up the grade. Worse yet, there was no place at all to pull off. So we struggled along, the engine choking and strangling even in first and second gears while the two Mercedes roared by on fresh rubber, really hauling the mail. We finally found a bare patch on the edge of a corner where we could pull off and have a looksee, and about then the first of the Stock Category cars came lumbering by, wallowed way over on their suspensions and tires squealing in agony. I popped the hood and went searching desperately around the Ferrari's fuel system, looking for the problem as Walt Faulkner's Lincoln, Pat Kirkwood's Chrysler, and the other team Lincolns of Bob Korf, Johnny Mantz, and Bill Stevenson passed by one after the other, some of them racing nose to tail and the whole lot covered by less than a minute! For sure those stock car guys were having a lot tighter race of it than the Sports Category cars. A *lot* tighter.

We didn't have much in the way of tools on board the Ferrari, but I made do with an adjustable crescent wrench and had already checked the strainer on the fuel pump and opened up the float bowls on the front carburetors before I happened to notice the real problem. The damn ground strap on the battery was coming loose, fr'Chrissakes! Why it didn't fall right off is a mystery to me (after all, if you've got no juice, you at least you know you should be looking at the electrical system, right?) and I had it fixed and the carbs back together in record time once I knew what was wrong. But we'd lost at least eight minutes, and Javier had himself wound up pretty tight when we jumped back in for that final charge over the top and descent into Oaxaca. Before the problem, we'd kind of hit a rhythm where Javier and the road were getting along pretty well with each other and I was almost used to his driving. But now he was pressing hard again and it was scaring the bejeesus out of me. Especially on the downhills where we had old Mom Nature's gravity pull along with every single millimeter of the

Ferrari's gas pedal travel working for us. Finally Javier overcooked it into a sweeping horseshoe right and I felt the back end start to come out from underneath us. I braced myself and clenched my teeth as I felt that unmistakable sensation of a car slipping away from its driver and into the hands of pure physics. But we got lucky and it just swapped ends in the middle of the road and collected a little wooden cross marking the spot where some other poor fish hadn't been so lucky. Javier stared at me sheepishly and shrugged.

"Hey, it's a long race, okay?" I told him reassuringly. "This is just the first leg. Let's think about making it all the way to the finish."

He nodded, took a deep breath, and stuck it in gear. And that's about when Sammy Speed's Nash came hurtling through the corner only to find us dead in the water smack dab in the middle of the road. On the one hand, I was thrilled to see Sammy running so good. On the other, I wasn't real happy about being caught directly in his cross hairs and about to get killed. Sammy reacted instantly, his hands a blur on the wheel as he somehow managed to swoop around us on the high side, climbing a good three feet up the rock face in a shower of stones and flint chips and missing all but the last little bit of the Ferrari, shattering the taillight and wadding up a few hundred dollars worth of hand-rolled aluminum while putting a healthy crunch in the Nash's left front fender. Right next to the big, bloody donkey impression and the smaller, mixed-breed dog dents under the headlight. Unfortunately, the hit was just enough to put the fender into their tire, and we heard it pop just a few yards down the road. As we sped away, we saw Sammy and Spud pulling over and scrambling to unpack all their tire-changing stuff (which, as expected, was already a total mess following two other tire emergencies). Turns out they were down to their last spare, too-one that they'd driven all the way down from Texas on with the cords already showing through. So Sammy and Spud had no choice but to take it real easy the whole rest of the way into Oaxaca. Especially on right handers. It was a real shame, you know?

But at least they made it. And so did we. And that was a hell of a lot more than you could say for many of the crews. Bonetto had rolled his Lancia and then it caught fire so he was out, two Mexican guys were in the hospital after chucking their Oldsmobile off the side of a mountain, and Bob Korf's riding mechanic got banged up when he fell out the side window of their Lincoln trying to fix the auxiliary fuel tank while the car was in motion. But the main topic on everybody's lips was what happened to Karl Kling's co-driver, Hans Klenk, in their 300SL gullwing. Seems they came blasting over a rise doing something over two miles a minute only to find a couple buzzards feasting on a little fresh armadillo meat served up by their teammate John Fitch just a few moments before. The buzzards made their usual lazy, lumbering, slow-motion liftoff to try and get out of the way, but one of them just wasn't quick enough and his whole filthy, foul-smelling, feather encrusted body-imagine something twice the size and weight of your average Thanksgiving turkey-came smashing through the windshield, cold-cocked Hans Klenk, and went crashing out through the back window in a shower of bloody, feathered meat chunks and broken glass. I guess Klenk's face was pretty cut up and he was plenty dazed, but he was a good soldier like all the Mercedes guys and insisted that Kling keep the throttle buried and get them the hell to Oaxaca. Which he did. Afterwards, he made a few sick jokes about it and allowed as how the worst part by far was the smell. Which made sense, since buzzards aren't especially persnickety about their sanitary habits or how long their food sits out before supper. Fact is, he said he never would've made it except that the shattered windshield and rear glass made for quite a substantial improvement in flow-through fresh air ventilation. To say the least. You really had to hand it to them for grit and team spirit, and it was amazing that they finished up third overall that day in spite of the buzzard encounter.

By 5:30 the next morning, the Mercedes crew had replaced the glass front and rear, cleaned out the interior so there wasn't so much as a busted feather or a glop of vulture residue, and installed a row of steel "buzzard bars" across the windshields of both 300SL coupes. Those guys were *good!*

When the time sheets were tallied, Jean Behra's amazing little Gordini was out front at an astounding 3 hours, 41 minutes, and 44 seconds, breaking the previous year's record by a full half hour and averaging damn near ninety. Wow! Five-and-change minutes back was yellow dot-artist Giovanni Bracco in his special lightweight Ferrari, then Kling's windowless Mercedes another 2:24 behind Bracco, Italian ace Umberto Maglioli in the supercharged Lancia, and the Chinetti in the first of the Ferrari Mexicos after team leader Ascari rolled his into a ball and the distributors shook loose on Villoresi's, costing him forty minutes and dropping him down to eleventh place. Fitch and Lang were well up in the other two 300SLs, running to a quick but conservative pace, and I was sad to see Creighton Pendleton's California-hotrod Ferrari just ahead of Phil Hill's more standard version. But Phil had also run into tire problems on the abrasive volcanic blacktop, and he wisely chose to baby it in to Oaxaca with his last fresh spare on the left rear and the other three skins worn clear down to the canvas.

While the Sports Category cars were fairly strung out, the stock car guys were at each other hammer and tongs the whole way, and you could throw a damn blanket over the top five (four of which were Lincolns, natch) who were separated by barely a minute after a whole day's racing. Boy, those guys couldn't relax for a second! It really said a lot for the kind of drivers you had tearing up the state fairgrounds and Saturday night bullrings back home in the U.S. of A., and, even though I considered myself more of a sportycar guy, I must admit they made me proud as hell to be an American. Fact is, they weren't all that far off the overall leaders in the bucks-up sportycar class.

Javier and me wound up 13th in the Sports Class and just outside the top twenty-five overall, and we were pretty damn pleased with that. Especially after that dumbass "fuel feed" problem that turned out to be nothing but a loose battery cable. You couldn't help wondering where we would've been if that little gremlin hadn't showed up-particularly on our rugged Mexican tires-and, best as Javier and I could figure, we would've come maybe 10th in class and sixteenth or seventeenth overall. Not that it mattered any, since the first thing you had to learn on a race like *La Carrera* was that you've got to keep focused on what's coming up next and forget the hell about anything in your rear view mirror. Even if it includes watching Skippy Welcher and Milton Fitting barreling off the edge of a cliff in their C-Type Jaguar.

But there must be a god who watches over infants, drunks and idiots, and so who should come rolling into Oaxaca just after dark in a wobbly, beat-up Mexican tow truck with about sixty percent of a Jaguar C-Type hanging off the back but Milton and The Skipper. They looked pretty banged up, too, what with Milton's arm in a sling and a thick wad of tape around his ribs and Skippy's face all bruised and lumpy underneath this strange, cockeyed head bandage-I swear, he looked like the fife player from *The Spirit of "76!*-plus the middle finger he had so prominently displayed while plummeting over the edge now held permanently erect with a flat metal splint. Turns out the Jag hit a big rut not far down the hill and both of them got tossed clear out of the car, landing reasonably softly in a clump of foliage. The bad news was that it was mostly brambles, so they got scratched up pretty bad, and it seems there was a beehive in it, too. But they made out better than the C-Type, which continued on down the hill, barrel rolling and tumbling end-for-end like one of those carefully staged, off-the-cliff crashes you see in Hollywood movies. About the only thing that Jag didn't do was catch fire. At least until it got to the bottom, anyway. In any case, the remains hanging off the back of that tow truck looked more like metal scrap metal on its way to the smelter than the latest hot new Jaguar racing car, and no question The Skipper was pretty damn upset about it.

In fact, he came looking for us.

Javier and I were over in the Ferrari compound in the middle of downtown Oaxaca, where I was busily putting on a fresh set of Mexican Goodrich tires and doing a general nut-and-bolt inspection while he carried on about the day's events with Villoresi, Chinetti, and a couple of the Muscatelli brothers in a mongrel blend of Spanish and Italian. That was fine with me. I'd rather see him with those guys, having a nice glass of wine and maybe a little dish of pasta than over at some local bar drinking his way down to the worm in the bottom of a bottle of Mescal. Anyhow, about then Skippy and the tow truck come wobbling up to the door, and before you could even think about it The Skipper had his chin clear up Javier's nostrils, screaming and cursing and showering Javier's face with a fine coating of spit while he was at it.

It's probably fair to say that hitting a man with a big, fresh bandage around his head and a splint on his middle finger would be frowned upon in polite company. And Javier was far too much of a gentleman to even think of such a thing. But the Skipper was making himself pretty hard to ignore, burrowed up until he was damn near inside Javier's shirt collar, shrieking and hollering and poking him in the chest with that metal-splinted finger of his. Finally Javier'd had about enough and shoved him away. But The Skipper came right back at him, this time with a nasty little shove of his own. Once again, Javier managed to refrain from punching Skippy right in that spit-spewing, gold-toothed mouth of his. But then The Skipper shoved him again-harder than before, and right in front of all his friends and *compadres* on the Ferrari team!-and this time Javier had no choice but to retaliate. So he slapped The Skipper right across the face. Like you would to a little kid. Only *hard!*

Skippy's eyes about came out of their sockets, and you could see the old primeval juices rising up in him like they were spurting up his spine. When they reached the top-Skippy's face puffing up the color of beefsteak and eyes bulging with rage-The Skipper's hands flashed out like two snakes striking and grabbed Javier around the throat. Except for that one middle finger, anyway. So Javier kneed him in the balls. And I mean *hard!* Skippy doubled over instantly, and that's when Javier followed up with a stylish, perfectly executed opposite knee to the chops that laid The Skipper out cold. I guess they didn't exactly play according to the Marquis of Queensberry rules wherever *'Poco Loco'* Premal learned how to fight....

Later on, Skippy came back with a couple local policemen-apparently to have Javier arrested for attempted murder or something-but I guess he forgot about all that Home Court Advantage/When-In-Rome stuff you need to remember whenever you're out of your own neighborhood. Turned out that Javier's second cousin was the brother-in-law of a friend of one of the bigshot local city officials in Oaxaca, and they'd even been to a few weddings and cockfights and funerals together and how was the old trouser snake anyway and why didn't they ever see each other anymore and why don't you guys all go out and have a nice dinner and a few expensive girls on me-the whole police force, sure!-and the upshot was that poor old Skippy wound up spending the night in the shithouse for assault. Straight middle finger and all.

On our way back to the hotel, we found Spud and Sammy Speed doing a little impromptu bodywork and thumb-and-eyeball alignment job on the Nash, and I was a little worried when Javier walked over to them and drew Sammy aside. I mean, I'd already seen him lay one guy out that evening, and Lord only knows what he thought about the little run-in we'd had with Sammy's Nash up in the mountains. But he spoke very quietly and respectfully and even put his arm around Sammy's shoulder. I guess he must've been apologizing. Then he reached in his pocket and pulled out a silver money clip stuffed with large notes, discretely peeled a few off, and whispered a little homegrown Mexican advice in Sammy's ear. The next morning, Spud and Sammy's Nash showed up with a brand new set of Mexican Goodrich tires.

I tried calling Julie from the phone in the hotel lobby, but there was a long line and I was feeling pretty exhausted, and about then the Muscatelli brother who was riding with Creighton Pendleton-I think it was Giuseppe-brought over a couple shots of tequila and offered up a toast. "To tomorrow, ey?" he grinned, and we clinked glasses and tossed them off. To be honest about it, he'd never been particularly social with me before, but I was beginning to understand the special brotherhood that develops between the idiots who do *La Carrera* in the seat with no steering wheel or brake pedal in front of it. Like maybe we'd be awarded our own special wing in a mental hospital or something. Or the other hospital, even.

It was coming on towards midnight when we finally turned in-I still hadn't gotten through to Julie-and, exhausted as I was, it was still hard to drop off to sleep. I swear, it seemed like somebody was shaking me awake no more than five minutes after I dozed off.

We were well up in the mountains and it felt plenty chilly the next morning, then got even colder as we charged north up another mountain range from Oaxaca to over seven thousand feet above sea at Yanhuitlan, then down into another low valley at Tehuitzingo, then climbing back up into the mountains to the end of the day's first leg at Puebla. It was only 256 miles and the surface wasn't nearly so rough on tires, but the turns seemed tighter and trickier and more deceptive than the day before. There was a sense of flow and rhythm to the highway on the first day, but on the second leg we'd crest a hill and the road would suddenly twist to the left or yank to the right without warning. And the corners seemed to close and open at odd, unpredictable angles, so you couldn't just swoop smoothly through them like the bends on day one. Or maybe we were just tired and a little off our game. For sure those yellow "Bracco Dots" were a huge help here. At least if you knew what the hell they meant, anyway. All the factory team Ferraris were going really quickly now, with Bracco's semi-privateer 3-liter holding a solid second overall to Behra's Gordini and Villoresi really putting the spurs to the big 4.1 Mexico, trying to claw his way back up the leaderboard after his distributor problems on day one dropped him back in the field. In fact, he set quickest time on each of the next three legs. But you had to be careful about trying to use the Bracco Dots if you didn't know the code. We noticed they'd put more than a few phonies down, so if you got to thinking you knew what they meant and started relying on them, every once in awhile you'd find yourself braking for a blind hill that was actually flat out in top or sweeping over to the exact opposite side of the road from where you wanted to be heading into a hidden hairpin. You've got to hand it to those Italians-they were pretty damn shrewd about keeping their little club exclusive.

A little locally-manufactured trouble hit many teams through the village of Acatlan near the bottom of the descent to Tehuitzingo. Seems the center of town had been closed off during the practice weeks, supposedly to keep the cars from tearing up the newly repaired pavement. Or maybe there was another, slightly more sinister plan at work. In any case, nobody had much seen the central plaza in Acatlan, where the road emerged from between two tall, white adobe buildings and made four sharp 90-degree bends-*LEFT! RIGHT! RIGHT! LEFT!*-around the plaza before snaking out of town. They were really 30 mile-per-hour corners-*maybe* 35-covered with loose dirt and surrounded by high curbs with the town plaza fountain/water supply/all-purpose washtub right there in the middle. And most of the racers were entering it totally blind after flying across mostly open-road landscape at eighty, ninety, and a hundred-plus miles per hour. It was tailor made for disaster, no lie. Which also meant it was tailor made for entertainment (remember, this is a country where slaughtering beef is the great national pastime and the locals would sooner bet on which chicken can peck the other one to death than which baseball team is going to win the world series!). So the townspeople turned out in force to sit on makeshift, wooden crate bleachers all day long, hooting and clapping and passing the odd bottle of distilled cactus juice back and forth and making occasional side bets as to whether the next car was going to make it through without hitting a building, curb, or the fountain (with, I think, a triple-double bonus parlay for clobbering all three). To make it even more interesting, some local police types (who, in typical Mexican fashion, were maybe the brothers-in-law or second cousins of the major Acatlan bookmakers) stood at the entrance to town enthusiastically waving the cars on. *"Andale! Andale! All clear ahead! Andale!"* directing them fast as possible into that narrow, high-walled adobe tunnel leading to the plaza.

For whatever it's worth, I think they picked especially hard on the Americans. Or maybe it was just that our guys were a little more gullible than the Europeans, who had maybe seen this sort of thing before on the *Mille Miglia* or *Targa Florio.*. In any case, Creighton Pendleton smacked the curb and bent up a few yards of hand-rolled aluminum bodywork, and poor Phil Hill did even worse, suffering through a hair-raising Slide For Life across the loose dirt and clouting the fountain, which pretty much pretzelized the left front wheel and bent the spring, too. They managed to get a new wheel on, but the front end was all out of whack and they had to settle for a sort of slow hobble the rest of the way into Puebla, dropping them well down the charts. And there were plenty of others, too. Much to the delight of the crowd.

As you might expect, the experienced open road warriors on the Ferrari team (including Bracco, who was essentially a team member except that he didn't have to take orders from anybody-not that any of the Italian drivers much did) all smelled something fishy and wisely backed off. Coming from Europe, they knew all about blind, narrow pathways between buildings, and how some of them tended to have a pretty serious cork in the end. Likewise the Mercedes team avoided trouble since they'd reconnoitered everything from the air and even sent a few scouts in on foot to check out what was lurking beyond the barricades. In fact, a few unkind tongues suggested that the Mercedes guys had spread a few pesos around to promote a little bounty on anything painted red. Being the sportsmen they are, I'm sure that rumor is no more true than the one about the Ferrari team manager offering a thousand lira reward (which worked out to about a dollar-fifty Cash American) for every time a car from the Mercedes team was accidentally delayed.

But of course all that stuff was way off base, on account of the simple country folk of Acatlan weren't really interested in whether Mercedes beat Ferrari or Ferrari beat Mercedes. Oh, sure, they had sentimental favorites. And most of those sentimental favorites were ragged old roosters with grisly pet names who were doing well at the local cockfights. If there was one thing fixed dead-center in the minds of most Mexicans, it was that *La Carrera* was a once-a-year blowout festival that, like most things in Mexico that seemed too good to be true, would soon fade into a once-in-a-lifetime memory to tell the kids and grand-children about. In fact, that was the really big difference I noticed between life in the states and Mexico. Even more than the clothes and food and language and dirt-eater economics, Mexicans seemed to understand the temporary nature of things much better than we do up in Jersey. But then, they live a lot closer to it. Up in the states, we tend to keep death under wraps in squeaky-clean hospital wards and velvet draped mortuaries, but down in Mexico, it happens right out in the street. So Mexicans seem to understand and accept that nothing in this life is permanent-and especially anything good-and that you'd better enjoy what you can while you can because we all wind up as food for worms sooner or later.

Which is maybe why you couldn't blame them for waving and cheering when Creighton Pendleton and Phil Hill and anyone else dumb enough to get sucked in too fast clouted the local architecture. Hell, it was the best entertainment they'd ever had. And winning a bet on a bent Ferrari was something you could brag about all year long. Maybe even longer.

Like everybody else, Javier saw the policemen waving us on as we swooped into town and instantly backed off. "What's up?" I asked.

"You'll see, *amigo,*" he laughed. "This is for the *gringos.*" And sure enough he was right, as we motored gently out between the white adobe walls to find Phil Hill and his mechanic hard at work trying to get their car disentangled from the fountain. They couldn't accept any sort of local help or they'd be disqualified. "You see how it is, *amigo,*" Javier grinned through his switchblade smile. "We are a poor country, but we know how to make use of our opportunities. *Cigarillo, por favor?*" So I lit him one of his skinny black cigarettes and passed it over. We were doing up over a hundred now, rocketing full speed out of Acatlan, and it didn't bother me at all.

Fact is, Javier's driving was actually a little subdued on the second leg, and I thought maybe the initial rush of juices had worn off and it was starting to dawn on him just how bloody damn far it was to Juarez and that both he and the car would need a little pacing to make it that far. Not that he was exactly stroking along, as the occasional little peaks in the upholstery under my butt would surely attest. What I didn't know at the time is that he was saving himself for the day's second leg, a balls-out, eighty mile blast from Puebla to Mexico City, going over the highest pass of the race at 10,482 feet and then plunging just as steeply down into the nation's capital. It was a stretch of road Javier knew intimately, and, although he didn't come right out and say it, it was the place he figured to put his mark on *La Carrera.* Or die trying....

Had I known, I would have been worried.

Not that it would've done me any good.

Meanwhile, Jean Behra was absolutely flying-and flying solo, at that-in the lightweight blue Gordini, whipping through the mountains like a hound on the scent, still gaining fractions and even whole seconds on his pursuers through every twist and switchback. And then the inevitable happened. We arrived at a short descent leading into yet another roundhouse, bootlace left hander just shy of Puebla-not much different than a hundred other corners we'd seen-only this time there were two ominous black streaks heading straight-on over the edge. Down at the bottom, upside-down in a deep, rocky crevice with its wheels still slowly rotating, was Jean Behra's Gordini! He'd either left it a fraction too late or maybe his brakes were getting iffy, but the end result was the same. With over *TEN MINUTES* in hand over Bracco's second place Ferrari, he'd thrown it all away. But that's the price you pay when you linger too long out there on the ragged edge. Behra was pretty banged up, too, but you had to figure he was lucky. After all, it easily could have been fatal. Still, it was a crying damn shame after the incredible run he'd put in. But it was one of those deals the smart money had more or less expected.

Everybody got a short layover in Puebla to grab a bite to eat, give the cars a quick once-over, and make emergency repairs before the difficult, eighty-one mile afternoon sprint up to 10,000+ feet and back down the mountains into Mexico City. A pretty stiff wind had come up, and I must admit I didn't much like the look in Javier's eyes as we waited in line for the start. It reminded me too much of the way he looked before we left Tuxtla Gutierrez, and also the way he looked just before he kneed Skippy Welcher in the balls.

Thanks to our problems the previous day and Javier's surprisingly conservative pace on the morning run from Oaxaca to Puebla, we were down in sixteenth overall with the fastest of the stock cars (including the whole damn Lincoln team!) up ahead of us. Just a few places behind us were Sammy and Spud in the Nash-I was really happy to see them doing so well, but still hoped we could stay ahead-and a few spots further back was the Porsche of that nose-in-the-air Prince von Metternich guy. Shit-don't-stink blueblood or not, you had to give him his due for running so well in an underpowered car.

We watched Marshall Teague's Hudson, Bobby Unser's Chrysler, and Bill Sterling's Cadillac take off one-by-one ahead of us, and I was very nervous indeed watching Javier grind his teeth between puffs of his skinny, black cigarillos. He looked pretty on edge, no lie, and maybe that's why I decided to join him and try smoking one myself. I can't say as my insides much cared for it, and the taste reminded me of licking one of those ancient, petrified Aztec mummies Hank showed me in his guide book. I guess they were pretty much the tobacco industry equivalent of Mescal. By then we'd worked our way up to the head of the line, and there was nothing but empty roadway and the rapidly disappearing taillights of Bill Sterling's Caddy in front of us. I swear, Javier must've touched his St. Christopher's medal and crossed himself a dozen times and mumbled a few full rosaries in machine gun Spanish during that last half-minute before the start. I had a nagging feeling this was going to be about the wildest damn ride of my life!

I was not disappointed. In fact, I believe I held my breath from the moment we squealed away from the start line in Puebla to when we swooped down into the huge, seething festival crowd on the outskirts of Mexico City less than an hour later. Javier scared the living shit out of me for the entire eighty-one miles, charging full tilt into blind corners I'd never seen before and skating right out to the edge of the pavement with nothing but empty air and a hard, unforgiving drop to the bottom if he misjudged it by even a few inches. But he knew that road, all right. And, except for a few rough edges, he knew how to drive it, too. But he had his teeth clenched the whole way and he was holding the steering wheel so damn tight I was amazed the wood didn't just splinter in his hands. We caught all the stock car guys except the four team Lincolns, passing inside, outside, wherever there was room-and sometimes even when there wasn't!-and left Spud and Sammy's Nash far behind. I could see Javier was having trouble with the brakes towards the end, and he was double- and triple-pumping them to get the car hauled down for the next corner. I can't tell you how many times my hand reached for the door handle and my feet involuntarily braced themselves against the floorboards, getting ready to jump ship like a bullfrog off a burning lily pad if it looked like we were going over the edge. Unlike that airplane ride down to Mexico, I sort of figured I'd do better taking my chances on the other side of the door, you know?

But the skull-faced little sonofabitch made it. Lord only knows how. And the feeling when we finally zoomed across the finish line on the outskirts of Mexico City was almost worth the terror. Almost. There was this huge sea of people shouting and waving and cheering and throwing their hats in the air, and at first I thought we were going to plow right into them-hell, we hadn't even reached the official finish line yet!-but, like a synchronized school of fish working in perfect unison, they swept aside at the last possible instant to create a terrifyingly narrow tunnel of hands and legs and arms and torsos and wildly waving sombreros all the way to the checkered flag. Javier Premal was about the biggest damn hero in Mexico right then, and it made me realize all over again how blessed sedate we are up in Passaic.

But the *real* party was just starting. After all, it was not only *La Carrera,* but also the forty-second Anniversary of the Mexican Revolution, and we were paraded into town like Rose Bowl floats while the crowd pressed in so tight I was afraid for the car. As the top-running Mexican, Javier was right up there with the cream of popular local saints, great matadors, and heroes of the revolution, and I was a little worried that we were going to get crushed to death in the stampede to congratulate him. I swear, the whole blessed population of Mexico City was there!

When we finally made it through to the Ferrari garage near the hotel, Javier was instantly surrounded by a locust swarm of clicking camera shutters and swept away in a human tide of friends, well-wishers, media types, local dignitaries, and high priced call girls. He wanted me to come, too, but I begged off. I wanted to give the car a little once-over and most especially take a serious looksee at the brakes. Besides, I thought I might be way overdue for a shower and a change of underwear. Hank Lyons dropped in while I was crawling through the brakes and topping up the fluid levels-he'd managed to hitch a ride with the Lincoln support team-and right away he wanted to know what happened to Jean Behra and the Gordini. So I told him about the skid marks and the little blue car upside down at the bottom of the ravine, and he thought it over and decided it was still likely to be the high point of the whole Jean Behra/Gordini story from day one to infinity. Hank had checked the time sheet, and, with Behra out, it was Bracco's semi-privateer factory Ferrari out front with Kling's Mercedes running second, about three minutes back. The other two 300SLs of Fitch and Lang were third and fourth, and you got the feeling old Alfred Neubauer's boys were running at a cool, carefully controlled pace. Their tire troubles were behind them now, and Hank thought maybe they were just trying to stay close and remain in formation until they got through the mountains and hit the long, fast sections across the flatlands. Especially the final three legs from Durango to Juarez. Then he'd turn them loose. Umberto Maglioli was way up in sixth in the little supercharged Lancia thanks to a trouble-free run and some really magnificent driving. Hank said Maglioli was without a doubt one of the best damn open road racers on the planet, and the little Lancia would never be able to run up there with the likes of the Ferraris and Mercedes team cars without him.

Chinetti and Villoresi in the two factory Ferraris were next, and you really had to hand it to Villoresi, who wasn't even in the top twenty-five at the end of the first day and had been driving flat out to make up time. In fact, Hank said they about had to lift him out of the car after he crossed the finish line in Mexico City. But he'd earned it, seeing as how he'd set top time on both the morning and afternoon legs, underscoring that Ferrari's big 4.1 Mexicos were without question the fastest cars in the race. But you need more than just the fastest car to win a race like *La Carrera,* and Villoresi was still a solid thirty-seven minutes behind the leader. I was disgusted to find that Creighton Pendleton was way up in fifth thanks to having a fast car, driving pretty well, and being luckier than shit, while poor Phil Hill and his mechanic were down in ninth after their crash in the Acatlan plaza and working hard at the layover with some Mexican mechanics to rebuild the whole left front suspension on their car. As for Javier and me, we were up to fourteenth, just behind the factory Lincolns, and Javier had set fifth best time overall on the run from Puebla to Mexico City. Hell, he'd beaten Creighton Pendleton by over two minutes! Suddenly all that bug-eyed terror seemed worth it....

But the *real* battle royal was going on between the stock car guys. By now the superior preparation and organization of Bill Stroppe and Clay Smith's Lincoln team had established them solidly at the front of the field. Sure, some other cars managed to cop quick time on the second and third legs, including the old Italian "Silver Fox" himself, Piero Taruffi, who had originally brought Ferrari to *La Carrera* the year before but had accepted a large bag of gold to drive for Oldsmobile 1952. And he showed he was worth it, too, winning the stock car category outright on the short, twisty mountain sprint from Puebla to Mexico City. But the factory Lincolns were already comfortably out front on overall aggregate. The problem was the little matter of precisely *which* Lincoln it would be. And none of those guys was much accustomed to running second. So the top four-Stevenson, Faulkner, Mantz, and Korf-were still covered by a hair over a minute *after nine hours and over six hundred and sixty miles of racing.* That was pretty damn amazing, no lie!

In spite of their problems, I was thrilled to see our buddies Sammy Speed and Spud Webster had somehow managed to keep that bustle-backed Nash in the top twenty-five, and Hank said they'd run completely out of brakes on the last, steep downhill stretch into Mexico City. "We about had to open up the doors and drag our feet," was the way Spud put it.

I asked about Big Ed, and Hank allowed as how he was over at the hotel Monte Cassino and still feeling pretty rocky, so I made a point of skipping the big blowout party and going over to see him when I was done with the car. But of course he wasn't there, so I went back to the race party. It was held in this big civic amphitheater they use for musical concerts and boxing matches and stuff, and, sure enough, that's where I found Big Ed. Drinking margaritas with Carlo Sebastian and the Muscatelli brothers. "Hey," I said, "I thought you were still a little under the weather."

"Yep, still am," Big Ed agreed. "Hell, I think I shit twice my body weight inna last two days." I had to admit, he was looking a little thinner than the usual pear-shaped Baumstein profile. I noticed he was kinda pale, too.

"Shouldn't you be, you know, maybe taking it a little easy?"

"I *am* taking it easy, Buddy. Hell, this is only my fourth drink."

I should mention that the glasses they were serving those margaritas in were about the size of your average goldfish bowl.

Most of the really serious racers had left by the time I got there. Under team orders, the Mercedes and Lincoln guys came early, shook hands, made small talk, smiled for the cameras with assorted bigwig government officials, and took off for team meetings and an early curfew. They also stuck strictly to Cokes or bottled water. The Ferrari team allowed themselves a glass or two of wine, but of course they're Italian so it's mom's milk to them. Everybody else went pretty much nuts. No question Javier Premal was the belle of the ball for all the homegrown Mexican fans, and you couldn't miss all the pretty, leggy, bosomy, and incredibly eager young señoritas crowding in around him and generally making themselves available. Javier called me over and introduced me around and a couple of the girls even looked mildly interested in the *gringo* riding mechanic-I mean, there certainly wasn't enough of him to go around-but it was all machine-gun Spanish and I couldn't understand a word of it. Besides, I wanted to call Julie.

And this time I finally succeeded. Once the guy at the reception desk found out I was riding in the Ferrari with *'Poco Loco'* Premal, he couldn't do enough for me, spending a good forty minutes on the phone alternately asking, demanding, pleading, arguing, and mostly just waiting in order to make the connection. And the whole time he kept apologizing for the delay and explaining as how the local phone system was really very good and it was not usually this difficult, but, what with all the racers and the anniversary of the revolution and-he rolled his eyes-"…you understand, *señor.*"

What I understood was that, on a good day, you could maybe make a five minute phone call out of Mexico City in a half an hour or so. But finally his face blossomed out into a huge, toothy smile. *"Bueno!"* he beamed triumphantly, and handed me the phone.

"Who the hell is this?" Julie's mom hissed into the other end of the line.

Oh shit.

"Uh, it's me. Buddy." I gulped and let it sneak out. "Julie's, um, *fiancée.*"

"You know what time it is, gas station boy?"

Obviously being engaged to Julie didn't cut much ice with her mom.

"Uh, I've, umm, sorta been in a car all day. I couldn't get to a phone."

"You been inna car until two inna morning?"

I could hear Julie in the background, asking for the phone. But her mom snapped, *"I'm not done yet!"* and then they got into quite an argument about it and also about how her mom should maybe talk a little nicer to me. It sounded an awful lot like me and my dad yelling at each other over at my folks' house. Finally her mom's voice came back to the mouthpiece. "Here's Joolie," she growled. "Nice talkin' t'you."

The receiver changed hands. *"Buddy?"* Julie asked, her voice sounding tired and terribly far away.

"Yeah. It's me."

"How come you haven't called?"

"Well, see, we're down in Mexico and..."

"You really should've called."

"Well, I tried a couple times, but..."

"They have phones in Mexico, don't they?"

"Uh, sure they got phones. But I've been pretty busy, see, and..."

"Because I want you to understand this is *not* the way it's gonna be. Not in this lifetime. I'll be damned if I'm gonna sit here by a damn phone that doesn't ring for three days after we're married."

"Three days? Has it really been three days?"

"You bet your ass it's been three days." You could tell she was really warming up to the subject. "And I'm not about to put up with it. You understand me, Palumbo?"

I told her I did.

But she repeated it in five or six more variations just to make sure I got her drift. To be honest, it didn't make sense to me to spend an entire long distance phone call that it took me over forty minutes to place explaining why I hadn't called before, but I'm sure any guy living outside a cloistered monastery will understand and sympathize. At least she said she loved me at the end, and that was nice. Even if it didn't exactly sound like she did.

I guess the party didn't break up until well past midnight (although some people-including Javier Premal and his squealing, highly animated female entourage-obviously had other places to go) and, come the next morning, a lot of the local drivers were looking a tad green around the gills as we gathered for the start at around eight ayem. Including Javier Premal. His complexion had gone a little olive on him and his breath smelled like garlic and hot peppers floating in shellac. He even coughed when he fired up one of his skinny black cigarillos, and I didn't much like the way the match shook in his hand. Or the way his fingers trembled when he reached out to touch that St. Christopher's medal on the dash. Not to mention the gray cloak of fog we could see clinging to the hillsides on the climb up towards Las Cruces. But everybody said the hard part was behind us, and that the next section from Mexico to Leon was mostly long straights with a few fast, open bends and just one difficult section of mountain switchbacks at the very beginning. And of course that's where everything went straight to shit for us.

Javier was driving a lot like he did on the Oaxaca-Puebla leg the previous day, taking it easy on both himself and the car. But you could tell he was a little shaky and off his game, because he'd turn in way early for a lot of the bends and had to lift way off or even dab the brakes to gather it up and square off the end of the corner. Which, as anybody who knows anything at all about racing will tell you, is a bad way to do it. To compensate, Javier tried braking sooner and harder and slowing down more for the turns, but he was pretty ragged-chirping the tires from jumping on the brakes too hard and fluctuating hard-soft/hard-soft with the pedal while he fought to find the right speed. At least he knew the road pretty well. But then one of the stock cars came roaring up behind us-I think it was Marshall Teague in the Hudson-flashing his lights and honking his horn at our Ferrari. And I guess that's when 'Poco Loco' decided it was time to come out of his shell and get on with it. Sure enough, he lost it in the biggest possible way at the very next bootlace. We were on a steep downgrade and I could see he was maybe coming into it too fast, and when he jumped on the brakes I felt the rears lock and knew instantly we were going for a very ugly ride. Like always in racing accidents, it all took place in agonizing slow motion. First the rear slewed out and I watched in horror as Javier steered desperately into the skid. But he was getting further behind the car every instant and we both knew it was liable to catch traction in a heartbeat and snap back the other way. And at that exact moment, still steering like mad, Javier turned to me and yelled *"GET OUT, AMIGO!"* Without even thinking I activated the escape-hatch procedure I'd rehearsed in my head so many times the previous day, yanking back on the handle, banging the door open with my shoulder, pushing off the transmission tunnel with my legs and diving out sideways onto the pavement. We must've been going about sixty or so and I remember hearing a loud *crack!* when I hit and then this terrible grating, grinding, clattering subway noise as I skated across the road with the texture of the blacktop flashing past my eyes, all the time trying to slide and not roll like all my motorcycle friends had cautioned me. I hit a dirt berm that catapulted me into the air, and it was right there-flying through space!-that I saw Big Ed's Ferrari go hurtling over the edge with *'Poco Loco'* Premal still at the wheel.

Next thing I knew I was flat on my back with a few Mexican locals and Marshall Teague's riding mechanic looking down at me. "You all right?" he asked impatiently. I really wasn't sure, but I kind of half nodded. *"Don't worry,"* he yelled over his shoulder as he raced back to his car. *"Somebody'll be along for you soon!"*

To tell the truth, I didn't exactly know who or where I was. There was a hollow roar like the ocean in my ears and everything looked strange and far away and distorted, like I was looking through the wrong end of my mom's binoculars. Then I tried to move and felt this sharp, fiery pain in my side. Oh *shit* it hurt! There was another one, too. In my wrist. And something wet was running down my forehead and into my ear. Jesus, I was *hurt!*

And then I remembered the indelible sight of Javier and the Ferrari going over the cliff, and knew that, no matter what, I had to get up. It took a couple tries and hurt like hell, but two of the Mexicans helped me and I finally got to my feet-*Jesus Christ, I've busted all my ribs!*-and staggered across the road to where those final, lock-'em-up skid marks disappeared at the edge. I peered over and damn near lost my balance. Geez, it was a long way down. Way at the bottom, like a kid's toy, the Ferrari was flattened upside-down on top of a boulder with the two lefthand wheels torn off. You could see smoke from a little oil fire going on someplace under the oil pan, and then, right while I was watching, it got to the fuel that had to be spilling out all over the place and there was this soft, almost whispered *ka-whumpf* and the whole thing was on fire. I remembered Javier's face as he yelled *"GET OUT, AMIGO!"* Especially his eyes. I think they were the saddest eyes I'd ever seen.

All of a sudden there was a horn blasting behind me and I wheeled around-*ARRGGHHH! STABBING PAIN IN THE SIDE!!!*-and here came Sammy and Spud shooting down the mountain in that stupid Nash with some other guy in a Chrysler right on their ass. Sammy got hard on the brakes (of which there obviously weren't much left) and slowed enough for Spud to holler *"YOUOKAY?WE'LLSENDSOMEBODY!"* out the window as they swooped past. I gave them a feeble wave with the wrist I could still move and just sort of stood there like a deer frozen in the headlights while the Chrysler damn near took my kneecaps off.

"You bedder geddout of the road, *amigo,*" a familiar voice advised, and I wheeled around again-*SHIT THAT HURT!*-and who should be standing there but *'Poco Loco'* himself. My God, he was *alive!* Sort of. He had a big gash from his cheek to his forehead and another clear through his lip, his nose was broken and pushed to one side, there was blood all over his clothes and he was standing kind of funny with one shoulder drawn up to his ear and the arm dangling at a weird, scary angle. He was also missing one sock and shoe. Don't ask me how. Apparently he'd bailed out just as the car went over the edge and took a bloody, bone-cracking, skin bruising tumble down the hillside and surely would've been killed if he hadn't smashed face first into some scrub bushes that decided to put their roots down in exactly the right place. We heard another pair of race cars squealing down the mountain above us. "C'mon, *amigo,*" Javier said softly. "Out of the road, eh?"

The two of us looked like we were walking barefoot on broken glass as we hobbled across to the opposite side. Some Mexican spectators were standing there, mouths dangling wide open, staring at us like we were one of those holy visions you hear about from old ladies at church (but that nobody you actually know personally has ever seen). "You okay?" Javier asked as we reached the other side.

To tell the truth, I hurt as bad as I ever had in my life. But no question Javier was worse off than me. "Nah, just a little banged up," I told him.

"Yeah. Me, too," Javier lied. His dangling arm was about turned around backwards from how it should have been and he was bleeding all over the place. A Packard and a Hudson scrabbled through, fighting for traction on the loose gravel our tires had kicked up. The Packard was a Mexican entry and the driver flashed Javier a respectful salute as he shuddered passed.

Jesus, my ribs hurt!

Javier said something to the Mexicans in Spanish and one of them nodded and walked over to the burro he had parked up on the hillside. He reached into a woven knapsack and pulled out a fat ceramic jug with no label on it, walked back down the hill, and handed it to Javier. But of course there was no way to pull the cork out with his wrecked arm. "Here, lemme help you," I offered, and between our two remaining good hands we got it open and traded off quick slugs one after another after another until it was all gone. The stuff tasted a lot like paint thinner, but thankfully it was *very* high octane.

"I'm sorry about your fren' Big Ed's car," Javier sighed, passing the bottle back for about the fourth or fifth time.

"Ah, that's okay," I told him, trying to shrug only it hurt too much. "He would've wrecked it himself sooner or later. Probably sooner...."

We were laughing about it by the time a Mexican Army ambulance came and picked us up about a half hour later. Honest we were.

There was a lot of rapid fire discussion at the crash site about where we should be taken, and the ambulance crew was pretty sure they were supposed to continue on in the race direction and drop us at whatever medical facilities might be available in the next town. But Javier was adamant that we should backtrack over the top at Las Cruces and on into Mexico City, on account of there were better hospitals (not to mention his own personal doctor) plus it was home for him anyway and the best place for me to catch up with Big Ed after the race was over and find a flight back to the states. For sure we wouldn't be driving back in that Ferrari as originally planned. I don't have any idea what was said, but it went from dickering to some pretty heated exchanges and then everybody was all smiles and it wouldn't surprise me if a few pesos didn't change hands.

The ride back to Mexico City was about the most painful experience I ever had, and I would be willing to bet that ambulance had solid chunks of angle iron where the springs and shock absorbers should have been. The liquor wore off on about the first hard bump, and, although the medics bandaged us up a little and gave us some pain tablets, they really didn't do much good. But then that's the way things were in Mexico. If you got hurt, you were supposed to just keep quiet about it and gut it out. And if you got killed, well, what did it matter? You were going to die sooner or later anyway. It reminded me of the story Javier told the first time I met him. About the bandits who used to rob the payroll gold on its way to Tampico and how when they got caught, the *Federales* made them dig their own graves before they shot them.

The hospital they took us to in Mexico City was pretty nice as hospitals go, and it turned out Javier's doctor had gone to medical school in the States and spoke perfect English. The report card on my injuries was that I had three cracked ribs on my right side, a dislocated shoulder, about a third of my right cheek ground off, a gash that took eight stitches right through my eyebrow, a nice collection of bumps, bruises, pavement rash, and black-and-blue marks, and a pretty clean break in one of the bones in my right wrist from when I probably put my hand out to cushion the impact when I hit the asphalt. I don't want to go into how much it hurt when they popped the shoulder back in, but the general gist of things down there was that anesthetics were for sissies. They had to shave one eyebrow to do the stitches, taped up my ribs, and put a plaster cast on my wrist and my arm in a sling. Then they gave me something to make me sleep and stuck me in a room where all I could do was lay there and hurt and then hurt some more. I thought I ought to call Julie, but I really didn't know what to say ("Hi, honey. I'm in a hospital in Mexico City…") but I was real groggy from whatever they gave me and didn't feel much like talking anyway. Not that I could make the nurses or doctors or any of the orderlies walking past my door-way understand what I wanted even if they'd bothered to look in. In that respect, it was exactly like hospitals in the States.

But mostly I just hurt. If I closed my eyes, I saw the hard, pebblegrain texture of that pavement rushing by my face like a subway train screaming past my eyelashes and heard that terrible grating, grinding subway tunnel noise-it went on and on like it would never stop!-and then, every once in awhile, I'd hear these strange, heavy iron bells ringing someplace way off in the distance and see a slow motion replay of Big Ed's Ferrari doing its graceful swan dive off the edge of the cliff.

It was almost like ballet.

Big Ed came to see me, still looking pretty washed out himself, and told me he had his travel agent making arrangements to get us home. That's when I had to ask what day it was. "It's Sunday," he told me like it should have been obvious. "Can'tcha hear the church bells?"

Oh. That's where the bells were coming from.

"You were pretty much out of it yesterday. I guess they gave you something." And right away it occurred to me that-*at that very instant!*-even as I lay there in that hospital bed trying not to breathe because it hurt too much and while most of Mexico City was gathered in churches with their hats off and heads bowed, the last leg of *La Carrera* was still going on and guys like Giovanni Bracco and Karl Kling and John Fitch and Phil Hill and Walt Faulkner and Bobby Unser and Sammy Speed were flogging their cars flat out and Wide Fucking Open across that fast, straight final leg towards the finish line at Juarez. At least if they were still running, anyway. So I asked Big Ed what was going on in the race.

"Ah, I dunno," he said listlessly. "I guess that Bracco guy in the hotshot Ferrari had everybody pretty much covered, but then he dropped out."

"He *what?*"

"Yeah. He broke down." Big Ed made a thumbs-down gesture and that was pretty much all he had to say on the subject.

God, I was dying to know the details!

That came when Hank showed up late the following afternoon to check in and see how I was doing. He'd been up at the finish in Juarez, of course, and then the Mexican officials (who'd been great to everybody if not exactly always in control) flew him and the rest of the press corps back to Mexico City for the big prize party. Free. Can you believe it?

"At the end of the third day Bracco had a seven minute lead over Kling's Mercedes," Hank told me excitedly, "with all the really difficult mountain driving behind them. But he'd been pushing pretty hard the whole way and maybe winding it up a little tight. And Kling set fastest time on the last leg of the day from Leon to Durango. Almost 112 miles an hour. It was the first leg Mercedes had won. What *nobody* knew was that the Mercedes mechanics had gone into their garage in the middle of the night and changed axle ratios for the fast, straight runs across the desert to Juarez."

That was a pretty smart move, you had to admit.

"Kling kept it up, too. He won the next morning's run from Durango to Parral, and suddenly Bracco's lead was down to under three minutes."

"Wow."

"Plus the Ferrari wasn't sounding so good. You could hear it."

"Y'know what it was?"

"Yep. Bracco dropped out with a bunch of broken valves not more than forty miles north of Parral."

"Geez, that's a shame. He drove one hell of a race."

Hank shrugged. "He drove one hell of a *three-quarters* of a race," he corrected me. "The whole point is to be around at the finish."

"Still, it doesn't seem fair. To run that hard and that well and then have nothing to show for it."

"Oh, he'll have something to show for it."

"How's that?"

"Assholes like me all over the world'll sit down at their typewriters and make him look like a hero."

I had to admit, that was worth something.

"So how'd it end up?"

"Well, it should've been Mercedes 1-2-3, but Fitch had some front end problems and somebody who wasn't supposed to helped work on the car or something and he got disqualified. It was a pretty shitty deal, too, since they let him keep running and he even set the fastest time of anybody on the last leg to try and catch up. They didn't tell him he was out until after the finish."

"That kind of stinks."

Hank shrugged again. *"You* try organizing a race like this. See how well you do. Besides, Mercedes still finished up 1-2 even without him. That's not too shabby."

I guessed not.

"Villoresi dropped out with mechanical problems, and so Chinetti wound up third in the only Ferrari Mexico still running. They won't be too happy with that back in Maranello."

"I'm sure they won't."

"Maglioli came fourth in the Lancia-he really did a hell of a job-and then it was your old buddy Creighton Pendleton just ahead of Phil Hill."

Damn.

"But don't worry about it. Everybody knows Phil can drive rings around that guy. Creighton just got luckier than shit and had a trouble free run. There's nothing you can do about stuff like that."

"Yeah. I guess not." For sure we'd be hearing plenty about Creighton's big "victory" over Phil Hill for the next few hundred years.

"What happened with the stock car guys?"

"It was the full steamroller, no lie. The Lincolns finished 1-2-3-4, with Bill Stevenson beating out Johnny Mantz by just sixteen seconds. Can you believe it? *SIXTEEN SECONDS!* And that's after *two thousand miles* of racing!"

"Wow."

"Yep. Stevenson set a new record at twenty-one hours and fifteen minutes, and there was a lot of grousing the last three days about just how 'stock' those Lincolns were. Hell, they were topping two-miles-a-minute on the straight stretches. You ever see one off the showroom floor that'd do that?"

I shook my head.

"But they passed inspection. Clean as a whistle."

You really had to hand it to Bill Stroppe and Clay Smith. They knew how to build a damn race car. And not get caught with their fingers in the cookie jar along the way. I got the feeling there might actually be something to this stock car racing game one day. "What happened to Spud and Sammy Speed?"

Hank sighed and looked at the floor. "Unfortunately, that's another crew assholes like me'll have to make heroes of."

"But they're okay, aren't they?"

"Yeah, they're okay. Physically, anyway. But they'd worked their way up into the top ten in the stock category by the time they came down out of the mountains. But then it was all over. The Chryslers and Caddies and especially the Lincolns just *smoked* 'em across the desert. And then Sammy swerved to miss a damn burro that'd wandered into the middle of the road and he rolled it over into a ditch."

"Aw, geez. I hope they weren't hurt."

"Not too bad. But the story's not over."

"It's not?"

"Nope. They couldn't accept help from any of the locals or they'd get themselves disqualified. But somehow-don't ask me how-Spud and Sammy got some planks and fence posts and barrels and stuff and got that Nash rolled back on its wheels and kept going."

"No!"

"Yeah. Can you believe it? No windshield. No goggles. The roof all caved in. The radiator leaking. Right across the desert with one front wheel pointed at Texas and the other one towards the Pacific Ocean. And they were sick, too. Both of 'em."

"The *touristas?*"

Hank nodded. "They made it all the way to the final leg from Chihuahua to Juarez-just 230 miles to go!-and halfway home the radiator finally split wide open and they cooked the motor."

"Oh, that's awful. What a raw deal."

"Well, that's *La Carrera* for you."

And it sure as hell was.

25¢

June 6, 1953

The Weakly Journal for Gearheads & Grease Monkeys

CUNNINGHAM
Scores First Big
International
WIN!

FERRARI - MERCEDES
SHOOTOUT
IN MEXICO!

SCOOP!!!

PEGASO:
HOT NEW
SPANISH
FLYER!!

HUMBER'S
TOP SECRET
SUPER SNIPE GT?

Plus +++ ☠ **Black Day at Bridgehampton** ☠

Vukovich Wins Indy 500! Put a Willys in your TC

New Healey Hundred Wows New York International Auto Show

Quality Breeds Speed

The ruggedness, road holding and steering of the famed type 300SL sports cars are to be found also in the new Type 180 . . . The amazing family type sedan that provides new standard of comfort, space, performance and economy. Here, for only $3350, you can secure one of the most satisfying Mercedes-Benz models ever built . . . the latest in a long line of the World's greatest motor cars. The Type 180 . . . A family car with sports car characteristics . . . The proud little brother of the great 300SL.

─MONTEZUMA'S FERRARI─

ADVERTISERS

Age & Treachery Racing
Skip Barber Racing Schools
Baurle Auto Sport
Dave Bean Engineering
Blossom Motorsports
Bond Corporation/Crystal Tack Cloth
British Car Magazine
Brumos Motor Cars/Porsche
Lee Chapman Racing
Chateau Dekon
Steve Cohen • Veronica DeGuenther
Alan Christian Motorcars
Classic Impressions
Columbia College
Comprep
Continental Motors
Cope Motor Sports
Cope Machinery Company
Donovan Motorcar Service
Fourintune
Harry Gaunt Jewelers
Glenspeed.com
R. Harrington Photography
Historic Sportscar Racing, Ltd.
Homeland Legacy Atlanta
Lawyers Without Borders
Dan Hayes • Jeff Hailand
Lexus of Dayton

Magnum Pads
Mercedes-Benz USA, Inc.
MG Magazine
Monoposto Register • Formula 70
Moss Motors
Muller & Company
Munchwerks (Road America)
MWE (Marcovicci-Wenz Engineering)
Parish Insurance
Passport Transport
Dale Phelon Motorsports
Physicians Without Fenders
Marty Bagby • Sharon Frey
Marv Primack • Barry Rosenblum
Shiffmayer Plastics
Seneca Lodge, Inc.
Siebkin's Resort
Terry's Jaguar Parts
Think Fast Ink
Friends of Triumph
Triad Consultants
Turtle Wax
Vintage Motorsport Magazine
• Vintage Tyres, Ltd.
• Vintage Racing Services
• John Welch • Rothschild Investments
• Bob Woodman Tires, Inc.
• Yard Racing

SPONSORS

Bob Akin Motorsports
The Atlanta Hawkes
Steve Brooks • Jack Velden
Baker Racing
Dick, Brad, Dean, & Duncan Baker
Bill Barry & John Semkus
Toby Bean
Bob Blain
Paul Boehlert
Gino Borghesa
Splinter Group Racing
"Super Dave," Marilyn, Stacey & Morgan Bondon
Phil Bradbury
Bobby Brown
Scott Brown & Carolyn Schaefer
Leroy Buell
Bob Colaizzi
B.F. Al & Lynne Cole
Phil Coombs
Dan Cotter
Walter Denahan
Jimmy & Ann-Marie Dobbs
Jack Douglas
Keith Dunbar
Jerry Etzel
Bob & Linda Feighner
Jim Freeman
Les Gonda
Jerry Gordon & Karen McRann
Peter Gulick
Steve Helveston
John Higgins
Joe Hish
Lotus Guy George Hovsepian
The HSR Timing & Scoring Crew
Ian Keith James

A Little O.F.F. (Old Fast Fords)
Ross Bremer • Karen Perrin
Ken & Lydia Kales
Steve Kibble
Tom & Kaye Kovacs
Dan Kubly
Jim & Paula Ladwig
Alan & Lillian Lewis
Barney Li
Southern Lotus Racing
Jim Williams, Robert Wyatt & Joe Allen
The Lucurell Family
Bill MacEachern
Ray & Janet Mulacek
Barb & Bernie Nevoral
Al & Anne Petkus
• The Pumpkins
John & Lisa Weinberger
• The Alex Quattlebaums
• Pat Ryan
• Joe Sexton
• Jeff Snook
• Robert F. Snodgrass, Jr.
• Michael Stott
• John Targett
• Team Deep Steam
Brian & Maura MacEachern
• Tom Veale
• The Vintage Connection
John Harden • Chris Campbell • Crane Eveland
Ken Morgan • John Washam
• Duck & Sue Waddle
• Herb Wetanson
• Court Whitlock
• Bob Woodward
• Tom Yeager & Scottie Ullring

AutoWeak design & photography by Art Eastman Graphics

HISTORIC SPORTSCAR RACING, LTD. ⌷⌷⌷

Atlanta • Daytona • Palm Beach • Savannah • Watkins Glen
FOR MORE INFORMATION CALL: (888) 477-5999 • FX (813) 935-9564

ROLEX

OFFICIAL HSR SPONSORS

MCIWORLDCOM

Allard J2X

Jaguar XK 120

Jimmy and Anne-Marie Dobbs'
favorite neighbor
Bob Fergus
in his new Jaguar C-type

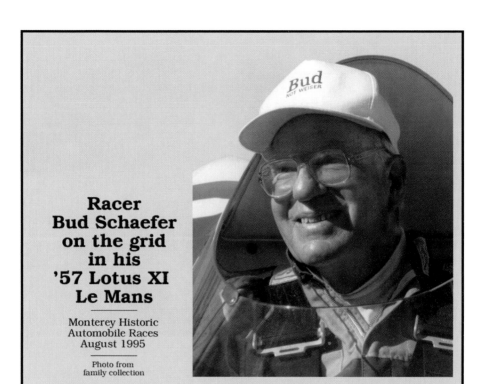

Racer Bud Schaefer on the grid in his '57 Lotus XI Le Mans

Monterey Historic
Automobile Races
August 1995

Photo from
family collection

Excalibur J

Mercedes-Benz 300SL

DaimlerChrysler Classic Archives photo

Karl Kling and Hans Klenk service their car on the way to victory in the 1952 Carrera Panamericana

NOW THAT YOU'VE PREPARED YOUR VINTAGE RACER--
PREPARE YOURSELF

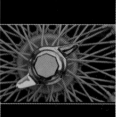

RACING OUR CARS WILL HELP YOU WIN IN YOURS.

- FOUR REGIONAL CHAMPIONSHIPS AT OVER 20 TRACKS NATIONWIDE--ONE WEEKEND OR YEAR ROUND--IT'S UP TO YOU.

- THE OPPORTUNITY TO LEARN NEW TRACKS WITHOUT THE EXPENSE, MAINTENANCE, LOGISTICS AND PREP TO YOUR OWN CAR.

- FORMULA DODGE RACE CARS THAT ARE SENSITIVE TO DRIVER INPUTS, AND PROGRESSIVE IN THEIR FEEL. A PROVEN RACE CAR TO TRAIN THE DEVELOPING DRIVER.

- SUPERIOR INSTRUCTION FROM DRIVER COACHES WITH BACKGROUNDS RANGING FROM FORMULA ONE, CHAMP CAR TO INDY LIGHTS, ATLANTICS, IMSA GTP AND SPORTSCAR/USRRC WORLD SPORTS CARS.

- WE OFFER COMPUTER CARS EQUIPPED WITH DATA ACQUISITION TO HELP EVALUATE YOUR PROGRESS.

- HOSPITALITY, DRIVER SEMINARS, FULL TIMING SHEETS, AND DRIVER SOCIALS ARE OFFERED AT EACH RACE WEEKEND.

- THE MASTER'S DIVISION RECOGNIZES AND REWARDS THE TOP 40+ YEAR OLD TALENT IN EACH CHAMPIONSHIP.

Skip Barber Race Series
800.221.1131
www.skipbarber.com

Pegaso Z-102

Kurtis 500S

Frazer Nash Le Mans Replica

LAWYERS WITHOUT BORDERS
ST. LOUIS, MISSOURI USA

Jeffress B. Hailand
LOTUS LANE
RACING

IRISH RACING
Daniel B. Hayes

R. Harrington
Photography

Quality Vintage Race Photography
Phone/Fax 905-332-7889   E-Mail: rharring@idirect.com

Jowett Jupiter

after a long, hot, hard day's racing
the smart set relaxes at

CHATEAU DEKON

home of the finest dialect comedy in motor sports

your hosts
STEVE & VERONICA

Lowell Blossom
Tony Spencer
Dan Quillen

Garagemahal (317) 873-5064 • 7950 Hunt Club Road, Zionsville, IN 46077

Classic – A creation of enduring value,
a standard, a perfect specimen.

Harry Gaunt
J E W E L E R S
Woodfield Center, 86th & Keystone, Indianapolis

Flawless Diamonds in 18K Gold
from $2,500

SENECA LODGE

South Entrance, Watkins Glen State Park

**The Glen's Unofficial
Race Headquarters**

The Best Prime Rib,
Steaks & Seafood

Bench & Bar
Tavern Room

Motel • Cabins
Chalets

607-535-2014

MOTOR SPORTS

Manufacturer of the

*Accessories & Custom
Components*

1007 Richards Street
Dalton, GA 30721
(706) 226-0989
Fax (706) 226-9772

Larry Cope (706) 278-1406
Home Phone

Mercedes-Benz 300SL

Karl Kling and his navigator
Hans Klenk cross the finish
line at Ciudad Juárez,
winning the 1952 Carrera
Panamericana for Mercedes

DaimlerChrysler Classic Archives photo

Crosley Hot Shot

Compensation Consulting Services

Since 1986

TRIAD CONSULTANTS, INC.
175 OLDE HALF DAY ROAD
LINCOLNSHIRE, ILLINOIS 60069
847.634.8300 / triadcons@pop.net

A good chassis technician sets the suspension by combining science and his senses. A race mechanic feels failures before they occur. Trackside engine tuning combines years of experience with an understanding of weather, the drivers style and engine specification. A well trained fabricator's welds outlast the tubes they affix. If you want this level of expertise and care brought to your restoration, repair, or track support, please consider Vintage Racing Services, Inc.

Please call for our brochure or for additional information.

1785 BARNUM AVENUE, STRATFORD, CT. 06497
203-377-1658   FAX 203-386-0486

LEE CHAPMAN RACING

For all your Lotus and Chevron racing needs

860.354.4479

MARCOVICCI-WENZ ENGINEERING

Formula 5000
BMW, COSWORTH MAE, SCA, DFV, BD, FERRARI, COVENTRY CLIMAX

Ted Wenz   516.467.9040

We ♥ love ♥ racing with Lee and Ted

Gary Fairbrother
Jan Giles
Peter Gulick
Burt Levy
Peter McLaughlin
Phil Meany, Jr.
Stirling Moss
Peter Schultz
Scottie Ullring
Tom Yeager

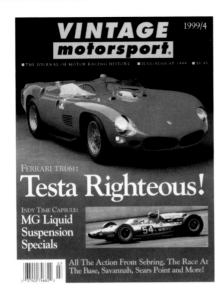

Allard J2X

Jaguar C-type

ENTERTAINMENT | SPORTS | MULTIMEDIA

w w w . m u l l e r c o . c o m

Congratulations to Burt Levy
Story Workshop® Alumnus
First Published in
Don't You Know There's a War On?
Story Workshop Anthology
Fiction Writing Department
Columbia College Chicago

MG TC

Siata 300BC

Real enthusiasts understand that fast, beautiful racing machines can only be appreciated in motion and close to the limit. It's a shame when they waste away in silent, musty reverence where their voices can no longer challenge the hills or delight the fans who love them. So here's to genuine enthusiasts like Rick Grant, who share rather than hoard and still pursue all the speed, noise, risk, and excitement that made them more than base metal in the first place. **We thank you!**

Jaguar XK 120

Lancia Aurelia

Aston Martin's Sebring Challenger

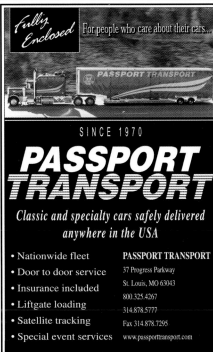
Ferrari 250 M

Cunningham C4R

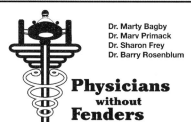

OSCA MT4

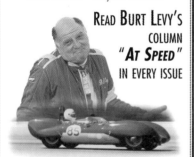

Mercedes-Benz 300SL

LUCK, GUTS and REACTION TIMES. . .

the three things racing drivers rely on when they haven't planned ahead!

In motor racing as in investment management, sustained success can only be achieved through experience, strategy, clearly defined objectives, and well informed choices. Rothschild Investment Corporation has had sustained success at earning and keeping their client's confidence since 1908. If you believe in planning ahead, consider Rothschild for the professional management of your portfolio, pension, or IRA rollover.

Contact: John Baker Welch at 312-983-8980
Rothschild Investment Corporation
A fee based registered investment advisor since 1908

World's **Fastest** *Sports Car*
— *with touring car comfort*

THE JAGUAR XK-120

LET'S LOOK AT THE RECORD:

- Le Mans, France, 1953: Placed 1st, 2nd, and 4th in the world's toughest endurance trial. Covered 2539 miles in 24 hours at an average speed of 105.8 m.p.h.

- Jabbeke, Belgium, 1953: 141.8 m.p.h. for new speed record.

- Montlhery, France, 1952: XK-120 Sports Coupe averaged 100.31 m.p.h. for 16,851 miles, breaking all speed records.

- Montlhery, France, 1950: 107.46 m.p.h. average for 24 hours.

Combine these achievements with the safe, road-hugging ride, the direct, positive steering, the smooth power of the twin overhead-camshaft engine, and you'll know why Jaguar is—*the finest car of its class in the world.*

JAGUAR

Westbridge Motor Car Company, Ltd.

Thoroughbred motorcars for discriminating drivers

Colin St. John, proprietor

Wear a *REAL*
CRASH HELMET
Like Race Drivers and Jet Pilots
Tough, rugged plastic helmet in red or white colors, cushioned with soft sponge-rubber. Is adjustable for perfect fit. Protects against hard bumps while riding motorcycles or driving Hot Rods and Sports Cars.
Wear It for Safety

Wal-Nut Products Company
10023 N. St. Lopez Ave.
Chicago 32, Illinois
only **$2.98**

Put the famous
BERMUDA
★**BELL**★
in *your* car
$9.95 ppd
Bert Feltoni
5858 Van Nuys Blvd.
Van Nuys, Calif.

Cadillac-Healey
Ex-Cunningham 1949 Healey Silverstone - extensively modified including a strong, race-prepared Cadillac V-8. Great competition history - In fine fettle and race-ready.
$1250 - Ted Jones, 4 Mission Drive, Palm Beach, Florida

A Triumph on Castrol
124 m.p.h!
by Triumph Sports Car

using **Castrol**

At Jabbeke, Belgium (20/5/53), the low-priced Triumph Sports car, in speed trim, was officially timed both ways over a measured mile at an average speed of 124 m.p.h. **THE MASTERPIECE IN OILS**

Making Time...

with **EDELBROCK** *POWER-SPEED!*
Time and distance are no match for EDELBROCK. To *make time* . . . to get there ahead of the crowd, install EDELBROCK power-speed equipment.
EDELBROCK EQUIPMENT CO.
4921 W. Jefferson Blvd. • Los Angeles 16, California

Ferrari 340 Mexico
Ex-Works Ferrari Mexico
Less than 3000 miles
Contact Carlo Sebastian

*providing fantastic finishes
for over 50 years!*

MONTEZUMA'S
FERRARI

*W*hen I first had the idea of funding
the production costs of this book with
sponsorships and advertising, I wasn't
sure it would work. After all, it had never
been done before, and we had less than
eight weeks to go before our scheduled
press date.

*T*he outpouring of support and
enthusiasm from my racing friends,
fellow gearheads, and the greater automotive
community was genuinely overwhelming,
far surpassing my wildest dreams.

Thank You All!

Burt "BS" Levy

Chapter 6: Home for the Holidays

Needless to say, my short-time fiancée and longtime, all-purpose girlfriend Miss Julie Finzio was not particularly thrilled when I came back from Mexico with my arm in a sling, my wrist in a cast, my ribs all taped up, and a bunch of Frankenstein Monster sutures for an eyebrow. Not hardly. *"MY GOD, WHAT HAVE YOU DONE TO YOURSELF?!!"* was I believe the way she put it when she first laid eyes on me at the airport. Fact is, I was kind of flattered that she'd taken the bus ride all the way over from Passaic just to meet the plane. It wasn't really necessary, you know? But I guess I'd let it slip that I'd run into a few little difficulties and wound up sort of laid up in a hospital ward down in Mexico. Now that we were engaged and all, it was apparently no longer just my business what kind of stupid, idiotic, hair-brained and potentially dangerous stuff I did with my own personal body. *"YOU'RE SUCH A FRICKIN' IDIOT!"* she said loud enough that people taking off in planes could hear. *"WHAT IF YOU GOT KILLED, HUH? WHAT THEN?"*

She was obviously glad to see me. You could tell.

We all rode back together in the big black Caddy Big Ed and me had left at the airport what seemed like a million years ago, and I had to sit up front with Big Ed on account of he always drove with the seat way back and I needed the room on account of I was stiff and sore as hell after the wreck and the long, cramped, bumpy plane ride home and none of my joints wanted to bend again. Ever. By that point Julie had calmed down a few notches and even had herself a little sniffle-cry about how could I do this to her and almost make her a widow before we were even married-before the wedding even!-and Geez, did it hurt much, honey, and you go ahead and sit up front and was the weather real nice in Mexico and *Oh God, I'm glad your home!* That's when she leaned forward, nuzzled her head into the good side of mine and kissed me softly under the ear. Geez, that felt great. But then my eyes kind of peeled over towards Big Ed and I felt my cheeks heating up when I noticed the smirk spreading across his kisser. But it felt good anyway, you know?

I was really looking forward to spending a little time with Julie alone, even though I wasn't real sure what good it would do. After all, my ribs still hurt something awful every time I made a quick move or breathed too deeply, and heavy breathing was one of our Main Attraction activities whenever Julie and I were alone together. No question I was going to be out of commission for awhile except for maybe holding hands and a little kissy face.

A lot had gone on in the two weeks since I'd left town. Julie said my mom had called and invited her and her mom and even Old Man Finzio over to Thanksgiving dinner (my God, it was the very next night and I'd forgotten all about it!) and Cal Carrington dropped by the station once or twice to see if there was any news from Mexico and so did Carson Flegley and of course Old Man Finzio had fired Butch a few times-but that went without saying-and, oh yes, Barry Spline from Westbridge called to say the rest of the parts had come in for Big Ed's Jaguar engine.

That got me to thinking about the bind I was in, seeing as how I had all this sports car work lined up at the Sinclair (and more sure to come as the weather got colder and all those Lucas batteries, starter motors and generators -not to mention the cold-start solenoids for our Jaguar customers-started to play up) and I couldn't even hold a damn wrench in my hand or apply more than a few measly inch-pounds of torque without causing my one remaining eyebrow to damn near shoot off my face and drooling blood through the stitches where the other one should have been. It occurred to me that I was going to have to find some help-and *fast!*-and right away I started having these ominous memories about all the ham-fisted, bolt-snapping, dent causing, gasoline and electrical fire generating, and all 'round talent-less succession of would-be grease monkeys I'd seen come and go at Westbridge like it was a blessed revolving door. To tell the truth, I was pretty much a lone wolf sort of operator and could only work around a guy like Butch because he was pretty much a lone wolf, too. The idea of hiring people I didn't know and then trying to ride herd on them to make sure they did things the right way and didn't put a clutch in wrong or burn up the wiring behind some ear, nose, and throat doctor's dashboard or drop one of Big Ed's Jaguars off the lift didn't appeal to me at all. But I was going to have to do it-like it or not-and right away I felt older in all the worst possible meanings of the word. But at least we had Thanksgiving, and, if I let myself sneak the Friday and our usual half-day Saturday off, that gave me until Monday morning to get it all sorted out.

I figured I owed it to myself, you know?

Thanksgiving was always a certified Big Deal around our house, even though my mom always felt bad about the turkey (you know how she is about birds-even big ugly ones with strange, Technicolor goiter arrangements like turkeys) and so she'd always pick one that was old and about ready to die anyway. Which is why the huge, heaping mound of turkey meat on our Thanksgiving platter was always a little on the dried out, stringy side. But she'd make up for it with her succulent and delicious pineapple glazed ham (thank goodness pigs didn't fly!) and sweet potatoes with plenty of butter and brown sugar and gooey marsh-mallow topping and green beans with pearl onions and slivered almonds and regular Idaho mashed potatoes, too (with her trademark creamy giblet gravy, natch) and pumpkin and mincemeat pies from the Swedish bakery that had been in the same location on Front Street for at least a million years and even liver dumpling soup from a recipe the old Bohemian widow down the street gave her along with homemade buttercrust dinner rolls if she really got things cranked up full blast in the kitchen. And this year she was in top form, seeing as we were having actual *company* over besides the usual once-a-year onslaught of family. Fact is, my mom was fluttering and twittering all over the house like a flock of her favorite chickadees, basting turkey breasts and poking forks in drumsticks and ironing dear little table doilies to go under the nut and candy dishes and hanging fancy guest towels that nobody was ever supposed to use in the bath-room and laying out little arrangements of perfumed, flower-shaped guest soaps that nobody was ever supposed to use either next to the hot water tap and fussily plumping up every blessed pillow in the house. Even in bedrooms that nobody would ever see.

Both my married sisters were coming with their husbands and kids, and even the youngest one, Mary Frances, had agreed to join us even though she was convinced that Thanksgiving was a decadent, bourgeois capitalist holiday dedicated to the ongoing oppression of the working class. None of us were real happy about that egghead N.Y.U. crowd she was hanging around with in that apartment she shared with three other girls in Greenwich Village. Not that any-body said too much about it. Of course my sister Sarah Jean would be there because she lived at home and didn't have much of anyplace else to go, and somebody would naturally have to go pick up my Aunt Rosamarina on account of she was afraid to walk the lousy six blocks to our house by herself and would certainly be in no shape to go back home by herself once she'd reacquainted herself with my dad's supply of Asti Spumante and after-dinner Anisette. And then there were the guests of honor: Julie, her mom, and Old Man Finzio. To tell the truth, I wasn't much looking forward to it. Not hardly. First off, no question Julie and me were going to be the focus of everybody's attention, the main subject of conversation, the object of every wink, nod, and sly, behind-the-hand comment, and the recipients of more blessed advice than you could find in the Bible. And I'm talking both Testaments, too.

About the only good news was that Old Man Finzio begged off because he had to go have some tests or something at the hospital. Or at least that's what I told my mom after I took the call about eight ayem Thanksgiving morning.

What he actually said was "I got better things t'do than t'hang around all day with a bunch of assholes." But you needed to be able to interpret and translate a little when you were dealing with Old Man Finzio. Especially ever since he'd been having the health troubles he never said a word about but made damn sure everybody knew about just the same.

"Ohh, that's too bad," my mom said in her even-more-singsong-than-usual holiday voice. "We'll have to be sure and send him a platter later this afternoon. It's a shame he's not feeling well. He's such a *pleasant* man."

And that, in a nutshell, should tell you something about what planet my mother lives on and how far it may be from the old *terra firma* you and I are familiar with. But I guess that's why she's been able to stick it out with a pill like my dad for all these years and raise a litter of kids who, in spite of everything, didn't turn out much worse than anybody else's. In fact, I'd say we actually ended up better than most.

My sister Tina and her loudmouth, wholesale paint salesman husband Roy were the first to arrive, with three cranky kids in tow and carrying a lopsided jello mold that looked about half melted plus a fourth new baby that badly needed a diaper change. You couldn't miss the smell when you leaned over to kiss her. "My goodness, what *happened* to you?" she asked as soon as she saw me. That was the first of about umpty-kazillion times I heard that same exact question throughout the afternoon and evening.

"Uh, I had kind of a little accident at this, umm, race down in Mexico."

"Oh yeah. *Suuure,*" Roy said, his eyebrows pumping up and down. "You probably got a little rambunctious with one of them Mexican señoritas I heard so much about. I bet she bucked you off like a damn bronco."

"Oh, *please,*" Tina groaned.

"Hi, Roy, good to see you again," I lied.

"*Ride 'em, Cowboy!*" Roy whooped as he oozed past on his way to the liquor cabinet. Somehow, the idea of a jerk like him having sex with my sister made me want to punch him in the nose. In fact, that's probably why I never cared all that much for their kids.

A little later my sister Ann Marie and her two kids arrived complete with her nebbish raw-materials-inventory-clerk husband with the perpetually watery eyes and that awful cabbage, bean, and peanut butter casserole side dish that she inevitably brought to every single family gathering. "You just need to pop it in the oven and heat it up," she called into the kitchen. Even cold, it smelled worse than the baby's diaper. "Jesus, Buddy, what happened to *you?*"

"Aw, I got in a little car wreck. That's all."

"You and those cars of yours." She shook her head. "If *I* was your wife, you'd never get away with it." You could see in a second who wore the pants around Ann Marie's house.

"That's why I'm so glad you're my sister and not my wife," I snickered. "Besides, I'm not even married yet."

"But I hear you're going to be." She gave me a dry, birdlike peck on the cheek. "Congratulations."

"Yes, congratulations," her husband said meekly, but she glared at him anyway, just to make sure he didn't think he was getting away with anything. I tired to remember his name because I knew I'd have to introduce Julie and her mom around later, but it was hard to do. He was just so forgettable.

"Jerry, take the children's coats. And wipe Melissa's nose, it's running."
Jerry! That was it.

My dad left in the two-year-old Mercury he was so proud of to go pick up my Aunt Rosamarina, and meanwhile my mom and sisters gathered in the kitchen the way female types always do at family holidays and left me alone in the front room to entertain Roy and Jerry and a couple of their kids. Not that it was difficult, since all you had to do was keep Roy's glass full and he'd provide all the necessary chatter. You could pretty much ignore Jerry. In fact, getting ignored probably felt real pleasant to him. And of course the kids were fine so long as they had things to break and spill. So it was really no problem.

It just wasn't much fun.

Roy said he wanted to hear all about that race down in Mexico, and Jerry actually looked pretty interested, too. "It sounds so *exciting!*" he whispered, like he was afraid a certain pair of ears in the kitchen might hear. You couldn't miss how he was inching forward on his chair. But of course there was no way to get more than a half-sentence out at a time with Roy on hand. Every other word reminded him of another south-of-the-border Dirty Mexican Hooker joke or Pus Oozing Venereal Disease joke or combination plate special Dirty Mexican Hooker/Pus Oozing Venereal Disease joke. I was plenty relieved when he finally asked me to go out in the kitchen and get more ice.

My dad returned with Aunt Rosamarina, and, like always, she made a beeline for the little green chintz chair off all by itself near the front window and waited there with a desperate smile frozen across her face for somebody to offer her a glass of Asti Spumante. I was happy to oblige. Weird as she was, Aunt Rosamarina never made me feel itchy, bored, and uncomfortable like some of my other relatives. Especially Roy, who made sure to take his dirty jokes down to a heavy stage whisper once my aunt was in the room, pretending to keep it quiet so as to spare her tender ears, yet making absolutely sure it was loud enough that she couldn't miss a word. It really made his day when he saw her flinch, gag, or blush.

Julie and her mom showed up a little late on account of the buses don't run especially regular on Thanksgiving. I would've gladly offered to go pick them up, of course, but I really wasn't in much shape to drive (plus it could go either way about my dad letting me use his precious Mercury) and it didn't even occur to my jerk father to get them when he went to pick up my aunt. But they finally made it and Julie looked just great. She was wearing that clingy yellow angora sweater I loved so much and a matching band of yellow ribbon across her hair and of course that flashy new sparkler on the third finger of her left hand. She was all smiles when she came through the door, too, even though I could tell she felt a little nervous. Me, too. And immediately we went through one of those wrong-end magnetic pole feinting matches where we didn't know whether to shake, hug, peck, kiss, or wrap ourselves around each other and play advanced tonsil hockey in front of the rest of the family. Then I had to introduce her around-Jerry, yeah *that* was his name-and I wound up saying "and these are their kids" because I could never keep them all straight except by description (this is the one who always has snot running out of his nose and this is the one who needs a diaper change and that's the one who bites) but Julie had them all figured out in a few minutes. I think women are just plain genetically superior to men at that sort of thing. As we passed by Roy and his third drink, he leaned in close and whispered *"Boy, she's got one hell of a set of knockers, don't she?"* loud enough for everybody to hear.

I also had to introduce Julie's mom around. She was wearing about a half pound of bright pink rouge and a fresh jet black spray paint job on her hair, and she had one of those pastel Vogue cigarettes with the gold tips lit up before I even had her coat off. It was beaver or raccoon or something and she told me in no uncertain terms to be real careful with it on account of it once belonged to Marlene Dietrich. Which I guess was just another way of saying she got it second hand. Julie's mom was one of those people who could smile and still look like she hated your guts, and her eyes always reminded me of a cornered rat. Or maybe something bigger, like a ferret or a possum. And I know what I'm talking about, because the neighbor's dog cornered a possum out behind the trash cans one night when I was in high school and I went out to see what was going on and shined a flashlight in its face. I still get the creeps when I think about it.

Anyhow, I knew her name was Rosa, but didn't know if I should be that familiar. So I tried, "and this is her mother, Rosa Finzio," and that really didn't feel right either. It was going to be one hell of a job to ever get around to calling her "mom." And of course I had to take both of them on the whole *"hello"-* *"hello"-"so nice to meet you"-"so nice to meet you, too"-"I've heard so much about you"-"I've heard so much about you, too"-"oh, and congratulations"-* *"thank you"* tour around the living room.

Then I got to my aunt Rosamarina on her perch over by the front window. "And this is my aunt," I explained as we presented ourselves in front of her. "I don't know if Julie's told you, but my apartment is over behind her house. Her name's Rosamarina, just like yours."

Julie's mom gave me the cornered possum glare. "My name's Rosa, not Rosamarina," she hissed. Then she leveled her very best howitzer look at Aunt Rosamaina. "And I never t'ought young boys oughtta have dere own apartments, eh? Dey get inta too much trouble."

Aunt Rosamaina looked at her like a refugee who didn't speak English.

Oh, great.

To get away, I ushered Julie into the kitchen where my mom and sisters were fluttering over the salads and side dishes and talking a blue streak about Julie and me. I knew that was true because they all clammed up and looked guilty as hell as soon as we got within earshot. Julie's mom chose to stay out in the living room, taking up a high ground position in the lone chair on the other side of the window from my Aunt Rosamarina, close enough to watch everybody but far enough away not to be roped into any unwanted conversations. And there she sat, like a hawk on a perch, twitching her head from side to side and flicking her eyes around the room while she chain-smoked those fancy Vogue cigarettes and quietly disapproved of every last thing she saw.

My mom and sisters were real sweet to Julie when I brought her into the kitchen, just like I knew they'd be. Especially my mom. In fact, it wasn't three minutes before I realized *I* was the blessed outsider there, and that what women do and talk over in kitchens on Thanksgiving and Christmas makes what guys do and talk over in garages, locker rooms, and neighborhood bars pale by comparison. Sure, guys think they have more fun and enjoy more true palship. Like we *belong* to something, you know? Something old, righteous, gamy, and noble. But it's the women who have the *real* insiders' club-maybe because they all share the same susceptibility to stupid love affairs, dumb pregnancies, convenient and inconvenient marriages, and all their associated social fallout. As a result, they seem to share the same tendencies towards clever schemes, grand plots, bitter disappointments at the hands of the very men they themselves built up to be more than they ever were, and long, unforgiving memories of all of it.

What goes on in those aromatic holiday kitchens is a blood ceremony-don't fool yourself-and the one thing you need to understand if you're a guy is that you'll never understand any of it.

After five or ten minutes of feeling like the fifth wheel in a kitchen with four perfect strangers I grew up with and one I was apparently planning to marry, I finally excused myself. "Make sure you see if my mom needs anything," Julie reminded me as I left the room.

"Yes, Buddy," my mom added. "Be a good host to Mrs. Finzio."

I would've rather brushed an alligator's teeth.

Meanwhile, my dad was down in the basement pretending to be chopping ice or something, but what he was really doing was hiding out. And I couldn't much say as I blamed him. In fact, for once in my life, I actually *respected* him for that. Oh, I guess I got along with my sisters and their families well enough. But they weren't exactly the First Choice People I'd pick to get stranded on a desert island with or even just hang around for a good time. Plus the holidays at our house were always the same old story-or same old *stories,* to be more precise-and you could almost write the script beforehand about *remember how the pan juices lit up in the oven one year and the kitchen stove caught fire?* Or:

the year of the freak snowstorm? Or:

the year everybody had the flu? Or:

the time Roy was showing us that Russian sailor dance and split his pants?

Of course Roy was wild shitass drunk when it happened, and wound up puking on his shoes like a high school kid on his way out to the car.

Sure, it was fun for five minutes. But then it was like the last few miles of a marathon run over and over and over again. Except for the women out in the kitchen, that is, where a lot more than coffee was usually brewing.

Anyhow, I did as I was told and asked Julie's mom if she wanted anything. "I like-a Campari," she hissed. "But I'm a-shu you no gotta any'ting like dat."

"I'll go check."

"No, donna go check. I don' wanna be bother."

"It's no problem. Really it isn't."

She made a sound like a car with a low battery trying to start on a frosty morning. "You jus' getta me whatever you want, garage boy. I'll-a be happy."

"I'll take one of those, too," Roy chimed in. And he meant it.

My Aunt Rosamarina didn't say a word, but I knew it would be wrong to opt her out of the round. So I went downstairs where my dad was busy rewiring the transformer on the electric train I hadn't used in twelve years. "Where do you keep the hard stuff?" I asked.

"Who wants to know?"

"Well, Roy, of course. And Aunt Rosamarina's just about used up the Asti Spumante. But mainly it's for Julie's mom."

"Whadda's she want?"

"She said to get her whatever I wanted."

"Hmpf," my dad snorted. "How about rat poison?"

For the very first time, I got the notion that there was maybe some dark, long-lost past history between my dad and Julie's mother. The idea made the tissue on my stomach lining go all dry and flaky. "Say, do you *know* her?"

"*Sure* I know her," he growled. "Hell, I've lived in this godforsaken town all my life. Why *shouldn't* I know her. We probably went t'grammar school together. Or maybe high school. So why the hell shouldn't I know her, huh?"

Now that might not sound like much to you, but, for my old man, it was just about the Gettysburg Address, and right away I got this feeling there were powers at work here that could do nothing but bring me grief. "Gee whiz, I'm just trying to get her a drink," I said lamely.

"She likes Campari," he said without looking up from the transformer. "But we don't have any. So give her vodka with a slice of orange. She likes that, too. The vodka's next to the good scotch and bourbon behind my bowling bag in the front closet where that asshole Roy won't find it. Pour the bitch all she wants."

"Geez, dad," I said like we were actually talking to each other, "you don't gotta talk about her like that."

He looked at me with his best hard-ass Union Boss sneer. "Just remember this, Buddy: *If the shoe fits....*" and went back to rewiring the transformer.

So I found the good hooch behind the bowling bag in the closet and poured Julie's mom one stiff enough for a root canal without anesthetic plus a weak, watery one for old asshole Roy and another stiff bolt for Aunt Rosamarina. Fact is, I was always amazed that my Aunt Rosamarina never looked drunk. No matter how much she sucked up. Of course, the other side of the coin was that she never looked particularly sober, either.

"Here y'go," I said cheerily, passing the drinks around.

"Boy, that Julie's got one hell of a playground," Roy reminded me in a stage whisper as I served him a watery gin-and-ginger ale. *"I bet it's fun twirling those babies around."*

I kind of wondered how big a dent my cast could make in his forehead.

Eventually suppertime rolled around and we all sat down around the dinner table, squared off against an unbelievably huge assortment of appetizers, soups, salads, roasted turkey, freshly carved ham, sweet potatoes, green beans, free form side dishes and multiple desserts that outweighed the whole lot of us by fifty or sixty pounds. My mom called downstairs and my old man reappeared for the first time in an hour and sullenly took his place at the head of the table. "Say grace, dear," my mom told him.

"Jesus Christ, let's eat!" he shouted like it was funny as hell and dug into the sweet potatoes.

My mom turned her empty, fluttering eyes to me. "Maybe *you'd* like to say something, Buddy?"

"Huh?"

"I thought, well, being engaged and all, maybe you'd like to say something. You know, to the *family....*"

I felt my insides ice over. But Julie was sitting next to me, and it reassured me a little when her fingers laced themselves quietly into mine. "Ah, er..." I began, leaping instantly to the bottom 100 list of great family orators. "Well," I started up again, "I, uhh, don't really know how much I got to say..." Julie kicked me a shot down where nobody could see. "...except to say that, umm, a bunch of you have found people to have families with," I looked at Tina and Ann Marie and right past their husbands, "and maybe now I've found one, too...." I looked around and it was obvious nobody figured I was done. "...so here's to the girl I've always, y'know..." I could feel the heat coming up on my face again, "...Julie, okay?"

There was a moment of rocklike silence followed by a round of faint, feeble applause. But Julie squeezed my hand a little tighter under the table and her mom even looked at me for a second like she wasn't about to go out and hire somebody to run me over with a road grader.

"Let's *eat!*" my dad said, leveling the first heaping mound of gravy slathered almond/raisin dressing at his kisser, and an instant later everybody was shoveling food in like they'd been stranded on a lifeboat in the middle of the Pacific for an entire lunar cycle. It was carnage, all right, and there was nothing but clattering serving spoons, loud slurping of gravies, soups and beverages, and sparks flying off both forks and bicuspids for the next twenty minutes without letup. About the only conversation (between mouthfuls, natch) was about passing the spuds or sweet potatoes and where my renegade sister Mary Frances might be. After all, she'd told everybody she was coming and knew from a lifetime of training when the show was scheduled to start at the folks' house every Thanksgiving. And yet here we were, well into the turkey and green beans, and she hadn't showed up yet.

Then, without anybody planning it, everything got real quiet.

Too quiet.

It was like a cloud passing over the sun.

"Oh, I heard about your husband being killed in the war," my mom finally blurted out like it'd just happened last week. "I'm so sorry."

"He got it inna Soloman Islands," Mrs. Finzio beamed triumphantly, her lower lip curling with pride. "Machine gunned dead by a Jap pillbox."

Lucky bastard.

"I gotta letter anna medal from President Roosevelt. *Personal,* too."

Thankfully, that's when the doorbell rang. It was Mary Frances, all right, wearing a big khaki army coat that was about two sizes too big for her over a standard Greenwich Village-issue black turtleneck sweater and slacks so tight I wondered how she ever got in them. God help her if she ever went down to Mexico, caught a dose of the *touristas,* and had to take an emergency dump. Hell, it'd probably crush her to death before she ever got them down over her hips. "Sorry I'm late," she said airily as she swirled into the room, "but there was a film showing I just *had* to make. Oliver's teaching an advanced seminar in post-revolutionary Russian Cinema and *Ten Days That Shook the World* was playing. I just couldn't miss it. I mean, Sergei Eisenstein simply wrote the book when it comes to *montage.*"

The amazing thing was that she said it like we all knew what the hell she was talking about. To be honest, I'd always liked Mary Frances a lot-because of her guts and her snotty sense of independence most of all-but right away I noticed as how she wasn't wearing any makeup and looked awful pale and drawn. Not that the women in my family ever wore a lot of makeup (or at least not so's you could tell) but all it takes is one bare naked female face to tip you off that either *they're* a corpse or everybody else has been spending a little primp-up time in front of a mirror. The other thing I wondered is who this "Oliver" character was. When you've got yourself a free-spirited sister, you tend to get a little nervous when they mention some name you've never heard before like it's one you've known all your life....

I must admit the rest of the dinner was pretty entertaining, seeing as how Mary Frances immediately started going off like a small town fireworks display about all the wonderful things she was learning and doing and all the incredible people she was meeting in "the Village" and how she'd really been nothing but an *embryo* before this all happened and most of all how this "Oliver" character had opened her eyes to the world. Oh, and incidentally how he was surely going to be the greatest writer/philosopher/abstract political thinker since Lenin,

Socrates, Plato and Descartes combined. And that might well have been true, since I didn't really know any of those guys and had no proof whatsoever that they didn't share but one brain between them.

Truth is, I was a little worried about Mary Frances. If there was one thing my short life had shown, it was that I didn't know shit about anything, and that most of the people I'd met who *did* think they knew shit about anything (my old man and Charlie Priddle, for example) were bound to be chock full of shit themselves. Right up to the hairline. So when my sister started spouting off (again, between mouthfuls) about all the fantastic things she'd learned and all the great, true meanings of life she was now coming to understand, my instant gut reaction was that some N.Y.U. guy with an itchy zipper and overdeveloped brain convolutions was whispering the truths of the ages in her ear just so's he could climb into her underpants.

It made me a little pissed off. More than a little, even.

So I was plenty curious when Mary Frances came up to Julie and me after dessert and said, "We're all having a little New Year's party down at the apartment. Actually, it's more like *three* apartments. In fact, it's all the people on our floor except that Czechoslovakian family from Prague. They pretty much keep to themselves. But the two guys across the hall are in off-Broadway shows sometimes and there's a jazz drummer and his girlfriend at the top of the stairway and I think the rest of his combo is maybe coming. Why, just *everybody* will be there. You guys should drop by."

"Really?"

"Yeah, really. Heck, you were always my favorite brother."

"I was always your *only* brother."

"So? You think that makes a difference?"

"What should I wear?" Julie asked.

Mary Frances leaned in nose-to-nose and giggled, *"Come naked!"* Then added breezily, "Or maybe just one of those metal Viking hats with the horns coming out the sides. You know, like those booming, *zaftig* heroines in all those Wagner operas." It was occurring to me that, even speaking primarily English, my sister had switched over to as foreign a language as my Mexican friend Javier Premal ever used in Spanish.

By this time dessert was long over and the kids from my other two sisters' marriages were running all over the place in states of destructive terminal boredom, so naturally it wasn't long before the first plate got broken and Roy's ashtray got upended on the carpet my mom had just spent half a day on her hands and knees cleaning. And, as always seems to happen in cases like this, the upshot was a nasty argument between the husband and the wife about exactly who's fault it was that their kids were such loud, clumsy, devilish, impolite assholes and precisely what punitive measures should be taken. Meanwhile, the kids had quietly disappeared outside (without their coats, natch) where they were feeding leftover turkey bones to the neighbor's grinning Labrador Retriever through the fence. Julie and I saw them doing it when we took the garbage outside. And there on the back porch, for just a moment, we realized we were finally alone. In fact, it was even quiet out there (at least if you ignored the muffled cracking and grinding noises coming from the big turkey leg bone in the Labrador's mouth) and there were even a few stars up in the sky over Passaic. I looked at Julie and she looked back at me as we put the lids back on the trash cans. "How're you holding up?" she asked.

"Okay, I guess. How 'bout you?"

"I've seen worse."

"Me, too."

Then there was a brief scream and scuffle from the fence, where Roy's oldest kid was trying to force his little sister's hand between the fence slats in hopes that the neighbor's Lab would mistake it for another turkey part. In a flash of crystalline uncertainty, I started to wonder if maybe getting married and having a family was really what I wanted out of life. And I could tell that Julie felt the same thing, too.

"Do you know any happily married couples?" I asked out of the blue.

Julie lifted her eyes from the kids pummeling each other against the fence with the neighbor's turkey-stuffed Lab barking excitedly on the other side and looked up at the stars. "We'll be *different"* she said with quiet conviction.

"Sure, we will," I agreed, slipping the fingers of my good left hand gently into hers. "Sure we will."

But that's what everybody thinks, isn't it?

Back at the Sinclair, my first order of business was to find some decent wrenching help while I was laid up with the busted wing. I got Butch back right away-he knew I'd come for him as soon as I got back in town-but he was pretty much a full-time cripple himself and so there was only so much he could do. Having been a first-hand witness to all the problems Old Man Finzio and Barry Spline had gone through with ham-fisted strangers who thought owning tool boxes made them mechanics, I didn't much want to simply hang a sign in the window or take out a blind ad in the Sunday newspaper. No, there was only one surefire way to land an ace mechanic. You had to poach one from another shop.

That's the only way you could be sure what you were getting. But doing that sort of thing was considered dirty, sneaky, rude, and all-purpose back stabbing within the greater Car Shop community, and you could make enemies for life if you got caught doing it.

Still, everybody did, and about the best damn foreign car mechanic I knew was Sylvester Jones. And no question he wasn't particularly happy over at Westbridge and had a future that amounted to MORE OF THE SAME in all capital letters as long as he stayed on there. So I went over on Monday to pick up Big Ed's engine parts-I had to borrow his black Caddy sedan for the trip on account of it had an automatic and no way could I operate a stick shift-and of course I timed it right around noontime so's I could have lunch with Sylvester out in the alley behind the Westbridge shop.

"Y'know," I told him as he unscrewed the top off his paper bag and drank his appetizer, "you really oughtta think about quitting this shithole and coming over to Jersey t'work for me."

"You?" he gagged. "Sheee-*it*, Palumbo. You jus' a damn *kid.* "

"Maybe I am," I argued, "but I got more damn sports car business than I can handle, Sylvester. Really I do. An' Old Man Finzio ain't gonna be around forever." Frankly, I was amazed at the words coming out of my mouth. "That shop is gonna be mine one day. You just watch." I meant them, too.

Sylvester shrugged and took another long, slow pull off his lunch bottle. "So whut if it is? That don't mean shit to me."

"Listen," I told him. "In my book, you're one of the best damn foreign car mechanics around."

"The best," he corrected me.

"Okay, *the* best. At least when you want to be."

He gave me a dirty look.

"But you'll never be more than a damn porter here at Westbridge. Even if you wind up fixing every damn car in the shop."

I could see he was rolling it over in his mind. "Yeah? S'how would it be any different working over by you?"

"At *my* shop," I said proudly, "you'd be a *full-fledged service technician.* " I tried to make it sound like a rocket scientist or something. "And you'd get a piece-work bonus, too."

I saw his eyes light up a little at that. See, there's two main ways to run a car shop. You can pay your mechanics on punch-in, punch-out, time-clock hourly like Colin and Barry did at Westbridge, and then just ride herd on them to keep their noses to the grindstone so they get the work out and make money for you, or you can put them on as minor-league partners where they get a percentage of the actual hours they bill according to the flat rate manual. Now this is a great deal for an enterprising mechanic who likes to hustle, but only if the shop stays busy enough to supply him all the work he needs. I swear, some of these guys will have three, four, five, or even six cars apart at one time! The bad part is that it tempts them to cut a few corners and resort to a few occasional short cuts in order to bill more hours. So the quality of the work can suffer and neatness tends to go right down the toilet. Why, I heard about one guy over at the Caddy dealership whose idea of a new car Pre-Delivery Inspection was to check the tire pressures, lift the hood, and spit on the air cleaner. Hell, he'd book a whole hour for that, and you had to get a little suspicious when a two-armed, two-legged, one-headed grease monkey managed to book 150 or more Flat Rate hours in a single 40 hour work week.

Believe me, it's been done.

But the deal I was offering Sylvester was the best of both worlds. He'd get a guaranteed weekly salary no matter what (and I made sure it was a little more than he was making at Westbridge) *plus* a bonus each week on hours billed. To tell the truth, I wasn't sure I could really afford it. And no question Old Man Finzio would have a fit. But it was one of those things I just *knew* I had to do. After all, if you can't get the damn cars fixed, you might as well just give up and take down your shingle.

Sylvester mulled it over. "Ah dunno, man," he said slowly. "It's way th'hell over in Jersey, and Ah don't think they likes mah kind over there."

"They don't like your kind *here,*" I reminded him.

"Yeah, but tha's different. At least they's *used* t'me here."

I could feel him wavering the other way. "Look," I said desperately, "you'll never get anywhere here at Westbridge, right?"

He nodded slowly.

"Then this is your chance. Your *opportunity.* I know how good a wrench you are. I *believe* in you." He still didn't look convinced. "Why, we could maybe even be partners one day."

He looked at me sideways, like he knew exactly how desperate and full of shit I was. "Don' ever try t'bullshit a bullshitter, Buddy," he laughed. "B'lieve me, you ain't about to save my life and I sure as shit ain't about t'save yours." He took one long, last pull off his paper bag. "Y'all jus' need a l'il wrenchin' help right now is all."

I tried to come up with something, but couldn't think of a thing.

"Look, son, how long's yo' wing gonna stay busted?"

"I dunno," I said glumly. "The doc says six, maybe eight weeks."

"Tell y'what. Ah b'lieve Ah got me a l'il vacation time coming…" to be honest, Sylvester *always* thought he had vacation time coming at Westbridge "…an' it's been sorta slow 'round here right now…" you could see he was thinking it over pretty carefully, "…an' mebbe Ah could see m'way clear to help y'all out here an' there for a couple weeks. Jus' sort of a l'il evening an' weekend side job for a l'il surprise Christmas money fr' mah kids."

My head bobbed up and down instantly. "Geez, that'd be *great!*"

"But don't be gettin' no big ideas about it, son. It's only temporary, see."

That was okay with me. In fact "temporary" was just about perfect.

As you can imagine, there was simply no end to the shit storm I stirred up by asking Sylvester Jones to do a little wrenching at the Sinclair. Freelance or otherwise. *"I ain't havin' no damn nigger workin' here!"* was the way Old Man Finzio put it, even mustering up some of his old piss and vinegar for the occasion. *"An' that's FINAL!."*

But I kept working on him. Especially since I knew he didn't have a lot of staying power any more. Why, I'd already gotten Butch back on the payroll, and that only took me half the morning.

"But Sylvester's the best guy out there," I pleaded from under the hood of Big Ed's Jaguar while Old Man Finzio sorted and straightened old cotter pins on his workbench. "He knows how to fix the damn cars."

"I don't care," the Old Man growled.. "I got *standards*. I don't want anybody sayin' I hired the first damn nigger garage mechanic here in Passaic. Besides, he'll steal us blind."

"No he won't," I shot right back. "I *know* I can trust him." Or at least I was pretty sure I could.

"Hmpff," the Old Man snorted.

"And it's only for a little while. Just till I get my wrists and ribs working again. I mean, just look at all the damn cars we've got to finish." I swept my good hand around the shop, where we had both of Big Ed's Jaguars and Carson Flegley's MG TD in various states of disassembly and even more sportycar work lined up outside. "With Sylvester here, we can turn all this into *cash money*. And *quick!*" I could see the Old Man thinking it over. "And I can have him come late and work evenings so nobody ever sees him."

"Hmm," he muttered, rubbing his chin. "Those colored boys *are* hard to see after the sun goes down." That was as close to cracking a joke as Old Man Finzio ever got, and he awarded himself a little half-chortle.

"Then it's settled?"

The Old Man slowly shook his head and spit on the floor. "Just don't have him here while I'm around, unnerstand?" he said in a voice you could barely hear. "I don't want anybody gettin' the wrong ideas. An' be sure and keep an eye on him, too. You mark my words, them tar babies'r sneak thieves before they leave their mama's belly."

"You got it," I agreed solemnly, trying not to sound excited.

Turns out old Butch wasn't real thrilled with the idea, either. In fact, it was about the only thing he and Old Man Finzio had ever agreed on. "He better stay th'hell away from my toolbox," as all Butch had to say on the subject, but you couldn't miss the fierce look of betrayal in his eyes.

But I was sure I could make it work. And that just shows you the difference between a young punk kid full of faith, enthusiasm, and bright ideas and somebody who's been around and learned better.

So Sylvester agreed and came to work late afternoons and evenings at the Sinclair. More or less. He showed up real late his second day and didn't even show up at all his third, and I began to understand that, although he maybe had decent intentions, Sylvester wasn't about to blow off his sure, steady thing at Westbridge for some wild-eyed kid's pie-in-the-sky mechanic's position all the way over in Passaic. So he'd drop by whenever he finished up early at Colin St. John's shop or if he took one of his frequent sick days (which, to be fair, he seldom ever did if he had an important customer's car to finish) when work was slow in Manhattan and came over to work with us. Whenever he did show up, he'd work at his usual disgruntled, steady and relentless pace, and no two ways about it, he got the cars done. And done *right* 99 times out of 100. That was important. But he was no way reliable-not that he ever promised to be-and I got to the point of seeing Sylvester as a whole lot of frosting without too much cake underneath, if you catch my drift. I was glad to have him when he showed because he could get the cars fixed, but no question he didn't share my interest, enthusiasm or desperate sense of urgency about what got finished when. And why should he? After all, he'd said at the very beginning that this was only temporary, and no way he was ever going to treat this as anything more than a few-extra-Christmas-bucks side job.

My problem was that I had a little stardust in my eyes and it was screwing up my vision, on account of I had this hair-brained notion that I'd somehow talk Sylvester into staying on at the Sinclair and even relocating his family someplace close by (not that anybody in our neighborhood would even *think* about renting to a colored guy) and then of course he'd quit the drinking and the all-night dice games with his broken-down Harlem buddies and settle down to a cleaned-up, respectable life here in Passaic with that enormous fat wife he couldn't stand and the two sets of brawling, bawling, foul-smelling twins that could all hide behind her backside without so much as an earlobe, elbow, or pinky finger showing.

That's how dumb I was.

But there were good things that came out of it, too. Like a few days later when our old pal Skippy Welcher showed up out of nowhere (and still looking pretty banged up) and demanded his old Jaguar back. That would be the much abused ex-works, ex-Creighton Pendleton, ex-everything else XK-120M that Big Ed bought off him (and against my better judgement) just to run that dumb SOWEGA airport race down in Georgia after he'd blown the engine in his own Jag at Watkins Glen and I couldn't get it rebuilt in time. Of course, at the time Skippy figured he didn't need his old XK-120 anymore since he'd bought Creighton Pendleton's slightly second-hand C-Type, which was a faster, lighter, more powerful, and far sexier car in every respect. Or at least it was until he and Milton Fitting went over that cliff with it at *La Carrera*. The remains of the C-Type had been sent back to England in quite a number of separate crates to be rebuilt at the factory, but it was going to take more than a short while to get it back. Much more. So Skippy figured he had a right to get his old car back in the meantime. Especially seeing as how Big Ed almost sort of owned the Ferrari that forced him off the road in Mexico. Or that was the way he saw it, anyway. Not to mention that I was riding shotgun in the Ferrari at the time, which, since I was sort of Big Ed's version of a Milton Fitting-style squire and sidekick, made him even more responsible.

Personally, I thought it was a grand idea, and I rang Big Ed up right away and told him to get his ass over to the Sinclair pronto so's he could dump The Skipper's oft-crashed XK-120 right back in his lap. I'd never trusted that car from the beginning, and now that Big Ed's own car would soon be done (and with a brand new, Buddy Palumbo Signature Edition racing engine, no less), I figured Skippy's car was just so much extra baggage. And for once Big Ed agreed with me. After all, he was going through some minor negotiational problems with Carlo Sebastian concerning who actually owned the flattened, burned-out Ferrari we'd left upside down in the bottom of a ravine in Mexico. Carlo had assured him that his money was safe and that the factory in Maranello would rebuild it better than new for him (*...and remember, you may not find another opportunity to buy such a car...*) but it would take a little time. And maybe a little more time after that. In any case, Big Ed agreed that his second-string Jag was better turned into cash, and hightailed it over as soon as he hung up the phone. Of course, the real frosting on the cake was the opportunity to make a little money off The Skipper while selling him back his own blessed car. That was too tasty to miss.

"I've had Buddy put a lot of work into that car since I bought it from you," Big Ed said grandly, really enjoying being on the seller side of a car deal for a change. Truth is, most of what I'd done is straighten out the damage from where Big Ed hit the haybales at that race down in Georgia. But The Skipper didn't have to know that. "It's a *much* better car than when I got it from you," Big Ed continued, patting the Jag on its freshly repainted fender. "Besides, I'll be racing my own 120 again next year. Why would I want to put a dangerous contender like you into a faster car?"

Why indeed?

"Maybe what I should really do is sell you *my* car and keep yours for myself. After all, these genuine *ex-works* cars are mighty hard to come by."

He had the Skipper's face popping and sputtering like molten lava.

"Yessir, they're mighty hard to come by, all right. Don't think I've ever seen another one like it. At least not here in the states, anyway...."

In the end, Big Ed made a quick couple hundred on the deal, and that's over and above the money he'd just paid me and the body shop to straighten out the crash damage.

Then Sylvester got into the act when The Skipper noticed that the valve stem caps were missing. I'd just been setting the pressures is all. But Sylvester pulled The Skipper aside and explained as how he'd come into possession of some genuine, Le Mans-issue *Jaguar Competition Department* valve stem caps. "Ah gots a set," Sylvester told him confidentially, "but they don't come cheap." He disappeared out back and took the four chrome auto parts store stem caps off his rusty old Plymouth and brought them in. "These here'r the special, *lightweight* ones," he told Skippy, and I swear The Skipper wound up paying him a buck each for them. Can you believe it?

But Sylvester wasn't exactly what you could call Steady Help around the Sinclair, and by now the weather had gone cold and so we had the usual winter influx of choke cable repairs and starter motor and battery replacements on your rank-and-file Fords, Plymouths and Chevvies on top of all the long-term sportycar and race car projects we had torn apart all over the place. Like Butch after his accident, I was slowly discovering there was a lot of stuff I could still do even with my featured wing in a cast. But there was even more I really couldn't. So, against my better judgement, I put Old Man Finzio's "MECHANIC WANTED" sign back in the window and waited to see what the breeze would blow in.

In the meantime (and likewise against my better judgement) I rang up my old buddy Cal Carrington, who had already proven beyond doubt that he was no way an automobile mechanic when we worked on his ratty old '47 MG TC together in my Aunt Rosamarina's garage. But he was an extra set of working hands and legs, plus I knew he'd be available since he didn't do much of anything anyway and would most likely appreciate the feel of a few extra Lincolns, Hamiltons, and even the occasional Andrew Jackson folded up in his pocket. No question he could do a lot of stuff on a monkey-see, monkey-do basis if you showed him real careful and then kept an eye out to see that he did it the way you said. But Cal was by nature a terrible angle shooter and short cutter-the kind you see a lot around car shops-who'd stare at a thirty minute job for twenty minutes trying to figure out how he could maybe get it done in fifteen. And of course it never works out. Or almost never, anyway. One thing genuine professional mechanics learn over time-and most usually through bitter experience-is that The Long Way is not only very often The Short Way, it is also, in many cases, The Only Way.

Cal didn't understand that, and he was just green enough and just cocky enough and just enough of a smartass to think that he could always find some trick new Easy Way to do stuff that experienced, grunt-level mechanics like me and Butch and Sylvester and all that went before had been doing the same damn way since the passing of the horse and buggy.

What did he think we all were, stupid?

Truth is, Cal Carrington didn't have the feel, patience, knowledge, theory or mechanical sympathy to work on cars. Not hardly. In fact, he didn't much like the notion of work in general, since it always seemed to include ugly provisions like getting up in the morning and only getting Sundays (or maybe Saturdays and Sundays) off. It offended his sense of *noblesse oblige.* Or that's what he told me, anyway. But, as a favor to me, he said he'd do it. And also a little because he was still on the outs with his folks, who were off someplace in the Caribbean and had made sure all the usual Castle Carrington nooks and crannies were devoid of folding money or even the jingle of loose change.

So Cal came to work at the Sinclair a few weeks before Christmas, to sort of be my arms and legs while I was healing up, and also maybe learn a little something about cars and even earn himself a few honest bucks by way of honest labor (which was, I believe, an entirely new experience for him) not to mention easing the standard-issue Morbid Racer's Boredom that is always a big part of the off season for anybody who's got the racing bug.

Things got pretty crazy around the Sinclair about then, what with the Old Man showing up every morning to skulk around the office for an hour or two in those same old blackened coveralls with the front pocket ripped off, muttering to himself while he went through the bills or sorted hardware at the workbench or maybe took something apart in one of the service bays that one of the rest of us would have to put back together. Or sometimes he'd just go lock himself in the john and stare at his reflection in the cracked, discolored old mirror over the sink for a few hours. Then he'd take off for some doctor's office waiting room or some hospital clinic waiting room and lots of times he'd never come back for the rest of the day. I felt really sorry for him, if you want the truth of it. But there wasn't much of anything you could say

Mean Marlene would drop Butch and his wheelchair off-he'd pretty much given up trying to get around on his crutches-around ten on her way to work. She'd landed herself a cocktail waitress job on the lunch and early dinner shift at some dimly lit joint in Englewood Cliffs that catered to the kind of 80- and 100-proof businessmen's lunches that sometimes went on well into late afternoon and yielded excellent tips whenever they did. Meanwhile Cal would roll into the shop an hour or so later, driving his mom's shiny new two-tone Packard with the spare key he'd had made on the sly. He was about the only damn apprentice mechanic I ever saw who drove himself to work in a four thousand dollar Packard Patrician. And then Sylvester might drop by later in the afternoon on the days he actually decided to show up, and he'd pitch in and help me finish up the cars that had to go out the overhead door that night.

To keep all the able hands working and things running smoothly as possible, I'd often as not wind up going on the parts runs myself. That way I could keep feeding my guys the hardware they needed to finish their jobs. Old Man Finzio usually took care of that sort of thing, but he was turning out to be even less reliable than Sylvester. Oh, he was *there* all right. Every morning at 6:30 sharp. But he just didn't much care about getting things done anymore.

To be honest, I enjoyed going on parts runs. It was a chance to get out of the shop-to break *free,* you know?-and it was always a challenge to organize all the places you had to stop in a logical order. Fr'instance, I might have a cylinder head that needed a valve job or a flywheel that needed resurfacing to drop off over by Roman Szyzmanski's machine shop, and then maybe a leaky radiator or heater core at the radiator shop plus a tread or two to pick up at the tire buster, a quick stop at the hardware store, the usual shit list of overpriced sportycar stuff from Westbridge, and a bunch of rank-and-file dealership and parts store stock for the Sinclair's longtime American sedan customers.

And I loved doing parts during the holidays. Every frosty windowpane had Christmas lights and a little fake tree or a cardboard cutout of Santa and his reindeer displayed inside-probably the same exact one that'd been taken out of mothballs and just as carefully packed away after the holidays for the past umpty-dozen years-and everybody seemed extra cheery the closer you got to Christmas. Although I had to restrain myself from bashing a deep dent in the dashboard with my cast when they played *I Saw Mommy Kissing Santa Claus* for the umpty-gazillionth time. But holiday music was all part of it-it was *everywhere*-and so were the decorations. Even in the parts stores, where the well-endowed dolly on the girlie calendar tacked up next to the phone was always dressed for the season, generally in something the nature of a white rabbit fur bikini (the top looking much like a seven-year-old child's earmuffs) along with matching fur cuffs, a bright red Santa hat, and dear little rabbit fur boots with four-inch stiletto heels. I always kind of wondered what those girls were dressed for, you know? Especially since they were usually carrying an industrial-size power rodder or a shiny new monkey wrench big enough to unscrew a damn sewer pipe. But they sure got your attention, and I guess that was the whole idea. Wasn't it?

Everybody behind those counters was extra friendly around Christmas time, too. Maybe it was the pine smell off the air fresheners or something, but they always looked happy as hell to see you. Although in my case it helped that everybody'd seen my cast and heard all about my harrowing, over-the-cliff Ferrari adventure in Mexico. And if they hadn't, I made sure they did! But it was nice, because all of a sudden I had a little minor league celebrity status going and that meant all the tire busters and parts countermen wanted to chew the fat with me. Like I was *somebody,* you know? So, between picking through parts pages and ordering up points sets, spark plugs, condensers, caps, rotors, and carb kits, we'd exchange views on Marciano's upcoming rematch with Jersey Joe Walcott and all those poor young guys fighting the Reds over in Korea-*Did'ja hear? Ike's going over there for a personal looksee before his inauguration!*-and that Jew-Commie Rosenberg couple they were going to fry in the electric chair for spying. Oh, and how're things going with that girl you got engaged to and where are you planning to spend Christmas, huh?

But, without question, the hottest topic of conversation the last couple weeks before Christmas was that Christine Jorgenson person who used to be a guy-a damn G.I., in fact!-but apparently didn't much like standing up to pee and flew over to Europe-Copenhagen, I think-to get a bunch of operations and hormone shots and stuff to turn him into a her. It was unbelievable, you know? Or at least that was the general opinion at the parts counters, machine shops, and tire and radiator shops around town. Most all the countermen I ran into thought it was a sickening, ugly, disgusting and perverted thing to do. Hell, that went without saying. But the question that really had everybody stumped was *why?* Even the mothers, wives, sisters, and girlfriends of the guys who worked in the parts stores figured that men had it made in this world compared to women. I mean, we pretty much got to run things, didn't we? Why anybody would want to roll that over just to cook pot roast, put curlers in their hair and wait for the damn phone to ring was beyond us all. It's like we felt, I don't know, *betrayed.* And it gave us the creeps, too.

I suppose if I hadn't had a small dose of ambition, I could've been perfectly happy as a parts runner. You had friends at every stop and you could shoot the breeze with every one of them about all the interesting stuff going on in the world. Your opinions would be respected, too. At least so long as they weren't too outlandish and your checks didn't bounce.

But I *did* have ambition. Or maybe it was just a shot of guilt dressed up to look like ambition. But, whatever it was, I'd catch myself in the middle of some deep philosophical discussion about Christine Jorgenson's downstairs plumbing or whether the Detroit Lions had a chance in hell against the Cleveland Browns and realize that, hey, I had to be on my way and get back to the shop. After all, we had a pretty ragtag bunch working there, and it was my job to keep feeding them parts and running around trying to sort the work out and be everybody's backup and keep the customers happy and put out all the inevitable fires. It didn't even occur to me that I was pulling thirteen and fourteen hour days damn near every day of the week and maybe that's why I felt like I'd been run over by a dump truck all the time.

The worst of it was I could tell Sylvester wasn't happy working at the Old Man's Sinclair. Sure, the extra money was nice, but it was also quite a haul back and forth from the edge of Harlem every day (or at least every day he felt like doing it, anyway) and besides, moonlighting in Passaic was seriously cutting in on his usual evening drinking, socializing, and dice games. Plus we seemed to be arguing all the time about his bonus money and exactly how many billable hours he had coming. Truth is, I don't think he much liked having some young punk kid telling him what cars to fix and handing him his pay packet at the end of the week. Even if it was me. And Old Man Finzio was grousing all the time about how he was missing some of his tools ever since Sylvester came to work at the Sinclair. Not that you could ever tell the way he left them scattered all over the whole blessed shop.

It all finally came to a head one Saturday when Sylvester showed up around lunch time all wobbly and disheveled after an all-night dice game and right away got into a big fight with Old Man Finzio about some missing socket wrenches. He came up to me a few minutes later, smelling of liquor and kind of wavering back and forth. "This ain't workin' out, man," he told me point blank. "Ah cain't do this shit no more."

I started to try to talk him out of it, but he stopped me before I had the first few words out.

"Nah, it ain't no good, Buddy. Ah jus' don' fit in here, see? An' if Ah try t'keep it up, you an' me ain't gonna git along anymore."

And I knew he was right.

"Oh, mebbe Ah'll still do a l'il side job every now an' then. But Ah sure as shit cain't work here steady no more. Nossir."

"But it's a better deal for you," I pleaded lamely.

"Never beg the hired help, son," Sylvester advised, patting me on the shoulder. "Iff'n you're gonna run a car shop business, y'gotta learn t'be a damn *boss!* Y'gotta hire and fire. Y'gotta learn t'be a grade-A asshole like Colin St. John an' Barry Spline." He looked me right in the eye. "Y'gotta be *tough.* There's plenty guys out there know how t'fix the damn cars. Or kin learn t'fix 'em, anyways. But they's gotta think of you as the *boss,* Buddy, an' Ah just cain't do that." And with that he turned, walked over to his old, rusty Plymouth, and drove off in the general direction of Manhattan.

I couldn't help remembering what he told me the day I asked Sylvester to come to work for me at the Sinclair. *"You ain't about t'save my life and Ah sure as shit ain't about t'save yours."*

But at least we were still friends.

Sort of.

Over on the hearth-and-home front, Julie and me were discussing "setting a date," which is a very big deal in the engagement and wedding business since there are so many clergymen, caterers, limo drivers, seamstresses, hall owners, tux renters, florists, second rate bands, and wedding cake bakers with their hands out who, as far as I can tell, only want to know two things. When and How Much. Of course the women look at it differently, and where I saw only a column of figures and a lot of boring sitting around, Julie and her mom and (get this!) my mom and sisters and even my Aunt Rosamarina were busily offering suggestions and making recommendations and burrowing their noses into Bridal magazines as if anybody with any sense at all really cared whether the bridesmaids' satin sashes were pink or aquamarine or pale violet. I mean, far as most guys are concerned, it's all over in a couple hours and everybody's generally stiff well before that, so what's the big deal?

Julie thought it was that I couldn't be bothered.

I didn't dare tell her that I just didn't much care.

"You just couldn't be bothered, could you?" she said angrily as we headed out to the drive-in together in Big Ed's black Caddy sedan. He'd been real good about lending it to me since my shifting arm was in a cast.

"No, it's not like that at all, honey," I answered lamely. "It's just that you've got so much, you know, better *taste* than I do."

"Hmpf," she snorted. "And what about setting a date?"

"Well, ahh…" I mean, it's not like I was *avoiding* picking a date. Even if it may have looked like that a little. Okay, maybe even more than a little. "Geez, I dunno, Julie. Whadda *you* think?"

"Well," she said, peeling off like a dive bomber on a strafing run into more of that Women's Club bridal mumbo jumbo, "Spring weddings are nice-you know, with all the flowers starting and all-but we don't want to make it too soon or people'll think, you know, that we *had* to. And summer's nice, too. But not late July or August, 'cause it's just too damn hot." She leaned in a little closer and sent a salvo of zingers up my cracked ribs.

"OW!"

"Sorry."

"That's okay," I grinned through clenched teeth.

"Anyhow, I'd kind of like to get married maybe earlier rather than later."

"Me, too." Fact is, I thought I felt pretty comfortable with the notion of being married to Julie-you know, having dinner together and having breakfast together and all the sweet, sweaty private stuff that's none of your damn business that I hoped would go on in between. It sounded like a pretty good deal to me. But the idea of the wedding itself filled me with dread. Maybe it was something about the church, seeing as how I never felt real comfortable in church. Not that you're supposed to. And for sure it was something about the family. The *big* family, I mean. You know, the one that comes marching down the aisle with every bride and bridegroom like an anchor chain fastened to a graveyard. And then there were all the damn wedding day complications I didn't much care about but didn't dare let on. In short, I felt like a doomed stink beetle under some little kid's magnifying glass on a hot summer sidewalk. Yeah, that was it. I'd been avoiding setting a date because of all the effort and nervous anticipation that was bound to escalate into sleepless nights and dumb arguments about seating arrangements and which band to hire and a kajillion other things. And then it would all be over in an afternoon and evening, and no matter how many people told you afterwards *"oh, how beautiful everything was,"* it'd still feel empty and strange and way off kilter.

Or at least that's what I thought, anyway. Hell, if it'd been my choice, I would've run us out to some renegade justice of the peace, had ourselves a quick civil ceremony, checked into a fancy hotel, and been in the sack by ten and up enjoying the kind of big, room service breakfast you need to satisfy a couple of happy and contented young honeymooners by ten the next morning. Then we could take all that stupid money we would've blown-hell, no way could her mom afford to pop for the wedding-and buy ourselves some things we really *needed*. Like a drill press or a Lincoln arc welder or maybe even a new hydraulic lift. But of course I knew better than to mention such a thing.

That stupid I was not.

Christmas Eve rolled around on a Wednesday that year, and by that time Julie was dropping by the Sinclair for an hour or so every afternoon to help out here and there and talk things over and maybe even get a little cozy now that my ribs were feeling better. By now we'd set a date (or rather, *she'd* set a date and I sort of nodded and um-hummed my way along) and the late word out of Passaic was that we'd tie the knot on Sunday, June 21st, and that of course meant that the whole blessed groaning, gibbering, gyrating Women's Club Wedding Plans Luxury Cruiser had been officially launched out of my mother's kitchen and woe be to the poor naked soul who lay in its path.

But I must admit it was nice to have Julie around every day, and especially to have somebody I could really count on at the Sinclair. She was a hard worker, no two ways about it, and pretty good with the customers, too. Plus she'd really let him know it whenever she saw Cal Carrington slacking off (which was any-time I wasn't lurking directly over his shoulder, to be honest about it) and I could see where she was going to be a genuine asset at the gas station, even though she figured it'd be better if she kept her job at the Doggy Shake and have two incomes so's we could maybe struggle up enough for a down payment to get our own house one day and settle down to raise a family. I hadn't really thought that far ahead. And for a very good reason, too. Thinking about stuff like that made me distinctly uncomfortable. And I'd bet I'm not the only guy who ever felt that way, either.

But, like I said, it was nice having her around, and except for the times she got a little too bossy and made my life miserable, she brought a nice, gentle, feminine touch to the Sinclair that it'd never had during the Old Man Finzio regime. Fr'instance she painted the bathroom and had me put up a new mirror and even hung some stuff in there that smelled nice so the place didn't look like the closet where Count Dracula sucked marrow out of his victims' bones anymore. For the holidays, she put up this sweet little Christmas tree with bubble spiraling candy cane lights and a wreath with a red velvet bow and some bells on it that jingled like Santa's sleigh whenever somebody opened the office door. To be honest, I was worried that she'd spend too much money on that kind of fluff (Old Man Finzio got mad at her about it, too) but I must admit it had a real nice effect on our customers.

To be honest, what with running the station and taking up the slack after Sylvester left and riding herd on Cal Carrington and keeping Butch and Old Man Finzio from killing each other and still nursing my wrist and listening to all of Julie's wedding plans, I kind of let my Christmas shopping slide a little. Which is why I got a little panicky when Julie dropped by Christmas Eve morning just as I was pulling Mrs. Muccianti's Pontiac into the service bay to fix a bum thermostat and asked when we were going to exchange presents. "Uhh, well...," I sort of mumbled, "...how about tomorrow afternoon?"

She shook her head. "That's no good. My mom and I have to go into town to see my cousins."

"Oh."

"Want to come along?"

"Nah," I shook my head. "I got stuff I gotta do." In fact that was a lie. But only a small one. I figured I'd better be right back here at the station by Christmas afternoon. My family always went to church in the morning-even my dad-and then had a big midday meal and exchanged gifts right afterward. By that time, he and I figured to have had at least one major fight and the gas station looked like a fine place to hide out. Plus I'd finally be able to get a little decent shop work done while it was empty and quiet. The notion of passing up all that holiday fun just so's I could feel clumsy and uncomfortable in front of another fresh crop of relatives I really didn't want to know didn't sound real appealing. "You know how it is with family."

"So when should we do it?" Julie asked again. "I can go get yours right now if you want..."

"Ahh, well, that won't work, see. I mean, I don't have your present, um, *here* right now." Her eyebrows arched suspiciously. "Listen, why don't I stop by your mom's place later on."

"Gee, I thought we could maybe, you know, be *alone* when we exchange gifts." She kind of snuggled up against me. *"So, whad'ja get me?"*

"Oh, umm, I can't tell you *now,* Julie," I said lamely. "It's a *surprise.* "

Naturally she caught a whiff of what was going on and I immediately witnessed a strange and frightening transformation as the happy light dancing in her eyes turned into a cold, hard glare. "So when do you think you want to get together?" she asked in dangerously measured tones.

"Uh, err, how'bout later on today. You know, after work."

"You got any special time in mind?"

"Oh, well..." I was going through the time gymnastics in my mind, trying to figure out how quickly I could get through the thermostat job-after all, I'd *promised* it back for Christmas, and no way could I count on Cal showing up on Christmas eve and Butch and Marlene had gone off to spend the holidays with her awful white trash family down in Tennessee-and then sneak away to do a little blitzkreig Christmas shopping and get all the gifts I needed before the damn stores closed and be back in time to meet Julie. "You want to maybe meet back here around five or so?"

"Not earlier?"

"Uh, no. I've got some things to do, see...."

No question she knew exactly what was up. And that was pretty scary, knowing she could see right through me like that. But it was also kind of comforting in a way, too.

So I fought my way through that damn thermostat job and then called Mrs. Muccianti and told her I'd maybe drop it off for her seeing as how it was Christmas eve and all (when what I really meant was that I needed it to do my shopping, since I could work the 3-speed column shifter on the Pontiac a lot easier than the floor shift on the tow truck with my bum arm) so long as she could drop me back at the station afterwards. Then I popped the phone off the hook, scooped a fistful of folding money out of the till (although I made sure to leave an I.O.U. that was almost nearly accurate) and took off to see what stores were still open. The first one I found was the F.W. Woolworth five-and-dime, and that figured to be perfect since they not only had all kinds of gifts, but gift wrap, tape and ribbon, too. But they were due to be closing in about half an hour, so I really had to get hustling. I bought my mom this pretty apron/oven mitt set with bluebirds and daisies all over it and a little fruit pattern sewing kit with a silk strawberry pin cushion inside for each of my sisters (I'd learned years before that the only way to avoid trouble was to get them all the same blessed thing, even if they didn't like it) and I was stumped for awhile about my dad. I mean, what he really *needed* was a length of barbed wire to run up his ass. But they were all out of stock at Woolworths. He didn't smoke a pipe or like cigars or play golf and he didn't have anything much in the way of hobbies except for bullying, and you don't really need any special gift equipment for that. So I finally broke down and bought him yet another gift set of after shave and cologne like I do every year-it was kind of a tradition, really-and hoped like hell it wasn't a duplicate of something I'd already gotten him. Fact is, the top shelf of our medicine cabinet looked an awful lot like the men's cologne and after shave section at Woolworth's.

But what could I get Julie? Time was desperately short as I combed up and down the aisles, searching frantically for something to beam out from the shelves and counter tops like a lighthouse beacon on a foggy night and save me. And then, right there in the costume jewelry section, I saw these two little fake diamond ear studs on genuine silver-plated posts that (to my eyes, anyway) looked like a perfect match for that expensive finger sparkler I'd bought her at the jewelry store. I couldn't believe my good luck. The only problem was they were too cheap. I mean, I had to spend more than three bucks on her, you know? Right on cue, the store manager's voice came crackling over the loudspeaker system: *"WOULD EVERYONE PLEASE BRING YOUR FINAL SELECTIONS UP TO THE CASH REGISTER..."*

Shit!

"...AND A VERY MERRY CHRISTMAS TO YOU AND YOURS FROM ALL OF US AT WOOLWORTHS."

I suppose I have no choice but to share with you how crazy stupid a frantic young guy's brain works. And no, I can't understand or explain any of it. But with time pressing down on me like a thumb on a grape and the last few lonely grains of sand running through the skinny part of the hourglass, I came to the terrifying realization that the company buyers who procured all the stuff on the shelves and bins and tables at Woolworths knew a hell of a lot more about value than I did-hell, they were *professionals*-so if my mom rated a six buck set of kitchen mitts and apron and my dad was into me five-fifty for the cologne and after shave he'd never use, then I somehow needed to blow *at least* a tenspot on Julie. I mean, that went without saying. And that's about when they flickered the lights to get all the last-minute jerkoffs like me the hell up to the registers. And right smack-dab in the middle of that desperate, momentary darkness I caught the flutter of gold out of the corner of my eye.

Over in the pet department.

I must admit that Mrs. Muccianti's husband dropped me off a little late at the Sinclair. But it wasn't entirely his fault. It'd started to snow a little and the roads were getting slick, and of course it was dark as midnight by five o'clock at that time of year. Plus they had some people over-family and relatives, you know the

Holiday drill-and nothing would do that I join them for a quick, high-octane eggnog or two and how was my mom and that nice young girl they'd heard I was going to marry and, oh yes, my father and old Mr. Finzio, too? Not that I much minded, since I needed someplace indoors to wrap up the silver stud earrings like they came from some fancy store and also that other present so's it wouldn't freeze to death.

It was damn near six-fifteen by the time I finally arrived at the Sinclair, and I remember there was a thin, brilliant white carpet of snow on the ground and Julie's spiraling candy cane Christmas tree lights were winking joyfully through the glass like something in the holiday windows at Macy's. But Julie herself didn't look joyful at all, seeing as how she was standing outside in the cold carrying a long, flat hanger bag over her shoulder. She didn't have her own key. "Geez. Sorry I'm late," I apologized through the haze of a few stiff egg nogs. "I got a little tied up."

"That's all right," she chattered through lips more blue than red, "I've only been waiting forty-five minutes." I could see she was shivering something awful-she must've walked all the way over from the Doggy Shake and then just waited for me-and it looked like she was too cold to be angry. That would come later. And no question this would go into the safety deposit box. Every woman has one of those. That's where they bank all the little shreds of anger, disgust, disappointment, doubt, and hatred that they are just too worn out to put a match to at the time so they may be taken out and rekindled many times over on appropriate future occasions.

But, it being Christmas eve and us being engaged and all and having just freshly set a date, Julie was willing to be a little pliable and forgiving. The space heater helped, too. "So, what time do you have to be at your folks?" she asked, just trying to be polite while her blood thinned out.

"I guess I oughta be there pretty soon. My sisters and their families are supposed t'be coming in tonight. But with the weather and all, I bet they don't show up till later." That was always one of the goofy things about the holidays. You didn't see these people all year, saw plenty enough of them to last another whole year at Thanksgiving, and then had them right back on your doorstep four weeks later for Christmas. In fact, you got them for the full tilt triple-header at Christmas, what with pastry snacks, pies, ice cream and coffee with *anisette* when they arrived on Christmas Eve, then breakfast, church, and presents on Christmas day, followed by yet another groaning board turkey dinner that left you wallowing in an overstuffed chair with your belt and the top button of your pants undone just so's you could wheeze. To tell the truth, I figured I was lucky to be sleeping in the apartment over Aunt Rosamarina's garage, since our house got awful crowded and noisy at Christmas and no question the bed was a lot more comfy than the basement couch at home.

"So?" Julie said, obviously starting to feel a little thawed out. "What did my favorite Buddy Palumbo get me for Christmas?"

"Oh, no," I told her. "You first."

"That's not *fair!*" she pouted. "I asked you first."

Then she drew in real close and took the collar of my jacket in both hands. She had such lovely skin. "I want you to show me first, Buddy. After all, this is our first real Christmas together." She wriggled her nose up to mine and whispered: *"C'mon. Whad'ja get me?"*

"Well," I said, kind of clearing my throat and circling the wagons. "You know how much I think of you, Julie. I mean, you're about the most precious thing there is...."

"You're really full of shit, Palumbo," she giggled.

"No, *really,*" the eggnog said. "So I knew I had t'get you precious things."

"You *did? Really?*"

"Sure I did! Nothing's too good for you."

"I can hardly wait!" I watched a shiver of anticipation shoot through her.

"Just feast your eyes," I told her, and pulled out the little wad of wrapping paper with the five-and-dime earrings in it out of my shopping bag. *"Look! Diamonds! Silver!"* and then I pulled out the other, much larger bundle of red and green wrapping paper. It looked roughly the size of a bowling ball. "And GOLD, too!"

You could've illuminated the whole blessed East Coast with the fireworks twinkling in her eyes. Which, to be honest, lasted until she had the first package about halfway unwrapped. "You bought me jewelry at *Woolworth's?*" she asked in amazement, not sounding entirely impressed.

"Well, I thought it kinda matched your ring, Julie, and..."

"Please," she said flatly. "Stop. And don't even tell me what's in this one." She picked up the larger package. "God forbid you should ruin the surprise."

'Well, it's just..."

But by then she had the paper pulled back and saw those two big, satiny goldfish swimming around in their brand new bowl. And they weren't any of those nickel and dime jobs, either. No, sir. They were both strictly top-of-the-line when it came to Woolworth's goldfish; a pudgy guy with stubby orange and black fins and a permanently sour expression on his face like Edward G. Robinson and a slightly larger and terribly elegant female (or at least I hoped she was a female) in flowing wedding-gown white with orange speckled trim and the prettiest damn eyes you have ever seen on a goldfish. Honest. Hell, they cost damn near five bucks between them, and that's not even counting the blessed fishbowl! Plus I bought a bag of orange, black, and gold cat's-eye marbles for the bottom, which the saleslady in the pet department assured me would look nice and do a swell job of hiding all the goldfish poop.

"Do you *like* him?" I asked hesitantly.

For a moment she didn't say anything. Not one single word. "I'm over-whelmed," she finally declared, and I must admit it sounded like she meant it. Just maybe not in the most flattering or enthusiastic sort of way.

"So," I said. "Now it's my turn. Whad'ja get *me?*"

Julie kind of shook her head and looked at the toes of my shoes. "It's noth-ing, really," she almost whispered.

"Nothing?" I snorted. "It sure doesn't *look* like nothing." And that's when I plucked the hanger bag right out of her fingers and yanked the zipper down, figuring I'd maybe I'd find a Dodgers' windbreaker inside. Or maybe some-thing with "MG" or "Jaguar" on it from that mail order house in California.

But imagine my surprise to find a brand new, single-breasted Brooks Broth-ers dress suit-so deep and serious a blue that you could almost mistake it for black in formal light-complete with a white shirt, striped silk tie, and belt and socks to match. Jesus, it must've cost her eighty bucks!

We stood there for quite awhile in absolute silence, with just the invisible sound of the snow falling outside and the faint whoosh of the gas through the space heater for company. "I guess my present wasn't exactly what you ex-pected, huh?" I said apologetically.

"I guess not," Julie sighed. "And mine wasn't what you expected, either."

"Whew. Not hardly. I mean, it's a *lovely* gift…" I knew I had to say this just right, "…*too* lovely, in fact. I mean, I hate t'see you spend so much money on me, Julie…."

"But I *want* to, Buddy. It's important for you to look *nice.*"

"But, geez, where the heck is a guy like me ever gonna *wear* it?" Boy, was that ever the wrong thing to say!

"Oh?" Julie's eyebrows shot up. "And I suppose I should've gotten you a plastic ring out of a damn gum machine and a couple nice tadpoles."

"Those're goldfish, not tadpoles," I pointed out. "And they were the best two in the whole damn store. Just *look.*" Right on cue, the two goldfish swam grace-fully towards each other and gently bumped noses.

Julie had been looking at me like she was about to take my head off. But then, almost in slow motion, her face melted into a big, helpless smile and she started to laugh. "I guess we're pretty different people, aren't we, Palumbo?"

"Yeah." I admitted. "I guess we are."

"Well, you better pray that old saw about opposites attracting is true."

"Oh? Why's that?"

"Why's that? I'll tell you why's that. Because otherwise I'm going to wind up murdering you in your sleep one night. Just like that. And you're so frickin' dumb about stuff you'll never even know why."

"Yes, I will," I protested.

"No," Julie laughed, "you most definitely will not." And then, for reasons I would never even pretend to understand, she gave me the nicest, softest little kiss right on the end of my nose.

"What's that all about?"

"I dunno. Maybe that's how goldfish do it?"

"Must be," I agreed, and kissed her back on the end of her nose, too. "So, have you thought any about what you're gonna name 'em?"

"It'll come to me," Julie assured me. "It'll come to me."

I sure hoped that saleslady at Woolworth's knew what she was talking about when she told me they were a male and a female, you know?

Christmas Day 1952 turned out to be a certified big deal around my folks' house, on account of that's when my old man finally broke down and bought us a television set. To tell the truth, it had to rank as about the worst kept secret in the entire history of our neighborhood, seeing as how he showed up while it was still light out Tuesday afternoon with this big corrugated box with "Zenith" printed all over it stuffed in the trunk of his Mercury-hell, it was so big he had to tie the damn lid down-and another long, skinny carton with the antenna in it sticking out the side window. And of course he made a big show of sneaking it into the garage so my mom and Sarah Jean and the neighbors all up and down the street would be sure to see it and marvel over how big it was. Then he'd go out every once in awhile to check on it with the garage door open and his beloved Mercury pulled way over to the side so's people could see it from the street. And come sunup Christmas morning, nothing would do but that we lug it inside and take it out of the box and right away put the antenna up on the chimney even though it was cold and wet and windy outside. That of course took a little doing since I still couldn't climb too well with my bum arm and my old man is pretty much useless around a set of tools. Although not to hear him tell it.

Anyhow, it was at least as good a show as anything that came over the airwaves-especially when he slipped on a slick patch and took a flailing, scrabbling, top-of-the-lungs cursing ass-ride down the slant of the roof that ended right at the very edge when he dug his heels in and knocked off a truly impressive length of gutter-but I have to give the old sonofabitch credit, he eventually managed to get it done. Even if he did get a little impatient and ran the wire right down the blessed chimney and out through the fireplace. Hey, he was in a hurry to see it work, you know?

My old man tossed my mom's favorite Venetian glass candy dish, Irish lace doily, and ceramic bluebird figurines off the coffee table in front of the couch, shoved it out of the way, and lovingly moved his brand new Zenith console model to the most prominent position possible, directly in front of the fireplace. I helped him do up the wires-I was a little excited myself, if you want the truth of it-and then everybody gathered around in their robes and slippers and held their breath as he reached out to turn it on....

It was only five to seven in the morning and the only thing on was the early Christmas edition of Sermonette on Channel 4. But that was followed up at seven by the Today show with Dave Garroway, and it was really something to see it all happening live right there in front of us in glorious black and white. Especially for me, since I knew Dave Garroway was not only a big TV and radio star, but also a confirmed sportscar nut. In fact, I'd seen him myself a time or two at the races, and started telling everybody the story about how he had this elegant SS-100 Jaguar that he wanted desperately to win the *concours d'elegance* car show competition at Watkins Glen. So he had the engine all dolled up with a gold-plated valve cover and reupholstered the interior in genuine imported ostrich skin. I kid you not. But of course car stories aren't really too interesting to anybody except car people, and everybody was telling me to "sshh" before I even got to the part about the ostrich skin. Fact is, getting "sshh'd" so people could watch TV became a real regular thing around my folks' house from that moment on.

Anyhow, my mom brought a tray of coffee in and then made everybody one of her trademark Sunday ayem breakfasts with sliced oranges topped with powdered sugar and scrambled eggs with cheese and sweet peppers and mounds of hashed brown potatoes and a platter of sausages and thick-sliced bacon accompanied by malted pecan waffles with real maple syrup that Cal gave me to give to her plus a basket of her famous homemade blueberry muffins. Meanwhile everybody kept their eyes glued to that slightly fishbowl- shaped screen in front of the fireplace, and watched in dumbstruck awe while Dave Garroway and his guests-including that crazy chimpanzee of his, J. Fred Muggs-talked on and on about how all the people at home that morning were celebrating Christmas. Following Dave Garroway at nine o'clock was a Christmas music show with Morey Amsterdam (plus a kid's show called "Wonder Boy" on the other channel) and, come ten o'clock, Channel 7 joined in with the Gracie Square Boy's Club Christmas Party. But we decided to watch Arthur Godfrey instead. Channel 5 came on with chapel services at eleven opposite a live broadcast of the Christmas church service from Washington Cathedral on channel 4, and that reminded my mom that it was time to hurry and get dressed so we could make it to eleven-thirty mass.

We hadn't even opened our presents yet, you know?

My sister Mary Frances showed up from Greenwich Village by the time we got back from church, and of course she took a heaping dose of shit about missing mass from the old man (who, by the way, had nodded off and snored his way through the entire service). But she came right back at him with this pinko/egghead Greenwich Village stuff about how "religion is the opium of the people," and of course that didn't go down well at all with the rest of the family. So for a change it was Mary Frances instead of me getting into a top-of-the-lungs yelling match with my old man and storming out of the house. Although I wasn't so sure I liked that "opium of the people" talk, either. I mean, church had always seemed kind of harmless and boring to me, but no question it did a lot for people like my mom and my sister Sarah Jean and poor old Mrs. DeMarco, who had lost both her parents plus a son killed on patrol in Korea and a husband in the hospital fighting a losing battle with leukemia. People like that need a place to go with their troubles, you know? And I guess church is as good a place as any. Even if the sitting and standing and kneeling and mumbling stuff that didn't make any sense to me or was in a language I didn't understand over and over and over again sometimes struck me as a whole lot of hokum.

But I knew better than to say anything. I mean, *who knew,* right? And, as little as I went to church-mostly just Christmas and Easter, really-it didn't bother me much to simply shut up and go along. Besides, I'd felt pretty chummy with that St. Christopher's medal on the dash of Javier Premal's Ferrari a couple times down in Mexico, and it sure as heck couldn't hurt to be on God's good side if he was in fact up there someplace and actually paying attention like all those good people in church seemed to think.

Unfortunately, my sister Mary Frances had picked up strong and highly unattractive opinions about damn near everything that had to do with anything from that egghead crowd of hers over in Greenwich Village, and it wasn't her style at all to shut up about it. In fact, it was a little scary to me that anybody could be so blessed positive about stuff that nobody could ever know for sure.

In fact, she was an awful lot like the church people that way.

Anyhow, Mary Frances hadn't been home fifteen minutes before she and my dad were screaming at each other and she stormed back out again-setting, I believe, a new household record-and I ran out after her to wish her a Merry Christmas (even if she didn't believe in it) and give her the little sewing kit I'd bought for her at Woolworths. "You know," I told her, half-mad and half-laughing, "you really didn't have to yank his chain like that. Now he'll be pissed off at the rest of us all afternoon just because we're related to you."

"I don't care!" She said defiantly. "He's been bulldozing us our whole lives, Buddy, and I'm just not about to take it anymore." Geez, you should've seen the look on her face. Why, her eyeballs were damn near vibrating. "That's what's wrong with this stupid world," she continued, shaking her fist in the air like a one-woman political rally. "People need the guts to stand up for what's *right!"*

Personally, I'd always figured *knowing* what was right seemed a lot more complicated than standing up for it. And I told her as much. But it was like peeing on a bonfire.

"You need to come down to our New Year's Eve party in The Village," she informed me, her eyes almost blazing. "You need to see what's *really* going on in this world."

And I decided maybe I ought to go. I mean, it's important to know what's going on in this world.

Isn't it?

Chapter 7: New Year's in New York

I kept thinking about my sister's party in Greenwich Village that whole dead, draggy week that seems to always come between Christmas and New Year's Eve. And this one was even deader and draggier than most on account of there was a standard-issue Saturday/Sunday weekend thrown right in the middle of it. It's the sort of time when you just don't feel like doing much of anything, you know? Luckily things were slow at the Sinclair, and that was good since nobody except Old Man Finzio and Butch were showing up for work, and then only for a couple hours a day. About the only positive thing was that I saw the doctor New Year's Eve morning and he decided to finally cut the cast off my wrist. Boy, was that ever a relief! Especially being able to scratch my arm again. "It's still a little tender yet," he cautioned me, "and I don't want you to put too much strain on it or you'll crack the bone again. But I think it should be all right."

I remember it was a cold, drizzly kind of day, and I'd driven over to the doctor's in Mr. Altobelli's Plymouth on account of Butch had just rebuilt the generator and so I thought it might require a professional sort of test drive. Not to mention it had three on the tree and was a bunch easier to shift with the cast and all. But as soon as I got back to the shop I borrowed Carson Flegley's MG and took myself a quick spin around town. Just to see what a sports car felt like again, you know? Even on a wet, crappy day and with nothing more than the standard issue, hamster breath MG heater for company. But even though the windshield wouldn't stay defogged, it was a heck of a ride. Sylvester'd just finished bringing it up to Stage 1-A tune according to the hop up article Carson and all the rest of the MG guys on the planet had seen in the August issue of *Road & Track.* He'd pulled the cylinder head and sent it over to Roman Szymanski to have 3/32nds milled off to raise the compression ratio to 8.6-to-one, had him polish and match all the ports and fit larger valves (including special, sodium-filled exhaust valves so's it could still run on pump gas) and stiffer, competition-grade valve springs, then topped it all off with larger 1½" SU carburetors with needles from the Stage 2 kit, a reground Harman and Collins camshaft Carson had ordered all the way from California (mostly, I think, because he liked the cartoon hula girl in their magazine ad), a set of "straight-thru" mufflers from another ad that promised "a pleasant, resonating, mellow exhaust note," and a pair of shiny chrome "Flo-Thru" air cleaners. It cost Carson quite a bundle, and it was precisely the kind of work I wanted our shop to do because there was plenty of hand labor and machine work involved and not one minute of it was listed in the flat rate manual. So you could make a pretty good profit on that kind of stuff so long as you knew how to do it and knew how to charge. And that last part was something I was learning more about every day. Especially since Julie'd been counting up the cash in the till every night and I was the guy passing out the pay packets every Friday afternoon. You get a pretty good feel for what's left in the kitty once you start handling that end of a business. Any business.

Anyhow, it felt great to get back into a sports car again and really be able to stir my way through the gearbox rather than clubbing at them with my cast. And no question you could really feel and hear the difference in Carson's TD. Without question we'd taken an agile, fun, and marginally peppy little British sports roadster and turned it into something you could barely live with on the street anymore. It didn't like to start and it popped and banged and backfired something awful during warmup. And even once it was warm it was all fluff and stumbles below about 3,000 rpm (which is really where you needed to be most of the time in actual city traffic) after which it would kind of clear its throat and make a balls-out, banzai charge up to the recommended 6,000 rpm redline. Which pretty much insured we'd be seeing Carson back at the shop for valve or bottom end work before many months elapsed. Or maybe both. And, as to that "pleasant, resonating, mellow exhaust note," it sounded more like a Gatling gun firing wooden bullets and caused people to come to their windows all up and down Pine street to see what all the racket was about. Even second and third story windows. And, loud as it was, the harsh new bark out the exhaust still couldn't overwhelm the great, sucking rush of air through those shiny chrome "Flo-Thru" air filters and oversized S.U. carbs.

In short, it was exactly what Carson was looking for.

As I said, I was curious about that New Year's Eve party at the apartment my sister shared with those three other girls in Greenwich Village, and I'd even asked Julie and Cal if maybe they'd like to go along. I mean, except for a few oddball racing parties here and there, Julie and I didn't really have what you could normally call a social life. Not hardly. And Cal didn't figure to have anything special planned for New Year's except maybe undoing the hinge screws on his old man's padlocked liquor cabinet again. Besides, Cal still had that bootleg key to his mom's new Packard, and no question it would be nice for Julie and me to travel in style-with a real, live chauffeur, no less-to some lah-de-dah New Year's party in Manhattan.

It was cold and damp with a light, rainy snow falling by the time Cal swung his mom's Packard up the driveway of my Aunt Rosamarina's house, running his usual forty-five minutes late. But at least he'd scrounged together a reasonably believable chauffeur's uniform, including a peaked cap complete with a genuine New York Taxi Driver's badge on top and a blue uniform jacket with two rows of brass buttons down the front like ushers wear at the movie theater. It was wise never to ask my friend Cal where he came by such accessories so as to avoid becoming an accessory-after-the-fact, but it was still generally good for a laugh. Seeing as how I'd finally gotten that damn cast off my wrist, I decided I'd surprise Julie by wearing that new Brooks Brothers monkey suit she'd bought me for Christmas. And the truth is I looked pretty damn classy in that outfit, even if the tie and buttoned-up shirt collar felt like one of those iron neck rings the galley slaves have to wear in all those big Hollywood bible extravaganzas.

As usual Julie'd read my mind, and she was all dolled up herself in this bright turquoise spaghetti strap evening gown and matching shoes that she'd borrowed off one of the other girls at the Doggy Shake. If you want the truth, I think it was somebody's prom dress or something. But it really looked swell on her. Especially since the other girl must not have been quite as big as Julie, so she was strapped in real tight and skinny around the waist and kind of overflowing a little up at the top. "Hey, put'cher eyeballs back in your head, okay Palumbo?" she snapped as soon as she saw the arch of my eyebrows. But you could tell she was real pleased with my reaction. I noticed she was even wearing those cheap Woolworth's five-and-dime ear studs I'd bought her, which I considered a really nice gesture. And they *did* match her engagement ring. Perfectly, in fact. At least if you squinted a little.

Of course nothing would do but that I come inside so's her mom could snap a few pictures, and then she gave Julie this dumb flower print cardigan sweater to cover up some of the meat and potatoes. "I won't have no girl a'mine runnin' aroun' like-a dat!" she insisted, sounding angry and yet proud at the same time.

"But *Mom!*" Julie protested while her mother did up the buttons. "This looks absolutely *ridiculous!*"

She was right, too.

"You'll catch-a *cold* inna dress like-a dat."

"But this looks..." she looked in the mirror and gasped, "...*ohhh, Jeez, Mom! This looks AWFUL!*"

Julie's mom hesitated for a moment, then went to the closet and brought out a big, white box that smelled of mothballs. Inside, under several layers of tissue paper, was the beautiful, full-length brown fur coat she'd worn to my folks' house on Thanksgiving. You remember, the one that used to belong to Marlene Dietrich? And maybe it did. I mean, at the very least it was mink or sable or raccoon or muskrat or something. Julie's mom gingerly unfolded it and held it up to the light. "I guess you can a-wear dis," she said uncertainly, handing it over to Julie. "It'll look a-nice." Then she leveled her eyes at me. "You make sure nuttin' a-happens t'dat coat, gas station boy."

"You can count on me," I told her through my best Eagle Scout smile.

She made a noise at me like a dog passing wind. It didn't exactly sound like a vote of confidence, you know?

I took the fur coat in my hands like it was the blessed infant Jesus and held it up so Julie could slip her arms inside. It would've been nice to take a little peek down over the collar while I was at it, but I felt her mom's eyes on me like the crosshairs of a gun sight and didn't dare. As we turned to leave, I couldn't help noticing that Julie had the goldfish prominently displayed on the mantle in the living room next to all the fancy china that was too good to eat off. "I see you gave our fish a nice spot," I said once we were in the car.

"Yeah," Julie laughed. "They're the first pets my mom ever let me keep. She always said she was allergic to fur so she wouldn't ever let me have a dog or a kitty or anything. You know how it is."

"They're probably a little more fun than goldfish."

"Oh, I don't know. I've already taught the little guy how to heel and fetch and get the morning paper."

"Really?"

"Um-hum," she nodded. "But it's gonna be tough to get him to beg or roll over. That's difficult for a goldfish."

"How about the other one?"

"Oh, she's not so athletic. You know. Likes to cook and sew and sit around in her dressing gown reading romance novels...."

Cal was looking at us like we were nuts in the rearview mirror.

"So," I continued, "did'ja ever pick names for them? I thought maybe we could call 'em 'Buddy' and 'Julie.' Just like us, y'know?"

"Nah," Julie shook her head. "I thought about that, too. But it'd get too confusing. Especially for you. And it's too ordinary, too."

"'Buddy' and 'Julie' are too ordinary?" I didn't particularly like the sound of that. "So whad'ja decide t'call 'em?"

"Oh, I figured the big, showy white one needed something, you know, *glamorous*. So she's Veronica Lake."

"I see. And the little guy?"

"Well, remember you said he looked like Edward G. Robinson?"

I nodded.

"I thought so, too. So I named him 'Rico.'"

Cal peeled instantly into his best Edward G. Robinson imitation. "As in *Enrico Caesar Bandello?"*

"Yeaaaah," Julie topped him, *"Little Caesar. Yeaaaah...."*

Cal drove us southeast through Clifton, Nutley, Belleville, Newark, Jersey City, and down into the Holland Tunnel to cross into Manhattan, and traffic was heavy with everybody honking their horns and blowing on noisemakers to get the New Year's celebrating in gear. You couldn't miss the rush of excitement and anticipation as we headed through that gleaming white tile tube into the city. Neither Julie or I had ever been in Manhattan on New Year's Eve (although we'd heard it broadcast live from Times Square on the radio a dozen times each) and it was amazing how urbane, grown up, and thoroughly sophisticated I felt right then. Iron slave collar and all.

We followed the directions Mary Frances gave me to a two-story corner building on Bleecker street with a darkened book store and barber shop on the first floor and all hell breaking loose on the second. Or at least that's what it looked like from the street, since the side windows were open for ventilation and you could hear a live jazz combo playing inside and people talking and laughing on the fire escape. "This must be the place," I observed..

"Either that or a riot on a cell block," Cal observed. It was raining, and seeing as how Julie had her mom's fancy fur coat on, Cal offered to drop us in front and go look for a parking place. Naturally I rushed around and got the door for her. I mean, you do that sort of thing when you're all dressed up. And that's when we heard a round of whistles and catcalls from the local Greenwich Village types enjoying a little smoke out on the fire escape. Apparently they weren't used to seeing anybody dressed up nice or being chauffeured around in a fancy new Packard in this particular neighborhood. Not even on New Year's Eve.

"I'm not sure I like this place," Julie whispered as we tried the door. But it was locked. So I buzzed Mary Frances' apartment and we stood there in the drizzling cold for quite some time before a shadowy form appeared at the top of the stairs and ambled slowly down. "Who is it?" a man's voice with a thick middle European accent demanded from the other side.

"Buddy Palumbo and Julie." I told the voice.

"Who?"

"Buddy Palumbo. Mary Frances' brother." I mean, I couldn't believe how particular this guy was being about who he let in. Hell, it sounded like they had half of Greenwich Village up there already.

"You're the automobile mechanic?" the voice asked.

"Jesus! We're about freezing to death out here, okay?"

We heard three separate latches undo and the door opened a narrow crack with a chain lock still across it. A strange, bloodshot eye with tiny little pupils peered out from beneath a scraggly eyebrow. "You don't *look* like an auto mechanic," the eye said suspiciously.

"Would you like me to rebuild a carburetor for you?"

"No, I suppose not," the eye chortled. "But you just can't be too careful these days. Can't be too careful at all." The eye looked us up and down again. "Especially the way things are...."

I made sure to look back like I understood whatever the hell he was talking about. I mean, it was pretty blessed damp and uncomfortable out there in the rain. Plus I was beginning to smell the wet fur on old Mom Finzio's ex-Marlene Dietrich fur coat.

"...and just look at the way you're dressed. My, my, my. Not like an auto mechanic at all."

"Pretend we just came from a costume party, OK?"

Right on cue Cal showed up behind us in his fake chauffeur outfit and the door just about slammed in our faces as soon as the guy got a load of the badge on Cal's cap. But Cal passed it through the crack so the guy could see it was just a taxi driver's badge-and most likely a stolen one at that-rather than the sort you found hanging around the local precinct station. He was a fleshy little college professor type with scraggly gray hair growing like unclipped shrubbery around his face and nervous, ferret-style eyes that kept looking us up and down from beneath his shaggy eyebrows. But he finally decided to let us in. "Like I said," he explained as he re-latched the door behind us, "you just can't be too careful the way things are these days."

We followed the little guy up the darkened stairwell to a door with frosted glass on top like in a doctor's office, and you could hear all sorts of music and noise and jabbering coming through from the other side. "The party's kind of a free for all," the little guy told us. "Your sister's place is around to the right. She's probably in there with Oliver and some of the other political science and philosophy people. I'm down on the end with the literary crowd. If you'd like to, drop by a little later." He looked up at us hopefully. "We're discussing existentialist story lines. Kafka and Camus, mostly."

"Gee. Thanks."

I'd have to say this was the first party of my life where I felt under-brained and over-dressed. Fact is, Julie, Cal and me stuck out like we were wearing clown noses and illuminated dunce caps. Which, to be honest, is about how we felt. Ahead of us was a long, shadowy hallway with a row of open doors on either side, and behind each of those open doors was one of the many distinct literary, political, philosophical, sociological or all-purpose artsy-craftsy or revolutionary academic sects that made up the special little world of N.Y.U. and Greenwich Village. And the amazing thing was how they all seemed to think-seemed to *know,* in fact-that it was the nerve center of the whole blessed universe. These were genuine, genius-grade people up here-no doubt about it!-and every one of them fierce, diehard believers in either The Common Good or Free Will. Or both. And they went on and on about the perils of conformity. Maybe that's why they dressed all the same. Either that or there must've been one hell of a sale on black turtlenecks at some store nearby, you know? At least Cal could take off his cap and usher's jacket, roll up his sleeves and blend in a bit, but everybody stared at Julie and me like we'd just dropped in from Jersey. Which, in fact, we had.

As we headed down the hall to my sister's apartment, you couldn't miss picking up choice tidbits of conversation filtering out into the hall:

"Have you seen *Forbidden Games* over at the Little Carnegie?"

"Oh, *yes!* Isn't it *marvelous?"*

"But it's much better in the original French, don't you think?"

"Oh, definitely. The subtitles just *ruin* it...."

Next doorway:

"Do you think the Rosenbergs will go to the electric chair?"

"No right-thinking government could ever conscience such a thing."

"Oh, I *agree.* Why, it's Sacco and Vanzetti all over again..."

Next doorway (with a high, sarcastic, singsong lisp):

"First he said I had the part, so I turned in my notice at work. But then the producer backed out at the last minute and the whole thing fell through."

Even higher and more singsong: "So what are you going to doooo?"

"Go back to waiting tables again I guess."

"As usual."

"Yes. As usual...."

There was jazz music coming from the doorway across the hall, and I craned my neck around the doorjamb to get a quick peek at the band. It was just four guys-two white and two colored-crammed into a little bay window area with a piano, a bass, a saxophone and a drum set. The skinny little white guy with the sax had thinning reddish hair and wore dark sunglasses so you couldn't see his eyes, and you couldn't miss how he swayed back and forth on his heels while he soared through a long, haunting solo. He looked like he was maybe on something to me. The black drummer was just taking it easy right then, softly swirling his brushes around on the top of his snare drum while he quietly chatted up this pale, slinky white girl in a black leotard who looked like she might be a dancer. I thought I smelled something funny coming from the fire escape. Like maybe somebody was burning a rug out there.

My sister's apartment was way at the end of the hall, and they had the door almost closed so the light from the naked bulb in the hall fixture and the music from the jazz combo wouldn't overpower all the candlelight and heavy duty conversation going on inside. There weren't but four tiny rooms-a little living room/dining room deal next to an even smaller kitchenette plus two little bedrooms and a john about the size of your average clothes closet-and nothing but the glow of cigarettes and a few scattered candles for illumination. I swear there must've been fifty people crammed in there, all jammed nose-to-nose, glass to glass, and cigarette ash to cigarette ash, carrying on the most amazing collection of political, philosophical, art/literary/film critique and current events discussions I had ever heard in my life. On the one hand, it made me feel like a crude, boorish, uneducated New Jersey slob. On the other, I was sorry I hadn't brought my old man's rubber hip boots from the chemical plant, because you have never seen bullshit flowing so thick or deep. "Most of these people start out with a BS degree," Cal whispered in my ear, "and you know what that stands for."

I nodded.

"Then they get an MS degree, for 'More of Same.'"

That made sense.

"And then, finally, after years of study, they get their Ph.D. And you know what that stands for?"

I shook my head.

"Piled Higher and Deeper."

That made even more sense.

Still, it was kind of fascinating to just sit there and listen. The hottest topics on the political/current events front seemed to be the upcoming Rosenberg spy case executions and that British physicist, Dr. Alan Nun May, who had just been released from prison for giving atom bomb secrets to the Soviet Reds. A surprising number of people in my sister's apartment seemed to think it was the right thing to do, can you believe it? There was also a lot of talk about Tailgunner Joe McCarthy's loyalty oath crusade and the professor from Columbia and the other one from Haverford who were busy denying they'd ever been communists in front of the House Un-American Activities Committee hearings. "It's an abomination!" the shaggy little literary guy who had originally let us in announced, pounding his fist against his hand. Apparently he'd drifted over from his literary bunch at the other end of the hall when they, as he put it, "got bogged down in *Being and Nothingness* again." You couldn't miss how he was a nervous, skittish type-you know the kind-and my sister explained as how he was a modern lit professor at N.Y.U. and had written a few articles on great communist authors, artists, and thinkers and was a little worried about being called before some committee himself.

"You mean he's a *communist?* " I said incredulously.

"Of course he is," Mary Frances answered, like it was nothing at all. "A lot of the people here are. Or at least they're sympathetic...."

I couldn't believe my ears. *Commies! Right there in the same damn room with me!* The amazing thing was that they didn't look any different or have horns and tails, you know?

"Come into the kitchen," Mary Frances said, tugging my arm. "There's somebody I want you to meet." So we kind of waded through the darkened sea of arms and legs and torsos, Mary Frances more or less pulling me along while I hung onto Julie's hand and dragged her behind us. Lord knows what would've happened to her if I ever let go! Cal tagged along, too. I don't think he wanted to get stranded out there in the other room by himself.

I have to say I spotted the guy Mary Frances wanted me to meet the instant we rounded the corner. And the dislike was immediate. He was a tall, slender, tweedy-looking type with a receding hairline and a neatly trimmed goatee, terribly disappointed eyes, and an accusatory smile that he flashed like an exclamation mark whenever he made a telling point in conversation. Which was often. He was more or less holding court next to the sink, explaining to a packed house of about a dozen people "the failure of the Stalinist regime to *capitalize* (if I may [short insider laugh] *use* such a term in this context) on their opportunities to advance the cause of Marxist-Leninist communism." After which he presented about five or six specific and thoroughly obscure examples that I don't think anybody in the room had ever heard of-God knows I hadn't-complete with times, places, names, dates, sources, footnotes and appropriate cross references. It was almost like he was having a damn conversation with himself, you know? But the really sick part was the way everybody was lapping it all up. Especially Mary Frances.

"Excuse me, Ollie," she broke in when he paused for a rare intake of breath. "This is my brother Buddy." I stuck out my hand like you're supposed to and he looked at it for a moment like he was trying to discern what it really *was* and what I actually *meant* by offering it to him before deciding if he should shake it. I swear, his skin felt like a dead frog.

"I'm Oliver Cromwell," he announced like everybody who was anybody already knew it. Then added with a wry, witty chortle, "But, of course, not *that* Oliver Cromwell."

There were a few polite titters from Mary Frances' roommates, two of whom were auditing his Philosophy of Politics seminar at N.Y.U.

"Nice t'meetcha." I told him, already feeling like a complete rube even though I hadn't said anything yet.

"Ahh, you're the automobile mechanic, aren't you?" He said it like maybe I wasn't. Like it was all just a diabolically clever smokescreen to cover some sinister true identity.

"Yeah," I said, and held up my fingernails as proof.

He looked at them and seemed somewhat satisfied that I might, in fact, actually be telling the truth. Of course, there was always the possibility that I'd *purposely* wedged grease under them to fool people. "So," he said, "you're the one who races, aren't you?"

Finally. Something I could talk about. "Yeah. Kind of, anyway. Fact is, I just got back from a race in Mexico a few weeks ago."

"Really?" he said, sounding terribly interested. "We were just discussing Mexico. *Fascinating* country. But terribly feudal, don't you think?" He flashed me his best weasel smile. "Tell me, how did you find it?"

I went to Texas and turned left, jerkoff is what I felt like saying, but instead I kind of hemmed and hawed through some bullshit about how we were really going pretty fast and working on the cars a lot and so I didn't really have time to pick up on much of the, umm, cultural or political stuff.

"Stuff?" he asked, his eyebrows arching steeply. Then he swept his eyes around the little personal peanut gallery he had gathered in the kitchen and stroked the edge of his goatee. "Speaking of Mexico, did any of you catch the story in the *Times* about Diego Rivera?" He looked right at me. "You *are* familiar with his work, aren't you?" He didn't even wait for me not to answer and rolled right on. "He's a marvelous painter-a genuine national treasure in Mexico-but a terribly troubled soul politically, I'm afraid."

You could see Mary Frances and her two roommates were hanging on every blessed word.

"He's a pure Marxist, of course, and that's led to no end of problems with the party." Oliver sadly shook his head. "Like all artists, he's too much of a free spirit for his own good."

How could anyone argue with an unbreakable chunk of truth like that?

"And of course he was overzealous in his loyalty to Trotsky."

Oh. Without a doubt.

"But now," Oliver sighed, stroking the edge of his goatee again, "he wants the party to take him back-*come home, prodigal son, all is forgiven*-but I doubt they'll have him." He slowly and deliberately laced his fingers together and looked down at the tops of his knuckles. "His paintings are wonderful, of course, but he's just too much of a liability."

Class was over.

But only momentarily, since this Oliver Cromwell guy obviously enjoyed being front and center in the spotlight. His eyes rose gently from his knuckles and did a slow, studious rotation around the room-tank turret fashion-finally coming to rest on Julie. "Ahh, and you must be the intended, *n'est ce pas?"*

"Yeah," Julie nodded. "We just got engaged."

He clapped his hands together. "Oh, splendid. Just splendid," he said like he was reading a soup can label. "Mary has told me *so* much about both of you…" he shot Mary Frances one of those sly, Insider Eyeball things, "…and your families, too."

That kind of hung there awhile, and for once I almost felt like sticking up for my old man and giving this guy a poke. I already wanted to sock him for what I was sure he was planning to do with my sister. Or maybe already had. And that's not even mentioning the other sock in the nose he had coming for messing up her brain. But I just kept quiet and let it slide. After all, people are going to be how they're going to be-even if they're your sister-and the more you wail and argue about it, the less good it'll do. You just wind up losing a friend. Or at least that's the way I've seen it happen.

"Ollie's an assistant professor at N.Y.U.," Mary Frances beamed proudly. "He's going to be a brilliant writer one day."

"Oh, *please,"* Oliver blushed, pretending to be embarrassed while quite obviously urging her on.

"Oh?" Julie asked, sounding entirely too impressed. "What does he write?"

"Oh, nothing *you* can read," Mary Frances laughed. To tell the truth, I felt pretty damn insulted. Not that either Julie or me figured to be particularly interested in anything this Oliver Cromwell character might have to say. But it's not like we were illiterate or anything, you know?

"Oh, don't take it the wrong way," Mary Frances explained immediately. "See, Ollie's quite sure English is a dead language."

"It is?" I mean, that was news to me.

"Dead as Latin," Ollie announced calmly, clearly pleased once again to be agreeing with himself.

"And so are French, German, Spanish, Russian, Chinese…." Mary Frances continued while Oliver gave her a proud, approving smile "…*SO OLLIE'S WRITING NOVELS IN ESPERANTO!"* She seemed terribly excited about it.

"In *what?*" I asked.

"Esperanto," she said like everybody ought to know. "It's going to be the universal language."

Hell, I'd never even heard of it.

Oliver cleared his throat. "In another twenty-five years," he proclaimed, oozing confidence from every pore, "everyone on this entire planet will be speaking, reading, teaching and writing in Esperanto."

"They will?"

"Absolutely," he nodded. "It only makes sense."

Geez, this was going to be news to an awful lot of people.

"Although," Oliver admitted cautiously, making a slow, seesaw motion with his hand, *"maybe* it'll take as long as thirty years."

This guy was really full of it, you know?

"So!" he said suddenly, clapping his hands together, "enough about me. Tell us all about the dark, mechanized nether world of automobile racing."

"Well, to tell the truth," I told him, "I do mostly wrench work-you know, preparing and fixing the cars and stuff-Cal over there," I nodded in Cal's direction, "he's actually a driver." Oliver looked terrifically unimpressed, so I added, "And a pretty damn good one, too."

Oliver swept his eyes over to where Cal was standing. "So *you're* a racing driver?" He said it like it was a felony.

Cal shrugged. "Yeah, I drive a little."

"How positively Neanderthal."

Cal bristled at that. He didn't like this guy's tone any more than I did.

"Please tell me, I'm curious," Oliver continued through a Cheshire Cat smile. "What drives you to do such a thing?"

"I dunno," Cal shrugged. "Do I really need a reason?"

"But *of course* you need a reason," Oliver informed him. *"Everybody* needs reasons for what they do."

Cal thought it over for a moment or two and volleyed back that great old philosophical ace-in-the-hole that never, ever falls short of the mark: *"Why?"*

Out-maneuvered in front of his own home crowd, Ollie quickly changed directions. "So tell me, are you really any good at it?"

"Yeah, I guess some people think I'm pretty good."

"I think he's pretty good," I chimed in.

Oliver looked at me like I was an uninvited guest with bad breath. Then he focused his eyes back on Cal. "But what do *you* think? That's the important thing, isn't it?" I swear, having a conversation with this Oliver Cromwell jerk was like going through the third degree.

"I dunno," Cal answered casually. "Are you any good at what you do?"

That took old Ollie Cromwell by surprise. The last thing he expected was for some Neanderthal race car driver to start putting him on the intellectual defensive. "But come now," he continued condescendingly, ignoring Cal's question and playing to the small crowd in the kitchen like they all knew, understood, and agreed completely with what he was saying. Which, excepting for Julie and me, I guess they did. "Isn't racing automobiles *frivolous?* "

"I don't think so," Cal said matter-of-factly.

"I don't either," I piped up without thinking. Immediately a whole collection of unsympathetic eyes rotated in my direction and I decided I'd feel more comfortable if I just kept my mouth shut. I mean, there was no chance for a guy like me to out-argue a guy like Oliver Cromwell any more than there was a chance I could out-drive a talent like Cal Carrington. They were just *better* at it, plain and simple. The good part is I was smart enough to know it.

"I see," Oliver nodded, evaluating Cal and me like a tasty appetizer. "But when you strip all the colorful trappings away, isn't it just a bunch of self-styled gladiators with a serious death wish problem and an over-developed supply of masculine hormones running around in endless circles while beating each other with mechanical clubs?"

"W-well…" I began. I mean, how do you respond to something like that?

"Although I'm sure they must be *lovely* clubs," he allowed through that awful, exclamation-point smile of his.

"I don't have a death wish," Cal said bluntly. He didn't like this Oliver Cromwell character's tone or arrogance one bit. And he was enough of a privileged, upper-crust society rich kid to not be intimidated by it. In fact, in his own spoiled, smartass way, Cal could act just as damn cool, calm, and Unquestionably Superior as Ollie could. And he could do it without having to say or explain much of anything at all, which you could see was pissing old Ollie Cromwell off more than a little.

You could feel the tension building as Ollie took a long, slow intake of breath and kind of drew himself up for another onslaught. "You say you don't have a death wish," Ollie said carefully, like he was pouring a foundation, "but yet everyone *knows* automobile racing is terribly dangerous.…"

"I dunno," Cal answered back. "I mean, *everything's* dangerous, isn't it?"

"But not like *that.* "

"Look," Cal shrugged, "none of us get out of life alive. If I want to race cars, it's my choice. Why should you or anybody else give a shit?"

"Ah-ha!" Oliver said grandly, stroking the edges of his goatee. "You believe in Sartre's concept of free will."

"No," Cal corrected him. "Just my own."

Oliver's lips parted like he was going to respond, but, amazingly, no words came out. In fact, all of a sudden you could feel how quiet it'd become. "Say, listen," Julie broke in. "It's almost eleven thirty. Does anybody wanna head over to Times Square to see the ball drop?"

"Sure thing," I nodded. After all, I'd never been there, and the conversation around the sink was showing every evidence of turning nasty.

"Sounds terrifically dull," Ollie Cromwell yawned. "Just a teeming crowd of drunks and idiots with nothing better to do." He rolled his eyes slowly up to the ceiling. "A spectacle full of sound and fury, yet signifying nothing."

"I don't know, Ollie," Mary Frances pouted. "It sounds like fun."

"Suit yourself," he said like she was just some stupid dumb broad from Jersey without a brain in her head and that he moreover couldn't care less where the hell she went or what the hell she did when she got there. Geez, I was really getting to hate this guy!

"I'll get the car," Cal offered, and we were on our way.

It wasn't all that far from Bleecker Street in The Village to Times Square, but it was slow going on account of the streets were packed with people-even though it was raining-so we were barely creeping along. Cal's mom's Packard was packed like a sardine tin since Mary Frances picked up a few undiscovered artists and unpublished playwrights and left-leaning Fellow Travelers on our way down the hall-including those two prissy actor/waiter types and a couple of their friends, some of whom seemed about ready to float right up out of their shoes. But they were all laughing and joking and having a good time, and everybody seemed to agree that going to Times Square to celebrate the stroke of midnight on New Year's Eve was a *marvelous* idea. Including this strikingly beautiful young Italian girl from Brooklyn who'd been taking acting lessons and ballet lessons and voice lessons and such from some of the people in those apartments and so got herself invited to the party that night. I swear, she was absolutely radiant, what with shimmering black hair and perfect, creamy skin and a waist so tiny you could about put your thumb and forefinger around it. Not that she was especially skinny other places, if you catch my drift. But the amazing thing was her eyes. They were deep and green and glistened like emeralds in oil. In fact, they had that same distant, unholy combination of fire and ice I saw from time to time in Cal's eyes, and you could almost feel sparks fly and sense the pull when those two came face to face for the first time in the hallway.

Her name was Angelina Scalabrini, and even though she was kind of quiet, she didn't seem at all out-of-place or nervous. There seemed to be this calm, focused, determined streak in her, and again it reminded me a little of Cal and the way he was about his driving. Cal picked up on it, too, and made sure she was pressed in next to him in the front seat on our way across town. When Cal asked her, she told him she was going to be a movie actress one day. She said it with a perfectly straight face, too.

Of course there was no place to park when we got to Times Square, and, seeing how it was getting near midnight, Cal told us to all bail out and he'd go around the block a few times and meet up with us after. So we all climbed out of the Packard and headed up Broadway towards Times Square. All except Angelina, that is, who stayed behind to keep Cal company. I noticed she never moved over towards the door after everybody got out. "Make sure you're here afterwards," I reminded Cal. After all, I knew he wasn't always the most trustworthy guy in the world. And that went double when he had something on his mind.

"You can count on me," Cal assured me through his best rich kid grin, and I almost believed him.

I'll never forget what it was like in that huge Times Square crowd when 1952 slowly rolled belly-up and 1953 burst out of its shell. It was quite an experience. And it was especially nice to be there with Julie. Oh, sure, it was cold and damp, but at least the drizzle had slacked off and there was a lot of energy that almost felt like heat coming off all the people crowded together there blowing horns and noisemakers and waving soggy paper party hats while enormous search-lights with steam rising off their lenses swept wildly across the sky. Everybody around us was shouting and whooping and passing little nip bottles back and forth-even to complete strangers-and there was music from Guy Lombardo boom-ing out over the loudspeakers so you could almost hear it and right in the middle of all of it I was standing there holding Julie's hand like we were the only two people in the whole damn world....

So much had happened that year! Why, when it started, I'd never really spun wrenches for a living, never been out on a date with Julie, never driven a sports car or seen a single blessed race. It was like a whole different lifetime, you know? I couldn't even recognize that kid I saw in it. And looking ahead seemed even stranger. I swear, it was like the curb I was standing on was the edge of the Grand Canyon, and for just an instant I felt that cold, hollow breeze of vertigo through my guts like when you look down off the roof of a twelve-story build-ing. It was the same sensation I'd had when that Pan Am Stratocruiser's wheels lifted up off the runway for the very first time.

About then they started the countdown and that big New Year's ball started descending from the top of its tower. I felt Julie's fur coat pressing in close against me and that cold, hollow thing inside me faded away. She squeezed my hand. Geez, it was nice not to be alone. Then the ball hit bottom and of course we kissed while corks popped and sirens wailed and noisemakers blew and Guy Lombardo played *Auld Lang Syne* over the PA system. It was a long, dreamy, faraway sort of kiss-you know, the ones that make your toes curl inside your socks-and when we finally came up for air, fireworks were exploding all over the sky above Times Square. It was a great moment to be alive. But of course the trouble with New Year's celebrations is that the energy eventually peters out after awhile and there you find yourself, rolled over into a new year that doesn't look or sound or smell or feel one iota different from the old one you rolled out of just a few moments before. Fact is, it feels a little hollow afterwards in the slipstream, you know?

We managed to find most of the people we came with and then went looking for Cal and the Packard, but of course he wasn't where we'd agreed he was supposed to be (not that I could completely blame him, since the streets were packed solid with people and buses and cabs and cars and cops on foot and horseback trying to get everybody to keep moving along) and of course that's when it started to rain again. "Jesus, what the hell are we gonna do *now?*" Julie wailed. Mary Frances and her twinkletoes friends from the theater/drama apartment figured it wasn't all that far and we could just hoof it back to the party. But they weren't dressed like we were. *"I can't walk fifteen blocks in these damn shoes and my mother's coat is getting ruined and I'm freezing my ass off, Palumbo!"* Julie screamed at me like there was something I could do about it.

"Cal'll show up," I said lamely, praying it was true. "Let's go over here out of the rain." So we stepped back into the doorway of a little storefront. Believe it or not, it turned out to be that friend of Colin St. John's *"LOST OUR LEASE- EVERYTHING MUST GO"* jewelry store where I almost went to get Julie's engagement ring. One thing I was already beginning to understand about Julie was that she'd get mad and explode and yet still nurse a long, simmering anger about it afterwards. Sometimes for weeks or months at a time. But there was always this one, desperate escape hatch out of such situations if I could just get her to see the humor in it and laugh. So I told her about Colin's friend and the jewelry store we were huddled in front of and how he was forever losing his lease and going out of business and burning roof shingles in the back room to get an authentic smell whenever he felt like having a fire sale.

"Maybe this is where you should've bought my earrings, huh?" Julie snorted. But then she thought about it and it turned into a laugh, and right away I knew I was home free. Wet fur coat and all.

About then Cal showed up, inching the Packard along in heavy traffic with Angelina still right there beside him and Mary Frances and the other theater types crammed in the back. They'd run into each other crossing the street about a half block up. So Julie and me piled in front with Cal and Angelina, and it was really a tight fit and Julie pretty much had to sit on my lap. Which was okay with me, except for the smell off the wet fur.

We got back to the apartment building on Bleecker Street around 1:30, and apparently the cops had been there a time or two to quiet the music down and so the guys from the jazz combo were just leaving with their instrument cases. "Listen, Buddy," Cal said as we piled out of the car, "I told Angelina I'd take her home, OK?"

I started to say something but never got the chance, as Cal reached across in one smooth motion, pulled the door shut, and nailed the gas. And that's about when we realized the hem of Julie's mom's wet fur coat was caught in the damn doorjamb. *"JESUSCHRISTSHITALMIGHTY!"* I hollered at the top of my lungs, pounding on the side window to the accompaniment of a long, drawn out, and thoroughly mournful ripping noise.

Oh, *SHIT!*

Well, Cal hit the brakes and we were able to rescue the renegade piece of fur from the Packard's door sill, but it looked terminally mangled to me. Cal kind of rolled his palms up-*what can you do?*-and left to take Angelina back home to Brooklyn. So Julie and me headed upstairs with everybody else, feeling pretty sick over the whole thing. Her mom was gonna skin us alive.

But it turned out one of the, umm, "friends" of the actor/waiter guys who went to Times Square with us worked as a dress designer and fabric grader in the garment trade over on 53rd Street. "Let him take a look at it," one of them said in a high-pitched, whiny voice. So they led us inside the apartment and introduced us to this slender, willowy kid with clear, sad eyes and a flop of pale blond hair that he was forever sweeping off of his forehead. His name was Paul, and he sure did know a thing or two about fabric and stitching.

"Well, this is thoroughly hopeless," he sniffed, holding the ragged piece up next to the rest of the coat and staring at it like the last part of a jigsaw puzzle that wouldn't quite fit. Then he looked at the coat again. "My Gawd, this style went out with garters and rubber girdles," he clucked. "How often does she wear this awful thing, anyway?"

"Not very often," Julie answered.

"I've only seen it once before," I added. "At Christmas."

"Hmmm, I see…" the blonde guy said, rolling it around in his head like Sherlock Holmes. "Think she'd notice if the hem was a little shorter?" You could tell he was enjoying the attention and challenge of it.

"How should I know?" Julie answered, looking to me for an opinion.

"Well," I observed, "we're sure as hell dead in the water like this."

"Very well," Paul announced, *"prepare for major surgery!"*

So Mary Frances brought over that dumb little sewing kit I'd bought her for Christmas and somebody else brought a fresh pack of Gillette blue blades, but, after looking things over, Paul allowed as how he really needed a sewing machine to do the job right.

"I've got one over by the window in my apartment," a sort of puffy, pasty-faced guy with thinning hair and a shaggy black beard offered, "but I don't think it works. Or at least I've never seen it run ever. We use it as an end table. The cats like to stand on it so they can look out at the street." So, while Paul the garment designer started slitting and basting the hemline of Julie's mom's supposedly ex-Marlene Dietrich secondhand fur coat, I went down the hall to see what I could do with a fold-up table model Singer sewing machine that dated back to around the discovery of electricity.

"This is real nice of you," I told the guy with the shaggy beard as I moved a few curious cats and some even more curious looking plants out of the way.

"Hey, no problem at all," he said with a goofy, high pitched laugh. "We don't always like to admit it here in The Village, but we all have parents back home and families to deal with."

"Yeah," I agreed, folding the sewing machine part up out of the table and rolling the big, cast metal flywheel on the end over a few times to satisfy myself that the needle did indeed go up and down. "So, where do you come from?" I asked, just making conversation.

"Me?" he said. "Oh, I'm just an ordinary, left-wing Jewish atheist from a Russian family background."

"You come from Russia?"

"No, not me personally. My grandparents came from there. I'm actually from Paterson, New Jersey."

"No kidding? I'm from Passaic."

"You're the car mechanic, right?"

"Yeah." I stuck my hand up. "Hi. I'm Buddy Palumbo."

"Hi," he said through a sheepish smile. "I'm Allen Ginsburg."

Turns out the sewing machine was an easy fix-just a frayed wire inside the plug, thank goodness-but I knew enough about mechanics to check the belt tension and even put a little oil on all the stuff that either spun or moved up and down. And I had to use blessed popcorn oil since nobody on that whole entire floor had ever heard about Routine Household Maintenance or kept any 3-in-1 Oil handy. Not that it came as any big surprise. But the popcorn oil worked, and, in about an hour, Julie's mom's coat looked good as new. Or better, even, since now you could see a few more inches of leg, and Julie had herself one genuinely shapely set of calves.

"Hey, thanks a whole lot," I told Paul, the blonde dress designer guy.

"Oh, it wasn't anything," he shrugged, looking kind of embarrassed. "Maybe one day you can fix a car for me or something."

"I hope I get the chance." I told him. And I meant it, too.

By then it was well past three and Julie and me were pretty done in. But of course my buddy Cal was still missing in action, so there was nothing to do but head back over to Mary Frances' apartment and sit on the carpet in the main room with the rest of the sleepy-eyed stragglers, half-heartedly listening to Ollie Cromwell and that bushy-haired communist literary type from down the hall arguing about whether Uncle Joe Stalin's Soviet communism was any better or worse than Mao Tse Tung's Chinese version, along with a few well-documented footnotes about the off-brand, half-breed version that Marshall Tito guy was fooling around with in Yugoslavia. And then-out of nowhere and without any provocation whatsoever-the conversation would take a weird half gainer into whether some French writer/philosopher guy named Jean Paul Sartre had actually stolen all his ideas from some other writer/philosopher guy named Soren Kierkegaard and if Albert Camus was the Real Thing or just a fool's gold flash in the pan. In a strange way, it reminded me of listening to one of Skippy Welcher's discombobulated monologues, you know? Except as a duet instead of a solo. By then we were back to a rerun of "resolved: that the Mexican communists should re-admit Diego Rivera to The Party" and it was pretty amazing how they could just keep going 'round and 'round even though there didn't seem to be any point or beginning or end to it. Except for maybe impressing the small remaining gallery of bored-looking spectators lolling around on the rug in front of them.

Fact is, if you listened carefully, you couldn't miss how those two would make sure to pick opposing positions-on virtually *any* sort of motion, notion or proposition!-just so's they'd have something to argue about! And I must admit my feelings about The Great Communist Menace changed drastically that night. I mean, how the hell were these people going to rule the world? Far as I could see, they couldn't even agree on whether they wanted a roll of toilet paper to unwind in a clockwise or counter-clockwise direction!

Chapter 8: The Future Beckons

The S.C.M.A.'s big annual meeting and banquet was held at the Henry Hudson Hotel in New York City sometime around the middle of January, and although I didn't go (fact is I wasn't invited, and neither was Big Ed) I was flattered to hear there were lots of eye-bugging, jaw-dropping stories about my near swan dive off a cliff in what was almost Big Ed's new Ferrari during *La Carrera Panamericana*. There were also a few wild tales from the mid-December race event out at Torrey Pines in California, where the weather lets them just about race all year. Lucky bastards. Phil Hill continued to make a name for himself by running away with the San Diego Cup feature in Ernesto Julio's silver C-Type after Jack McAfee's 4.1 Ferrari (which looked to be the only real threat) blew out a universal joint on the starting line. And to think I helped get that silver Jag halfway across country to California! There were also a bunch of long, dull meetings about schedules and rules and venues for the upcoming season plus a few hush-hush, behind-closed-doors caucuses where Charlie Priddle and his upper echelon of armband types tried to figure how the hell they could keep people like Big Ed Baumstien out of their events without appearing to be par-ticularly narrow minded or, worse yet, attracting any adverse publicity. I guess a few of them were worried about that pack of noisy Jewish lawyer types from the B'nai Brith Anti-Defamation League, and especially the way they were all so obviously in cahoots with the liberal hebe press in Manhattan. Not that Big Ed had much in common with those guys (or ever once asked anybody to fight his battles for him) but his last name *was* Baumstein, and, as far as some of Charlie Priddle's Mayflower Money wolf pack were concerned, that would prob-ably be enough for those bleeding heart hyenas from the newspapers.

But the hottest topic of conversation was the upcoming twelve-hour endur-ance race at Sebring, Florida in March, which would be the first fully F.I.A.-sanctioned, World Class Professional sports car event ever held on American soil. Needless to say it was something of a sore subject with many of the hardcore tight-asses on the S.C.M.A.'s various steering and ruddering committees, see-ing as how it offered real Cash American prize money and also served as the first round of the F.I.A.'s new World Sports Car Championship, which meant a few genuine European factory teams and some genuine, world class profes-sional race drivers might be involved, and this went against a lot of the hal-lowed, devoutly amateur "gentleman racer" bullshit that a lot of the old line S.C.M.A. types espoused as a way to keep the riff-raff out.

And especially the *fast* riff-raff.

I guess the whole thing started with some hotshot New York promoter named Alec Ulmann, who liked sports cars and had this bright idea about holding a race down in Florida in the middle of winter. I mean, a lot of your wealthy black sheep S.C.M.A. types were down there anyway, soaking up sunshine and afternoon cocktails while working stiffs like me were shoveling snow out of driveways and drying our gloves out on the space heater afterwards. Anyhow, this Ulmann guy had a pretty good idea about where to throw this car party of his, too, since there was this big old worn-out military airport just a few miles outside the little town of Sebring, right smack-dab in the middle of Florida, where a graveyard of derelict World War II bombers and cargo planes sat rotting in the sun, surrounded by scraggly acres of orange groves growing up out of the sand.

Carson Flegley told me the first Sebring race was held on New Year's Eve day, 1951. It was a six hour deal that was scored according to this weird French formula called Index of Performance, which is a thoroughly incomprehensible handicapping system that takes distance traveled, engine capacity, and maybe even the drivers' hat sizes into consideration and generally picks a winner from among the little tiddlers scrapping around at the back of the field where nobody ever pays much attention. Tommy Edwards said the whole idea was for some dumb little blue car that couldn't beat anybody on sheer speed to actually win something. And he could never understand how the French came to rule international racing after the war, anyway. I mean, sure, they had *Le Mans,* which everybody pretty much agreed was the biggest damn sportycar race in the world. But they didn't really have much in the way of major league, homegrown contenders. Then again, maybe they just stumbled into it by default seeing as how the British, Italians, and Germans were too damn busy building neat race cars and couldn't be bothered.

In any case, that Index of Performance deal worked exactly as planned, and this dinky little Crosley Hotshot (which looked like a kid built it out of an orange crate and a set of roller skates and couldn't go much faster) was declared the winner-much to the consternation of the few people who actually watched the race-even though Tommy Edwards and his old buddy Eddie Dearborn covered by far the most distance in Eddie's Cad-Allard. In fact, they were *twenty-two laps* ahead of the "winning" car at the end. But who cared, you know? It was all just a fun winter lark in Florida. In fact, Tommy used to laugh like hell when he told the story about how that little Crosley belonged to some guy named Vic Sharpe from Tampa, who just drove down to Sebring to deliver some tires to a friend who was running the event and maybe stick around and watch if it looked interesting. But then he got into the paddock and the old buzz got going, and pretty soon Tommy Edwards and Eddie Dearborn and a bunch of other guys around the beer keg started telling him that his Crosley had a really good shot at winning the damn race on account of the handicap. Hell, it just had this wheezy little 724cc peanut of an engine-by far the smallest in the field-and that could amount to a tremendous advantage if you were looking at things through the wrong end of the binoculars like those Index of Performance handicappers were. But this Vic Sharpe guy from Tampa had never been in a car race (although how could you ever tell in a Crosley Hotshot?) and so Tommy and Eddie scoured around the beer keg until they came up with two likely prospects to drive the damn thing-Fred Koster and Bobby Deshon-and even put up the entry fee the next morning so the Crosley could run the damn race. Naturally the owner was a little worried about having enough car left afterwards to drive back to Tampa, but everybody assured him they would take it real easy and just go out for a Sunday morning drive (or, more properly, a Sunday afternoon and evening drive) and the only thing they did to prepare that car for the race was to slap an extra leaf in the front spring. Seems one of the drivers went out for a few practice laps and discovered that the Crosley wanted to roll right over on its nose whenever you bent it into a corner at anything more than a brisk walking pace.

So it was just a big joke, you know, and then an even bigger one when the blessed thing "won" on Index and my friend Tommy and his co-driver Eddie Dearborn came home a distant eighth in spite of covering the most miles. "It was bloody *perfect!*" Tommy laughed. "We must've passed that little bugger every third or fourth lap. And to think we paid the bloody entry fee!" Then he leaned in and whispered. "But Eddie and I knew who'd *really* won, even if it wasn't on the bloody scoring sheets. Beat Creighton Pendleton's Ferrari by three laps-fair and square-even though they wound up ahead of us on that blasted Index of Performance thing."

In any case, everybody seemed to have a swell time-hey, what's not to like about shirtsleeve weather, palm trees, and plenty of engine noise and cold beer in the middle of winter-and the following year the event was moved to March, lengthened to twelve hours, and drew a much larger crowd of both entrants and spectators. It was still scored on Index, so a lot of the cleverer S.C.M.A. guys brought (or bought!) smaller displacement machinery to run at Sebring. As a result, there were more in the way of Siatas and MGs and Crosleys and such than Jag XKs and Ferraris (although there were certainly some of those) along with these two strange, tubby little French roadsters called Deutsch-Bonnets. They had tiny, air-cooled two cylinder engines and front wheel drive, and made a sound (at least according to ear witnesses) like a pair of geese with serious gastric distress. Even so, they were sort of quick (at least in the Extreme Tiddler sense of the word) and quickly earned the nickname "Douche Bags" around the Sebring paddock.

To be honest, French cars had always been kind of a mystery to me, and I sometimes got the impression they did things just to be *different,* you know? Or maybe they just looked at what the British were doing and said, *"Zut Alors, we cannot copy the Rosbifs!"* and then looked at what the Germans were doing and say *"Sacré Bleu, we cannot copy Le Boche!"* and then looked at what the Italians were doing and remembered which side they fought on in World War II (at least at the beginning, anyway) and then designed their cars according to whatever was left. Or, as Barry Spline put it, *"When y'think about it, mate, all yer best French cars came from two bleedin' Eye-talians and a bloody Brit!"*

Still, they were quick for their engine size and one of them wound up winning the first Sebring 12-Hour on Index (for the glory of France, natch) just the way those F.I.A. handicappers in Paris had hoped and schemed from the beginning. Only this time, the Sebring race attracted a lot more attention from everybody-entrants, fans, and press alike-and a lot of your pencil-and-typewriter types had a little difficulty understanding how a car that covered 676 miles in twelve hours could possibly finish ahead of one that did 754. Especially when it made a noise like sick geese. So many of the race reports from Sebring listed the Frazer-Nash Le Mans that actually covered the most distance as the winner. In fact, it was the exact same car I saw parked inside the Westbridge shop the very first time I went there in the spring of 1952. I remember it was the first real racing car I'd ever seen, and felt the very first tinges of the old racing disease when I was standing there beside it.

The much-reported "win" by that Frazer-Nash caused a lot of consternation among the old line S.C.M.A. types who wanted to keep everything fun and low-key and anything but serious at Sebring, and it got even worse for '53 when Alec Ulmann wheeled and dealed the F.I.A. into awarding The Twelve Hours of Sebring full international status. That was a hell of an accomplishment for a three-year-old race on a decaying old airport somewhere out in the orange groves in the middle of Florida. But it was the off season over in Europe and maybe some of the lads would like a little trip someplace down a bit closer to the equator? Plus everybody and his brother had an eye on the American market, and what better way to show off your wares (or sell off last year's hot new model to some rich, wild-eyed Yank) than to parade them around someplace in the middle of Florida during the height of tourist season when a lot of the ermine and emerald crowd were already down? Although, to be honest, Sebring was quite a distance-in every imaginable way!-from Palm Beach, Key West, Miami Beach and Miami.

A major skirmish ensued between promoter Alec Ulmann and certain members of the S.C.M.A. hierarchy (led, naturally enough, by Mr. Charles Winthrop Martingale Priddle) the upshot of which was that Alec told Charlie and his boys exactly what they could do with their beloved Amateur Status and signed up the Triple-A (who ran most of the professional oval track racing in the U.S. of A., including the Indianapolis 500) to sanction the event. In retaliation, Charlie Priddle threatened to yank the amateur standing of any S.C.M.A. driver who ran the Sebring event (which would mean they couldn't run any of the regular club races anymore) but soon realized that damn near all the big wheels and top cars planned to go anyway, and so he quietly pulled in his horns. I guess that's what made Charlie Priddle such a strong and dangerous force inside the club. He never took on a face-to-face fight unless he was pretty damn sure he could win it, and he didn't have any trouble at all slinking away with his tail between his legs when things started stacking up against him. He'd be back. That was for sure. And he'd *remember,* too....

Anyhow, everybody was pretty torqued up about this big new international race in Florida, and of course Cal Carrington was absolutely frothing at the mouth to go and even Carson Flegley was pretty excited (or about as excited as he ever got, which was not very) about trying out his freshly hopped-up MG, and it wasn't two or three rounds of drinks later they'd shaken hands on running it together in Carson's car. So Cal showed up at the Sinclair bright and early the next morning (or bright and early for him, anyway, since it wasn't even noon) and explained as how we were all going down to Sebring, Florida, to run the twelve hours with Carson's TD.

Once again it sounded like a hell of an adventure-major races in faraway places always do!-but it seemed like it was getting tougher to get sucked into these deals without thinking it over a little first. Truth is, I was worried about what would happen to the shop while I was away. Can you believe it? But you couldn't count on how Old Man Finzio would be, and Butch was not exactly what you would call topnotch customer service or management material. Not hardly. And you just can't take off and leave a business like a gas station to run itself. Somebody's got to be out there at the pumps making neighborhood chit-chat and wiping bug splats off your regular customers' windshields every day or they'll find someplace else that will. Lord knows there are plenty of gas stations around. The service work has to get done, too. You can't tell somebody with a simple, fifteen-minute thrown fan belt or cracked distributor cap that you're sorry, but the mechanic's down sunning himself in Florida and they can't have the car back for a week. That's just no way to do business.

Besides, I wasn't real sure how all this would go down with Julie. I mean, here we were engaged and all and spending a lot of time together and the last time I went out of town, I came back with no right eyebrow, a couple cracked ribs, and my arm in a sling. I had the feeling she was not going to be exactly overjoyed about this.

But then everything changed when Big Ed got wind of that race down in Florida, and especially how it was a Triple-A sanctioned event. See, Big Ed didn't have an S.C.M.A. license, but he *did* have one from the AAA (and, no, I don't know how the hell he ever got it, since as little of an amateur race driver as he was, he was even less of a professional one) and so this looked like a perfect opportunity to get a little wintertime sun, get another race under his not inconsiderable belt, and chat up the other S.C.M.A. racer types to get them on his side for the inevitable showdown with Charlie Priddle.

"Geez, Big Ed," I told him, "I'm not real sure I can just, you know, *take off* for a couple weeks."

"Sure y'can, Buddy," he grinned, flicking a clump of cigar ash through the window crack on the black Sixty Special sedan. It was wintertime, and the new white Eldorado convert was most likely going to stay packed away in the garage until spring. "See, it's like this," he told me, his cigar kind of rolling around in his mouth, "y'gotta unnerstand that this here is your *business,* see?"

"I know. In fact, that's exactly why I think I gotta stay."

"Nah. Lissen t'me, Buddy. *THIS* is your business. Sports cars. Race cars. Takin' carra guys like me who're gonna buy these here expensive cars and have the damn money t'*race* 'em and fix 'em when they're busted." He took a long, thoughtful drag on his stogie. "Hell, *anybody* can run a damn gas pump, Buddy. You got somethin' *special* here. Believe me, I know this stuff."

"I dunno," I shook my head, "I mean, it all goes to shit if I'm not here."

"Then *hire* somebody. Hell, hire *two* people."

"It's not that simple. After all, it's not my place. It's Old Man Finzio's."

"Screw him. Besides, he ain't never around anymore."

"He's here mornings most days," I told him. "And it's still his damn business, even if he's not here all the time."

Big Ed's cigar started into one of its figure-eight rolls.

"Besides," I added, "you don't know how damn hard it is to find decent mechanics. Just ask Colin St. John and Barry Spline. And *honest* decent mechanics who actually bother t'show up for work every day are even tougher."

Big Ed's cigar stopped dead center then and went into a slow, up-and-down bobbing motion, like a bottom fisherman jigging off the Jersey piers.

"The worst is I couldn't afford it even if I found somebody good. Butch pretty much earns his keep but he can't do a whole lot of stuff. And Cal…" I choked down a crude laugh, "…Cal just doesn't care. Not unless there's a race in it, anyway. If I'm honest with myself, he's pretty much useless. Fun to have around, but useless."

"And Old Man Finzio?"

I thought it over, trying to be fair. "About the only thing he does around here anymore is straighten out bent cotter pins and take money out of the till."

"I see," Big Ed said absently, staring out past the hood ornament to where two little kids were packing snowballs on the sidewalk. "Tellya what," he said finally, still looking off into the distance. "Lemme think it over, OK? Maybe I'll have some kinda idea t'work things out…."

"Sure, Ed," I agreed half-heartedly. "But what could *you* do?"

"You never know, Buddy," he grinned around both sides of his fat Cuban cigar. "You never know."

So imagine my surprise when Big Ed showed up at the Sinclair at 7am the next morning and offered to take Old Man Finzio to breakfast. I mean, *nobody* ever asked Old Man Finzio to eat with them. Much less to pay for it. And that was just fine with the Old Man, because he didn't much fancy company. "People are fulla shit," was pretty much the way Old Man Finzio felt about his fellow man, "and them are the nice ones."

But Big Ed was an awfully good customer-our best, in fact-and so there was no way Old Man Finzio could turn him down. I remember I was putting the finishing touches on Big Ed's Jag engine back in the service bay that particular ayem, but came down with a severe dose of curiosity and kept sneaking out by the pumps even when there were no customers, just so's I could peel an eyeball over towards the little coffee shop across the street. I could see the two of them in the window there, the Old Man all stern and quiet and backed up as far away from the conversation as he could get, while Big Ed was leaning forward across the table like an insurance salesman, burrowing his way in, a confident grin on his face while his hands made pictures in the air and the tip of his cigar added little whips and loops for punctuation. They were in there an awfully long time-till almost ten, I think-and, by that last half hour, I could see that Old Man Finzio was leaning forward a little across the table, too. I think they maybe even shook hands at the end. Really.

Naturally I was dying to know what happened, but Big Ed just breezed right by me and climbed into his black Caddy sedan. "Gotta have some papers drawn up…" he mumbled without looking up. "I'll talk t'ya later, OK?" And with a screech of rubber he was gone.

I found out three days later that all Big Ed did was become a not-so-silent partner in Old Man Finzio's gas station. Can you believe it? Only I guess "partner" would be far too simple a word, since Big Ed had to make Old Man Finzio comfortable on a whole big assortment of sticking points and Big Ed was moreover no dummy when it came to business deals and he sure as hell knew the difference between assets and liabilities. Not to mention the difference between long term and short term versions of each. I don't pretend to understand all the reams of legal stuff his lawyers spit out, but it was full of *parties of the first part* and *parties of the second part* and *whereases* and *ipso factos,* but the general gist of it was that Big Ed forked over a tidy little chunk of front money (which I guess Old Man Finzio could really use so's he could get himself a better class of hospital treatment than they had over at the V.A.) and also snuck him sideways onto the payroll at one of the scrapyards-like he'd been there awhile, you know?-which happened to come with a nice little hospitalization policy. Big Ed knew all about such things since rumor had it one of Frank Costello's top lieutenant's worthless cousins and the even more worthless son-in-law of some hotshot on the local zoning board were both enjoying the same sort of deal for many years, even though neither one bothered to show up for work. Ever.

So Old Man Finzio still got to hang around the Sinclair as much as he wanted (which, thankfully, wasn't all that much anymore) and keep half the profit from the gas pumps as long as he was there. I guess he was real stubborn about that, even though I figured leaving a complicated and expensive wrench job to go out and pump gas at twenty-nine cents a gallon amounted to a major pain in the ass. Especially in wintertime. In return for the money, Big Ed got some kind of five-year lease on the gas station business with an option to buy whenever the Old Man didn't want it or didn't need it anymore. It looked like one hell of a deal for Old Man Finzio, since it not only guaranteed him a little more than he was already taking home, but also that he'd get it no matter if things continued to go well or the business fell on hard times. And occasional hard times-whether they came from illness, mistakes, family problems, good weather, bad weather, tight money, loose money, or just the wrong phase of the moon keeping all your customers' cars running fine-were always a big part of the gas station business.

Far as I was concerned, the important part of the deal was that Big Ed was putting me in charge as what he called his on-site manager, and that meant whatever I said went once you were inside those overhead doors. Truth is, it wasn't all that different from what was already going on, but getting it all on paper put a whole new light on it. And I think there was some kind of built-in buyout clause, too, although Big Ed didn't say anything about it and I knew better than to ask. Personally, I couldn't see how he was going to come out. I mean, I was already at the limit of what I could do with just two hands and two feet and we still seemed to be scratching to meet payroll every week. Not to mention that all the long-term race shop work in the back always seemed to take twice as long as I'd estimated. Or maybe three times. Oh, the racing customers would pay the extra hours-almost to a man-but big projects torn apart all over the place take time and floor space away from the bread-and-butter tune-ups and oil changes and brake and muffler jobs you need to keep rolling down the road to keep the cash rolling in. "I dunno, Big Ed," I told him. "I mean, I'm really grateful for what you did and all-I mean *really* grateful!-but I'm still not sure this was such a smart thing to do with your money."

Big Ed clapped a dinner plate-sized hand on my shoulder. "Lissen, Buddy, you already seen I ain't particularly chickenshit about how I spend my money. What's the diff t'you if I blow it on a car shop or the next friggin' divorce lawyer, huh?" Then he leaned in close so I could see the street-hardened glint in his eyes. "Don't be fooled, Buddy. I don't go off half-cocked." He tapped his finger against his temple. "I *think!* And, believe me, I generally make my partners and me some pretty important money."

"You do?"

"Yep," he nodded, biting down on his cigar. "And so I'd hang on real tight if I was you."

"Why's that?"

Big Ed looked me square in the eye, then leaned over and whispered in my ear, *"Because this time, Mr. Buddy Palumbo, YOU'RE my friggin' partner."*

"G-geez," I gulped. "And you think we can really make *money* off this?"

He shot me a wink. "You just watch us."

I told Julie about Big Ed's deal when she stopped by later that afternoon to go through the bills for Old Man Finzio and do a little tidying up, and right away I saw her jaw take a set and her eyes narrow down. "You really think that's such a good idea?"

"Geez, Julie," I tried to explain, "I didn't have anything to do with it."

"Hmpf," she snorted.

"No. Really," I protested. "Big Ed made the deal with your uncle. Honest. Across the street in the coffee shop. I saw the whole thing." Have you ever told the God's Honest truth to somebody-and most especially a wife or steady girl-friend-and had it sound like absolute lying bullshit even to your own ears?

"You just wait and see," Julie warned, the possibilities rolling over in her head. "He's gonna start taking over. You'll see. And then he's gonna think he should get his frickin' work for free. And he's our best customer."

I had to admit that notion never crossed my mind, and all of a sudden I was seeing this partnership with Big Ed in a new and unflattering light. "Gee, d'ya think he'd actually *do* that?"

Julie looked at me like I was too blessed dumb to pull a wagon. "Sure he would. In a second." She thought for a moment. "Only not right away. He's gotta let a little time pass first and do it little by little so's you don't really notice. Remember, what he's really after is *you.*"

"Me?"

"Sure you. He knows you got the magic touch when it comes to workin' on those frickin' MGs and Jaguars. He wants you workin' on his cars, and he wants to make money off the talent you got workin' on other people's cars."

No way could I believe my good friend, best customer, part-time mentor and traveling companion Big Ed Baumstein would do anything like that. Still, what Julie said made sense in a shrewd, slimy, scheming kind of way. To tell the truth, I was pretty naive about that sort of thing, and, like most regular guys and in spite of a mountain of evidence to the contrary, I tended to trust people and take them at face value until they'd proved me wrong. Usually by stealing me blind and then shitting all over me. Several times, in many cases. So I got to thinking it was really good for me to be hooked up with somebody like Julie, who, even moreso than most other women, tended to think the worst about everybody she wasn't absolutely sure about and even then sensed all sorts of ulterior motives, hidden agendas, simmering envies, and secret, long-held grudges swirling in the mist behind what appeared to me to be normal, everyday acts and meaning-less conversations.

I always figured she was being paranoid, you know?

But now it was occurring to me that there was a nice balance between my easygoing nature and Julie's hard-edged and suspicious view of things. Sure, we'd fight about it. Plenty, in fact. But, deep down inside where I never planned to let her see it, I was beginning to realize she was my first and last defense against all the sneak thieves, con men, fast talkers, rat-finks, skunks and wea-sels of this world who eat dimbulb grunts like me for breakfast.

"So whaddaya think I oughta do about it?" I asked, trying to sound like I was just humoring her. I mean, a guy's gotta keep his pride in tact, you know?

Julie thought it over for a moment. "You gotta talk t'him. You gotta tell him right out what you're worried about-that he's just taking advantage-and that you'd always figured this was gonna be *your* frickin' business one day after…well…you know what I mean." Julie wasn't about to say "after my uncle croaks," but I knew what she meant.

I must admit, the idea of going head-to-head with Big Ed Baumstein didn't much appeal to me. But no question Julie was right. After all, we were telling everybody we were going to get married on June 21st (not that it had really sunk in between my particular pair of ears) and this gas station and car repair business represented a big, economy-sized chunk of our future. Plus Big Ed didn't exactly strike you as the kind of true blue, long term, grind-it-out, nose-to-the-grindstone/shoulder-to-the-wheel partner you really needed in anything like a garage business. He was more your spur-of-the-moment, seat-of-the-pants, got-a-hunch/bet-a-bunch Wheeler Dealer type of individual, and, if you weren't careful about it, you might also pick up this nagging notion that he was exactly the sort of person the police might someday find folded up in the trunk of an abandoned car with no plates on it over behind the docks or buried in a shallow grave somewhere in the marshlands north of Newark. "Okay," I finally mumbled, "I'll talk to him."

"And don't be chickenshit about it," Julie warned with a threatening edge to her voice. "Remember, now that he's gone and got himself a foreign car repair business, *he* needs *you* more than *you* need *him!*"

It was a scary, giddy sort of feeling knowing she might actually be right.

"And there's one more thing you gotta do," Julie added in the same tough, unwavering tone.

"What's that?"

"You gotta get rid of Cal."

"WHAT??!!"

Julie nodded. "I know he's your friend and all, but he's lazy and he doesn't show up and you just can't count on him."

That was all true enough. Fact is, Cal had gone missing more days than he'd worked ever since he'd met that beautiful and mysterious Angelina Scalabrini from Brooklyn at the New Year's Eve party in Greenwich Village. Plus he was turning out to be a real liability sometimes even when he did bother to show up, seeing as how the novelty had long since worn off and he'd pretty much lost interest in what he was doing and stopped paying close attention to the jobs in front of him. Truth is, we were getting an awful lot of comebacks on his work and complaints about cars that weren't ready on time. Dammit, she was right again. Worse yet, I now had two of the toughest tongue-dancing jobs I'd ever attempted in my life on deck and nobody but Julie behind me for backup if I got in over my head. And she wouldn't be there. It made me want to just go back into the shop and fix a broken car. At least that was something I knew how to do.

But firing Cal didn't turn out to be near as tough as I expected. The next day he bothered to show up (which turned out to be sometime after lunch the following Thursday) I told him I needed to talk to him and even offered to take him across the street for a doughnut and a cup of coffee. Since this was highly unusual behavior, Cal knew for sure something was up. But when I finally got him eyeball-to-eyeball in the farthest back booth at the coffee shop, I found my conversation kind of hemming and hawing and stumbling and staggering all over the place. That's when Cal smiled that million-dollar rich kid smile of his and put his hand on my arm. "You're trying to fire me, aren't you?" he said, almost laughing about it.

"Well, er..." I started in, "...it's not, umm..."

"Hey, don't worry about it," he grinned.

"Really?" I couldn't believe it. "Are you *sure?"*

"Hell, *yes!* Shit, I've been trying to find a way to tell you I want to quit for a couple weeks now."

"You're joking."

Cal shook his head. "Not a chance. See, I got this surprise little influx of cash," he pulled a Big Ed-sized wad of greenbacks out of his pocket, "and I thought it might be a good time to, umm, *explore other opportunities....* "

Why, there had to be a couple hundred bucks there! Maybe more. And of course I was curious as hell about where and how he came by it. But I knew better than to ask where any of Cal's flash-flood surpluses of folding money came from. That was always the sort of information you were better off not knowing. Not that he'd ever tell you the truth about it anyway.

"Fact is," he continued, "I was only hanging around because I knew you were in a jam and needed help. I wanted to help out, see."

"Don't worry," I laughed, "you weren't that much help."

Cal actually looked a trifle apologetic for about two-tenths of a second. "No, I guess I wasn't, was I?"

"Hey, that's OK," I told him. "You weren't around very often."

"Yeah," Cal's face brightened. "That was a good thing, wasn't it?"

"Yes," I had to agree. "It was." We were both getting a pretty good rise of the whole thing, you know? "So," I asked him, "what exactly are these *'other opportunities'* you're planning to pursue."

"Beats me," Cal shrugged.

"Could any two of them be named Angelina Scalabrini?"

Cal gave me a sheepish smile. But then his face darkened. "To be honest, I haven't seen much of her lately."

"Lately? Hell, you only met her three weeks ago."

"Yeah, I know. I called and went over to see her a couple times, but she's got this real cracking bitch of a mother."

"You can't tell me one damn thing about girlfriends with bitchy mothers."

"Oh, no," Cal assured me, "this one's a grand prize winner. She's wants Angel to be an actress real bad-I mean *real* bad!-and doesn't want her wasting time running around with guys who can't push her career. Not at *all."*

"So now it's *'Angel,'* huh?"

Cal looked down at the remains of his doughnut and I swear for a second I almost thought he blushed. Almost. Then he looked back up at me, only real serious this time. "But now they're gone."

"Gone?"

Cal nodded. "I guess her mom was going through a divorce or something, and it must've got settled because all of a sudden there was no answer on their phone anymore and then it was disconnected."

"Disconnected?"

"Yeah." Cal nodded and looked back down at his plate. "I went over there a couple days ago, but their place is pretty much cleaned out."

"D'you know where they went?"

Cal shook his head again. "Who knows? Maybe even Hollywood?"

"You could check with the phone company. Or even the post office?"

"Nah," Cal said, not sounding too sure about it. "I'm not gonna go chasing after her. It's not my style. And it's a waste of time, too. Hell, she knows I'd like to see her and she knows where to find me." He gave a weak little shadow of a shrug. "I mean, it's not worth it, you know?"

You had to respect Cal for his spoiled, rich kid self-centeredness. It made him pretty damn invulnerable. "Well, good luck, ey?"

"Thanks. And the coffee's on me, okay?"

"Sure. It's about time you picked up a damn check."

"Well, don't hold your breath for it to happen again any time soon."

"You planning to run through your wad that quickly?"

"Always managed to in the past."

"Geez," I shook my head. "I don't know if I could ever live like you do."

"You couldn't," Cal said matter-of-factly. "You gotta be born to it and have a whole damn *bunch* of money slip right through your fingers before you stop feeling it anymore."

"Easy come easy go, huh?"

"Yeah," Cal grinned. "It's a gift...."

The meeting with Big Ed was a tougher nut to crack, and I have to admit I felt like a double-dip cone with a heaping scoop of stupid on top of a heaping scoop of nervous when we sat down in the coffee shop together a couple days later. To be honest, I really wished Julie was there with me. But I swallowed hard, set my jaw, dug my heels in down under the table where he couldn't see, and let it all out about how Julie was worried that he was just using me and how Julie was afraid he was going to take advantage of me and want all his work done for free and then got to the hard part about how Julie thought it was just naturally going to be *our* gas station business after, well....

"After the Old Man kicks the bucket," Big Ed interjected, completing the thought with his usual charm and delicacy.

"Yeah," I kind of mumbled, looking down into my lap. Geez, I felt miserable. Like I was some kind of ungrateful, chickenshit traitor, you know?

It was quiet for awhile, and then Big Ed struck a stick match to his cigar and sucked a few times to get it fired. "So," he said slowly, "your girl Julie thought all that up by herself, huh?"

Now I felt like an even bigger chickenshit for saying they were all Julie's notions. Even though they were.

"Hey, it's OK, kid," he told me. "Don' worry nothin' about it." And then he reached out and patted me on the arm. "That's one hell of a sharp little girl you got there. No shit."

"You think?"

Big Ed nodded. "She's sure'n hell lookin' out fr'you, all right."

"But you weren't really planning t'*do* all that stuff," I asked, then heard myself add, "were you?"

Big Ed shook his head. "Nah. 'Course not. But lemme tellya something, kid. Intentions don't mean dick in this world. If your friggin' future's at stake, get it down on paper in black and white. Y'gotta remember, things change...."

"Yeah," I agreed. "I guess they do."

"In fact, that's about the only friggin' thing you can count on."

So Big Ed agreed to have his pack of eagle-eyed (not to mention hawk-nosed) lawyers draw something up for me-I think he called it an employment contract-and advised me to get some other lawyer to look it over before I signed.

"It'll be fair," he told me, "and it'll make it so's you can buy the place out from me after the Old Man croaks."

"Geez, that's really awful nice of you."

"Think nothin' of it, Buddy. Your girl's right about you. It's like you got a special magic when it comes t'sports cars. You're a hard worker, too. And honest on top of it, at least far as I can tell."

"Thanks."

We shook on it.

"Y'know," I said, "I trust you, too, Big Ed. Seems t'me like shaking hands oughta be enough."

"Nah," Big Ed sighed. "Not in this friggin' world. You gotta protect yourself, see. The guy you shook hands with might have a change of heart, or get some hot new dolly who wants it all for herself whispering in his ear. He could even get run over by a dump truck or hit by a freight train or find himself in the path of a stray bullet and wind up on the cold side of the grass. You tell me: what's his friggin' handshake worth then?"

I thought it over. "Nothin's my guess."

"Yep," Big Ed nodded. "That's about the size of it."

That was a good thing to know, even if it wasn't particularly nice.

"And one more thing," Big Ed continued.

"What's that?"

"Don't ever even *think* about divorcing this girl."

"Jesus, Ed, we're not even married yet!"

"All the same, you lissen t'what Big Ed's tellin' ya. Don't you ever even think about it."

"Why's that?" I wanted to know. I mean, this came from a guy who'd had more divorces than most people have new cars in their lifetime.

"Because first off she's a good one. There ain't many like her out there, b'lieve me. An' besides," he advised through the center of a perfect, bluish-white smoke ring, *"by the time she was done with you, Buddy, there wouldn't be nothin' left but th' bones...."*

But the real surprise came a few days later, when out of the clear blue this beatup Ford pickup pulls in off the street and two leathery-looking Italian guys clamber out dressed like they're going deer hunting. Before I know it, they're running tape measures lickety-split around the building and staring into the service bays and arguing with each other in a rapid-fire mixture of English and Italian. Each time they get done arguing, one of them makes a few notes in a little spiral notebook with the broken-off stub of a carpenter's pencil held in fingers gnarly enough to be tree branches. Naturally I'm curious, so I leave the valve adjustment I'm working on and go outside, but by then they've climbed back into the pickup and taken off. As they wheel past the door, I notice *Graziano Construction-General Contractors* painted on the side of the pickup bed. And underneath, in smaller script letters, it says simply: *"We Can Build It."*

The next Monday they show up again with yet another guy dressed for deer hunting-you know, flannel lumberjack shirt, quilted vest, and one of those goofy, army-issue bombardier hats with the fleece lined earflaps-and the three of them start laying out sticks and string and poking holes in the damn asphalt. Before I can even throw my coat on to go see what's up, one of them opens the office door a crack, hollers, *"you moova da cars, eh?"* and goes back outside.

Turns out he wants all the cars out from behind the building, and this is really quite a request since many of the cars parked around the perimeter fringes of every repair shop fall into the Hopeless Case category or are torn seriously apart and waiting for machine shop work to be done or are sad old rustbucket beaters that have been abandoned by owners who can't afford the bill. And many of those are inevitably listed over on two or three flat tires. But when I asked the guy what was up, all he said was *"Signore Big Ed, he's a-say moova cars"* and went back to his measuring and stringing.

"Look, I'm kinda all by myself here," I tried to explain. "I mean, the guy inside's in a wheelchair and all and…"

The head deer hunter guy actually looked up at me for a split second. *"Ey, you needa help?"*

"Yeah," I said, sounding a little embarrassed. "I could use a little help."

"Well why you a-no say so, ey?" And then he gave me this wide, leathery smile with all the background molars missing.

I may be prejudiced, but I reckon you can't beat Italians when it comes to construction work. I mean, they built the blessed Colosseum and the Roman Aqueducts and Ebbett's Field, and no question they all pride themselves on working at a furious, relentless pace until a job is done. Or at least the non-union ones do, anyway. And the weather never bothers them. Hell, it was freezing cold outside, but the four of us had all the derelict cars moved in less than twenty minutes. Plus it was entertaining, seeing as how the whole operation was orchestrated with plenty of nonstop hollering and swearing and rude Italian hand gestures. These guys were something else.

Big Ed dropped by a little later that day and had himself a short huddle with the head guy from Graziano Construction, then came inside to talk to me. "Well, whaddaya think?" he asked, unwrapping a fresh cigar.

"I dunno," I told him, sounding more than a little peeved. "Could'ja maybe tell me what the hell you're doing?"

"Building us two more service bays," Big Ed grinned like it was obvious. "An' I think I'm gonna have 'em push the back wall out to the fence and maybe cover that area over there," he pointed to where we had several of the dead cars huddled together along the edge of the lot, "so's the cars don't gotta sit outside in the weather."

I felt my legs wobble like shaky bowling pins. *"You're WHAT??!!"*

"You heard me, din'tcha?"

Well, a whole express train of thoughts rushed through my head right then, including how much we could use the space on one hand and why didn't Big Ed bother to talk it over with me first on the other. Not to mention how the hell I was going to keep the damn shop operational while all this construction work was going on.

"Don' worry about it, Buddy," Big Ed assured me. "They're just layin' foundations and ordering materials an' stuff now. I'm havin' 'em do all the heavy shit while we're down in Florida next month."

"But, I mean, gee whiz. Shouldn't you have at least *asked* me?"

Big Ed looked puzzled. "You mean you don't like it?"

"Sure I like it. I mean, what's not to like. It's just..." I swept my eyes around the shop, "...I mean, *I'm* the guy who's gonna be working here, right? Shouldn't I have a little say-so about how things are gonna be and what's gonna go where?" Believe it or not, I was feeling pretty damn angry about it.

"Hey, cool down a little, huh?" Big Ed grinned, calmly putting a fresh match to his cigar. "Of *course* you're gonna be involved, Buddy. Wouldn't think of doin' it any other way. You just draw my boys a little picture of what you want and where you think you want it."

I felt my knees wobble again. "You mean I can have another hydraulic lift if I want one?" Anybody who's worked under a car on the floor (or, worse yet, out at curbside with rainwater draining in your ear) knows the value of a lift. It puts your work right in front of you and takes all manner of dirt out of your eyes, kinks out of your back, and cramps out of your muscles.

"Sure, you can have another lift," Big Ed nodded."

"I can even have *two?"*

Big Ed looked at me a little sideways. "Let's not go nuts yet, okay?"

So I sat down that very minute with a pencil and a ruler and started laying out the kind of shop I wanted on the back of the month of January off the big girlie calendar Julie let me keep tacked behind the door so long as I kept the door open when she was there so's she didn't have to look at it. I remember it was February 2nd that particular Monday-I don't think I'll ever forget it-so I really didn't figure to need January any more.

Even if she was a real doll.

Big Ed kind of hovered there over my shoulder looking satisfied as a well-fed tomcat while I drew and scratched and erased-lift here, hoist here, press here, tire balancer here, work benches, power outlets, air lines, parts cleaning tank-I felt like a kid on Christmas morning, you know? And then something frightening occurred to me. "Saaay," I asked Big Ed, "Just where am I gonna find the kind of mechanics I'll need and all the new cars and customers to fill all this space?"

"Don' worry. You got this kind of place, you'll find the damn mechanics. Trust me, *they'll* come to *you!* An' if you got the right damn mechanics, the customers'll find you, too." Big Ed laid a meaty hand on my shoulder. "You got to take it one step at a time, Buddy. You can start lookin' fr' wrenchin' help right away. But don't be in no hurry. And Jesus, don't be offerin' 'em too much at first and givin' the damn store away."

Big Ed obviously had a pretty good bead on the sort of businessman I was.

"In fact, I think I'd let Julie do most of the hirin' and firin' if I was you."

That was a bitter pill, but I was surprised at how easy it went down.

"An' remember. Don't get distracted with all this shit. I want that friggin' Jag a'mine warmed up, ready and waiting when first practice starts fr'that twelve-hour Sebring race down in Florida."

"Of course it will," I told him without thinking. "Piece of cake."

Chapter 9: Goin' South

To be honest, there wasn't all that much to do to get Big Ed's Jaguar ready for Sebring. I'd already about finished up the motor and put in a new clutch and a new second gear and synchronizer sleeve as long as I had everything apart. No matter if he was going up or down through the 'box, Big Ed had a habit of being pretty brutal on second gear. But it was done and back in the car and I'd gone through the brakes and given all the suspension stuff a serious nut-and-bolt. Plus I'd talked Big Ed into a switch to wire wheels on account of they'd keep the brakes cooler and be a lot more convenient on pit stop tire changes during a twelve-hour race. Not that, based on past experience, Big Ed actually figured to be running that long. But it really hurt me to shitcan those neat looking rear fender skirts. They really *made* the XK-120, you know? But they just wouldn't clear the knockoff ears, so they had to go. I wrapped them real carefully in an old wool army blanket and promised Big Ed they'd go back on the car (along with the bolt-on disc wheels) when his Jag went back to regular street duty after Sebring. If, in fact, it ever did. To top it off, I had the Greek at the body shop touch up all the Jag's assorted battle scars and then apply a bumper-to-bumper Simonize wax. That was really the sort of thing I preferred to do myself-that's the only way you know it's done right and that spots aren't skipped or residue isn't left lurking in all the seams-but I was way too pressed for wrenching time to be doing cleanup work any more. And of course the kid at the body shop did a thoroughly half-assed job and I had to take it back and make him go over the spots he missed and get all that leftover wax residue out of the seams. People just don't care, you know?

It occurred to me that what I really needed was some after-hours high school kid to drop by the way I used to and help out here and there with the wax jobs and oil changes and gas pumps and those long, finger withering sessions at the parts cleaning tank. I also needed at least one more mechanic. A guy who knew the cars and knew how to fix 'em and could be trusted to show up every day-and on time, too!-and moreover be conscientious about what he was doing and really care about the customers and the way their cars ran when they left the shop.

In other words, I needed about two more of me.

Especially after it began to dawn on me what was involved in trying to run two of my best customers (including my new partner!) in a twelve-hour endurance race at a track none of us had ever seen in a place none of us had ever been damn near half a hemisphere away in Sebring, Florida. At least money wasn't a problem, since Big Ed peeled me off a couple hundred bucks in cash-just like that!-to cover travel expenses. "Make sure y'save all the friggin' receipts fr' Uncle Sam," he told me. "An' pick up a few blank spares whenever you get th' chance. They come in real handy around April 14th."

The problem was figuring out how to get all the short term work done and delivered in time while gathering up everything we might need in Florida and puzzling out how the heck we were going to carry it all in an XK-120 and an MGTD-plus our personal gear-and then how the hell three guys were going to drive two cars all the way down to Sebring, since Big Ed wisely decided it sounded like a pretty boring trip. So even though he told the current (and, at that point, I think soon-to-be-ex) Mrs. Big Ed he was going with us, he was actually planning to fly down to Havana where they had some very interesting stage shows that a well-connected guy like Big Ed could have encored later in the privacy of his own hotel room (with himself as a participant) for a slight additional fee. In any case, he was planning to hook up with us again for practice the day before the race. Then there was the little problem of me being the only available pit crew for a two car team, and that certainly wasn't going to work, either. It was dawning on me that I was at least two good hands and sixty-odd cubic feet of luggage space short of what I needed.

I talked to Julie about it-I mean, who else did I have to talk to?-and she was pretty damn definite that nobody was probably better than somebody I didn't know or couldn't trust. I'd thought about taking her, but she was going to watch over things for me at the Sinclair and put in just enough hours at the Doggy Shake so she wouldn't lose her job. Not that the manager there would ever fire her, since I'd seen the way he looked at her out of the slimy little corners of his eyes and knew he liked having her around. Truth is, I wanted to pop him one for it-especially when she wore those clingy sweaters of hers-but, like Julie said, it was job security.

I could tell Julie was not particularly thrilled about my taking off on another extended, long-distance motor sports adventure-especially after the way I came back from Mexico-and she made it crystal clear that this was not the way the way things were going to be once we were married. "I hope you're not thinkin' about traipsing all over the whole frickin' globe to car races and leave me stuck back here in Passaic like a dog tied to a frickin' tree."

"Gee whiz, no, Julie. It's just I gotta, you know, take care of my sports car customers. Heck, they're the best ones I got. Besides, most a'those races are a whole lot closer to home."

She didn't look particularly convinced.

"Besides, I was hoping maybe you could start coming with me."

"Oh, great. So I can spend my frickin' weekends watching you fix busted race cars. What more could a girl ask for?"

"Geez, Julie, there's a lot more to it than that."

"Oh. Yeah. I forgot about listening to you *talk* about cars while you're drinking beer with all your car crazy buddies."

The bare fact is that there are people whose eyes light up when you mention winding roads, Weber carburetors or Watkins Glen and people who couldn't care less, and if you're a member of that first group you sometimes tend to forget that the second group even exists. Or that it's maybe slightly bigger than the Weber carburetor/Watkins Glen crowd. Unless of course it's somebody you're around all the time-like fr'instance somebody you're engaged to-who makes a real point of reminding you about it. Constantly, in fact.

There was also the little problem of finding a co-driver for Big Ed. Of course the perfect choice would have been Cal Carrington. But he'd already made a deal with Carson Flegley to co-drive the TD, and I was hesitant to dangle the carrot of a Jaguar drive in front of him when he'd already agreed to drive with my second-best customer. Especially since I knew he'd want to snap it up in an instant. But I did talk to him about it, on account of I wanted to be a fair, honest and open kind of guy.

I wonder how long it takes you to grow out of that stuff?

"Oh, *PLEASE!*" Cal groaned. "Get me out of the thing with Carson so I can drive Big Ed's Jag. Oh, sweet Jesus *PUH-LEEZE!*"

"You can't do it." I told him. "It's not right."

"Who *cares??!!* This is the Goddam opportunity of a lifetime!"

"No, it's not. If Big Ed spends any time behind the wheel, odds are you won't even finish. I think you've got a better shot with Carson. Honest I do."

"But it's a damn *Jaguar,* Buddy..." If a man can salivate from the eyes, Cal was doing it. "I've never even *driven* one before...."

I shook my head. "Listen, Cal, there's lots of stuff at stake here. And not just for you. You'll get your shot in Big Ed's car. I promise I'll find a way."

"You will?"

I was frankly amazed how certain I was. "This just isn't the right time, Cal. And besides, you already accepted the deal with Carson. Believe me, he's put a lot of good stuff in that car."

"He has?"

I told him about all the fancy hopup parts I'd tucked under the TD's hood, and no question Cal's eyes brightened up considerably. "Besides," I added, "you've gotta honor your commitment, don't you?"

"I do?"

"I've heard that's the way it's done among civilized people."

"That's the way it always is," Cal groused. "There's always some sneaky, back-handed catch to all that damn 'civilization' stuff."

With Cal off the short list and Tommy Edwards back over in England someplace and all the other reliable hotshoes either unavailable or already committed or unwilling to partner up with Big Ed, I had a real hard time figuring out who to recommend. And then it dawned on me. Sammy Speed.

"But he's a friggin' oval track racer!" Big Ed snorted. "And he don't know nothin' about Jaguars."

I told him I reckoned Sammy could figure it out. "Look how good he did in Mexico with a blessed *Nash!*"

"Well, yeeeeaaah," Big Ed said, pulling the word out like taffy while he rolled the idea around in his mind.

"He'll do great!" I assured him. "I'm just sure of it." Then I shot Big Ed a little weasel look. "And you can bet the S.C.M.A. guys will be pissed as hell if you bring him." Like I explained, the S.C.M.A. didn't much like either pro drivers or American oval track types.

"Yeah, they will," he mused. "Won't they?"

"Bank on it."

"You know where to find him?"

"I think I can figure it out."

"Well," Big Ed grinned, firing up the second half of his latest cigar, "give the S.O.B. a call. Lessee if this guy can turn both ways."

It took a little doing and a whole morning on the phone, but I finally managed to locate Spud Webster down in Fort Worth and he managed to put me in touch with Sammy up in Indianapolis, where he was making the rounds of all the local race shops and car owners' offices (and believe me, there are a bunch of them in Indianapolis) trying to line up a quality ride for the 500 on Memorial day. Preferably in one of those new Kurtis roadsters. But it wasn't going all that great and there was also a late winter blizzard going on in the Midwest, all of which made for pretty tough sledding for a driver who only had talent and desire to sell and hadn't really made a huge name for himself. At least not yet. Plus he had a terrible cold and maybe even a little fever on account of he only had a few bucks in his pocket and had to walk or take the bus from one race shop, garage, or office to the next.

Sammy'd never even heard of Sebring, but I explained as how this was the first year it was running as a *bona fide* F.I.A. international event and a lot of the heavy hitter teams from Europe might be there.

"Yeah?" he said, his teeth chattering against the receiver (I think he was in an outdoor phone booth). "Is the car any good?"

"It's a Jaguar 120 Super Sports, Sammy. I just finished going over it, and I think it's pretty damn good as far as XK-120s go."

"What kind of chance does it have to win?"

"None, really," I told him. "But it might do well in its class if you drive like I think you can and Big Ed doesn't screw things up too much."

"Class win, huh. What's that pay?"

I had to admit I didn't know. "But I'm pretty sure I can get Big Ed to pay you something just to come down and drive."

"Oh yeah? How much?"

"Oh, say…" I really had no idea, you know? "…a hundred bucks?"

"A hundred bucks to do a sportycar race in Florida?" I heard him start to haul back for a sneeze on the other end of the line.

"Yeah. Sure. Why not?"

"I'll…be…*there!*" he gasped, and sneezed so hard into the mouthpiece I was surprised I didn't get an earful of snot.

The plan we worked out was that Sammy and Spud would meet up with us at this hotel called The Harder Hall that Big Ed's travel agent had found in Sebring, and I reckoned that having Spud along would take care of most of my pit crew problems. Far as I could see, there wasn't much of anything that he and I and the two spare drivers shouldn't be able to handle. But that still left the little problem of getting Big Ed's Jag and Carson Flegley's MG and all the tools and jacks and spare tires and extra parts and stuff down to the middle of Florida. But Big Ed came up with a solution. "Why don'cha just use one a'my trucks?"

I had a few misgivings about that, since Big Ed's trucks were either open top haulers like you'd use for gravel or dump trucks, and those had all hauled some pretty nasty stuff over some pretty nasty terrain over the years and looked, smelled, and ran accordingly.

"Nah," Big Ed told me, "I got a brand new one on order that'll be in the week before the race. A genuine virgin without a mark on it. Maybe you guys can break it in for me."

And that's how Cal, me, and Carson Flegley wound up driving down to Florida in a strange-looking caravan made up of a freshly rebuilt, creamy white XK-120 Jaguar, a shiny black MG TD with a somewhat fussy but satisfyingly crisp-sounding motor, and a brand new, hot-off-the-assembly-line Mack dump truck painted deep maroon with *Baumstein Trash Packers* lettered on the doors in fancy gold script and a heavy duty flatbed trailer stout enough for earth-moving equipment hitched on behind. Since both the TD and the Jag had fresh engines that could certainly use a little break-in mileage, I figured we'd lash one of 'em to the trailer and drive the other one for the first half of the trip, then switch 'em around somewhere-say maybe Richmond or so-and having three able-bodied drivers and only two vehicles figured to mean that somebody could always be catching a little shuteye. That way we could round-robin the driving and try to make it straight through. Or that was the plan, anyway.

My best guess was that we should leave right around the crack of dawn on Thursday, March 5th, and that it would take us roughly thirty-six hours to cover the 1200-odd miles from Passaic, New Jersey, to Sebring, Florida, which, even with stops for food and fuel and maybe even a few hours of shuteye, figured to get us down there in plenty of time to register, get our pit and paddock spots squared away, and be ready for first practice bright and early Saturday morning. Of course, I'd never seen any of the roads we'd have to travel or knew which route we should take or anything, but I'd looked at a map once or twice and Carson even called the local AAA auto club and got a bunch of these nifty "Trip Tik" route cards they'd make up just for the asking so long as you were a member. We figured to need 'em, too, since Carson had no idea where we were going even with his fancy route cards and Cal had always either flown or ridden in the back with his sister when his folks went down to Palm Beach (at least until they stopped taking him, anyway) and so he wasn't much use, either. But they were both still better off than me. Outside of that recent trip to Mexico, I'd never been any further south than the south end of the boardwalk in Atlantic City.

As is typical the first time you try to organize one of these deals (or, to be more accurate, most *any* time you try to organize one of these deals) everything started going straight to shit before we even left Passaic. Carson and his AAA route cards showed up right on time, of course, and he immediately drove me over to the Mack garage in Hoboken to pick up Big Ed's new truck. I'd wanted to pick it up the day before, but it seems the sign painter had misspelled "Baumstein" on the doors and so had to re-do it and they wouldn't let us touch it until the paint had dried overnight. Then they couldn't find the damn keys and papers and sat us in this dreary little truck dealership lunch room with a pot of bitter coffee, a plate of stale, day-old doughnuts and a copy of the *New York Times* for company while they tried to round everything up. "Jesus, did you see *this?*" Carson gasped, pushing me the front page of the *Times*. "Uncle Joe Stalin had a stroke yesterday."

"A what?"

"You know, a brain hemorrhage." Being in the funeral parlor business gave Carson a little professional familiarity with that kind of stuff, although not so much as a medical doctor or anything. He read on a little while I looked in over his shoulder. "It says here he's 'gravely ill,'" Carson said with an insider nod. "That's what they usually say when it's, you know, *about that time....*"

"Hmm. Wonder who's gonna take over?"

"They got a couple different names here. Malenkov. Beria."

I'd never heard of any of them, but I was pretty sure a spirited debate on the subject was taking place that very moment up and down that second floor hallway where my sister Mary Frances lived in Greenwich Village.

In other news, that loose cannon Senator Joe McCarthy was grilling some poor bastard from "Voice of America" in front of the TV cameras and Sabre Jets were battling MiGs over North Korea and Martin and Lewis had a new movie out. I can only take so much of the front page before I flip over to the funnies, sports, or the movie section. And I bet I'm not the only one.

They finally came up with the keys and papers (they were right over the sun visor!) and it was almost ten by the time we hustled ourselves back to the Sinclair. Then there was the little problem of trying to pack all the shop gear and spare parts and such inside. Dump trucks are not exactly designed to haul anything but loads of scrap, waste, and trash, and that stuff generally seeks its own level and tends to stay put thanks to a consistency like furniture stuffing and sheep shit with the occasional brick, anvil, or phone pole thrown in. But racing spares and shop equipment are a decidedly different deal, since you really don't want them crashing and banging all over the place trying to seek their own level every time you go over a bump or drop a wheel in a pothole. Not hardly. Plus there was so damn much room in the back-squeaky clean, but vast and dark, too-that I was tempted to turn the Sinclair inside out and take everything but the blessed hydraulic lift along with. I mean, I'd already learned that all-important racing lesson at Westbridge:

If you take it with, you most likely won't need it.
But if you leave it behind, you are sure to need it desperately.

Then Cal called and said his folks were coming back while we were going to be away and he couldn't exactly have the Packard missing in action when they arrived. Oh, *great!* So Carson had to shoot over and pick him up while I loaded up all the tool boxes and crates of spare parts and cases of 40-weight Castrol (like they didn't have any motor oil in the whole blessed state of Florida, right?)

as best I could and tried to put Big Ed's XK-120 on the trailer all by myself. This turned out to be a lot tougher than I thought, seeing as how I'd never done that sort of thing before and didn't realize it was not especially brilliant to try and load an automobile onto a trailer before the trailer is hitched to the tow vehicle, on account of if you do, the trailer tries to shoot out from under the car like seeds out of an overripe grape. Apparently I was going for honorable mention as shop doofus that morning and solved the problem by wrestling the tongue of the trailer over against the outside wall so it couldn't move. And how I ever figured to turn it around again with a 2800 lb. Jaguar lashed on top was beyond me. Although I must admit it never even occurred to me until I had it tied down....

About then Cal and Carson showed up-it was almost noon, and already I was feeling this slow, agonizing itch of desperation about getting down to Florida on time-and helped me load up the heavier stuff like the oxygen and acelylene welding bottles into Big Ed's new dump truck. Then the three of us attempted to get hernias in unison trying to turn that damn trailer around and get it hitched up with the Jag still on it. And of course that's when the nose wheel on the trailer got levered over at a bad angle and more or less collapsed, the whole thing smashing hard into the pavement and damn near amputating a few sets of toes. Which, if you think about it, would've made a nice package deal with the hernias in the emergency room. By now I'd arrived at the conclusion that we really needed to take the Jag back off the trailer before hitching it up to the dump truck, but of course now the whole thing looked like the aftermath of a plane crash, what with the the trailer nose-down into the concrete and several inches of daylight showing under the rear wheels. To be honest, I'd have to say I didn't understand very much at the time about trailer towing and tongue weight.

Anyhow, there was nothing for it but to get our very biggest floor jack out of the shop and crank the nose of the trailer back up in the air, and I almost convinced myself we could maybe move it around like that and hitch up. But the pavement was real uneven where the slabs came together and we damn near dropped it again, so we finally piled a bunch of cinderblocks underneath, undid all the ropes and chains and turnbuckles, pulled the ramps out, and unloaded the Jag. And that's precisely when Mrs. Muccianti's Pontiac pulled in with a short in the horn button wiring that made it go off all the time like a dive alarm on a Submarine. It was not the sort of sound a professional car mechanic could ignore. So I went looking for the short-it was hidden down inside the damn steering column, wouldn't you know?-while Cal and Carson and the floor jack wrestled the gimpy trailer over and tried to hitch it up to the back of the truck. But they weren't having much luck, and it wasn't until after I came over to show them how it was done (and also failed) that Butch rolled out of the shop and casually observed as how the ball on the hitch was the wrong size for the cup on the trailer. It took him a little while to explain on account of he was laughing so hard. So Cal and I took an emergency run over to a trailer place in Big Ed's Jag to get the right size hitch ball, and of course Cal got stopped for speeding not more than a block away from the shop. It was a good thing, too, since Cal was still accelerating full throttle when the gumball lights came on and if the cop had been just another block further on we probably would've gone to jail. Naturally the cop wanted to know just who we thought we were and whose car it was and blah, blah, blah, and he didn't show much in the way of sympathy when we tried to explain what a monstrous hurry we were in to get to Florida. Especially since we were heading north when he pulled us over.

In the end he didn't believe us, and wound up calling Big Ed from the phone at the Sinclair after he'd looked over the title and registration. I guess he figured we were nothing but a couple gas station kids out for a joyride in a customer's car. Can you imagine? He spent a long time on the phone with Big Ed, and I remember looking at the clock and seeing it was already 2:45 and feeling very desperate indeed about just how the hell we were going to get to Sebring on time. Big Ed was in a hurry himself since his flight to Havana was scheduled to depart later that afternoon, but he made a few calls and managed to diffuse Cal's speeding ticket thanks to his finger-in-the-pie downtown connections. The cop didn't look real happy about not running us in. "You just better watch it, buddy," he growled at Cal as he gathered up his paperwork, "I've got my eye on you."

"He's Buddy," Cal corrected him, like he was trying to be helpful.

Some day that guy was going to get us in *serious* trouble.

And most likely soon.

It was getting on towards rush hour by the time we finally got the hitch ball mess straightened out and the Jag back up on the trailer and ready to roll, and of course that's when Cal decided he was hungry. *"Jesus, Cal, we gotta hit th'damn road!"* I almost whimpered.

"Five minutes won't make any difference," he told me. "I'll just get something to go from the place across the street, that's all."

"Dammit, Cal!" I heard myself scream. You can really get impatient when it's already disastrously late and you're trying to get on the road and then some smart aleck rich kid has the nerve to want to eat.

"Hey, take it easy, huh? I haven't eaten anything all day."

And that's about when I realized that I hadn't either (at least if you didn't count the bitter coffee and petrified doughnut I helped myself to at the Mack

Truck dealership that morning). There was nothing to do but give in. "Okay," I sighed. "And get something for me, too, willya? And coffee. In fact, make that *two* coffees, okay?"

"Sure thing," Cal grinned. And then came the inevitable: "You got any money on you?" Cal had apparently run through the flash flood cash influx he was enjoying when I fired him. Or maybe it was just force of habit. When you were around Cal Carrington, all ready cash was considered fair game for anything Cal decided the group needed to do, eat, drink, or buy, regardless of whose pockets it arrived in. Why, he was damn near a communist that way.

Wouldn't you know it, they were putting together a big catering deal for a local bowling league at the sandwich shop across the street, and it took them almost twenty minutes to come up with a hamburger, a cheeseburger, and an oliveburger deluxe plus a couple orders of fries and three coffees, and it was damn near five o'clock and coming on dusk by the time we finally hit the road. Which put us right into the teeth of the great commuter exodus from Manhattan when we linked up with US1 southbound at the Newark airport.

If you like, you can follow US1 all the way from the heart of New York City to the tip of the Florida Keys, and some folks might think it would be the best way to go since it's well marked and well traveled. But I knew it would be choked with car and truck traffic that slowed and sped up and slowed again like a giant accordion the entire fifty-odd miles from Newark to Trenton. And that was just the first fifty miles. Plus Carson's hot-rodded MG didn't much like traffic, alternately fluffing up the plugs or running on the brink of the red zone whenever we got stuck in a sea of taillights. So we took the New Jersey Turnpike south out of Elizabeth-all four beautiful lanes of it-and did a nice end run on all the stop-and-go congestion in Trenton and Philadelphia. It was the long way mileage wise, but, like so many other things in life, the long way often turns out to be the short way.

I was meanwhile discovering that Big Ed's new dump truck was not the easiest thing in the world to drive. With all the shop gear packed inside and Big Ed's Jag hitched behind, it had about the same accelerative capacity as Butch's wheelchair. Only not quite so quick off the line. And it didn't really have much in the way of a boulevard ride, either, so Cal and I both got a lap full of hot coffee over every bump from the Sinclair's driveway to the city limits. By which time our cups were pretty much empty. To be honest about it, Big Ed's dump truck was a lousy support vehicle. But then it was never really designed or geared for highway travel, and it took maybe a half hour for your eyeballs to stop jiggling whenever you got out from behind the wheel. Plus there was no way to fasten all the stuff down in back, so all the jacks and tools and spare tires and gas cans and umbrellas and tarps and folding chairs and God-only-knows what else tended to jiggle and shift and bang and clunk around back there like a big, noisy pile of junk.

But it wasn't so bad on the turnpike, which was smooth and swift and not bad at all once traffic lightened up after about 6:30. I even got to where I could cruise at damn near a mile a minute so long as I kept a death grip on the wheel and resisted the temptation to react to every little twitch and sashay I saw the trailer do in the side mirror. Not that I could feel it much in the seat of my pants or anything, since that Jaguar/trailer combination was like a little tin dinghy tied to the stern of the Titanic. Still, I figured it was maybe a good time to back off whenever I got a good view of the Jag's profile. Which of course only made things worse. In fact, it wasn't until Cal took over that we realized you had to put your foot *into* the gas rather than lifting off (or, worse yet, going for the brakes) when you needed to straighten things out and whip that trailer back in line. And that was just one of the many ass-backwards lessons we all had to learn about hauling a trailer.

Backing up doesn't even bear mentioning here....

Anyhow, we crossed the Delaware River on the big toll bridge just south of Wilmington about 10:30, and it was quite a sight, even at night. But then it was back to two-lane highway on Route 40 as we headed on towards Baltimore to rejoin US1. And right about then is when we got shagged by the police for the second time that day-something about no lights on the trailer-and I quickly realized that there was no blessed wiring connection on the back of the dump truck. I mean, who tows with a dump truck, right? By that point I was pretty cold and tired and miserable and so I started to plead with the cop to let it slide on account of we just *had* to be at this big, international car race in the middle of Florida in another thirty hours. But he said he couldn't (you know how cops are-especially when they see that you're on the defensive and getting all whimpery about it) so I had to face the prospect of opening up the blessed tail lights on the truck and running jump wires all the way back to the lights on the trailer. It wasn't really that tough a job, but the tools and wire and everything were buried someplace in the deep, hollow darkness inside that damn dump truck. Not to mention it was pitch black dark and the one flashlight we had outside the tool box was a faithful old olive drab Boy Scout model Carson kept in the door pocket of his MG. But when he flicked it on, all we got was that pathetic, golden-yellow glow that indicates you should have replaced the batteries a month or two ago.

Right on cue it started raining.

Well, I knew the cop didn't like standing there in the rain any better than we did, so I tried again. "Say, lissen," I pleaded. "How'bout if I just turn on the Jag's taillights, huh?"

"Yeah," Carson chimed in, "and I *promise* I'll run right behind him in the other car so people can see my brake lights and turn signals."

It started to rain harder then. You could feel it.

"And I *promise* I'll fix it once we find a place to stop...."

"Aww..." The cop said, sounding a little disgusted. Geez, it was *really* pelting down. "...Aww, all right," he finally grumbled. Then added, "But you be sure to get it fixed!" as he beat a hasty retreat to his squad car.

Cal and Carson and I stood there by the side of the road with the rain coming down in buckets as the rising and falling glare of the headlights passed by us on US1. "So," Cal asked with a perfectly straight face, "who forgot to bring the picnic lunch?"

I think that first night on the road to Sebring had to be the longest night of my entire life. With all the delays and stuff it was well past midnight by the time we reached the outskirts of Baltimore, and naturally we missed a turn someplace and got lost trying to find the junction with US1 in the middle of town. It's amazing how simple it looks on the damn map, you know? But we made excellent road time over the next stretch from Baltimore to Washington on account of it was four lanes again and there was hardly any traffic at that time of night. In fact, Carson was having to drive a little bit quicker than he wanted just to keep up with Cal in the dump truck. Naturally I couldn't get much in the way of sleep because Cal was buzzing that blessed truck up to seventy or more on the straight stretches-and believe me, that was all it had!-and between the bouncing and the tortured drone off the engine and worrying about cops or the damn trailer jack-knifing I didn't dare close my eyes. Or even blink. But that was okay, since now there was no alternative to flat-footing it all the way to Florida with only gas and pee stops along the way if we were going to have any chance at all of making it. There was no radio in the truck-not that we could've pulled in much but some fuzzy, all-night gospel preaching on local stations-so I amused myself doing drawn out, soulful renditions of *"Do Not Forsake Me Oh My Darlin'"* from *High Noon* and Hank Williams' *"Your Cheatin' Heart"*. That last one always made my guts quiver because it reminded me of that cheap, scummy night with Sally Enderle up at Elkhart Lake. And it was even sadder since I'd heard that Hank Williams cashed his final chips in a few months before. But the worst part was I could never remember all the words, so I'd wind up singing the same blessed line or two over and over and over again, just varying the pitch or fade or adding a little vibrato (or what I thought was vibrato, anyway) to enhance the feeling. Probably the only thing that kept Cal from strangling me is that the engine was so blessed loud he couldn't hear much of it except when I was in full crescendo mode. At least the rain had slacked off and you could even see the glimmer of a couple stars if you squinted your eyes just right. Or maybe that was just glare from the passing headlights. It gets hard to tell when you've been on the road a long time in the middle of the night.

We needed to find a gas station since there didn't figure to be any open on the 105-mile run from Washington down to Richmond, and this time a cop actually helped us out. I saw his squad car parked in front of one of those cheesy little all night diners made out of a railway car, and I had Cal swing the rig around so we could stop and go inside. It was a good time for a men's room break and another refill on coffee anyway.

"Well," the cop said, "if y'go down here to Florida Street and angle left-not the *hard* left but the *angle* left-and then go down about…oh, hell, wait'll I finish my pie and you can follow me." That was mighty nice of him, you know? But then he probably recognized the dazed, road-weary look in our eyes and figured we'd never find it by ourselves. See, the city of Washington, D.C., is kind of tough to find your way around on account of it's got all these straight streets and angle streets and traffic circles and stuff that are supposed to make perfect symmetrical sense but really don't at all unless you live there. Cal said it was a lot like what goes on in Congress.

Anyhow, Carson and Cal followed the cop down about three straight streets and two angled streets to a Standard Oil station that was open all night, and we figured this would be a good time to swap the driving around a little. Cal said he was fine and I knew he was, and that of course meant Carson said he felt fine, too. But he looked pretty beat-especially his eyes-and I very diplomatically suggested that we really needed him to bat cleanup when we got a little further south and both of us were tired. I knew Cal would've rather driven the MG-hell, who wouldn't?-but he also knew we'd make better time with him in the truck. So I settled in for a stint in the MG, and, after riding in the dump truck, that hot-rodded TD felt almost luxurious by comparison.

Naturally we got lost trying to find our way back to US1, and would've spent half the night going straight up the angled streets and angling down the straight streets if we hadn't passed that same cop again (while we were traveling, I might add, the wrong way on a one-way street) and he not only let us off but

211

once again led us through the maze and back on our way. "Say, thanks a bunch," I yelled over, giving him a big thumbs-up as we tooled onto US1 at Rhode Island Avenue.

"Have fun in Florida," he called back. It sounded like he wanted to go, too.

Even after we found the highway again it was tough getting out of Washington, what with all the damn squares and malls and traffic circles and stuff, but it was neat because it was the middle of the night and there was nobody but us and the cops and the street sweepers out-it was still too early for the milk men and newspaper trucks-and you wouldn't believe how they keep everything lit up at night. We passed by the Washington Monument and the Jefferson Memorial before crossing over into Virginia, and I'd have to say Washington DC was the most beautiful city I'd ever seen. It made me feel kind of small and proud and hollow inside-like a kid in church-looking at all those famous buildings and memorials I'd only ever seen in school books.

It was coming on three by the time we crossed the Potomac River into Virginia, and that's when it dawned on me that we were now guests of the Confederacy. In fact, the land we were traveling through was where a lot of the Civil War was fought, and though we never think about that too much up in Passaic, they think about it all the time down there. In fact, it's pretty much the local religion. It was hard to believe that you could drive down US1 from the Union capital in Washington right to the old Confederate capital in Richmond in less than three hours. They were that close. It was a good road, too-four lanes all the way-and I was really enjoying Carson's MG. Especially the way it had a little snap when you put your foot down, even in top gear. An engine builder could feel pretty damn proud of a job like that.

It seemed like we'd been on the road just about forever, and I had to admit I was getting pretty tired. Time does funny things when you're alone on the highway in the wee hours of the morning, and it can get to where every mile seems to take absolutely *forever* to roll through the odometer. You catch yourself starting to nod off and jerk yourself awake only to find you've only gone another three-tenths of a mile since the last time it happened. So I tried keeping myself awake by biting my lip and pinching my cheek and running through my entire repertoire of old Southern favorites, which basically amounted to two verses of *"Dixie,"* a chorus and a half of *"In the Evening by the Moonlight,"* a few choice bars of *"Swing Low, Sweet Chariot,"* and to the end of the first run of "doo-dahs" in *"Camptown Races."*

Then I'd start over again.

But finally the sky started getting light to my left-from pitch black to shadowy purple to flat, eerie gray-and it always gives you a shot in the arm when you see those first rays of sunlight venturing up over the horizon. We stopped at a little roadside gas station/café in Petersburg just as dawn was breaking, and inside we found a couple local farmers fueling up for a day in the fields and conjecturing about how the crops were going to go in and what was likely to happen "over there in Roosha" now that old Uncle Joe Stalin had finally kicked the bucket. I guess that was big news everywhere that day, but it still sounded strange-to my ears, anyway-to hear those guys jawing about world affairs in just-fell-off-the-turnip-truck southern drawls. But then I'd never been anywhere south before, and I suppose you really need to *go* someplace-to look and listen in person, you know?-before the locals turn into anything more than colorful extras in some movie you've never seen.

Cal and Carson and me were feeling pretty done in after driving all night and decided to treat ourselves to a little sit-down breakfast. Hell, twenty minutes wasn't going to make any damn difference. So we ordered eggs and biscuits and sausage, and when the plates came I wanted to know what the little pool of white stuff that looked like Cream of Wheat was between my eggs and sausage links. "Them are grits," the guy behind the counter explained.

"Grits? What are grits?"

The short order cook looked at me like I'd just arrived from outer space. "They made outta hominy," he said, as if everybody and his brother knew what the hell 'hominy' was. But they tasted okay if you doctored 'em up with a little butter, salt and sugar like he said. Better than okay, in fact.

I'd always figured we'd take US1 the rest of the way to Florida, but Carson had been thumbing through those route cards of his and explained as how we could lop off a few miles and miss going through Raleigh and Columbia by taking 301 south through the Carolinas, picking up US15 where it crossed the bridge over Lake Marion at Santee, continuing on 15 down to Walterboro, switching over to Alternate 17 and following that until it linked up with regular 17 just outside Pocotaligo, which would take us into Savannah. I was a little leery about it, since US1 looked like a safe, sure bet all the way, and, seeing as how we'd already gotten ourselves lost a couple times, I wasn't sure I wanted to go messing around with any "Alternate" highway routes or towns I'd never heard of with names like Santee and Pocotaligo. "Well, whadda *you* think?" I asked Cal.

"He thinks it'll be quicker and take some miles off," Cal shrugged. "What the hell, let's give it a shot." Race or not, we were all so blessed exhausted we didn't much care. It was also time to swap drivers around again, but, to tell the truth, I was a little nervous about putting Carson at the helm of the dump truck with Big Ed's Jaguar on the back. Not to mention that it figured to about halve our average speed. "Hey, I'm not tired at all," Cal grinned. And, for that one instant, he almost looked like he meant it. So Carson got back into his MG and I climbed up into the passenger side of the dump truck next to Cal.

"You really think we're doing the right thing getting off US1?" I asked.

"Who knows?" Cal answered. "But I sure as hell wouldn't worry about it."

"Jesus, you don't worry about *anything!*" I snapped angrily.

"Well, you worry about *everything!*" Cal snarled right back at me.

Truth is, your nerves can get a tad raw after twenty-four hours without sleep. And especially when you figure you've got another twenty-four to go.

We pulled away without another word and drove in stony silence for the next few miles, but then the first rays of sun broke over the clouds and slanted in through the side window so we could feel them all warm and golden-orange on our skin. "Hey, listen," Cal offered through an exhausted smile, "let's just take it a little easy and enjoy this beautiful day, okay?"

"Suits me," I mumbled.

"And don't be so glum, huh?"

"I got lots to be glum about," I reminded him.

"Nah, you don't," Cal grinned, gunning the engine. "Trust me, Buddy, it's all downhill from here...."

And that got me thinking. "Say," I asked. "What exactly does that mean?"

"What does what mean?"

"You know. What you just said. *'It's all downhill from here?'*"

Cal registered a blank look.

"See," I tried to explain, "it could mean that everything's going to get much easier from here on in, or it could mean just the opposite, that everything's going straight to hell."

"Well then," Cal beamed, "I'd be right either way, wouldn't I?"

It was all two-lane stuff after breakfast, which meant slow going whenever we'd get stuck behind a delivery truck or a rubbernecking family of tourists, and I still couldn't sleep what with all the noise and rocking and bouncing. But I could kind of loll my head over against the seatback with my eyeballs slid over sideways to enjoy the passing scenery while I repeated the title line of Rosemary Clooney's *"Come On a'My House"* a few hundred dozen times. It was real pretty country-all low, rolling hills covered with meadows and farms and hardwood forests as we headed south through the towns of Stony Creek, Jarratt,

Emporia, and Skippers, then on into the tobacco plantation country of North Carolina at Pleasant Hill.

Only it wasn't so pleasant when Cal overheated the brakes trying to play Boy Racer on the way south from Rocky Mount-floorboarding it on every empty stretch and then braking hard for curves and towns and such-and you couldn't miss the odor of singed brake linings in the cab. But I didn't say anything, seeing as how it was the only way were going to make Sebring in time. Or at least I didn't say anything until I noticed we were gaining speed quite impressively on this slightly downhill stretch even though Cal was pumping hell out of the brakes. He might as well have been knocking on the door to an empty house. "Oh, *SHIT!*" he said through clenched teeth. You could see there was a pretty serious look in his eye.

Gravity being how it is, we were nudging towards eighty about then. Not that you could really tell, since the Mack's speedo ran out of numbers at 70 and the needle was just kind of quivering there at the end of the dial like it was ready to fall out onto the dash. There was a fog of brake dust inside the cab and the engine sound resonating through the firewall reminded me of a cement mixer full of ball bearings-neither of which, I'm sure, were recommended break-in procedures according to the Mack Truck owner's manual.

At least the road was fairly straight.

But it was downhill. *Steep* downhill, in fact.

And of course that's when our *third* set of flashing red lights appeared in the rear view mirror. "Oh, shit," I groaned. "You probably better pull over."

"That's easy for you to say," Cal grimaced, pumping even harder on the brake pedal. But he'd obviously boiled the fluid, and, seeing as how gas compresses while a fluid does not, he was pretty much stepping on a balloon. I guess the cop thought we were maybe trying to make a run for it, so he put his siren on, too. Just to show us he was serious. Jesus, were we ever gonna catch hell. *"Stop using the brakes for a minute!"* I yelled at Cal, rightly figuring they needed to cool off a little. There certainly must have been a nice, healthy breeze down there to do the job. Meanwhile the trooper swung out into the oncoming traffic lane, pulled alongside, and motioned for us to pull over. Cal did his best mouthing the words and using sign language to explain as how we didn't have any brakes, and I'm sure the officer appreciated the part where Cal took both hands off the wheel to give him the old palms-up New Jersey shrug. And that's precisely when another truck-this time one of your over-the-road, semi tractor varieties-appeared over the next rise heading in our direction. Given his fifty or so miles-per-hour and the eighty give-or-take-a-few we were doing, the distance between us was closing rapidly. *"Jesus, try the brakes again!"* I hollered. And naturally that's exactly what the cop tried to do, too. For a moment it was like a hellishly dangerous version of the old "You first. No, *you* first" vaudeville routine. But our brakes were still super hot, and the Mack only slowed a little before they faded again and the squad car was able to slot in behind-lights still flashing and siren still wailing-with a hundred yards to spare. Okay, maybe more like fifty. Meanwhile the truck coming the other way had thrown out all the anchors and you could see a stream of blue smoke pouring off the rear tires. I swear, I thought he was for sure going into one of those awful tank-slapper deals that get worse and worse with every pendulum swing and wind up with the trailer jack-knifing across the road and chopping off the oncoming traffic at about door handle level. Unless of course that oncoming traffic happens to be a runaway dump truck full of auto shop equipment with an XK-120 Jaguar hitched on behind, in which case you have a wreck large enough to set off the earthquake sensors at every geological laboratory on the eastern seaboard. But the semi driver knew his stuff and put his foot back into the gas as soon as he saw the opening, and he had it about two-thirds under control as he flew past us, steering like mad. But he did take just the flash of an instant to look over as he went by, and I do not believe I will ever forget the mixture of rage, fear, amazement, contempt, and sheer, utter disbelief boiling in his eyes.

Who could blame him?

About then the road passed through the bottom of the dip and started to climb again, and that of course started bleeding off the speed in a hurry. Why, we were even back on the speedometer again! Once we got down to about 40 Cal tried the brakes again and now there was actually some semblance of feel in the pedal (at least after about three pumps) and Cal managed to get us over to the side and stopped before we crested the next hill. Thank goodness.

As you can imagine, the State Trooper was not in particularly good humor when he asked us to "please get y'all down outta that truck now, heah?" in that drawled-out, fake-as-hell easygoing tone they use down south when they're getting ready to rip your liver out and eat it for lunch.

"It's the brakes...." I started to tell the cop, but he waved me off. He was a big, rotund bruiser of a guy with one large, soft roll hanging over his belt buckle and a smaller, matching roll overflowing the back of his shirt collar.

"Ah know all about y'all's brakes, son," he said, walking up and down in front of us like an angry school principal. "Ah didn't get borned yestidday. Ah saw them taillights flashin' off an' on." He looked at Cal. "Y'all musta been doin' quite a l'il dance there. Quite a l'il dance indeed."

Cal nodded, trying out a smile. "I was working up a sweat all right."

"Ah 'spect you were. Ah 'spect you were." He cocked his head and looked into Cal's eyes. "Y'all surely wouldn't a'been goin' any over the speed limit before them brakes failed, now would y'all?"

"Oh, no sir." Cal assured him.

"Hmmm," the cop said, not sounding one tiny bit convinced. "An' tell me now, jist where is it y'all boys're goin' in such a great, all-fired hurry this fahn mawnin,' hmm?"

So we started telling him about the race in Florida and all our adventures along the way and especially about that nice cop who helped us out in Washington, D.C., and that's about when Carson came tooling over the hill doing a giddy mile a minute or so in the black TD. It looked to me like the cop had never seen an MG before. "What th'hail *is* that thang?" he chuckled as Carson pulled up beside us. "Y'all steal that l'il doodlebug off one a'Santa's elves?"

"It's an MG," I explained.

"MG, huh? Whassit staynd for?"

"Morris Garages," Carson said proudly in his little pipsqueak voice.

"Morris Garages, huh?" the cop repeated, starting to laugh. "That's one hell of a sweet name now, iddn' it?"

"That's where they come from," Carson said sheepishly. "It's in England." Then added: "They're not very fast."

The trooper looked at Cal and me. "Ah 'spect not. But whut's that other 'un y'all got taggin' on behind?"

"It's a Jaguar XK-120," I told him. "And it *is* fast."

"Oh really?"

"You bet."

"Would you like to take a little spin?" Cal asked. Boy, I thought we were in for it. But the cop looked pretty interested. "I mean," Cal looked at me, "we were planning to swap the cars around anyway, weren't we?"

So Cal chatted up the cop as only he could while Carson and me unloaded the Jag, unsnapped the tonneau, and wiped it down a little to get the dust and rain streaks off. We had to jump the battery, of course, but then Cal and the trooper took off-can you believe it?-and we had the truck's brakes bled and the MG loaded up and ready to go before they got back. In fact, I was starting to worry a little about Big Ed's car (not to mention ever getting to Sebring on time) when they finally showed up again, coming over the hill behind us at a hundred or so with that oversized Carolina State Trooper behind the wheel. I swear, he was grinning from ear to ear.

"That's one hell of a car y'all got there," he said as he waved goodbye. "But y'all be careful with it heah in Nawth Cah'lanna, y'heah?"

Around noon we crossed the bridge over the Cape Fear River just outside Fayetteville and continued south on 301 through Roslin, Oakland, Lumberton, and Raynham before crossing into South Carolina at the little town of Hamer, which was easy to miss if you blinked at the wrong time. Then it was a long, pretty haul down 301 to 15 at Santee and on to 17A and 17 the rest of the way into Savannah, just like Carson's AAA route cards said. We didn't get lost once, can you believe it? Highway 17 kind of follows the Atlantic coastline and what they call the "intracoastal waterway system" down through South Carolina and Georgia, and right through the heart of grand, weary old southern towns like Ridgeland, Hardeeville, and especially Savannah. You really got the feeling people lived a different way of life down there, and also that it'd maybe been around longer, too. Everything looked somehow older and softer and slower and maybe even a little worn out, what with faded, sagging old mansions and rickety wood-and-tarpaper shacks where the "po' folks" lived kind of sprouting out of the loamy soil around them like mushrooms. In the yards were heavy limbed trees draped in shrouds of moss that reminded me of ghosts and funeral veils and cobwebs. Or maybe it was just the light, since it was coming on towards dusk and everything had that shadowy, deep-orange glow it gets around that time of day.

Come nighttime we switched off driving again, me in the truck with Carson riding shotgun and Cal tooling along just ahead in the Jag-he'd driven every single mile except for that very first stint out of Passaic-and we'd been on the road about twenty-nine hours straight and had fallen into a nice, steady, thoroughly exhausted sort of rhythm where the time passed without much effort and another hundred miles didn't seem like anything at all. "We've got our long legs now," was the way Cal put it when we filled up, drank another cup of coffee, and peed out a half gallon more just outside Brunswick. I think that was the very first time since we'd left Passaic that I actually felt like we were going to make it. In fact, it gave me a little boost to realize we were almost to Florida, and I was doing a particularly tender and soul stirring rendition of Eddie Fisher's *"Oh! My Papa"* (over and over again, in fact) as we crossed over the state line a little before midnight.

By God, we were gonna make it after all!

But confidence always turns out to be the big traitor in these deals, and sure enough we ran into a plague of Florida jackrabbits on the short crossover to Highway 301 just north of Jacksonville. That's right: *jackrabbits*. We were going across this low, flat scrub country (which is really most all they have in

Florida once you get north of the palm trees and away from the beaches) and I swear, one after another those damn jackrabbits came cannonballing out of the darkness and bounded across the roadway right in front of us. Instinctively Cal would swerve to miss them and I'd instinctively try to follow him, but they were so blessed quick they'd be out of the line of fire by the time you got there and meanwhile I'd be steering up a damn storm trying to keep the truck and trailer out of the ditch. Cal figured it was some kind of kamikaze rabbit death squad trying to get even for all their buddies who'd already wound up as furry little grease smears on the asphalt, and no question they awarded each other points for every car or truck they sent slewing off the road sideways, along with bonus scores for rollovers and gasoline fires. Why, I could even *hear* the little bastards out there in the darkness, chuckling through their damn Bugs Bunny buck teeth about all the terrified tourist skid marks they'd left careening off the highway. But then I was pretty tired, you know?

Still, it was a nice, warm Florida night and we were running with the windows down, and as I slalomed my way through the rabbits and worked on a few choice choruses of *"I Been Workin' on the Railroad,"* I thought about how nice it was to be down here in Florida with my racing buddies when everybody back in Jersey was still wearing wool hats and mittens. And that's when I heard this horrible screech followed by a loud snapping noise and a heavy wobble coming up through the seat cushion. So I looked in the rearview and here was the damn trailer wagging all over the road like a downed high tension wire with sparks showering off where I was pretty sure a wheel had been just a little while before. I immediately flashed the lights to signal Cal we were in trouble and eased the rig to a halt about halfway off the road.

It was eerie out there in that flat, dark Florida scrubland in the middle of the night. There were all these strange, creepy chirps and grunts and slithery rustles coming out of the bushes. "They got any alligators up here?" I asked Cal as we surveyed the damage.

"Nah, we're too far north," he assured me. "Up here all they got is bats, rats, and water moccasins."

"Great."

The problem with the trailer looked pretty damn terminal. Apparently the wheel bearing had overheated from all the hours of high speed running and turned itself into sort of a molten glob of metal about two seconds before everything locked up solid and parted company from the trailer, including wheel, tire, lugnuts, hub, and about three inches of stub axle. "What are we gonna do now?" Carson wanted to know.

"Well," I told him, "I believe this trailer is pretty much parked where it is."

"Look," Cal said. "There's three of us. Why don't we just unload the MG, unhitch the trailer, and be on our merry way again?"

I shook my head. "I can't leave Big Ed's trailer just sitting out here in the middle of nowhere. Besides, we gotta get it fixed anyway in case we need it to haul one of the cars back to Passaic."

"Then we've gotta split up," Cal reasoned. "Two of us have to take the cars on to Sebring along with whatever we absolutely need out of the truck, and the other guy's got to run into Jacksonville and find somebody who can rescue the damn trailer, then continue on down by himself and meet us there."

I knew I didn't have to ask just who that person might be.

Well, it wasn't as bad as it might have been. I got Cal and Carson on the road with their helmets and race entry paperwork and a few carefully selected spares-not that they'd know what to do with them-and insisted that Cal let Carson drive the Jag as otherwise he'd get there about two hours ahead of the TD. Then I got the roller jack out, unhitched the wounded trailer, and headed into town. There weren't any signs of life-hell, it was four thirty in the damn morning!-but I eventually found a Greyhound station and, wouldn't you know, there was some guy out back in the shop working on a Scenicruiser bus with transmission problems. It was perfect! I mean, the guy was a fellow grease monkey first off, and, sure enough, he had a buddy in the towing business who had a rig big enough to handle semis and buses. No question that's what we were gonna need to pick that one-wheeled trailer up off the asphalt and haul it back to town.

We made a deal on the spot for one of Big Ed's twenty dollar bills, and I was off for Sebring again just about the time the sky was getting light. I swear, I was so damn tired that the palm trees all had faces like Julie's mom and Old Man Finzio and my Aunt Rosamarina-why, some of them even looked like giant St. Bernards! Fact is, it's a wonder I didn't get myself killed. But fortunately Florida is the tourist trap capital of the entire universe, and although there was no way I could stop at any of them, I was fascinated by all the signs for famous attractions like Circus City *("world's biggest sideshow")* and Mike Jackson's Reptile Farm *("500 Rattlesnakes! All bare handed!")* and Fruitland America (where you could buy and ship oranges or grapefruits anywhere in the whole blessed world and also be amazed by the world's largest ball of string *and* the world's biggest wad of tinfoil) not to mention *"Live Native Alligator Wrestling every half hour"* at Gator Land and *"Authentic Indian Handicrafts"* at the Seminole Village or *"Amazing Apes and Gigantic Gorillas"* in the Monkey Jungle and *"Secrets of the Sea"* at Aqua World and *"Parrot Mountain"* at Fascinating

Birdland and the glass bottomed boat rides at Silver Springs. I knew Julie would've really wanted to stop at that one on account of her friend Serafina Massucci went to Florida on her honeymoon and sent Julie a picture postcard from Silver Springs that said "having a *wonderful* time on our honeymoon in Florida" but really meant *"nyah-nyah nyah-nyah"* and this would be a great chance to get even. I made a mental note to stop there and at least get Julie a few postcards on the way back.

But of all the tourist traps and sucker attractions advertised on highway 301 (and later on US27 heading south from Ocala), none got my juices flowing like *The Atomic Tunnel.* Those guys really knew how it was done, no lie. It started way up around Highland, just outside of Jacksonville, where a billboard the size of a small apartment building read:

ATOMIC TUNNEL
100 MILES

That was all it said. In huge yellow block letters against a shiny black background. It sure got you wondering all right. And of course you came on another one just as big about forty minutes later that read:

ATOMIC TUNNEL
75 MILES

Only the second one had a little extra starburst tacked on top that read: *"DON'T MISS IT!"* As you can surely imagine, there was another sign at fifty miles. And then they started coming up every ten miles until the twenty-five mile mark. And then every five miles. And then every blessed mile of the last ten. Each one had a *"DON'T MISS IT!"* or *"YOU WON'T BELIEVE YOUR EYES!"* or *"THE POWER OF TOMORROW!"* starburst tacked on top, and not one of them said a single damn thing about what The Atomic Tunnel might be about or have hidden away inside.

Boy, was I ever dying to check it out, you know?

But there was no way since I was running way, *way* behind schedule and not making very good time on account of all the slow moving traffic down 301 and 27. Going my way it was mostly over-the-road semis hauling food and fuel and television sets and pre-fab furniture along with sedans and station wagons with license plates from Illinois and Michigan and New York and Ohio and Pennsylvania and Minnesota carrying numb-looking moms and dads and back seats full of noisy, sticky, bored, antsy kids who were surely in the midst of asking, pleading, begging, crying, screaming and outright demanding that their parents stop at that Atomic Tunnel. I knew just how they felt, too.

But the worst of it was the little old tanned retirees who'd taken their life savings, pension money, and social security south to live out their golden years in sunny Florida. You always knew when you were behind one, because their cars were always three or four years old but spotlessly clean-hey, they had plenty of time for washing and waxing, right?-and they'd be wheezing along at a giddy thirty-eight miles per hour with their nose jammed into the steering wheel and their bony knuckles clutching the rim in a death grip. In fact, sometimes that was all you could see. Just the knuckles. Or sometimes you'd also make out a tiny little bun of white hair-like a Q-tip, you know?-poking up over the seat back. In any case, it was tough getting stuck behind one (or, worse yet, getting stuck behind a row of trucks and out-of-state travel trailers stuck behind one) because they'd just motor merrily along like there was nobody else on the whole blessed planet and you took your life into your hands if you dared try to pass in something as heavy and sluggish as Big Ed's dump truck. The road was narrow and flat as an ironing board and the edges generally dropped off into a shallow ditch on either side, and there were *always* caravans of trucks loaded with oranges and grapefruits from the groves further south coming the other direction. And, if you got really impatient and decided to plant your foot to the floorboards and risk it anyway, they'd look up at you angrily from behind their bifocals, curse through their dentures, and shake a thin, bony fist out the window at you as you went by.

Chapter 10: Sammy Speed Goes Sportycar Racing

I finally arrived at Hendricks Field about three in the afternoon, and, just like always, the sound of racing engines echoing down the straightaways put a fresh shot of adrenaline in my system and woke me right up again. That's just the way it is when you've got a dose of the old racing disease. Truth is, Hendricks Field looked to be a pretty awful place to hold a motor race. It was just an old, worn out airport that seemed a hell of a lot bigger than it needed to be on account of the Army used it to train bomber crews and as a dropping off point for aircraft on their way over to Europe and the Pacific during the war. Then the war ended and left this huge, empty network of concrete runways with heat waves shimmering off them, dotted here and there with rusty metal hangar and barracks buildings and surrounded by narrow blacktop access roads running every which way around the perimeter. Along the flight apron on the far side, a junkyard chorus line of derelict B24's, B25's, DC3's, B17's, C46's and PBY's sat abandoned in various stages of neglect, cannibalization, and decay.

Sure, a few planes still taxied for takeoff and landed with a thump and a patter of tar strips, but they were mostly private jobs carrying orange grove owners and fruit fly inspectors and wide-eyed real estate developers. When the Army decommissioned Hendricks Field, they turned the keys over to the local Sebring Firefighters Association for safekeeping-hell, nobody really knew what to do with it-and it was nothing more than a huge, Godforsaken slab of concrete out in the middle of nowhere that nobody much wanted or needed. And that made it just about *perfect* for a sportycar race, seeing as how it had pavement and plenty of space and not much in the way of neighbors to get upset by the noise. Plus it was just southeast of the little town of Sebring, which sat around a big and rather pretty inland lake (at least if you didn't mind all sorts of slithery reptiles and bug swarms that could get downright opaque on towards evening) where entirely too many rooms were going unoccupied at the Kenilworth and Harder Hall hotels. Truth is, Sebring had seen better days as a tourist spot, and naturally there were sad stories that went along with the change.

Like the Harder Hall, for example, which was this huge, four-story apartment building done up in fading flamingo pink and surrounded by tennis courts with grass growing through the cracks and tropical gardens that were choked with weeds. It was originally built by the Singer Sewing Machine company back around the turn of the century as a place for favored employees (and even more favored customers) to take their winter vacations. I guess Singer was the first and by far the biggest sewing machine company in the world, and they had no trouble filling the place up to overflowing during tourist season. But things changed. The first war came, then the depression, and it was no longer necessary to pass out posh winter vacations at big pink hotels in Florida when the threat of a simple pink slip would do just as well.

So, just like Elkhart Lake and Watkins Glen, the local innkeepers, bartenders, restaurateurs and chamber-of-commerce types were only too happy to hear this Alec Ulmann guy's pitch for a sportycar race at Hendricks Field. After all, those people had *money,* and knew how to rent rooms. And eat supper. And have a few drinks before dinner. And most usually a few drinks after dinner, too. And the local chamber-of-commerce types went even more gung-ho when Ulmann's race grew a little each year and especially when he wheeled and dealed his way into making it a full-blooded FIA international championship event in 1953.

But it was still a pretty lousy excuse for a race track, what with skinny little blacktop access roads dumping out onto bomber squadron-sized runways that were almost as wide as they were long and looked like enormous concrete deserts. Oh, they'd marked out the so-called "race course" with a bunch of leftover 55-gallon oil drums, but it was all flat and empty out there on the runways and it was hard to get any sense of perspective. Plus it was rough as hell, since the big concrete slabs that had originally been poured perfectly flat with neat, pinstripe little tar joints in between had been thrashed by torrential tropical storms and baked under relentless tropical sunlight and pounded by squadron after squadron of heavy, groaning aircraft all through the war years and then just been left to settle, which they did at some highly awkward angles. Like I said before, the state of Florida isn't much more than a big, soft sandbar that's only about one deep tide from becoming a giant saltwater marsh full of alligators, egrets, and needlefish. So it was no surprise that there were a lot of stress cracks and chunks of old concrete breaking loose all the time, leaving ledges tall enough to be classified as curbs in most cities.

On the other hand, maybe that's what made Sebring such a worthy place to hold an endurance contest. If your car could take twelve hours of pounding around those jagged concrete runways, hell, it could take damn near *any*thing. It was tough on drivers, too, since it was usually plenty hot during the day (even in the shade-of which there wasn't any) and it could get plenty cold at night, too. Plus there was wind and grit and sand and no place to hide from any of it, and if you got real lucky, you'd set your stuff up on top of a colony of fire ants, who would calmly and quietly climb all over your ankles, wait for a signal only fire ants can hear, and all sink their teeth in at once....

But, like my English friend and fighter pilot/racing hero Tommy Edwards always said, "Hey, it's the same for everyone, sport. That's what makes it so bloody interesting." And what a surprise when I ran into him when I went looking for our guys along pit row. Geez, it was great to see him again.

"HEY! TOMMY!!" I hollered over the roar of the engines.

He looked up and this really grand smile spread out under his salt-and-pepper mustache. "Well, if it isn't the young master mechanic from New Jersey." He stuck out his hand. "Bloody great to see you, sport. Bloody great indeed!" I was glad to see he was carrying his old green racing helmet and looking fit, sharp and happy. The last time I'd seen him was at that Halloween party where I proposed to Julie, and he'd been drinking a lot and agonizing over his marriage coming apart and losing his S.C.M.A. license for a year on account of that accident Skippy Welcher'd put him into at Watkins Glen where that poor little seven-year-old boy got killed. "So," he asked, "what brings you to the sunburn and stinging insect capital of the world?"

"Oh, Big Ed's got his Jag 120 down and Carson and Cal are gonna co-drive in Carson's TD."

"And you get to play nursemaid."

"Yeah," I nodded, "I guess that's about the size of it."

"And who's the lucky devil sharing the drive with Mr. Baumstein?"

"Sammy Speed. He's mostly an oval track guy we got to know down in Mexico during *La Carrera.* You probably never heard of him."

"Like hell I haven't. In fact, he made a bit of a name for himself in the morning practice session."

"He did?"

Tommy nodded. "Unless I miss my guess, he cut second-quick time among the One-Twenties first crack out. Just behind Walt Hansgen. Caused quite a stir with some of the Jaguar regulars, as I understand it."

"Wow. He's never even driven one before!"

"Word is he looked pretty lurid doing it, too."

"Well, I prob'ly oughta be finding them. But I'll see you later, right?"

"Count on it, sport. Where are you staying?"

"At some place called the Harder Hall, I think."

"Splendid. So am I. In fact, so's the whole bloody team."

"Oh? What team is that?"

"Aston Martin. They brought a couple DB3's over to have a bit of a go and were nice enough to ask me along."

"Tommy!" some tall gent with a British accent called from trackside, *"It's your turn rolling around."*

"Gotta run, sport," Tommy grinned, pulling on his helmet. "But I'll catch up with you in the bar."

"Promise?"

"Bet your life on it."

I finally located my guys down at the far end of pit road, and it was kind of neat that you could split up hundreds of miles away and even have one guy coming in from Fort Worth and another from Indianapolis and Big Ed flying up from two nights of wicked fun in Havana and still all come together on a little corner of this huge, noisy patch of concrete in the middle of Florida that none of you has ever even seen before. It's a feeling you don't find anywhere else, believe me. Naturally Spud had done a good job filling in while I took care of the trailer business up in Jacksonville, and he'd got both cars out by the middle of the first practice session and then made sure everybody got a few laps in to figure out which way the track went. That was important, since night practice was coming up after supper and there was no way in hell to find the track at night unless you already knew which way it went.

Big Ed and Carson were out in the Jag and the MG, and Cal and Sammy were sitting on a couple spare tires at the back of our pit area, exchanging notes about the circuit. "So," I butted in, "howzit goin'?"

"Hey," Cal grinned, "if it isn't the prodigal son."

"Nice to see you again," Sammy nodded, looking serious as a gunfighter..

"So, what's it like?" I wanted to know.

Cal and Sammy looked back and forth at each other. You could tell they were already on their own special wavelength. "Well, those oil drum track markers are pretty damn stupid," Sammy observed.

"Guys're runnin' into 'em and knocking 'em out into the middle of the road," Cal agreed. "And the surface is just plain awful."

"Yep. It's gonna be pretty hard on the cars," Sammy said matter-of-factly.

"Yeah, but not near as hard as your co-driver," Cal added through a reptile grin. "Too bad we can't get Carson and Big Ed to share one of the cars and let Sammy and I have the other."

That made too much sense to even think about. "So," I said to Sammy, "I heard you went pretty quick in practice."

"I'm gettin' the hang of it," he nodded, barely concealing a smile. "Old Cal here did okay, too."

"Fastest of the MGs," Cal beamed. "Although this Bob Fergus guy from Ohio is only a heartbeat behind. He finished third last year in a Siata."

I'd only been there two minutes and already I was starting to worry. "Lissen," I told them, "this is only *practice,* okay? Let's be sure we leave ourselves enough automobile left to do the damn race."

"Hey, don't tell *us* about that," Cal snorted.

"Yeah," Sammy chimed in. "Tell *them.*" He pointed out at where Big Ed was wailing by at about ninety in top and made a jagged, tire screeching downshift for turn one before he ever touched the brakes. I swear, that brand new motor of mine must've kissed 6000 rpm. Geez, what an animal! And he was *still* seven whole seconds off what Sammy'd done in the car. No question Carson looked to be a little easier on his equipment, but he was nine seconds behind Cal's pace in the black TD.

"This could be one real long weekend," Spud said wearily, shaking his head at the stopwatch and writing the time down on his clipboard.

"Long laps generally make for long weekends," Sammy observed.

Cal took me by the elbow and looked into my eyes. "Listen," he said, "y'gotta do your best to keep those two out of the cars as much as you can."

"But it's *their* cars," I reminded him. "What can I do? I mean, they're my two best customers. How the hell am I gonna say, 'uh, sorry, but I don't think you oughtta drive your own damn car because you're too damn slow.' Hell, I got a *business* and a *future* to think about here, you know?"

"Yeah," Cal agreed miserably, "I know."

After practice we unloaded all the stuff from Big Ed's dump truck and set up our pit area, and it occurred to me that I'd brought about five times too much in the way of spares and general shop equipment and not nearly enough in the way of tarps and tent poles and picnic coolers and water jugs and camping things, since you were on your own to set up a weekend field bivouac at Sebring, and, if you didn't bring it with you, you pretty much did without. But then I didn't know, and the truth is I'd never been much of an Eagle Scout anyway. Still, it was nice having a lot of hands for a change and Spud was a really big help on account of he'd done this sort of thing at dirt bullrings and county fairgrounds weekend after weekend and season after season and knew all the ropes. Even Big Ed lent a hand, although you couldn't miss he seemed a little weak-kneed and unsteady following his two nights in Havana. In fact, he looked awful pale for a guy who'd just spent a couple days in a tropical paradise. Maybe even a little bloated, which was a hard thing to spot indeed on a guy the size of Big Ed Baumstein. "Boy, this is a tough damn place," he wheezed, wiping a half-cup of sweat off his brow. "It's bumpy as hell and sorta hard t'find your way around." He fished around in his pockets for one of his brand new favorite Cuban cigars.

"And some a'those European guys, *whew!*" he shook his head. "They go by you high, low, in the dirt, through the grass…it just don't matter t'those guys!"

That reminded me about my friend Tommy Edwards, and, seeing as how we were about done unloading and arranging things, I excused myself and took a little meander through the paddock to see what was up and maybe try to find him. I'd been awake so damn long and I was so blessed tired and worn out that it was almost like when you're sick and running a fever and it feels like you've got pillows under your feet when you're stumbling to the can to throw up again. Only I didn't feel sick, just terribly weak and lightheaded and like if I didn't hang onto things, I might just float off into space like some kid's helium balloon. Still, it was neat to see all the activity going on in the paddock as the teams got ready for night practice. It was quite a mix of cars, and also entirely different from what I'd seen in Mexico just a few months before. Neither Ferrari or Mercedes sent factory teams over-I guess they didn't figure Sebring was all that important in 1953-but there were several privateer stateside Ferraris, and the general opinion around the paddock was that Creighton Pendleton's big 4.1 out of our neck of the woods ought to be the quickest. Especially since Carlo Sebastian had brokered a deal where Phil Hill was co-driving with him. I guess it was a hard thing to put together on account of Creighton was maybe a little uneasy about co-driving with somebody who might easily turn out to be quicker in his own damn car, but Carlo convinced him that a 12-hour race was more about maintaining a decent pace and avoiding rather than cutting fast laps, and that having a savvy guy like Phil on the team really gave them the best chance of winning. And winning *always* appealed to Creighton Pendleton. Besides, only team insiders ever really know which driver is in the car.

But the smart money was on the Cunningham team. They had Johnny Fitch back behind the wheel of one of those brutal, Chrysler-powered C4R's, and he was sharing it with that Phil Walters guy I'd seen race and win in Briggs Cunningham's hotted-up Porsche at Brynfan Tyddyn. They only had one car available in the aftermath of the six-hour S.C.M.A. race at MacDill Strategic Air Command base up by Tampa two weeks before. Fitch and Walters each had a C4R for that one, and Johnny Fitch went on to win after yet another great cat-and-mouse duel with Creighton Pendleton's Ferrari. But Walters' car broke and they couldn't get it repaired in time for Sebring. That was too bad, since Cunningham had been running his cars over in Europe (and done pretty damn well against the best they had to offer) but, although they'd come close, they'd never quite managed an outright win, and it would be really super to pull it off right here at the first-ever bigtime international sportscar race on American soil.

228

Briggs himself was driving this gorgeous little jewel of an OSCA MT-4 that the Maserati brothers put together over in Bologna, Italy. It was only 1340ccs, and, seeing as how his co-driver was a very decent and experienced 'shoe by the name of Bill Lloyd, Briggs was keeping his eye peeled for that Index of Performance trophy.

Up against the Cunninghams were a trio of privateer Jaguar C-Types, and I was amazed to see that one of them was the same blessed car that went over a cliff with Skippy Welcher and Milton Fitting inside it down in Mexico. The factory in England had done an absolutely amazing job getting it straightened out in just three months' time-especially with the holidays and all-and it looked to me like they'd just about jacked up the radiator cap and driven a whole new car underneath. Why they would want to bust their tails for a no-talent idiot like The Skipper was beyond me, but I guess money talks and Colin St. John put a word in to hustle things along since he was making a nice slice on the deal and wanted to be sure Skippy had the car back in time for the 12 hours of Sebring so he could wreck it again. Plus Colin had put together a rather lucrative little side arrangement to get this rich kid from Kansas City the co-driving duties in The Skipper's Jag. The kid's name was Masten Gregory, and he was a scrawny, pasty-faced little runt who looked more like a world class stamp collector or a high school math whiz than any kind of racing driver. But he sure must've had himself some deep pockets, because Colin St. John was all ears when he said he might just buy himself a C-Type or two if he liked the way they drove. Masten was one of those infuriating Lucky Sperm Club types who come out of the woodwork every now and then, flash an enormous family fortune, rent top rides or outright buy the very best machinery available, and then wreck most of it while they try to learn how to drive. It was a perfect fit, really, since Masten had the right kind of money and Skippy had the right kind of car and moreover the kid had just come on the scene and didn't know much of anybody and so had no idea that nobody who knew The Skipper really wanted to drive with him. Not even in a damn C-Type! Personally, I thought it was disgusting that a young punk kid could have that kind of money to spend. Especially one who wore thick, heavy glasses and had this high little pipsqueak voice that made you wonder if his balls had dropped. But I guess they must have, because you should've seen that sonofabitch drive. Oh, he was plenty wild and didn't have much in the way of style or grace like Phil Hill or Cal Carrington. But he sure wasn't afraid to put his foot down! In fact, I don't believe that Masten Gregory kid was afraid of *anything.* Or maybe he was just a little short on imagination, you know? In any case, he struck me right off as the kind of race driver Tommy Edwards said the cemeteries were full of.

Besides the Ferraris and C-types there were several S.C.M.A. Cad-Allards that didn't figure to be on the pace (or go the distance, take your pick) plus a whole passel of more-or-less standard issue XK-120s-including our car-and legions of spear-carrier MGs and Siatas and such duking it out for class honors or just for the fun of it. There were some sixty entries all told, but the wild card had to be that Aston Martin team from England that my friend Tommy Edwards was driving for. I didn't know much of anything about Aston Martins, and figured they were pretty much like Jaguars only nobody'd ever heard of them. At least not over here in the States, anyways.

"Good Lord, don't ever let David Brown hear you say that!" Tommy laughed. I guess Aston Martin had been around a long time-lots longer than Jaguar, in fact-and had a lot of competition history in the old days back in England between the wars. And you know how Englishmen are about their history and bloodlines and fine old traditions and such. But Aston was kind of like the Maserati brothers down in Italy on account of they always seemed to have a hard time keeping the wolf away from the door. Then, finally, this big industrialist guy named David Brown more or less bought Aston Martin out of bankruptcy-lock, stock, and barrel-and set out to make something out of it. The idea was that Astons were going to be a cut above Jaguars in the price, performance, finish, tradition, and exclusivity departments-more in the Ferrari and Maserati league, really, but *British!*-and this David Brown character could afford to tread water in the deep end for a long, long time in order to make it happen.

The two cars they sent over for Sebring were Aston's new DB3 racing models, which, according to Tommy, were mostly just a rehash of some old, prewar hardware dressed up in new, low-slung bodywork with sleek fenderlines and this massive, awkward-looking grille on the front that was kind of a cross between a grouper's scowl and a steel girder railroad bridge. It sure was distinctive, though. The Aston DB3s only had 2.9-liter engines (compared to 3.4 for the C-Types and a whopping 5.4 for the Cunningham!), but they were pretty light and had a very sharp and experienced team behind them. Head man was this tall, severe looking gent named John Wyer, who'd been hired on personally by David Brown as team manager and took his job *very* seriously. He was an efficient, organized, no-nonsense sort of guy equipped with a cold, withering glare that could turn your spine to jelly if he leveled it at you. Behind his back, Tommy and the other team members called him "Death Ray." But you could tell they respected and believed in him, and moreover knew he'd put one hell of a driver lineup together. Tommy was sharing a car with an English driver named Reg Parnell, who'd been around for quite a while and was already something of

Reg Parnell, who'd been around for quite a while and was already something of a legend over in England, while the second car was for a hot young prospect named Peter Collins and famous Brit motorcycle champion Geoff Duke, trying his hand at four-wheel racing for the very first time. They were all the McCoy, every one of them, plus they'd all had plenty of experience on airport circuits since that's mostly all they raced on in England after the war. If there was one thing you could find plenty of over there after 1945, it was decommissioned bomber bases. And what better place to stage a motor race? So wartime airfields were transformed into race tracks like Silverstone, Goodwood, Aintree, Snetterton, Ibsley, and Castle Coombe, and that's where these guys drove on a regular basis. So it was no surprise to learn they were the exact same drivers Big Ed complained about who were passing him "high, low, through the dirt, in the grass." You got the notion they maybe took their racing a little more seriously over on the far side of the Atlantic. Or at least a little closer to the edge. In fact, Tommy surprised me by saying he was afraid he was "going to wind up the slow bloke in this bunch."

"Really?" I couldn't believe it, you know?

"Oh, yes," he said matter-of-factly. "These are some bloody quick fellows. Bloody quick indeed. Especially Reg-he's raced about everything back in England-and that young comingman, Peter Collins." I could see by the look in his eye that Tommy was serious. And maybe even a tiny bit awed, too.

"Oh, you'll do all right," I assured him.

"I suppose. But I reckon Aston only invited me because I've been here and know where all the decent pubs are." He looked off to the west, where a huge, orange-red sun was just touching down against the top of the orange groves. "But it'll come right. After all, a race like this isn't about going quickly."

"It isn't?"

Tommy shook his head. "No, you've got to concentrate on just *finishing* the bloody thing before you ever start worrying about coming home first." He shook his head. "There are just so many ways to *lose....*"

"There are?"

"More than you could ever imagine, sport," Tommy laughed. "Races like this are generally not *won,* they're *lost.* It's seldom your quickest driver or fastest car that gets the job done for you. No, it's always the slipup. The weak link. The botched pit stop or the third gear that wasn't hardened properly at the factory or the bloody fool who tries to go just that little bit too fast and either breaks the car or smashes into something. At a race like Sebring, you try to run a fair pace and get through traffic as best you can, but you always need remember the two cardinal rules of endurance racing."

"And those are?"

Tommy held up his index finger. *"Don't hurt the bloody car,"* he said solemnly, then uncoiled the next finger. "And *don't hurt the bloody car...."*

Back over at our end of the pits, we gassed up the cars, checked fluid levels and tire pressures, and then pretty much waited around for night practice to begin. I guess that's the first time I really took any notice of the team in the pit next to us. It was the Excalibur bunch out of Wisconsin, and boy, did they ever have some cool-looking race cars! They reminded you a little of fighter planes-Sabre jets, in fact-even though a close inspection revealed they weren't much more than ordinary, everyday, sheep-in-wolf's-clothing Henry J sedans in racy, two-seater bodywork. The guy behind the whole thing was an bright, enthusiastic, well-connected young industrial designer from Milwaukee named Brooks Stevens. He couldn't drive himself on account of he had polio when he was a kid and wasn't really up to it physically, but he loved sports cars and had done quite well for himself designing steam irons and outboard motors and everything from the shape of the diesel locomotive to the brass buttons on the conductors' uniforms to the cocktail napkins in the glass domed club car for the Milwaukee Road railroad. Brooks also drew up a lot of automotive stuff, including the jaunty little civilian-issue Willys Jeepster after the war and the Manhattan (which, if you bothered to notice, was really a damn fine looking sedan) and Henry J for Kaiser. That's where Brooks' pet idea came from about building something over here to compete with MG and Porsche and Jaguar. I mean a real, honest-to-goodness, all-American sports roadster you could go buy off the showroom floor at your local Kaiser dealership. He kept pestering and pestering William Kaiser about it until he finally shipped Brooks three new Henry J chassis just to shut him up. Free for nothing! And the cars he turned them into took your breath away. Even if they weren't all that fast. But they could hold their own against an MG (even if they couldn't catch an exhaust whiff off a Jaguar) and they were showroom detailed right down to fancy Excalibur badges on the sides and these nifty, gunsight-style Excalibur hood ornaments on the nose. Plus you had to like Brooks because he was lively and fun type of guy to be around and never put on airs like you might expect from a world famous, well-connected industrial designer from Milwaukee.

He had some pretty decent drivers, too. Nothing like the genuine English pros over at Aston Martin, of course, but I noticed that Dick Irish guy who'd run away with the little formula car race at Brynfan Tyddyn and came third at Sebring the previous year co-driving his Siata with Bob Fergus. I knew Tommy Edwards always thought a lot of both of them. Dick's co-driver was a tall, square-jawed guy from the Chicago area named Hal Ullrich, and I understand he and his brother did a lot of the building and fabrication on the Excaliburs at their shop in Evanston, Illinois. "They never answer the phone when I call down just to see how things are going," Brooks laughed. "But I always get through in a hurry when they need more money."

I discovered that you always get to know the folks in the next pit during an endurance race-you can't help it, really-and I figured we were pretty lucky to be pitted next to those guys. I mean, besides the Cunninghams, they were the only genuine American cars in the race. Plus they were really nice people. Especially Brooks Stevens. Like I said, he was a pretty important and high-powered sort of guy, but he still wanted everybody on the team to call him "Kip" (which I guess was his nickname ever since he was little) instead of "Mr. Stevens." Although he owned the team and did everything from drawing up the cars to signing the checks, Brooks Stevens struck you more like some wide-eyed kid who was happy as hell they just let him hang around.

Another car that caught my eye-and everybody else's-was this brand new, silvery gray Austin-Healey One Hundred they had tooling up and down all over the paddock. It was just there to show off, not to race, and Geez, was it ever a sharp looking thing! It had low, sleek fenderlines and this handsome, fan-shaped front grille, and struck you like sort of a small-caliber Jag 120, only with a big, gutty grin on the front instead of that snooty, look-down-the-nose Jaguar sneer. Sebring was the first time anybody in America had seen the new Healey Hundred, and the rumor going around was that it wouldn't cost much more than an MG. No question a sizeable chunk of the MG owners on hand-including Carson Flegley-got the notion they were carrying the keys to last year's automobile.

Night practice at Sebring was one of the most amazing things I'd ever seen. It started with all the cars and crews and drivers gathering in pit lane while the lower half of a huge, blood red sun settled slowly into the orange groves, painting the sky with neon blues and purples and magentas. Meanwhile the drivers climbed in and engines fired and headlamps flipped on all up and down pit road, and an instant later, they were roaring past and peeling off onto the Sebring runways like a squadron of wingless night fighters off for a midnight raid on Hamburg, Dresden, or Berlin. It was awesome....

You could listen to the cars accelerating through the gears and watch them sweep into the wide, gentle left of turn one and disappear behind the big, rusty block of the hangar building. But you could still hear them, braking and downshifting for turn three, accelerating towards the Amoco Chicane, braking again, accelerating through a long, sweeping right, then back on the brakes and down through the gears for Warehouse Hairpin, which everybody said was the tightest damn corner on the face of the earth. Then you'd kind of lose them as they accelerated out of the hairpin, and there would be a long, uneasy wait before you heard them again, echoing down the long, fast straightaway behind the paddock, downshifting for the fast, wide, bumpy U-turn called the K.L.G. Curve, and came pounding down the pit straight again. The Sebring race circuit was a whopping 5.2 miles around, and it took even the fast guys more than four minutes per lap. The slow cars could be a minute or more behind, which meant that lapped traffic got to be a problem in short order. But slower traffic was nothing compared to visibility. With every passing lap, the lingering remnants of sunlight faded and the colors in the sky faded into deep, shadowy shades of gray.

In a few more laps the sky was black as the inside of a dresser drawer, and fierce yellow pairs of headlight beams came sweeping out of that last corner like miniature searchlights and squinted their way down the runway towards turn one. The drivers were squinting, too, trying to find the right way to go out in the darkness, and one after another brought their cars in to have its lights adjusted. The savvier teams had extra driving lights-the Cunninghams wearing a pair of kazillion candlepower aircraft landing lights flanked out on either side of the grille, while the Aston Martins mounted one huge, Cyclops-style Lucas Flamethrower right in the middle-but no matter how many lamps you have or how carefully you aim them, it doesn't do much good if there's nothing out there for the light to reflect off of. And that's the big problem at Sebring. Out on those vast, wide-open runways, there's not much between you and the horizon but bleak, black emptiness.

You might as well point a flashlight into the sky....

Spud and I wanted all our drivers to get a taste of night driving, since Sunday's race was scheduled to start at noon and run till midnight, so damn near half of it would happen after dark. Naturally Big Ed and Carson took the first stints while there was still a little light in the sky, and it became obvious pretty quickly that neither of them felt real comfortable about racing at night. Big Ed kept coming in to have the lights adjusted, but still managed to drive off the track someplace or other almost every single lap. Not that I knew it at the time, since all I could do was wait there helplessly in the pits with Spud and Cal and Sammy, looking at my stopwatch and wondering where the hell our Jag had disappeared to whenever the small hand ticked much past five minutes. But, to be fair, Big Ed was hardly the only guy with those kind of problems. A lot of drivers went missing now and again during night practice at Sebring. Eventually they'd show up again, flashing their high beams or pumping the brake lights incomprehensibly when they powered past to let their crews know that either something had gone terribly wrong or that everything was okay. It was hard to tell which. For sure there'd be plenty of wild stories and/or excuses heard later around the bar. "Y'know," Sammy observed, "it wouldn't hurt if we got ourselves a couple extra lights."

"Maybe we could find some at a parts store or a truck stop?"

Spud shook his head. "We're out in the middle of nowhere. Ain't nothin' but the bars gonna be open by the time night practice is over. And tomorrow's Sunday. Everything'll be closed."

"Don't worry," Cal told us. "I'll come up with something."

And that's about when Big Ed stopped coming around.

Period.

Oh, shit.

But all we could do was stand there, waiting and wondering while we watched Carson puttering around at what must've been genuine white knuckle speed for him. Even if it was bog slow compared to most of the other MGs. Let alone the Cunningham, the Astons, and Phil Hill in Creighton Pendleton's Ferrari, who was really hauling the mail. After twenty-five minutes or so I waved Carson in so Cal could get a few laps in, and of course he was right on the pace by the second lap and thoughtfully brought the TD in after three or four more circuits so that Sammy could try a few laps. Just so's he could see what it looked like and figure out which way the road went in the dark.

"Did'ja see Big Ed out there?" I asked Cal as soon as he got his helmet off.

"Hell, no. Shit, you can't see much of *anything* out there."

"Boy, I'll say," Carson agreed with a hint of swagger in his voice.

Practice ended a couple laps later and afterwards we waited for damn near half an hour before a tow truck finally appeared at the end of pit road with Big Ed's Jag hanging off the back. Fortunately the damage wasn't too bad-just a flat tire and a pretzelized front wheel-and Big Ed explained as how he'd gone off course and actually got lost out there in the darkness. And he was hardly the only driver to have that kind of problem. In fact, it was pretty easy to drive right off the racing surface at Sebring without knowing it. I mean, it wasn't like going off a road, because you were still on concrete. About the only way to tell was that all of a sudden you were alone and there weren't any other cars anymore. Plus little indicators like bits of trash and concrete chips scattered around in your headlight beams along with scraggly, foot-high weeds sprouting up out of the expansion joints. Assuming you were paying attention. Otherwise, you could drive a long, *long* way before you ran out of pavement.

Which is precisely what happened to Big Ed ("Jesus, it's so friggin' dark out there y'can't find yer own friggin' asshole," was the way he put it) and there was nothing he could do except stop and wait for another race car to go by and try to follow the searchlight sweep of its headlight beams and the red flicker of its taillights back onto the race course. And that's how he happened to the huge, jagged pothole he never even saw and wrecked the right front wheel. "Think y'can fix it, Buddy?" Big Ed asked sheepishly.

I knew I could, but, now that the engines were quiet, it was occurring to me all over again how utterly exhausted I was. It was the kind of tired you can't resist. The kind that makes your head floaty and fingers weak and seeps in through your skin like the chill off wet clothing.

"Hey, don't worry about it," Spud said, clapping a hand on my shoulder. "Me'n Sammy'll take care of it. You look *beat.*"

On the one hand, I figured I ought to stay there and do it myself. I mean, *I* was supposed to be the big Jaguar expert, right? On the other, I'd been up about seventy-five hours straight as far as I could figure, and our so-called "endurance contest" wasn't even slated to start until noon the following day.

"You sure?"

"Sure!" Spud grinned. "No problem a'tall. After all, it's just four damn wheels and an engine, iddn'it?"

I somehow fell asleep in the dump truck on the way back to the Harder Hall, and kind of wished Big Ed'd just left me there on account of once he woke me up and dragged me and my duffel bag inside to the registration desk, I heard all the racing people laughing and jabbering and the glasses clinking over in the bar, and so I was all wound up again by the time I got up to the room. "Look, I'm gonna take me a shower," Big Ed allowed. "I think I maybe still got a li'l Havana on me down where it don't show with my clothes on. You go down and get somebody to sneak ya a drink in the bar, okay? I'll come down and get'cha when it's your turn in the can."

So I did. And who should I run into just inside the double doors but Hank Lyons, fresh in from California on the Greyhound (or, more correctly, a whole series of Greyhounds) and scribbling away furiously in one of his ever-present stenographer's notebooks. "Hey," I said, "what's the good word?"

"Smith," he said without looking up from his notepad.

"Smith?"

"Sure." Hank continued, finishing up the last line. Then he smiled up at me. "Wordsmith, get it?" I think he was expecting more of a reaction than just staring off into space. "Are you okay? You look like shit."

"Then I look like I feel."

"You sick?"

"Nah. But I think I been up since the middle of February."

"Tired, huh?"

That observation should've easily won Hank a prize for Understatement of the Century. But I was too bushed to tell him about it. "It'll be sack time for me as soon as Big Ed gets done in the can so I can take a shower."

"Just stay down wind until that happens, okay?"

"I really look that bad, huh?"

"You smell that bad, too."

"It's nice of you to tell me."

"Hey, truth in reporting, right? That's me all over."

We got ourselves a couple drinks-the hostess didn't even ask if we were old enough-and I couldn't help noticing the dangerously beautiful Miss Sally Enderle up at the end of the bar with Creighton Pendleton and two of the Muscatelli brothers. She was wearing one of her revealing sleeveless halter tops with plenty of skin showing, and she'd obviously been down in Florida for awhile since every smooth, gorgeous inch of it was tanned to a perfect, golden brown. Hank's eyes followed mine over to Sally's exposed midriff and came to a screeching halt. "Jesus," he wanted to know, "who the hell is that?"

So I told him all about the rich, tanned, snooty, spoiled, achingly gorgeous and thoroughly unpredictable Miss Sally Enderle and her occasionally steady-date relationship with the equally rich, tanned, snooty, spoiled etc. Creighton Pendleton the Third. But I was careful to leave out the part about the chunk of night we spent together at Elkhart Lake. I liked Hank and I trusted him, but I knew enough about reporters to know that no story is ever really "off the record" where those guys are concerned. Especially a really juicy one. They just can't help themselves, you know?

Besides, he never would've believed me.

Hank was still staring at Sally's midriff. Him and every other guy who didn't come in with a seeing eye dog. She was leaning back with her elbows propped up against the edge of the bar so her amply-filled halter top and smooth, golden stomach were displayed to their best advantage-she really knew how it was done, no lie-and her long, elegant neck tilted back so her perfectly chiseled chin and even more perfectly chiseled nose were pointed in the general direction of the sign over the men's room door. Without really meaning to, I caught myself trying to remember that night in Elkhart Lake and what it was like to have her naked underneath me. But it was like a dream you can't quite recall, you know?

Or maybe a nightmare. And afterwards all that's left is this little empty space you can't get to anymore. Looking at her up at the bar with her dark eyes flashing and her chestnut hair tossed back-laughing and teasing and laughing again- I couldn't believe I'd actually been with her.

"So what brings you to Sebring?" I asked, trying to change the subject.

"Oh, I'm covering it for *Road and Track* magazine."

"Really? Geez, that's a hell of a neat deal."

"Yeah, I guess," Hank laughed. "If I don't eat anything but Bologna sandwiches and potato chips on the bus ride back to California, I probably won't lose more than ten or fifteen dollars on the whole thing."

"Sounds like it pays almost as good as being a race mechanic."

"It's about the same sort of deal. You get to hang around the fringes of all the fun and money and excitement. You can even kid yourself that you're a part of it. But, except for the occasional free hangover and lots of excellent free meals, none of it ever rubs off."

"Yep. Sounds like the same job exactly."

Still, it was neat that Hank was getting paid to cover the races-even if he wasn't getting paid very much-and I knew he'd do a good job of it because he was as sick with the racing disease as any of us. He knew his stuff, too, and was right on the money when he guessed the race was going to boil down to a battle between the Cunningham and the Aston Martin team with maybe Creighton and Phil Hill in the Ferrari as a dark horse and the Index of Performance scrap coming down to that little supercharged French Douche Bag *(nobody* called them Deutsch-Bonnets) or Briggs Cunningham's exquisite little OSCA. About then Big Ed showed up and bought another round, but I begged off. But he insisted it'd help me sleep (like I needed any help, right?) so I wound up carrying a double Rusty Nail up to the room. And that's only because they didn't have any Mescal.

Upstairs I took a scant swallow or two from my drink and a long, hot shower-just standing there with the hottest water I could stand streaming over me until I couldn't keep my eyes open anymore. Then I went to bed and tried to think about Julie as I fell off to sleep. But I kept getting this picture of Sally Enderle instead, leaning back against the bar with her perfect nose, chest and chin angled up towards the ceiling fixtures in the far corner of the room.

Laughing.

Big Ed rolled me out about six-thirty, and, if anything, I felt even weaker and more worn out than I had the night before. That's what happens when you get into one of those race weekend sleep imbalance deals, where you owe your body more shuteye than you will ever be able to pay back before you're dead, and your body repays you with all the wit, spark and willingness of a flat battery. But a ham and cheese omelet with bacon on the side (and grits instead of hash browns!) plus a tall glass of that great, fresh-squeezed Florida orange juice that had been on the blessed tree the night before-not to mention about a half quart of black coffee-were all it took to jump-start myself back to life again. Over breakfast, we talked about pit stop schedules and race strategy (like we actually had any) and what we could do in case one of our cars got stranded out on the backside of the course in the dark like Big Ed had the night before. "It took 'em twenty damn minutes t'find me an' get me out," he grumbled. "An' that's *after* practice ended." He shoved a whole slice of buttered raisin toast in his mouth, chewed twice, and swallowed. "Hell, if the damn lights'd gone out, they would'a *never* found me. At least not till sunup, anyway." He devoured another slice of toast for emphasis. To be honest, watching Big Ed eat was like watching a train wreck. You wanted to look away, but you just couldn't.

He had a point, though. We had no way of knowing where the cars were stranded or what had happened to them or even if the driver was okay when one of them stopped coming around on schedule. Especially at night. All we could do was sit and wait. And, if it was something simple, the driver could work on it and fix it out on the course and bring it back in. Of course, if anyone tried to help out or if anybody except the driver worked on it, the car would be disqualified. But that didn't mean a sharp mechanic couldn't go out there and offer a little advice. "I guess we need some kinda signal," I told Big Ed without thinking too much about it.

"Yeah. A signal. That's *it!*" Big Ed agreed, unwrapping his morning cigar.

We headed out to the track to see how Spud and Sammy made out with the Jaguar's wheel and front end, and I was actually a little concerned about it. But I shouldn't have worried, because Spud was the genuine article and knew how to get the job done no matter what when the green flag is scheduled to fall at precisely straight-up noon the following day. "Aw," Spud said like it was no big deal at all, "the rim was junk an' I didn't wanna take a chance on the tire-I felt one a'those little goiter bulges where the cords are maybe broke when I ran my hand around inside-and Ed got himself a nice little tweak in the alignment, too."

"But it's okay now?"

"Right as rain. Or at least I think so, anyway. We found out they got a warmup practice at 8:30 an' I'm gonna have Sammy take it around just t'make sure everything's okay. At least if that's okay with you."

"Hell, yes." It was really nice having somebody around I could count on. In fact, I couldn't help thinking how great it would be to have somebody like Spud working at the Sinclair, you know?

But I got worried all over again when Sammy pulled Big Ed's Jag back into pit lane after just two laps of the warmup practice. So I ran right over to see what was up. "What's wrong?" I asked him.

"Nothin,'" Sammy shrugged, waving me off. "Nothin' at all. But any car's only got so many laps in her, and I figger we oughtta save ours for the race."

Meanwhile Cal was out circulating in Carson's MG, and right there was the big difference between Sammy and Cal-even though they were both great drivers-and also, in a way, the real difference between a genuine professional and a wet-behind-the-ears amateur. If you turned Cal loose on a race track, he'd run until he ran out of gas or something broke or they checkered the session. He just flat loved to drive-he couldn't help himself!-and he'd obviously need to grow a little patience and savvy to go with his natural speed if he was ever going to run with the big boys in Europe. Not that I doubted for one second that he had what it took to get there.

After practice Spud and I went over the cars one last time-fluid checks, tire pressures, loose connections under the hood, general nut-and-bolt under the fenders, topping up the fuel tanks-then went over our pit stuff again-fuel cans, water bucket, oil, brake fluid, gear lube, stopwatches, clipboard, pens, signaling board, chalk, knockoff hammer, tool boxes, floor jack, jack stands, spare tires, a cooler of sandwiches and cold pop, two umbrellas, the boxes of assorted MG and Jaguar parts I'd brought along as insurance so at least those things wouldn't break-all of it laid neatly out in perfect, ready-to-grab order that would turn into absolute chaos by the second pit stop. Only we didn't know that yet. Spud had even rigged up this canvas tarp on a couple lengths of steel conduit to create a makeshift canopy and hung two headlamp bulbs up at the corners that we could run off the dump truck's battery so we could maybe see at night during pitstops. But of course we were really bush league compared to guys who'd done this before-particularly the Cunningham and Aston Martin teams-who had tool benches and welding rigs and partitioned parts, hardware, and electrical boxes with designated places for everything. Hell, they even had their own generators.

Still, I was pretty proud of what we'd done.

And the race hadn't even started yet!

Then there was the little matter of driver strategy for Team Jersey (as I'd decided to christen our effort when nobody was looking) and it was sort of a delicate situation in that everybody knew Sammy and Cal would be fast as stink and wouldn't likely screw up, while the exact opposite was true of the two car owners. Spud and I talked it over, and we had to weigh the fact that the really important part of *any* race is the moment when the checkered flag comes down, and, if you're in a position to make up time and challenge for position there towards the end, you really want your very best 'shoe in the car. Especially at night, when the difference between an ace and a muddling duffer about doubles. On the other hand, the most hectic and dangerous part of every race is at the start. Especially here at Sebring, where they were using a LeMans-style start. This involved lining all the cars up along the pit side of the main straightaway, parked side by side and angled out so's they're ready to peel out onto the race-track. Then they line the first-stint drivers up in these stupid little painted circles on the other side of the road, about twenty-five or thirty yards away. I know it sounds dumb-and particularly for a race that lasts one whole rotation around the clock, but when the flag drops, the drivers sprint over to their cars, jump in, fire up, and, unless they're first or second man away, charge flat-out into the teeth of the most hellacious high speed traffic jam you have ever seen in your life. Tommy Edwards told me it usually sorts itself out pretty well after a couple of laps, but anything can happen in that mixed bag, foot-to-the-floor feeding frenzy right there at the start. "Adrenaline's pouring out of everybody's ears and the bloody tiddlers are shuffled up every-which-way with the big iron and everyone's scrapping and scrambling for the same bloody bit of road...it's rather amusing, actually," Tommy explained through a helpless smile. "Of course, the night before over drinks everybody talks a bloody marvelous game-all about taking it easy at the start, running to a safe, sane, and sensible pace, taking care of the bloody car-oh, you should hear it."

"Then what happens?"

"Oh, then they sit out there in those stupid little circles getting all wound up-other drivers on either side of them and that big crowd pressing in against the fences and it's so bloody quiet you can hear the pennants snapping in the breeze and your own sweat splattering against the concrete..."

I could almost *feel* it, you know?

"...and then the starter raises the flag and the drivers who've been to a bloody track meet once in their lives get down on all fours-even the really fat ones-and inevitably one clever bloke who doesn't want to get stuck in the jumble makes a break for it..."

"You mean he jumps the start?"

"Oh, bloody hell *yes!* In fact, that new boy Stirling Moss is downright famous for it."

"But doesn't he get penalized?"

"No, not really. There's not much the bloody stewards can do."

"Why's that?"

"Because as soon as anybody takes so much as a step-why, even a healthy flinch will do-it's a bloody jailbreak stampede and everybody's off for the cars. If the starter's any good, he'll have the flag dropped and be getting out of the way before they're halfway across."

"I dunno, Tommy," I told him, "It sounds a little, umm, *stupid* to start a twelve-hour car race with a twelve-second foot race."

"Oh, it *is!*" Tommy laughed. "That's the whole point. It gets everybody all revved up and all the cars shaken up in a bag so there's plenty of opportunity for murder and mayhem on those first few laps. Makes for good spectator value. And it's kind of fun in the cars, too. But you *do* need to be careful."

With that in mind, Spud and I figured the best deal would be to have Cal and Sammy start. It only made sense. The hard part was convincing Carson and Big Ed. Especially Big Ed. But once he saw the cars being pushed out to their side-by-side starting slots in front of the pits and that flat, naked, unforgiving slab of concrete the drivers had to run across from their little painted circles and the throng of spectators packed in tight against the fences-Geez, it was a hell of a crowd!-he thought better of it. Running a foot race in front of a couple thousand strangers is a little like stripping down to your skivvies at the beach on Coney Island. Only the lucky few-the Creighton Pendletons and Cal Carringtons and Sally Enderles of this world-look any good doing it. The rest of us-and especially a fleshy, uncoordinated mountain of a guy like Big Ed-would just as soon keep that stuff out of the public eye. And God forbid if a driver stumbled and twisted his ankle or something on the way over. They'd wind up picking him out of somebody's grillework. Besides, Sammy was a wiry, tightly coiled little guy, and, in spite of a slightly bum leg from the night he went through the fence at Ascot Park a few seasons before, he still figured to have the Jag fired up and away before Big Ed even got the blessed door open. Not that it made all that much difference in a twelve-hour race. But the quicker you got away, the better your chances of running clear of that mad stampede of mismatched machinery and drivers with adrenaline gushing from every pore and heart rates well up into rabbit and hummingbird territory. Or, as Sammy put it, "The best place to be in a racing wreck is in front of it."

Sunday, March 8th was a gorgeous, sunny, Chamber-of-Commerce perfect Florida day, and while they got the cars lined up in front of the pits-fifty-four of them all told, with the fastest ones up front and the tiddlers down at the far end-a few dignitaries whose names you couldn't catch were introduced and a bunch of speechifying you likewise couldn't understand crackled over the PA system. Once the cars were set, the brass section from the local high school marching band-all six of them-accompanied some lady from a nearby church choir who apparently had delusions about performing at the Met one day through a particularly desperate rendition of *The Star Spangled Banner.* Then Donald Healey himself took some local race official bigwig on a final, pre-race "inspection tour" of the course. Personally, I think it was just another excuse to show off that new Austin-Healey One Hundred roadster in front of the crowd. But it sure was pretty to look at, no lie. After that, this classy and refined-looking English gent named Captain George Eyston (who had a couple World Land Speed Records to his credit and had been invited over to serve as official starter) climbed to the top of this rickety, two-story "observation tower" they had overlooking the start/finish line.

Meanwhile the race cars sat there, glistening in the sun, while the crowd pressed in against the fences and their drivers stood in their stupid little painted circles, fidgeting with their chinstraps or tugging at the wrists of their driving gloves or checking the hands on wristwatches that never seemed to move. There were only a handful of moments to go, and I swear the closer we got to straight up noon, the quieter everything got. In fact, if you listened past the rush of the air up your nostrils, you could hear your own heartbeat....

"Thirty seconds," Captain Eyston said into his microphone, and you could almost see the sparkplug banners flutter from the mass intake of breath.

"Twenty."

At the far end of pit lane, I heard a socket wrench fall and roll across the concrete. From the sound, I'd guess it was a 14mm or a 9/16ths deepwell.

"Ten...nine...eight...seven..."

Somewhere between *"four"* and *"three"* I noticed the first tiny flinch of movement, but, before you could catch who it was, the stampede was on. It looked a little strange, really, these guys in goggles, gloves, and helmets scampering hell-for-leather across an airport runway and jumping into their race cars. But that all changed when the patter of little feet became the grind of starter motors and then this avalanche of sound as one engine fired and then another and then absolute bedlam as the whole field exploded away in a shock wave of rubber smoke and Castrol fumes. First away was Erwin Goldschmidt's older-style Healey Silverstone with a Caddy V-8 stuffed inside and then that wild rich kid from Kansas City, Masten Gregory, right on his heels in The Skipper's freshly rebuilt C-Type, Phil Walters in the Cunningham C4R, Peter Collins in the first of the Aston DB3s, and the rest, well, any way you like. Of course our eyes were fixed on Big Ed's creamy white XK-120 not quite a third of the way down the field and Carson Flegley's black TD another twenty-odd positions back. No question Cal was one of the first guys across (I'm sure he wasn't the first to jump, but it wouldn't surprise me a bit if he was the second) and he made a perfectly-timed little leap over the door and had it fired, in gear, and away before most guys even sat down. But he was way down the field and, knowing that even the fastest TD on earth was no match for the big iron ahead of him, he wisely swung way wide so as not to get nailed broadside by faster cars with slower, less coordinated drivers behind the wheel. No question he was first MG across the stripe. Sammy wasn't quite that fleet of foot and elected to actually go in through the door because of his bum leg. But he didn't fumble or get flustered like a lot of guys, and squealed smartly out into traffic just ahead of mid-pack. In fact, for just an instant, he was door-to-door with Cal in Carson's TD. And right then, with cars dodging and feinting and broadsliding every which way and everybody barreling foot-to-the-floor, redline-*shift*-redline towards corner one, Sammy gave Cal a little one finger salute and Cal flicked him a "thank you" one right back-like it was all happening in slow motion, you know?- and about then the Jag's power advantage got the better of Cal's superior momentum and the Jag drew slowly away. And right there was the difference between those two and their car owners standing on either side of me in pit lane.

Meanwhile the rest of the herd thundered past like a runaway freight train. All except that Reg Parnell who was sharing the second Aston DB3 with Tommy Edwards. Based on the sooty clouds coughing out the side pipes, I figured it was most likely flooded-maybe some over-zealous crew member squirted a little too much joy juice into the carbs for a quick getaway-and I could see Tommy standing there in helpless agony, shoulders forward, spine taut as a bowstring, trying to *will* that damn car into starting. Even the last, straggling tiddlers had long since disappeared behind the hangar and you could hear the thundering echo of the main pack spitting out downshifts as they braked for Warehouse Hairpin and then fade into the distance as they accelerated off towards the far reaches of the circuit. One of the Aston mechanics started to make a break for the car, but John Wyer's hand shot out like it was on the end of a tempered steel trap spring and stopped him in his tracks. He knew if anybody except the driver so much as *touched* the car while it was on the race course, they'd be disqualified on the spot. Without completing so much as a single blessed lap. Then, just when it seemed hopeless, the DB3 started to catch on one cylinder. And then another. And then maybe one or two more joined in and the second Aston stumbled away, spluttering and banging as the engine tried to choke down its oversupply of raw fuel. It disappeared like that behind the hangar building, but then you could hear it clear its throat and come on song as it accelerated out of the long, sweeping right heading towards the hairpin, accompanied by a mass sigh of relief from the Aston Martin pit and a smattering of applause all up and down pit lane. Even from the Cunningham team. And that's when I first experienced that special, strangely two-faced glow that goes along with endurance racing. On the one hand, you want to beat the other guys. Want to beat them so badly you'll take bold gambles and silly risks and push yourself and your machine to the limit-and beyond!-to try and get it done. And yet there's also this other part of it. This strangely communal sense that *"we're all in this together."* I can't really explain it, but you could feel it roll down pit lane like a warm, gentle breeze floating on the fingertips of that applause.

For the first hour or so, an endurance race feels an awful lot like a sprint. You can tell who's where and which cars seem to be the quick ones and how you're doing compared to the rest of the entries in your class. And I must admit Team Jersey was looking pretty good. Sammy was running second among the regular-issue XK-120s and about thirteenth or fourteenth overall, holding a nice, steady pace and keeping the class-leading Jag 120 of Walt Hansgen more or less in sight. Cal was doing even better, running ahead of all the other MGs and maybe even going a little faster than I would have liked at this stage. But he wasn't twisting its tail or slamming his way through the gears (or at least not down the pit straight where I could hear it) and he was one of the few guys who never lifted-not even for the flutter of a heartbeat-through those fast lefthand sweepers just past the pits. In any case, I was pretty damn proud to see two cars that I'd worked on powered by two motors that I'd built with my own two hands doing so well in such an important race. At least early on, anyway.

Meanwhile there was a hell of a battle going on at the front of the pack, as Masten Gregory made a wild bid for the lead ("too clever by half" was the way Tommy described it) and looped The Skipper's C-Type at the hairpin on the very first lap. He was lucky and didn't hurt the car, but had to sit there by the side of the road, grinding his teeth into powder while the whole blessed field streamed past before he could rejoin. Phil Walters in the lone Cunningham used that enormous Chrysler Fire Power under the hood to power into the lead down the two long straightaways out on the backside of the course. But he had company, as Peter Collins in the lead Aston Martin wasn't far astern, and those two continued to keep each other company, lap after lap, while they simultaneously eased away from the rest of the field. You could see the Cunningham had more in the way of sheer grunt, but the Aston was lighter and seemed to handle a little better. And, just like Big Ed said, the Aston drivers would go for any opening anywhere once they got into lapped traffic, while Walters preferred to play it safe and wait for the straightaways where he could just power effortlessly by rather than risk trying to go under slower cars in the corners. Then again, Peter Collins, Reg Parnell and Geoff Duke had never raced against most of the Americans, while all the Cunningham guys had plenty of experience running with the rank-and-file S.C.M.A. types, and knew that some of those guys never so much as *glance* at a mirror once they're done with their morning shave.

Creighton Pendleton rose to fourth in his 4.1 Ferrari and looked to be running pretty well, but the real star at that stage had to be Reg Parnell in the second Aston, who was carving his way up through the field like nobody's business after being stranded at the start. Masten Gregory in The Skipper's C-Type kind of hung onto his tail for awhile, trying to follow, but you could see he was in over his head and finally looped it again (and again without damage, the lucky SOB) and lost touch. After that Masten actually settled down and drove pretty well. He was quick, too. No two ways about it.

About a half hour in, the Frazer Nash that won the '52 race stopped out on the circuit with some kind of mechanical gremlin or other, and the driver couldn't find it so he had no choice but to push the car all the way to the pits. It was over three quarters of a mile and he was "pretty well knackered" (as Tommy put it) by the time he got there. And all for nothing, since it turned out to be a busted timing chain. So the previous year's winner was out, not forty-five minutes into the race! Not that he could've run with the Cunninghams and Astons anyway. But it was still kind of sad, and you felt a little communal sense of loss flow through the pits as the crew sadly pushed their silent Frazer Nash back into the paddock. They were the first retirement, but everybody and their brother knew they would not be the last.

Just before one o'clock Collins' Aston Martin saw an opportunity in heavy traffic and snatched the lead from Walters' Cunningham, and they went back and forth like that for most of the next two hours, the Aston sneaking away a bit in traffic and through the corners, the Cunningham content to reel it effortlessly back in down the straightaways, but not attempting a pass unless momentum just carried it on by. Then the Aston would generally nip right past again under braking for the next corner. As you can imagine, the spectators were loving it (and so were the pit crews!) but you got the notion that both drivers were keeping a little in hand so there would maybe be some semblance of an automobile left at the end of twelve hours. Reg Parnell had absolutely streaked through the field in the second Aston, and there was a modest cheer from the far end of pit lane when he caught and passed Creighton Pendleton's Ferrari for third place. It was quite a drive, no question about it.

Meanwhile Team Jersey made plans for our first-ever pit stops. The rules said you had to complete twenty laps (or about a hundred miles) between fuel or oil stops, and that you had to shut the car off while it was sitting in the pits to reduce the fire hazard, and then it had to restart under its own power. Spud and me figured the MG was good for at least thirty laps and the Jag, with its big 17½ gallon fuel tank, maybe a safe four or five more. But you never know how a car's going to pick up those last few gallons-especially through sweeping turns where the fuel may slosh away from the pickup-plus our Jag figured to be at least a lap ahead of the MG by that point, and we sure didn't want both cars in at the same time. Not hardly. And naturally Carson and Big Ed each had their own ideas about who should be in when and the more we puzzled and planned and argued and figured the more complicated and impossible it got. Geez, we were only an hour into the blessed race and already we were yelling at each other, you know? I decided to maybe take a short hike down to the Aston pits to check in with Tommy Edwards and see how those guys handled pit stop strategy. Not that it figured to do much good. But at least it would get me away from Big Ed and Carson, both of whom were wound up tighter than a hairpin valve spring and changing their minds every two seconds just to blow off some of the tension. I guess the prospect of hopping in a front-running race car and knowing there's no way you can keep up the pace is a little intimidating. Maybe more than a little, even.

Things were much calmer up in the Aston pits, where John Wyer sat on this tall chair looking out over everything like a hawk on its perch, only pausing to glance at his clipboard and jot down times when his two team cars went by. I found Tommy back behind the tires, sneaking himself a quick smoke. He looked a little tense, which was unusual for him. At least I'd never seen it before. "You guys are looking pretty good," I told him.

"It's early days yet, sport." He snuffed out his cigarette. "Early days."

"Yeah, but you got both cars running in the top three. I mean, you couldn't ask for much better'n that."

"Touch wood." He rapped his knuckles on an orange crate full of oil and brake fluid cans. "But it does put a bit of pressure on."

"Oh, it's just another race, Tommy. You've been in a million of 'em."

"True enough. But these once- and twice-around-the-clock marathons are something else. You're not just out there by yourself in these things."

"You're not?"

"No," he shook his head, "here you're carrying the whole bloody crew on your shoulders. You don't want to be the sorry bloke who lets them down."

"Oh, you'll do fine," I assured him. "You always do."

"I surely hope to. I understand there was quite a bit of discussion about which bloody drivers to bring along for this race. My name wasn't exactly at the top of everyone's list."

"Well, it should've been."

"That's kind of you to say," he said, patting me on the arm. "I think it's maybe even worse for poor old Geoff Duke."

"How's that?"

"Oh, some of the factory people don't fancy him much. Of course, he made a fabulous reputation for himself on motorbikes-can't tell you how many bloody championships he's won-but a lot of so-called experts believe cars are a different kettle of fish entirely."

"Whadda *you* think?"

Tommy shrugged. "I think he'll do a bloody good job. After all, he's a *racer.* Through and through. No bloody question about it. But so much can happen in one of these things..." he looked off into the distance "...you just don't want to be the poor, sorry bloke behind the wheel when it does." And that's when I got my first inkling about the one great, unwritten law of endurance racing-*If you're in the car, it's YOUR fault!*-no matter if you get smashed into by another car or the crankshaft breaks because some idiot at the factory didn't torque the bolts properly or a bolt of lightning shoots out of the sky and zaps you halfway down the backstraight or a rhinoceros escapes from a local zoo and charges you broadside from behind the next corner station, if it happens while you're at the wheel, it's somehow your responsibility. And you feel it, too. Even if you know there was nothing on God's green earth you could do. After all, everything was running fine until *you* got in....

"I'm sure it'll work out fine for both of you," I told Tommy, and of course that's precisely when Cal came sputtering into pit lane with Carson's MG running on maybe two-and-a-half cylinders. *"Jeezuschristalmighty!"* I yelped, and dashed lickety-split down towards our end of pit row. By the time I got there, Spud had the hood up and the distributor cap off-like Butch Bohunk always said, *"always make sure yer sparks'r in order before y'start fucking around with the carburetion"*-but I saw right away that the jet tube on the rear S.U. had dropped down so it was running like it had the choke full on. I reached in and pushed it back up, and promptly burned the hell out of my wrist on the exhaust manifold. I could even smell it. *"I need some wire over here!"* I hollered, yanking my hand out of there. A moment later, Spud was shoving a roll of 10-gauge electrical wire in my face. *"No, not that kind!"* I yelled. *"I need MECHANIC'S wire!"* I watched Carson tear desperately into our parts boxes-rolls of tape and squirt cans of oil and collections of wire connectors flying in all directions-and quickly decided I was better off doing it myself. *"GET OUT OF THE WAY!"* I yelled at him. *"You and Big Ed put the fuel in! Then get your helmet and gloves on! Spud! Put the damn distributor back together and check the oil and water!"* I found the wire. *"The brake fluid, too! Check the brake fluid! And the tires!"*

Well, it was a Chinese fire drill and seemed to take absolutely forever, but, in the end, we had Carson's MG fixed up and back on the track in less than seven minutes. Which was one hell of a good job for a crew that hadn't so much as cleaned off a windshield together before. In fact, I was thinking we ought to buy Team Jersey team jerseys for everybody, you know? Just so people would know who we are. Why, even Big Ed did okay, except that he got caught watching Sammy Speed tool by in his Jaguar rather than keeping an eye on the MG's gas tank and spilled about two gallons of high test all over the place. The bad part was we'd lost at least a lap on the new class leaders, and Carson certainly wouldn't be much help running ten or more seconds slower per lap than Cal. Plus the spilled gas meant I couldn't do any decent calculations on fuel consumption, but my seat-of-the-pants best guess was that the early stop would mean we'd have to make one extra pit stop near the end in order to go the distance. Assuming we made it that far.

Fortunately Sammy was still running smooth, clean, and strong in Big Ed's Jaguar-holding a solid second among the regular XK-120's with the leader well in sight-but I noticed Big Ed getting more and more nervous and fidgety as the time for the Jag's first pit stop approached. He was sitting there on the spare tires with his helmet on, staring down into his lap while he tugged his driving gloves on and then pulled them off again a couple dozen times. "Y'think maybe we oughta leave Sammy in a little longer?" he finally asked as we got down to the last few minutes.

"I dunno," I told him, avoiding his eyes. "It's *your* car, after all. Whadda *you* wanna do?"

"Well," Big Ed mused, still fooling around with his gloves, "it's just he's doin' so *good,* you know?"

"Yeah, he is," I nodded.

"But maybe he's tired. He's been out there more'n two hours."

I allowed as how I doubted a pro like Sammy Speed would be tired.

"We're runnin' second in class now, aren't we?"

"Yep. And maybe tenth or eleventh overall."

"He sure is doin' *good,*" Big Ed repeated, slowly shaking his head.

I scribbled an "IN" sign on our chalkboard and showed it to Sammy on his thirty-fifth lap, and just over four minutes and ten seconds later he came barreling down pit lane and brought the Jag to a screeching halt directly in front of us. Spud and Cal gassed it up while I checked under the hood and Sammy started to clamber out of the car. "You feelin' OK, Sammy?" Big Ed asked.

"My leg's a little stiff an' I could do with a drink of water. But aside from that I'm feelin' pretty good."

"Hm. Think y'could maybe pull another shift?" Big Ed asked sheepishly. "You're doin' *awful* good out there."

A big smile spread out under Sammy's goggles. "I was hopin' you'd ask."

"Okay, then," Big Ed said, patting him on the helmet, "try another spin and lessee what happens."

Sammy climbed back behind the wheel and Spud handed him a paper cup full of water. "How'r the gauges running?" he asked.

"Oil's not too low and the water's not too high."

"That's what we like to hear."

Cal got the last drop of the last gallon in, fastened the cap down, and we waved him off. I think the whole thing took less than four minutes. Then we looked back up pit lane where that Walt Hansgen's Jag was in and he was handing over to his co-driver, a guy named Don McKnought. I didn't figure he'd be as quick as either Walt or Sammy. And that was good, since we'd need ourselves one hell of a lead before Big Ed got in the car.

Big Ed knew it, too.

Then we started to notice an ominous little cloud of oilsmoke following Carson's TD every time it went by. It wasn't one of your huge, opaque, mosquito abatement varieties, but more one of those little nagging wisps that just refuse to go away and get you wondering just where the hell it's coming from and how much oil might be left in that wonderful new engine of mine. Carson wasn't due in for at least another hour, but I finally worried myself down to where I called him in to check it. I popped the hood and gave everything a quick once-over, and right away saw as how there was oil all over one side of the engine. So I gave the oil filler cap and the two valve cover hold-down nuts a frantic, make-sure twist-one of them didn't feel exactly right-before realizing that the dipstick was missing and that's where the damn oil was coming out. Lord only knows where it'd gone! So now I had two problems to deal with. I had to somehow stop the bleeding down there and then figure out how much oil to add without the blessed mark on the dipstick to guide me. And, as always in an endurance race, the clock was running.

Spud found a piece of rubber fuel line that was about the right diameter and I shoved it down in the hole and kind of tied it on with some mechanic's wire-poking the wire through the rubber and twisting it around two of the oil pan bolt heads-then made kind of a chimney out of it by running the tube up the side of the engine and lashing it to one of the valve cover hold down nuts. It wasn't pretty, but I figured it ought to work (at least until I sent Cal around to scrounge up another dipstick) and the only thing left was to decide how much oil to put in. "Whaddaya think?" I asked Spud. "One quart or two?"

"I dunno," Spud shrugged. "Why not split the difference?"

So I added a quart and a half and sent Carson back out again to finish his stint. We really should have topped up the fuel before we sent him back out, but of course I didn't think of that until he was pulling away. The good news was that the oil cloud diminished significantly the next lap and was gone entirely a few laps later. And of course Cal had no problem borrowing us a replacement dipstick from a blown-up TC a few pits down whose owners were already well into the beer frame.

Right at three hours all the leaders came in for their first stops, and by that time you could see that many of the cars were sporting dings here and there from banging into those stupid steel drums or rudely colliding with one another while disputing the same chunk of pavement. First in was Reg Parnell's Aston at 2:57pm, and John Wyer's team did a topnotch job of refueling that big, thirty-gallon gas tank, changing all four wheels and tires, and getting Tommy Edwards into the car and off in a cloud of dust in just a tick over three minutes. Wow. Tommy gave me a hearty thumbs-up as he charged past us and out of the pits.

Sally Enderle had been giving pit signals to Creighton Pendleton in one of her typically jaw-dropping halter top outfits, but she really outdid herself when it came time to call the Ferrari in for fuel, tires, and to hand over the driving chores to Phil Hill. Out of nowhere, she strode proudly out to the edge of the track carrying the "IN" sign while wearing a red and white polka-dot bikini with matching headband and five-inch spike heels. Honest to God she did. Why, you could hear wrenches, screwdrivers, and globs of drool hitting the pavement all up and down pit lane.

I guess Creighton'd been having some sort of brake problem where he had to pump the pedal a few times to get the pressure up, and so the Muscatelli brothers swarmed all over the car to see what they could do while their geeky brother

Sydney put the fuel in and Creighton pulled Phil Hill aside to tell him about it. Then the last of the fuel went in and Phil got in the car and everything seemed set except one of the Muscatelli guys was still stuck underneath, working away desperately at the right front brake adjuster. At times like that, with the car still hung on the jack and the rest of the cars roaring past and the race seemingly slipping away, it's like everything peels into agonizing slow motion. *"What the hell's wrong under there?"* Creighton demanded angrily.

Giuseppe Muscatelli's head came out from under the fender. *"She's a-no adjust, ey?"* he screamed at Creighton. *"She's a-spin and a-spin and a-spin, but she's a-no adjust!"*

"Then leave it! Phil'll just have to pump the damn things same as I did." And he leaned over to yell as much into Phil's ear while the car came down and an instant later the Ferrari was roaring out of the pits and back into the fray. With, I noticed, the brake lights flashing on and off as Phil Hill wisely checked out the pedal feel before he actually had to call on them in earnest. Personally, I thought they maybe should've taken a little more in-depth look at the problem before they sent him back out. I mean, there are lots of things you can soldier on without in a race, but brakes and steering aren't exactly among them. Anything else goes wrong and you at least have a shot at getting the car over to the side and out of harm's way. But lose the brakes or steering and you're pretty much turned into a passenger on what usually turns out to be a pretty ugly ride.

The second Aston and the Cunningham came in for service a few minutes later-Geoff Duke and Johnny Fitch taking over, respectively-and by this time most everybody else had stopped for fuel and driver changes, too. And not three laps later, poor Geoff Duke got caught with a round in the chamber in the Russian Roulette game of lapped traffic heading into the Warehouse Hairpin. Most of the eyewitness accounts had him coming up to lap (who else?) Skippy Welcher in his C-Type as they both bore down on a pair of tiddlers engaged in their own battle. At first it looked like The Skipper was going under them both before the braking zone-so Geoff naturally pulled out to follow the faster car through-but then apparently Skippy chickened out and decided to swing back over behind the smaller cars again. Geoff of course went for the opening, and he was about a third of the way alongside The Skipper's C-Type when Skippy had another change of heart (I'm sure he had *no* idea the Aston was even there!) and jinked out to the right again, leaving the Aston absolutely no place to go. Geoff instinctively swerved to avoid a collision, glanced off the Jag's fender anyway, and went bounding across the grass and sand on the inside of the corner, airborne most of the time according to eyewitness reports. And everyone knows your brakes don't do much when your blessed wheels are off the ground! The Aston shot back across the track just as the first of the tiddlers rounded the corner, collecting him broadside and spinning them both *hard* into the haybales on the far side. Meanwhile Skippy and the other tiddler just motored on through with hardly a scratch. Can you believe it? But of course that's one of the things you learn about racing; that you can very easily have somebody else's accident for them. It happens all the time. And, as so often happens, The Skipper continued blithely on with no more than a slightly bashed fender and a thoroughly out-raged bar story about "that God-damned idiot English motorcycle jockey who ran right into me."

There is no justice in this world.

Geoff Duke did manage to untangle the Aston from the haybales and limp back to the pits, but it only took a single, withering glance for John Wyer to see that the rear axle was too seriously damaged to continue. Geoff started to ex-plain what happened, but Wyer waved him off. The car was finished and that was that. There was really no point knowing anything more.

Turns out it was one hell of a motor race at Sebring that year-a real cat-and-mouse game between the John Fitch/Phil Walters Cunningham C4R and Reg Parnell and Tommy Edwards in the remaining Aston DB3-but I really didn't know a lot of the details until I heard all the bar stories afterwards and read Hank Lyons' race report in *Road and Track* a few months later. But that's just what happens in endurance racing. What starts out like any other race turns into a kazillion little individual events and episodes all around the circuit and up and down pit lane, and pretty soon it's the old "can't see the forest for the trees" routine when you've actually got a car or two in the race. You can't help being preoccupied with what's happening to your own car, and you also can't avoid getting sucked into what's happening to the team right next to you in pit lane. It doesn't take more than a few hours and a handful of major scares and minor emergencies before you've completely lost track of the bigger picture. And, once that's happened, it's damn near impossible to get it all knitted back to-gether again in your mind. Of course the big teams-at least the *experienced* big teams, anyway-have special people who do nothing but keep lap charts. Lap after lap. Hour after hour. Pit stop after pit stop. And not just their own cars, either. They keep track of damn near everybody in the whole blessed race. Or at least in their class. That's because otherwise they'd be at the mercy of the so-called "official standings" the stewards at the pre-race drivers' meeting *prom-ised* would be posted on the bulletin board behind race control absolutely every half hour without fail no matter what. Which all by itself should've been a serious tipoff that no way in hell would it ever happen. The experienced guys knew all about it, too.

Carson came back in and handed the MG over to Cal-the car was running pretty decent but no question we were well down the standings-and then I brought Sammy in and again Big Ed asked him if he wanted to stay out a little longer and again Sammy said "fine with me," took a drink of water, and headed back onto the circuit. We were a solid first in class at that point, and I figured we were damn near a half lap ahead of the next XK-120. Then one of the Excaliburs sputtered in trailing a thick cloud of steam, and it must've been a head gasket because it erupted into a damn geyser when they took off the radiator cap. That was it for them, and Carson, Big Ed, and me helped them push it back into the paddock. They were really nice guys-especially that Brooks Stevens character who designed the cars-and I really hoped the other one would go the distance. I think that's all they really wanted, you know?

Briggs Cunningham and his co-driver were running unbelievably well in that elegant little 1350cc OSCA, but they were still second on Index to that goofy little French Douche Bag with its popcorn popper 745cc engine. The supercharged D.B. was being co-driven by the French guy who built them, Rene Bonnet, and an American guy named Wade Moorehouse, and I swear the racket it made would just about crystallize the wax in your ears. Even Briggs Cunningham admitted it was a shoo-in for the index prize if it just kept motoring along to the finish.

It was no surprise to see Phil Hill doing a hell of a job in Creighton Pendleton's Ferrari-wonky brakes and all-holding down a smooth and secure third overall even though he had to pump the pedal four or five times before every corner and yet still running a second or two quicker than Creighton. That had to be eating Creighton alive, and I'll wager I wasn't the only guy on pit lane who thought it couldn't have happened to a nicer guy. Not hardly. And then Phil went missing. The Ferrari was only a few pits down from us, and I could see all the questions and concern swirling around in their eyes as Creighton and the Muscatelli brothers watched the seconds tick away and wondered where the hell he was. One of them ran down towards race control to see if they knew anything, and you could see the brows furrowing and frowns growing longer as thirty seconds late stretched into a minute. Then one minute into two. Then three. Then four. Sally Enderle looked *very* unhappy about the situation. Creighton just looked mean.

About fifteen minutes later Phil appeared, walking slowly towards pit lane from the general direction of the esses, shoulders slumped, eyes downcast, and helmet dangling limply from his hand. I felt all empty inside as he trudged past us, still looking at the ground. Creighton Pendleton was standing there waiting for him like a concrete bridge abutment. "What the hell happened to my car?" he demanded in one of those icy, irritated voices that are often worse than actual screaming.

"It's wrecked," Phil said miserably. "It's over in the sand at the entrance to the esses. The brake pedal went right to the floor...."

"I told you to pump them!" Creighton howled, his voice climbing a few notches and wavering ominously.

"I did pump them," Phil said evenly, looking back into the glare from Creighton's eyes. "But it went to the floor anyway." He looked down at the ground again. "We're finished. I'm sorry."

Boy, you could tell how lousy he felt.

There wasn't much of anything more to say, so Phil went behind the pits to get some water out of the cooler, and I decided to sneak back myself and maybe have a word with him. "Geez, that's a tough break," I said.

"Oh, hi, Buddy," Phil answered listlessly, rummaging through the cooler.

"What happened out there?"

"Oh, we'd had some sort of brake problem where you had to pump them a few times to get the pedal up. And then all of a sudden there was nothing. I pumped like hell and that was it. *Nothing!"*

"So what happened?"

Phil's eyes got big. "It just went straight off. There was no way I could make the turn at that speed..." I saw a tiny, almost invisible little shiver go through him. "...then it launched off a little rise or something and went flying through the air-I must've been ten feet up!-and came crashing down into the foundation of some old army barracks they used to have over there." He shook his head and sighed. "The car's a mess." And then, out of nowhere, he let out this faint, helpless little laugh, as if there was something amazing and funny and remarkable about the whole thing.

"Well," I reminded him, "at least it wasn't your fault."

Phil Hill looked at me like I was speaking a foreign language.

It's amazing how a race that starts out like a flat-out, balls-to-the-wall sprint slowly, almost imperceptibly fades into an endless, numbing, endurance grind. But it does. You just can't hold that hot buzz of energy and excitement-that *edge*-for twelve solid hours. Besides which pitstops and retirements and mechanical gremlins and slower drivers paired with faster ones tend to spread things out so that leads that were once only a sliver of daylight inevitably stretch out to a handful of seconds, the length of a straightaway, more than a minute, more than a lap. And still the cars drone on-each one going 'round and 'round every four or five minutes or so-and all you can do is stand there in the pits sipping old, cold coffee, marking the times down, and worrying a little if they're too slow and even more if they're too fast. I guess you might say it's boring. Only it's not really, because the unexpected is always lurking out there-every single second of every single lap-and you've seen it happen often enough up and down pit lane to know that the racing gods are just *waiting* up there, hidden behind the clouds, snickering behind their hands and making little side bets with each other, ready to squash you in an instant if they catch so much as a whiff of confidence.

Like that tiny little Douche Bag that had run without a hitch and was leading easily on Index. But then the clutch started to slip. They brought it in and you could smell it was maybe a bum seal leaking oil onto the clutch. They looked pretty frantic about it, running around and wringing their hands and shouting helplessly back and forth at each other. Then one of the mechanics in the next pit suggested they could maybe get most of the goo cleaned off the disc by spraying a carbon tet fire extinguisher into the bellhousing. It was really a pretty good idea if you thought about it. But they grabbed the first fire extinguisher that fell to hand, and unfortunately it belonged to the pit lane safety steward officials rather than the team and was only to be used in case of genuine fire emergencies. They were disqualified on the spot. At least their teammates were still running in the supercharged car with the highly irritating exhaust note, and they instantly took over the lead on Index even though they were more than a whole lap behind.

Our friend Skippy Welcher was out, too, after co-driver Masten Gregory retired in rather lurid fashion when he went straight off at the hairpin his first lap back in the car. Not that it was entirely his fault, since I understand The Skipper neglected to tell him that he'd pretty much used up the brakes and you maybe had to pump them a couple dozen times to make them work. In any case, Masten came flying into the hairpin quite a bit faster and deeper than Skippy, and imagine his surprise when he went for the brake pedal at his customary Last Possible Instant and felt it plunge all the way to the floorboards. Realizing he was in a potentially ugly situation (and to the utter amazement of the spectators and corner crew!) Masten Gregory actually stood up in the blessed seat and bailed out over the side! Can you believe it? He got away with it, too, suffering no worse than a sore shoulder and a little nick on his elbow. Fact is, Masten Gregory became pretty famous for that kind of dismount as the years went by. Meanwhile, Skippy's brakeless and driverless C-type smashed through the haybales, bounded through a ditch, crossed the highway bordering the track property, entered the trailer park across the way, tore through four lines of drying laundry, and nosed into an abrupt halt broadside against a derelict Ford pickup some guy had up on blocks in his yard.

It was actually kind of funny.

Especially since nobody got killed.

Not even experienced hands were immune to the perils of Sebring. Poor Tommy had to take evasive action to avoid a spinning car and glanced off one of those awful steel marker drums lining the course. The damage wasn't bad, but it smashed up the right-hand headlight, and the Aston team knew they'd have to replace it before night fell. They'd wisely set their lights with the right one angling left and the left one angling right-cross-eyed, you know?-and that big Cyclops central light aimed right down the middle of the road. So losing that right side light would make them pretty much blind in left hand corners. But John Wyer had put together a really crack crew, and they got it repaired during their next fuel stop without losing much more than an extra thirty or forty seconds. Still, those seconds ultimately add up, and it was enough to put them out of touch with the leading Cunningham as the sun began to slowly ease its way down towards the top branches of the orange trees.

We were having our own troubles, too. The TD was smoking again, trailing an ominous little wisp of bluish-white smoke behind it as it Cal powered down the pit straightaway in front of us. Carson saw it, too, but neither of us said anything. It was like if we ignored it, maybe it would go away? Or at least not get any worse.

But the toughest deal of all happened to Dick Irish and the remaining Excalibur from the pits next to us. You could feel the numbing wave of worry and disappointment when all of a sudden it stopped coming around. It'd been running like a damn train all day-not terribly fast, but terrifically steady-and then, out of nowhere, it went missing. They sent a runner down to race control to try and find out what happened, but before that drama ended Cal was back in the pits trailing a pretty significant cloud of oil smoke. Oh, shit.

"It's pushing a bunch of oil out someplace," Cal hollered over the engine noise. *"I had to come in when I saw the pressure drop."*

I reached in and switched the key off. It looked pretty certain this would take awhile. But a quick peek under the hood proved it wasn't so bad after all. The valve cover had somehow shaken itself loose and dumped oil out all over the place. And I mean _ALL_ over the place! Including the exhaust manifold. So *that's* where the smoke was coming from! The bad news was that the valve cover gasket was pretty beat up, so I had to take the cover off and do my best to re-fit the pieces (slathering on a half tube of Permatex for good measure) and every-thing was going well until I tried to tighten it down, gave that iffy rear hold-down nut just that one little tweak too far, and stripped the threads.

Oh, *SHIT!*

It was probably just waiting to happen, too, since we'd all gone over every-thing a hundred dozen times before the race to make absolutely *sure* everything was snug, and then I'd tightened it again (and with commendable ferocity) when we suffered through that little dipstick problem earlier in the day.. In any case (and as anybody who knows anything about MG's can tell you) the valve cover hold down nuts on an MG engine are rather special bits that you can't exactly replace out of Old Man Finzio's coffee can. Or not easily, anyway. So I topped up the oil-it took almost three quarts!-and sent Cal back out to do one slow, careful lap while we raced around trying to locate the hardware we needed.

The guys in the Excalibur pits had a pretty nice collection of nuts and bolts, but it was all American S.A.E. and U.S.S. thread and we needed British Stan-dard. Fortunately that Hal Ullrich guy who built and co-drove the missing Excalibur for Brooks Stevens was a very clever mechanic, and he helped me cobble together some rubber seals and a couple big washers to move the nut further up the threads where it might find more to grab onto. At least until we managed to cannibalize the real stuff off one of the retired MG's. Hal was happy to help, too, since he figured he had plenty of time on his hands. While I was under the MG's hood, Cal told the Excalibur guys he'd seen Dick Irish pushing the missing car out on the furthest backside of the course, a good three miles from the pits. No question it was going to take Dick Irish quite awhile to make it in. If he even could.

Cal went back out and did a couple more laps while we scrounged around for a redundant MG-wouldn't you know, there was a TD with a fresh, gaping hole in the block just a few stalls down pit lane!- then brought him in again, replaced the whole valve cover, gasket, and stud assembly with the parts off the dead car, and added yet another quart and a half of oil. According to the rules, you were supposed to go at least twenty laps between fuel or oil stops, but Carson and Big Ed and all the Excalibur guys kind of huddled around us in pit lane so that none of the officials could see us. Cal was ready to let Carson back in-I mean, we were well out of it by now-but the sun was down into the tops of the citrus groves now, a dazzling ball of blast furnace yellow-orange staring the drivers right in the eye as they wailed down the backstraight into the K.L.G. Curve or tried to line themselves up for the Warehouse Hairpin. "Maybe you'd like to go out again?" Carson said meekly, shielding his eyes from the sun. I'd always had the impression that Carson's eyesight was nothing real special, you know?

"Sure. Why not," Cal shrugged, and hopped back into the TD. But he was in again the very next lap. *"I think maybe we hurt something inside the motor when the oil was low."*

"What's it doing?"

"Well, the oil pressure's down to thirty pounds. And that's if I'm lucky."

I looked over at Carson and explained in as few words as possible that we stood an excellent chance of blowing his expensive new motor sky high if we kept on running.

He thought it over for a moment or two. "Is it for sure going to blow?" he wanted to know.

"Well," I answered, trying to be as honest as I could, *"nothing's* for sure, Carson. We might be able to baby it home. And then again we might not. You just never know. But it'll for sure be a lot safer and cheaper to fix if we switch it off now."

Carson ran his tongue nervously across his lips. "But we *might* be able to make it to the finish, right?"

"Yeah," I admitted, "we might. But it's one hell of a risk."

He hesitated for a minute, teetering on the brink, but then you could see his eyes narrow down and jaw take a set. "What the hell," he finally said, "let's *do* it! We didn't come all the way down here to Florida to just tuck our tails between our legs and run home."

"You *sure?"*

Carson nodded. "Yep. Let's try to *finish* this thing. Either that or we'll just run her till she blows." I must admit I really admired the look in the little pipsqueak's eye.

Cal did, too. "Why don't you do the honors, then," he said, clapping an arm around Carson's shoulder.

"You think I can?" Carson asked, squinting into the sun.

"Not a doubt in my mind," Cal assured him. "You just get on out there and show everybody how a *real* man babies a sick car around."

So Carson climbed in and took off, and as soon as he left Cal and I looked at each other and broke out laughing. We couldn't help ourselves, you know?

Meanwhile poor Dick Irish was out there somewhere, pushing, pushing, *pushing* that silent Excalibur back towards the pits as the sun dropped lower and lower into the trees and a mean evening chill crept into the air.

By this time Sammy was due in with our Jag. He'd driven the whole damn race so far, and was still leading the regular XK-120 class by about a minute and a half as best I could figure. This time he bailed out of the cockpit as soon as the tires screeched to a halt and ran around behind the pits to, well, let's just say he was under a little pressure after more than six straight hours in the car. The tires looked pretty ragged-he'd been working 'em *hard* through the corners, even though he was going easy as possible on the engine, brakes and gearbox-and I decided this was maybe a better time to change them while we still had a glimmer of twilight left than to try and do it at night. So Cal ran the jack up while Spud and I wielded the knockoff hammers and put the new set of skins on, and this time there wasn't any discussion at all when the Jag came down off the jack. Sammy looked at Big Ed and Big Ed nodded and Sammy climbed right back in the car. He was some kind of race driver, all right.

About forty-five minutes later Dick Irish and the dead Excalibur appeared up at the far end of pit lane, advancing at no more than an exhausted, agonized crawl through one pool of light after another as he pushed that car through the glare of still-active pits and the deep patches of darkness where teams who were out of it had already packed up their stuff and gone home. The Excalibur crew knew that nobody could help him or they'd be disqualified, but they ran up to him and walked alongside, encouraging him and urging him on as he pushed and strained and stumbled to try and get the car up to their pit. He did it, too-took him almost two hours all told-and you had to love his sense of humor when he finally arrived. "Brooks?" he asked softly, standing there shivering in a pool of his own sweat. "Exactly who was it wanted our space way up at this end of the line?"

Turns out the diff had busted-you could hear all this nasty stuff gnashing around inside when they jacked it up and turned the rear wheels-but there were apparently a lot of teeth still left on the gears (or pieces of teeth, anyway) and that Hal Ullrich guy had the bright idea that they could maybe fill it up with a sort of vomit paste of heavy grease and wood chips and tiny nuts and bolts and little bits of metal and God-knows-what-else to jam up the gaps and make it to the finish. They did, too. Dead last, but they made it. And, come the awards party Monday night, they awarded Dick Irish a special sportsmanship trophy. He really deserved it, too.

Nighttime at Sebring was downright eerie. I don't think there's anyplace on earth as deep and black and empty as those runways at night. It was also cold and windy, and you felt your teeth chattering as you stood there in the pits punching the stopwatches and writing down times that really didn't mean much of anything anymore. Barring incidents or problems, the order was pretty much set. At the top of the charts, Fitch and Walters in the Cunningham had eased away from Reg and Tommy's Aston by the better part of a lap (which, when you think about it, is still unbelievably close after nine solid hours of racing) and everybody else was pretty much soldiering on and trying to hold station to the finish. Or maybe trying to creep up on the next guy in class if they looked like he was having a problem. Those of us who were left had been together for two solid days now, and the pairs of headlights sweeping out of the last turn that had looked so similar and anonymous the night before each had their own personalities now. Tommy's Aston with that big Cyclops eye in the middle and one headlight askew. The Cunningham with the two small, brilliant aircraft landing lights inside the regular beams searing into the darkness. The fanfare blare of the Aston's straight six compared to the deep gut-rumble of the big Chrysler Hemi in the Cunningham. And the staccato beat of their tires over the tar strips told you they were still-by far- the two fastest cars out there. In fact, you could recognize every single car, from the close-set eyes and corn-popper shriek of the Index-leading Deutsch Bonnet (it didn't deserve to be called a Douche Bag anymore) to the sick sputter and pirate leer of a C-Type with valve problems and a smashed headlamp, just trying to limp home and score a finish. I could tell our MG and XK-120 from any of the other MG's and XK-120's as easily as a momma sheep can pick out her own lambs from a flock of strangers.

We were doing pretty good at that point, too. Carson's MG was still out there, circulating regular as clockwork every five minutes or so and holding close to thirty pounds on the oil pressure gauge at full throttle, while Sammy and the Jag were now the better part of a lap ahead of the second place XK-120 and looking pretty well set for a well-deserved class win. The only problem was that Big Ed was going to have to get in the car sometime if he wanted to be classified in the results, and you could see he was plenty nervous about it. Especially now that it was full dark.

"Look, maybe you could just leave him in till the finish?" I suggested. I mean, Sammy'd driven himself one hell of a race-his first-ever sportscar race, too!-and I figured he deserved that class win. But it *was* Big Ed's car, and I had to bear in mind that Big Ed was not only my friend and best customer, but also sort of my business partner now, too.

Big Ed thought it over and shook his head. "Nah, I can't do it," he finally sighed. "Everybody'll think I'm some kinda puss if I don't get out there and put some laps in."

I looked at Carson and Spud and they looked back at me. "Look," I said, "I gotta bring him in for fuel in a couple laps. But it won't be quite enough to get us to the finish. I figure we'll have to stop again for a quick splash with maybe about fifteen or twenty minutes to go. How about waiting till then?"

I could see Big Ed was mulling it over.

"And remember, that second place XK-120 only has to stop once, so we'll lose a little time to them in the pits…" It was pretty obvious I wanted to steer Big Ed towards that last stop-just trying to push it as far off into the future as possible, you know?-but it was obvious Big Ed didn't feel real comfortable about letting Sammy run the whole damn race and then hopping in at the last minute to hog the glory part at the end. And I had to give Big Ed a lot of credit in the character department for that. But I also figured leaving Sammy in was still our best shot, and I told Big Ed as much.

"You're afraid I'll fuck things up, arent'cha?" he growled at me. "Ain'tcha forgettin' whose damn car it is?"

"I'm not forgetting anything," I told him, looking him square in the eye, "but Sammy's a genuine pro-caliber driver and that's all there is to it." I could see that hurt him, and I felt pretty lousy about it. "Geez, Ed, this is about the biggest, most important damn race we've ever been in and we got a chance for a good finish here-I mean a *really* good finish-and wouldn't it make Skippy and Charlie Priddle and Creighton Pendleton and the rest of those stuck-up S.C.M.A. bastards eat their livers to see you drive it across the finish line and into victory circle?" You could see from the roll of Big Ed's stogie he was conjuring up the picture in his mind. "First in class," I added, just to turn that shot from black-and-white into color.

"B-but won't they know I was just in for the last couple minutes?"

"Who the hell knows anything in a race like this," I lied. "Once it's dark and you can't see the helmets, how d'ya know who's in *any* of the cars."

"Hmm," Big Ed nodded, rolling the notion around in his head.

"If you want, you could maybe even smear a little dirt and grease on your face or even do a few pushups or something to work up a sweat. Just to make it all look legit."

Big Ed looked at me like that was the most disgusting, dishonest, and thoroughly magnificent idea he'd ever heard in his life.

"I'm bringin' him in next lap," Spud yelled over from trackside.

Big Ed looked down at his shoes. "Okay," he kind of half-mumbled. "You're a smart kid, Buddy. You got a deal." Then he thought of a way to save a little face. "But if Sammy says he's getting' tired," he added bravely, "I'm takin' over."

The odds on Sammy Speed admitting he was tired were as long as on our parish priest announcing he'd had sex with barnyard animals. It just wasn't in the cards, you know?

So we brought him in and Spud and Carson gassed him up while I checked the tires. They were nothing special, but they were at least as good as what we had left on the other spare wheels. Boy, you could really feel the heat off the brakes. Sammy looked pretty damn bushed, but he knew how close we were to the end and recognized without being told what was going on with Big Ed. "How's the car?" I asked him.

"Ahh, the brakes've been a little soft for the past couple hours-I gotta pump 'em a few times to get enough pedal for the hairpin-and the left front's grabbing a little, too."

"Anything else?"

"Oh, yeah. It pops out of third gear when you ease off the gas. You gotta kinda hold it in with your hand."

"But everything else's okay?"

"We got a little clutch slip going into fourth. But it's okay if I baby it."

I nodded. "How about the gauges?"

"How would I know?" he laughed. "The goddamn dash lights haven't worked since the last pitstop."

Probably a fuse I thought as Sammy roared off into the night. He appeared again some four minutes and eighteen seconds later-drifting smoothly and sweetly out of the K.L.G. Curve and onto the pit straight-just like clockwork.

The tough part was going to be explaining all the things that were going wrong with the car to Big Ed, and somehow giving him enough coaching so he could nurse it along to the finish. "You got to back off real early for the corners and pump the brakes a little to build up the pedal," I told him. "And it pulls to the right when you get on the brakes hard. And you gotta remember to hold it in third gear or it'll pop out." Geez, I sounded like a little league coach talking to a rookie relief pitcher just before the ninth inning of a tie game. And I gotta give Big Ed credit. He was listening just as hard as he could. Even if I got the feeling it was all just swirling around in his head a few times before leaking out his other ear. "Oh," I remembered. "And the dash lights are out, so you can't see the tach or the gauges."

"I never look at 'em anyway," Big Ed admitted proudly.

Well, at least that was one less thing to worry about.

With a little under two hours to go we brought the gimpy MG in for its last stop. The oil pressure was reading less than 25 now, and a sharp mechanic could smell and even faintly hear the beginnings of the terminal rod bearing death rattle that would inevitably spell the end of one pretty damn good MG motor. But it looked like we were getting the slow, agonizing brand of deterioration rather than the Cataclysmic Fragmentation Bomb version, and I actually held out slim hopes that we might make it to the checker. Cal climbed out to hand it back over to Carson, but Carson didn't look real eager about it. "Y-you want to get back in?" he asked in his little pipsqueak voice. I guess he figured Cal had that special, sixth-sense mechanical sympathy about race cars. Or at least more of it than he did. Not to mention that Cal could certainly see a lot better out there on the runways at night. But Cal surprised the shit out of me when he said he wouldn't hear of it.

"Nah," he said. "You got us this far, Carson. I think *you* oughtta be the guy who takes us home."

"R-really?"

Cal nodded. "No question about it."

So Carson hopped in and took off, and right away I walked up to Cal and shook his hand. "That was a damn nice thing for you to do."

"If you say so."

"Whaddaya mean, 'if I say so?' You made him feel like a million bucks."

"Well," Cal said sheepishly, "the truth is that I don't figure it's gonna last much longer-the needle's about falling right off the gauge whenever the revs drop-and I didn't much fancy the idea of hiking two or three miles back to the pits. It's *cold* out there."

"Y'know, Cal," I said disgustedly, "you really didn't have to tell me that."

"Sure I did," Cal grinned. "I can't have you walking around thinking I'm a nice guy or anything. It'll only get you disappointed later on."

As always happens in endurance racing, the tiny, almost invisible advantages the Fitch/Walters Cunningham had piled up one on top of another over Tommy and Reg Parnell in the Aston throughout the day and evening had added up to an insurmountable lead. So long as things continued according to plan, anyway. Still, I felt happy as hell for Tommy. Barring any blind-side blow ups or screwups in the last forty-five minutes, their Aston would come home second overall and first in class (not to mention second on Index thanks to their 2.9 liter motor) and that was one hell of a fine result. Not to mention that he'd held his own with some of the best drivers in the whole damn world. And believe me, there's never any tougher, more troubling competition in all of motor sport than a quicker teammate....

I was proud of the Cunningham, too. Even though there were no factory teams from Ferrari or Jaguar or Mercedes Benz at Sebring that year, it was still a genuine World Class event, and, for the first time *ever,* an all-American car was going to win! It made you swell up a little inside, you know?

Still, I was nervous about that last stop for our Jag and handing it over to Big Ed, and I calculated and re-calculated how much fuel we'd used so I could leave Sammy out there until the last possible moment. But eventually, with just shy of twenty minutes to go, I had to bring him in. The good news was that the other Jag had a wheel jam on the splines when they were trying to put fresh rubber on so Walt Hansgen could put on a final sprint to the finish, and then, somehow, the knockoff got kicked into the darkness and they couldn't find the damn thing even after they'd decided to just leave the old tire on so's he could get back out there. It wound up costing them more than a lap, so now the pressure was off and all Big Ed had to do was stroke it home.

"All you gotta do is stroke it home," I told him confidently while crossing all my fingers behind my back. My toes in my shoes, too.

"Y-yeah," Big Ed mumbled, not looking all that convinced. As I'd suggested, he'd gone behind the pits and dirtied himself up a little so he'd look convincing. But he'd done a typically Big Ed job of it so he looked more like he'd come second best in a fight with a lube rack than someone who'd spent four or five of the previous twelve hours out racing around the runways of Hendricks Field.

"And remember about the brakes," I reminded him for the umpty-hundredth time. "And the clutch. And about holding it in third."

Big Ed nodded each time, but I don't really think he heard me.

Sammy pulled gently to a halt right in front of us and switched off. Cal and Spud put five gallons in the tank while Big Ed and I helped him out of the car. It was like lifting a sack of potatoes. "You okay?" I asked.

"Just a little stiff, that's all. But forget about me, huh? Get that big guy in the car and get him the hell out of here."

So I pushed Big Ed into the car and watched him take a deep breath and hit the starter button and...

Nothing!

"JESUSFUCKINGCHRIST!"

"WHAT THE HELL'S WRONG?"

"I DON'T KNOW!"

"TRY IT AGAIN!"

Nothing.

"TURN OFF THE LIGHTS!"

"THEY ARE OFF!"

"THEN TURN THEM ON!"

Big Ed looked puzzled.

"TURN THE DAMN LIGHTS ON! I NEED TO SEE IF WE GOT ANY JUICE LEFT IN THE BATTERY!"

Big Ed flipped the lights on. They looked fine. But then he hit the starter button again and they dimmed down to almost nothing.

Shit!

Well, the rules were pretty specific that cars always had to start under their own power-you couldn't push them or anything-and you couldn't hitch up a booster battery unless you had one on board. Here we were, just over fifteen minutes from the end of the damn race-*TWELVE FREAKING HOURS!*-and we were licked by a damn dead battery. But then I had a thought. Maybe it *wasn't* a dead battery. Maybe it was just a loose connection or a short or something in the starter motor or the ignition switch. So I dove into the passenger seat and undid the two knurled nuts that hold center dashboard in place while Cal jacked up the side so Spud could scramble underneath to check out the starter motor. And meanwhile the seconds were turning into minutes and those were ticking away one after another after another. *Damn! We've got to get this thing rolling!*

"*TRY IT AGAIN!*" Spud yelled from under the fender as the other XK-120 sped past down the pit straight. Now they were back on the same lap with us.

"*JESUS! JUST A SECOND!*" I had the inside of the dashboard spread all over my lap. "*OKAY. HERE GOES.*"

I hit the button and the engine whoomped to life. But I still had to get the dash screwed back in place. Or enough back together that something wouldn't fall out or short and make the car quit someplace out on the circuit. And of course that's when Cal dropped the jack and the car crashed down on the pavement and those two stupid little knurled nuts that hold an XK-120's dash panel in place fell down into the passenger side footwell.

"*SHIT!*"

"*WHAT?*"

"*NEVERMIND!*" I tore wildly at the floorboards and finally came up with one of them-*that would do!*-then fumbled with clumsy, shaking fingers to screw it back in.

"*GOT IT! IT'S FIXED!*"

"*THEN GET THE HELL OUT OF THERE!*"

Oh. Yeah. I was still in the car.

I bailed out over the side and Big Ed damn near ran me over as he squealed out of the pits. I swear, I was trembling like a little kid when I got up off the concrete and dusted myself off.

"Well," Spud grinned, "that was pretty exciting, wasn't it?"

"Yeah," I agreed shakily. "A little *too* exciting if you ask me."

"But we got it *done!*" Cal whooped, punching his fist into the air. "That's the really great thing!"

"Yep, you boys did a nice job there," Sammy Speed said in a weary, rasping voice. "Even if it *did* look a little like a old Buster Keaton movie."

That's when I turned around and really looked at Sammy for the very first time. The lines in his face looked like greasy leather crevices and you could see in his eyes that Sammy was still out there on the runways, chasing that frail, vibrating blob of headlight beam like he was falling down a hole with no bottom. He looked exhausted. Fact is, we *all* looked exhausted. But it was that good, fulfilling kind of exhaustion you get when you know you've run the last mile, cleared the last hurdle, fought the good fight and survived. Why, even Carson in our walking-dead MG was still out there circulating.

It was a miracle, you know?

And of course that's when the MG reappeared at the far end of pit lane, barely creeping along with the lights off, the right front tire flat and wobbly, and the fender over it pointing towards the sky. "Jesus, what the hell happened?" I asked as Carson pulled up in front of us.

"The damn lights went out! All by themselves! I didn't do ANYthing!" You could tell by Carson's voice that it must've been pretty exciting. *"Then I was fooling with the light switch and I hit one of those stupid steel drums!"* Geez, he was damn near crying, you know? *"I was trying to slow down,"* he whimpered, *"but I just couldn't see!"*

"Hey, don't worry about it," I told him, then added what I hoped was a reassuring pat on the shoulder, "Let's have a look."

Well, the headlights turned out to be simple enough-the blessed fuse had managed to pop loose after twelve hours of pounding-and while I tracked that down and fixed it Spud put one of the used spares on the left front and we got him back out there in less than five minutes. Spud and me were getting pretty good at this stuff, no lie.

And that's when Sammy told us he hadn't seen Big Ed come around....

We looked at each other, but nobody said anything. And that's when this bright red-orange rocket of an emergency flare shot up someplace behind us and popped into a feeble little red-orange umbrella in the sky.

"What the hell was that?"

"I'm not sure." It was way off in the distance, somewhere around the fast, third gear sweeper where the two long runways came together. And that's when I remembered what Big Ed said about getting some kind of signal to use if he got stranded out there on those runways at night.

"Oh, God! It's Big Ed," I moaned. And I was sure of it. Turns out Big Ed arrived at the Dunlop Turn where the two longest straightaways come together only to find the same exact steel drum that Carson had hit rolling down the middle of the roadway. It was just dumb, shitty luck that Big Ed happened to be the next car around. And you'd have to say Big Ed was doing pretty well up to that point. Hell, he'd gone more than two-thirds of a lap, remembering about the brakes pulling and babying the clutch and even holding it in third gear. But then his headlight beams swept through a fast corner and revealed this lumpy old oil drum rolling across the road right smack dab in front of him! He instinctively swerved and lifted off the gas, and of course as soon as he lifted the gear lever popped out of third and he immediately started to lose it. There was a long, screeching slide, somewhere in the middle of which he jammed on the brakes, and naturally the left front locked solid and yanked everything back the other way into yet another endless, tire-rending screech across the concrete. But he was bleeding off speed all the time and it most likely still could've been just a harmless little spin even then. Only when he finally went off, it was still kind of sideways and the wheels dug into that soft, sandy soil and rolled the car over.

Luckily Big Ed wasn't hurt-it was one of those slow, stupid, Vaudeville Pratfall kind of roll-overs that wound up depositing him in the grass like some college frat prankster had pulled a chair out from under him. It was a good thing that Big Ed packed that signal flare into the door pocket before the race started (although he could have remembered to tell us about it!) on account of the weeds were about neck high out where he was overturned and they never would've found him till sunup without it.

Sure, we were all disappointed. Devastated, in fact. But you'd have to say it wasn't entirely Big Ed's fault. That oil drum could've popped up in front of anybody. Although you couldn't avoid the ugly suspicion that maybe, just maybe, Sammy Speed would've found a way to miss it. In his defense, Big Ed never for an instant believed he was in the same league as Sammy, and besides that he'd jumped into a car with all sorts of stuff going wrong with it and maybe the best damn XK-120 driver in the country trying to reel him in. Plus our electrical problem panic in the pits must've put him in a pretty frazzled state of mind even before he went out. And he hadn't really had much in the way of night practice, either. Or at least those were all the things I kept telling myself over and over so I wouldn't say anything I'd be sorry for later. Besides, you could tell Big Ed felt plenty awful about it already.

And who could blame him?

All I know is that I've never experienced anything like the way we all felt when we realized the Jag was out of it. It was like somebody'd opened a tap on our heels and just let all the juices drain out.

But there's always a bright spot somewhere-even if it's in another blessed county-and we could take some small measure of pride in the fact that Carson's MG somehow failed to blow on schedule and actually managed to finish the damn race. Why, we even beat somebody! Fact is, when the provisional results were posted, Carson and Cal were listed in thirty-second position out of thirty-three finishers, just ahead of that last-place Excalibur in the pit next to us that Dick Irish had spent almost two hours pushing in from the furthest reaches of the circuit after the diff started to pack it in.

As a result, Team Jersey and the Excalibur crew wound up enjoying a heck of a non-victory celebration over our gallant battle for last place back at the Harder Hall. It lasted till damn near dawn. I mean, we were all so damn exhausted, who the hell could sleep?

I remember we awoke in a gritty, grimy fog at the Harder Hall sometime around one p.m. the next day. Not that the sun wasn't shining. In fact, it was beaming down from a clear, picture-perfect azure sky like a damn travel poster. Only we were in no shape to appreciate it, thanks to a few minor-league hangovers, the cumulative effects of too many days without sleep and too many miles without rest and too many desperate adventures-inevitably punctuated with wild, exhilarating peaks followed by dark, debilitating valleys-not to mention the usual post-checker letdown that comes creeping through your system after every race, when you know the last opportunities have slipped forever down the drain and you can feel the dull, comparatively pointless pressures of everyday life bearing down on you like a slow freight carrying sad-eyed old beef cattle and terrified, squealing piglets off to the slaughterhouse. There is no Morning After like a race Morning After, and you can generally multiply the negative residual after-effects by the length of the race, the number of disappointments endured, and the distance traveled to get there. Squared.

But the amazing thing about the Indomitable Human Spirit is that it simply doesn't know any better, and so you find yourself brushing the teeth and combing the hair of the dead-eyed zombie staring back at you out of the mirror, pouring a half-quart of coffee down its throat, and heading back out to some godforsaken place in the middle of a tangled sea of orange groves to gather up the bits and pieces of a once-promising two car race team from a worn out, run down old Army airport named Hendricks Field. On the way out, it occurred to me that they ought to give you your tetanus boosters at times like these. Why, you'd never feel a thing.

I won't bore you with all the locational and logistical hassles we had on tap, what with one slightly rolled Jaguar and one barely ambulatory and surely soon to be deceased MG in Sebring and our only trailer-and a one-car unit at that-supposedly under repair several hundred miles due northeast in Jacksonville. But these things always seem to have some strange, inexplicable way of working themselves out, and the first surprise was that Big Ed's Jag wasn't nearly as bad as we thought. Oh, it was a mess, all right, what with the right side kind of steamrollered and most of the lights broken and big, lumpy divots in the hood and front fenders like somebody'd been wailing on it with a twenty-pound sack of nickels. Not to mention that it'd been inverted for quite a spell, so most of the engine oil, transmission fluid, coolant, rear end grease, brake fluid, etc. had spilled out all over the place and mixed with the local dust, grit, sand, and smaller edition uprooted plant life to create a most unappealing paste-like substance. But there didn't seem to be any structural damage, and, once we'd got it wiped down and re-filled all the important juices, that old dog fired right up and ran like a charm. At least if you ignored the clutch slip and the way the brakes pulled to the left and how the transmission lever popped out of third gear any-time you lifted off the gas pedal. But I reckoned it would easily make it as far as Jacksonville to get it on the trailer (assuming the trailer was actually fixed) so long as we got new bulbs in and the lights working again and didn't catch too much flack from the cops.

Carson's MG was another matter, however, since a morning start-up indi-cated about zero oil pressure at idle and both Spud and I recognized the sound of a little dwarf with a ball peen hammer hard at work down in the oil pan. It was a miracle right up there with the loaves and fishes that the blessed thing had finished the damn race, you know? And of course that's when Big Ed came to the rescue by palming Spud and Sammy a sizable lump of cash to "help us get the cars back to Jersey." And I could tell by Spud's eyes that it was a hell of a generous wad, too. But you could tell Big Ed still felt bad about what happened, and I guess he figured this might in some small way make up for it. Or at least some of it, anyway.

So Spud looked over the front end of Carson's MG and the back end of his dusty old ¾ ton Ford pickup, and then he was off into town to find the stuff he needed to hustle up a satisfactory tow hitch. And I've got to give him credit. When he returned later on that afternoon, he had an Army surplus Jeep towbar that he'd picked up for three bucks and bent and welded so it matched right up to the MG's front bumper brackets. And I mean first time, too. Plus his timing was about dead-nuts perfect, since we'd gotten everything loaded up into Big Ed's dump truck by that time and were all ready to roll.

There was a big awards party dinner in town Monday evening, and Big Ed insisted that everybody on Team Jersey should come as his guests. Personally I was getting a little anxious about returning to Passaic and finding out what exactly might be going on at the Sinclair, but Big Ed was pretty persuasive about how we'd been in the damn race and so we really ought to be there. Especially since it represented a swell opportunity to do a little ground-level lobbying among the S.C.M.A. rank-and-file for his licensing/membership show-down with Charlie Priddle that would most certainly be coming up later that spring. Big Ed knew enough about big, noisy parties in big, noisy rooms to realize that you really needed a home table-a "base of operations," you know?-and that the best one possible would have to be the biggest, busiest, noisiest damn table in the hall. One right next to Tommy Edwards' corner of the official Aston Martin table with all the Team Jersey irregulars plus the entire Excalibur crew in attendance would do nicely. Especially after Tommy and some of the other Brits got a few gin-and-tonics under their belts and started lobbing dinner rolls in the general direction of the podium. Emphasis on "general." In any case it was a lot of fun. Particularly when a small but particularly stale three-week-old sesame bun ricocheted smartly off Creighton Pendleton's forehead-I swear it left a mark-and *ker-plopped* into the deeply scooped neckline of Sally Enderle's elegantly sequin-trimmed cocktail dress. Where it remained-wedged in solidly!-through a round of raised eyebrows, a flutter of stifled laughter, and the pop of at least half a dozen flashbulbs. She was not amused.

As always at one of these deals, the main topics of conversation were week-end war stories, assorted rude comments about other drivers at the table (and even ruder ones about those not present) and discussions of upcoming events. Dick Irish was passing out mimeographed copies of the S.C.M.A.'s summer schedule, and no question I was going to have to get my butt in gear to have Carson's death-rattle MG and Big Ed's crumpled XK-120 and all my other sportycar customers' cars ready in time for the race at Bridgehampton on Satur-day, May 23rd, followed just a week later by an event at Thompson Speedway up in Connecticut, and then a few weeks off to repair the inevitable damage before the Mount Equinox hillclimb up in Vermont on Saturday, June 20th, and Sunday, June 21st. And right away I got this nagging buzz of a notion about how I might actually have something else planned for that particular weekend. Not that I could remember what it was.

In any case, we stayed and partied and congratulated Tommy and the rest of the Aston crew and commiserated over toasts to our epic battle for last place with the Excalibur guys, and meanwhile Big Ed ran quick reconnaissance sorties out from the table and back again (each time bringing a fresh load of drinks, natch) all the while reminding us that we had a long way to go the following day and certainly didn't *have* to stick around until the last keg was emptied and the last blessed dog was hung. "Juss shink how mush *better* you guy'shl feel tomorrow," he slurred through a broad, beery grin, "Schtarting off early after a good night'sch schleep...."

With such a wise and reasonable plan in the works, it should come as no surprise that we were the last table out of there and didn't hit the road until well past ten-thirty the next morning. And every last man jack of us felt like dog shit all the way to Jacksonville. The good news was that our lumpy Jag made it without incident, the trailer was ready as promised, and then it was down to just Sammy, Spud, Cal and me in the two tow vehicles while Big Ed caught a plane and Carson had to go with him on account of an unfortunate natural gas leak at an old people's home in Weehawken over the weekend had put his whole blessed embalming staff on overtime. Truth is, I didn't do much more than sleep and stir and stretch and sleep some more all the way back to Passaic. Even in Big Ed's bouncy-jouncy dump truck. While Cal just drove and drove and drove. But that's what he was good at, you know?

There was a lot of interesting stuff waiting for me when we finally got home late Thursday afternoon. As promised, Big Ed's construction crew had been hard at work while we were down at Sebring, and there was a brand new service bay tacked onto the end of the Old Man's building-complete with a hydraulic lift!-plus a little free-standing tin awning over at the end of the lot so's you could park three or four customer cars out of the weather while they were waiting for service. That was a pretty good idea, since most of your bucks-up sportycar types don't like to see their cars left out in the rain. And if you ever owned a car with a Lucas ignition system, you'd know why.

But the best part was having a brand new, freshly painted service area that had never been used before. Service bays tend to accumulate stuff (boy, do they *ever!*) even when a good mechanic works there. It can't be helped. Just like my Aunt Rosamarina's garage, all the nooks and crannies start filling up with stuff that's of no earthly use whatever, but still seems way, *way* too valuable to throw away. Especially orphan machinery like old Butch habitually collected in his scrap-heap front yard. You know, motors and generators and widgets and whatsits that needed "just a little fixing up" to be "good as new again." Plus there's always a clutter of stuff from cars that died on the operating table and half-finished, Money Evaporated projects that would never see the light of day along with the internal organs and amputated extremities of long-gone automobiles that somehow seem to curl up and go to sleep in the dark, hidden spaces under work benches or behind the parts tank or stuck to some unused piece of wall like it's made out of flypaper. And it gets even worse when you've got a cheapskate old parts hoarder/cotter pin straightener like Old Man Finzio around.

But now we had this brand new, virgin space that didn't have so much as a lonely fuzz ball of lint in the corner, and I immediately staked my claim and had my tools moved over there and my girlie calendar and mimeographed copy of the S.C.M.A.'s summer schedule tacked up on the wall just as soon as we got the cars unloaded. Spud looked pretty impressed by my new lift and service bay, and allowed as how he'd like to have a setup like that for himself one day. "Y'can get petty tired of crawlin' around on the ground like a damn reptile alla time t'get stuff fixed. That's a fact."

"But you get t'work on race cars all the time," I reminded him. "And you get t'go to all the races."

"Oh, yeah," Spud grinned. "That's a real four-star plus, isn't it?" He looked down at the dirty, tired, worn out body beneath him that hadn't had more than one good night's sleep, two showers, and three square meals in more than a week. "In fact, that's why we do it. That and the glamour...."

"Yeah," Sammy nodded wearily, "You can't forget about the glamour."

It was damn near eight o'clock by the time we got everything squared away at the Sinclair, and naturally I asked Spud and Sammy if they'd like to stop over by my place, such as it was, to clean up a little and maybe even catch forty winks on the floor before taking off for Texas. But they said no, since they'd just as soon get on the road and the hell out of the greater New York metropolitan area as soon as possible. So I said goodbye and we all shook hands and I told Sammy one more time what a heck of a swell job he'd done-better than swell, even-and what a damn shame it was that it all came to nothing in the end. Oh, our buddy Hank Lyons wrote a few nice lines about it in his magazine article, but that didn't appear in *Road and Track* until June and even then it was just a half sentence or so since he had to reduce everything that happened in twelve hours down to two pages. With pictures

"Hey, that's the way it goes," Sammy shrugged. You could tell from his voice that he'd been there before. Lots of times. "And thanks fr'thinkin' of me in the first place, eh?"

"Hey, no problem. Happy t'do it."

"Well, it was still real nice of you."

I felt the color coming up on my face. "Who knows, maybe we can do it again sometime?"

"Sure thing, Buddy. Anytime at all. You know where to find me."

"Yeah," Spud chimed in. "Just follow the smell of exhaust fumes."

So they took off into the night in Spud's old Ford pickup and I knew before they were even out of sight that I'd see them again. I couldn't help thinking what a damn, unfair shame it was the way things turned out at Sebring after all their hard work, and I sure as hell hoped Sammy'd get the break he deserved some day. He was one hell of a race driver-just like Cal-only Cal could always fall back on being a spoiled, black sheep of a rich kid if he felt like it. Sammy Speed was out there without a net.

Chapter 11: Back to Reality

There was another surprise waiting for me back home at the apartment over my Aunt Rosamarina's garage, where I discovered that Julie had been hard at work while I was down in Florida, cleaning and scrubbing and ironing and folding and generally trying to neaten the place up a little. Why, there was even a little vase of flowers sitting on an Irish lace doily on the windowsill over the sink. But I guess it was during that cleanup time in my apartment that she decided my cheesy little tarpaper pup-tent of a room over my aunt's garage was definitely *NOT* where we were going to live once we were married. And she let me know about it in no uncertain terms when I saw her the next day at the Sinclair. I remember distinctly it was Friday the 13th.

"If you think I'm gonna move into a shithole like *that,* you've got another think coming, Bub!" was I believe the way she put it.

To be honest, it wasn't something I'd done a lot of thinking about.

"...I'll be damned if I'm gonna have my friends and the girls at the Doggy Shake see me living in a frickin' *garage,* Palumbo," she said between her teeth. It was obviously something she'd been chewing on for several days. Or it'd been chewing on her. Take your pick, it amounted to the same thing. "It's bad enough I'm marryin' somebody who *works* in a damn garage."

"Geez, Julie," I started to say. I mean, the last thing in the world I wanted was an argument. I was just too worn out and used up to manage one properly. And that's when you know in advance that you're destined to come out on the losing end

"Lissen, Buster," Julie continued, making her index finger do a nasty little corkscrew under my nose. "You asked me to marry you and I said 'yes,' and I'll tell you right now you'll never find anybody-and I mean *anybody*-who will work harder or stand by you better than I will."

"I know th-" I started to say, but she cut me off again.

"But I'll be damned if I'll be made a fool of, Palumbo. We're gonna have us a real, honest-to-goodness *home,* unnerstand? A place where I can cook a nice dinner or have friends over if I feel like it. A place where I'm not ashamed to have my mom over for coffee after church. A place where I'm not smelling old kitty litter all the time or taking showers in the middle of the damn living room."

Thinking it over, I had to admit that the apartment over my Aunt Rosamarina's garage didn't seem particularly suitable for a young married couple. Not unless they were squirrels or ferrets or something. "Well," I said in my most reasonable and accommodating manner, "you've obviously been doing a lot more thinking about it than me. Where exactly did you have in mind?"

"Weeeeell," she said with a dangerously sweet, singsong lilt to her voice that I soon came to recognize as a signal that plans had already been finalized and I was merely getting my marching orders. "I understand the people living downstairs from my mom have been arguing a lot lately..."

The hairs stood up on the back of my neck. "Oh? How do you know that?"

"We can hear it upstairs."

"You can?"

"Well, you can if you get your ear right down against the floor..."

The hairs on the back of my neck went into a Calypso dance.

"...and sometimes it's loud enough you don't even need to."

"Really?" I said like I had absolutely no idea where this was going.

"Yeah, really. Anyhow, the guy's lost his job or something and she's been talking to her mother about moving back home with the kids..."

"You heard all that through the floorboards?"

"No, we got a party line, too."

"That's awful!" I said disgustedly.

"Yeah., I know. But the guy's a bum anyway. She's probably better off."

"That's not what I meant."

"Oh?" Then the singsong voice came back. "Anyhow, I was thinking about how *perfect* it would be if they moved out and *we* could move in downstairs from my mom..."

The hairs on the back of my neck caught fire.

"...Oh, I know she can be kind of a pain sometimes..."

Boy, that went without saying.

"...but she *is* my mom. And I've been worrying a lot about leaving her all alone after we get married..." Julie ran her hands around the back of my neck and pulled me in close to her. Geez, did that ever feel good. "...Besides, you'll be going off to races sometimes on the weekends. You don't want to be leaving me behind all by my lonesome, do you?"

"Well," I said, nuzzling into her hair and thinking about that cozy little cabin I stayed in at the Seneca Lodge at Watkins Glen the year before, "I was kind of hoping you'd come with me sometimes." I could look up past the wonderful smell of her skin and hair and see that mimeographed copy of the S.C.M.A. race schedule taped to the wall.

"Oh, I *will*..." Julie assured me. "...sometimes...." She kissed the bottom of my earlobe and then started nibbling on it just a little. And of course that instantly started stoking up the old fire down in the boiler room. She pressed her hips in tightly against the heat. "Oh, Buddy," she breathed into my ear, "I just can't *wait* 'till we're married…" then ran her tongue once or twice around the inside for good measure.

The rest of me caught fire.

"…it's just a hundred more days, Buddy," she whispered into my cheek and sideburn, "I've been counting. Oh, everything's going to change for us come June twenty-first. I'm sure of it."

At the mention of that date, my entire body went rigid. Or all except the part that was already rigid, which did the opposite. I mean, that S.C.M.A. race calendar was staring me right in the face. "Uhh, Julie?" I gulped, kind of backing away. "There may be a little, uhh, *problem* with June 21st, see…."

Lightning bolts shot out of her eyes.

"….I mean, I didn't plan it or know about it or anything, but there's this S.C.M.A. hillclimb in Vermont that weekend…."

She let loose another volley, and no question I felt the jolt.

"….and you know all my guys will want to go…."

Now she was the one who was on fire. And not the good kind, either.

"….and, well, that's really gonna be our future here at the shop. The sports car people, I mean."

Speaking of mean, I'd never seen such a slow, simmering hatred in anybody's eyes before. Not ever. And it immediately occurred to me that Julie and I were about to have our first major fight. Oh, I'd *thought* we'd had major fights before. But they were going to be nothing compared to this. And the worst part was I could see it coming and yet there wasn't a damn thing I could do except brace myself, batten down the hatches, and try to weather it out.

"Let me get this straight," she hissed through clenched teeth. "You're planning to cancel our wedding so you can go to a car race?"

"Geez, not *cancel,* Julie," I tried to explain. "I was just hoping to, you know, *reschedule* or something…."

"I see," she said cold as death itself. "After the date's been set and the church is all arranged and a hall's already been rented…." Her voice raised up that first, scary notch. "You have any idea how *hard* it is to find a frickin' reception hall in June, Palumbo?"

Now I knew that last part wasn't true. My old man had insisted he could get us a cheap deal on his union hall for the reception, but they were still dickering over the price and there was a little bit of a scheduling conflict with the Chemical Workers' Union bowling team, which always celebrated the beer frame over at the hall after their Sunday morning league games and regularly stayed until closing time. Or later. And of course my dad's solution was just to invite them, too-hey, they were all good union guys, right?-but the rest of us thought a bunch of sweaty drunks in iridescent gold satin bowling shirts with purple trim might clash a bit with the rest of the wedding crowd. But the point is that I knew the last thing Julie said was pure bullshit. And I'm proud to say I had the good sense and fledgling matrimonial seasoning to keep my mouth shut about it.

Meanwhile Julie's voice climbed up to the next rung. *"You just don't do this to people, Buddy!"* And the next. *"And you sure as hell aren't doing it to ME! DO YOU UNDERSTAND ME, PALUMBO?!!"* It would be hard not to. Not even from two blocks away.

Judging from Julie's complexion, she would never need to buy rouge again.

"L-look, Julie," I pleaded, trying to calm her down, "it's not just because there's a stupid race or hillclimb or anything. Honest it isn't."

She folded her arms across her chest and fixed me in the crosshairs of a cold, withering stare.

"I mean, these people are more than just my customers, Julie. They're my *friends,* too." She didn't even flick an eyelash, so I swallowed once for luck and kept going. "I want them to be there *with* us, you know? In fact, I was even thinking of asking Cal to be best man." The truth is that I hadn't thought about it even once until just that instant. But Julie didn't need to know that, did she? *"I mean, Geez, Julie, who else have I got?"* I wailed in an absolutely perfect Betrayed Victim voice. "I grew up in a house with four sisters and I sure as hell don't want one of my asshole brother-in-laws as best man. Or worse yet one of my dad's jerkoff union shop buddies. Hell, I don't even *know* those guys...."

I could sense her starting to soften just a little. Like from hard as the diamond I'd bought her to something around granite or thereabouts. But then her eyes flashed tough again. *"Go to hell, Palumbo!"* she spit out unexpectedly, then spun on her heel and stalked out of the shop.

And there I stood, arms outspread towards the warm, empty hole in the air where she'd been standing.

It wasn't until later that I realized Julie had plenty enough of the old female matrimonial instincts to know better than to just melt down and compromise on the spot over such a heavy duty issue. No, there had to be a proper dose of rage and suffering first. A week or so on the pillory would do. And then the Pound of Flesh. There always had to be a Pound of Flesh. In fact, I bet it's written down someplace and hidden away in the back of a sock drawer where men never get to see it. Or maybe tucked between the pages of *Good Housekeeping* cookbooks or wedged under the pin cushions of little gift sewing kits like the ones I bought my sisters for Christmas.

I'm sure of it.

In any case, I wound up walking on eggs for several long, agonizing days while we worked our way towards a solution. Julie had some mystical female hormone thing about needing to be a June bride, and the weekend after the Mount Equinox hillclimb was no good on account of there was going to be a brand new open road race out by the Delaware River in Sullivan County at someplace called Callicoon, and I was dead sure my guys would want to go. Plus the week before June 21st was no good because I'd for sure find myself stuck under a bunch of cars when it would be infinitely better for my health and peace of mind to be away on a honeymoon someplace with Julie. But fortunately that never came up on account of the church was already booked that weekend. It was supposed to be booked up the weekend before, too, but I got lucky when it turned out one of Big Ed's many scary-looking "business associates" turned out to be a big contributor to some Archdiocese building fund or other (in return, I believe, for having the chapel of a new church named after his father, who was most unfortunately blown up by a car bomb-very likely the handiwork of the Muscatelli brothers' own dear departed old man-back in the twenties) and so had quite a bit of suck with our local New Jersey wine and wafer hierarchy. At any rate, he was able to tweak a few schedules around and bend a few arms (but hopefully not to the breaking point!) and got the decks cleared for us at our own, local parish church at 9:30 in the morning on Saturday, June sixth. I know that seems a little early in the ayem for a wedding ceremony, but there was another group coming in at 11:30 (they'd originally been scheduled for 10) and another at 2:30 (originally set for 1pm) and it just wouldn't do to get married at night. Of course Julie was upset about the time and also about how everybody-and especially all her girlfriends at the Doggy Shake-were going to think we *had* to move the date up (if you know what I mean) but I told her two weeks wouldn't make much difference anyway and, if they were really her friends, why would they ever think such a thing anyway. I also offered to tell each of them personally that Julie was most definitely not giving out any free samples before the big day-I'd even swear on a Bible or take a lie detector test if they wanted-but somehow she wasn't real enthusiastic about that idea.

Slowly but surely, Julie started to come around. But she still knew she had to make it tough on me. Just to set the right kind of precedent, you know? The final kicker was when Big Ed got one of his other connected buddies in the pasta and ptomaine business to offer us a really nice hall in this fancy Italian restaurant at a really reasonable price-antipasto, minestrone soup, salad, a family-style dinner with chicken, steak, green beans, stuffed shells and manicotti, a four-story wedding cake, coffee, tea, or cappuccino, a few gallons of spumoni ice cream (with real pistachio nuts, no less) along with all the beer, wine, and cheap liquor we could drink included. It was a hell of a deal, no lie.

So Julie and me shook hands, exchanged a wary kiss, and agreed that we'd be married on Saturday, the sixth of June, 1953, at 9:30 in the morning at St. Jude's Catholic church just a block up from the Doggy Shake, followed by a blowout noontime-to-whenever luncheon reception at Pete and Pasquale's Palermo Room Pizzeria and Pasta Palace over on Polk Street. We even had a live band lined up called The Monotones, who had been recommended as "absolutely dreamy" by one of Julie's girlfriends at the Doggy Shake, although we found out later that the drummer was her second cousin or something and he was only trying to make it in the music business on account of he couldn't cut it as a fry cook over at his uncle's bar and grill.

But it was great to finally have it all set, you know? Except for the Pound of Flesh part, of course. And that amounted to, God help me, agreeing to move into the bottom floor apartment of the duplex where Julie's mom lived. I admit, it was like trading the crackle of a lone skyrocket for what amounted to life as a galley slave, but, to tell the truth, I figured I was going to wind up living there anyway-I had faith in Julie, she'd find a way-and so I wasn't really losing anything, you know? Or at least nothing that wasn't lost already.

Meanwhile, back at the Sinclair, I was up to my ass in sportycar work and wondering how the hell I was going to get it all done without more help. It took one whole day and most of a night to haul the engine and transmission out of Big Ed's Jag again for the umpty-eleventh time (it's definitely a bad sign when the heads on the motor mount bolts are getting rounded off from over-use) so's I could fix the slipping clutch and third gear synchros while the carcass went over to the skinny little Greek's body shop again for more pounding, filling and painting. And of course there were a kazillion interruptions during the day, what with people pulling up to the pumps and our regular American sedan customers who needed this and that and the phone ringing every five minutes and some traveling woven label salesman who needed a jump start for his brand new Studebaker Commander hardtop just up the street on account of he'd accidentally left his lights on while he had a two-hour, three martini lunch with a prospective customer discussing all the important business aspects of how tough Rocky Marciano was, the prospects for the Dodgers new pitching staff, and what was going on inside the waitress' blouse. So he was naturally in a big hurry. He was one of those antsy, impatient types who hover there like a damn horsefly in your ear until you finally drop whatever the hell else you're doing and go help them out. That's really pretty rude, you know? But I must admit that new Stude hardtop was a stunning looking automobile. They called it the Starliner, and it was just as smooth and sleek as anything you ever saw out of Europe. Even if it was just all the same old Studebaker nuts and bolts underneath. Brooks Stevens told me a guy named Bob Bourke from Raymond Loewy's studio in South Bend designed it. I'd never heard of either of them, but Brooks allowed as how Loewy was a pretty well known industrial designer and had his own in-dependent design shop right there on the premises at the Studebaker factory. His staff did just about all of Studebaker's cars-the good ones as well as the prime crapola-and the '53 Starlight Coupes and Starliner Hardtops were meant to be a little special since it was Studebaker's 100th anniversary. Apparently the com-pany started out building Conestoga wagons back when the forefathers of all the S.C.M.A. bigwigs were busy shooing Indians off the land they'd lived on since the dawn of time so's we could have our cities, suburbs, schools, hospitals, post offices, gas stations, all-night grills, candy factories, tractor plants, slums and dry cleaning establishments out where the Indians only saw forests, plains and grazing land. I guess they just didn't have any imagination, you know? But the main idea is that Studebaker went back a long, long time in these United States, and the Loewy Studio's new Starliner hardtops and Starlight coupes were kind of a proud cornerstone to mark their 100th year. Or maybe headstone would be more like it, the way things turned out. But they sure were some beautiful cars-lovely from any angle-and I remember reading where they won some kind of academy award medal for design. It was well deserved, too, and represented one hell of an improvement over those old bullet-nose, "which way is it going?" jobs Studebaker was foisting on the American public a few years before.

But, much as I liked the shape of that new Studebaker, this particular situa-tion was just one more instance of a really nifty car belonging to a Grade A asshole. And then the sonofabitch didn't want to pay me a lousy dollar for the jump once I got it running. Can you believe it? "I thought you guys did that sort of thing for free," he said, kind of glowering at me from beneath a single, shaggy black eyebrow that went all the way across his forehead.

"You giving any free labels this week?" I asked him. You think I'd know better than to try arguing with a guy who had a three martini head start on me.

"Okay," he said belligerently, curling his lower lip out, "you just tell me what the hell ever happened to the 'service' in 'service station,' huh? You just tell me that." He was kind of swaying back and forth against the Stude's side mirror while he spoke, and I couldn't believe it when the damn thing snapped clean off and deposited him right on his kisser in the middle of Pine Street.

It's times like that you realize there is a God after all.

But the point is I needed more help at the Sinclair, and when I put the old "EXPERIENCED MECHANIC WANTED-MUST HAVE OWN TOOLS" sign in the window, I was praying that same God would send me somebody with the foreign car savvy and mechanical sympathy of a Sylvester Jones, the stamina and work ethic of a healthy Butch Bohunk, and the innocent, homespun good nature of Will Rodgers. It wouldn't hurt if he'd work cheap, too.

Instead I got Raymond.

Raymond Tuttle came to New Jersey all the way from the rural outskirts of Dubuque, Iowa, on account of the company his dad worked for transferred him to a new job over in Nutley, and, things being how they were, he dragged his whole blessed family along with him. A brother, two sisters, six rooms worth of priceless family heirlooms and worn out, hand-me-down furniture, a few feeble house plants, and an over-sexed Beagle-mix hound with a perpetually infected left ear named "Barney." Raymond was just heading into his junior year in high school when the transfer came through, and I'm sure it must've been tough on the kid to leave the house he grew up in and all the neighbors who used to shoo him out of their yards and all the friends he never made in school. It's not that he wasn't *likeable*, you know? It's just that he had the general luster and personality quotient of a stalk of celery. He was one of those geeky, awkward, gee-golly-gosh farm town kids who wear a constant look of bewildered amazement, work hard and diligently, and seldom get anything right the first time. Or the second. But, of all the other prospective wrenches I interviewed-and there must have been at least two-Raymond Tuttle impressed me with the fact that he seemed too damn simple and heartland straight to try and cheat me. Which was a constant problem with the available mechanics from our own, home-grown New Jersey workforce.

Plus he'd work cheap and could start right away.

The story on Raymond was that he finished high school in Nutley, and, in spite of his obvious qualifications as a target for bullies and the butt end of jukes, managed to establish himself as a guy who was too dull to even pick on. Not enough entertainment value, you know? After high school he took some Diesel Truck Mechanics correspondence course like you read about on the inside of matchbook covers with the idea of maybe someday going back to Dubuque to work on bulldozers and farm tractors and such. But he didn't really have the money or the imagination to go back to Dubuque on his own, so he took a job as an apprentice maintenance mechanic at an old and well established stock pot and teapot lid factory in Elizabeth. But over the years, control of the factory had passed from its original founder to his two bickering sons-one of whom finally bought the other out after he came into possession of some particularly embarrassing photographs of the other brother with a hat check girl in Atlantic City-and then it eventually passed down to the remaining, sole owner brother's son-in-law, who had previously made a career out of flunking out of college. Anyone who is familiar with these handed-down-family-business deals knows it's a lot like that old "three on a match" thing from the foxholes of World War I, and the third generation can most usually be counted on to screw up, dissipate, and destroy whatever's been built up over the years. It's a basic law of American business, I think.

Anyhow, it should come as no surprise that the whole shebang folded up less than eight weeks after my boy Raymond landed a job there, and it was just sheer chance that he was hanging around picking up his tools (all of which, by the way, fit into a box that could easily be mistaken for one of the standard-issue lunch buckets the union guys at my old man's chemical plant carry to work) when Big Ed Baumstein happened by to look over the used machinery and see if there were any bargains to be had. And he picked up right away that Raymond was a straightforward, forthright, earnest young man of the type you don't usually find around the Hudson River unless they're floating downstream on top of it. Of course, Big Ed didn't know if Raymond knew one damn thing about fixing automobiles-not that Big Ed could've spotted such a thing if it were displayed on a silver platter directly in front of his face-but he knew I was looking for help and he knew Raymond was (or soon would be) looking for a job, and if there's one sure talent Big Ed always had in spades, it was spotting likely deals and putting them together.

So he sent Raymond Tuttle over for an interview, and since the only other prospective talents who'd bothered to wander in were that second Hugo character who used to work at Westbridge (and who I already knew to be a cheat, a butcher, a short-cutter, and a hasher) and this terrifically friendly *"hey, just a-between a-you anna me, ey?"* local *paisan* named Dominick who'd been working at the local Lincoln dealership but got recently relieved of duty for curbing cars. "Curbing" is a very popular pastime in the retail car dealership business, and the fact that it's highly profitable is somewhat offset by the certainty that you *will* get fired if anybody catches wise. The way it works is this: A guy comes in to sell or trade a car or have some major repair work done, and the sale or service manager gives him the dealership's version of their very best price on the deal. And, most usually, that's when the really smart shoppers spin on their heels like toy tops and start running-not walking-towards the nearest exit. But of course that's all part of the game, isn't it?

"Curbing" involves following that prospective customer out to the curb (and likewise out of sight and earshot of the other dealership personnel) and offering a better, "just a-between a-you anna me" price on the car he wants to sell or trade or the repair work that needs to be done if he'll just come around to your private office in the alley behind your brother-in-law's second cousin's garage with cash in hand. "Curbing" is a truly unforgivable sin in the retail automotive business, and, like all unforgivable sins, there's an awful lot of it going on.

So I picked Raymond.

And I prayed.

And, surprisingly enough, it didn't turn out too bad. He showed up on time and he worked hard on whatever you gave him to do. At least until he got stuck, anyway, in which case he'd quietly fuss and fume and figure and frown and put together and take apart and scratch his head and travel up every blind alley known to man just to keep from embarrassing himself by having to ask for help. He could waste entire days like that if you didn't keep an eye on him. But Butch could help out a little there, and I asked him to make a point of wheeling past Raymond's stall in the service bay every so often to make sure he wasn't beating his head against a brick wall. And of course old Butch knew how to handle the situation with tact and diplomacy if Raymond needed a little expert coaching: *"Hey, you stupid asshole, what th'hell ever made you think you were a mechanic in the first place, huh?"*

"Well, gee whiz, Butch, I was just starting out as a apprentice, y'know…"

"'Apprentice?' Is that *exactly* the same as 'asshole' or a little different?"

But of course then Butch'd show him what to do-just like he did for me when I was first starting out and didn't know anything-and you got the hopeful feeling that, just maybe, Raymond Tuttle would work out. Especially since he was honest and reliable, and honesty is something that simply cannot be bought. It likewise cannot be sold, in case you're ever trying to get a decent price for it on the open market. But it does give you a certain sense of security to know that you will only be skewered on a spit and roasted to a cinder in the fires of hell for *honest* mistakes and fuckups rather than the scheming, venal, dishonest variety you know well enough to look out for.

Even if Raymond Tuttle was a mixed blessing as a mechanic, he could run out to the pumps to take care of gas customers and clean off their windshields and make a little small talk-so long as it was very, very small-and that alone freed up a lot of wrenching time for me. The week after I hired Raymond on I got that death-rattle engine out of Carson's TD torn apart, had Butch order what we needed to fix it, and then attacked the transmission on Big Ed's XK-120, which needed just about everything replaced except maybe the drain plug. No question Big Ed was a pretty brutal guy with the shift lever, and I got the feeling that what happened at Sebring with it popping out of gear had been sort of waiting in the wings since the first time Big Ed rolled that car into the station. The good news was that the clutch slip was just from a leaky seal on the first motion shaft coming out of the transmission, and, although I promised myself to have a little peek anyway, my best guess was that the motor was still fine.

That was a relief.

But we still had a problem getting parts, on account of I really needed to keep my hands around the shop to get the work done and I really needed Raymond there to take care of what he could and clean windshields out at the pump island and Butch to watch over Raymond's shoulder and do a little unit work at the special bench we'd set up for him and order our parts over the phone and even handle some of the incoming calls from customers when he wasn't feeling too belligerent. But we really needed somebody to make parts runs, you know? When you're working on a customer's car-or, even more particularly, several customers' cars at once-a steady supply of necessary hardware is absolutely essential if you want to get your projects finished on time and not have the shop cluttered up chock full of dead, disassembled automobiles you can't do anything with.

It used to be I could count on Old Man Finzio to do the parts runs, but he just wasn't around enough any more. Oh, he'd be there at 6:45 every morning -rain, shine, sleet, earthquake, tidal wave, or nuclear missile attack-but after he'd gone over the service appointments and fussed around at his tool bench for awhile, he'd generally be off to get some sort of treatment or to wait in some doctor's office reception area for most of the rest of the day. And, on the days he was around, you could tell he was getting tired even by the time lunch rolled around. It was a different kind of tired than I'd ever really seen before, and I have to admit I found myself worrying over and feeling sorry about the Old Man's condition-even if he was the meanest, orneriest sonofabitch the good Lord ever put on this earth-but about the only thing you could do for him was to make sure everything kept running and that there was cash in the till at the end of the day and, aside from that, just generally stay the hell out of his way. Which wasn't hard since he really wasn't around all that much.

It was Raymond who finally came up with the grand solution to our parts runner problem. Seems he had a two-year-older brother who was between employment positions at the time, had his own vehicle, and liked to sleep late on account of he had a little minor league career going as a pool hustler. "Hell, he could come by, sure," Raymond said through that earnest, open-mouthed look of yokel bewilderment he always wore.

"And he's got a car?"

"Yessir."

"And he knows his way around?"

"He's the one who got us here from Dubuque," Raymond said proudly. "He can read maps and everything."

Hell, how could you go wrong with a recommendation like that?

So Raymond's older brother showed up around noon the next day (which, I would soon discover, was destined to be his regular starting time), buzzing into the Sinclair in a rusty and dilapidated little 1947 Crosley station wagon with the exhaust pipe dangling from a length of plumber's strap and a telltale trail of wispy, bluish-white smoke coming out the end. Crosleys were odd, tiny, Kiddie Car-looking cars built in Marion, Indiana (of all places) and had about the same sort of styling and construction values as a corrugated tin outhouse. But I guess that only made sense, since the company that built them was really in the radio and refrigerator business and obviously knew a lot more about making radios and refrigerators than building cars. Or maybe they just didn't see much difference, since Crosleys were built and styled an awful lot like a Motorola, Kelvinator, or a Frigidare. Still, they were kind of clever, what with spot disc brakes before anybody else ever heard of them in 1950 and tiny, economical little 44-cubic-inch motors featuring copper-brazed, stamped sheet metal engine blocks more along the lines of a refrigerator condenser than your normal, everyday cast iron variety (although they had a bad habit of springing leaks like a damn steam boiler and Crosley finally switched over to cast iron in 1949). But those engines were small and light and revved like crazy on account of they had a genuine overhead camshaft just like a blessed Ferrari or Mercedes Benz. Although you'd have to say the similarities ended about there. A lot of the tiddler sports cars like Siatas and such used Crosley engines for those very reasons. I guess Crosleys sold pretty well right after the war when anything with four wheels and a few wheezing hamsters under the hood could find a home, but it didn't last once the rest of the American motor industry got up off its fanny and Crosley finally gave up and went back to radios and refrigerators in 1952. Still, they were kind of interesting (in a carnival freak show kind of way) and parts were never, ever a problem. The junkyards were full of them.

But the amazing part was that, even Kiddie-Car tiny as Crosleys were, you still couldn't see much more than the very top of Raymond's brother's hairdo over the windowsill when he putt-putted into the station. It was done up in a kind of an orangey-red sculptured pompadour effect like a cross between a wood duck and an Irish setter, and I swear it didn't rise much more than a few inches when he got out of the car. I don't want to say that Raymond's brother was exactly a side show midget or a dwarf or anything, but he was sure as hell knocking on the door. Oh, his head was damn near regular-issue human size and he was really a pretty good looking guy-in fact, with his big smile and all that gleaming, orange-red hair piled on top, he looked like one of those country singers out of Nashville with the gold-sequined satin jackets and solid gold guitars. But the body under that head was maybe less than four feet at the shoulder, and, even with the big head and big hair on top of it, he wasn't hardly five feet tall. Even in cowboy boots. And they had thick heels, too.

"Buddy," Raymond said proudly, "this here's my brother, Tater."

"Tater?"

Raymond nodded.

"As in *'potato?'*"

Raymond nodded again.

"Pleased t'meetcha," Tater said out of an easy, confident grin. "Ray's said a lotta nice things about'cha."

"Well, geez, thanks." I looked at Tater with his big, country western grin, and then past him at that sorry looking Crosley wagon. "That your car?"

"Yessiree," Tater said proudly. "She gets damn near 30 miles to a gallon."

"I see," I nodded. "But is that gasoline or oil?"

"Lately both," he laughed, and right away I started thinking he might work out after all.

Things actually started running pretty smoothly around the Sinclair for a while after that. We had plenty of business-almost too much, in fact-what with the racing season coming up and the shop getting a reputation around New York and New Jersey as a place that did decent work and would actually try to get your car finished sometime around when they said they would. I'd show up every morning around seven and try to keep Old Man Finzio from pissing off too many customers while we wrote up the day's work orders, and then I'd generally sneak across the street for some coffee and a sweet roll (or even eggs or pancakes if I thought I had the time) and think about what we had to do. I'd make sure and be back by eight when Raymond showed up-always right on the dot-so's I could get him started on something, see to it that the Old Man had something to fool with if he felt like it, and start in on whatever project or projects I had going. Mean Marlene would drop Butch off around ten on her way to her lunchtime/dinnertime cocktail waitress job, and right away he'd wheel his way into the service bays to have a look at what Raymond was stuck on and make a list of parts he needed to order. Butch was one of those invisible assets that you never fully appreciate until they're not around, and it came into focus real clear on the rare days when Marlene was off work and took him over to the V.A. hospital for the therapy treatments on his legs that never seemed to do much good. When he was gone, I'd notice how much time it took to make all those blessed phone calls. You can spend absolutely for*ever* waiting for some parts counterman to look something up, especially when he's got three or four live customers in front of him at the same time, and I could never even come close to Butch when it came to getting the right part for the job on the very first shot. He had a real knack that way, you know? So I'd have to say I wasn't too upset when Butch decided to say the hell with it and quit going to the V.A. for therapy treatments anymore. I mean, what was the point?

Tater'd come rolling in a little after noon, often looking a trifle shaky if he'd had particularly good or bad luck around the pool table the night before, and Butch would be ready with a list of stuff to get and the addresses and phone numbers of where to get it all. But he didn't exactly know his way around like a local resident, so there were a few false starts. In fact, Tater's first four parts runs included getting lost twice, backing into a police car while trying to park in a no parking zone, and becoming sidetracked when he walked into a corner tavern to ask directions, saw they had a pool table, and wound up making fifteen bucks and spending the night with a large blonde working girl with breasts as big as his head. Or at least that's what he claimed when he showed up early (it wasn't even eleven!) the next day and apologized. I was plenty pissed, of course, but Tater Tuttle was one of those guys who you just can't stay angry at. In fact, he was a little like Cal that way. He'd give you that big, warm smile and shrug those tiny little shoulders-*hey, what can you do?*-and you'd feel all the venom melt out like there was a leak someplace on the back of your shoe. But I made it real clear he'd be between positions again if he ever pulled another stunt like that, and I'm proud to say he kept it down to once every two or three weeks after that. And never when we had anything really crucial going on.

Some days Tater would bring the old family hound with him. It's name was Barney, and it was about the horniest, randiest, nosiest, worst-smelling old four-legged fleabag you ever saw. Far as I could tell, Barney didn't do much except eat, shit, and lick his privates, but both Raymond and Tater seemed really attached to that randy, smelly old butt-sniffing hound. At first I insisted that they tie him up whenever they brought him around the shop, but Barney didn't much like that-he was obviously one of those lone wolf, independent, free ranging types-and so he'd stand back there on all fours with his nose and tail pointed at the ceiling and just howl. And howl. And howl.

It was not the kind of noise you could ignore. Not even with practice.

"He'll be good iffen y'let him run," Tater told me. "We allus let him run back home. He'll be fine."

So, against my better judgement, I let Tater take the clothesline off Barney's neck one day when it was quiet and not too much was going on. And right away Barney was off around the perimeter of the shop-nose down, tail straight out behind him-sniffing and snuffling into every nook and cranny the way only hounds can do. It turned out you could pretty much trust Barney-sort of-and he'd be careful to stay out of the way when you were busy doing something and even take himself little side excursions into the neighborhood, disappearing for hours on end sometimes but always coming back well before closing. And he *never* missed lunch. I swear, that dog could smell a roast beef sandwich through three layers of tinfoil and hear the rustle of waxed paper from clear across the street. And he'd eat *anything*. Garbage day came every Thursday in our part of Passaic, and Barney would vanish all morning and come back around lunchtime with an exhausted grin on his face, a big, swollen belly, and smelling worse than a sewage treatment plant during a stomach flu epidemic. I'd make Raymond or Tater take him outside and hose him down-which he obviously hated-but you could bet he'd be gone on his regular weekly garbage raid the following Thursday just the same.

Barney was actually kind of lovable sometimes. He'd come over and lay that big, velvety head of his on your knee and look up at you with those big, sad, hound dog eyes-especially if you were eating something-and he'd just quietly stay there until you broke down and gave him a morsel or scratched him a little behind the ears. He was smart, too, and really picked up a lot about what was going on around the shop and the neighborhood in general. Like that Thursday was garbage day or that there was a fence he could jump with a hot little Pomeranian on the other side whose owner swore she was going to feed Barney poisoned meat one day but never did. And his sense of smell was truly uncanny. He'd put that nose of his up in the air and know in an instant when they were tossing out the chicken carcasses they used to make soup at the restaurant across the street, and he always seemed to know when women who came into the shop were having their time of month. In fact, you had to keep an eye on him or he'd put his head right up under their dresses to check it out. And he had the sex drive of an entire high school football team. Honest to God he did. Whenever he could get at her, Barney would hump that poor little Pomeranian until her eyes rolled back into her head. And the same thing with the toy poodle two blocks down. And the standard poodle a half-block the other way. And the Scottie and the Wire-Haired Fox Terrier and the old lady German Shepherd and the hot redhead Irish Setter and the Lab and the Golden Retriever and the Spaniel and the Spitz. Not to mention the legs of damn near every sweet smelling lassie or gamy little kid who happened into the shop. Or passed within nose-shot of the front door. I swear, I'd even seen him hump thin air. Not that he was totally indiscriminate, since he'd never even think of humping Raymond, Tater, Butch, or Old Man Finzio. And he'd only do it to me once every morning by way of saying hello. Then it got to be every other morning. And then once every few days. Or even less.

I was starting to think he didn't care any more, you know?

But there were so many other legs to consider. And though I will never be able to fathom what his standards or reasons might have been, some people did nothing whatsoever for Barney. He'd just lay there like a rug with his head down on his paws, watching them stroll by without so much as blinking. But then one of the Chosen Many would pass by and you'd see his nose take a quick sniff of the air, his ears perk up, and in a flash he'd come up off the floor like he had J.A.T.O. assists. Next thing you know, he'd have somebody's leg in a death grip and be giving them the same sort of treatment that made that Pomeranian's eyes roll back into her head. Old Man Finzio thought that was funny as hell, and took quite a shine to Barney one day when he was arguing with some cheap mooch customer over the price of a new radiator hose and the guy started getting really nasty with him. Instantly Barney was right there beside the Old Man's leg, bearing his teeth and growling menacingly, the fur standing on end all up and down his back.

The Old Man started bringing him treats after that.

Easter Sunday fell on April 4th that year, and, for reasons I will never completely understand, my mom decided that she was going to have Julie and her mom and all the damn relatives over again after church so we could all have another nice meal together and get to know one another a little better and blah blah blah. I was beginning to see that the whole family/relative/get-together deal that went along with getting married had every potential of turning into a colossal pain in the ass. I mean, it's not that I didn't love my family (there were really only two or three I really couldn't stand) but I had a life of my own to live and a gas station and repair shop to run and, Geez, we'd just gotten everybody together for Thanksgiving dinner and then again at Christmas a few months before. Heck, I knew how important all that family stuff was (or at least that's what I'd heard, anyway) but I just didn't feel the need to be around them in one large, concentrated group more than once or twice a year. Say Christmas and the

4th of July. That would be fine. And I knew from the frozen, Death Mask smiles they wore as they traipsed through my folks' front door-at least the husbands and the kids, anyway-that they'd just as soon be going in for a root canal.

But I guess the women feel differently about things like that. Especially after they get married or when they're about to. Right away they develop this instinctive, deep-rooted sense about what families *ought* to do-even if it's no fun for *any*body-while men generally prefer to behave like they always have since they were little kids and gravitate towards whatever looks good, tastes good, or figures to feel good when you do it. Like fr'instance going to the second annual International Motor Sports Show at the Grand Central Palace exhibition hall in Manhattan that was going on the same exact day.

I mean, as a bona fide *professional* in the foreign car business, and, as such, I figured it was my sacred duty to take a little Easter jaunt across the old George Washington Bridge and take a looksee at all the hot new models from Europe. Besides, it sounded like a lot of fun. But, what with all the work we had piled up in the shop and all the heavy duty MG and Jaguar racing projects we needed to get back together in time for Bridgehampton on May 23rd, there was no way I could even think about sneaking away any day except Sunday. And, wouldn't you know it, that was Easter.

I should have known to keep my mouth shut about it, too.

"You're not skipping out on our family Easter to go look at *cars?*" my mom asked, sounding all hurt that I'd even think of such a thing.

"You're not skipping out on our family Easter to go look at CARS!" my dad hollered, making it plain that there was no room for negotiation.

"You're *not* skipping out on our family Easter to go look at cars." Julie said flatly. "So don't even think about it, Palumbo."

No question about it, I was surrounded, out-manned, and outgunned. But I guess that's just something you have to get used to if you're planning on getting married.

I talked to Cal and he wanted to go, too, so we decided to set up a little end run maneuver so I could maybe do both. The car show in Manhattan ran from one to ten on Easter Sunday, and I figured if we all went to mass together in the morning like my mom wanted to, I could buzz through the family meal deal, politely shoot the breeze for awhile, and then maybe say I wasn't feeling well or something and sneak out in time to meet up with Cal and make it over to Manhattan in plenty of time to see the show. But I didn't tell anybody about it-not even Julie-since I knew it was a vile, sneaky, underhanded and heathen thing to do, and, whenever you're contemplating stuff like that, it's important to stay focused on the sneaky part or everybody will find out about the vile, heathen, and underhanded parts that go along with it.

So Easter Sunday rolled around and I put on that handsome blue Brooks Brothers suit Julie bought me for Christmas and showed up bright and early at St. Jude's like I was supposed to for 10:30 mass. Julie was waiting outside with her mom, looking absolutely radiant in this pretty new yellow-and-white Easter dress with matching hat, purse, and shoes. Geez, did she look great! Although I must admit some little Married Male hormone in my system immediately started wondering about how much she might have spent for an outfit she was only going to wear once a year. Or maybe just once, period, since Easter is tradition-ally the time when women show off their latest finery while all those dress, hat, shoe, and purse manufacturers (many of whom do not celebrate Easter, if you catch my drift) take a drive over to Long Island to look at bigger houses or head over to the International Motor Sports Show to see if there's anything exciting on display.

But those are the kind of thoughts you're best off left to bury-after all, they can't do anything except get you in trouble-so I kissed Julie and told her how swell she looked and then lied right through my teeth and told her mom the same thing. Julie's mom shot me the kind of smile you save for clumsy doormen and bad waiters and turned her cheek up with the obvious intention that I should kiss it. All I could think was that it looked like the skin on an elephant's ass, only powdered up like it'd been dredged in peach-colored flour and then topped off with enough rouge to bury a bowling ball. But I took a deep breath and did it-Julie was watching me, I could feel it-and I think it's a real credit to me that I didn't cough or gag or have my lips fall off.

My folks showed up a little after that with my sister Sarah Jean and my Aunt Rosamarina in tow, and we all went in and found seats together well down towards the front. Not that we much wanted to sit that close, but the back rows always fill up first in church-it's sort of a tradition, especially at Christmas and Easter when you've got overflow crowds-and the smart folks who don't want the priest to be able to make eye contact (or, worse yet, see them dozing off during the homily) either show up early so they can sit way in the back or show up late after the place is already full and get to stand against the back wall or out even out in the entrance hall.

I guess I must be a pretty lousy Catholic on account of I never seemed to get all that much out of church. I mean, if God is really all-knowing and can read your innermost thoughts every second of every day, what the hell's the point of getting all dressed up to go someplace special to pray to Him. I mean, He already knows the whole story, right? And it's not like He's going to be impressed. Plus I could never help wondering about all those Baptists and Lutherans and Methodists and Presbyterians and Greek Orthodox and Russian Orthodox and Church of England types who, at least according to our guys, had it all wrong. And that's not even considering all the Jews and Buddhists and Muslims and Hindus and Confusionists who were going straight to the fires of hell-Do Not Pass "GO," Do Not Collect $200-the instant their hearts stopped beating. It just didn't seem fair, you know? Although maybe it was some sort of real estate deal. If only good, practicing, churchgoing Catholics who had never committed any mortal sins could get into heaven, you really wouldn't need much space. Not much space at all. In any case, I figured I was damned (in more ways than one, maybe) if I was going to believe in any God who could be that unreasonable. But don't get me wrong. Far back as I can remember, I've always been rock-solid certain there's something bigger and more important in this universe than people. It's just that, being people, I don't especially think it's our place to understand it. In fact, I think it seems a little bit arrogant to think we do.

But church never bothered me much. Especially seeing as how I didn't go real regularly. Just a couple times a year, really, like most of the other Catholics I knew. But I liked the fact that you could count on getting out in less than an hour-Christmas, Easter, weddings, baptisms, first communions, confirmations, funerals, or regular Sunday Mass-while I'd heard those beanie-head Jews over in Brooklyn stayed at it all day. And sometimes they wouldn't eat on top of it. Plus I liked the idea of confession, even though I never went. The notion that you could patch things up with God even after you'd done mean, cruel, unspeakable things was an unbelievably good deal. In fact, it was one of the things that got me suspicious about church in the first place.

I could go, though. Just to keep peace in the family and keep my mom happy. I'd sit there and add up the pieces of red glass and green glass and yellow glass and royal purple glass in the stained glass windows or count the little sculptured hiccups in the masonry moldings along the tops of the walls or the gold fleur-de-lis patterns on the carpets and tapestries. Or wonder why you had to sit and stand and kneel and stand and kneel and sit at various times during the service. Did that mean something special to God? Or was it, as my dad said, "just to keep everybody awake." But it was nice being in church with Julie. Really it was. She sat right next to me and we held hands and she played a little bit with my fingertips until I started noticing the warmth of her all up and down against me and, God help me, I started to get these terribly impure thoughts. Right there in church, you know? And of course then it seemed like everybody was looking at me and knew exactly what I was thinking-especially the priest!-and that's when Julie leaned over and whispered in my ear, *"You're blushing, Palumbo!"* She sounded like she was just a little proud of it, too.

I remember the homily that day was about "Do Unto Others," and no doubt I will roast on a spit in hell with all the Jews, Buddhists, Muslims, Hindus, Confusionists, bad Catholics and off-brand Christians for what I was thinking of doing to Julie and praying she would be doing right back to me in the very near future. But at least I was praying, and everybody knows that's what you're supposed to do in church.

Naturally my married sisters and their families got there late-going anyplace is always directly proportional to the distance involved and quantity and ages of the people who have to get ready divided by the number of available bathrooms-but they made it in time to get in the communion line, and there's definitely a well-entrenched school of Catholic religious thought that believes God doesn't do His head count until then, so if you slide in under the wire for the cookie, you're safe.

After church we headed back to my mom's place for another monstrous holiday dinner-only this time at noon-complete with a big Easter ham and sweet potatoes and egg bread and my sister Ann Marie's perpetually disgusting cabbage, bean, and peanut butter casserole. Naturally everybody said it was delicious. Mary Frances showed up just as we were sitting down and of course caught a heaping dose of shit from my old man about missing church. And of course she countered with that same old line about "religion being the opiate of the people," but I noticed she didn't deliver it with her usual fire and indignation. In fact, she seemed kind of dull and listless about it, and for sure wasn't taking her usual relish in pissing oiff the old man. Something had to be bothering her. I could tell.

Without Mary Frances and my old man hollering at each other it was a pretty quiet meal. At least until everybody got around to the subject of Julie and me. Then it was "when is the rehearsal dinner" and "who's doing the flowers" and "have you met with the priest yet" and "where are you going on your honeymoon" and a kajillion other questions that seemed terribly important to everybody else but which I figured would more or less take care of themselves. In any case they'd become distinct non-issues entirely by sometime around midnight on Saturday, June 6th. I mean, I figured what was really important was what was going to happen *after* we got married. And I don't mean *just* after, either (although you can bet I was spending a lot of time thinking about that, too). It seemed to me that the days and weeks and months and years after the wedding were what would really tell the story. To tell the truth, I was a little uneasy about it. Maybe more than a little, even. Especially since Julie and my sisters and my mom and Julie's mom and even my Aunt Rosamarina were all focused in on our wedding day like it was the blessed Second Coming of Christ, you know? Although I think that's just something women do in order not to think too much about what comes afterwards. Plus they want to be damn sure the guy involved understands that this amounts to an iron-clad, no-cut contract, and-so the logic must go-the bigger a deal the wedding is, the more obvious that becomes.

After we ate, my Aunt Rosamarina sat in the front corner by the window all by herself, just like she had at Christmas, knocking down glass after glass of Anisette while Julie's mom chainsmoked those gold-tipped, pastel-colored Vogue cigarettes directly across from her, kind of perched up all funny on her chair while her head rotated around the room in tiny, erratic little jerks, keeping an eye on everybody like an damn owl on a tree limb. Boy, what a swell pair of bookends those two would've made. Particularly with the collected works of Edgar Allen Poe in between. Meanwhile my dad showed off his new-at-Christmas Zenith TV, and we all sat around watching the Easter Parade live from Fifth Avenue. It was on three channels. I personally thought it was pretty dull, but the ladies all seemed interested in the clothes and celebrities and stuff, and all my dad and brother-in-laws were really interested in was opening up their belts and the top buttons of their pants to make a little more room so they could drink a few more beers or cups of coffee with a little spike in it and shove a few more slabs of coconut-frosted lamb cake or a half-dozen more cannolis in their faces.

By prior arrangement with Cal, my headache and severe case of stomach distress came over me in a sudden, overpowering wave at precisely two-thirty, and it took me less than twenty minutes to apologize to everybody (making sure to look like I was about to puke on their shoes) and excuse myself from the proceedings. But, right there at the last minute, Julie threw me a curve. "You've got a car, don't you?" she asked innocently.

"Sure. I've got a customer's Nash. Why?"

"You're gonna get in trouble some day drivin' all over hellan'gone in other people's cars!" my dad hollered over from the couch. He'd had a few drinks, and that always brought out the uglier sides of his personality.

"Oh," Julie said innocently, "I was just hoping you could maybe drive my mom and me home."

"Well, ahh, I'm feelin' pretty sick, see...."

"But you have to go right by there, Buddy." Her voice was all sweetness and cream, but the look in her eyes made it clear that this was not a negotiable request. So I drove them home. What else could I do? And then, when we got to her house, she threw me the second curveball. She told her mom she was going to go on back to my apartment with me just to make sure I was okay. And of course her mom had no sooner disappeared into the house than Julie fixed me with a withering stare. "You're going down to that stupid car show in Manhattan, aren't you?"

"Well, I, er, uhh…." There was no place to hide, you know?

Needless to say, Julie thought it was pretty damn stinky of me to break up our big family get-together just so I could go down and look at some fancy chrome grilles and bumpers-no matter where the heck they came from-and it didn't matter a bit that the family wasn't going to do anything more than sit in front of my dad's new Zenith for the rest of the afternoon watching *Victory at Sea; Roller Derby; Kukla, Fran, and Ollie; Super Circus;* and Jackie Coogan in *Cowboy G-Men.* To tell the truth, both my folks had kind of turned into television addicts. It was an easy thing to do. My old man liked it for the ball games and the prize fights and the war shows like *Victory at Sea,* while my mom loved the Milton Berle, Sid Caesar and Ernie Kovacs variety shows, panel quiz shows like *What's My Line,* Skippy Peanut Butter's popular *You Asked for It,* and that little pipsqueak Wally Cox as *Mr. Peepers.* Imagine my surprise when Chuck Day casually mentioned that Wally Cox raced motorcycles out in the California desert. Wally Cox, can you believe it? But the point is my folks were glued to that flickering gray tube just about all the time, and it was no surprise that people who came over by the house fell under its spell, too. Like I said, it was an easy thing to do. And there they'd sit, with their mouths hanging open and eyes glazed over, watching any damn thing that came on like rodents mesmerized by a snake. So why the heck should I have to hang around just to do that? Especially when I had more important things to do. And I told Julie as much.

"That's not the point," she said. Which, based on an informal, thumbnail survey of other married or soon-to-be married males I've known, is exactly how most wives, fiancées, and steady-type girlfriends tend to respond after you've made a typically Guy Style honest, fair, and thoroughly reasonable assessment of a situation. But I knew better than to argue, since I was wrong going in and therefore destined to lose regardless of the merits of my case.

So I took another approach. "Say, why don't you come with? It'll be *fun.* "

She looked at me kind of sideways. "Are you trying to make it sound *fun* to go look at cars?"

"Sure."

Julie gave me that terminally exasperated grimace women save up for just such occasions. "Look, Palumbo, let me explain it for you. Going to a show is fun. Listening to live music is fun. Going out to parties is fun. Even just having a nice meal in a nice restaurant is fun. But looking at frickin' cars is just looking at frickin' cars. Understand?"

I pretended to understand.

"And look how I'm dressed..." She still had on that pretty, yellow-and-white, wear-it-once-and-pay-for-it-over-the-next-twelve-months Easter dress, complete with matching hat, shoes, and purse.

"You look *great,* honey," I gushed. "And I bet *lots* of people at that show will be coming directly from the Easter Parade on Fifth Avenue." She didn't look particularly convinced. "And look how *I'm* dressed, too. Why it'd be a damn shame not to go out someplace and parade ourselves around a little as long as we're all spiffed up like this."

"You mean someplace like a car show?"

Obviously I needed more ammunition. "Howabout if I throw in dinner?"

She mulled it over. "At a nice restaurant?"

"Absolutely at a nice restaurant. Cloth napkins and everything."

"You're sure your stomach is up to it?"

She really knew how to put the blade in and twist it. Honest she did.

"And a downtown movie, too?"

"Sure, if we have enough time."

She thought a moment more. "Okay, Palumbo, you got yourself a deal."

I was pleased to witness the mature, adult way we'd been able to negotiate our way through the situation. That was an important thing. Although I was already starting to worry a little about how much money I had in my pocket-it was a good bet Cal wouldn't have anything but moth holes and dust bunnies in his-and whether it would stretch far enough to cover my side of the bargain. And I decided maybe it would-*just!*-so long as we ate cheap, tipped even cheaper, and parked on the street.

But what a surprise when we rolled into the Sinclair and found Carson Flegley's family's funeral parlor's black Caddy limousine parked out front with the motor running, Cal behind the wheel, and Carson sitting next to him fiddling with the air conditioner controls and radio knobs. Seems Cal's folks had gotten wise to the old phantom spare key trick on his mom's Packard, and now that was gone and Cal was officially grounded until the second coming of Christ or when the Giants won the pennant. Whichever came first. But it turned out that Carson wanted to go, too, and of course there were no funerals on tap on account of you just don't go planting stiffs on Easter. So not only did Julie and me get to ride around like a couple of swells in the back seat of a Caddy limousine (which only had a very small line of *Flegley Funeral Home* gold lettering on the sides), but Carson also figured to have a little cash on him so I wouldn't have to spend the whole evening steering us away from fancy appetizers and whipped cream desserts and secretly counting the nickels left in my pocket every time somebody wanted another cappuccino.

Plus it was nice for Julie to get to know Cal and Carson a little better, since, by default as much as anything else, they'd really become my best friends. But that's just the way it is. You get involved in cars and racing and it just doesn't leave a lot of time left for anything else, you know? Julie understood that, too (boy, did she *ever!*) and so regarded Cal and Carson with a hint of well-deserved suspicion. Fortunately Cal was always a real smooth talker, and all the way into Manhattan he tried his best to make Julie feel like she belonged. "Boy, I can sure see why Buddy never brings you out to the races!" he started in. "A beautiful girl like you would sure get a lot of attention from all those rich playboys."

"Like you, for instance?"

"Oh, not *me*. Far as I'm concerned, you're Buddy's girl. I'm real particular about those kinds of things." Cal swiveled his head around and grinned into the back seat. "But if you ever get tired of this bum, give me a call, okay?"

"I'll keep it in mind."

"Hey," I interrupted, "I thought you guys were my friends."

"You've got to understand, Buddy," Cal explained over the seatback, "there are no such thing as friends where beautiful, sexy women and fast, sexy sports cars are concerned."

"How on earth can a *car* be sexy?" Julie wanted to know.

"Well, just like a woman," Cal said without even thinking about it. "The first part is how she looks and carries herself."

"Y-yeah," Carson timidly agreed. "Y-you see something like a Jaguar or that n-new Austin-Healey and it just, I dunno, *does* something to you...."

"So it's all about looks?"

"Not at all. Like I said, that's just the first part. Then comes the best part, where you finally get it in your hands and feel the power and balance and the way it responds," Cal inhaled like he was smelling sweet perfume. "Like I said, a great car is like a beautiful, sexy woman. Better, even."

"Oh. I see," Julie said playfully, right in the spirit of it. "A sports car is *better* than a beautiful, sexy woman."

"Certainly. At least if it's a good one, anyway. See, a good car always does what you want it to and never gets cranky or has headaches or needs you to scratch its back or hold its hand or spend more time with it."

"So a car lets you come and go as you please."

"Sure. And it never holds anything back, either. If you ask it for a hundred percent, it gives you a hundred percent. No questions asked." Of course all of this was bullshit. Cal and I knew better than anybody that cars-and especially sports cars and even more especially race cars-were subject to nasty personality quirks and ugly mood swings and violent fits of temper as sure as any creature of flesh and blood. But he was just making conversation, you know? And doing a damn good job of it, too.

"So when you drive fast it's like making love?" Julie asked.

Cal started to rip off another smart remark, but then he stopped. It was like the shadow of a cloud passed over his face. "There's a big difference between *driving fast* and *racing,"* he said thoughtfully. Then added: "And all that bull about driving being like sex is just an old wives' tale."

"It is?"

Cal nodded. "Whoever thought that one up has either never raced a car or never been with a woman."

"Oh, and you've got so much experience with both," I tossed in, trying to lighten things up again. But Cal was onto something and didn't want to let go.

"No, really," Cal said softly under misty, faraway eyes. "One's cool and calm and relaxed when it's good and the other's just the opposite-all urgent and hot and sweaty..." his eyes flicked to the rearview mirror and I think he saw Julie blushing. Or maybe it was me. "...unless you drive like that asshole Skippy Welcher, that is."

Carson and I both burst out laughing.

"Who's this Skippy Welcher character?" Julie wanted to know.

All three of us started to explain, but thought better of it and gave up before the first word came out. I mean, where on earth did you start on a monument to bad taste and idiocy like The Skipper. "You really need to see for yourself," Cal finally said. "Words fail me."

"Words fail *you?"* Julie gasped incredulously. "That's hard to believe."

We all got a good laugh off that, and I was really pleased that we were all getting along so well. I mean *really* pleased.

"Seriously, you ought to make Buddy bring you out to the races sometime and see for yourself."

"I keep asking her to go with, but she never does."

"Why don't you come up to Bridgehampton with us the 22nd and 23rd of May," Cal offered. "It's right close by. Out at the end of Long Island. In fact, that's where I met this bozo for the first time."

My mind swirled back to that spring day at Bridgehampton, when Big Ed and I drove out in his brand new Jaguar to see our very first sports car race and I met Cal and started working on his ratty, broken-down MG. It was hard to believe it was only a year ago. So much had happened in between.

"Hmpf." Julie snorted. "My mom would really go for that. She'd have herself a conniption fit if I asked to go on a frickin' overnight with three boys."

"But you guys are going to be *married* in a couple more months."

"That's different. But only *after* we're married, understand. My mom's kind of old fashioned about that sort of thing." Julie swiveled her eyes over to mine. "And so am I, Buddy Palumbo, even if I don't always act like it."

I gave her a little kiss on the cheek for that. She deserved it.

"That's so sweet I may vomit," Cal choked, and made an elaborate puking commotion into the seat between him and Carson.

"Hey, watch it!" Carson squealed.

"That's *really* disgusting," Julie observed. She looked over at me. "You have such refined friends."

"Well, they may be awful," I admitted, "but at least they're mine."

"And you're welcome to every frickin' one, Palumbo," she whispered so Cal and Carson couldn't hear it.

We were just peeling off the George Washington Bridge into Manhattan traffic when Cal suddenly snapped his fingers. "Hey, I've got a great idea. You'd like to bring Julie to the race at Bridgehampton, right?"

"And?"

"And I bet I can fix it so it's okay with her mom."

"Hmpf," Julie snorted. "I can tell you've never met my mother."

"No, really," Cal insisted.

As you can imagine, I was all ears.

"See, my folks have this summer cottage on the shore in East Quogue. They hardly ever use it, and it's not far from Bridgehampton at all."

"So?"

"So we could all stay there."

Julie looked at Cal like there was wind whistling between his ears. "And what makes you think my mother would go for that?"

"It's a pretty big place. Why, you could have your own room. You could even bring a friend or something."

Julie shook her head. "Nah, I just can't see it," she said. But you could see the wheels were turning.

"I got it," I said. "Howabout if one of my sisters comes along. They never let me get away with anything."

"You mean Mary Frances?" Julie snorted. "Why, she's just about *living* with that stuffed shirt Ph.D. jerk in Greenwich Village. And you want *her* to be our chaperone?"

"No. Not Mary Frances. Sarah Jean…" I could see Julie's eyes start to light up, "…I mean, she's damn near a nun."

"It'd do her good, too," Cal chimed in.

"Y'know," Julie nodded slowly, "it just might work."

So we made plans right then and there to go to the races at Bridgehampton together on the 22nd and 23rd of May and stay overnight at Cal's folks' place in East Quogue and ask my stay-at-home sister Sarah Jean along to make sure everything stayed strictly on the up-and-up since it would still be two weeks before our wedding day. Boy, was I ever excited! It sounded like one of those dreamy, faraway romantic adventures you read about in books or see in the movies that never actually happen to real people.

The International Motor Sports Show at the Grand Central Palace in Manhattan was quite a fancy deal, and naturally Cal wheeled the limo right up in front like we were royalty or something. I was about to say something-I mean, I didn't want to get arrested or anything when I was supposed to be back at the apartment over my Aunt Rosamarina's garage hugging the damn commode-but when Carson scurried out in his best black funeral suit and opened the door for Julie and me, it seemed to be catching and right away the fat guy at the front entrance with the gold braid on his cap and cuffs bent into a little bow and swept the door open for Julie and me like we had pockets overflowing with gold, frankincense, and myrrh. Even though Julie was trying to be nonchalant about it, you could tell she was enjoying all the respect and attention. "You know," she whispered in my ear, "it's nice being on the other side of the tray of French fries for a change."

So Julie and me strolled into the Grand Central Palace like it was the foyer of our own private villa in Monte Carlo, and right away we were smitten by all the gleaming, foot-deep paintjobs and glistening chrome trim shimmering all around us. Not to mention all the latest, hottest cars from England and France and Germany and Italy and everywhere else you could think of, including makes and models neither of us had ever heard of before. The first one to catch our eye was the brand new Alpine sports car from the British Sunbeam company, which the guy on the stand explained had built some very famous and successful race cars back in the teens and twenties but fell on hard times and finally got swallowed up by the Rootes Group before the war. Anyhow, the new Alpine was a high, handsome thing that looked more like a pint-sized version of a Rolls or a Bentley convertible than any kind of sports car. It was done up in creamy white with red leather upholstery, just like Big Ed's XK-120, and the sales brochure bragged about how well Sunbeams had done in European rallies and made an especially big deal about how Stirling Moss had driven one at over 120 miles-per-hour on some closed-off highway in Belgium. But I'd been around the block enough times regarding genuinely stock vs. sneakily modified automobiles to guess that an Alpine fresh off the showroom floor would never go anywheres near that fast unless you pushed it off a damn cliff. Still, it was pretty nice to look at and certainly had a lot more interior room and luggage space than your average two-seater sports car.

Across from Sunbeam was the Porsche exhibit, and the centerpiece was a gray 1500 Super convertible with upholstery the color of Spanish tile. It really looked pretty sharp, but it was hard explaining to Julie why it cost damn near as much as a Jaguar. "It looks like, I don't know, such a *lump....*" she said, being careful to keep her voice down so none of the sharp-eared, taut-jawed Porsche factory representatives could hear her. Oh, I tried to tell her about Porsche's advanced design and lightweight construction and independent suspension and air cooling and all that stuff, but it didn't sound real convincing on account of I felt pretty much the same about Porsches myself. I mean, they just didn't have *style* like a Jaguar or a Ferrari. Even if they did go like stink on a race track. "Well, they may be wonderful cars," Julie whispered, shaking her head, "but they remind me of melted gumdrops."

"Thanks a lot, Julie. Now I'd never be able to look at another Porsche without thinking of melted gumdrops."

Just past the Porsches was the Jaguar display featuring four sparkling XK-120s-two roadsters, a coupe, and one of their new "drophead" convertible versions with genuine burl walnut veneer interior trim and real crank-'em-up glass windows-surrounding one of their sleek-yet-stately Mk. VII sedans on a big, rotating turntable. That one was done up in a stunning shade of iridescent blue and fitted with the newly available Borg Warner automatic transmission. "Now *that's* a car for me," Julie sighed. "It's just beautiful, isn't it?"

"Someday I'll buy you one," I promised her. And, at least right at that very moment, I meant it.

In front of the turntable was a highly polished Jaguar engine on a special display stand-it was still about the handsomest damn automobile engine I'd ever seen-and off to one side was a marble pedestal with the impressive first-place trophy the C-Type had won at Le Mans on its very first attempt in 1951. And of course Colin St. John from Westbridge was right there in the thick of things, chatting up the crowd and telling the better-heeled prospects about the exciting new "Jagyewahr drophead" that offered the finest in civilized top-down motoring and the equally thrilling new Mark VII luxury sedan with automatic transmission that would be just the thing for the little woman (or the girl the little woman didn't know about) to take tooling down Fifth Avenue. Only you really needed to get your deposit down immediately in order to secure your place on the waiting list, since it was already *quite* extensive....

Same old Colin.

He noticed us standing there and excused himself from a certified non-prospect in a four year old Sears Roebuck suit. We were buying parts pretty regularly from Westbridge by then, so Colin walked elegantly over and gave us a grand smile. "And how is the young motoring entrepreneur from New Jersey today?" he asked in that tweedy British accent of his.

"Okay, I guess." Julie gave me a little jab in the ribs. "Oh, and this is Julie Finzio. I think you maybe met her at the costume party last year."

"Of course. Absolutely lovely." He kissed her hand. "Charmed, my dear."

You could tell Julie was enjoying this kind of treatment.

"You're the intended, are you not?"

"Yeah," I told him. "We're planning t'get hitched in June."

Julie glared at me, then rolled her eyes at Colin. "You have to excuse Buddy. He doesn't know anything about the social graces yet."

"Oh, but I'm sure you have enough for both of you, my dear."

You have to admit, that Colin St. John was one smooth talker. But then, that's what he did for a living.

"Oh, Buddy," Colin added, "there's someone you might wish to meet over there." He took us over by the Le Mans trophy and introduced us to these two tall, well-dressed English gentlemen. "This is Mr. Ernest Rankin, who designed this lovely display for Jagyewahr, and this is Mr. William Lyons, who designs and builds the cars."

I just about fell over. *"You're* the guy who designs Jaguars?"

"I'm afraid Mr. St. John is being overly polite," he chuckled. "It's my staff who design and build the cars. I don't do much beside hold the tiller and crack the occasional whip."

WOW!

"W-well, I sure love your cars," I said lamely.

"Thank you very much."

"Geez, I work on them all the time over at my shop."

"I'm sorry to hear they require so much attention."

"Geez, that's not what I meant," I sputtered, "I mean, it's…"

"Oh, that's all right," he laughed. "You just make sure to keep them running properly, all right?"

"I sure will."

"And now, if you'll excuse me, I'm afraid I have to meet with someone from the newspapers. It's been a pleasure meeting you, young man."

"Geez, me, too."

Then they took off and left us standing there in front of that big first place trophy from the twenty-four hours of Le Mans. Wow. The head man from Jaguar. In person. Cal and Carson were never gonna believe this.

Naturally that had to be the high point of my entire day, but we found lots of other neat stuff at the show, too. Right behind the Jaguar display Mercedes had their full line of 170, 220, and 300 sedans and convertibles (but no 300SL sports car, which I couldn't figure) and further down the aisle was this big, dangerously sleek yet unmistakably elegant and refined Bentley Continental coupe. I observed that it looked perfect for some rakish Duke or Earl to drive off into the countryside with a succulent and thoroughly underage young stablehand's daughter at his side. Julie liked that one, too. Except for the part about the stablehand's daughter, anyway. "Your mind's a frickin' sewer, Palumbo," was I believe the way she put it. And I had to agree.

Gathered around the Bentley were an Aston Martin DB2 coupe, a seven passenger Rolls Royce limousine, and this flamboyant Daimler Special Sports sedan called the "Silver Flash," which was about as swoopy and slinky and dramatic as anything that big could possibly be. "It looks like something Jean Harlow would drive," Julie whispered in my ear.

"Hell, it looks like Jean Harlow, period!" And it did.

Around the Bentley and Rolls stand were an outer circle of less expensive, lower-class sports and touring models from MG, Riley, and Morris, all of which seemed pretty dull in such company. Across the way, Allard had one of their Cadillac-powered, four-seater K3 touring models and one of their new "Palm Beach" sports cars-neither of which had the raw appeal of the cycle-fendered J2X models like Tommy Edwards and Eddie Dearborn drove. Or at least I didn't think so. But between them was one of the sleek, low, envelope bodied J2X "Le

Mans" versions in a deep metallic red, and it looked pretty slippery for such a big old monster of a car, what with slick little plexiglass covers over the headlights and a wide, menacing bulge in the hood to clear a hot-rodded Oldsmobile V-8 with Hilborn fuel injection on top. Nasty!

Further on we came to a pretty little coupe version of the Deutsch Bonnet that won the Index prize at Sebring, and I made the mistake of telling Julie what everybody up and down pit lane called the little French car at Sebring. "I don't think that's funny at all," she said, and proved it beyond question by not looking in the least tiny bit amused.

Behind it we came to the Momo stand, which was really more or less the Cunningham setup seeing as how Alfred Momo was the ace wrench and key organizer who looked after the Cunningham race team and all of Briggs' other automotive enterprises. They had this stunning, Vignale-bodied Cunningham "production" coupe on display that Colin St. John said was built as much to keep the I.R.S. happy as to actually sell any cars, and next to it was an 1100cc OSCA similar to the one Briggs raced at Sebring that year. I guess Momo had some sort of side deal as the OSCA importer, and they were really wonderful little cars-beautiful to look at and beautifully built as well. Speaking of nifty Italian cars, Tony Pompeo was there as the SIATA importer and had their new 2-liter roadster on a rotating turntable, while Alfa Romeo unveiled this incredibly wild and slippery coupe called the "Disco Volante" ("Flying Saucer") that looked about the right kind of sports car for Buck Rogers or Flash Gordon to use for tearing around the solar system.

English makes I'd never even heard of like Alvis and Armstrong-Siddeley displayed formal, upright, old fashioned-looking sedans that were a healthy notch or two down from Rolls or Bentley money but still had lots of that stiff-upper-lip stuffiness people seem to want and expect from British automobiles. The Bristol aircraft company showed off a smooth, slippery sports coupe sporting the same rugged six cylinder engine that powered the Frazer Nash sports car and many English racing specials (although Barry Spline told me later it was really a knock-off of an old prewar BMW engine that got taken back to England-along with its designer-as spoils of war after the Armistice).

And who should we run into near the end of the aisle but our friend Brooks Stevens and the Excalibur that we'd pitted next to at Sebring. "Hey, Buddy," he said, warmly shaking my hand. Like I said, he'd had polio, so he didn't have much of a grip. "It's great to see you again."

"Good t'see you, too." And then I remembered before Julie even had a chance to jab me in the ribs. "And this is my fiancée, Miss Julie Finzio."

Julie gave me a look of amazed approval.

"Well, congratulations," Brooks beamed. "Although why anyone would want to marry a greasy paddock rat like this fellow is beyond me."

"Oh, it's his charm, Mr. Stevens," Julie replied. "Can't you see? He's just terribly irresistible."

"It's a shame about your eyes," he laughed. "And call me 'Kip,' all right?"

Julie gave him a big, warm smile. She sensed right off that he was really a nice sort of person to be around.

"So," I asked, "you selling any cars?"

Brooks looked at the Excalibur squatted on the carpet behind him. "Not really. But then, I'm not much of a salesman. Don't really have the stomach for it. Besides, Bill Kaiser's given Dutch Darrin the nod on a new sports car, so I'm not really sure I could get the chassis even if I had orders to fill."

"But you're here anyway?"

"Well, the space was already paid for and all the travel arrangements had already been made, so why not? Besides, I had a few meetings planned in New York, anyway. A few new design projects to noodle on. And I always love going to the car shows. Just to see what everybody's up to."

"And who's Dutch Darrin?"

"Another designer. Really quite good sometimes. At least if you like his style. Take a look." Brooks pointed and directly across from us one of the brand new Kaiser Darrin sports cars. I didn't think it was nearly as sporty or original or all-American futuristic as Brooks' Excalibur, but it did look a little more like a real, everyday car. Brooks said the body was made out of fiberglass, which was a first, and the doors slid back into the rear fenders on tracks instead of swinging open like on normal cars. "What's the point?" I asked.

Brooks shrugged. "I think it's one of those handkerchief-up-the-sleeve High Fashion things, but I couldn't be sure."

But of all the unique features of the new Kaiser Darrin, none was as striking as the front end. Especially the grille. Julie stared at it awhile and then whispered, "It looks like Marlene Dietrich putting her lipstick on."

Brooks Stevens laughed out loud. "Oh, that's *perfect!*" he cried, clapping his hands together. "In fact, I think maybe it *is* Marlene Dietrich putting her lipstick on, isn't it? Oh, that's *priceless.*"

"Y'know," I told him, looking back and forth from the Kaiser Darrin to the Excalibur, "I can't believe they picked that one over yours."

"Oh, I suppose they thought Dutch's idea was a little more practical for everyday use. Besides, if there's one thing I've learned in this business, it's that there's no accounting for taste." He looked at us with a sad, experienced smile. "After all, that's why there's chocolate and vanilla, right?"

I looked down at my watch. "Geez, we'd better be getting along. I promised Julie dinner and a movie after this, and we've still got more stuff to see."

"You make it a *good* dinner now, not one of those cheeseburgers," Brooks warned playfully. "A girl like this deserves the best."

"In that case, what am I doing with him?" Julie shot right back.

"That, I'm afraid, is destined to be *your* problem."

As we walked away, Julie leaned over and whispered, "what a *nice* man." He really was, too.

It was getting late and we knew we had to find Cal and Carson, but I told Julie I couldn't possibly leave without seeing the Ferrari stand. It was over in a far corner, almost hidden away, and of course Carlo Sebastian was there with his elegant mane of silvery-white hair, klieg light smile, and a perfectly tailored, cream-colored Italian silk suit that probably cost more than my old man's Mercury. He had two stunning Pinin Farina coupes and one Vignale roadster on display, and even Julie could tell these were some very special automobiles. And she was pretty impressed when Carlo waved us over and put his arm around my shoulder. "So," he said, looking extremely serious, "have you been driving over any cliffs lately?"

"Nah. I'm trying to keep that to sort of a one-to-a-customer deal."

"An excellent idea."

"But I am getting married."

"Ahh, the biggest cliff of all."

"And this is her. Julie Finzio, meet Carlo Sebastian."

He bowed from the waist. "A pleasure, I'm sure."

You could see she was a little awed by him. But who wouldn't be?

"How's the show going?" I asked, just trying to make it look like Carlo and me were genuine chums.

"I don't really know why we come," he sighed dramatically. "All the cars are sold before I get them, of course, and then I can't get any more."

"Geez, that's a shame," I told him, even though I wondered just a little if it was really true.

"Oh," he allowed, "one gets used to it."

"And the show?"

Carlo shrugged. "The factory wants people to see the cars. What can you do? And of course you need to keep your eye on the competition." I followed his gaze across the way to where three cars the likes of which I'd never seen before

307

were on display. They looked a little like Ferraris, and, just like on the Ferrari stand, there were two coupes and a convertible. One coupe done up in a dazzling, eye-gouge yellow was up on an elevated, rotating turntable with a big "SOLD" tag stuck under the windshield wiper.

"What the hell are those things?" I asked Carlo Sebastian.

"Pegasos!" he spit out. "They are made in Spain by truck mechanics."

"Truck mechanics?"

Carlo made a face like he'd eaten a bad clam.

Naturally we wandered over to take a look, and Julie and me about fell over backwards when we saw the price tag: TWENTY-NINE THOUSAND FIVE HUNDRED DOLLARS! Can you believe it? Why, it was more than twice as much as a Ferrari and *four times* the price of a Jaguar! Which seemed like an awful lot of money for a sports car built by some truck company in Spain. Especially considering nobody'd ever even heard of a Pegaso before. But it sure was dazzling, no doubt about it, what with a beautifully finished, hand-built Italian body and a perfectly fitted, hand-tailored leather interior. And it figured to be pretty fast, too, since under the hood was a specially built, double overhead camshaft V-8 engine with a supercharger perched on top. I went back over by Carlo Sebastian and asked him about it.

"It's really something, isn't it?" he laughed. "If it makes anywhere near as much horsepower as headlines, it can't help but be an outstanding success."

"Where'd it come from?"

"Wilfredo Ricart designed it, so you know in the beginning it has to have everything. In fact, that's likely going to be the problem."

"I don't get it."

"Ricart used to work with Ferrari when they were at Alfa Romeo together during the war. That was before Ferrari had his own company." Carlo Sebastian shook his head and sighed. "They never got along."

"They didn't?"

Carlo pulled me in a little closer and whispered: "Ferrari told me Ricart wears shoes with thick rubber soles in order to cushion the shock to his brain stem when he walks."

"That sounds a little nuts to me."

"Then you understand perfectly, my friend."

"But where does Pegaso come in?"

"It's very simple. Pegaso is a Spanish truck manufacturer who wanted to build something extravagant to show the world what it could do, and they hired Ricart to design it because he'd been head engineer at Alfa Romeo and got credit for a lot of Ferrari's work there. And Vittorio Jano's before him." Carlo made a nasty little cat spit noise between his teeth.

"So what happened?"

"Ricart gave them what they asked for. More of everything than anybody ever dreamed of before. State-of-the-art or beyond in every department. A car on the leading edge in every possible way." He started to laugh again. "The only problem is that it's fiendishly complicated, designed by a man without a single thing that ever worked right in his portfolio, and built by a bunch of Spanish truck assemblers who have never so much as even visited a race track or driven a lowly MG around the block so as to understand what sports cars are all about." He gave me a thin, insider smile. "Outside of that, it's perfect."

But it still looked pretty imposing. And you had to be impressed with the price. Not to mention that they'd actually sold one there at the show. To Rafael Leonides Trujillo, no less, who'd been in the papers quite a bit since he'd left his position as political leader, military strongman, and all-purpose dictator of the Dominican Republic. I guess there must be a lot of money in the Retired Dictator business.

Anyhow, Julie and me gawked at that Pegaso for quite awhile (no matter what, your eyes kept going back to the price tag!) and then went looking for Cal and Carson, but we kept getting snagged every fifteen or twenty paces or so by some new grille grinning our way or some new headlamp giving us the eye. And one that really caught Julie's fancy-don't ask me why-was the lowly little Volkswagen Beetle. I explained to her as how it was designed by the same guy who did the Porsches she didn't much care for (in fact, there's an awful lot of common blood between the two, even if the Porsche types don't much like to admit it!) but none of that mattered to Julie. "It's *cute!*" she declared, and that was about as enthusiastic as she'd gotten over anything at the whole blessed show. So I asked the salesman to pop the rear deck so I could have a looksee and even carefully got down on my hands and knees in my new Brooks Brothers suit to take a peek underneath. Even though it was cheap, you could see it was screwed together pretty good, and, like I said, it had a lot of the same exact design features as the Porsche. But the thing I liked best about it-and I could feel the old wheels starting to rumble and spin between my ears-was it was *simple.* Heck, here was a car even Raymond Tuttle could learn to work on. That was a pretty big deal if you owned a car repair shop, believe me.

We finally located Cal and Carson over by the Jowett stand, where Cal was working some poor English guy over about maybe driving one of the new Jupiter sports models for them at Bridgehampton. Just to show everybody what it

309

could do, you know? And, believe it or not, the guy was more or less listening to him. Carson was throwing in a little support here and there, telling the guy what an ace driver Cal was, and I tossed my own two cents-worth in and was frankly amazed when the guy actually said he'd think it over, gave Cal a card, and told him to call in a week or so. Can you believe it?

On our way out, nothing would do but that Carson had to stop one last time at the turntable with the new Austin-Healey Hundred on it that we'd seen down at Sebring. Cal said it was about his fifth or sixth trip back. And he was hardly alone. No question that new Austin-Healey was attracting more interest than just about anything else in the hall. In fact, it won the grand prize for best design in the show that year. And it was easy to see why. It was low and wide and sleek and handsome, with smooth, sweeping fenderlines balanced by a jaunty, defi-ant-looking Bulldog sneer on the front. But the main thing about the new Aus-tin-Healey was that ordinary people like Carson Flegley could actually afford one. That alone made it one hell of a lot more appealing than Colin St. John's waiting-list Jaguars or Carlo Sebastian's Ferraris that were already sold or that unbelievable Diamond-As-Big-As-The-Ritz Pegaso that only a retired dictator could ever hope to own.

No, the Healey Hundred was a home run, all right, and I could see in the soft, gentle yearning glistening in the corners of Carson Flegley's eyes that he'd indeed fallen in love. "I've just *got* to have one of those," he whispered achingly as we took him by the elbows and led him gently away from the Austin-Healey display. "Really I do."

He was hardly the only guy to fall in love with that Austin-Healey at the International Motor Sports Show that year.

We got out of the show a little after seven and we were all pretty tired and hungry, and that's when Cal suggested we tool all the way across town into Brooklyn to go to this little Italian pasta and pizza place he knew about. It seemed like an awful long way to go-I mean, there *are* a few restaurants in Manhattan-but as usual Cal was driving and so there was no use arguing about it. And it was actually kind of nice riding in the back seat of that plush Caddy limo with Julie. I cranked up the divider window and pulled the pleated wool curtain across it and it was like we were in our own cozy little upholstered cubbyhole with the nighttime lights and street corner sights of downtown Man-hattan gliding by on either side. I had my arm around Julie's shoulders and she had her head leaned over on mine, and every once in a while we'd do a little kissing. And then maybe a little bit more. And it didn't take long before the windows were getting steamy and I was right back to feeling like I had in church that very morning. "Hey, take it easy, Buster," Julie whispered as I tried to sort of lean us over. "Remember where the heck we are." But she didn't sound mad about it or anything, and that was really nice.

It turned out the restaurant Cal was taking us to was way over in hell-and-gone someplace in the old Italian section of Brooklyn, and it was obvious he didn't know the place all that well on account of we got lost once or twice trying to find it. And, once we got there, it didn't look all that special to me. I mean, it was just a little neighborhood storefront joint in an area where you'd maybe think about locking your hubcaps in the trunk just to keep temptation away from some of the more enterprising young street toughs who hung out at the candy store across the street and spent their evenings smoking cigarettes and pitching pennies on the sidewalk.

"How'd you find this place?" I asked as climbed out of the Caddy.

"Oh, I was here once or twice before," Cal said vaguely.

But of course that wasn't the whole story. It turned out the name of the place was Scalabrini's, and of course it belonged to the father of the beautiful Angelina Scalabrini Cal met at the blowout New Year's Eve party in Greenwich Village. He'd gone out with her a few times after that, but I guess she had this thing about becoming a movie actress-or maybe it was her mother who had it for her-and then there was some trouble between her folks and Angelina and her mom pretty much disappeared. Maybe even out to Hollywood. Cal hadn't heard a thing from her since, and for sure the real reason he brought us to Scalabrini's was to do a little casual sleuthing to see if he could find out where she was. But the waitress didn't know much except that Mr. Scalabrini never talked about it-not *ever*-but he made a habit of coming out of the kitchen every once in awhile to pass out freshly-baked *calzone* and chat up the customers, and Cal could ask him personally then if he wanted to.

So we had salad with olives and red onions and artichoke hearts and some good garlic bread and then split a huge pizza with everything but anchovies on it. And I must admit, it was pretty damn good. About halfway through, the old man Scalabrini came out of the kitchen with a tomato sauce-stained apron wrapped around his middle and started making the rounds of the tables. He was a big, sweaty, Southern Italian *paisan* with dark skin and sad eyes and a carpet of coarse black hair all over him, and you could sense a little tension behind the smile he beamed at each individual customer around a table. When he got to us, Cal stood up and reached out to shake his hand. "I don't know if you remember me or not, sir, but...."

"Shu' I 'member you," Scalabrini said in a thick dago accent, not sounding too happy to see Cal at all.

"Well, I was just wondering…."

"Yeh?"

"….if you have any idea where Angelina is?"

Scalabrini's eyes narrowed and you could see a little twitch working away at the corners of his mouth. "She's a-witt'er mudder."

Cal waited for more, but there was nothing else coming. "Well," he finally asked, "do you have any idea where her mother is?"

Scalabrini glared at him. "I'm a-hope she's a-rot inna Hell," he whispered through trembling lips. "An' now, iffa you 'scuse me, I needa go back inna kitchen." And then he turned and walked slowly away from us, his head hung down between his shoulders, staring at the floor. I really felt sorry for the guy, you know? We all did.

It was well past nine by the time we finished at the restaurant, and we were all feeling pretty pooped. But I'd promised Julie a movie if we had the time, and, wouldn't you know it, there was a late show of that new 3-D thriller *House of Wax* with Vincent Price playing at a theater in Manhattan. "Aw, I didn't mean a movie like *that.*" Julie protested. But of course Cal was driving and he and Carson and I were all real eager to see it, so that's where we went. The 3-D part was kind of phony, if you want the truth of it. Especially where this guy playing paddle ball in front of a theater bounces it right at the camera. I mean, geez, nobody even ducked. And it wasn't real scary, either. Honest it wasn't. Except for maybe the part where this deformed, shadowy character in a black cape and mask and a big black hat is stalking this beautiful, frightened girl through these wet cobblestone alleys in the fog.

We joked about how fake and hokey it was afterwards, but I don't think any of us slept really well that night.

Chapter 12: Lost on Long Island

I was really excited about Julie coming up to Bridgehampton with me and especially how all of us would be staying at Cal's family's summer place in East Quogue, and I swear I had so much energy that I was just whistling right through all the stuff we had going on at the shop. You get into rare periods like that from time to time, when it's like you're riding the crest of a damn wave and everything you touch gives up without a fight and does what the hell you want it to. It was catching, too, and even Raymond was doing work that seemed to come out right the very first time. Of course, I'd learned that there were practical limits to what he could handle-you really didn't want him adjusting valves on a Jaguar or trying to track down an electrical short or tearing a transmission apart to replace the synchros (unless of course you *wanted* little detent springs flying all over the place and the specially-sized, impossible to find ball bearings that sit on the end of them rolling down the nearest available floor drain)-but he could swap tires and do grease-and-oil jobs and screw in spark plugs without stripping the threads. It even got to where he could replace brake shoes and repack wheel bearings or even swap fuel or water pumps without messing up too badly (at least on cars he'd done once or twice before, anyway). So long as I stayed careful about what I gave him, he was working out fine. And, in the weeks leading up to the race at Bridgehampton, the gods of the sportycar repair business and all of our local Passaic Ford-Chevy-Chrysler customers were serving up an ideal mix of work that kept the cars rolling in and out and the cash register ringing like a blessed slot machine hitting the jackpot every single evening.

Julie seemed pretty excited about Bridgehampton, too. Or maybe it was our wedding two weeks later she was really focused in on. It didn't matter. Far as I was concerned, they were about the same thing, and that long, convoluted day we'd spent together on Easter had convinced me even more that I was doing a very wise thing getting hitched up with her. She'd drop by the Sinclair after work to tidy up the office and put numbers in the account books like she always had for Old Man Finzio, and her eyes would be all sparkly and alive and we'd talk about all kinds of stuff that we had to do or ought to do or should forget about doing, and I really had this sense that we were becoming a genuine *team,* you know? And it didn't even bother me that the people living downstairs from her mom had indeed busted up and moved out and so it was pretty much set in stone that we were going to live there after we were married. But I'd already given up on that deal when we swapped for the wedding date change, so there wasn't really any shock value.

Just a vague sense of dread.

Oh, my sister Sarah Jean was kind of a hard sell on the Bridgehampton deal. At least at first, anyway. She was always awfully shy-especially around strangers, you know?-but then out of nowhere my sister Mary Frances said she wanted to go, too, and all of a sudden it was all set. And even Julie's mom went along with the idea once she knew my two sisters were coming along and that they'd all be bunking in together with Julie. Especially after Cal had his folks' chauffeur call, pretending to be his father and explain to Julie's mom that everything would be properly chaperoned and on the absolute up-and-up. I guess Cal had come into possession of some moderately inflammatory New Year's Eve nightclub photos of the chauffeur drinking champagne out of his older sister's shoe at one of the tables when he really should've been waiting patiently at the curb outside. They gave him quite a bit of leverage where the chauffeur and his sister were concerned.

So everything was going swimmingly. Plus I'd have to say I was in love, since I can't think of any other infection that makes it so you can't hardly wait to see the other person again even after you've just left them and can't wait to dial their number again even after you just hung up. Even if it's just to hear them breathing on the other end. And it's my experience that times like that are few and far between, when the world is full of bluebirds and sunshine and everything seems so blessed effortless that it moves along without trying. The only bad part is you get lulled into this feeling that things will go on like that forever. Which of course they won't. But it doesn't do you any good to spoil things by thinking about it. What for? So go ahead. Enjoy yourself. Pretend the ride will never end. At least you'll have something swell to remember when you find yourself back in life's outhouse again.

Big Ed dropped by the station a few weeks after the International Auto Show to check on how his Jag was coming and chew the fat about the cars he'd seen there. And I suppose I shouldn't have been too surprised that he thought that new Kaiser Darrin "sports car" was really something special. "Boy, did'ja see how those doors slide back into the fenders?"

I allowed as how I had.

"Boy, that was *neat!*" Big Ed took a long draw on his stogie. "Y'know, I was thinkin' about maybe gettin' me one a'those things...."

Of course I didn't care much for the Kaiser Darrin and was about to tell Big Ed as much, but I thought better of it. The truth of it was a guy like Big Ed Baumstein was probably better off in a phony boulevard sports car like a Kaiser Darrin than a truly fast and serious piece of machinery like an XK-120. Or, worse yet, a Ferrari. Besides, like 'Kip' Stevens said, there's no accounting for taste, and that's why there's chocolate *and* vanilla. So I changed the subject. "Say, did'ja see that Pegaso thing over by the Ferrari stand?"

"Whoo-eee," Big Ed exhaled, shaking his head. "Thirty grand? For a God damn *car?*" He shook it again. "That's *house* money, not car money...."

"But did you like it?"

He thought it over. "I liked the *color,* but I'd still rather have a Ferrari."

"Me, too."

So we shot the breeze for awhile about the cars in the show and I walked him over to see the engine and tranny out of his Jag that were all completely back together and ready to slip right in just as soon as we got the rest of the car back from the body shop.

"And when's that?" Big Ed wanted to know.

Well, it was supposed to be in just another day or two, but experience had led me to understand that body shops generally adhere to the same sort of free-form, thoroughly elastic promise dates and completion deadlines made famous by Colin St. John and Barry Spline over at Westbridge Motor Car Company, Ltd. Still, you didn't really mind if they did good work. "The end of next week," I told him, hoping I'd included enough bullshit excuse leeway for the little Greek guy who ran the body shop.

"Good. I wanna be sure that thing's ready for Bridgehampton." There was a very determined look in Big Ed's eye, and it wasn't until later that I found out the licensing/membership battle with Charlie Priddle and his tight-assed, Anglo-Saxon wolfpack on the S.C.M.A. membership committee was building up for a showdown at Bridgehampton. Turns out Big Ed somehow managed to get hold of an entry form (which were supposedly only mailed out to certified S.C.M.A. competition license holders) and made sure his was one of the very first in. Certified mail, too. But of course the problem was he was ineligible, since he wasn't a club member and likely couldn't join on account of his last name ended in one of the Forbidden Eastern European Syllables such as "stein," "baum," "blum," "witz," and "berg."

Only turning him down was not the sort of thing the S.C.M.A. membership committee wanted to do right out in the open. Especially since Big Ed had already finessed his way into the Triple-A license he ran on at Watkins Glen. He'd also used it to run with many of the S.C.M.A.'s star competitors (and without seriously killing anybody) at the 12 Hours of Sebring. And that was a real can of worms, since Charlie Priddle's armband crew had repeatedly warned all license holders that the S.C.M.A.'s 6-hour deal at MacDill Air Force Base on February

21-22 was the only genuine *approved* sports car race in Florida that spring, and anybody who had the temerity to run the unseemly 12-hour *professional* grind at Sebring two weeks later stood an excellent chance of having their ticket pulled. But Charlie and his guys hadn't really thought that one through, since one of the key factors in getting people to obey orders is remembering to order them to do whatever they were already planning to do in the first place.

It makes you look really powerful that way.

It likewise makes you look pretty lame when everybody listens to what you have to say, hears all the warnings loud and clear, and then pretty much shrugs and yawns and goes off to do exactly whatever the hell they were planning to do anyway. And that's precisely what happened in Florida, as most everybody whose car was still running (plus a few more) headed straight for Sebring after the S.C.M.A. race at MacDill (with maybe a few beach days in between, natch) to run that "outlaw" F.I.A. pro race. The result was that Charlie's guys had to be real careful about how they handled this licensing thing with Big Ed. I mean, the whole art of bullying is based on singling out the lame, weak and friendless, and Charlie's guys couldn't very well make an example out of Big Ed when a lot of their own heaviest hitters had done the exact same thing. Plus Big Ed had made a few friends around the paddock (or at least got a few of the right people not to think of him as an enemy) and even scored himself a few genuine, stand-up-and-be-counted supporters like Kip Stevens and Tommy Edwards' Chicago-based fellow Allard racer Eddie Dearborn. And it certainly couldn't have hurt when he had a well-connected New York lawyer fire a warning shot across the S.C.M.A.'s bows in the form of a very friendly letter pointing out the many negative aspects of litigation.

But it was still touch and go as to whether they'd accept his entry and let him run at Bridgehampton, and I understand there were even a few side bets going around among the more sporting members of the club. Big Ed was pretty sure he was going to win, and even got some friend of his with a more acceptable last name to arrange a room for him at one of the swankiest places out towards that end of Long Island. I'd mentioned to him about Cal's folks' place-I figured I had to, you know?-but was really sort of pleased he'd made his own plans for a place to stay. Which of course meant he wasn't planning to come alone, if you catch my drift.

Then one day I got a call out of the blue from Spud Webster. "Hey, you old pit rat," I told him, "it's good t'hear your voice."

"Yours too. How're things up there in the New Yawk sportycar business?"

"It's New *Joisy,* not New Yawk," I reminded him.

"New Joisy. New Yawk. What's the hell's th'difference? None of you guys talk so's an ordinary citizen can understand."

"You mean there's actually people *living* out there beyond the Hudson?"

"Yeah, there is. I'm in Indianapolis right now, and they've got real stone buildings and paved streets and everything."

"Do tell."

"In fact, that's what I called you about."

"How's that?"

"Weellll…" Spud paused for a second and I could tell right away something big was up. "…it looks like we maybe got Sammy a ride in the 500…"

"The *Indianapolis* 500?"

"That would be the one."

"Wow. That's *great!"*

"Well, maybe it is and maybe it isn't."

"I don't get it."

"See, we were knocking around trying to line up a ride, and we happened to hear some scuttlebutt about this old Indianapolis race car tucked away some-place in a garage or barn or something just outside of town. There's lots of stuff like that hidden out around Indianapolis, believe me."

"So?"

"So we found out where it was and went to take a look at it, and it was really in pretty decent shape."

"What kind is it?"

"It's a Lugi Lesovsky chassis with Riley carburetors-a dirt track sprinter with solid axles all around like they run on the fairground circuit-and it's all there and all in one piece. Real nice car, too. Except for the paintjob."

"So what's it doing in a barn?"

"Well, turns out it belongs to the widow of this Marshall Winston guy who used to run a car at Indy every single year before the war-just that one race, every year-and he went at it again when the racing started up again after the war was over in '46."

"So this is a car from 1946?"

"Oh, no. It's a '49," Spud said proudly. "In fact, the guy'd just bought it from the previous owner a couple winters ago when he suddenly up and died from a heart attack."

"That's too bad."

"I s'pose. Anyhow, it's been sittin' ever since. I guess the wife never had much use for racing."

"I hear there's a lot of that going around."

"Yeah. Always has been."

"I dunno, Spud," I told him, "The 500's an awful big deal and everybody shows up with the latest stuff. Sounds t'me like that car's maybe a few too many years out of date." I didn't know all that much about speedway racing, but I did know that Bill Vukovich showed up at Indianapolis with a fuel-injected engine and Frank Kurtis' new roadster-style chassis in '52 and pretty much ran away from the field until a steering bolt broke and he brushed the wall. Surely there'd be a whole passel of new Kurtis roadster chassis and fuel injected engines down at The Brickyard this year. Not to mention all the S.C.M.A. types frothing at the mouth about the hot rumor that Ferrari was sending a special Indianapolis car over for Alberto Ascari to drive, and the general consensus around sportycar paddocks from Bridgehampton to Pebble Beach was that Ferrari could comfortably be expected to show all those gee-whiz Midwestern yahoos in Gasoline Alley a thing or two. Squared off against that sort of opposition, I didn't figure an old fairgrounds-style dirt car was going to have much of a chance. And I told Spud as much.

"Oh, we know all that. But we're not tryin' t'*win* the damn thing. Hell, Indy pays plenty good just t'qualify. Especially compared to the Triple-A fairgrounds circuit. And there's a lotta publicity, too."

"Yeah, that's true," I agreed. *"Everybody's* heard of the Indianapolis 500."

"That's right! It can do a driver a lot of good just t'be there in pit lane and rub elbows with all the crews and team owners and maybe even get a crack at qualifying a *real* car when time starts runnin' out."

This was pretty exciting stuff-even if it was a longshot-and I really felt good for Spud and Sammy. "So what's the plan?"

"Well, we got us a little team put together with two money guys Sammy's been working on for months. One of 'em owns a racetrack back in Texas we ran at alla time when we was just starting out-we still go back there and run once or twice a year-and the other guy owns a bunch of car dealerships here in Indianapolis and is always lookin' for a cheap way t'strut up an' down pit lane like he owns th' place in front of his customers."

"Sounds like you're pretty much set."

"Yep. We got our entry in on time and everything."

"Boy, that's really something, isn't it."

"Yeah. We only got one problem left."

"What's that?"

318

"Well, it seems we're a little short on crew people. I mean, we got *lots* of guys we can have if we want 'em-the guy with the car dealerships'll give us his whole damn service departments if we want-but that's just not the same as havin' somebody who's been around a little and knows the ropes." There was a short pause at the other end of the line. "That's where you come in."

"I do?"

"Yeah, you do. Sammy and me were kinda hopin' you'd come on down to Indianapolis for qualifying and then maybe th'race if we manage t'make the field. And I figger we got a pretty good chance, too. This same car sat on the fourth row in 1950."

"It did? Really?"

"Sure did."

"Geez," I said, letting it all tumble over in my mind, "it sure was nice of you guys t'think of me." I was really flattered, you know? And the thought of going to-no, actually being a *part* of!-the biggest damn race in the world....

"Mind you, we don't have a lot of extra cash, see, and about the best we could do is take care of your room and board and maybe send you a bus ticket if y'need one. And a'course you'd get shares on the prize money after the checker when everything's wrapped up."

Boy, I wanted to go something awful. I mean, it was the Indianapolis 500, for gosh sakes! But already I was thinking about all the other stuff I had going on in my life-the gas station and repair shop business I had to run and the wedding to Julie I had coming up and all the cars I had to get race-ready for Bridgehampton-not to mention that the schedules really butted head-on, what with some dumb sports car rally out on Long Island that a lot of my best customers wanted to go on the same exact Sunday as the first weekend of qualifying, then Bridgehampton the very next Saturday during the final weekend of qualifying, and then a New York Region S.C.M.A. time trial up at Thompson Speedway in Connecticut the same blessed weekend as the 500 itself.

"Gee whiz, Spud," I groaned into the receiver, "I don't think I can come."

And right at that instant is when I realized what it meant to be grown up.

I didn't like it much, either.

Meanwhile there was a lot of heavy discussion going on between Julie and me about where exactly we should go for our honeymoon, and I think it says something about the differences between the male and female sex in that the male doesn't generally worry too much about such things until the proper time arrives-say the night before-while women are all concerned about planning and plotting out itineraries and leafing through a hundred kajillion travel brochures just to make sure everything's going to be absolutely *perfect*. Which of course it never is. But that's women for you. Personally, I didn't see how it made all that much difference where we went, you know? Especially seeing as how I hoped we'd be spending most of our time indoors. Not that I could tell Julie that. Plus everybody and his brother (and sister) were giving us advice. A lot of people recommended Niagara Falls, on account of just about *everybody* went there for honeymoons. "You know *why* everybody goes there?" Cal asked one afternoon.

I told him I thought because it was so romantic, what with all that majestic natural scenery and all those hundreds of thousands of tons of crashing, tumbling, cascading water and all the rainbows in the mist and all.

"Nah," he sneered, "People go there because the noise from the falls drowns out all the pounding and banging from the next room."

But Niagara Falls seemed like an awfully long way to go. We'd have to spend at least one entire day-and I mean one long, grueling, six ayem to twelve midnight grind-driving there (assuming I could come up with a car someplace) plus another day shot coming back, and, seeing as how we agreed we couldn't really afford the time or money to be away for more than five days total, that didn't leave much honeymoon time in the middle and pretty much guaranteed that we'd arrive all worn out and get back home in about the same condition. I kind of half-heartedly suggested Watkins Glen, on account of it was only about half as far and really had some nice lodges and tourist cabins and real pretty scenery. But Watkins Glen only meant one thing to Julie-*racing!*-and her response to that idea didn't amount to much more than a bull snort and a highly sarcastic laugh.

Big Ed suggested a place he'd been to once or twice up in the Catskills, but when I called it sounded awfully expensive. And when I asked why, they explained as how their kitchen was famous the world over for their chopped liver and beef brisket and matzo ball soup, and that I could also rest assured it was kept *strictly* Kosher. And I couldn't help thinking it was maybe not the right sort of spot for a couple greaseball Italian kids from Passaic. Although I'm quite sure it's very nice.

One of my old man's union buddies put a plug in for Lake George way up north of Albany, but that was kind of a long haul, too, and I was pretty suspicious of any place one of my old man's union chemical plant guys thought was pleasant. I mean, what the hell could they possibly know about pleasant? Just look where they worked!

Big Ed tried again with Atlantic City, and that almost got the nod because it was close and had the seashore and the boardwalk and all-not to mention it was cheap-but then Carson Flegley of all people suggested Cape Cod, and, for reasons that are probably best understood by the chamber of commerce types who put together those travel brochures, the words "Cape Cod" set off little harmonious, tinkling chimes inside Julie's head. Mine, too. Especially after Julie picked up one of those brochures at the travel agency over on Grant Street and brought it over by the Sinclair. "Oh, just *look* at this!" she gushed, pointing to a picture of this absolutely adorable little white clapboard shore cottage with handsome green storm shutters, bright red geraniums sprouting out of the window boxes, and a perfectly sculptured privet hedge out front.

"It looks like a house," I deadpanned. Sometimes you just can't resist that urge to piss them off, you know?

But it really did look lovely. And so did the ocean seashore and the old antique shops and sidewalk vendors in Provincetown and the thought of fresh oysters and lobster dinners I could actually afford. Plus Julie found out there was this car ferry you could take from the tip of Long Island, so you could maybe spend a little of your travel time snuggling up in your stateroom rather than getting stuck behind a garbage truck in Providence, Rhode Island, or following a couple churchgoing retirees in a four-year-old Oldsmobile halfway across Connecticut at not a fraction over thirty-nine miles per hour.

So we settled on Cape Cod-it sounded really nice, honest it did-and I did my best to help plan everything and take part in all the decisions exactly the way Julie wanted me to by mostly nodding my head and agreeing with every single thing she had to say. "It's so nice we're doing this *together,*" she'd tell me with a wonderful, warm glow in her eyes.

"Yes, it sure is," I'd agree, and go back to the carburetor or camshaft or whatever I was working on.

"And the boat ride will be *so* romantic...."

"Boy, will it ever."

"We can go antique shopping in Provincetown."

"I'm looking forward to it."

"Of course, we won't *buy* anything."

"Oh, of course not."

"But we'll just look."

"Yeah. We'll just look."

"Unless we see something we really, *really* like."

"Yeah." I agreed. "We'll just look."

Big Ed finally got his entry back from the S.C.M.A. the end of the first week in May, and he was pretty thrilled about it since it looked like we were in. Sort of. What it amounted to was that the Competition Committee (Charles Winthrop Martingale Priddle, chairman) had indeed accepted Big Ed's entry fee and he would indeed be listed as a driver in the race program. But he would be listed as "an *alternate,*" seeing as how the race was already over-subscribed, and, safety considerations being what they were after the unfortunate incidents at Grand Island, Elkhart Lake, and especially Watkins Glen the previous year, it was important to limit the number of competitors on the track at any one time, and certain considerations also had to be given to seniority among the membership when evaluating entries and blah, blah, blah.

"What does it mean in plain English?" I asked Big Ed.

"Well," he answered slowly, unwrapping a fresh cigar, "I think it means I'm *in...* " he fired up the stogie and took a long drag, "...only I'm *not.* "

That was exactly the way I saw it, too.

But it wasn't like he was the only one. With some justification, the S.C.M.A. had set a limit of thirty-five cars for each of the three races on the schedule at Bridgehampton on May 23rd, and they had forty-three entries for the Wilcox Trophy race and a whopping forty-nine for the Bridgehampton Cup feature. As you can imagine, there were a whole bunch of disappointed and/or highly pissed off "alternates" as a result, and so there was no way Big Ed could say he was being singled out or picked on.

"So what are we going to do?"

"Oh, we're gonna be there all right. You bet your sweet ass we are. An' we're gonna be *ready,* too."

"Even if you don't get to race?"

"That's not the point, see." I could see his cigar starting to rotate.

"It's not?"

"Nah. This is just one l'il battle, not the whole friggin' war."

"I don't get it."

"It's simple, see." He took his stogie out and used it for a pointer. "They wouldn't let me join their friggin' club last year, so there was no way I could get a competition license, right?"

"Right."

"So I got a Triple-A license, an' they had t'let me race at Watkins Glen."

"Yeah. So?"

"But I still couldn't get in the damn club, right? So I went down and raced at Sebring two months ago with all those S.C.M.A. guys."

"But still on your Triple-A license."

"Right."

"And now they won't let you race again at Bridgehampton."

"You are so dumb, Palumbo. The important thing is that *they accepted my friggin' entry,* see? And I'm gonna show up, too. With bells on."

"Even if all you get t'do is stand around with your face hanging out?"

"Who *cares?* Now that they've accepted my entry once, they'll have t'do it again next time. And the time after that. Besides, maybe they'll let the alternates practice or something on Friday. And, with assholes like our buddy Skippy out there, they may bend or blow up enough cars that I'll get in." Big Ed looked at me like I should think it was a genius sort of plan, but I have to be honest that it seemed like an awful lot of effort to go through to most likely not even get to drive. "Look at it this way, Buddy. It's a foot in the door. That's all a guy like me needs. In fact, that's what all those tight-assed, skinny-nosed pricks are worried about."

And they were, too.

By this time I had Big Ed's Jag back from the Greek at the body shop-he did a good job, too, especially considering the fenders on Big Ed's car were by now close to forty percent lead and filler putty-and had just about finished dropping the freshened up engine and tranny back in. And that's when Big Ed suggested we take it on this car rallye he'd heard about out on Long Island the weekend before Bridgehampton. It was being put on by something called the Long Island Sports Car Club, but there were sure to be a bunch of S.C.M.A. people there, and Big Ed figured it might be a perfect opportunity to do a little socializing with the right sort of people and check the car out to make sure it was ready for Bridgehampton.

Now I'd never been on a sports car rallye (and neither, it goes without saying, had Big Ed) so I asked around about what it was like. Carson Flegley wasn't exactly sure, but he was planning to take his TD in order to break in the new rings and bearings I'd put in after Sebring, and Cal was tagging along as his co-pilot and navigator. Turns out Cal had actually been on a rallye once before. "It's kind of like a treasure hunt," he explained.

"Oh? What's the treasure?"

"Aggravation, mostly. Sometimes divorce."

As usual, Cal was dead on the money.

The deal with sports car rallies is that they give you a list of instructions, such as "Turn Right at Third Stop Sign" or "Bear Left at Intersection" or "Go Straight at Cemetery" or "Turn Right, Bear Left, and Go Straight 1.456 miles after PLUMBER." Only they don't tell you what "PLUMBER" is. It could be the name of a road. It could be an actual plumbing shop. It could be a name painted in ¾-inch high letters on the backside of a rusty tin mailbox stuck on a post at the side of a beautiful country road you're screaming down at damn near the speed of sound since you already missed a sign three instructions ago, got lost, and are hustling like mad to make up time.

I didn't tell you about the time part, did I?

See, it isn't bad enough that you're trying to follow this route you've never seen that was laid out by some sadistic guy who probably spends the rest of his free time pulling wings off flies. Oh, no. You've also got to maintain a highly specific average speed. Say, something simple like 37.654 miles per hour. In order to do this, crack rallye teams bring along stopwatches and clipboards and slide rules and logarithmic tables and notebooks full of scratch paper and plenty of nice, sharp pencils. And then, while all of this is going on, right between the "Turn Right" and the "Bear Left" and the "Go Straight" and the PLUMBER sign you missed three times before you finally saw it and the average speed worked out to three decimal places, the instructions will tell you to "Change Average Speed to 43.36 MPH at DEW DROP INN," which is invariably a quaint little lakeside tavern where all the really smart rallye teams will spend the balance of the afternoon with their nose stuck in a beer bottle.

But of course we didn't know any of that.

Although we soon found out.

We had to leave Passaic right around dawn to make sure we arrived at the starting point at Brightwaters (which is about halfway out Long Island) in time for the drivers' meeting at ten ayem, and right away we realized that we weren't very well prepared, since, like I said, everybody else had stopwatches and clipboards and slide rules and even these strange, circular-looking Blackwell average speed calculators specially designed for the job. All we had was Big Ed's gold watch (which at least had a second hand) and an old estimating notebook from the body shop that had somehow found its way into the trunk. We had to borrow a pencil from some guy with a Porsche who had at least six of everything. And I noticed that his wife had at least another half dozen more. Of *everything*. They looked pretty damn serious to me.

It was obvious that this rallying stuff attracted a slightly different crowd from actual racing (to say the least!) and you had to be impressed by how many engineers and Ph.D.s and math professor types were on hand. Or at least that's what they looked like, anyway. But they had some awfully nice cars; Jags and Porsches and MGs and even more exotic stuff like Lancias and Aston Martins and such. And then who should roll up but Charlie Priddle in this beautiful, deep red Maserati. Hell, I never knew he owned a Maserati. But Charlie owned a lot of cars, and he always made a point of bringing the exact right one to every event. Like the time he brought his 1922 Rolls Royce to the hillclimb at Giant's Despair so he could win a beautiful first place trophy in the "vintage" class that nobody else was even entered in. Or the time he trucked his antique Stutz Bearcat most of the way to Elkhart Lake and then secretly unloaded it and drove it into town as if he'd driven the damn thing all the way from Connecticut just so's he could award himself the big first place trophy for the Rallye to Elkhart Lake when all the scoring went up for grabs and the scoring committee (Charles Winthrop Martingale Priddle, chairman) decided to give it to the oldest car that had covered the longest distance. Which, to no one's surprise, turned out to be Charlie's 1914 Stutz.

And now, here on a quiet Sunday morning out in Brightwaters, Long Island, Charlie wowed 'em once again by showing up for a genteel sports car road rallye in a balls-out Maserati racing car. Why, you could hear the thing coming a half mile away! But a fast car doesn't really do you much good on a road rallye (unless you get lost and fall behind) and so Charlie also brought his other ace in the hole in the form of a navigator who also just happened to be a tenured math professor at M.I.T. and likewise just *happened* to fly down for a weekend on Long Island as Charlie's special guest.

Right.

Anyhow, they handed out some general instruction sheets and we stood around for awhile drinking carry-out coffee and shoving carry-out doughnuts in our faces while the officials began waving the rallye cars off one minute intervals. Why, it was a lot like the start of the *La Carrera* legs. Only without the crowds, noise, or excitement. Pretty soon it was time for us to get in line and a few minutes later we got to the front and the starter guy counted off "five...four...three...two...*GO!*" and we were off.! And screwed up right away. The very first instruction said to "Turn Left at 2/10ths of a mile," and Big Ed never bothered to zero the trip odometer at the start.

"Well, zero it NOW!" I told him.

"Right now?"

"YES!"

"What's my next instruction?"

"Turn Right at THE CANDLE SHOP."

"Is it a PLACE or a SIGN?"

"How the hell should I know?"

"I think we just passed it."

"Are you SURE?"

"Hell, no."

You get the idea. And it only got worse after the first checkpoint when we'd finally gotten on top of it enough to start worrying about time, too.

"Are we ahead or behind?"

"How many miles have we gone?"

"Since the beginning or since the last checkpoint?"

"No. Since we changed our average speed to, let's see here, thirty-four-point-oh-four-six miles per hour...."

"When the hell was THAT?"

"Back there by COBBLER'S CHICKEN RANCH," I answered sheepishly. "I guess I forgot to tell you."

"GODDAMMIT!!!" Big Ed bellowed, slamming on the brakes. "That does it! YOU drive!"

So I took over at the wheel-can you believe it?-and Big Ed buried his not inconsiderable nose in the route instructions and timing calculations. And he was pretty damn good at it, too. Once he got the hang of it, anyway. He was incredibly quick with numbers-I guess a guy in his line of work had to be-and he had a good sense of what to do whenever the rallymaster tried to trip us up. Which was always. Like when we hit a series of instructions that were all written in gibberish, such as "Het eeiionnttrsc fo dOl woTn dR dna leBoy odaR." I would've given up on the spot. But Big Ed looked at it for a second and snapped his fingers. "It's 'the intersection of Old Town Road and Boyle Road,'" he yelped triumphantly. And sure enough it was.

Personally, I didn't think rallying was especially the best way to spend a nice sportycar afternoon out in the country. Heck, you were too damn busy and on edge to enjoy it. But I could see where certain types of people might really enjoy the challenge. Not that you'd ever want to have lunch or dinner with them. Far as I could see, the best part was when you got lost and got a little behind and had to drive like a damn maniac to catch up. Which we were doing on a fairly regular basis. And the amazing thing was that Big Ed was really into it and would be yelling at me to "give it the gas, Buddy!" and "get the friggin' lead out!" in his own damn car. Which, as you can imagine, I was only too happy to do. But you miss stuff when you're traveling too fast, and sure enough we went flying right past this one gravel side road and Big Ed yelled, "That's IT, dammit! That's Derbydale Road!"

So I dropped down a gear, reached for the handbrake, cut the wheel and yanked. The Jag snapped around in an absolutely perfect half-spin and we were off in the opposite direction and sweeping onto Derbydale Road in a shower of stones before you knew it. "Where in the name of hell did you learn *that?*" Big Ed asked, his eyes bulging with anger, fear, awe, and amazement.

"Sammy Speed showed me how to do it. It's called 'a bootlegger turn.' He said they use it down South if they're haulin' moonshine and the cops're after 'em. You just turn the wheel and yank up on the handbrake. See?"

"Yeah. I see. Do me a favor, okay?"

"Sure."

"Don't do it again."

"But it worked perfect," I protested.

"So will cutting your head off and using it for a bowling ball."

In any case, we made it to the end (which was more than you could say for a lot of the entrants) and both Big Ed and I were thrilled when we actually zeroed the final checkpoint. Right on the button. And I'd have to admit that was a pretty spectacular feeling. Even so, I couldn't really recommend sports car rallying as a steady Sunday afternoon pastime. And I sure as hell never wanted to go on one with Julie. Not on your life. In fact, not even if you gave me that $29,000 Pegaso from the New York International Motor Sports Show to play with and paid me, to boot.

I'm just not that stupid, see.

Chapter 13: Two Different Shades of Black

While Big Ed and me were out thrashing around Long Island getting repeatedly lost in his Jaguar, a car drama of an entirely more serious sort was being waged around the vast, two-and-one-half mile stadium bowl at the corner of 16th and Georgetown streets in Speedway, Indiana. Pole qualifying for the 1953 Indianapolis 500-the biggest damn race in the world according to most people!-was underway, and I knew my friends Sammy Speed and Spud Webster were there someplace with all their hopes and dreams wrapped up in that antique, 1949 Lugi Lesovsky upright sprinter with Riley carburetors on the engine, trying like hell to make the field.

Spud was using the shop of that rich car dealer guy who was putting a few bucks into Sammy's deal in return for a fistful of pit passes, and he sneaked into the office and called me once or twice during the week to let me know how things were going. I mean, who was gonna question a few extra long distance calls on the boss's private line, right? And I wasn't really surprised when he said Sammy was having a little trouble getting the car up to speed. "Hell," I told him, "what do you expect from a 1949 automobile?"

"Nah, I don't mean up to speed with the front runners. I mean up to what the fastest guys were doin' in cars like this two r'three years ago."

I found that a little hard to believe. "Is there something wrong with it?"

I could sense Spud pulling in a little closer to the receiver so nobody else could hear. "It's this place," he whispered. "The Brickyard. I think it's got him a little spooked."

The idea that anything-and particularly anything to do with racing!-could spook Sammy Speed was simply not possible. I mean, I *knew* Sammy, and I'd personally seen him slay dragons with a penknife and leap bare-assed through rings of fire. He was braver than Dick Tracy, no two ways about it. "That's pretty hard to believe, Spud," I told him. "No way in hell's a guy like Sammy scared of any damn racetrack."

"I *never* said 'scared,'" Spud whispered even lower. "I said 'spooked.'"

"What's the difference?"

"'Scared' is when you're afraid of something an' wanna go hide under your bed with your eyes closed until somebody makes it go away. 'Spooked' is when you're out there doin' a high wire act on a thin strand of wire that just might break at any moment. And if you make just one tiny screwup, everything you've worked for is right down the toilet. Just like that. And maybe you wind up all busted up in the hospital, too."

"But it's just another racetrack, isn't it?"

"Yeah, it's just another racetrack. But Sammy says it's a place you gotta sneak up on. You start trying t'show this place who's boss and it'll bite'cha."

"Because it's so fast?"

"Yeah, I guess. And that concrete wall don't help much, either. It takes an awful lotta not lookin' to see it's not there."

I tried to visualize it in my mind, you know? Tried to imagine what it might be like to come sliding out of a broad, sweeping corner at well over two miles a minute and come so close to that gray blur of concrete that you could almost reach out and touch it. But that's what the *fast* guys did at Indy.

They had to.

"Sammy's not th' only one havin' trouble," Spud continued. "That John Fitch friend of yours who drove for Cunningham and Mercedes had a hell of a time. Couldn't get up to speed."

"Johnny Fitch?" I mean, I couldn't believe it!

"Yep, the same. Guess he just couldn't get comfortable out there. Had one of the newer cars, too...."

That was even more unbelievable. I'd seen Johnny Fitch race lots of times - and *win* lots of times-and I knew him to be both bullet fast and a genuinely cool customer in any kind of racecar you could think of. "There must've been something wrong with the car," I told Spud.

"Nah, there wasn't," Spud said flatly. "He just couldn't get comfortable. Don't think he ever broke much over 130. So they put one of the Indy regulars in and he was up to decent qualifying speed in a couple laps. Think he did over a hundred-thirty-six with it."

I couldn't believe what I was hearing. "But look what Johnny Fitch did at *La Carrera* and Sebring," I protested. "You saw it yourself."

"Don't get me wrong," Spud quickly agreed, "John Fitch is one *hell* of a race car driver. But, like I'm trying t'explain, this place is just, well, *different.* All that braking and downshifting and 'clipping the apex' stuff you sportycar guys go on about just don't work here. Sammy says it's like threading a damn needle, four times a lap. And without ever leaving any slack in the thread...."

Again I tried to imagine a race track so intimidating it could spook somebody like Sammy Speed and make a cool, experienced wheel man like Johhny Fitch feel uncomfortable.

"Nobody goes quick here right out of the box," Spud continued, "and if they try, they usually wind up in a little different kind of box. A pine one...."

But things got better. Sammy kept working at it and working at it as the week went by, going out every session he could, trying to get used to the sheer, eyeball flattening *speed* of the place and learn how to focus so hard and so far ahead that he wouldn't much notice the wall. He said the real trick was learning how to finesse your way through those long, sweeping corners-each one just a little different from all the others-until you found that smooth, clean, effortless glide that brought you right out to where you could *feel* the wall but not actually see it or touch it.

And he was getting there. Getting used to the long front straightaway with empty grandstands towering over it like a gray tidal wave. Getting to know all the minute little cracks and bumps and ripples in the pavement. Learning to gently roll out of the throttle for the corners instead of lifting off suddenly and unsettling the car. Forcing himself *not* to clutch the wheel in a death grip or hold his breath through the turns. Creeping his way up to speed. Cutting it a little closer and a little smoother and a little finer every lap. And the stopwatches showed he was getting it, too. Oh, he was still well down to the latest cars with their low slung roadster chassis and fuel injected engines. In fact, it was touch and go whether he'd be fast enough to qualify. But he was going faster than anybody ever had at the Speedway with an old upright sprinter.

And people were taking notice, too.

Or at least he hoped they were.

So of course I was dying to know what was going on at Indianapolis that particular Sunday afternoon on Long Island. Only none of the sportycar rallye types seemed particularly interested in the Indy 500. Especially now that the much-ballyhooed Ferrari entry for world champ Alberto Ascari (the one that was going to show those Gasoline Alley yokels what a *real* race car was all about, remember?) failed to materialize. In fact, it never even showed up. So who really cared? And of course you couldn't get anything over the blessed radio except a rare side remark that they'd had a little rain and Bill Vukovich qualified on the pole in the same exact *Fuel Injection Special* Kurtis chassis he'd damn near won with the year before. I read in the paper the next day that Vuky averaged a whopping 138.392 miles-per-hour on his four-lap, ten-mile qualifying run, and that amounted to the second fastest qualifying speed ever recorded at the Indianapolis Motor Speedway. But Indy veteran Chet Miller had run 139.034 in one of Lou Welch's monstrous Novi V-8s on the final weekend of qualifying the year before, and that still stood as the official track record. Of course even I had heard of the Novis, and how they were hands-down the most powerful cars at the Speedway and had been for years. But, fast as they were, the Novis were also big and heavy and hard on fuel and tires, and never managed to put it all together when it counted on race day. Plus they always seemed to be kind of snakebit at Indianapolis, and bad luck in racing-and most especially at the Indy 500-is something you don't want to believe in but learn better than to ignore. Spud told me the Novis were really awesome in person, and made a noise that would just about crystallize the wax in your ears. And, what with record holder Chet Miller back in one again that year, a lot of scribes and Gasoline Alley insiders figured him for a pretty good shot at the pole. Hell, Chet Miller had been in every blessed Indy 500 since 1927 and had driven more laps around the Speedway than anybody on the planet. Which is why the biggest news coming out of that first weekend of qualifying-and the one thing that made *all* the papers-was that Speedway veteran and official record holder Chet Miller was killed while looking for even more speed in a practice wreck on Friday.

Like Spud said, the Speedway was a place that could bite you.

The little blurb I found hidden away in the back of the *New York Times* sports section said only seven drivers had qualified before rain hit and shut everything down, and that's pretty much what Spud had to say when he called me at the shop to fill in the details. "We mostly just waited in the qualifying line," Spud said listlessly. "We could see the weather front moving in and pretty much knew we wouldn't have a chance. But you don't dare give up hope, you know?"

"Yeah. I know. So what happens now?"

"Well, we just gotta do it next weekend. Us and a hundred other guys. But Sammy's doin' real good with the car now. He's got that look back in his eye and that chip back on his shoulder. If the track's good and the car doesn't screw up, I figure we qualify easy next weekend."

"Geez, I wish I could be there with you guys."

"Hey, we each got our own roads to hoe, Buddy. That's the way life is."

"Yeah, I guess."

"But keep a good thought for us, okay?"

"You know I will, Spud. You know I will."

Meanwhile we were busy as hell at the Sinclair trying to get everything ready for Bridgehampton. Between finishing up the final few tweaks on our customer cars and loading stuff up and getting things organized at the shop between Butch, Raymond, Tater and Old Man Finzio so work would actually get done and nobody would get a shiner, split lip, slugged, stabbed, shot, or fired on the spot in my absence was quite a project. And then, clear out of the blue, Cal tools into the station driving that Jowett Jupiter sports car we'd seen on the floor of the

International Motor Sports Show at Grand Central Palace. I didn't know much about Jowetts-hell, *nobody* did here in the States!-but I guess Cal'd been getting the whole nine yards from the Jowett guy we met at the auto show who he'd been working on mercilessly for the previous few weeks. Turns out the Jowett brothers came from someplace in England called West Yorkshire and built their very first automobile way back around 1906. They got kind of a reputation between the world wars for building slow, cheap sedans whose mainline sales slogan was: *"Jowetts never wear out, you leave them to your next of kin!"* It was the kind of advertising someone in Carson Flegley's line of work could really appreciate, you know? Anyhow, after the armistice they dusted off their last prewar sedan, tarted it up a little, and released it as the new Jowett Javelin. And I guess it must've been pretty good, because Jowetts won themselves a few races and rallies right after the war when competition, to be honest, was pretty thin. And then some British scribe named Laurence Pomeroy wrote something about how England should really be building and exporting sports cars, and the Jowett people got wind of it and decided that, indeed, it might be a jolly good idea to have something a little sportier in the showrooms. Especially over here in the States, where Americans were on top of the world and hungry for fun, and moreover had the sort of fat wallets you needed to feed such appetites.

So Jowett entered a deal with a racecar company called E.R.A. to turn the Javelin into a two-seater sports car, and I guess the thing they came up with didn't please anyone. So there was a lot of arguing and finger-pointing and everybody walked away mad, but in the end the car got built and it wasn't half bad. A quarter bad would be more like it. Or maybe just *odd* would be closer to the truth. The styling looked sort of smooth from some angles (at least if you squinted hard) and ungainly and dumpy as hell from others. Julie said it reminded her of the duck-billed platypus she'd seen in the zoo.

Like the Javelin sedan, the Jowett Jupiter sports car had an opposed four-cylinder engine that was flat as a suitcase-kind of like a Volkswagen or a Porsche-only water cooled and way up at the front of the car. Almost ahead of the front wheels, even. With the radiator stuck behind it. Which naturally put an awful lot of weight on the nose, and weight was kind of a congenital problem with Jowett Jupiters in general. Not to mention that the slightly raised compression ratio put in to give them "real sports car performance" tended to make them blow head gaskets with chronic regularity. And, if you were lucky enough to keep that under control, the head studs would usually start cracking their way out of the block. But the chassis was kind of neat-if a little on the hefty side-and Cal said a Jowett did manage to win its class at Watkins Glen in 1951. In 1952, the factory entered three cars in the 1500cc Production Car class at Le Mans, and, although two of them snapped their crankshafts (which, it turns out, was another all too common problem with Jowetts) the third one soldiered on to score a fine class win. Unfortunately, the 1100cc Porsches running a class down from them were *much* faster and finished way ahead. So the handwriting was pretty much on the wall that the Jowett Jupiter's career as a fast, exciting new smallbore sports car was pretty much finished.

Which was really a problem for the guy Cal met on the Jowett stand at the International Motor Sports Show, on account of he had a modest sized garage down by the docks crammed full of unsold Jowett Jupiters, and so he was all ears when Cal told him he could do a good job with one at Bridgehampton. After all, the cars weren't exactly going anywhere. And the worst that could happen would be Cal might get killed in a wreck (in which case maybe the insurance company would pay for the car) and, if he did well, it might impress people enough that a few of those unsold cars would go away. "So you're gonna race this thing at Bridgehampton?" I asked.

"Yep," Cal grinned. "They're even paying the entry fee."

"Boy, that's quite a deal you got," I said respectfully. "How'dja swing it?"

"It's simple, Buddy," Cal explained through his best rich kid smile, "I have a golden tongue and a silver mouth."

He did, too.

"So," I asked, "how does it handle?"

"Weellll...," he started in, kind of circling around the answer, "...of course it's hard to tell from just driving around on the street, y'know...."

"Cut the bullshit, Cal. What's it like?"

Cal looked at me sheepishly. "It's like an arrow, Buddy?"

"An arrow?"

"Yeah, an arrow. An arrow with a lead tip on one end and nothing but feathers on the other. It just wants to go straight."

"Even when you turn the wheel?"

"Especially when I turn the wheel."

"Hmm. So it's maybe a little heavy in the nose?"

"You could say that." He looked up at me with the usual Cal Carrington sparkle in his eyes. "In fact, you could say that twice."

I ran my eyes up and down the Jowett. Julie was right. It *did* look like a duck-billed platypus, you know? "So what're you gonna do?"

"Do? I'm gonna *race* it, Buddy. Just like I said I was. And afterwards, I'll give it back to him in one piece. Just like I promised."

"But don'tcha think the Porsches will beat you?"

"Hell, *yes* the Porsches will beat me. Unless they maybe put Helen Keller in one, anyway. But that's not the point."

"It isn't?"

Cal shook his head. "The important thing is I got myself a drive with some-body else footing the bills. *That's* the hard part, Buddy. Hell, if I can just beat all the MGs I'll be happy. And so will that Jowett guy from the auto show, believe me. After all, you're never gonna get a guy with a Porsche to move down to a Jowett Jupiter."

"No, I guess not."

"But you could just maybe get a guy with an MG to move *up* to one. At least if you beat him bad enough." He motioned me to lean in a little closer and added, "After all, not everybody *likes* German cars...."

That was true enough. A lot of people still had this nagging prejudice against Germans simply because they'd tried to conquer the whole damn world, laid waste to Europe and a good chunk of Russia, fought to the grim, bitter end against an entire generation of young soldiers, sailors, and aviators from the allied countries, and enslaved and/or slaughtered millions of helpless civilians less than ten years before. Can you imagine?

But, like Cal said, the important thing was that he got the drive.

"Hey, it's all downhill from here, Buddy," his golden tongue told me from its home in his silver mouth. "I've got my first shot. My first sponsored ride. I'm on my way." He gave me a wink that went off like a flashbulb. "Trust me, Buddy. It's all downhill from here...."

Thanks to the blue laws out at the far end of Long Island, Saturday was always race day at Bridgehampton, seeing as how Sunday was the Lord's day when the righteous and worthy went solemnly off to church while everybody else more or less slept off Saturday night. As a result, the S.C.M.A. had their registration and practice scheduled to start bright and early Friday morning, and we wisely elected to travel out to Cal's folks' shore cottage near East Quogue on Thursday afternoon so's we could be all chipper and ready to go first thing in the morning. Although there was also the feeling, on many of our parts, that Thurs-day evening might also develop into a hell of an impromptu racing party. Im-promptu race weekend parties are always a distinct possibility on such occa-sions. Especially when they've been meticulously planned.

Big Ed and the mystery date we all figured he had were planning to travel out by themselves in the white Caddy Eldorado with a bunch of our bigger stuff like spare tires and floor jacks and such in the trunk. Cal, Carson, Julie, my two sisters and me were hauling a bunch of smaller shop stuff along with our clothes and other Necessary Weekend Paraphernalia in the Jag 120, the Jowett, and the MG. Or at least that was the plan until I saw all the luggage the three girls were carrying. I mean, this was just a damn overnight, you know? To be fair, my sister Mary Frances had some basic understanding of how to travel light and was only carrying this one fold-over hanger bag and a little makeup case. But Sarah Jean and Julie looked like they were planning to do a trunk show. "Look," I said as diplomatically as I could, "the cruise ship doesn't depart until *after* the trip to Europe and the Asian railway excursion. So could you maybe leave those things here? Just until we get back from the race at Bridgehampton the day after tomorrow, okay?"

"Real funny, Palumbo."

"Oh, I *know* I packed too much," Sarah Jean admitted like it was something she'd have to tell the Father about in confession. "But I just didn't know what to leave behind. I, uhh, I don't get to do this sort of thing very often. Not since pajama parties, anyway...." I could see Sarah Jean was in quite a state, and realized that I'd kind of taken her part in this deal for granted and not thought about how nervous she might be about going away on a race weekend with a crowd of strangers like this.

Why, I'd only been thinking of myself!

But then, what are brothers for?

"Listen," I explained, "these are little bitty cars with little bitty trunks and there's just no way we can carry all that stuff along with the food and the car parts and the drink cooler and the racing gear...I mean, it just won't all *fit*."

"So what'll we *do?*" Sarah Jean whimpered, her lower lip trembling. I was really starting to think I'd made a big mistake, you know. But then Mary Frances came to the rescue.

"Hey, it's no big deal, all right? Julie n'you can put the stuff you really need together in one bag." Julie and Sarah Jean looked at each other skeptically, then back at Mary Frances. "Look, I'll help you," she told them confidently. "Trust me, it'll be a breeze."

"Sure," Julie agreed, putting her arm around Sarah Jean's shoulder. "Like your sister says, it'll be a breeze." Then she fixed me with an accusing glare. "Y'got anyplace *private* around here, Palumbo? Someplace where a few proper young ladies can attend to business?"

"Well," I said, "there's the parts room."

"Hmpf," Julie snorted. "But I guess it's better than the can."

Mary Frances laughed and I saw this wonderful flood of relief gushing up in Sarah Jean's eyes. And it occurred to me all over again as I helped them drag Julie's and Sarah Jean's luggage into the parts room that I was real fond of all three of them and real happy to see them getting along.

I must say I was proud of the way I got everything organized and sorted out and packed away into the trunks and door pockets and behind the seats and shoved into every available nook and cranny on those three sports cars. And especially the way I got it all handled in time for us to be out of the shop and on our way by two-thirty Thursday afternoon. In fact, I deserved some sort of medal for it. But I was motivated. I knew we needed to get in the wind early so's we wouldn't get mired in rush hour traffic crossing Manhattan and Brooklyn. Especially since Big Ed's Jag and Carson's MG were both honed a little fine and wound a little tight for inching along bumper-to-bumper in heavy traffic. Plus I had this tingling urge to get Julie and me out to that cottage on Long Island together as fast as twelve wheels and fourteen stout British combustion chambers could haul us. I mean, we'd never been away anyplace together or anything, and I had this little itch of an inkling something special was maybe going to happen out there. It's like I could feel it all over my skin like the static electricity off my old wool army blanket.

Of course it went a little awkward just before we left trying to figure out who should ride with whom. Julie and me were a lock, of course, but somehow we had to sort out Cal, Carson, Mary Frances and Sarah Jean. The two girls couldn't ride together because neither of them was real comfortable with a floor shift, and, as a professional sportycar mechanic who had ridden with both of them at one time or another, I had to agree. Although there was probably a clutch job in it for me someplace if they did. So everybody just kind of stood there frozen for a moment-like when two people meet head-on in a narrow hallway-but, before it could get genuinely uncomfortable, Mary Frances settled it by hopping into the Jowett with Cal. "I'll take the handsome blonde guy with the ugly car," she winked at Sarah Jean. "But he'd better keep his damn hands to himself."

"Hey, no problem," Cal grinned. "I need 'em to shift and steer."

"Yeah," Julie tossed in, "but watch it when we get out on the highway."

That left Carson and Sarah Jean sort of standing there by his MG, and right away he scooted around to the passenger side and opened the door for her.

Geez, I wished I'd thought of that.

For a change we crossed into Manhattan through the Lincoln Tunnel so's we could pick up Route 27 on the New York side, and of course the girls all complained about driving through the tunnel with the tops down on account of all

337

the fumes and grit and dust in there. And it was pretty awful. But it got better when we came out on the other side and wrestled our way through heavy traffic down Canal Street and across the Manhattan Bridge onto Flatbush Avenue in Brooklyn, then headed east on Atlantic until it turned into the Sunrise Highway out towards Idlewild Airport. And no question our little sportycar parade turned quite a few heads along the way. We finally broke free as we crossed over into Nassau County, and I must say it was a truly beautiful sort of late spring/early summer afternoon and absolutely perfect for a top-down drive out to East Quogue. The sun was still high in the sky even though it was well past five-don't you love it around that time of year, when the evenings linger on till damn near nine o'clock?-and Julie and me were holding hands down on the transmission tunnel and not saying much of anything as the scenery whispered by and the wind spilling over the top of the Jag's windshield played with our hair.

It was one hell of a nice time to be alive.

When we got close to East Quogue, I waved Cal's Jowett around so he could lead the way, and of course I should've known better because once we left the main highway the race was *on* and it was all I could do to keep up. Even in a hot-rodded Jaguar. Naturally we'd lost Carson and the MG completely, but Cal kept his foot in it, scything through turns and switchbacks and giving that panting little four-cylinder all it could take on the straight sections. I flashed my brights and honked the horn for him to slow down, but I might as well have been addressing a garage wall, you know? Then again, what would you expect from a guy like Cal Carrington on a beautiful summer afternoon with a brand new sports car in his hands, a great road beneath its wheels, and a pretty girl to impress at his side?

So I let him go (like I had a choice, right?) and watched that strange, bustleback rear end of the Jowett slowly ease away through the twisty stuff and then just used the Jag's massive horsepower advantage to reel him back in again once the road straightened out. Or at least that's what it looked like from my perspective. Judging from the bulge in Julie's eyes and the way her fingers were dug into the dash cowling and her feet were braced against the floorboards, things maybe looked a little different over on her side of the car. To say the least. And that made me wonder what my sister Mary Frances must've been thinking. I mean, I'd ridden in the shotgun seat with Cal a bunch of times, and, even through I trusted him completely, I knew it was not for the faint of heart.

Up ahead there was this worn out little country grocery store off by the side of the road, and, without warning, Cal dabbed the brakes, double-clutch, heel-and-toe downshifted, and executed an absolutely stunning powerslide into its parking lot, showering gravel in all directions. It was all I could do to lock up all four and come to a screeching, shuddering stop some fifty yards further down the road. Julie looked at me disgustedly and rolled her eyes. "You guys and cars," she said, shaking her head. "You're just big, overgrown kids with big, overgrown toys."

As I backed up to the front of the store, it occurred to me that I couldn't have said it any better myself. "I gotta get some stuff inside," Cal called over as he leaped out of the Jowett.

"What about Carson and Sarah Jean?"

"Don't worry," he grinned. "They'll be along soon. There's no other road to take once you get off the highway."

The screen door banged behind him, and all of a sudden I realized how blessed quiet it was with the engines switched off-just the sound of the dust settling and a few birds chirping and a slight wind through the trees-and how strange and tingly it felt not to be moving anymore. "Wanna get out and stretch your legs?" I asked Julie.

"Sure thing, Barney Oldfield. And, if there's a ladies room on the premises, I think I'll just go clean the crap out of my pants."

"Oh, it wasn't that bad, was it? I was taking it *easy....*"

"Then do me a favor, okay?"

"Sure."

"Take it even easier, huh? Like maybe save killing yourself for when I'm not in the frickin' car." I could tell from Julie's voice that she was kind of half serious and half jerking me around, and didn't know for sure herself which way she meant it. No question that seat without the steering wheel and brake pedal in front of it can be a pretty tough place to sit. Especially when it's in a fast sports car and the guy next to you is showing off.

Sure enough Carson and the MG rolled up a few minutes later, and he was a little upset at the way Cal and me had lit out on him. "That w-wasn't very nice," he pouted. And I had to agree with him. But it sure was fun.

By that time Cal was done with his shopping and had us help him out with about six bags of groceries and two big, sweaty blocks of ice in a cardboard box. "It's just down the road a ways," Cal told us, slipping on those stolen aviator sunglasses he'd gleeped on our way to Grand Island. "Follow me."

So we headed down the paved road about another mile and then followed the Jowett onto this narrow, unmarked gravel drive that went right through the damn woods. It was almost like a tunnel made of trees and ferns and dense green foliage, and a lot of it had grown over the winter so that new, small branches snapped against the windshield frame on either side. You could smell old pine needles and fresh, wild onions floating on the damp salt air off the ocean. We broke out into a shallow, sandy depression full of rye grass and shore reeds, then rolled over one final crest to find ourselves on top of a sand dune with a spectacular, wide open view of the Atlantic Ocean. It was pretty damn impressive, no two ways about it, stretching out so far into the distance that you couldn't really make out where the blue of the ocean faded into the slightly lighter blue of the sky. Looking out at it made you feel tiny and empty and insignificant, but also strangely satisfied.

"Hey, where the hell are we going?" I finally yelled up to Cal.

"I don't think these cars can make it down our driveway. Follow me."

And so I followed him, the Jowett and Big Ed's Jag and Carson's MG forming a single file conga line with the endless expanse of the Atlantic to our right and the late afternoon sun beaming down over our shoulders so the cars cast long, misshapen shadows ahead of us. Seagulls hovered in the wind overhead, calling to each other, while foot-high whitecaps rolled gently in and pointy shorebirds skittered after them, picking at the wet sand. It was like something out of a movie, you know? In fact, it was better. It was like being *in* a movie. And naturally Cal made it all the more interesting by inventing his own little game of "sea chicken" based on what the birds were doing. As each wave rolled in and then back out to sea, Cal's Jowett would chase after it, following the receding water line and then (hopefully, at least) swerving away just in time before the next one rolled in. Carson and me picked it up right away. The idea was to stay as close as you could to the water's edge without ever actually getting in it and kicking a telltale roostertail of water up off the tires. Now for Cal and me this was a pretty dicey sort of game to be playing, seeing as how we were in other people's cars. And particularly other people's cars with Lucas electrical systems, which have never exactly been noted for their moisture tolerance. But stuff like that just never seemed to bother Cal Carrington. As I've said before, he never suffered any kind of shortage in nerve or confidence departments, and, if you were lucky, it was catching.

Of course all the girls got angry at first, shaking their fingers and howling about getting wet or getting stuck in the sand or falling clear out of the car if one of us turned too sharp. Which was all nonsense, really. What they *should* have been worrying about was having the wheels dig into the sand and rolling the car over on top of them. But women generally don't have that good a feel for vehicle dynamics, you know? And besides, they started to enjoy it a little in spite of themselves, shrieking in mock horror when the car they were in got caught in a roll of surf and squealing with delight when it happened to one of the other two. In fact, we got so involved we drove right past Cal's folks' place and on for at least another mile before we finally turned around and headed back. We were all pretty well soaked, if you want the truth of it, and no question the Jowett, the MG, and Big Ed's Jag were going to require an extensive drying out period. But we were all laughing like hell....

The Carrington family's shore cottage sat up on a low bluff overlooking the ocean, and you had to be pretty damn impressed by the sort of place the Carringtons referred to as "a cottage." Hell, it was bigger than the house my sisters and I grew up in. Not that it was real fancy or overdone or anything. It was just a big, comfy old frame house with green storm shutters, a blackened stone fireplace in the living room, a large, homey kitchen, a big brick barbecue and jungle gym out back, and dormer bedrooms up in the third floor attic for the kids. But I think my favorite part was the front porch, which ran all the way across the front with hurricane lamps fastened to all the support posts and a big chunk of whalebone nailed over the front door. If you felt like it, you could lean over the railing and stare out to sea with your nose splitting the air like a damn ship's prow aimed towards Africa. Or you could plop down on an overstuffed wicker couch and pull my old wool army blanket up around you against the chill. Or you could rock awhile on the rocking chair or, better yet, glide back and forth with somebody you liked on this old slatted porch swing they had hanging from the ceiling. It was a pretty special sort of place.

The inside of the house was neat, too, and a quick tour left no doubt that Cal's mom surely enjoyed her antique hunting while his dad really got a charge out of all that salty, heave-ho, seafaring stuff. In fact, the place was chock full of oil paintings of great sailing ships and rope-knot wall hangings and other assorted nautical doodads. Like lobster pot planters and old wooden ship's wheels and glass front display cases filled with antique brass telescopes and compasses and sextants and such. I tried to imagine what it must be like, having enough money to simply peel off the bills for any neat old piece of junk that catches your eye. But I didn't have a good enough imagination.

Speaking of which, I got to thinking maybe Cal was in one of his flash-flood wealthy stages as we unpacked the groceries, since it looked like Cal had bought about one of everything they had in that little store. Only it turned out he'd told the grocer his folks were on their way up and just to put it on the old family tab. Typical. But otherwise he never could've got us the two cases of Knickerbocker or the bottle of Bacardi or the fifth of his old man's favorite Pinch scotch whiskey. Although I couldn't so much as be in the same room as a bottle of Pinch without recalling the Fourth of July Fireworks Disaster Cal and I ignited in my Aunt Rosamarina's garage. Which, time having passed, was always good for a few hearty toasts.

It was decided that the girls would share Cal's folks' master bedroom on the second floor, which had its own bathroom, a great big four-poster bed with a flower print canopy over it, and a roll-out trundle bed underneath. Me and Cal and Carson would make do with either the downstairs couches or the guest bedroom on the second floor or the kids' dormer bedrooms all the way up on the third floor, depending on how steady our legs felt or where and when we passed out. Then it was on to chopping the ice and putting the food away and getting a fire started in the barbecue out back so's we could grill up the hamburgers and hot dogs Cal's parents had no idea they were treating us to for dinner. Meanwhile, upstairs, I could hear the girls talking and giggling and carrying on the way only girls can do. Besides our wedding, it sounded like the hot topic of conversation was the upcoming coronation of Queen Elizabeth over in England, which had been getting a lot of press coverage and was apparently considered an astonishingly big deal even to a lot of people here in the States. Most of whom, it should come as no surprise, were either loyal British subjects or women. In any case, I was happy to see that Julie and my sisters were getting along so well. It meant a lot to me. It really did.

We had a pick-at-it barbecue dinner along with an adult-style round or three of cocktails while the sun oozed slowly down into a smoky gray horizon somewhere off in the general direction of New York City. It was one of those long, slow, lingering summer twilights, and we all just sat out in the back yard around an old wooden picnic table and talked about this and that. And one of the main topics of conversation was the difference between what males and females of the species like to talk about. "Take it from me, I know" Mary Frances proclaimed, pointing her index finger up in the air for all to see, "men only have one thing on their minds."

"It's not like that at *all,*" Cal shot back, folding his arms across his chest. It sounded like there'd been some discussion on the subject already during their drive across Long Island in the Jowett. "It makes me sick when I hear women say that men don't think or talk about anything but sex."

"Sex??!!" Julie hooted. "She's talking about *cars!"*

Well, maybe we did talk a lot about cars. I mean, it was just such a fascinating subject, you know? And surely more interesting than a bunch of stuffy English folks getting dressed up in Lord and Lady Halloween costumes just to watch some big, slow-moving coronation ceremony where the high point of the whole proceeding is when a young lady with blood the same general color and temperature as the Atlantic Ocean puts a fancy jeweled hat on top of her hairdo. I mean, who cares? Far as I could see, it was like having the Rose Bowl Parade without the damn football game, you know? Still, I wanted to be fair, and so I made it a point that we spent some time discussing the wedding. Especially seeing as how both my sisters were standing up and Cal was going to be best man and of course Carson was in on it, too. But we had to be careful about it, since women can go on for absolutely *ever* once you get them started on the subject of weddings. I swear, they're worse about it than we are about cars. Really they are. Not that any one of them will ever admit it.

Later on the girls cleaned up the dishes while Cal and Carson and me sat out on the front porch smoking some fancy cigars that Cal'd gleeped out of his old man's humidor in the den. Truth is, I'd never been all that big on smoking cigars. Maybe on account of I'd spent so much time downwind of Big Ed, and had come to the sorry conclusion that the more he spent on his high class imported stogies, the worse they smelled. But somehow they seemed just right this particular evening. Especially when accompanied by a few snorts of his old man's favorite Pinch whiskey served up in genuine after-dinner-drink brandy snifters. In fact, it was amazing how much more relaxed, grown-up, worldly-wise and cosmopolitan we were feeling with every puff and sip.

About nine a few other racer types started showing up. Most of them were guys we'd met at Watkins Glen or Brynfan Tyddyn, and I found out what Cal meant about the driveway since one of them got high-centered on the crown and a bunch of us had to go up there in the dark and lever him off. Wouldn't you know, it turned out to be none other than Tommy Edwards riding with that Eddie Dearborn guy he'd introduced me to at Siebkens bar in Elkhart Lake. And you should've seen the car he was driving! Why, it was the same exact metallic red Allard J2X Le Mans model I'd seen on the stand at the New York International Motor Sports show just a few weeks before. "Hey, great t'see you again," Eddie grinned, slapping his arm around my shoulders. "Guess I maybe shoulda brought th'Jeep." You could tell this was hardly his first party of the evening.

"Good to see you, old sport," Tommy said, clapping his arm around my shoulder. "I see you've fully recovered from Sebring."

"Yeah. More or less."

Eddie Dearborn climbed back into the car and fired up the deep, gut-trembling rumble of the fuel-injected Olds V-8 under the hood. *"You guys be careful where you grab and push, okay?"* he shouted over the din. *"It's all aluminum, see, an' you can leave a dent if you so much as breathe on it hard. It'd cost a friggin' king's ransom t'get the damn thing straightened out. And Lord knows they'll never match the paint. See my helmet here?"* He reached into the passeneger side footwell-even while gunning the big Olds engine and sending off an impressivly helpless shower of sand from the right rear wheel-and produced a brand new fiberglass racing helmet painted the exact same shade of deep metallic red as the car. *"See here,"* he hollered over the bellowing exhaust, *"They hadda paint it three friggin' times t'get it right!"*

The car hadn't budged an inch.

Eventually somebody had the bright idea that we could maybe use some wood planks or something under the wheels, so Cal went up and ripped all the slats out of the picnic table in his parents' back yard. Just like that! Can you believe it? But it did the trick and we got Eddie Dearborn's brand new Le Mans Allard off the hump and safely back down the drive. And we left it there at the bottom, parked crosswise and blocking the way so we wouldn't have to rescue any more low-slung sportscars as the evening wore on. "If I'd a'had my old J2X, it woulda cleared easy," Eddie puffed as we climbed back up the hill. "This new baby sits one hell of a lot lower." He'd decided to wear his new fiberglass racing helmet to the party-hey, it was a *racing* party, wasn't it?-and, considering his condition, it didn't look like too bad an idea.

"So," I asked him, "is it *fast?"*

"Shit, *yes!"* he grinned enthusiastically. "That Olds is one hell of a damn motor, b'lieve me. Why, I was even hoping your asshole buddy Tommy here could get that stupid license crap of his cleared up with the S.C.M.A. just so's I could rub his nose in it a little."

"Oh, and I'm quite sure you would have," Tommy said sarcastically. Then he leaned over and stage whispered: "You know, Eddie's driven some of his most brilliant races at the party the night before."

"I can see...."

Meanwhile more sportycar people were arriving all the time, bringing even more booze and food with them, and by the time we got back to the house every light in the place was lit and there were shouts and snorts and laughter spilling out of all the open windows. Eddie and Tommy headed inside and it wasn't five minutes before Eddie Dearborn-metallic red crash helmet and all-had parked himself and two full beers in front of this old player piano in the den. And it wasn't five more minutes before he had it cranked up full blast and got everybody in the room singing along with him on old piano roll songs like *Alexander's Ragtime Band* and *A Bicycle Built For Two*. He was quite the party character, no two ways about it.

But it'd been a long day and I didn't really feel like all that raucous noise and singing and banging on the piano, so I was happy to find Julie all by her lonesome in the rocking chair on the end of the porch. "You okay?" I asked.

"Sure. I'm fine," she said softly, looking out over the ocean. "It's just way too noisy in there."

"Yeah, it is, isn't it." If you turned your head just right and craned your neck away from the den window, you could make out the waves rolling in over the sand. "Say, you wanna go for a walk or something?"

"That'd be really nice," Julie said, and the way she said it made me feel all warm and cozy inside.

So I went in and gleeped us a couple bottles of Coke with about a half-pint of rum split between them, grabbed a flashlight out of a kitchen drawer, and put my old wool army blanket over my arm in case we wanted to sit ourselves down someplace and look at the stars. "Ready?"

"Sure," Julie said. "Why not?"

It was amazing how the party noise faded into the night and the sound of the ocean lapping at the sand replaced it as we meandered our way up the beach. Turned out we didn't hardly need the flashlight, since there was a fat, first-quarter moon hanging in the sky like a spoonful of quicksilver, and, once we got away from the house, it and the starlight were plenty enough to see by. Without even trying to we walked side by side and barefoot across the sand, kind of letting our hands dangle between us with the fingers barely touching, heading off who-knows-where in the general direction of Gibraltar. We didn't talk much. Julie asked me if I worried about getting married, and I lied and told her not at all. Or maybe it wasn't really a lie, since I hadn't really been thinking about it much. Not really "I don't know," I told her, "It just seems like the right thing t'do and the right time t'do it, you know?"

"Yeah, I do," she told me. "I guess I feel the same way, too."

"Oh, I know it'll be a struggle sometimes..." I allowed, taking another slow pull off my Coke bottle.

"It is for everybody."

"...but we'll get by..."

"I know we will."

"...if we just stick by each other..."

"If we just stick by each other."

We stopped and faced each other, and I decided to pull a deadly serious look down over my face like a windowshade. "Julie?"

"Yes"

"I forget what comes next. Is it the 'in sickness or in health' or are we all the way up to 'till death do us part?'"

"You're such a jerk!" Julie laughed.

I gave her a little kiss. "Wanna go for a swim?"

"You're outta your mind, Palumbo. That water's gotta be cold as ice."

I walked over and put my toe in. She was right.

"You wanna sit down then?"

Julie shrugged. "I guess that'd be nice."

So I walked up the sand dune and spread my old army blanket out barely over the crest, out of the wind, and we sat down and leaned back on our elbows with our eyes just high enough to still see the surf rolling in under the moonlight. Then, after awhile, we stretched out on our backs and looked up into the sky. It was deep and black and so empty and full of stars at the same time that it went on and on forever. We were holding hands between us and then we were kissing and I could feel her all up and down against me and then it got to where I couldn't tell where I ended and she began anymore. I wanted her so badly it was like a hollow, pounding ache inside the heat. And I could tell she felt the same way, too. *"We really ought to,"* I whispered desperately into her ear. *"We're gonna be married in two weeks anyway, Julie, and no way could it ever be this perfect again."*

I thought sure she'd get angry and tell me to get lost, but instead she pulled me in even closer. *"Oh, what the hell, Buddy,"* she whispered back through urgent, trembling lips. *"Go ahead...."*

And so I did. Or, more accurately, *we* did. And it was like nothing that had ever happened to either of us before. Not that it's any of your business. But it's like we got so close to each other we seemed to be melting together, straining and pulling and pushing like we were trying to get out of something and into something at the same time, all the while tumbling free-fall down this deep, black hole with a bucket of skyrockets at the bottom that spiraled up our spines and exploded into a shimmering, multicolored gush of hot lava on the inside of our eyelids at the end. Or at least that's what I thought. *"Gee whiz, Julie,"* I moaned into her hair, *"that was...that was...just unbelievable!"*

"You done already?" I heard her whisper from someplace far off in the distance inside my head.

I felt my eyes slide open. "Ahh, well, geez, Julie..." I heard myself saying, "...if you'll just, uhh, *wait* a minute or two..."

"Nah," she kind of chuckled. "That's okay." And she started to push me off from on top of her.

"No, *really,*" I insisted. "If you just wait a sec..."

"No, I mean it, Buddy. It's okay. Really it is." She rolled me over onto the blanket next to her. "It was *nice.*"

"Yeah," I sighed. "It was nice, wasn't it?"

"Yeah, it sure was." She sounded pretty proud of it, too.

Then we just kind of laid there side by side on the blanket, looking up into that black velvet sky that went on forever and ever. I could feel her there next to me-like she was *more* of me-even though we weren't actually touching. We stayed that way a long time, just looking up at the stars and listening to the surf rolling in. "Gee whiz," I repeated to the stars in the Big Dipper, "that was *unbelievable!*" I reached out just a little so our fingertips were touching. "Y'know, it's almost like we're floating, isn't it? Like it's after a shipwreck or something and we're floating on one of those blow-up inflatable life rafts out there in the middle of the ocean with nothing around us for thousands and thousands of miles in every direction...."

"Yeah, it's nice, all right." Julie agreed, propping herself back up on her elbows. "But I think we better get your pants back on and fold this raft of yours back up before one of your racing buddies happens by in a rowboat."

"Aw, c'mon, Julie..." I leaned up to start kissing her again.

"Hey, that's enough, Palumbo," she laughed, pushing me away. "After all, we gotta save *something* for the wedding night."

"There's no way it could ever be better than this."

"Yeah." She agreed, giving me a soft little peck on the eyebrow. "I guess we did pretty good for first-timers, didn't we?"

I wasn't about to tell her that it wasn't exactly my first time, but I was pretty sure she was right, anyway.

So we got dressed and just sat around for awhile, polishing off the last of our rum-and-Cokes and watching the moon slink down towards the tree line behind us. Neither of us felt much like going back to the party, so we decided to walk down the beach a little further. And then a little further after that. I don't know how far we walked that night, but it wouldn't surprise me if we made it all the way out to the tip of Long Island and back. Or at least that's what it felt like, anyway. We didn't say too much, just kind of listened to the surf and smelled the salt air and watched the moon settle back behind the trees on our way back to the cottage. The party had thankfully died down a little by then and most of the people who could still stand or string words together were gathered in the kitchen and overflowing out the back door into the yard. I was pleased to see there was nobody on the front porch, so I went inside and got us a few more drinks and Julie and I sat on the swing for awhile, just kind of gliding back and forth with her head leaned over on my shoulder and my head leaned back over on top of hers. Believe it or not, we actually saw a shooting star. Or maybe I just made that part up. But it sure felt like we did and that's the way I always remembered it afterwards.

Chapter 14: Julie's First Race

I remember waking up about the time the first sliver of sunlight came peeking up over the horizon like a sleepy, yellow-orange eye. I was still out on the porch, stretched out on that old, overstuffed wicker couch with my wool army blanket pulled up under my chin. It smelled just a little like Julie's perfume, and when I slid my eyes over to the side, there she was, sitting up in the rocking chair with a knit afghan over her shoulders and a sketchpad in her lap. I guess she found it someplace in the den along with some artist's colored charcoals Cal's sister had started up with one day and abandoned just as quickly. "What're y'drawing, huh?" I asked her though a heavy yawn.

"Just some jerk car mechanic," she answered without looking up.

So I got up and stretched and looked over her shoulder, and wouldn't you know it, she'd drawn a picture of me. Sleeping. With that old blanket pulled up under my chin and the sweetest, most contented, even angelic smile on my face. It was a hell of a swell drawing, too. And then I noticed that she'd put in these two petite little devil's horns growing up through the skin at the top of my forehead. "What're those for?" I asked.

"I draw what I see, Palumbo. Don'cha think it looks right?"

I looked at the satisfied smile and the dreamily closed eyes and the wicked little horns again. "Yeah," I agreed, kissing the top of her head, "You've got me nailed dead center, all right. In fact, it's a perfect likeness."

Cal appeared in the front doorway a few moments later with a grim, hung-over look in his eye and a steaming mug of coffee in his hand. "We'd better get rolling," he said in a hoarse, uneven voice, "Carson and I are in the first practice group and registration's sure to be a mess." He took a sip from the mug and looked over at Julie. "You wanna try to get the girls ready?"

"Sure. How soon are you planning t'leave?"

"Fifteen, maybe twenty minutes."

"Jesus Christ!" Julie yelped, bolting up from the rocker. "That's not even enough time to put my frickin' face on..."

"There's coffee on in the kitchen if you want some...." Cal called after her as she scrambled up the stairs.

Cal took another sip of coffee and looked out towards the horizon. There was a misty layer of overcast that looked like it would soon burn off. "You guys have a good time last night?"

"Sure did. It was one hell of a swell party."

"I'm surprised you noticed," Cal continued, slipping me one of his patented insider winks. "Seems like you two went missing most of the night."

"We went for a walk on the beach. It was nice."

"I bet it was," Cal said under an accusingly arched eyebrow. I felt the color coming up on my face. "Anyhow, you look like hell this morning."

"What do you expect from a guy with horns?" I said to change the subject, and showed him Julie's sketchpad. Cal regarded it carefully.

"That's really good, isn't it?" he said.

"Yeah. It is. She really oughtta be doing stuff like this full time instead'a serving up hot dogs and burger platters at the Doggy Shake."

"I swear I'll murder the next person who mentions hot dogs or hamburgers," Carson's voice warned weakly from the other side of the door. Jesus, he looked even worse than Cal.

"You look like hell," Cal told him.

"I feel like hell."

"There's coffee and sweet rolls in the kitchen."

Carson's complexion went even greener at the thought.

So I went inside and fixed him one of Butch's morning-after cocktails, which amounted to three Anacin tablets washed down with a double-dose Alka Seltzer. I made one each for Cal and me, too. Not that I was really bad hungover, but that sort of stuff is catching. "I've got it!" Cal said suddenly. "Let's jump in for a quick swim. That'll shake out the cobwebs for sure!"

"You're outta your mind," Carson groaned.

"That water's gotta be forty degrees."

"No chance," Cal said confidently. "It's gotta be at *least* fifty. C'mon," he taunted, "don't be a damn sissy."

"Are you *daring* us t'do it?"

"I'm *double* daring you!" Cal shouted. And, as everybody in the civilized world knows, double dares go first. So he leaped over the railing in a smooth, graceful arc and took off lickety-split towards the water, windmilling clothes off in all directions along the way. *"Last one in is a monkey's uncle!"* he hollered back over his shoulder.

Carson looked at me and I looked at Carson and just like *that* we were off like a shot, running and stumbling towards the surf with shirts and pants and shoes and socks and even Carson's glasses flying in all directions. The only way to do it of course was to run right out into the water and dive head-first into the waves, and I'd have to say the shock was about equal to leaping bare-assed into a snow bank. And then it doubled when we heard some hooting and whooping behind us and turned around to see Julie and my sisters cheering us on from the second floor window. So there was nothing to do but make one of those tough, carefree, I-can-take-it Guy Show demonstrations of splashing around in the surf until our lips turned blue-it took all of thirty seconds-and then we had to kind of pick our way backwards towards the house, bodies shivering and teeth chattering, gathering up all the scattered clothing and fumbling to cover ourselves up as best we could along the way.

It sure woke us up, though.

We got toweled off and dressed and of course the girls still weren't ready, so Cal decided to cook us up a little eggs and toast and bacon while we were waiting. And so we ate that and naturally enough the girls *still* weren't ready. "J-Jesus, what's t-taking them so long?" Carson asked through teeth that were still chattering a little.

Cal held up his index finger and rolled his eyes towards the ceiling. "It is easier to pass a needle through the eye of a camel than to get three females ready to go someplace in the morning."

Carson looked at him blankly. "Why the heck would anyone want to stick a needle in a camel's eye?"

"Beats me," Cal shrugged. "It's an old Arab proverb."

"Must've been a *very* old Arab," I offered. "It doesn't make any sense."

"Maybe he's senile?" Carson chimed in. "That might explain it."

Well, it was good to see we were all feeling our old selves again, anyway.

But it was really starting to get late. "Look," I finally said, "you guys take off in the Jowett and get registered. We'll be along as soon as I can get those three organized upstairs.

"Who's gonna drive my MG?" Carson wanted to know.

"Either me or Julie. She's okay with a stickshift."

"I'd rather it was you."

"Suits me. She can drive Big Ed's Jag. She's done it before."

"Aren't'cha worried he'll get mad?"

"Not if you don't tell him," Cal observed, expressing my sentiments exactly. "Now let's get our butts out of here before we miss practice, okay?"

So Cal and Carson took off in the Jowett and, when Julie finally came down, I explained the new travel plans to her. "Sure," she said. "Don't think I'd mind tooling around Long Island in a frickin' Jaguar. Maybe I can pick myself up a rich guy or something?"

"You already got a guy."

"But is he *rich?*"

"He's rich in spirit."

"If you can't count it, it doesn't count. My mom always told me 'show me a man with no money and I'll show you a bum.'"

"Yeah, but I'm *your* bum."

"I'm so lucky."

Without thinking about it I leaned in close and whispered, *"That was really special last night, wasn't it?"*

"It was okay," she teased. But then her eyes got tough. "An' I don't want you tellin' all your buddies about it like guys always do."

"Why would I do a thing like that?"

"Why? Because you're a guy, that's why. Guys do stuff like that. It makes 'em feel like big shots."

"I'd never do anything like that," I told her. And I meant it.

"You sure as hell better not. Or last night will have to last you for a long time, Palumbo. And I mean an *awfully* long time...."

At that exact moment, I became aware that a terrifying new weapon had been added to Julie's arsenal. In fact, it was easily the Boy-Meets-Girl equivalent of a nuclear warhead.

Mary Frances and Sarah Jean came down a few minutes later and I quickly force-fed them the rest of toast and eggs and we took off for Bridgehampton, Mary Frances and me in the MG and Julie and Sarah Jean in Big Ed's Jaguar. Boy, did those two ever look neat together in that car. Scary, even, although I couldn't tell you exactly why. "So," I asked Mary Frances once we were on the road, "did you guys have a good time last night?"

"Yeah, I guess so," she sighed. "But it seems like all those people want to talk about is cars, cars, cars. It gets pretty boring after awhile."

"Too bad we can't have discussions about Mexican communists and novels in Esperanto like your uptown friends in Greenwich Village."

Mary Frances started to answer back, but then she stopped herself and let out another long, weary sigh. "To be honest, it was kind of nice to be away from that for awhile. Those people are just so *intense* all the time, you know?"

"I can see how they would be."

"I swear, it's like a damn contest sometimes. A big, stupid contest about who knows the most. About *anything*! The subject doesn't even matter, for gosh sakes. It's just about who knows the most about *everything.*"

"I bet your buddy Ollie Cromwell does pretty well on that score. He seems to think he knows everything about everything."

"He's brilliant," she said like it was a reflex action. Then she leaned her head back and looked up at the sky. "But let's not talk about him, okay."

"Is something wrong?"

She shrugged. "Why should anything be wrong? I just don't feel like talking about him, that's all. Don't worry, you'll see him at the wedding. And at the rehearsal dinner, too." You couldn't miss the hard, cold edge creeping into her voice. "Hell, If I knew you liked him so damn much, I would've brought him along this weekend...."

"Hey. Take it easy, huh? We don't have to talk about him if you don't want to. We can talk about my friends just as easy. How d'ya like Cal?"

"He's the worst of the bunch," she laughed. "He's thoroughly self-centered and completely obsessed with car racing. He could win a prize for it."

"You don't think he's good looking?"

"Of *course* he's good looking. He can even be charming when he puts his mind to it. But all he talks or cares about is car racing." She shook her head. "There's got to be more to life than that. Why, he's even worse than *you!*"

"How about Carson?"

"Boy, he sure fits the part as an undertaker, doesn't he? It's like they sent him over from Central Casting."

"He's nice, though."

"Yeah, once you get past the Bela Lugosi part. Did you notice he spent a lot of time last night hanging around Sarah Jean?"

I couldn't say as I'd noticed, seeing as how Julie and me hadn't actually been there most of the evening.

A little accusatory light went on in Mary Frances' eyes. "That's right. I remember now. You guys were gone for an *awfully* long time..."

I felt the color coming up on my face again.

"...You weren't doing anything *naughty,* were you?"

I glanced in the rear view mirror and saw I was about the same shade of red as Eddie Dearborn's new Le Mans model Allard.

Traffic got heavier as we got closer to Bridgehampton, and it was after ten by the time we met up with Cal and Carson in the paddock. But the practice sessions still hadn't started seeing as how the S.C.M.A. armband brigade weren't nearly done stacking up the haybales and blocking off the side roads to secure the circuit. It was hard to believe that I'd attended the very first sports car race of my life right here at Bridgehampton precisely one year before. I mean, so much had happened since then. Now I felt like an old hand who knew all the ropes, and it was really special to have Julie and my sisters there so I could show them around and explain things. I think showing somebody new around is almost as good as seeing it for the first time yourself. Maybe even better, since you get to see it though their eyes and through your own at the same time. Anyhow, you could tell all three of them were seriously impressed by all the people and cars and color and sheer human *effort* it took to pull off an event like this. I think they were also pretty impressed by how many people said "hello" to me or shook my hand or gave me a little shot in the ribs or clapped a hand on my shoulder as we walked through the paddock.

Or at least I hoped they were, anyway.

And then who should we stumble upon but that prize-winning asshole Skippy Welcher and his squire Milton Fitting, fussing around with the yet-once-again rebuilt C-Type that The Skipper drove over a cliff in Mexico and Masten Gregory bailed out of just before it jumped the track, crossed the highway, ran through two lines of drying laundry and crashed into an old derelict Ford pickup at Sebring. I figured Colin St. John had to be making a damn fortune off him just on parts. There was also a girl with them, a severe looking young woman with hard eyes and blond hair pulled back in a long braid. I'd never seen her before. Skippy saw me out of the corner of his eye, and at first it was like he didn't exactly recognize me. But then he flashed me that misshapen gold tooth smile of his and stepped into our path, his face popping and twitching like a busted valve spring. *"You need to get yourself one of these Amsterdam girls,"* he proclaimed, pointing his thumb back over his shoulder at the girl with the braid. *"They do what they're told."*

"Oh?"

The Skipper nodded proudly and puffed out his chest. *"Yes sir, they do! Why, when I say 'get down on your knees,' she gets right down there!"* I swear, he was talking loud enough that you could hear the sonofabitch all the way over in Nassau County.

"Jesus, who the hell was *that?"* Mary Frances whispered as soon as we were out of earshot. So I told them all the gory details about Skippy Welcher and his Welcher Waxout ear swab fortune, and also about his ex-everything XK-120M that he'd sold to Big Ed and bought back again and his Jaguar C-Type that I had personally driven halfway across the country and about the wreck he caused that got Tommy Edwards' license suspended at Watkins Glen the year before and about seeing him go over that cliff in Mexico and how he ran the car out of brakes for his co-driver at Sebring. "I don't get it," Mary Frances said. "If he's such an idiot, why on earth do they let him race?"

"That's a good question," I said. "In fact, it's a very good question. But I guess it's mostly on account of he's rich and he's been around about forever and he's pretty well connected with some of the bigwigs in the sport."

"They actually *like* him?"

"No, not really. But that's not the point."

"Well, then, what *is* the point?"

Don't you hate it when people ask you questions you've already asked yourself a kazillion times and have never been able to properly answer? "Weellll," I said slowly, "I guess the *real* point is that neat race cars don't have any control over who owns them, see? And it's hard to get somebody *out* once they're *in*. Especially if they've been around since the beginning."

"But wait a minute," Julie demanded. "Didn't they take your English friend Tommy Edwards' racing license away?"

"Yeah. They gave him a year's suspension. They really should've given it to Skippy. I mean, he *caused* the wreck..." I shook my head. "But it was a tough one to call, since Tommy's the one who actually had the crash. And I guess they figured they had t'do *something,* seeing as how a lot of people got hurt and a little seven-year-old boy got killed...."

"A seven year old boy got *killed?"* Sarah Jean gasped.

For just an instant the sight of that little boy lying there against the curb on Franklin Street like a heap of dirty laundry flashed in my head and sent a shiver clear through me. "Yeah," I nodded softly. "It was pretty awful."

We located Big Ed's white Eldorado convert over by the registration tent, and, true to form, he was having yet another heated argument with Charlie Priddle about getting a paddock pass sticker for his Caddy. "I got all kinds of jacks and tools and stuff in the trunk, see," Big Ed was saying, "an' you're gonna make us *carry* it all in?"

"The rules are very specific, Mr. Bomb-steen," Charlie explained without looking up from his paperwork. "If you'd bothered to read the supplementary regulations on the back of the entry form, you would've known that only *race* cars are allowed in the paddock."

"But what about that big semi rig the Cunningham team brought in? Or that panel truck the Muscatelli brothers have parked over there next to Creighton Pendleton's Ferrari?"

"That's different. Those are *support* vehicles."

"Well, we got three damn cars entered in this thing, an' my Caddy's gonna be our support vehicle. Now how about giving me a damn parking sticker?"

About then who shows up but Tommy Edwards and Eddie Dearborn in Eddie's new Le Mans-style Allard. Eddie was still wearing his new, metallic red crash helmet (although now with a couple scuffs and dings in the paint from bouncing off assorted doors, walls, and possibly even headboards the night before) but looking amazingly chipper for a guy who'd done so much high-octane partying the night before. At least except for the black eye and the fresh, raw bruise on the end of his nose. "What the heck happened to you?" I asked.

"U.P.I.," Eddie said simply.

"U.P.I.?"

"Yup," he nodded, flashing a big smile.

"What's that stand for?"

"Why, 'Unexplained Party Injury,' of course!"

"I'm amazed you were able to drive home at all last night," Mary Frances grumbled disapprovingly.

"Hadda drive," Eddie shrugged helplessly. "I was too damn drunk t'walk!"

"I drove," Tommy corrected him. "Eddie just doesn't remember."

"Good thing I wore my helmet, then." He rapped his knuckles against the shiny red fiberglass. Then he looked accusingly over at Tommy. "You didn't beat the crap out of my new car or anything, did'ja?"

"The redline's seventy-five hundred, isn't it?" Tommy needled. "Although I couldn't quite get it up there in top."

"The way I've heard it," Eddie volleyed right back, "you've always had a problem getting it up."

"Your wife would bloody well know."

"She's my ex-wife."

Tommy looked up at me and sighed. "There are actually several of them," he explained, looking painfully serious. "And they'd all bloody well know."

"Now LOOK!" Big Ed's voice bellowed from the registration table. *"You accepted my entry and my friends' entries an' I'll be damned if we're gonna carry all that friggin' stuff back t'the cars when you let everybody else an' his friggin' brother bring support vehicles in!"*

"What's the problem?" Eddie wanted to know.

"Oh, Charlie Priddle just likes to jerk Big Ed around," I told him. "You could say it's kind of a hobby of his."

"This guy a friend of yours?" he asked Tommy.

Tommy gave a curt little nod.

Without another word, Eddie climbed out of the Allard, walked over to the registration table, reached down and opened the little tin cash box right under Charlie's nose, took out a parking sticker, and handed it to Big Ed. Just like that. Then he turned to Charlie and gave him a big, neighborly smile. "We don't have to be assholes about everything, Charlie," he said soothingly. "It's just not necessary. Life's too short." And then he turned around and walked out of the tent.

Boy, I wanted to pin a damn medal on him for that. "He sure isn't afraid of Charlie one bit, is he?"

"No," Tommy explained, "he's been president of the Chicago region for quite awhile and so he's about the same level on the pecking order as Charlie. Plus he's a good sort of bloke and everybody pretty much likes him."

"That's a lot more than you can say for Charlie."

"He's also a bloody decent race driver."

"That's also a lot more than you can say for Charlie."

"Agreed."

Big Ed peeled the backing paper off the parking sticker and applied it to the Caddy's windshield, and about then his weekend "date" appeared following a visit to one of the makeshift outhouses they'd set up around the paddock. She was a big, tall, bosomy girl with a pile of brassy orange-red hair on top of her head, trashy makeup, gold high heels, and a wad of gum the size of a cue ball smacking between her lips. "That's the worst crapper I ever seen in my life," she whinnied at Big Ed. "An' I hadda wait in line for it, too."

"Meet Rhonda," Big Ed said around his cigar. "This here's Buddy an' his sisters an' his girlfriend, Julie."

"Actually, she's my fiancée." I corrected him, and Julie gave my hand a nice little squeeze of approval.

"Well, ain't that nice," Rhonda gushed. "I been married once myself."

"Big Ed's been married a couple a'times," I said proudly.

"Yeah. You could say I'm kind of an expert on the subject," he laughed. "Especially the alimony part."

We all wandered back into the paddock to unload the trunk of the Caddy and take all the stuff out of the three sports cars, then taped over the headlights and put racing numbers on the sides. Julie did all the numbers, and so they came out real professional and artistic and much better than they ever looked when I did it. Not that I'd ever tell her that. The armband crews had just about finished everything by then-they were only running two and a half hours late-and the call went up for the first practice group. That was for the smallbore cars in the Sagaponack Trophy race, including Cal's Jowett Jupiter and Carson Flegley's MG and all the other so-called "unmodified" production sports cars under 1500cc. Now that "unmodified" part was actually a teeny bit elastic, since a few of the entries-like Carson's TD, for example-had been tweaked and tinkered with and breathed upon by various wrench twisters-like myself, for example-with the express purpose of making them faster. But, since his car still *looked* pretty stock, he figured nobody would much mind if he ran with all the other supposedly stock MGs rather than jumping in with the stripped down, fire breathing, and even supercharged examples running in the second race. Where, incidentally, they didn't stand much of a chance on account of they were up against genuine, thoroughbred, purpose-built under 1500cc racing cars like Briggs Cunningham's gorgeous little blue-gray jewel of an OSCA (with Phil Walters driving) or West Coast Hotshoe John von Neuman in that much-modified tin-silver Porsche that almost won here the year before. Carson's car wouldn't have a chance in hell against stuff like that-in fact, it might even be hazardous to the other entrants if he got in their way-and so, to protect the safety and welfare of all concerned, Carson had selflessly (and silently) elected to run his car in the stock category. And don't think for one blessed moment that he was alone.

I decided to take the girls over by trackside so they could get an idea of what was going on, and along the way we saw Tommy and Eddie standing next to yet another dangerous-looking Le Mans-style Allard. It was just like Eddie's car, only white and with a hopped-up Caddy V-8 under the hood, and they were chewing the fat with its owner, a transplanted Brit from Connecticut named Lee Chapman. He was a hell of a nice guy and really savvy about racing cars, and apparently he and Tommy and Eddie knew each other from way back when. As they stood there talking, you couldn't miss that Tommy had the same desperate, furtive itch in his eyes Cal got whenever he was hanging around a racetrack with nothing lined up to drive. I guess nobody's immune to it once they get bitten by the racing bug.

I wanted to bring the girls right down close to the track where Big Ed and I watched from the previous year, but now they had big signs up saying NON-SPECTATOR TERRITORY and even a few armband people around to make sure you obeyed. I guess it was a good idea, even if it kept us a little too far away from the action. But the S.C.M.A. was getting pretty sensitive about such things following Tommy's terrible accident at Watkins Glen and the MG that brushed the spectator fence at Elkhart Lake and broke some lady's leg. So they'd put this grim little insert in the official race program at Bridgehampton titled *"See You Next Year?"* that encouraged spectators to *"read and learn 10 simple rules of safety for watching a sports car race."* It was mostly all basic, common sense stuff like *"STAY FAR AWAY FROM CURVES! A skidding car can come out of a skid and hurtle forward in any direction of the clock. It's not a nice way to die."* That was rule #2. Rule #10 said: *"A car traveling at 115 m.p.h. covers 168 ft. in a second. Before the race begins, test yourself to see if you can move faster on foot. If you can't, then go back and memorize the other nine rules above."*

"See," I told Julie and Mary Frances and Sarah Jean proudly, "they're really serious about making this safe for everybody." And right about then we heard the bumble-bee drone of the smallbore field pulling out onto the track for practice. They charged out of the paddock and came sweeping past us in a wild, feinting, snarling, downshifting gaggle of noise and color.

"It sure doesn't look very safe to me," Sarah Jean observed as the last car sailed out of sight. "Not very safe at all."

"Why?" I asked. "I mean, we're well away from the track."

"Not for us," she corrected me. "For *them.*"

Of course to me it looked pretty tame. I mean, I'd been around for a whole season and I'd seen the big cars run at Elkhart Lake and Watkins Glen and even ridden in the Suicide Seat with Javier Premal in what was almost Big Ed's new Ferrari on *La Carrera,* and so a bunch of supposedly stock smallbore tiddlers taking a flat and pretty much straightforward right-hander at a giddy thirty miles per hour or so didn't exactly make my heart pound or throat dry. But watching the three girls seeing it for the very first time reminded me of what it felt like when I was watching it myself for the very first time at this same exact corner precisely a year before. And *that* was exciting!

I tried to help them understand the differences in skill and style and technique between the quick guys and the duffers, and it was really easy to spot if you just knew what to look for. Cal was of course one of the best 'shoes out there, and he was really giving that dumpy-looking Jowett one hell of a ride. But you could tell it lacked for lightness and horsepower compared to the quickest Porsches, and it also seemed awful nose-heavy the way it blundered around with the front wheels cranked all the way over and the rear end just kind of tagging along for the ride. He was really having to work that car, no lie.

There was one other driver who caught my eye, a Navy dentist from Parris Island, South Carolina, named Dr. Richard Thompson. Or Lieutenant Dr. Richard Thompson, to be more precise. Anyhow, no question he knew how to drive a race car, and he had his Porsche right out on the ragged edge after just a few laps of finding his way around. In fact, I heard some of the other drivers grumbling afterwards that he was really pushing too hard and taking way too many chances. But they always say that about the really *fast* guys. From where I sat, I never saw him put a wheel wrong. Not once.

You could see Mary Frances was really drinking it all in. I think she liked the raw speed and excitement, and even more how it took skill and even a little subtlety to make a car go fast, not just brass balls and overblown bravado. Julie was more reserved, like she wasn't quite sure if she wanted to let herself enjoy it. And Sarah Jean looked terribly worried and apprehensive. Especially every time Carson's MG wobbled by doing a clumsy, irregular rendition of a four-wheel drift. You had to give him points for effort, though.

After the session we headed back into the paddock to see how our guys were doing, and along the way we saw the first female racing driver I'd ever seen in my life. Her name was Isabelle Haskell, and she'd showed up with two pretty little Siata roadsters, one for herself and one for a friend of hers named Perry Boswell. They were getting ready to run in the next practice group for modified under-1500cc cars entered in the Mecox Trophy Race, and you could really see Mary Frances' eyes light up when she saw her strapping on a helmet. Julie's too, in fact. "Geez, I didn't know they had any *lady* race drivers," Sarah Jean gasped.

"Neither did I," I admitted, sounding maybe a little too surprised.

"Oh? And what makes you think a woman couldn't drive just as good as a man?" Julie demanded.

There is never a good answer to a question like that. Especially when it's asked by your wife-to-be. So I just kind of pretended my hearing had gone bad. It was the wise thing to do.

We found Cal crouched down by the left front tire of the Jowett over by our spot in the paddock, and you could see he'd about worn the living shit off the outer edge of the tread and the sidewall. "So, how's it handling?" I asked.

"Like a damn garbage scow," he answered cheerily.

"You still looked pretty good out there."

"Oh, it goes around okay, I guess. But it plows something awful compared to the MGs I've driven."

"Hmm. Maybe we can do something about it?"

"Like what?"

"Well, first let's swap the tires around. Put that one on the right rear and vise-versa. And then let's maybe put a little more air in the fronts to keep them from rolling under so bad."

"Sounds like a plan. We've got another session later after lunch break and the big cars run. We'll try it then."

"Speaking of lunch...." Rhonda whinnied between gum smacks.

So Big Ed took us over to a food concession some local business whiz was running out of the back of his pickup truck and bought everyone a couple hot dogs, a bag of chips, and a bottle of warmish pop at something approaching double your normal, everyday retail pricing levels. Racetrack food vendors are pretty much legendary for their appreciation of captive markets and intuitive grasp of supply-and-demand capitalism. But it tasted good and was surely far from the most expensive meal Big Ed ever got over-charged for. Plus it looked like he was happy to have a bunch of people around him because, if you want my honest opinion, he was having a little case of the flutters and needed the distraction. Tommy'd come by and kind of talked him around the track and Cal had come over and done the same, but you could see in his eyes as the session drew near that Big Ed was really pretty wound up. "Hey, take it easy," Eddie Dearborn said, clapping a hand on his shoulder, "It's just a damn drive in the country. *Enjoy* yourself!"

"S-sure," Big Ed said, not sounding too sure at all.

"Just remember t'be a little careful coming off the far side of the bridge."

That was the same thing Tommy and Cal had told him. "That bridge over the Sag Pond is a real booger, even in a little car," Cal said while Big Ed was strapping on his helmet. "In fact, why don't we see if we can sneak back and watch from there during this session. It's gotta be a real Class-A handful in something like an Allard."

"Good luck, honey," Rhonda smacked, then gave Big Ed a sloppy wet kiss all over his lips just as he stuck the lever in first and tooled away.

"You wanna come with us?" I asked her, trying to be polite.

"Not on your life, honey," she told me. "My dogs are *killin'* me! I guess I shouldn't a'worn these damn heels." I looked down and saw the arch of her shoes had about the same profile as the first big dip on the Silver Flash roller-coaster at Coney Island.

"You sure?" I asked again.

"Hey, don't worry after me, honey. I can take carra myself. You just go on about your business."

So Cal, Carson, Tommy, the three girls and me all headed up the pit straight towards the final corner, crossed the road when nobody was much looking, and made our way up Bridge Lane past Highland Terrace to where the racetrack crossed the humpbacked bridge over the Sag Pond. It was a quiet, scenic little spot where local fishermen went after crabs most other weekends, but you could see right away how it might be tough in a racecar. The road was narrow and bumpy and the high crown in the middle turned it into a kind of launching ramp. "You just gotta remember to hit it square and keep your wheels straight while the car's in the air," Cal explained like it was no big deal. "The last thing you want to do is come down all catty-wumpus."

We heard the thunder of the big cars pounding out onto the circuit-the deep gut rumble of the hot-rodded American V-8s in the Allards and Cunninghams all muddled together with the six-cylinder blare of the Jaguars and the finely-meshed, animal howl of the Ferraris-and, just like the first time a whole year before, I felt my throat tightening up and my palms starting to itch just from the sound of it.

This was gonna be *good!*

The cars were still all bunched together and the drivers were wisely being a little tentative the first couple times through while they tried to get the feel of the place. But there was plenty of noise, and I felt Julie pull in closer next to me each time the field exploded past like a fast freight train passing six inches in front of our faces. "Jesus," I heard her whisper under her breath.

The next lap they were a little more strung out, and the next lap even more. Big Ed was well towards the back, thank goodness, and naturally The Skipper had already stopped at the pits to have some stray bits of hay cleaned out of the grille and wheel wells, so he was all by his lonesome back at the butt end of the field. As he should be.

Meanwhile the quick guys were starting to give it a little stick, and it was really something to see them come over the humpbacked crest of that bridge with damn near a foot of daylight showing under all four wheels. Then they'd come crashing down *hard* on their suspensions when they landed. It was pretty brutal, to be honest about it. And you could hear real easy which guys were keeping their foot in it and which guys were lifting when they charged up to that hump. Not to mention which ones were smart enough to feather it a fraction while the car was flying so the engine wouldn't over-rev and the rear wheels wouldn't overrun the car's speed while it was airborne.

And then Eddie Dearborn got it all terribly wrong. He'd just lapped Big Ed coming out of the right hander off Main Street onto Bridge Lane-no problem, Big Ed saw him coming and even waved him on by-but that put him a little off-line heading onto the bridge. Like he was coming in at a little bit of an angle and not quite perfectly square. But he kept his foot in it. And I guess the hump must've been real uneven when you hit it that way, because it launched that car way up into the air and turned all cockeyed, and you could hear that big, fuel-injected Olds revving like crazy as Eddie floored the gas to try and straighten out the skid he knew he'd be in as soon as the wheels came down. I saw the Allard kind of nose-over in midair and come down hard on the left front wheel, and Eddie must've instinctively turned the steering to try and straighten things out while it was still airborne, because it landed all catty-wumpus with the wheels pointed all wrong and then the outside tire bit and yanked the car around hard to the right. About then the back wheels came down-spinning at maybe a hundred and fifty miles per hour!-and sent the car careening into a wild, teetering slide. Eddie fought it all the way, his hands a blur on the steering wheel as he tried to steer into the skid, but then it caught traction and snapped back the other way so fast no mortal human could ever keep up. The Allard shot off the road, bounded through a shallow ditch, launched out the other side, and went cartwheeling into the trees. It hit one, flipped high into the air, and ricocheted off another. And that's when Eddie came out of the car like he'd been thrown by a rodeo bull. His body flew through the atmosphere like a kid's rag doll, arms windmilling helplessly in terrifying slow motion. But there was nothing to grab onto and nothing but empty atmosphere to break the fall as he smashed cranium-first into the base of a concrete driveway marker, cracking his brand new fiberglass racing helmet open like a melon rind.

You knew right away he was dead.

Chapter 15: An End, a Middle, and a Beginning

It took a long time to get the mess cleaned up at the bridge over Sag Pond, and the frantic rushing and scrambling and screaming and sirens that immediately followed Eddie Dearborn's crash quickly faded into a numbing, uneasy silence. I remember Big Ed was the next car by and he slowed to a crawl and looked through his racing goggles with huge, disbelieving eyes and a complexion the color of candle wax. Carson bolted and ran across the road almost immediately to see if there was anything he could do, and, when I thought about it afterwards-and I thought about it a *lot* afterwards-I was always proud of him for that. But the situation was way beyond help even before the Allard stopped rolling and came to rest in a weary, battered heap, upside down at the edge of the road with two wheels torn off and the other two slowly rotating. They had the red flags out around the course almost before it was finished, and, as the drivers pulled their cars over and shut them off, it got so quiet you could hear the hiss of steam from the Allard's fractured radiator core. And, just a few feet away, the body of Eddie Dearborn lay stretched out on the grass for a long, long time. It was like nobody knew what to do with it.

Finally the ambulance crew arrived and hovered over the body for awhile, trying to figure out what to do, and it was Carson who finally got a sheet out of the back and put it over what was left of Eddie's head. It was not really the kind of thing you wanted to watch, but you really couldn't make yourself look away, either. For sure I didn't want to catch Julie or Mary Frances or Sarah Jean's eye. Or Tommy's or Cal's, for that matter. I felt weak and sick and disgusted and stupidly giddy and ashamed. It didn't seem real, you know? It didn't even seem possible. But then all you had to do was look at that battered chunk of metal and the frail little sheet-covered mound just a few feet away from it and you knew it was nothing less than absolute reality.

The ambulance crew finally got Eddie loaded up and drove silently away, roof lights revolving but in no particular hurry, and then there was nothing to do but make our way back to the paddock-*g'wan, folks, there's nothing you can do here*-where we found Big Ed sitting on a spare tire with his knees splayed out and his arms dangling helplessly by his sides. Like I said, he'd been the next by and saw the whole thing happen, and no question he got far too good a look at it. It shook him right to the foundations, and I was pretty sure he'd even been crying a little. Carson held up amazingly well, but of course he was used to that sort of thing because it was around him every day of the year. Still, he looked a little pale and shaky. Somehow Cal managed to stay quietly aloof from it, as if it was something that happened out of sight and far away and never really touched him, while Tommy wore the face of marble military statue and didn't say a word. The three girls were in deep shock-especially Sarah Jean-and I could see that Mary Frances was angry, too, as if it were all some cruel trick played at her expense. I swear, she was wadded up like a fist. And Julie was deadly quiet, already a million miles away and slipping further all the time.

I was just dead numb.

There is no silence as huge, empty, and ugly as silence in a racing paddock. It usually means something terrible and irrevocable has happened somewhere out on the circuit. Then, slowly, bit by bit and whisper by whisper, the word filters around, and, soon enough, everybody is just helplessly hanging around like drying laundry that won't come clean and wondering what to do next. That's always the racers' way: *What do I do NEXT? What do I do NOW?* It's unbearable when there aren't any answers to those questions....

Tommy said he had to go back to the room he and Eddie were sharing to "take care of things" and call his family-somebody had to do it-and Carson offered to go with because he had all that professional experience with death and almost knew what to do. Meanwhile the word came around that the rest of the day's practice sessions were canceled-some of the racers were predictably and inexcusably upset by that-and everybody started slowly melting out of the paddock and drifting off someplace where they didn't really feel like they belonged. I know I didn't.

We had a clam bake planned at Cal's folks' house that night, and there was no choice but to go through with it since Cal had ordered these lobsters and clams flown in live from someplace in Maine and charged it to his parents' account, and there was really nothing to do but go pick them up at the little local airport or let them rot. So I busied myself building a charcoal fire out in the barbecue at what felt like the middle of the afternoon, then took the big metal lobster tin out of its barrel of dry ice, punched holes in the top like the instructions said to, and put it on the grill. It made my guts flutter that I could hear things moving and scraping around inside the tin when I did it.

Carson brought Tommy and his suitcase back to the cottage with him-we had plenty of space, and there was no reason for him to stay in the room he'd been sharing with Eddie-and we all sat down around the big oak dining room table to have dinner around eight o'clock. I remember it was dull overcast outside and just starting to spit rain.

The clams, lobsters, and corn on the cob were delicious, but there was no joy in it for anybody and it was one of the quietest dinners I've ever attended. Including meals I've eaten alone. We didn't talk about anything at all, just stared at our plates and avoided each other's eyes. A lot of the food went uneaten. But then, as the coffee and cake came around, Mary Frances suddenly slammed her palm down against the table. *"It's all so damn senseless!"* she spit out at us, her eyes sweeping the room. *"There's just no need for it!"*

The racers around the table all looked at each other, like we were trying to find a spokesman. "There's no need for anything, really," Cal offered lamely. "You just do what you have to do."

"But you don't *have* to do this," Julie told him in a sad, weary voice. "People get *killed.*"

"People get killed every day," Cal reminded her. "That's the way things are. *Everybody* gets killed eventually."

He didn't sound particularly convincing.

"But you don't have to go *looking* for it!" Mary Frances snarled. You could see she was really upset. "You're playing *'See If I Can't Be Killed'* like it's a fucking game of Russian Roulette...."

I'd never heard her use that word before. Not ever.

"No, we're bloody NOT!" Tommy said suddenly with an angry military clip to his voice. It hushed the whole table, and everybody's eyes swiveled around to meet his. They were hard and black and bright as star sapphires. "It's just not like that at all," he said softly, almost apologetically. "I mean, what's the whole bloody point of life, anyway? *Not to die?* Is that it? Well, that's pretty bloody foolish. We're all going to die. In fact, that's probably the only one true thing any of us know for certain."

"But, Jesus Christ almighty," Mary Frances shot back, "you don't have to go *chasing after it,* do you?"

Tommy glared at her. But then you could see his eyes slowly softening and the faintest little trace of a smile playing at the corners of his mouth. "Look," he said in a comforting, fatherly way, "racing is a dangerous sport. That's the way it's built. You accept that if you want to do it."

"But you can get yourself killed! Doesn't that *mean* anything to you?"

"Of course it does!" Tommy insisted with a rare crack of emotion in his voice. "In fact, I think that's the whole bloody point."

You could see Mary Frances didn't understand. None of the girls did.

Tommy thought it over for a moment, choosing his words carefully. "I suppose when you get right down to it, it's the danger-the *risk!*-that makes motor sport so different from other things. Take that element away and it's just another game. Like badminton or cricket or tiddly winks."

"But the danger is just so...so *pointless.* "

Tommy shook his head. "No, it isn't. It's a challenge. A test." He paused and thought about it a little more, and then continued in a soft, almost helpless sounding voice. "But it's more than that, really. Except for when I flew combat missions in the war, inside a racecar is the only time in my life when I feel like I bloody well know what I'm doing."

"So it's like war, then?"

"No," Tommy corrected her. "War really *is* pointless, isn't it? Racing is like the distilled-down challenge of mechanized combat-the best essence of what you can do with a decent pilot and a decent machine-but without all the bloody filth and death and political stupidity. I know what my machine should be able to do and my mission is simply to go out there and try to do it. Sometimes under strange or difficult or even terrifying conditions." Tommy took a long, slow breath and even more slowly exhaled. "When you strip everything away, I guess it's really all about grace under pressure, isn't it?"

"Yeah," Cal agreed cautiously from the other end of the table, "maybe that's it." He looked over at Mary Frances. "I never really thought all that much about why, but I've always known that doing this-and being really *good* at this!-was the most important thing in my life."

"M-me, too," Carson offered hesitantly. "Oh, d-don't get me w-wrong. I know I'll never really be any g-good at it. But just to g-get to be a part of it. To be out there t-trying my best and getting to hang around with p-people like Cal and Tommy and B-Buddy...."

"That is the other thing, isn't it," Tommy agreed. "We're our own little combat squadron, aren't we. Our own little community. We *depend* on each other, even when we're out there scrapping tooth-and-bloody-nail for the win. In fact, *especially* then." His eyes went around the table, pausing momentarily on each of the drivers. And me, too. "We take care of each other out there, don't we. We bloody well have to."

"But it's still just dumb luck if you don't get killed, isn't it?"

Tommy thought it over. "I don't think so. I mean, the odds are better than that, aren't they? And I've always felt there's an important distinction between luck and fate. Luck is a pure blind draw. The flip of a coin. The turn of a card. But fate has a bloody face on it. It can smile on you or eat you alive, but there's always some kind of meaning or irony or nobility to it...."

You could hear the rain pattering softly on the sand outside.

"....and there's something else, too," Tommy continued in a voice so low you had to strain forward to hear him. "No one on the outside would ever suspect, but it's tremendously peaceful and even serene inside a racing car. You're so wonderfully alone and isolated and consumed with what you're doing that nothing from the outside world can touch you." He let out a gentle sigh. "In fact, when things are running right and everything's going well, it's the most peaceful, comfortable place I know...."

It felt strange going back to Bridgehampton the next morning.

Everything looked the same as the day before except there were tons more people on account of it was Saturday and Race Day and thousands of fans had flooded in from every point on the compass to watch the races. But it was like all the racers and crews and armband people were sleep walking through the paddock with their feet barely touching the ground. At least until the engines fired for the Sagaponack Trophy Race at around 10:30 ayem-including Carson's MG and Cal's Jowett Jupiter-and the cars buzzed out onto the circuit. With all the problems in practice on Friday, grid positions were pretty much drawn out of a hat, and The Fates Tommy told us about the night before decided to put Carson Flegley on the very front row and Cal's Jowett well towards the back. "M-make sure somebody takes a p-picture!" Carson sputtered excitedly as he strapped on his helmet.

The race ran true to form after a few laps of shuffling and reshuffling. That Navy Lieutenant/Dentist Dr. Richard Thompson carved his way into the lead in his Porsche-driving like the dickens, believe me!-followed by four other Porsches at a respectful distance. Cal somehow managed to fight and finesse his way through all the MGs and the slower Porsches to take a solid, lonely, and more than respectable sixth overall. Which was really a hell of a performance, no lie! And Carson naturally plummeted down the field for the first few laps and then slid backwards more slowly from there, finally coming home twelfth out of eighteen and doing (for Carson, anyway) a pretty decent job.

Next up was the Mecox Trophy Race for modified smallbore cars, and it was an absolute runaway for Phil Walters in Briggs Cunningham's OSCA. In fact, he went so quickly he was invited to enter it in the big-bore Bridgehampton Cup feature race later that afternoon just to see what it could do. Which figured to be plenty on a tight, narrow, bumpy little circuit like Bridgehampton. A guy named Tom Luck from Philadelphia flipped his Siata during the race and had to be taken to Southhampton Hospital with a busted collarbone, but it wasn't real serious and fortunately happened way around on the other side of the circuit so the girls didn't have to see it.

During lunch I saw Tommy Edwards in deep conversation with that Lee Chapman guy who had the white Le Mans Allard, and I guess Lee was having a few second thoughts about running the car after what happened to Eddie Dearborn. Not that he was frightened or anything, but he'd drawn a front row starting position and didn't feel all that much like racing and no question a brute like an Allard was a real handful around a claustrophobic little circuit like Bridgehampton. In fact, there was a lot of loose talk around the paddock that day to the effect that Allards were "killer cars" and that Eddie Dearborn was dead because of it. I mean, didn't all the Allards withdraw from the race at Grand Island the year before on account of they were uncontrollable?

Tommy thought it was all rubbish, of course, and quickly accepted when Lee Chapman asked him if he wanted to drive. They fixed it up so Tommy would wear Lee's helmet and goggles, and, since Lee always raced with a bandana over his face to protect against dust and stones, they were pretty sure nobody would be the wiser. Like I said, Lee was an Englishman, same as Tommy, and he thought all that S.C.M.A. license suspension stuff was a bunch of hooey. "Some of these people are as soft as bloody grapes," was the way he put it. And good for him, too.

Meanwhile Big Ed didn't get in on account of there was only one slot to fill with an alternate-the place Eddie Dearborn would've occupied-and it went to a longtime club member in another Jaguar. Which didn't upset Big Ed one bit, since he was still pretty shook up and didn't feel much like racing.

So three o'clock rolled around and the big bore cars lined up for the Bridgehampton Cup race with Tommy masquerading as Lee Chapman in the white Le Mans Allard on the front row-right next to another Allard-but just behind was Creighton Pendleton's 4.1 Ferrari (the engine of which had now been massaged by the Muscatelli brothers to be exactly like the one he'd driven in Mexico) who would no doubt be a factor. But a lot of the smart money was on Phil Walters in that little 1380cc OSCA that won the Mecox Trophy race earlier in the day. It seemed perfectly suited to a tight, bumpy layout where the bigger cars couldn't really put their power down. He'd turned a couple laps at over eighty-three miles per hour car during the smallbore race, and that was easily as fast as any of the bigger cars had gone.

Tommy planted his foot and leaped into an early lead at the first flutter of green, but he ran into brake problems almost immediately-we hadn't thought to adjust and bleed them because the whole deal came together at the very last second-and he was having to pump them to get the pressure up from about the third lap on. Finally the pedal went all the way to the floor and he had to scoot up the escape road to keep from hurting Lee Chapman's car ("If it were mine, I might've tried to make the bloody corner. But I'm pretty certain I would've bounced off a few things, and that's just not the sort of thing one ought to do with someone else's car."). With Tommy out of the picture, Creighton Pendleton swept easily into the lead and looked to be pretty secure up on the point until you noticed how quickly Phil Walters and the OSCA were coming up through the pack. I had a watch on it and figured that he'd catch the Ferrari with at least two laps to go, and so I told Cal and Carson that we ought to batten down the hatches and get ready for one hell of an exciting finish. And that's when all the red flags came out and all the racecars pulled over and switched off and everything went ugly quiet again around the circuit.

Turned out it was Skippy Welcher. Again. But this time even I had to say it wasn't entirely his fault. Sure, he ran himself out of brakes again, shot up the escape road, and smashed his C-Type head-on into a fence. So what's new? But it wasn't his fault and there was nothing he could do about the four spectators standing there in the middle of the escape road, watching the cars go by in a place clearly marked as NO SPECTATOR TERRITORY. The Skipper's car scattered them like bowling pins, and it was just dumb luck that nobody got killed. As it was, there was a fractured leg and a crushed heel and severe lacerations and all four (plus The Skipper) had to be taken to the Southhampton Hospital. And that took quite a bit of time seeing as how there was only one ambulance left on hand since the other one had taken the guy with the busted collarbone to the hospital a little earlier. And that's about when the police and the race stewards put their heads together and agreed that we'd all done quite enough damage for one day-*G'wan home folks. There's nothing more t'see here*-and the balance of the Bridgehampton Cup race was summarily cancelled.

I remember we stood around for quite a long time after that, loading up our gear without saying much of anything and trying to figure out what to do next. In the end, Big Ed decided to drive Rhonda home-or wherever she was going-in the XK-120 while I took Tommy with Julie and me in the Eldorado convert. It was a very quiet ride, and I was glad the Caddy had such a good radio to fill up some of the emptiness. Even if none of us were in much of a mood to hear *"How Much is That Doggie in the Window."* But then they played *"Ebb Tide,"* and that seemed to fit a lot better. I dropped Tommy off at some swanky men's club in Manhattan where Eddie Dearborn stayed when he was in the city and took Julie back to her mom's place in Passaic and then went back to the shop to unload Big Ed's Caddy.

The phone was ringing when I got there.

It was Spud. "Well, Buddy," he said gleefully, "believe it or not, we're on the damn dance floor!"

"That's nice," I told him.

"Yessiree," he bubbled into the receiver. "Sammy went out and cut a 135 and change with that old turd. 'Course, we gotta sweat it out through bump day tomorrow, but I figure it's gonna hold up!"

"That's really great," I said without enthusiasm.

"It sure as hell is, isn't it!"

"Yeah. It sure as hell is."

"We're in th'gosh darn Indianapolis 500!" he yelped into the other end of the line. *"I just can't believe it!"*

"That's really great," I repeated. "It really is."

"Say," Spud said slowly, "is something the matter with you?"

So I told him about everything that had happened at Bridgehampton. It seemed to take a long time to get it all out. And I'm glad he couldn't see my face, because it was all I could do to keep from bawling.

As you can imagine, the hot topic of conversation all over the sportycar world was about the mess up at Bridgehampton and how it would likely be The Last Straw as far as racing on public roads was concerned. The New York legislature had already passed a law prohibiting racing on state highways after the terrible accident at Watkins Glen the year before, and the only way they'd been able to swing the deal at Bridgehampton was by running on county roads rather than state highways. Plus it helped that only rich, privileged types could afford to play around at sportycar racing or have summer places out at the end of Long Island, and those sort of people in general regard The Law as something that may or may not apply to them as they see fit. But now the shit was surely going to hit the fan-there was even a big, indignant, self-righteous, and thoroughly sanctimonious piece about it in the *Times*-and people like Cam Argetsinger and the local Chamber of Commerce types were fighting like hell to keep the races going in Watkins Glen by moving them up to a new and not nearly so dangerous (or exciting!) farm-country circuit well outside of town where the only likely casualties would be splattered bugs and a few unlucky field varmints.

But there were alternatives. Thanks to cigar chomping, sports car-loving, head man/commander-in-chief General Curtis LeMay of the Strategic Air Command, the S.C.M.A.'s 1953 race schedule already included quite a few events on the flat, safe, isolated, and sadly featureless concrete runways of S.A.C. air bases in Tampa, Florida; Austin, Texas; Omaha, Nebraska; Everett, Washington; Columbus, Ohio; Reno, Nevada; Albany, Georgia; and Riverside, California. Not to mention two other '53 events that were lined up at Naval Air Stations. How the good general managed to pull this off was quite remarkable, since certain dimbulb taxpayers might easily have taken offense to the notion that their hard-earned tax dollars should be used to pay U.S. servicemen to close down Top Secret air defense locations in order to put car races on for the benefit of a bunch of rich, black sheep playboys. But General LeMay had this idea that the spectator gate would go into a special fund to create "hobby room" workshops on the bases where his men could pursue healthy, constructive outside interests like taking care of the general's collection of sports cars. Or their own, if they could afford one. He also had this theory (which Tommy Edwards wholeheartedly endorsed) that driving in competition was a lot like dogfighting in fighter planes-that it called for a lot of the same command skills, judgement, and coolness under pressure-and so he strongly encouraged his pilots to take part in order to keep their reflexes sharp and hone their talents. Although the truth is not too many of them on Air Force pay could afford it.

The good part about airport racing was that the crowds could be kept well back and, airport runways being what they are, there wasn't much out there to run into except other cars and the pylons and haybales and such the armband people set out to mark the course. The bad part was that the tracks were all flat and featureless as an ironing board, didn't have so much as a blade of grass for shade or scenery, and generally baked under the heat of the summer sun like a pancake griddle in the desert. As you can imagine, this created a lot of all-purpose moaning and groaning throughout the S.C.M.A. membership about the loss of the beloved "natural" road courses and what to do about it. And the obvious answer was to go out and *build* a "natural" road circuit that would stay true to the sweeping, swooping, uphill-downhill lefts and rights of a favorite country road. Only without all the rgular country road hazards like ditches and telephone poles and trees and old stone bridge abutments to run into. Not to mention permanent fences all the way around to keep spectators a safe distance away, and especially doing it all on private land where you could pretty much do whatever the hell you wanted and thumb your nose at the local state legislature while you were at it.

But that kind of thing took time-not to mention a huge pile of money and a whole lot of organizing and coordinating-and we saw the first real evidence of what was coming when Big Ed, Cal, and Carson and me went up to the little S.C.M.A. regional event at Thompson Speedway the following weekend. Personally, I wasn't real keen on going, on account of I had all sorts of work backed up at the shop and, while Raymond was trustworthy as an old coon hound-say

Barney, for example-he was not exactly what you could call a self-starter. Or finisher. And, speaking of Barney, I worried about him getting a little too chummy with customers' legs if I wasn't around to shoo him off. Especially since Old Man Finzio got such a kick out of it and tried to encourage him by stapling pictures of good looking female Irish Setters and Golden Retrievers in appealing, suggestive poses over the rug Barney laid on when he wasn't leaping fences to service Pomeranians or rummaging through favorite garbage cans around the neighborhood. Plus Butch was all pissed off at Old Man Finzio over something or other (not that this was particularly unusual) and Tater had managed to run his Crosley into the back of a customer's Buick when he got a little too confident with the brakes, then borrowed another customer's Chrysler to take the Crosley's radiator in to have it fixed and got sideswiped by an egg truck driven by some young farm kid who didn't have insurance. So I had a lot of stuff to pay for all at once-not to mention the regular payroll blues that rolled around sure as death and taxes every Friday afternoon-and not near enough regular customer cash flowing in on account of I wasn't getting my usual amount of work out because I was off fooling around someplace at the damn races. Or that's the way it seemed, anyways.

And laid over the top of it all like a tasty shit frosting was the fact that my wedding to Julie was coming up in one more week and so I had a ton of family stuff to do and rings to buy and a priest to meet with and a tux to rent (not to mention making sure all the groom's men got theirs) and a rehearsal dinner to attend and a bachelor party to endure and then how the heck was I going to sneak away for a honeymoon in Cape Cod with Julie when all of a sudden the damn wolf was scratching at the door and I needed to be there to take care of it. Plus Julie had been acting kind of strange and distant in the aftermath of Bridgehampton-not that I really blamed her-and I felt like part of it was that she was starting to get the jitters about getting married, too.

I know I was.

And it only got worse when I asked her if she maybe wanted to go up to Thompson with me. She was ice cold to the idea-dry ice, even-and looked at me like I had to be certifiably insane to even think about it.

So, for the very first time, I was headed off for a race weekend I really didn't much want to go to. If I wanted to be anywhere at all that weekend, it was surely down in the pits at the Indianapolis 500 helping out Sammy and Spud. But instead I was headed up to the northeast corner of Connecticut to Thompson Speedway, which wasn't much more than a little podunk local oval track where two-bit stock car guys ran on Friday and Saturday nights. But it was a place to race, and the New York Region of the S.C.M.A. had been coming up there for years for time trials, sprints, and goofy car games like races where the slowest car was declared the winner or where you had to drive through an obstacle course backwards. It all sounded pretty lame to me, and I knew without thinking that Charlie Priddle had to be involved.

But Big Ed was all keen on going, especially seeing as how it was the first S.C.M.A. event he was actually going to be allowed to enter and run, and watching Charlie Priddle eat his liver about it would be worth the trip alone. Plus he wasn't planning to be alone, since he once again planned to have the brassy haired, big bosomed Miss Gum Smack of 1953 all over him like a bad skin rash for the entire weekend. The two of them were riding up in the Jag this time, so Carson and Cal took the TD and I got stuck making the trip solo in the Eldorado. Not that it's such a bad way to travel. I guess Cal had to give the Jowett back following his fine drive at Bridgehampton, and the story I got was that the guy actually sold that car to somebody who'd seen it run. But then there was some kind of major (not to mention highly timely and convenient!) garage fire at his warehouse and all of a sudden the guy wasn't stuck with a serious oversupply of unsold Jowett Jupiters anymore.

Hey, things happen, right?

Thompson Speedway was made up of two paved ovals-a quarter-mile and a half-mile, one inside the other-and you could see construction work was underway to add a misshapen ribbon of blacktop leading off the backstraight of the outer oval and out briefly into the countryside to turn it into a sort of half-assed road circuit out of it in time for the big S.C.M.A. National meeting scheduled for Labor Day Weekend. But it was nowhere near done, and so we spent all of Saturday morning watching dull, one-car-at-a-time standing-start time trials around the inner and outer ovals. If you ask me, it was pretty lame compared with real racing. Not to mention boring as hell. About the most interesting part was watching the person who waved the green and checkered flags, which was once again Sally Enderle of the breathtaking shorts and halter top. She was there alone, too, since apparently Creighton Pendleton looked down his nose at this sort of thing. And for once I agreed with him.

Skippy Welcher was on hand, of course, but driving the much abused, ex-everything XK-120 that he'd sold to and bought back from Big Ed seeing as how his C-Type was still laid up having its front end rearranged following the crash at Bridgehampton. That put him and Big Ed in the same class, and I didn't much like the look of that at all. Carson was nice enough to offer Cal a share of the driving in his MG, and it didn't surprise me a bit that Cal copped quickest time among the MGs. But not by much, since the cars started from a dead stop and it was nothing more than foot-to-the-floor acceleration all the way through the first corner and down the backstraight. Then you had to back off-a little or a lot, your choice-for the final turn before the checkered flag.

What a thrill, right?

By lunchtime nothing had broken, so we just hung around not doing much of anything except trying to find the Indianapolis 500 on the radio. But it was hard to do up in that particular corner of Connecticut. We finally located a station out of Providence way down at the end of the dial that at least had race updates every fifteen or twenty minutes-if you could make it out between the crackling and the static-but about all they talked about was how Bill Vukovich and the Fuel Injection Special were pretty much running away from everybody. Then there must've been a cloud shift or wind change or something over Providence and we lost the signal completely. Damn.

Meanwhile, at Thompson Speedway, they'd started up with the backwards slalom runs, pylon obstacle course, and Australian Pursuit races on the afternoon schedule. Those last were actually kind of fun. They'd start four cars spaced out evenly around the track, and when the beautiful Miss Sally Enderle fired a starter's gun into the air, they'd all take off lickety-split and start chasing each other around the track. If another car passed you, you had to drop out, and the race was over when there was only one car left. As fate would have it, Big Ed and The Skipper wound up in the same group and I was a little worried about what might happen, but, fortunately, they were about equally lousy drivers and that really quick Walt Hansgen guy was in with them and easily passed them both before they ever got close to each other. For which I was thankful.

By the end of the day I still had no idea what'd happened at Indianapolis, and it was about eating me up inside. Then Big Ed had the bright idea of calling up one of the news services in New York and pretending we were some little small town newspaper whose wire service machine was down with the flu. I watched Big Ed listening intently into the receiver and scribbling some incomprehensible brand of shorthand on the edge of a phone book, and then his face suddenly spread out in a pleasantly amazed smile. "Yer not gonna believe this," he beamed. "The little sonofabitch finished ninth."

"You're kidding!"

"Like hell I am."

"Boy, that's really something, isn't it. Ninth overall at the biggest God Damn race in the world!" I was happy as hell for Sammy and Spud, and really disappointed that I hadn't been down there to be a part of it instead of up at this two-bit S.C.M.A. time trial in Connecticut. Hell, if I'd been there with them, who knows? Maybe they could've finished eighth. Or even seventh.

I felt like I'd let them down, if you want the truth of it.

And maybe cheated a little bit, too.

Come evening there was a big weenie-and-bean and barbecue party over at some S.C.M.A. bigwig's Gentleman Farmer spread a few miles away, and it was your usual intimate little catered gathering for seventy or eighty close personal friends out in the yard beside his horse barns-*watch where you step!*-complete with hayrides and a bonfire and a fiddle band and all the food you could eat and beer you could drink. It must be nice to be able to afford that sort of thing. I bet you don't have to be nearly so nice to people in order to make friends. Then I found out it was actually Skippy Welcher's place (or one of his places, anyway) and I began to understand and appreciate why he had such godawful suck within the club. I guess he'd been throwing this particular party for years whenever the S.C.M.A. came up to run at Thompson, and everybody always enjoyed the heck out of it.

It's amazing what money can buy.

Anyhow, I was just hanging around all by my lonesome at the far end of the fence with a half-eaten sandwich in one hand and a half-empty beer in the other-my fourth or fifth, I think, but I couldn't swear to it-when who should come casually wandering my way but the beautiful Sally Enderle. She'd never done that before. I remember it was dark except for the flicker off the firelight over by the barn and believe it or not she came right up to me with such a huge, friendly smile plastered across her face that it made me look over my shoulder to see if there was maybe somebody behind me she genuinely wanted to talk to. But we were alone. "So, how are things going with you?" she asked like we were deep, dear old friends.

"Uhh, fine, I guess."

"I saw you at Bridgehampton. But you never came over and said 'hello.'" There was something wrong here and I knew it. Especially when I saw her starting to twirl her hair around her finger. That's always a danger sign.

"Well, uh, see, I was kinda *busy,* y'know?" She smiled and kind of cocked her head over to the side so I could get a little better look down her top. Geez, was she ever *gorgeous.*

"I saw you walking around with those *girls* all weekend," she said coyly.

"Uh, well, two of 'em are my sisters, see...."

"I see. And the *other* one?" She was using that same teasing, taunting, dangerously singsong voice I'd crumbled for at Elkhart Lake.

"Well, umm, that's sort of my girlfriend. Julie Finzio...."

"Your girlfriend? Really?" her eyebrows arched upwards. "I heard it was more like you were *engaged* or something." She pulled in a little closer. "So tell me. Is that true?"

"Well, uhh, yeah. It's true. In fact, we're, umm, sort of plannin' on gettin' married next week."

"Reaaalllllly," she breathed, stretching it out like taffy. Then she kind of gently reached out and wrapped her thumbs through my belt loops, flashed those luminous, catlike eyes right up at me and breathed, *"You know, Buddy, I've never forgotten about that night at Elkhart Lake...."*

I felt her hand slip down and brush across my zipper. There was something there for her to feel, too. No question about it. Sure, I knew she was toying with me. Just trying to see how well the old equipment worked, I guess. Maybe even looking for some droll form of amusement to fill up an otherwise boring evening when there was no Creighton Pendletons around. And maybe even break up a marriage that hadn't even happened yet in the process, which would doubtless make for a charming snippet of gossip to tell all her high class friends. "Look," I said, kind of backing away, "maybe this isn't such a good idea, you know?"

Her face went hard and cold as a marble tombstone. "No, maybe it isn't," she snapped, her nostrils flaring. Then she spun on her heel and stalked off towards the barn. And, as she moved away, a single bright, shining thought shimmered through my mind like the effervescent orange-red trail of a skyrocket.

Jesus, she had a great ass.

Come Sunday I was minor-league hungover and there were even more boring time trials and dumbass "novelty events" at Thompson Speedway all morning. Then finally, after lunch, we had the big feature events of the entire weekend: four-car, wheel-to-wheel sprint races around a sort of half-assed "road circuit" made up of pieces of both the inner and outer ovals. Once again fate and similar cars put Big Ed and The Skipper in the same group, and this time all my worst fears were realized as they screeched away from the starting line and headed into that first sweeping corner side by side. Much to my amazement, they made it all the way through, wheel-to-wheel and door-to-door with neither one giving an inch. But they were gaining speed all the time down the back straightaway, and there was no question that somebody was going to have to give way before they got to the next turn. But of course that could never happen if you knew anything about the two guys involved. So neither one backed off and they both arrived at the next corner going *way* too fast to make it through. Big Ed was on the inside and so naturally he lost it and skidded right up into Skippy just as The Skipper was losing it and skidding right up into hay bales the armband people had piled up against the low concrete wall around the outside of the turn. Thankfully the layout was short and tight enough so they weren't going all that fast-I'd guess they were both still in second gear-but it was messy as hell and there was a lot of tire squealing followed by ugly crunching, scraping, screeching noises of the chalk-on-a-blackboard variety followed by a final, thudding *KA-WHUMPF!* and an explosion of dust and flying hay at the end.

As you can imagine, Big Ed and The Skipper were out of their cars and squared off nose-to-nose (or more accurately nose-to-chest hairs, since Big Ed towered over The Skipper like the damn Empire State Building) with Skippy all bright red and hollering at the top of his lungs and shaking his fist under Big Ed's nose and showering spit in all directions. But Big Ed was looking even redder, growling and snorting and cursing right back at him, his hands clenching and unclenching menacingly at his sides. Lord only knows how he resisted the urge to grab that little jerkoff by the neck and squeeze his head clean off like pus out of a pimple. Fortunately a few armband types showed up about then and maneuvered in between them before anybody started swinging. And, to be honest, the damage wasn't really serious on either car. Just a few dents and scrapes in the sheet metal. Like I said, they weren't going all that fast, and Lord knows neither of those two Jags was exactly a stranger to body filler. Fact is, it turned out to be about the most entertaining thing that happened all day. Especially if you lucked into a ringside seat.

Back in Passaic, I right away called the little Greek guy who owned the body shop to see about getting Big Ed's Jag straightened out. Again. And then it was time to really get down and concentrate on the work in the shop and try to unbury myself and maybe even get a little ahead before Julie and me went on our honeymoon. But of course that was next to impossible on account of all the wedding stuff going on and interrupting me every five minutes or so. To be honest, I really didn't give much of a shit about what sort of green vegetable we were going to have or which lady from the church choir was going to sing the *Ave Maria* or who the hell sat next to whom at the reception party. But it was like The Most Important Thing In The World to Julie and her mom. And my mom. And my sisters. And all of Julie's girlfriends from the Doggy Shake. And, in some greater sense, probably every last female person on the planet, if they'd only known about it. In fact, I was noticing that the closer the wedding got, the further away I felt from Julie. I mean, we just didn't have any time to ourselves. Or at least none that wasn't chock full of little odds and ends we had to take care of or things we just *had* to do. I was starting to feel like a damn passenger in my own life, you know?

Or maybe I was just getting cold feet?

At least Spud called to give me the blow-by-blow on the 500, and it turned out to be mostly a case of Sammy just hanging around and keeping his nose clean and going as fast as he dared in one of the slowest cars to make the field at the Speedway that year. Plus they botched up a couple pit stops-*damn, that never would've happened if I'd been there!*-and Sammy had to soft pedal on the engine and tires because it was terribly hot. In fact, it was so hot that a driver named Carl Scarborough from Clarkston, Michigan, actually died after the race from heat exhaustion. Can you believe it?

But Sammy Speed soldiered on, slinging that old upright sled through the corners and pounding it down the straightaways with a firm but sympathetic touch. And the car took care of him. In fact, it wasn't a bad car at all. Just an old one. They slipped all the way to the bottom of the field after a first pit stop where everything went wrong and greenhorn crew people were tripping all over each other and running into stuff and damn near setting the car on fire with the fuel rig. But then things settled down and, slowly but surely, Sammy started climbing up towards where he belonged. That took over an hour, but he did it. And then he started climbing even higher. He was in a groove now, just like he had been in Big Ed's Jag at Sebring. Meanwhile the heat was taking its toll and a lot of guys were retiring or handing over to relief drivers. Like Carl Scarborough did on lap seventy, just before they rushed him to the hospital. But not Sammy Speed. No, sir. In fact, he got all the way up to sixth place at one point, but then they had a wheel nut jam up all catty-wumpus on a pit stop and Spud had to grab the guy by the shoulders and throw him out of the way so he could put it right before the threads got hopelessly buggered and put them out. It cost Sammy more than a lap. But he put it behind him and kept soldiering on like you have to in a race like Indy, going right back into his same, smooth, smart rhythm like nothing had happened. And, as more cars coughed and broke and died and drivers got worn down so far they busted their cars or choked and spun, Sammy kept working his way back up again. He was still climbing when the checker fell.

Ninth overall at the Indy 500!

That was something you could be really be proud of, no lie.

The wedding rehearsal at St. Jude's was scheduled for six o'clock sharp Thursday evening with a rehearsal dinner immediately following at Pete and Pasquale's Palermo Room Pizzeria and Pasta Palace over on Polk Street that you got almost free for nothing if you rented a room to have your reception there and particularly if you invited a lot of people who liked to drink hard liquor, since only beer and wine were included free. I figured it would be nice if I maybe brought Julie a big bunch of roses, you know? But imagine my surprise when I opened the cash register and found nothing but dust and a few cobwebs. And I knew right away what had happened. No question Old Man Finzio had scooped the drawer to rent his tux and maybe even buy us a wedding present, and didn't leave so much as a buffalo nickel behind. It really pissed me off that he'd beaten me to it, and it also worried me a little since I had a payroll to meet on Friday and nothing much on hand to do it with. Then who should show up just as I was getting ready to leave but that asshole Skippy Welcher and his ex-everything-and-then-some XK-120. *"Your friend Mr. Baumstein is responsible for that,"* he screeched, pointing at the two bashed-in front fenders that made his Jag look like it was puckering up for a little kiss. *"And I intend for him to fix it!"* He pounded his fist into his palm for emphasis and you could see he was pretty upset on account of his facial muscles were running all over the place like a wash bucket full of mice.

I explained as how he really needed to take that up with Big Ed, and also that, seeing as how it was the night of the rehearsal and dinner and such for my wedding, I really had to be on my way. And to make it clear, I started to close the door between the shop and the office.

"YOU'RE NOT GOING ANYWHERE, SONNY!" Skippy yelled, grabbing the doorhandle on the other side and pulling it towards him. Well, I'd had just about enough of his shit, so I braced my foot against the wall and yanked back the other way. And of course that's when the damn knob came clear off in his hand, sending The Skipper tumbling ass-over-teakettle backwards over the lift and depositing him in a crumpled heap in a patch of well-used oil-dri. It actually would've been funny except that the door-and it's one of those thick oak jobs, too-flew right back in my face, smashing hard into my cheek and forehead and damn near knocking me cold. *"I'LL SUE YOU FOR THIS!"* Skippy screamed from the greasy pool of gearlube he was sitting in. *"DO YOU HEAR ME, YOUNG MAN? I'LL SUE!"*

Jesus, they could hear him on Staten Island.

About that time Milton Fitting appeared at the door, looking even more dumbfounded than usual to see his boss planted ass-first on the floor. Apparently Skippy had him waiting by the curb in one of his other cars. "Look," I pleaded, "I really gotta get outta here tonight, Skippy. Really I do. Just pull the damn car in and leave the keys, okay? I'll figure something out."

"NOT UNTIL YOU PROMISE TO FIX IT!" he demanded from the general direction of the floor drain while shaking a pint-sized fist in the air.

"Yeah. Sure. Fine," I told hiom. "I'll fix your damn car."

"AND BAUMSTEIN'S GOING TO PAY FOR IT, TOO!"

"Sure. Anything you say." I could feel blood running down my cheek.

"Very well," Skippy said in a strangely dignified voice. Especially for somebody sitting in a puddle of grease and anti-freeze. "Very well indeed."

I was already fifteen minutes late for the rehearsal by the time I got back to my apartment to shower and shave and change into that spiffy blue Brooks Brothers suit Julie'd bought me for Christmas. And what a shock when I looked in the mirror. Jesus, I looked like one of Rocky Marciano's sparring partners! There was a big, ugly gash in my forehead, a purplish bruise on my cheek, and all the makings of a World Class shiner around my eye. Shit! I did my best to stop the bleeding and cleaned it up as much as I could, then jumped in and out of the shower (only using soap on the parts of my body that would show with my suit on) and then rushed down the stairs while trying to put my pants, shoes, and socks on along the way. Even so, I knew I was late enough to be in trouble with everybody from God on down before I even left the apartment.

And it wasn't even my fault, you know?

Sure enough I walked into a solid wall of ice inside the chapel at St. Jude's. Hell, even Cal was there ahead of me! And the worst part was that Julie acted like I'd somehow showed up forty minutes late, split open my own forehead, bruised my own cheek, and blackened my own eye on purpose just to spoil our wedding. Can you believe it? And nothing I could say seemed to help. Her mom was a real peach about it, too, *tsk-tsking* at her wristwatch and looking my shiner and then back over at Julie with one of those infuriating little *I told you so* future in-law smirks. And that's the woman we were going to live just an ear-to-the-carpet downstairs from, you know? There wasn't a thing I could do about that, either. So all I could do was robot-walk my way through the rest of our wedding rehearsal like some kind of mechanized Apology Dispenser, whispering *'Scuse me'* and *'Geez, sorry I'm late'* into every passing earlobe while every eye stared back at me like a locked closet door. Boy, did I feel like a creep.

And then it got worse.

We got to the part where Julie came down the aisle on Old Man Finzio's arm-I mean, she really didn't have anybody else, you know?-and he was hacking and coughing until he just about doubled up and had to sit down, and right then this little lightbulb came on for everybody that he was most likely not the best choice in the world to walk Julie down the aisle. But we had to just file that away at the time because *the show must go on,* and when Julie finally got up there beside me on the altar, I could see in her eyes that she was still fuming like hell. And not just about me showing up late or looking like I'd been worked over by one of Frank Costello's favorite henchmen. *"I can't believe you told him!"* she hissed into my ear when we leaned forward for the big payoff "and you may now kiss the bride" part.

I looked at her with one of those patented male "what the hell are you talking about?" expressions, and she responded with one of those sneering, cynical, women-only-need-apply "you know perfectly well what I'm talking about" looks that make the blood in your veins fizz like seltzer and the toes curl under inside your socks. But I couldn't say anything, because we were up on the altar with everybody looking at us and applauding and stuff, and it wasn't until we were walking back up the aisle together, arm in arm with everybody's eyes on us, that I could whisper back, *"What the hell are you talking about? I never said anything about anything to anybody."*

"Hmpf," she snorted back. And that was about it as far as an answer was concerned. Obviously she thought-or, correct that, she knew for absolute, rock-solid *certain*-that I'd told Cal all the grisly, glorious details about our night on the beach up at his folks' place in East Quogue. Which of course I never did. I mean, all I ever did was blush, you know?

But sometimes that's enough.

"Julie. Sweetheart." I whimpered as soon as we were safely out in the vestibule. *"I never said anything to anybody. Honest I didn't."*

She looked back at me with eyes as cold and clear and hard as the diamond on her finger. *"And it wasn't enough that you went braggin' to all your guy friends, either. You had to tell your frickin' sister, too!"*

Jesus, was I ever in trouble.

And I hadn't even *done* anything, you know?

Right away I got the feeling that this was going to be a truly unforgettable evening. In all the worst possible ways. And naturally I pulled Cal aside first chance I got to see just what the hell he'd said, and he gave me this typically blank Guy Look like he had no idea on earth what I was talking about. "I was just trying to make a little conversation to fill up the time because you were so damn late. That's all I was doing."

"But what did you *say?"*

"Nothing!" he insisted. "Unless maybe she took it the wrong way when I made some little wisecrack about this being maybe your *second* rehearsal for the wedding."

Yep. That would've done it.

"You *asshole!"* I snarled, grappling at his lapels.

"Hey, take it easy, huh? I mean, I was just trying to make a little harmless conversation is all…."

I turned around and stalked off to keep from socking him one. I mean, he was my best man, you know? Plus it wouldn't look too good if we *both* showed up with fresh shiners on Saturday.

As if that wasn't enough, I could feel a lot of strange, unidentified, free-form agitation floating around the wedding party, and most of it seemed to be between my old man and Julie's mom. I'd catch them staring at each other so hard their eyeballs were almost vibrating, but then, as soon as the other person so much as glanced in their direction, they'd quickly look away like little kids do when they get caught doing something naughty. I could tell there was something going on there, you know? And I swear I had no interest whatsoever in finding out what it was. Not that I wasn't curious. But it struck me immediately as the kind of thing I was better off not knowing about. Which meant, of course, that it was something I was unwittingly and inevitably destined to find out.

About the only person who didn't seem mad as hell at everybody was that literary philosopher communist creep Oliver Cromwell from N.Y.U. by way of Greenwich Village that my sister Mary Frances had meet up with us at the restaurant. He obviously got quite a charge out of hanging around with somebody who'd been in an actual fistfight. Probably because he'd never been in one himself. "It gives you a *valiant* look!" he proclaimed like some kind of half-assed Shakespearean oracle, and right on the spot I felt like fixing him up with a valiant look of his own. The truth is I didn't like this guy at all, and it really gnawed at me that Mary Frances apparently did. Otherwise why on earth would she bring him around to meet the family? And especially to a wedding, which is a tactic universally employed by single female types as a way of dropping a none-too-subtle matrimonial hint to a typically thick-skulled and insensitive person of the male persuasion.

Plus it made me sick inside when I thought about what I was pretty damn sure the sonofabitch was getting away with when the lights went out, if you catch my drift. Not with *my* sister, dammit! And it was even worse because Ollie'd been hard at work on his new book-which he went on and on and *on* about-concerning the classic, age-old struggle between the classes and how the new *inelligentsia* were destined to awaken the hearts and minds of the working class and spur them on to revolt against their *bourgeois* oppressors and seize control of their own destiny. Or maybe it was their future. Or maybe it was one for each hand: future in one fist, destiny in the other. But-and here was the really *fascinating* part!-he'd done it all in novel form based loosely on the ancient

Greek legend of Pygmalion. Best as I could make out (after you stripped away a few fifty-pound sacks of bullshit, anyway) it was about this benign and enlightened man of letters who takes a poor, dull, and thoroughly unenlightened working class girl under his wing and, through the application of ceaseless, selfless effort, endless hours of tutoring, and occasional mainline injections of pomposity, evolves her into a creature of admirable knowledge, inner wisdom, and shimmering intellectual brilliance.

He made it up himself, too.

And of course he was writing it all in Esperanto so that future generations could enjoy, appreciate, and learn from it. Why, even his everyday conversation was peppered with words and phrases in Esperanto. There was just no way he could help it, you know? Especially when he stood up to make a toast. "When Mary first brought these two to my humble abode," he began grandly, "I could see they were very much in *amo,* and that this wedding was surely *okazi."* Oliver let his eyes sweep around the table like a searchlight beacon, drained his glass, and threw it dramatically into the corner, where I guess it was supposed to shatter into a million glittering pieces. Only Pete and Pasquale had been in the restaurant business long enough to know that you're better off with the thicker variety of glassware that you don't have to replace quite so often, and so it kind of bounced off with a hollow *"thunk!"* and rolled under the table. It did leave a nice stain on the wallpaper, though.

"What the hell was he talking about?" I whispered to Mary Frances.

"He just said it was obvious you two were very much in love and that your marriage was meant to be."

"Oh."

Oliver leaned around both of us to look directly at Julie. I could smell he'd had a little something to drink. "From the first time I saw you, my dear, I was impressed by your beauty, your charm, and especially your *mamoj."*

"What did that mean?" I whispered after he sat down.

"It means he likes her tits." Mary Frances whispered back.

Boy, did I ever want to pop this guy one in the kisser.

I had my chance, too, when we wound up alone together just outside the door of the men's room. He was just coming out and I was just going in, and I kind of latched onto his sleeve and pulled him over against the wall. "I beg your pardon," Oliver said down his nose, only slurring his words a little on account of he'd been busy diving into the deep end of the wine carafes with my beet-faced boozer of a brother-in-law, Roy.

"Listen," I said, "I know it's really none of my business, but I'd kinda like t'know what your, umm, *intentions* are with Mary Frances." I looked up into his eyes and it was like he was peering at me through a microscope. Like I was a diseased gnat's testicle or some particularly amusing species of algae.

"Of course it's your business," he said like it was none of my business at all. And then the lecture began. "At first, we were just acquaintances. Then we became good friends. After that, your sister grew to become my *amatino*," he regarded me with the most condescending of smiles, "and now, with the passage of time, that relationship has blossomed in the fullest possible way. She has become my *kromvirino*."

With that he turned on his heel and unsteadily walked away. I wasn't sure exactly what he'd said, but I had a pretty good inkling of what it meant. And I didn't like it one little bit.

I went into the john and, as I stood there trying to make out the painted over graffiti just over the flush handle *("What are you looking up here for? The joke is in your hand!")* who should walk in but my old man. He'd had a few snorts himself, too. You could tell. There were only two urinals so he had to come over and stand there right beside me. We tried to ignore each other like guys always do in those situations, but then I heard myself say, "There isn't anything, you know, *going on* between you and Julie's mom, is there?"

He took in a long, slow breath and pulled his zipper down. It'd gotten so quiet that the sound echoed off the tiles.

He didn't say a word until he was done. "Well," he said as he zipped up, "I think we maybe went out a few times before I met your mother."

Instantly I was falling down a deep, black hole. *"Oh, my God!"* I groaned.

"Hey," he said, rolling his palms up. "Who *knew?*"

"Oh my God," I repeated. "You didn't, you know, *do* anything, did you?"

"Oh, 'course not," he assured me with his best Union Buddy shrug.

I let out a tightly held breath. "Jesus, that's a relief."

He turned the water on and washed his hands, then pulled a few feet of fresh towel down off the roller to wipe them. "Well," he said into the stainless steel towel dispenser, "except maybe that once."

Now the hole had no bottom.

Friday night they threw a bachelor party for me over at Carson Flegley's family's funeral home, and we had to have it kind of late on account of they didn't want to upset all the grieving relatives and friends who'd come in to look at the fresh stiffs being displayed in two of the chapel rooms. But that was over by 10, and promptly at 10:05 the party started in earnest down in the casket showroom where I'd proposed to Julie in the first place. I guess they all thought it was fitting, and I guess it was, but to tell the truth I didn't much feel like being there. I mean, Julie was mad as hell at me for something I couldn't help and something else I didn't even do, and the frost she was giving off had Glacial Ice Age written all over it. Not to mention that my old man had a big, grinning skeleton in the old family closet regarding my future mother-in-law (who was a pill already just on general principles) and I had serious money troubles over at the shop that I hadn't told anybody about and the wedding was sure to be a disaster on account of my black eye and Old Man Finzio's coughing fits and on top of that my favorite sister was messed up with a stuffed shirt commie literary philosopher creep who I couldn't stand and who I was pretty sure was only along for the damn ride in the first place.

So I had a lot on my mind.

But being around Cal and Carson and Big Ed and all my good car racing buddies cheered me up a little. Especially after a few rounds out of a very special case of private stock Mescal in these strange, amber-tinted bottles that my *La Carrera* partner Javier Premal had sent up all the way from Mexico just for the occasion. Which, of course, got everybody loosened up in a hurry. Especially after Big Ed showed them the part about eating the worm. *"'Ere's t'the next one t'die,"* Barry Spline toasted grandly while tossing off his fifth or sixth shot of the stuff.

"Hear, hear!" Colin St. John agreed.

"Don' worry abouda shing, Buddy," Big Ed advised, sloppily throwing an arm around my shoulder. I guess he'd gotten pretty chummy with the Mescal supply himself, and kind of wavered back and forth a little as he squared up to look me in the eyes. "You lishen d'me. Ever'thingsh gonna be jush fine."

And that's when it occurred to me about Skippy's Jaguar being over at the shop and how I'd sort of agreed to fix it and have Big Ed pay for it just to get rid of him. And it also occurred to me, drunk as he was, that this might be a perfect time to tell Big Ed about it. So I did.

"So thass how y'got th'shiner?"

I nodded.

He looked real serious for a moment, like he was thinking over something important, but then this smile started spreading across his face like an oil spill and not two seconds later he burst out laughing. *"Ahh, fuck that ashhole,"* he hooted. *"F'ggedaboudhim!"* Then he pulled me in real close so our noses were almost touching. "Thish ish *your* night, kid..." he told me, tears welling up in eyes that seemed to be pointed in opposite directions.

I let out a long, sad sigh.

"Wash d'madder, kid?" Big Ed wanted to know.

"Oh, lotsa stuff," I told him, and took a sad, helpless snort of Mescal. "Money's a big part of it. I haven't been getting enough work out of the shop on account I've been off racing all the time with you and Cal and Carson and now I'm supposed t'be going on my honeymoon an' I haven't even got enough dough back in the till t'meet payroll." I decided it was best not to tell him about Old Man Finzio beating me into the cash drawer.

"Thash *it?*" he asked incredulously.

It looked like a reasonably substantial problem to me. And I told him so.

"Well, howsh'aboud if I take carra th'payroll fr'you thish week, huh?"

My eyes flew open. *"Would* you?"

"Sshure I would, kid," he slurred, reaching in his pocket and pulling out a fist-sized wad of bills. He peeled about a half dozen off the top and pushed them into my shirt pocket. They were all *fifties,* too! Can you believe it?

"J-Geez, Ed, I...."

He waved me off. "Lesh jush call it a l'il wedding preshent, okay?"

Boy, was that ever a relief.

"An' thish here'sh jush fr'*you.* Jush 'caush you're such a nische kid..." he pushed another couple twenties into my shirt pocket. "An' now I godda liddle *shurprise* fr'you...." He walked me over to the exact same immense, creamy-white-with-gold-trim Lardbucket Edition coffin I'd actually proposed to Julie in during Carson Flegley's Halloween costume party back in October that seemed like a million kazillion years ago. I mean, an awful lot had happened since then. "SSSShhhhhh," he said with his finger over his lips. "Lesh'shee if anybodysh home?" He rapped his knuckles on the lid in the well-known ancient code: *"boomp-boo-pa-boomp-boomp?"*

And I about jumped out of my skin when it knocked right back:

"Boomp!-Boomp!"

And the lid slowly raised....

Trust a guy like Big Ed to come up with an astounding creature like Trixie Van Dash, who was a lovely and refined young thing with breasts like ripe casaba melons and a fetching little stage outfit made up of six sequins, two tassels, and a bead. She went over to this goofy little kid's portable Mickey Mouse phonograph she had hidden in the corner, put on a scratchy copy of *"It Takes Two to Tango,"* and immediately launched into a highly artistic little dance number featuring herself and a ripe banana. That was quickly followed up by a similarly choreographed interpretation of *"Mambo Italiano"* (only this time with a zucchini instead) followed by her grand finale, *"I've Got a Lovely Bunch of Coconuts,"* which included the most amazing display of variable pitch, in-synch and counter-rotational tassel twirling you have ever seen. To be honest, Ive always found such entertainment degrading and embarrassing for entertainer and audience alike. And I'd know, too, since I watched every bump, grind, twirl and wiggle of it. In fact, I don't believe Iso much as paused to blink for the duration of her performance. After the end of her dance show, Trixie Van Dash circulated around the room on a sort of free-form curtain call, collecting tips while demonstrating all the other interesting and enlightening things she could do with her various female parts, such as plugging up stray mouth, nose, and ear passages, picking up folding money, and making change.

Big Ed leaned over and put a fatherly arm around my shoulder. *"Y'cn' do any'shing y'want witsh her,"* he whispered in my ear. *"Any'shing ad'all."*

Well, I guess it was a hell of a nice offer. But I had to beg off. I mean, I just didn't feel *right* about it. Or maybe I was just scared. Or embarrassed. Or both. Or all three.

"You really are pusshy whipped, aren'sha?" Big Ed laughed. *"'ffit wash me, I wouldn't let an opportunity like thish push by, Buddy"* he advised wisely. *"Thish could be your lasht-ever chance t'get a deschent blow job...."*

Besides being our wedding day, Saturday, June 6th, turned out to be the hottest damn day of the year. The temperature climbed right up to 88 degrees and just kind of hung there like a damp sock on a clothesline. It also didn't help that I'd been a little too liberal with the Mescal the night before and was feeling somewhat rocky when Julie's mom rang me up at 6:30 in the freaking morning just to remind me that this was indeed the day I was scheduled to marry her daughter and that I had to make sure to be there on time-not late like at the rehearsal-and to make sure all the groom's men would be there on time as well. And dressed nice, too. And shaved. And also with their shoes shined. I told her "sure thing" after each item and tried my best to sound responsible and enthusiastic, but the truth was I had a splitting headache and her screeching into my ear wasn't helping it one bit. But I somehow avoided saying anything I'd be sorry for later by holding the receiver a healthy six inches away from my head.

I made myself a Butch Bohunk Signature Edition Morning After Cocktail, put a pot of coffee on, and started tidying up the apartment. The people living downstairs from her mom were supposed to have moved out by June first, but they'd been living there a long time and had accumulated an awful lot of stuff, and naturally there were the typical long, loud, threatening arguments over who belonged to what that are always an ugly bi-product of every broken marriage. I guess the husband hadn't been living there for awhile, but he came back for the move and it dragged on for several noisy, uncomfortable extra days. And then, when they were finally gone about mid-week, there was still a bunch of old junk like three-legged end tables and filthy wall-to-wall carpeting and broken baby toys and orphan left slippers and such scattered all over the place. So it was really in no condition to move into. As a result, I figured Julie and me would just naturally have to move into my apartment for a spell while we cleaned and fixed up and painted that downstairs apartment in her mom's duplex. And so I wanted my place to be as presentable as possible when we got back from Cape Cod. What I didn't know was that Julie had been doing a little thinking herself, and had decided we ought to move in upstairs with her mother on account of that would make it *so* much more convenient while we were fixing the place up. Fortunately I remained blissfully unaware of her plan until after the service.

Next thing I had to drop by the shop and make up all the pay envelopes for everybody and then leave them in the till for Old Man Finzio to pass out. But then I thought better of it, and just left the Old Man's in there. I put Raymond and Tater's envelopes in the bottom drawer of Raymond's toolbox and did the same with Butch's and figured I'd tell them where they were at the church service or afterwards at the reception. I also swapped the tow truck for Big Ed's black Caddy sedan, which he'd said we could use since it seemed a somewhat more dignified mode of transportation than the Old Man's tow truck. Especially for a girl in a wedding dress and a guy in a tuxedo.

Then it was over to pick up my tux from the rental place the moment they opened at 8 o'clock sharp, and it wasn't till I got back to my apartment that I realized they'd given me two left shoes. So I called the rental place back in a panic and they looked around for it and allowed as how, seeing it was June and they had so many weddings and graduations and stuff going on, they couldn't find a right one left in my size. But, if I hurried right over, they *did* have a perfect match in a size 11½, and maybe we could stuff a little tissue or something in the toe to make it work. Great. Just great. So I ran back and got the other shoe, and of course it was way, *waaay* too big. Not only was it an 11½ when I normally take a 10, but it was also a Double-D width when I've just got a regular, Average Medium Human Being sort of foot. So, as you can well imagine, my right foot kind of sloshed around inside that thing like water in the bottom of a patent leather rowboat and I had to be careful how I walked or it'd flop right off my foot. Which would be just great for *"dancing to the mellifluous melodies of the Monotones"* with Julie and her mom and my mom and all my sisters and every other blessed female person of any possible age, shape, weight or physical description who was planning to attend the reception. You're required by law to do that sort of thing when you're the guy getting hitched.

Shit.

Then, halfway to the church, I had one of those sudden panic attacks that splash over you like a bucket of ice water when you realize you've forgotten something terribly important. Like the little satin box with the wedding bands in it that was still sitting on the damn counter by the sink in my apartment. So I wheeled around in a desperate U-turn and promptly got pulled over by one of Passaic's finest, who had his nose all out of joint just because I damn near took the front bumper off his squad car in the process. I'd never even *looked* in the damn mirror, you know?

Anyhow, this chunky, beer barrel-shaped cop heaved his way up out of the squad car and kind of sashayed over to Big Ed's Caddy, obviously in no hurry at all. He was wearing a set of those mirrored aviator sunglasses so you couldn't see his eyes. "Lissen," I begged urgently, "I'm getting married in less than an hour, see, and I just realized…"

"Can I see your license, please?" he said from underneath those boilerplate sunglasses, and I could tell right away that he was one of those buzz-cut, by-the-book, frustrated Marine Drill Sergeant types that somehow seem to find their way onto police forces everywhere. And I could tell right away there was no chance of catching a break from this guy. Might as well plead your case to a marble headstone in a cemetery. So I handed over my license and he looked at it and studied it and turned it over like it was the missing clue to the blessed Lindbergh kidnapping. "This your car, son?" he wanted to know.

"No. It's Bi-I mean, it belongs to Ed Baumstein…."

"He know you're driving it?"

"Of course he does. He's my, uhh, *business partner,* see."

"You look pretty young to have a business partner, son. Exactly what sort of business is it?"

I wanted to say *'What business is it of yours?'* but thought better of it. "It's a car shop. Finzio's Sinclair. Over on Pine Street."

"The one with all those foreign sportscars in the lot?"

"That's the one."

He rubbed his chin for a moment and thought it over. "Never understood what anybody needed with a car that's faster than one of our squads."

"Listen, I just fix 'em," I said helplessly. Jesus, was this guy going to go through my whole life story? "Look, Officer, I'm on my way to get married this morning, see…"

"You just sit right where you are while I run a check on those plates and write you up for that U-turn, son. Don't worry, I'll have you on your way in a few minutes."

So all I could do was sit there, stewing in my own juices, while a guy who was undoubtedly voted Most Promising Bully and given the Slowest Penmanship award in his high school yearbook wrote me up. I swear, it must've taken him fifteen minutes. And then he followed me all the way over to my aunt's house to make sure I didn't speed. Guys like him just love to see ordinary citizens sweat and squirm. It's their damn nature.

The church was already filling up by the time I finally arrived, and of course Mrs. Finzio was standing outside with a brand new coat of spray paint on her hairdo and the most impatient and disgusted look you have ever seen plastered across her face. *"Ay! You supposed to be here an hour ago!"* she snorted, then shook her head and turned her cheek up for me to kiss. I swear, I would've rather licked a turd.

"Where's Julie?" I asked.

"She's inna special room inside. For d'bride. You not allowed t'see her now. Notta before the service. It's-a bad luck." She looked me up and down without smiling. "You gotta d'rings?"

I patted my pocket.

"At's a-good."

I stood there for a long moment feeling terribly uncomfortable, then finally excused myself to go inside. But she grabbed my arm as I was turning to go.

"You gotta take a-good carra my Joolie, now," she told me. "Or *else!*"

It sounded more like a warning than a request.

There were all sorts of people filing in and trying to find places to sit inside the church-relatives and racing people and good customers from the Sinclair and all Julie's girlfriends from the Doggy Shake-and I really didn't feel much like talking to any of them. So I kind of snuck out the side door and around the side of the building to a little rear door that led to a short flight of stairs up to the sacristy. And who should I find sitting on the steps, all by her lonesome, but my sister Mary Frances. Crying. Geez, she looked like hell. She was all tumbled down in a heap with her legs splayed out to either side, her pink satin bridesmaid's dress wadded up between her knees, and a fistful of Kleenex trembling in her hand. She was making these mournful, choking little sobbing noises while rivers of black mascara cascaded down her face.

"Geez, what's the matter?" I asked.

She looked up and tried to say something, but instead a whole new wave of tears welled up in her eyes and spilled over down her cheeks.

I sat down next to her and put my arm around her shoulders. "Is it that Oliver Cromwell guy?"

She shook her head. "He's...not...coming," she choked out between sobs.

"And *that's* why you're crying?" I asked her incredulously. I mean, him missing the wedding was the first good thing that had happened all day.

She shook her head. "I told him...not to come..." she forced the words out, "...don't want...anything to do with him...anymore."

I squeezed her shoulders. "Listen, Mary, I really think that's great news. Honest I do. I didn't feel right saying anything while you two were, you know, 'going out' with each other. But I always figured him for a pompous, arrogant, stuck-up jerk."

"He is...a jerk," she nodded with a kind of shudder.

"So stop crying, okay? You're better off without him. Really you are."

"That's not...why...I'm crying...."

"It isn't?"

She looked up at me with the two saddest eyes I had ever seen and slowly, almost imperceptibly, shook her head.

"Then what is it?"

I saw another flood of tears coming up in her eyes. "That sonofabitch..." she whimpered angrily, then dropped her head down between her shoulders again and spoke so low I could hardly hear. "...I'm pregnant, Buddy."

I should have seen it coming, but the news still about knocked me off the step. But I knew what to do. I pulled her gently over so she could rest her head on my shoulder, kept my mouth shut, and let her cry. It was like nothing I'd ever heard before. I could feel her tears against my cheek and the shudders that shook through her each time the full, crushing reality of it dawned on her all over again. It was awful.

"Hey, what's goin' on down there?" Cal called from the top of the stairs.

I tried to wave him off.

"You better get your ass up here and get married, dipshit. Everybody out there's waiting on you."

I looked over at Mary Frances. "Listen, I gotta go."

"I know." She took a deep breath, held it a few seconds, and let it out. "I'll be okay. Really I will." She gave me a brave little flicker of a smile.

"You sure?"

"Sure I'm sure," she nodded. "Now you go."

I looked at the black streaks down her cheeks. "You're kind of a mess..."

She swallowed hard. "Is there a john up there?"

393

"Yeah, I think so. It's for the priests, though."

"Don't worry," she said with a feeble little laugh. "I won't steal anything."

"And no trying on any of those fancy robes, either," I kidded her.

She leaned over and kissed me on my shiner. "You're one of the good guys, you know?"

"We'll talk later," I promised her. "Everything's gonna work out. You'll see. It always does."

"Yeah," she swallowed. "One way or another."

"Hey, Palumbo! You waitin' for an engraved invitation?"

"Go on, Buddy," Mary Frances urged. "You gotta go now."

So I helped her up and walked up the stairs in front of her so nobody in the wedding party could get a good look at her face.

"Hey, it's showtime, Buddy," Cal grinned. "And you've got lipstick and makeup all over you." He took the handkerchief out of his breast pocket and pushed it around my face. "You brush up against Julie's mom?"

"Nah. It's my sister's."

"You got the rings?"

I handed him the little satin box. The organist was already playing and I could see that everybody was already in their seats. And a moment later the priest was motioning for Cal and Carson and me to come out in front of the altar. I half-stumbled going out there on account of that stupid, oversized right shoe, and it didn't help any that my knees were knocking around like wobbly bowling pins inside my rented tuxedo. My mouth was dry and I was sweating like hell and I could feel the color draining out of my face like there was a leak on my heels as I turned to face the crowd. Geez, the place was packed and they were all just staring at me like I knew what the hell I was doing.

But then I saw Julie standing there in the doorway at the far end of the aisle, all perfect and radiant in white lace and satin. Only she had that damn veil down so I couldn't see her face, and I went into this spastic little panic that she was maybe a complete stranger-maybe someone I'd never even met before-and as I stood there, staring at her, it was like she was moving farther and farther away, until it was almost like I was seeing her way far off in the distance through the wrong end of my mom's old bird-watching binoculars.

I tried to swallow but there was nothing there but chalk and feathers.

What was I doing here?

I saw her mom next to her with those cold, angry eyes burning two perfect holes in my skull and Old Man Finzio on the other side hacking half his lungs into his hand and Big Ed in the back row with his soon-to-be ex-wife that I'd never even met before-she looked pleasant enough-and my two married sisters coming down the aisle in bridesmaids outfits while their husbands sat in the pews minding their kids, half-heartedly trying to keep them quiet, and my mom right up front starting to cry and my dad looking like he'd rather be drinking beer with his buddies over at the union hall. And I swear every pair of eyes in the joint seemed to be focused right at me, like I was some poor young buck frozen in the glare of a thousand onrushing headlights.

WHAT THE GOD DAMN BLOODY HELL WAS I DOING HERE?

Then the music started and everybody hushed and Old Man Finzio gave one more fanfare hack and started walking Julie jerkily down the aisle. And I suddenly got this wave of horror that he'd lift the veil and reveal Julie's mother's face underneath! *Oh, Jesus NO!*

Old Man Finzio stifled a wracking cough and a baby cried out in terror somewhere in the audience. The sounds echoed around in the chapel.

By then Julie and Old Man Finzio were right in front of me, and I could almost hear my knee joints rattling inside my pants. Then he lifted up the veil and-*THANK GOD!*-it was Julie's face after all.

Only she looked plenty scared. Just like me. And I swear I wanted for all I was worth to be able to dive into the pupils of her eyes and find that same warm, safe, dark, excruciatingly comfortable place we'd found together that night on the beach near Cal's folks' place on Long Island. That place where we were so wrapped up into each other it was like we were melted together and you couldn't tell where one of us ended and the other began.

But I couldn't get there. Julie's eyes were distant and flat and apprehensive, and the longer I tried to find my way into them, the more I felt like some scrawny, teeth-chattery kid stuck up on the top platform of a diving tower, staring down at Deep End water that seems to be getting deeper and colder and further and further away the longer he looks at it.

"Don't worry about a thing, Buddy," Cal leaned over and whispered in my ear. *"It's all downhill from here...."*